Luke Montgomery

A DECEIT TO DIE FOR

A Novel

ETHANDUNE PUBLISHING

Ethandune Publishing

www.ethandunepublishing.com

Copyright © Luke Montgomery 2012

ISBN 0615596940

To the Turkish people in grateful appreciation
for the warm hospitality and love shown
to a wandering stranger in their land.

ACKNOWLEDGEMENTS

Though it is my sincere desire to honor all of those who have helped shape this, my first novel, I must ask that you be generous in your forgiveness of omissions. Though this may be a work of fiction, the mind that created it was forged in the furnace of real life. Many have contributed either muscle or fire in the shaping of the mental metal.

First of all, I am indebted to many dozens, if not hundreds, of Turks, both friends and strangers, for sharing with me the complex nature of the Turkish psyche. There are too many to name here, but I will always carry them in my heart. My understanding of Islam in general and Turkey in particular was shaped significantly by my friends Fahrid, Cem, Zeki, Yusuf, Gökmen, Dave, Ali, and Ibrahim.

I also want to thank Gary, Don, Dale, John, and Grace for their many years of support and encouragement. Without them, this book would not have been possible.

Vivian did an outstanding job on the interior formatting and went above and beyond my expectations on a very tight deadline.

As every writer knows, feedback is essential for authors to overcome their many blind spots. All of the following "readers" were part of the cure for my literary myopia and tunnel vision: Barbara, Elizabeth, Dan, Michael, Mark, and Linda.

I also want to thank my wife for her unfailing support and encouragement, as well as my children—the two oldest for "hatching the idea" with me—and all of them for indulging my desire to write.

FACT

All references to historical events in this novel are accurate. The 16th century conspiracy which inspired the novel is true in its entirety. It has been preserved for posterity in a single complete manuscript currently safeguarded in Vienna at Österreichische Nationalbibliothek (The Austrian National Library).

"MEN NEVER DO EVIL SO COMPLETELY AND CHEERFULLY AS WHEN THEY DO IT FROM RELIGIOUS CONVICTION."

Blaise Pascal

THE BEGINNING

OUTSIDE OF MURCIA, SPAIN, 1612 Ibrahim twisted violently, straining every last sinew in a desperate, but futile effort to free his arms and legs from the battle-hardened hands of the two burly Spanish soldiers who had pinned him down on the floor of the blacksmith's shop. A third soldier grabbed the hilt of a sword from the glowing coals and straddled Ibrahim's body stretched out on the floor. The stench of wine, rancid sweat and pig fat was so nauseating Ibrahim began to retch uncontrollably, but nothing came up. The Spanish soldier cackled like a jackal and with all the hatred and malice of a servant of Satan, he said, "This is the last time you will ever speak Arabic, you filthy traitor. If the Inquisition had been run by soldiers instead of priests, this Morisco problem would have been solved long ago. I'm going to cut out your heretical tongue and brand your lips. For you, speech will be no more intelligible than the snorting of an old sow."

In a split second, faster than the soldier could react, the words Ibrahim valued above any earthly thing, the sacred confession of the oneness of God came rushing from his mouth, *"La ilaha illa Allah…"*

And, they were then cut short by searing, insufferable pain, and the smell of burning flesh…

Ibrahim woke to a muffled scream only to find that the hand covering his mouth was his own. He gasped for breath. *Another nightmare.* Every night brought a fresh horror provoked by the hatred his people endured daily.

Rolling over on the hard ground, he looked at his grandfather sleeping just a few yards away. Tears welled up in his eyes as he looked down at the pitiful rack of skin and bones clutching a tattered wool blanket beside the cold remains of last night's campfire. His white beard was stained again with fresh blood. For the last two days of their forced march to the coast, the withered old man had been so beset with coughing fits they had barely managed to keep up.

1

Ibrahim looked at the company of Spanish soldiers just beginning to stir in their camp a mere fifty yards away and his jaw hardened in anger. *Why? Why do they hate us?* He had been asking the question for months now. A Spanish cook was already making his rounds with a cup and a flask of wine. If it weren't for the unforgiving Toledo blades they all wore at their sides, he would've gladly rushed them with stones and a sling shot. Sentries on the outskirts of the camp gave three blasts on their horns, a signal to the ragtag group of exiles that camp would soon be struck.

The ordeal had begun two years ago in Valencia with the edict of expulsion, but now in every village and town they passed through, the decree of Phillip III was read publicly, ordering the Moriscos to depart from their beloved Spain. He knew every word by heart:

> Firstly, all the Morsicos of this Kingdom, men and women with their children, must within three days of the proclamation of this edict in their place of residence, leave their houses and embark from wherever the Commissar orders them to. They may take with them whatever goods and possessions they are able to carry and embark on the ships prepared to take them to North Africa, where they will be landed without suffering, either in their own persons or in what they are carrying with them. Any ill treatment or harm by word or by deed...

Another coughing fit seized his grandfather, and when it was over, he rolled towards the fire, almost too weak to expel the blood which had filled his mouth. The old man spit as forcefully as he could. Some of it still dribbled down into his beard. Ibrahim pulled a dirty rag from his sack to wipe it off, but his grandfather protested.

"That rag hasn't been washed in days. I can't stand the smell. Come and sit down. We must talk."

Ibrahim sat cross-legged in the dirt, careful to keep the soles of his feet away from his grandfather.

"My son, today you will continue your journey to the sea. The port is only a two-day march. There, you will board a ship for the lands of Islam. You will start a new life under the protection of the Caliph. If Allah wills, you will find peace. I am happy for you."

He paused to take a breath, which only triggered another round of violent coughing and more blood. Ibrahim waited patiently for his grandfather to catch his breath and he prayed. His grandfather spit more bright red blood on the ground and then continued.

"I remember how my own grandfather spent the last fifteen years of his life bemoaning the fact that his father had not thrown in his lot with the Jews in 1492 when they were expelled from the Kingdom by Ferdinand and Isabella. He always said no Muslim should have been naïve enough to trust a Catholic promise of religious freedom. He was right." Ibrahim nodded his head. He had heard the story many times and was in no mood to hear it again. His stomach growled with hunger, and he was eager to get their things packed before Spanish soldiers came prodding them with lances. His grandfather noticed.

"My son, I have lived in the House of War all of my life. We had hoped that Allah would restore Andalusia to the House of Islam, the house of Peace. For seventy years, we have hoped and prayed that God would strengthen the hand of the Turkish Sultan to restore our fortunes. Our prayers have gone unanswered, but Andalusia is still my home. I cannot survive the voyage and am too old to start a new life. I would rather be buried here in good earth, where my fathers before me fought, married, farmed and were themselves buried, than to be dumped overboard at sea. You must go on alone. "

"No," cried Ibrahim with a look of terror in his eyes "No, Grandfather. You're all I have. Please!" The desperation in the young boy's face grieved the old man, who stretched out his hand and put it on his head.

"If I am all you have, then you are poor indeed. Allah is your guide. I have spoken with your aunt Fatma. She has agreed to care for you."

"But, the soldiers will kill you if you refuse to march," protested Ibrahim. "The edict is very clear. Disobedience will be punished by death."

"I'm already dead. Better to die a martyr in glory than a sick old man in exile."

Ibrahim fought back the tears. His grandfather was about the only family he had. Both parents had died in the fighting that broke out in Valencia two years earlier when the edict of expulsion was first proclaimed. At the time, he had been with his grandfather in Castile, and he never saw them again. His younger brothers and sister had been taken by the church and placed with Catholic families because they had been baptized at birth and were therefore considered Christians.

"Listen, my son, you must be strong. I have several things I must give you. One is especially precious. You must guard it with your life."

Another horn blast shook the frosty morning air. Any minute now, the soldiers would be rounding them up. He pulled a leather string out from beneath his undergarment. Attached to it was a leather bag.

"Take it. It is all the gold I managed to hide from the soldiers. And this," he said, removing a bundle from the folds of his robe and extending it towards Ibrahim, "was entrusted to me by a holy man, a *mujahedeen* from Granada ten years ago. When he came to our village, he was leading a small band of warriors. They were organizing a revolt against the Crown with help from the

3

Huguenots, the Dutch and the Caliph. Their common bond was a hatred of Catholics, who either burn them at the stake for being heretics or launch crusades to displace our people."

Ibrahim took the bundle and held it reverently. It was quite thick and wrapped in fine, oiled sheepskin. His grandfather continued,

"We heard two weeks later that this *mujahedeen* had been arrested and taken before the Holy Office of the Inquisition. He was tortured for information and then burned alive. May Allah remember his sacrifice with favor. Like the other secret books circulated by our local imam, this too is written in Spanish with Arabic letters. The old man closed his eyes and rolled over onto his back.

"I can't read. What it is I do not know, but it must be very important, or the holy man would not have been so anxious for its safety. He told me that if anything happened to him, I must give it to a Muslim merchant with orders to deliver it to the sultan. This is a most sacred trust. He gave me the gold to ensure delivery. He said there was only one other copy and that it had been taken to the Netherlands."

Ibrahim had heard the stories for years now. The Netherlands were in open revolt against Spain for its idolatry. The Protestants were holding their own against the Church and moving closer to a pure religion that worshipped Allah and did not commit blasphemy by claiming that God had a mother. The Sultan had lent assistance to those in Hungary and Holland. The Dutch had even minted crescent-shaped coins bearing an inscription that read *Rather the Turk than the Pope*. This had given everyone hope. Hope that proved illusory. Hope that soured into bitterness. The descendants of the Muslim rulers of Spain were now being deported en masse. They faced starvation and servitude wherever they landed as they were forced to leave their lands and fortunes behind.

The old man looked at Ibrahim and his thin clothes.

"In my bag, you will find a robe I made just for you. Keep the manuscript concealed in the pocket I have sewn in the folds. The gold must be kept around your neck. The soldiers may search your bags before allowing you to embark."

Ibrahim opened the pack and quickly put on the robe his grandfather had prepared. It was made of fine wool and hung perfectly about his shoulders with large folds of fabric flowing down to the top of his ankle. Next, he put the leather string around his neck, tucked the bag under his shirt, and pulled out a packet of dried apricots for his grandfather, who gently pushed his hand aside.

"I shall not eat today. Prayer is the only sustenance I need right now."

Ibrahim pulled the prayer rug out of his bag and spread it on the ground facing east southeast. As near as he could tell, this was the direction of Mecca. His grandfather was now sitting up, and Ibrahim poured water into his hands so that he could wash before his prayers. The ice-cold water seemed to revive the old man, and he began muttering the Arabic prayers he had never under-stood, but had been taught from birth. When he was finished, he stood in front of the rug, crossed his hands in front of him, and continued with the ritual.

Several groups of people had already passed along the road looking nerv-ously at the ritual ablution. Groups of soldiers were yelling at everyone to get moving. One noticed the old man doing his prayers and came striding towards him like a bull elephant.

"You heard the horn! There is no time for prayer. Get moving!"

The old man turned towards Mecca and knelt on his prayer rug. This infuriated the soldier even more.

"Get off your knees, old man. You will be able to practice your heresy freely soon enough."

Still, the old man refused to acknowledge the fact that he was being addressed, but he turned his head ever so slightly towards Ibrahim and pointed with his eyebrows to the road. Grabbing his bag, Ibrahim ran to the road and mingled with a large group of the Morisco exiles. They had seen what was hap-pening and opened up to embrace him. The soldier was shouting now.

"Get up! Get up, you dog! Get up and go home." He kicked the old man violently in the ribs, knocking him off the prayer rug. Ibrahim did not want to watch; he couldn't bear it and yet he was transfixed by respect. He could not turn his back on his grandfather in this his greatest hour. He would bear solemn witness to the testimony of the man's faith.

Soldiers and travelers alike watched the scene unfold. Coughing and out of breath, his lips stained with blood, the old man slowly pulled himself erect before the soldier.

"I am an Andalusian," he said proudly. "This is my home."

"Not anymore," jeered the Spaniard. "This land belongs to the Crown and to the Church, not to Catholic pretenders who practice their witchcraft in secret."

"The Crown cannot take away my birthright. I am a son of Andalusia as much as you are," he replied. "I am not leaving."

"Not leaving?" The soldier retorted with a sneer. "Your schemes to con-vince the Ottoman Sultan to launch an invasion will come to nothing. And, whatever the case, you won't be here to join him if he does. Our spies have intercepted more than one of the desperate pleas your people have sent to the Port for assistance. Now move it!"

"I'm not going," the old man repeated softly, "I have decided to stay."

"Decided to stay, eh?" He turned to the people standing around watching. "Did you hear that? The old man has decided to stay." He turned back and looked with disgust on the blood-stained beard, the sickly frame.

"Well, then I guess you have decided to die," said the soldier with the glint of bloodlust in his eye. The newly risen sun flashed on a blade of Toledo steel, as it was suddenly whipped from its scabbard. The soldier placed the tip over the old man's heart."

"Move!" he fairly screamed.

The old man only smiled and said, "May Allah bless you, my son."

The soldier put his hand on the man's shoulder and with a quick shove thrust the tip home. His body jerked. The soldier twisted the blade. The man stood unmoving. Blood began to trickle from his nose and he whispered, *"La ilaha illa Allah..."*

Ibrahim could not hear the words, but he could read his lips and knew his grandfather was reciting the confession of faith. A violent shove sent the old man reeling backwards, and the soldier removed his blood-stained sword with a jerk. Ibrahim clutched his bundle even tighter as he watched his grandfather collapse in a heap on the sacred land of his fathers.

1

SATURDAY, NORTHERN COAST OF TURKEY Yusuf stood on a steep cliff in the pre-dawn stillness surrounded by hazelnut orchards overlooking the Black Sea. It was quiet, a quietness he knew would succumb to rowdy crews of Kurds hired out of the East by the locals to bring in the harvest. Yusuf had waited a long time for this day and never imagined the final operation would go down in a setting like this. For some reason, he had always pictured it happening in a ghetto quarter of Istanbul in the basement of a historic mosque, an urban shoot-out requiring that a whole block be cordoned off by the police.

His mind flashed back over the ten years of investigation—the sleepless nights, the weeks away from home, the near misses, the false leads and dead ends, and most of all he thought of the colleagues he had lost in this ideological struggle. The struggle to keep faith from being used as an instrument of oppression. His face was grim. He had on his game face, but inside he flirted with the idea of hope. He and his men were preparing to raid the villa that Bekir Kaya had reportedly entered upon his arrival in this small town. Yusuf thought it was a strange place to find the most wanted terrorist in Turkey, but then again this was probably how Bekir had eluded capture for so long. Doing what no one expected him to do.

A stiff breeze from the north had brought relief from the August heat. In the distance, he could see several drilling platforms flaring off natural gas. It was still dark, but the eastern sky showed the faintest hint of approaching dawn as the earth rotated to expose its uppermost crust to a blazing summer sun. Until recently, the small, sleepy town of Akçakoca had been primarily a vacation destination for the middle-class residents of Ankara, who had built summer homes on the steep slopes overlooking the Black Sea. The town boasted the closest beach to the capital city and so naturally it had attracted investment early on. The population doubled to more than seventy thousand in the summer months and became a bustling magnet for domestic tourists, but the tourist season was short.

The cool waters of the Black Sea were only warm enough to swim for two and a half months from mid-June to late August, so for nine and a half months, Akçakoca was practically a ghost town. That had changed slightly with the discovery of natural gas off the coast. There had been an influx of technical personnel working on the platforms and natural gas pipelines and this had brought new life to the city. All of these developments had been positive and welcomed by the residents, but now there was an evil in their midst that most knew nothing about.

A full moon danced on the silent waters below and Yusuf could just make out the villas and small multi-family residences built into the steep hillside. The policeman at his side pointed to a magnificent villa and though Yusuf could not see them, he knew that there were at least twenty plain clothes policemen and counter-terrorism agents hiding in the hazelnut orchards surrounding the building. He looked at his watch. In fifteen minutes, they would raid this building. The policeman began to lead him through the orchard to his position.

The capture of Bekir Kaya, one of the masterminds behind the Turkish arm of Hizbullah, would be the biggest break they had had since 1999 when Abdullah Öcalan, the leader of the PKK, the left-leaning Kurdish separatist group that had plagued Turkey for almost thirty years, was captured in Kenya. This time, their lucky break had come from an undercover agent working at the Harem bus-station in Istanbul, who had told them just last night that he had made positive identification of their quarry.

Yusuf had been tracking this man ever since the organization was crippled by a series of operations in 2000. One of the leaders, Hüseyin Velioğlu, had been killed in a police raid in Beykoz that led to the recovery of forty-one computer hard disks. However, twenty-four of these had been significantly damaged since they were riddled with bullets during the ensuing firefight, so the Turkish government finally requested assistance from the FBI, and eventually a significant amount of information was reclaimed. What they learned was shocking. Certain members of the intelligence community and the government had been working with Hizbullah to use its fanatical religious ideology against the leftist PKK.

Yusuf had known before he signed up to work in counter-terrorism that in Turkey it was an especially dirty business, but after his older brother was killed by the PKK in an ambush while doing his mandatory military service, he swore to his father that he would devote his life to the eradication of terrorism in their beloved homeland. Twenty years later, he wondered if it had been worth it, especially after learning how the state had itself founded or funded some of these terrorist groups either to create opposition to another group or to further its own interests through non-state actors. Like Joseph, his namesake of old, had found favor in the eyes of Pharaoh, Yusuf had somehow managed to rise in the ranks of one corrupt government after another. The reason was simple. He was a man of honor and virtue and even the most corrupt were in need of men with character. The real miracle was that he had remained untainted and uncompromised after all these years.

Yusuf looked down at his watch. It was time. The leaders of each team were fitted with an ear-piece and they all heard him give the command.

"Okay boys, I know you want to see this lowlife swinging from the end of a rope, but do your best to take Bekir alive. This does not apply to his comrades. In fact, he will probably be more willing to cooperate if he sees some of their brain matter splattered on the wall. Now, go!"

Yusuf heard a tiny explosion blow the lock on the front door and then it was pandemonium. His men burst through the door shouting, "Down, down, everybody down!" Before he even entered the building, the first thing he noticed was the screams of women. *What the hell is going on here?* The big open room of the villa was empty. He headed for one of the side rooms. It was full of scantily clad young women, some speaking Russian, but others speaking languages he did not know. They were all screaming so that he could not even hear his men. He told them to shut up in Turkish. This did no good. He went back into the main room and saw his men moving in pairs from room to room, weapons at the ready. One team was moving up the stairs. It was over in less than 3 minutes. Every room in the villa had been searched and there was not a man in the place, much less the terrorist they sought. Yusuf felt himself begin to lose control. Curses flowed like red-hot lava from his mouth. None of the team leaders dared to look at him. He spun around looking for the local police sergeant, "Son, did you bring me all the way from Ankara to raid a brothel? What in the hell is going on here?"

"Captain Demir, I can assure you that we saw Bekir enter this villa and no one has entered or left since then."

"Then why isn't he here?"

"I don't know."

"You don't know. Well, you had damned well better find out!"

Yusuf turned to his Lieutenant.

"Move all of the women into the main room. Have you checked the attic and the basement?"

"We have checked the attic and as far as we can tell there is no basement."

"Really? That is odd. So, why are all of these women here with no guards? They may be here for pleasure, but it is not their pleasure that keeps them here."

"Sir, all the windows are custom-designed with key locks on them."

Yusuf looked around the room. The young women were all crowded into the main room. They were clearly from several different countries and spoke different languages, but they had one thing in common. They were all drop-dead gorgeous. None of them looked older than twenty-five and several looked like they might even be teenagers. Most were crying, some were trying to communicate in broken Turkish, but they all had a look of desperation in their eyes. Yusuf raised his voice and asked in Turkish, "Where are the men who were guarding you?"

There was no response. Then he tried in Russian, "Где находятся люди, которые за вами наблюдают?"

Several of the women began speaking so rapidly he could barely follow. He silenced them with a wave of his hand and said, "Говорите, но не все сразу."

A tall, brunette stepped forward. She looked intelligent and when she spoke it was slowly and deliberately as if to make sure that he could easily follow what she was saying. He listened for a moment, asked one question and then began barking orders and walking toward a corner bedroom with the woman in tow. Most of the bedrooms were quite plain. White curtains on the windows, no paintings on the walls or decorations of any kind, a double-bed with large pillows and a small table beside the bed. This one, however, was much more opulent. The curtains were thick, green velvet. At the center of the room was a tall, four-poster bed, draped with beautiful tapestries. There was a long, but low chest of drawers opposite the bed with a huge mirror that covered most of the wall hanging above it. A gigantic Persian rug that looked like it might be hand-woven silk covered almost the entire floor.

The young lady pointed to the wardrobe in the corner of the room. It was an ominous piece of walnut furniture and was unusually wide. He ordered two of his men to move it, but the tall brunette walked up to the door, opened it and pointed to the floor. Yusuf followed her finger down to a steel trapdoor. The wardrobe itself was completely empty. In a low voice, Yusuf immediately ordered everyone out of the room. He left one man at the door to keep watch and walked back into the room where all the women had been gathered. He spoke briefly with the young woman who had directed them to the bedroom and then walked out of the building with his Lieutenant and two sergeants.

"If that son of a donkey is hiding underneath that door, there is almost no chance of us taking him alive. If we blow the door, then we are likely to kill whoever is down there and if we try to cut through it with a torch, then they are likely to blow the whole place up and kill themselves and a few of us."

He felt trapped. He felt cheated. His Lieutenant broke the silence.

"Sir, I know you want him alive, but if dead is the only option then we will have to settle for that."

"Believe me, I want him dead more than I do alive."

The Lieutenant nodded in agreement. "But, since those are not our orders, your only option is to get a torch and cut the hinges off. I'm sure there are internal bolts turned by the lock so it will be faster to work on the hinges."

Yusuf quickly weighed his options.

"I suppose you are right. Get a welder down here. Do we have anyone who can operate an acetylene torch?"

"Yes sir. Several of us can."

Yusuf managed a weak smile.

"Then, make sure you are not the one doing it. I can't afford to lose you. In the meantime, let's put up a few floodlights and make sure the perimeter stays tight. No one in or out without our knowledge. And, get a bullhorn in here so we can tell this walking dead man he is surrounded and he must surrender."

It was the Lieutenant's turn to smile.

"Oh, I'm sure he'll come right out with his hands behind his head."

"That would be too bad," said Yusuf coldly, "Because then we couldn't shoot the bastard."

Yusuf watched his Lieutenant as he walked towards the men. He was glad to be working with Murat again. They had met in university and taken Russian together. Transfers had kept them apart more than together. Fortunately, his rise in the ranks had given him the right to have a hand in shaping his own team and his first decision had been to bring in Murat.

He turned back to the villa and noticed that a number of women were on the porch and that the local police chief had just driven up. He hated dealing with officers in these small towns. They were usually pompous idiots, but he had to be professional, so he immediately walked up and greeted the man.

"Good morning, sir."

"Good morning, Captain. So, the man you were looking for wasn't there?"

"Well, we think he may be hiding in a basement."

The police chief looked surprised.

"Does the villa have a basement? The plans we obtained from the zoning office show it to be a simple two-story building with no underground structure."

"Well, we found a steel trap door in the floor so I assume it leads somewhere. We are bringing in a torch now to cut off the hinges so we can open the door."

"I see. What in the world are all of these women doing here?"

"I was about to ask you the same question. You're the law in this town."

The police chief faked a look of innocent ignorance.

"We've heard rumors of foreign prostitutes plying their trade here, but this is the first time we have actually had more than rumor to go on."

Yusuf struggled to control the anger he felt rushing into his brain. *You lying bastard. Over twenty foreign women held against their will, forced into prostitution, and you know nothing about it in a town this size?*

"Well, I think you need to see the situation for yourself," said Yusuf.

"Actually I have asked one of my lieutenants to handle these women. I assume they are all here illegally and without work visas, but we will need to document everything carefully. It is immoral sluts like these that corrupt our youth. They encourage drug use and spread STDs. This whole sordid affair will require an extensive investigation."

"Which is exactly why I think you should come inside and see the situation for yourself," insisted Yusuf again.

"I would love to, Captain," responded the police chief, "But, the governor of Düzce will be here shortly for a ribbon-cutting ceremony at the new pipe factory, and I am going to be personally overseeing security for his visit, so I really don't have the time."

He paused and then added with a jerk of his head towards the women, "It is sad really that the Europeans cannot keep their women."

"What do you mean?" asked Yusuf, fully aware of the direction the conversation was about to take.

"Well, you know what they say around here," continued the police chief, "'Keep a child in their stomach and a rod on their back.' That's the only way to keep a woman in submission."

Now, Yusuf was at the boiling point.

"Can you give me just a moment, Chief?"

"Of course."

Yusuf looked back at his men and saw Murat was still there. He shouted something in Russian to him and turned back to the police chief.

"Well, for my report, why don't you tell me briefly what specific instructions were given to the team guarding the house after you received word from my office."

Yusuf already knew what had happened because he had talked to both of the sergeants in charge, but he needed to keep the police chief here a few more minutes. He feigned interest as the police chief droned on about how seriously they had taken the orders from Ankara and about how they had followed standard protocol in setting up the watch. He was clearly concerned as he knew that any incompetence on his part in an operation as important as this one could cost him his job. Yusuf heard Murat address him in Russian from the front door and turned to see him standing there with the tall brunette and two other women. The police chief, however, kept talking and was facing away from the front door to the villa. Yusuf put his head down as if in thought and took several steps towards the villa. Then, he interrupted the police chief and asked, "Now, who did you say was on the team you sent?"

The police chief turned and followed him and Yusuf looked up at the Lieutenant standing in the doorway some twenty yards away. He saw two of the three women nod their heads vigorously. It was enough. He stopped and put his hand on the police chief's shoulder.

"I will be sure to put it all in the report. Thank you for your time. I know that you have had a busy day today."

"I wasn't quite finished."

"Of course, but the report doesn't need to have all the details, does it? Give my regards to the governor."

"Do you know him?"

"He was my classmate in high school."

"Then, I will be sure to convey your greetings."

Yusuf continued walking towards the villa and took the Lieutenant back into the main room.

"So, they're sure?"

"Yes, two of them. They're absolutely positive."

"Fine. Call Özer in Ereğli and tell him we want a bus, and we need it immediately."

He looked through the open door of the villa to see his men unloading oxygen tanks and torch equipment. He wanted these women out of the building. It might not be safe. He walked over to the couch and stood on it so everyone could see him and then, in Russian, he said, "We believe there is a terrorist hiding in the basement of this building. He may be armed, and he may have explosives. I need all of you to dress warmly and move outside. My men will assist you."

It wasn't cold out, but he couldn't remember the word for "modest" and he didn't want to expose them to the hungry stares of dozens of men.

Murat had brought in the torch, and his men were moving the acetylene tanks into the back bedroom.

He moved towards the men and said, "Remember, I only want three people in the room with me, one operating the torch, one with his gun trained on that door and one to help remove the trap door once the hinges are off. Put your headlamps on high-beam. If they are down there in the dark and don't blow us all to kingdom come when the door opens, they will be momentarily blinded when the door is jerked off and our light floods the basement. When I start talking into the bullhorn, you start cutting. I won't stop until you have cut off both hinges. With any luck, they won't be able to hear the torch over the bullhorn, and it will give us a tiny edge when we open the door."

They entered the room quietly. He took a deep breath, turned the volume on the bullhorn all the way up and nodded. Yılmaz lit the torch and Yusuf began what sounded like a sincere attempt to persuade the terrorist to surrender. It was not as difficult as he imagined it might be to keep the words flowing. He just kept talking about how escape was impossible and how cooperation and surrender were the best course of action. They had estimated it would take four minutes to cut through both hinges. It turned out to be about three and a half. Yusuf drew his sidearm, a Ghost TR01, and trained it on the door. The man at his side had a fully automatic H&K G3 pointed at what was about to be a cavernous black hole. Yusuf gave the signal and the other two men lifted the door and jerked it aside.

Yusuf had expected shouts of *Allahüekber,* gunshots, or an explosion, but they were greeted with silence, and their headlamps revealed only a steel ladder leading down into blackness. Yusuf continued talking through the bullhorn, telling Bekir and his men to lay down their arms while one of the men threw a canister of teargas through the door.

"It's a bloody tunnel not a basement."

Yusuf shouted for Murat while the three men pulled on their gas masks. They waited forty-five seconds and then descended the ladder. Murat rushed into the room.

"What is it, Captain?"

"It's a damn tunnel. That's what it is. I have a bad feeling about this. Call the Navy base in Ereğli. See if they have a chopper they can spare for us."

"A chopper?"

"Yeah, and a coast guard cutter."

"I don't understand."

"Well, this tunnel either comes out down by the shore or in a grove of trees somewhere. We need to have some eyes in the air as soon as the sun comes up and that means we have to hurry. I don't know if these low-life scumbags are on land or at sea, but they damn sure aren't underground."

"Right away, sir."

"And get a team up here to sweep the room for DNA samples. I want to know if Bekir was in this room."

Yusuf walked out into the main room and was about to sit down on one of the couches when he heard one of his men arguing with a local policeman. He wearily changed course and headed for the front door. When he walked out the door, there were several uniformed policeman trying to herd the women unto buses and one of his men was arguing with the police lieutenant.

"Good morning, Lieutenant. Would you mind telling me what the hell you think you are doing?" asked Yusuf.

"Good morning, Captain," replied the Lieutenant, "I have orders to take all of these prostitutes down to the station for identification and questioning."

"I'm afraid that isn't going to happen," said Yusuf matter-of-factly.

The Lieutenant was a heavy-set man with a huge nose. His accent told Yusuf he was probably from the Aegean region, either Uşak or Denizli.

"Sir, with all due respect, you are the Captain of a counter-terrorism unit. Your job is to capture terrorists. Our job is to deal with petty crimes and misdemeanors. Let us do our job. We have dealt with whores like these before. We will handle these sluts, and they will pay dearly for seducing our young men and corrupting our family values."

14

Yusuf felt his blood pressure rising again.

"These women may have valuable evidence regarding the whereabouts of our suspect. They will be transported to Ankara for questioning and issues regarding residency and work permits can be dealt with there."

The Lieutenant acted shocked.

"Sir, you can't be serious."

"About what?"

"About trusting an infidel, much less a prostitute to give you accurate information."

"Lieutenant, last time I checked, Turkey was still a secular republic that prohibited discrimination based on race, gender or religion. These people are human beings. They have rights and I have reason to believe that they were held here against their will."

The Lieutenant bristled. He was clearly unaccustomed to dealing with people like Yusuf.

"Captain, with all due respect, you know how loose and promiscuous these foreigners are, especially the women. They have no honor. It is a shame that they are allowed to enter the country at all. Just look at what they do!"

Yusuf lost it.

"'Look at what they do', you say? Who are they fornicating with, Lieutenant? Themselves? Every province in the country has at least one state-run brothel. How many have you visited?"

"A couple. Before I was married." He said it without any shame.

"And how many of those women were named Fatma, Ayşe, Ebru or Selin?"

"I'm not sure."

"Then tell me, you self-righteous, jackass, how many of them were foreigners?"

The Lieutenant looked down at the ground. Yusuf moved closer and fairly screamed in his ear.

"How many were foreigners?"

The Lieutenant shifted his weight uncomfortably and continued staring at the ground. In a flash, Yusuf drew his revolver, chambered a round and put it to the Lieutenant's head. Several policemen drew their weapons and shouted at the Captain to lower his weapon. Yusuf ignored them as he did the pleas from his own men.

"Answer me right now, or so help me God, I will blow your brains out."

"One. I only saw one foreigner."

"And did you sleep with her?"

The Lieutenant was shaking now and started babbling a prayer in Arabic, which infuriated Yusuf all the more.

"I'm only going to ask you one more time. Did you sleep with her?"

"No. She was too expensive."

"So, you were banging a good Muslim girl, huh? I thought it was these foreign women who had no morals. You know, the problem with people like you is your sense of honor is restricted to your own mother, wife and daughters. Lieutenant, it is people like you who give Allah a bad reputation and if there is a hell, I expect your little corner is particularly hot."

Yusuf lowered his weapon, leaned close to the Lieutenant's ear and whispered, "Two of these prostitutes have already identified your police chief as a regular customer. So, tell your boys to back off, load them up and go home right now, or Ankara and my friends in the army are going to make the torture of Laurence of Arabia look like foreplay by comparison. As for that lying son of a donkey you call a police chief, tell him I hope he enjoyed his time with the girls because I am going to see to it that he is surrounded by nothing but boys for the next ten years in a state penitentiary. Abuse of power and abetting organized crime are not going to sit well with a jury of good Muslims."

The Lieutenant turned to his men and addressed them in a shaky tone, "It's alright, men. The Captain is under a lot of stress right now. No harm done. Leave the women. They are material witnesses in the case. We'll let counter-terrorism take them back to Ankara."

The men grumbled, but put their weapons down. In two minutes, they had all loaded up in their white and blue mini-vans and were driving away. Yusuf turned back towards the villa just in time to see the first rays of the sun rising over the mountain.

"Murat!"

"Yes sir."

"What did the men find in that tunnel?"

"Sir, it comes out near the beach. The exit was very cleverly disguised as a culvert. There are footprints leading down to the beach and into the water. It looks like they may have boarded a boat."

"I'm not taking any chances. Any word from the Navy base?"

"There's a chopper on the way, and they have sent two boats. Özer says that the bus for the women should be here within fifteen to twenty minutes."

"Call the governors of Zonguldak and Düzce. I want roadblocks on every highway and have them send Bekir's picture to every roadblock team."

+===+

Twenty-five nautical miles north of Turkey's Black Sea coast, the sun rose on a small boat carrying eight men who pulled alongside a container ship under the flag of Qatar. The FAL rifles slung on their backs, the grenades on their belts and the wetsuits made them look like a team of commandos. A ladder was lowered over the side and one by one the men climbed up.

"As-salamu alaykum."

"*Wa Alaykum As-salam.* Thanks for picking us up ahead of schedule."

"My pleasure, Bekir. Run into a little trouble?"

"Yes, but with Allah's favor we gave them the slip."

"The favor and protection of Allah is the only thing that can explain why you're still alive."

"*Alhamdulillah.* May Allah be praised."

"So, what are our orders, Bekir? Do we head straight for Moldavia?"

"Yes. Can your crew be trusted?"

"All of the grunts are Gagauz Turks who graduated from our schools in Moldavia."

"So, they are all converts?"

"Yes. Our schools are tremendous evangelical tools."

Bekir smiled. "Every idea's time comes sooner or later. It's our turn now."

2

LONDON, ENGLAND   Raindrops raced chaotically down the window pane where Ian stood looking out on a grey sky. He stared broodingly at the tiny crumbs of water sliding in stalls and starts down the glass, gathering strength as they huddled with like-minded molecules until they finally gathered the critical mass that sent them plunging headlong to the ground. The rolling black clouds he watched through the ordered chaos of the drizzle splattered pane had blotted out a beautiful summer day in London. Normally, this would have been enough to dampen his spirits, but today his mood was an unusual mixture of melancholy and mirth.

Ian turned away from the window, stared at the wooden lockbox sitting on the table, and reached in his pocket for the key. This was what had buoyed his spirits. Yesterday's discovery had reignited his desire to complete a personal quest and renewed his enthusiasm. And yet staring out the window at the storm, he felt that the water falling from the heavens meant to douse his new-found fervor. Memories of the dreary, overcast day when his wife, Patricia, had passed away threatened to come rushing in like a flood removing the silt that had accumulated in his soul over the last two years and finally buried the grief of separation. For two years, he had muddled through his classes and shelved all his projects until time and numbness interred his sorrow.

He fingered the key in his hand. *What's the point if Patricia's not here to share it with?* It was a negative train of thought and he knew it wouldn't take him any-where worth going. He had been down that track before, had lived there for almost two years. He saw another train of thought going the opposite way and, with the desperation of a homeless hobo, he hopped unto it instead. *Your misery doesn't honor her memory. Get on with your life.* There was a fresh pot of Ceylon tea on the table and the whole afternoon to examine this miraculous find, the first lead he had had in years. But this train was suddenly thrown off track by a ringing doorbell. Ian sighed. Intrusion. Again. He sat motionless contemplating whether or not to answer it. A voice from the other side made up his mind for him.

"Ian, it's me, Judith."

One could hardly hope for a more charming intrusion. He walked quickly to the door, slipped the deadbolt and opened it in a crack.

"Judith? I had no idea I was expecting you." The feigned reproach made her smile.

"Were you expecting someone else?" she rejoined. "If you were, I need to know now."

Ian was accustomed to her directness.

"Of course not. Who would a grumpy old professor like me be expecting on a Saturday afternoon?"

He moved aside and opened the door. She entered like a cloud of honey-suckle and jasmine, hung her umbrella in the entry and slipped off a purple rain coat to reveal a sleek black dress that hugged a body toned by constant exercise. She was forty-nine going on thirty-five, almost fifteen years his junior.

"I'm surprised you braved the rain. It's been pouring," he said, trying to move the conversation to something safe and neutral while he cleared the fog that always descended on his mind when he was with her.

"It's rain, Ian, and I'm Irish."

If he hadn't known her better, the austerity dripping from her voice like a leaky roof would have felt like a slap in the face. It was all the harder to take coming from a creature of such surpassing beauty and it wasn't just her spar-kling blue eyes, or her curly locks of thick, black hair; it was her intellectual passion and boundless curiosity.

"You didn't think a little water falling from the sky could keep me from our weekly tea, did you? Besides, I'm dying to know what you found at the sale. It was awfully cruel of you to run off without me. Sending me a text on your way to the airport was absolutely heartless."

She smiled as she said it, her way of driving the knife edge of her displea-sure even deeper.

"Well, I only found out at the last minute myself. A friend of Charles heard about it from a bookseller in Amsterdam. Charles was in London, so he called in for tea and told me I should move on it immediately. I was on the evening plane. If I'd had more forewarning, maybe I could have arranged something."

"I'm surprised you didn't, knowing how much I love Amsterdam. Oh well, it can't be helped. I hope you have some tea on."

"As a matter of fact I do," he replied. She was already heading towards the kitchen.

"Well, are you going to tell me whether your week away from me was worth it?"

"Amsterdam was incredible. So vibrant, so full of energy and life."

"Did it make you feel younger than I do?"

Ian felt his cheeks getting hot. She continued. "Did you find anything in our field?"

"Our field…" His voice trailed off. "What could I find in our field? Our field is a dead end. If there is one thing I have often regretted, it is my choice of a field."

Her gasp literally sucked the oxygen out of the air.

"Ian, you can't be serious. History is a sacred trust. The future of civilization lies with those who have the keys to the past. We are the guardians."

"Are you sure that isn't just a mantra we keep chanting to our narcissistic egos in an attempt to put a good face on our irrelevance? History is important. It's Byzantine history that isn't. Think about it. Babylon predates the Byzantine Empire by one thousand years and wrote its history on clay tablets, yet there are more Babylonian sources than there are documents from the Byzantine Empire. Research requires sources, Judith, and we have none to speak of. Besides, you are hardly in the field anymore."

"Once a historian, always a historian. It's not my fault I was selected to be the UK special representative on the UN Committee for the Protection and Promotion of Diversity in Cultural Expression. That was a door that history opened for me. What is it you're always saying? 'History and philosophy are the prerequisites for policy and therefore politicians.' I'm sure you said it better."

"True enough."

"So, the trip was a waste?"

"Not exactly. I was able to purchase a collection of personal correspondence ranging from 1604 to 1738. They are mostly Dutch and Spanish, but there are a couple of interesting pieces in *Aljamiado*. I'll need to have them translated."

"What makes you think they might be relevant?"

"According to the bookseller, they were part of a private collection held by a Morisco descendant. He was unable or unwilling to provide further details."

"That sounds promising. Anything else?"

"Strangely enough, I also found a couple of Byzantine manuscripts."

"I hope you were able to acquire them."

"Yes, I was. Thanks to Charles, I was the first buyer to show up. It was weird though. If you recall, at every sale for the last three years, someone has beaten me to the punch, purchasing everything of interest before I was even able to view them. Well, thanks to Charles, this time I got there first. Still, when I arrived, the seller said he had only just published the details of the sale on the Internet and had received an offer almost immediately to buy everything—sight unseen for the full asking price. He only agreed to sell them to me because he had not yet responded to their email."

"Excellent!" Her enthusiasm charged the air with electricity. "I know how disappointed you were at missing the other sales. Maybe these letters will hold some clue."

"Maybe, but I'm beginning to wonder who these people are? It's not normal."

"Probably just some collector. You don't seem overly excited," she remarked as he poured her a cup of tea.

"The personal letters may prove interesting, but the manuscripts are known works. They bring nothing new to the field, and what we need is something new. The Roman Empire continued in the East for one thousand years after it had fallen in the West, and yet the northern Barbarians left more in Rome than was able to survive in Constantinople. Where are the archives of one of Earth's greatest empires? Less than two thousand works have survived the ravages of time and tyranny, and we must content ourselves with hashing them over and over and over again."

"We all share the same frustration, Ian, but there is nothing for it. We shall continue to labor on quietly in our little corner of academia, unappreciated and unknown. I used to resent it too, but not anymore, especially when I can work with you."

"It has been fun working together, but you spend most of your time sipping champagne. You rub shoulders with power-brokers in government, education and business, and conferences aimed at ensuring the values of the world's peoples do not result in conflict that leads to war."

"That is not a bad thing," she rejoined.

"No, of course not. The problem is most of the people you work with have no sense of value."

"Their work would be impossible without yours."

"Maybe. Whatever the case, I must be content with trying to ensure that the facts of the past are passed down to the next generation and occasionally indulging in a bit of historic sleuthing."

"Sleuthing? That is the most pathetic attempt at humility I've heard in a long time. More published journal articles than anyone in the department for, what is it, twelve years running? You have won two awards for distinguished history teaching on two different continents, three international awards for scholarly research and you've been nominated Historian of the Year twice in Britain. Sleuthing indeed!"

He smiled. It was meant to hide the shock he felt at how much she knew about his accomplishments. It didn't work.

"You think I haven't researched everything about you? I do not easily give away my affection and certainly not to some dark horse. I love your mind and your passion."

"Is that all?"

"And your blue eyes."

She sensed the all-too-familiar look of melancholy detachment settle over his eyes like a fog, turning them from cerulean blue to gray. She wasn't going to let this happen again.

"Tell me, Ian. What is the locomotive of human history?"

"Am I sitting for an exam?"

"Just play the game with me."

"Power, of course."

"True, but let's give it some nuance. Conquest, Ian. It's conquest, pure and simple. And, not just for men, but for women like me too. The thrill of victory, the sense of challenge, this is what fuels the human race. And women thrive on it as much as men do. I have never laid siege to a city and failed to enter triumphant."

Her lips pursed in a seductive pout, and she fluttered her eyelids to enhance the impact of her words. He stared into her eyes and she held his gaze. Then, he felt her hand touching his on the table and slowly the blue changed to sea green, her hair lightened until it was strawberry blonde, and he was startled to find himself looking at Patricia. The waking vision of his late wife startled him. He closed his eyes and sighed deeply.

"Ian, what's wrong?"

"Nothing."

"Come on, Ian! We can't get close if you don't open up."

"It was just a flashback of sorts."

"Of Patricia?"

"Yes, Judith, of Patricia."

He opened his eyes and looked back across the table. The same blue eyes were still staring back at him, but they were squinting ever so slightly, taut with resolve.

"She was a wonderful woman, Ian. You were a lucky man. Lucky to have had so many years with her. Lucky to have found a true soul mate. You should be thankful and cherish her memory, but, Ian, she is gone now. As historians, our job may be poking about the past, but you can't live there. Everything there is dead. Love and life happen in the present. You've got many years ahead of you. Give yourself a chance. Allow yourself to love your work again. I'm sure Patricia would want you to move on. If the tables had been turned, wouldn't you have wanted her to move on too?"

The question caught him off guard and the answer which flew to his mind like a lightning bolt startled his modern sensibilities. *No, I wouldn't. I would want her to go on loving me forever. What is love if it is not eternal?*

"I don't know how to answer that question, Judith. I guess I'm just not ready."

She caressed his hand.

"I understand and I'm here for you. Besides," she smiled again. "I enjoy the adventure, the mystery, how you keep stringing me along. The chase is just as fun as the catch. Now, let's get back to our dismal corner of history."

Ian sighed and forced another smile.

"The worst thing of all," she said exuberantly, "is the lack of respect we get." He noted her attempt to lighten the mood. "Even the name is an insult: Byzantine history indeed. Only here in the west. To all the eastern peoples, it was and still is called the Roman Empire. The empire of Rome that survived the fall of Rome by a thousand years."

"All that is water under the bridge now. Still, it's a shame that the quarrel between the Catholic and Orthodox should have ended by sacrificing one of the great cities of the world to an even more foreign culture. For eight hundred years, Constantinople held the Eastern flank of Europe and kept the warriors of the crescent from overrunning Europe. For eight hundred years, they fought a losing battle against an enemy with vastly superior resources. They bled out slowly, and then they were abandoned by the West at their hour of greatest need, giving the Turks one of the most geo-politically sensitive locations in the world straddling Europe and Asia."

"Politics, Ian. The politics of culture and religion. Why would the Papal puppets of the West come to Constantinople's aid against the Muslims? The Orthodox Christians were potential rivals for the allegiance of their subjects while the Muslims were merely the enemy. The spirit of Cain is part and parcel of any religion. Why am I my brother's keeper?"

Only an ex-Catholic could have said it with a cynicism as sour as that in Judith's voice. She continued.

"The armies of the Pope invaded Constantinople under the guise of the Fourth Crusade, ostensibly on a mission to repel Muslim armies and bring aide to Christians. Instead, they sacked the capital of the empire weakening it even further and contributing to its eventual demise. The Reformation came too late and Constantinople, which had formed a bulwark against the rising tide of Islam for over eight hundred years, was allowed to be destroyed by the most committed jihadists of all time—the Turks from Central Asia. Maybe the West thought the Turks would rid them of the Orthodox plague and that they would then drive out the Turks and retake the city."

"Or, maybe they just didn't care. Whatever the case, it was a strategic mis-calculation if there ever was one. It almost led to the defeat of Christendom, and it took four hundred and fifty years to free the European peoples, many of them Catholic, from the Ottoman yoke. History has come full circle. Southeastern Europe once again is faced with a growing threat from the Middle East."

"You can't be serious, Ian."

"I am."

"But, we have the U.N. Things are different now."

23

"I know you disagree, but you are blinded by your EU aspirations to the reality there. But, we've discussed this before."

He sat his tea down on the table, walked into the study and returned carrying one of the two manuscripts he had purchased. Judith's face lit up as he placed it reverently on the table in front of her.

"Αποδίξες Ιστοριών," she said softly.

"Yes, *Proofs of Histories.* Proof that the victor does not always write history."

Her smile was sardonic. "Laonicus Chalcondyles. Who can argue with his contention that the conquest of Constantinople was analogous to the fall of Troy? It was a dark vision heralding four hundred and seventy years of Ottoman rule."

"Like Jeremiah, the prophet of despair. Constantinople fell to the Crescent hordes and the Anatolian bastion of Christianity was lost forever. The Orthodox were almost entirely subjugated to Islam, the West shrunk, and a blood red moon rose on the Bosphorus."

"You paint such a dreary picture, Ian."

She gingerly opened the manuscript.

"This copy is particularly valuable," continued Ian. "It is a very early copy."

Judith carefully opened the book and began to turn the pages. Ian furrowed his brow as he lifted his teacup to his lips and then set the cup back down without taking a sip. He had spent his life studying the history of the Byzantine Empire, and now the same questions that had tormented historians and philosophers for years were gnawing at the corners of his mind, like a terrier worrying a bone. He watched Judith flip through the manuscript, but his mind was far away.

Why? No, not why. How? How could the experience of a Byzantine historian like Laonicus Chalcondyles be such a perfect mirror of what men and women throughout the centuries and around the globe in dozens of cultures and religious systems had endured down through the ages? How had history gotten into this rut of ruin and rubble, allowing religion to be an instrument of havoc and horror? Why had most of the unending stream of humanity flowing from the loins of men and women been destined for misery and hardship at the hands of imperial taskmasters? Why was oppression the hallmark of humanity? How could the few rule the many with such impunity for so long? With almost four thousand years of recorded history to work with, why were the mistakes of history still being repeated?

The questions had always been as troubling as the answers were elusive. He thought back to the conference held at his own university, King's College London, in January 2009 entitled "Authority in Byzantium." *Why is man so determined to rule his neighbor?*

He had examined the manuscript thoroughly before writing out the check on his retirement account, and had only convinced himself to splurge when he remembered what Patricia had always said, "Passion pays no heed to price tags." It was not in the best of condition. Much of the binding had deteriorated from excess humidity. Many of the pages were completely detached and had been haphazardly stuffed between other pages. Still, it was a prize find.

"This is wonderful, Ian. It needs some attention, but valuable nevertheless."

"Well, I had planned to spend the rest of the afternoon and evening restoring at least some sense of dignity by putting these loose leaves back where they belong. Would you like to help?"

"I'd *love* to," she said softly.

He picked up the manuscript and led her into his study, where she grabbed the stereo remote and turned on her favorite jazz station. For the next hour and a half, they rearranged the loose pages, putting them back in order. It was an enjoyable exercise punctuated by conversation that was professional and stimulating, directed almost entirely by the different passages they spotted on the pages of a book that not one person out of ten million had ever even heard of. He felt a twinge of guilt for finding so much pleasure in the rarified air of her presence.

As they neared the end of the book, where the pages were in particularly bad condition, he realized that two of the pages were stuck together. Experience had taught him better than to try and peel them apart. He walked over to a cabinet of dark oak behind his desk and rummaged around until he found a small box.

"What is that?" asked Judith when she saw something resembling a large ballpoint pen with a cord.

"It is a micro steamer."

He had performed this surgical procedure dozens of times. Judith watched intently as he set to work, but, five minutes later, he still hadn't persuaded the pages to forego their stubborn embrace.

"Maybe we should just leave those and come back to it later," suggested Judith. The same thought had crossed his mind and been immediately banished. Defeat was not an option.

"I thought you enjoyed a challenge?" he teased gently. "But if you have somewhere you need to be, I can continue on my own."

A wry smile slowly bloomed on her face.

"Would you like that?"

"No," he responded just a bit too hastily. "I just don't want you to get bored. It shouldn't take long now. The expansion and contraction caused by the application of heat and humidity should force the pages to loosen their grip soon."

"Then, books must be very unlike humans. Byron says a sultry climate has the opposite effect on us."

She never misses an opportunity.

"Actually I do have to leave in about twenty minutes. I promised Mother I'd stop by for dinner."

Ian turned back to his work. Ten minutes later, they were no closer to getting the pages apart than when they had begun.

"This is the darnedest thing I've ever come across. I've never seen two pages adhere to one another so tightly."

He unplugged the device, put it back in its box and stood there puzzled.

"Turn on that light," Judith said, pointing to an elegant art nouveau lamp on the other end of the desk. Ian reached over and switched it on. Judith held the page vertical to the book and flipped it back and forth.

"Am I seeing things or do the edges of these two pages seem to be slightly discolored? It is like an irregular border about a centimeter wide along all three sides."

Ian held the manuscript under the lamp.

"I believe you're right." He was irritated at himself for not noticing it earlier. He stood there for a minute and then turned abruptly, strode into the kitchen and pulled out a two-million-candle emergency flashlight. He turned off the overhead lights and switched on the flashlight.

"What are you doing?" she asked curiously.

He didn't answer. Instead, he held the flashlight up to one side of the page and looked at the other side to see how much light would penetrate. What he saw only served to pique his curiosity.

"Do you see that?" he asked. "There is noticeably more light coming through the outer edges than there is penetrating the middle. In fact, the demarcation is a perfectly straight line, but it doesn't correspond to the width of the discolored border."

He moved the flashlight back and forth, looking for clues that would help him.

"It's probably just a loose leaf, folded in half and stuck between the two pages," ventured Judith.

He turned the overhead lights back on and sat down to nurse his teacup.

"I would say you were right except for the uniform, discolored border you pointed out and the fact that we can't get the pages apart. What if…" but he never finished the thought. There was no need. Instead, he headed straight for the bathroom.

"Ian, what are you doing?"

He returned carrying his shaving kit. He had kept his father's straight-edge razor in that bag for nearly twenty years, and thanks to Gillette Inc. and its many imitators, he had never found opportunity to use it until now."

"Ian, are you going to tell me what is going on?"

"The uniform discoloration can only be one thing. The intentional application of some chemical substance to each of the three sides."

26

"You mean it was glued?"

"Exactly, which means that whatever is between those pages wasn't meant to be found."

He held the page straight up, perpendicular to the book and the razor sliced effortlessly through the thick paper along the binding to detach the two pages completely. He examined the edge he had just cut and his suspicions were immediately confirmed. He could see that the paper was not stuck together there. He held the pages horizontally in front of him and blew gently to force them apart; then he took a pair of tweezers out of his shaving kit and gently slid a piece of paper out from between the pages like he was pulling it out of an envelope.

Judith let out a low whistle. He laid the paper down on the desk in front of them. Judith knew, and Ian hoped, that they were looking at a clue.

"It looks like Arabic, doesn't it?" asked Judith.

"I'm not sure, but that would be my guess."

"This is incredible."

The script was flowing and ornate, written with a dark, high-quality ink. The instincts of a man who had spent most of his life in research swung into action and questions began racing through his mind. *Why had it been so carefully hidden inside an ancient manuscript? Who had put it there and when? Who had written it and to whom? What was it about? More questions without answers.* Ian glanced at the clock.

"Well, you had better be going. Your mother doesn't like to be kept waiting."

"Oh, we stumble on a perfectly delightful mystery, something that could be a clue, and you show me the door."

"The mystery will still be here tomorrow."

"Is that an invitation?"

"If you like."

"I'd take you up on it, but my daughter's new play opens tomorrow night and I promised I'd be there."

"Don't worry. It'll be our mystery and we'll solve it together."

"I'll hold you to that, Prof. O'Brien, but it will have to wait until I return from Brussels."

"The attacks in Germany?"

"Yes. The UN has asked three members of our committee to participate in the diplomatic meetings. We'll also be meeting with a delegation from the US led by Senator Tom Giovanni. They want to use the incident to show that this is no time for Europe to get cold feet. We must move forward with the interfaith dialogue initiative. It's the only way to achieve peace."

He walked her to the door; she gave him a peck on the cheek and squeezed his hand.

"Thank you for a lovely time, Ian."

"Give my love to your mother."

"I think I'll just keep it for myself," she rejoined with a smile.

Ian walked back to his study and stared at the piece of paper sitting on the desk. This was an enigma to be sure. As he sat down at the computer and his fingers began flying over the keyboard, he could almost feel the years falling off in the youthful joy of discovery.

The next time he looked at the clock it was almost midnight. He sighed. He still had to put the finishing touches on a paper he was presenting at a conference on Byzantine history Wednesday morning. For him, sleep was a wretched necessity, proof of a world gone wrong. Still, without it, he knew he would be worthless the next day when he needed a clear mind to work on his presentation. Time to turn in, he said sternly to himself.

It was the same game every night. Ian would patter around the apartment trying to put off going to the bedroom where his wife, Patricia, had succumbed to breast cancer two years ago. He knew it was childish, foolish for a grown man. Yet, her absence from that room more than any other reminded him of the hole she had left in his life. That had been their private sanctuary and now the bedroom was a bittersweet place he dreaded entering. He would probably never get used to her absence, but a man had to sleep, and so here he was again, alone with himself.

3

A glint of sunlight caught the concierge's eye, and he turned just in time to see the porter opening the door for Professor Zeki Öztürk. He pushed the button under the counter to let the manager know his VIP guest had arrived. He didn't know who Zeki was, and he didn't care. The hotel manager wanted to be on hand when the professor arrived, and he had been staked out in the lobby all day just to notify him of Zeki's arrival. He sized up the man walking across the marble floor of the hotel lobby. He was nothing like what he had been expecting. That morning, the manager had shown him a photograph of Zeki, proof that no picture could capture a person, much less a personality.

The man wore a pair of thin wire-rimmed glasses, but that was the only thing that fit the profile of a professor. Just under six feet tall with enough breadth in his shoulders to make a 34-inch waist look small, the man literally floated across the floor carrying a large piece of luggage and a laptop case in one hand and his suit coat in the other. His jet black hair created a striking contrast with the metallic silver Paul Fredrick dress shirt, which was a flawless accent to his muscular build. He looked like an Olympic gymnast showing up to practice a floor routine. But, it was the man's eyes that captured the concierge's attention. They were black as coal and shone with an eerie light. The man exuded confidence, his eyes danger.

"How can I help you, sir?"

"Zeki Öztürk," he said extending his passport. "I'd like to check in."

"Of course."

The concierge heard the door to the office open behind him.

"Mister Öztürk! *As-salamu alaykum.*"

"*Wa Alaykum As-salam.*"

"How wonderful to see you again."

"Your castle is my London residence."

Mustafa was a jovial Bedouin from Qatar who leveraged his cultural understanding of hospitality to tremendous profit.

"Where is your friend, Haluk?" asked Mustafa.

"He's scheduled to arrive on Sunday, I believe. I came early just to enjoy the last few days of summer weather here in London. The conference starts Monday."

"You have been preparing for quite some time now. How many esteemed professors will be attending?"

"I haven't seen a final list, but I expect there will be over a thousand people in attendance from thirty different countries. Not all researchers, of course. Your business is brisk, I hope?"

"Yes, partly thanks to your recommendation in the conference literature."

"I'm sure that has little to do with it."

Few people saw Mustafa as anything more than a personable hotel manager, but this was just an outward front. Zeki's instincts for people bordered on the paranormal. When combined with years of training in how to piece together random tidbits of information to draw ironclad conclusions, Zeki knew more about most people than they knew about themselves. He had friends who could confirm his hunches too. Mustafa played a dangerous game serving multiple masters. The man had connections with agencies across the Middle East.

"I have you staying in room 319, Mr. Öztürk," said Mustafa extending his key.

"You remembered?"

"I never forget a compliment or a customer preference."

"I did like the view," smiled Zeki in reply.

"A Mr. O'Brien has left a rather large package and a note for you. Shall I have it sent to your room?"

Zeki's face broke into a smile as he took the note from Mustafa's hand. It was just like the professor to do something thoughtful.

"Yes, please do," he replied, turning to follow the bellboy towards the elevator. Once inside the elevator, he opened the note:

Merhaba Dostum, I hope your trip was not too tiring. I look forward to seeing you at the conference on Monday. I'm sorry I will not be able to be there early, but let's have lunch together after the plenary session. The books are a small token of my appreciation for all of your help in Istanbul.

Sevgilerle,
Ian O'Brien

Zeki smiled at the Irishman's use of his own native language. *Is he studying Turkish at his age?* He felt sure that the largish package held under the bell-boy's arm contained the books Ian had referred to.

Zeki followed the bell-boy into his hotel room, fished a small bill out of his pocket and handed it to the young, dark-skinned man. *Probably Pakistani.*

Before the boy had even closed the door, he had pulled the curtains. The first thing he did was put on his slippers, open his suitcase and start hanging up his clothes. From Ankara, London was a short four-hour flight, but when you added the time it took to drive out to Esenboğa Airport and the traffic from Heathrow to his hotel, total transit time was almost eight hours. The older he got, the more he hated traveling.

He knew travel fatigue was simply lethargy caused by hours of inactivity, but it made him feel his age more keenly. He looked at the package wrapped in brown paper sitting on the chest of drawers. It would be some old book that Ian had found at an estate sale somewhere. He found a small Swiss army knife in his bag, cut the string and tore the paper away. He drew his breath in sharply as he very carefully picked up two bound manuscripts. Ian had clearly outdone himself this time. One was volume six of the eight-volume *History of the Wars* by Procopius of Caesarea, the most prominent early Byzantine historian. The second was *Arcana Histora* by the same author. *Ian must have noted their absence from my library last year when he was in Istanbul.*

He flipped open his briefcase and took out the brochure he had saved from the 21st International Congress of Byzantine Studies several years back. It was a complete list of the workshops and sessions, but the back cover included a list of select restaurants that had been carefully prepared by committee members intimately acquainted with the best dining in the area. He scanned the list for something on Southampton Row, the same street on which Bonnington Hotel was located. He needed the number for the Chanbeli Indian Restaurant and there could not have been a less suspicious way to carry it.

Istanbul was a cosmopolitan city, but Indian cuisine had never developed a following there. London was much further from India, but its colonial ties to the area had resulted in significant cultural exchange. The demise of the Ottoman Empire at the turn of the century had made the Turks very inward and hostile to foreign influences. It all began to change when Turgut Özal liberalized markets in the early 1980s. Still, Turkey had no organic connection with India, so curry was something known only to cultured members of the elite who had been abroad. London was the best chance he would have at a decent curry dish.

Next, he fished around in his suit coat for his cell phone, carefully removed the back of the phone to take out the SIM card and insert the new pre-paid one that he had bought at the airport. Five minutes later, he had confirmed his reservation; twenty-five minutes later he was at the door.

As usual the restaurant was dimly lit and Zeki waited a moment in the entrance for his eyes to adjust to the darkness. His nose, however, sprang to life, enjoying the olfactory feast of tamarind, saffron, turmeric, ginger and coriander. A waiter noticed him standing at the door and immediately came over to show him to his seat.

"Mr. Öztürk, *As-salamu alaykum*."

"*Wa Alaykum As-salam*. Abdullah. *Inshallah*, you are well."

"Allah is ever merciful. It is a pleasure to see you again. *Kısmet* smiles upon you. The chef has prepared a magnificent buffet of the finest Punjabi dishes."

"Well, the only thing better than a meal at Chanbeli is two meals at Chanbeli and a buffet is more like several meals rolled into one."

"Ours is to serve. We are slaves of the One."

The waiter showed him to his customary seat in the back corner where there was a table for two. The table gave him a clear view of the front door. As Abdullah stood pouring his sparkling water, Zeki asked nonchalantly, "Is there any news?"

"None that would serve your purpose."

4

SUNDAY, LONDON   Ian awoke early Sunday morning, determined not to let his curiosity about the mysterious document interfere with his work. After a breakfast consisting of one hard-boiled egg, a piece of toast and tea, he sat down to work on his presentation. It was futile. No matter how hard he tried to focus, the allure of a pristine enigma, a document that had remained hidden for perhaps hundreds of years, was too strong to resist. The vortex of the esoteric pulled at every other thought like a magnet snapping up metal filings. It was pointless to try to resist. He closed the plastic binder which held his speech, walked into the kitchen for another cup of tea, thinking over how it had all started.

His interest in George Sale had begun many years ago. The man had been an Orientalist of some reputation. He had worked on the ambitious Universal History project and completed one of the early English translations of the Qur'an. As a member of the Society for Promoting Christian Knowledge, he had edited the *Arabic New Testament.* Although he was a solicitor, he only practiced law out of necessity. The man was a true scholar. Unfortunately, he had died unexpectedly at the age of thirty-nine.

He respected Sale as an accomplished fellow historian and for the man's commitment to learning, which was why he had snatched up one of Sale's diaries at a private offering twelve years ago. The diary had lain on his shelf for almost five months before he had found time to read it. What he discovered was a man of deep faith violently opposed to blind tradition. The more he read the more convinced he was that Sale had been a kindred spirit.

Ian walked into his study, pulled the dusty diary off the shelf and sat down at the desk. The book fell open to a series of entries towards the end guided by memory creased into pages and binding. Over the last decade, these pages had turned into a hobby of sorts. Conspiracy and danger were not hard to spot in these short entries. They had led him on a journey of discovery that opened his eyes to the intrigues of culture, and its political value as a weapon. He knew the lines he had circled in red by heart, but read them anyway.

July 5th 1736. My meeting in Amsterdam with the Morisco printer was peculiar in the extreme. His lavish hospitality and overanxious manner made me apprehensive. When I inquired about his business and family, he was elusive. After some pleasantries, he quickly came to the point, offering me ten thousand guineas for my copy of the Spanish translation. It is impossible for me to conceive what purpose would warrant such an exorbitant sum. I asked for a few days to consider his offer, at which point he became very agitated and insistent. When I refused to budge, he dismissed me out of hand, saying I was a fool to even consider rejecting such a magnanimous offer. Needless to say, it is incumbent upon me to ascertain what his true purpose is. A friend recommended I contact an acquaintance of Eugene of Savoy, which I intend to do on my next visit to Amsterdam.

It had taken Ian several months to say with certainty what translation Sale was referring to. Ian flipped over four pages to a related entry.

September 3rd 1736. It is now two weeks since I sent the printer a letter informing him of my unwillingness to part with the Spanish translation in my possession. Now, for the last three days, I have been shadowed on the street by two men. I could swear one of them was present at my meeting in Amsterdam.

Ian turned the page to read the last entry Sale ever made about the manuscript.

September 29th 1736. I saw the two shadows again today in the market. This evening, Mr. Callamy informed me that several foreigners have been making discreet inquiries about me. I am more convinced than ever that this is a matter of State. It is imperative that I find out more. In the meantime, I must take measures to protect it.

A little less than one month later, Sale had been stricken with the fever and died. Within thirty years, his manuscript had disappeared forever; only a half-finished copy survived and it had remained hidden until 1974 in a private library in Australia.

Ian closed the diary, stood up in the center of the room and allowed his eyes to focus on nothing in particular until the whole room became somewhat fuzzy. He could imagine then that the books which lined the walls from floor to ceiling were actually a mural or wall paper instead of real books. This was the library of a historian, his private collection. It had taken years to build and was his most prized material possession. He gazed upon the books which chronicled

34

the story of mankind's triumph over the cruelty of the natural world, how he had tamed nature and transformed it into a farm, banishing hunger and deprivation, how he had created alphabets to facilitate communication and trade, creating the leisure time necessary to meditate upon and express sublime spiritual truth in art and literature. It was the story of mankind's triumph.

It was also a story penned in the blood of people from every tongue and tribe. The tale of humanity's fatal flaw, the irresistible allure of power, and the horrifying violence employed to obtain and keep it. He closed his eyes and allowed his mind to fly back through the pages of history and shuddered at the terror man had visited upon his brother. Horrors and suffering too vile to utter were buried in the volumes before him, silent testimony to the existence of evil.

His cell phone rang. He looked at the screen. It was Judith.

"Hello, Judith."

"Hi. How goes the sleuthing?"

"No progress yet. Too busy working on my presentation for the conference."

"You don't fool me, Ian O'Brien. You could lecture on any facet of Byzantine history without a moment's forewarning, and you've been working on this for weeks."

"Well, I was just considering a short break to do some background reading on the symbol at the top of the page, but I honestly haven't spent any time on it yet. The first thing I'll need is some help with the Arabic. I assume it is a Morisco document."

"Must be. Have you met Dr. Brown from the Mediterranean Studies department?"

"At King's College?"

"This will be his first term."

"I have not yet had the pleasure of meeting him. How do you know him?"

"Remember how they asked me to fill in for Dr. Humphries on the search committee while she was undergoing yttrium treatments for stage-three liver cancer. The man's credentials are excellent, top-notch scholar, already published in several journals, and classical Arabic was a special field of interest. Dr. Peacock over at University College London was his advisor."

"Well, that would be helpful indeed. I shall stop by his office on Monday."

"No need to rush. You promised this would be a team effort, remember. I'll be back on Thursday."

"I won't solve anything without you, just a little preliminary investigation and fact-gathering…"

"I'll call you when I get back."

"I'll be waiting."

5

ANKARA, TURKEY   He hated working on Sunday, but the disappointment over Bekir's escape was rubbing Yusuf like a pair of new shoes. They had lost him without a trace. There were too many loose ends and unanswered questions. He knew the answers were less important than the process of engaging the facts. This was what stimulated his investigative instinct. *Why had Bekir risked exposure by taking public transportation? There must have been something pressing and other arrangements had fallen through. What could be pressing right now?* Yusuf racked his brain for any significant developments. *Did this mean that the Turkish branch of Hizbullah was being resurrected? Why the Black Sea? He had almost certainly rendezvoused with a ship. Headed where? Georgia? Moldavia? Ukraine?*

Yusuf had gained a wealth of information from the women, none of which shed any light on these questions. Most of the women had come to Turkey after being promised house-keeping, home-care or nanny positions with wealthy Turkish families. When they arrived, however, their passports were taken away from them, and they were forcibly removed to one of several brothels in Istanbul. The very best were selected and then taken to the villa in Akçakoca. The small Black Sea town was really just a stopping place on their way to the Middle East, where they were sold to rich Arab businessmen as concubines. Every week between four and eight of the women had been taken away, never to be heard from again. They were auctioned to the highest bidder over the Internet and those who refused to perform for the camera were brutalized into submission. Then, before they were delivered to their new owners, they were kept busy serving patrons, not all of whom were local.

The most interesting discovery had been a metal safe in the wall of the tunnel under the villa. Bekir and company had made tapes, very revealing tapes of politicians, diplomats and even officials within the security directorate. Blackmail material. *Had Bekir used them?* He didn't know.

The whole thing made Yusuf sick. The white slave trade was rearing its

36

ugly head again. Human trafficking by the Turkish mafia had stepped up significantly in the last twenty years. The government had worked with international human rights organizations to put an end to it. The trouble was that it always involved local policemen bought off with money, sex or both. Now, a violent group of religious fanatics had decided they wanted a piece of the action. It was undoubtedly a lucrative business, and they needed cash to fund their operations. Young girls for fascist Arabs, filthy rich with oil revenues. It was an easy source of income.

Only three people even knew the tapes existed. One was Murat and the other was his friend Bülent in Istanbul. He couldn't afford to use them. The political firestorm it would ignite would certainly cost him his job. It wouldn't matter that he had simply been tracking a known terrorist and happened to stumble upon them. They might not have him fired, but his career would be over. They would transfer him to some hell hole like Şanlıurfa and let the remainder of his natural life serve as purgatory for the sin of exposing the emperor without his clothes. No, he would do his best to keep this evidence out of the prosecutor's hands.

Yusuf had put the tapes under lock and key, but he couldn't put the images out of his head. A female Lieutenant had conducted the interviews. Yusuf and Murat had watched from behind a one-way mirror hoping for clues to Bekir's whereabouts. The tales of brutality, humiliation and cruelty made him sick to his stomach. There was one girl in particular that stood out. She was only seventeen, a wispy blonde with bright blue eyes set like windows looking in on a cloudless soul. She had a dignified aquiline nose sprinkled with freckles. You had to look hard though to see this beauty, past the tears, past the fear that had extinguished her smile. She never stopped crying, a broken, violated and dishonored woman.

The Turkish branch of Hizbullah was not a group to be taken lightly. They had sympathizers inside the Turkish intelligence network. Until the ruthless group was crippled by a large-scale operation in 2000, it had engaged in a protracted intimidation campaign against their ideological enemies, the progressives and liberals in the country. They kidnapped key individuals and tortured them for months before killing and burying them in their own backyards. So many bodies had been dug up that their houses were referred to as "grave houses". Three reporters who had written about connections between the terrorist group and the state had been murdered on the street in broad daylight and the perpetrators were never found.

The idea popped into Yusuf's mind so suddenly it took him completely by surprise. *Damn it. Why didn't I see that before?* He picked up the phone and dialed a friend in Foreign Affairs, but was sent straight to voicemail. "Hakan, this is Yusuf from Counter-Terrorism. Look, when you get a chance, I'd love some detailed reports about the skin-head attacks on Turks in Cologne and

Berlin six weeks ago. We have an important development that I think may be connected. Thanks."

Could Bekir be planning retaliation for the attacks on Turkish communities in Europe? His gut told him it was a possibility and it seemed reasonable enough given the history of the organization. The attacks by Neo-Nazis had been headline news in Turkey for two weeks straight. Several apartment buildings inhabited by Turks had been set ablaze in the wee hours of the morning in Berlin and Cologne. Over thirty Turks had lost their lives and another seventy-five had been seriously burned. Swastikas and racist epithets had been written on cars in the parking lot. The Turkish government viewed it as a sign of rising xenophobia and an attempt to sabotage Turkey's bid for EU membership. Needless to say, relations between the governments were extremely tense. High-level diplomats in Germany had spent the last weeks bending over backward to assure Turkey that this was an isolated incident and promising to bring the perpetrators to justice. Turkish diplomats were publically angry while in private, they discussed how to best use the incident to pressure Europe into speeding up membership negotiations.

The Turkish Prime Minister had spent years complaining that the EU was a Christian club. His intent was clear. He wanted to make any rejection of Turkey look like it was religiously and racially motivated. It was psychological propaganda at its finest, a direct strike at the multi-cultural solar plexus of Europe. The continent, which had been plagued by war and intolerance for centuries, was desperately trying to atone for its witch hunts, its religious wars, the Inquisition, and the Holocaust. In spite of this, the Serbian ethnic cleansing of Bosnian Muslims had put yet another stain on Europe's image. It was only stopped by NATO intervention prompted by the US. It had been a grim reminder to the citizens of Europe and the rest of the world that tolerance was a fragile thing. It only served to strengthen European resolve to achieve its multi-cultural dream, regardless of the cost, and this helped Turkey tremendously.

Yusuf's cell phone vibrated on the table.

"Hello."

"Yusuf, this is Hakan."

"Hakan, thanks for returning my call. How are Derya and the kids?"

"They are all fine. What's up?"

Yusuf dove right in. "I'm trying to work out something and have a theory. Yesterday, Bekir Kaya managed to give us the slip in Akçakoca. I am sick over it. We were so close to capturing him."

"Kaya? You have to be kidding me? I thought it had been years since we had a lead on the guy."

Yusuf sighed, "We think he has spent most of that time in Egypt and Yemen rallying support and in Chechnya fighting the Russian occupation."

"So, why would he risk coming back to this country?"

"I'm not sure. We think he boarded a ship on the Black Sea. There were sixteen vessels within one hundred miles of Akçakoca in the 24-hour period before we raided the place he was staying. There was no way for us to effectively track every one of them."

"And what does this have to do with the attacks on our people in Germany?"

"You know how these religious nuts oppose Turkey's membership in the EU."

It was Hakan's turn to sigh. "Well not all of them, but the more mentally handicapped ones do for sure."

Yusuf understood the code all too well. There were plenty of devout Muslims who felt like membership in the European Union was the best way to reach that continent with their message, as it provided unrestricted flow of not only ideas, Europe had always been open to those, but also of people, most notably Muslim missionaries.

"The only thing those dimwits don't oppose," continued Hakan, "is a return to seventh-century Arab culture and a perpetual jihad. In their mind, Western society is a corrupting influence and we would be better off without the "inventions of the infidel," although I have yet to see one go without TVs and telephones. Nor, do they have a problem using American rocket launchers and surface to air missiles."

"Well, the timing of Bekir's arrival in Turkey and his boarding a ship in the Black Sea make me wonder if there could be a connection with what happened in Germany. Maybe he is planning a terrorist attack as a reprisal. It would certainly lead to a deterioration of relations and heightened tension. It might even inspire some of the more radical Turks and Muslims in Europe to conduct copycat attacks. It could spiral out of control very quickly."

"And it would put the brakes on what they view as an unholy alliance or at least slow down the process of negotiating Turkey's membership in the EU. Bekir would jump at the chance. Besides, revenge would certainly win them support here at home in some circles."

Hakan's stopped for a moment and then said, "How can I help?"

"Well, I know that the Ministry of Foreign Affairs is heading up both the investigation and the diplomatic efforts related to the attacks in Europe. A copy of the files would at least give me a starting place."

"Easy enough. Anything else?"

"Bekir is already being sought on a red notice. I think we should post an additional green notice now too. All of the countries on the Black Sea must be put on the alert through official diplomatic channels. I'm finishing up my report today. It will be on your desk in the morning and you can use that as a basis for any recommendation you want to make to the Minister."

"That is a pretty bold step. I'm not sure the Minister will agree, but I will look at the report."

"Look, I know there is a fair amount of conjecture here and this could be put down to coincidence, but, in my line of work, assuming coincidence can get you killed. My job is to prove coincidence, not assume it."

"I understand, but I may need more than this."

"Give me some time. Oh, and one more thing."

"Yes."

"If we could keep a really tight lid on this I would appreciate it. We all know that Hizbullah had people on the inside before we made the big bust in 2000. There may still be sympathizers in intelligence. Plus, underneath the brothel he was using as a safe-house, we recovered video of various officials in what you might call compromising positions. We don't know if they have been blackmailed and are working with Hizbullah, but we still have to be extra careful."

"I understand."

"Then, you'll understand why you must forget what I just said."

Hakan understood. "I don't know what you're talking about," he said, absolutely deadpan. "The only person I will talk to is the Minister. If he agrees with your plan, though, there will be a lot more people involved."

Yusuf had already checked and at least this Minister was not on any of the tapes.

"That's fine, but we need to keep this circle small."

"I agree, and he will too."

"Give my greetings and love to your family and my apologies for the weekend interruption."

"No problem, we'll talk soon."

6

Monday, London   Zeki reached for his cell phone in the dark to turn off the alarm. It hadn't gone off yet and wouldn't for another ninety seconds. He wondered why he even bothered to set it anymore. He had spent years in intelligence and had many deeply ingrained habits to show for it. One of these was the ability to allow himself only a certain amount of sleep. Still, he was a cautious man and knew that even when finely tuned, the brain was capable of a lapse, so he dutifully set his alarm any time he was traveling abroad. There was no muezzin to sound the call to prayer here in London, at least not one he would be able to hear from his hotel room, though that was likely to change soon enough. The first day of the conference was going to be busy, but he put all thoughts about his work out of his mind and turned his attention to his morning prayers.

＋━━＋

Ian was walking in what could only be described as Never Never land. A late summer sun shone brightly on grass of emerald green and the desire of his heart ran towards him with arms outstretched. How long had it been since he had seen her looking so fresh and pretty? Patricia's blue eyes fairly sparkled, accented by the string of pearls that hung around her neck. Her strawberry blonde hair was bouncing on her shoulders with every step. Something told him the white dress was special and he was irritated that he couldn't place it. He stretched out his arms to receive her when suddenly he saw only grayness, and the clanging sound of a telephone jolted him into a different state of consciousness. The real world. A world without Patricia. As his brain attempted to switch gears and bring him out of the REM-induced stupor, he groped for the wretched thief that had snatched this precious moment away from him. It was not every night he got a visitation from Patricia, but he whispered a silent prayer for one every time his head hit the pillow.

"Good morning."

"Good morning," he responded groggily, his eyes still closed.

"I hope I didn't wake you," said a vaguely familiar voice on the other end. Suddenly, he popped up as if he had been prodded with a poker. He opened his eyes to see if he might still be dreaming. The voice sounded just like Patricia's. Hope flooded his heart.

"Dad, are you there? Hello, can you hear me?"

"Gwyn, is that you?"

"Daddy, of course it's me. Have you forgotten what my voice sounds like?"

"How could I, darling? It's so much like your mother's."

"I hate to call so early, but I just got a text from Gilbert. He says he has a two-hour layover on Tuesday. Maybe you could steal away from the conference for a couple of hours, and we could meet him at the airport around three o'clock."

"He could have given us a bit of forewarning, don't you think?"

"Dad, come on, you know what his work schedule is like. It isn't easy being at the beck and call of the board of directors. They've run him ragged the last two months. I'm sure he only just found out himself."

"Just what an over-achiever like Gilbert needs, a slave driver for a CEO." *Are they any different from the Caesars, Emperors, Kings and Sultans?* "Wait a minute, I thought you were flying to Dallas on Wednesday and driving out to see family for your vacation."

"I am, but I changed my departure. I managed to get a seat on a Tuesday night flight as well, a couple of hours after Gilbert's departure, so I can just come early and hang out in the airport with you after he leaves. It'll give us a chance to catch up."

"I hate to skip out on conference sessions, but it's been a while since the three of us got together."

"Come on, Dad. It'll just be the afternoon."

"Okay. I'll be there."

"The usual place?"

"Yep."

"I'll send Gilbert a text right now to confirm."

"All right, darling. I'll see you tomorrow afternoon."

"Bye, Daddy. I love you."

"I love you too."

He hung up the phone, turned around and looked down at Never Never land. The sheets were a tangled mess. It hardly looked like the place of his dreams, but he only dreamed of her here in this room. He would have gladly lain back down and tried his luck again. It never worked. He knew that he would have better odds with a lottery ticket. He glanced at the clock. It was almost six. It was a bit early, but he needed to shave and shower. Besides, it wouldn't hurt to be there early to see if everything was ready for the conference. Maybe he could catch Dr. Brown and ask him to take a look at his mysterious letter.

He stood in the shower with his eyes closed just enjoying the jets of hot water pulsing against his face. He was replaying the dream over in his mind. Then, his face broke into a smile. He knew now where he had seen that dress she had been wearing. It had been her wedding dress.

7

Zeki had finished his prayers, taken his shower and reviewed his notes. The plenary address would be given at ten o'clock followed by a lecture on Byzantine graffiti, a sequel to the conference theme three years ago. Then, there would be a break for lunch, and he would be leading one of the break-out sessions in the afternoon. He had not even bothered to open the curtains, but the lack of light seeping in around the edges confirmed what the ache in his left shoulder had foretold the evening before. It was going to be another rainy day in London.

He placed his notes back in his briefcase, grabbed his navy blue overcoat and was about to head for the elevator when suddenly he stopped, took a piece of hotel stationary out of the complimentary folder on desk and tore off a piece no bigger than his thumbnail. *This is silly. There is no risk here.* He threw the tiny piece of paper in the bathroom trash and started to walk out the door, but when the paper hit the trash can, it exploded in his mind, sending him hurtling back to an episode that had happened on an August day over twenty years ago.

It was 1986 in Şanlıurfa, his first field assignment in the Southeast. The escalating violence was straining the resources of the Turkish intelligence infrastructure and analysts like himself were hastily pressed into field ops out of necessity. He had been given a short six-week crash course in field operations and put on a bus with a new identity card. The proverb 'haste is an invitation to the devil' proved once again its sagacity.

Their mission was to pinpoint the routes used by the PKK to transport narcotics, the primary source of funding for the Kurdish separatist group. The safe house he was using was on the second floor of a four-storey building. The knowledge that any of the people he saw on the street or even the doorman might in fact be with the enemy was unnerving, and it had taken some time for him to get used to it.

He had completed his casual reconnaissance in an area on the Syrian border where his cover was acting as a wholesale buyer of livestock for an Istanbul slaughterhouse. He climbed the stairs and was pulling the key out of his pocket when he saw that the tiny piece of paper he had slid into the door jamb just below the hinge was lying on the floor. The memory was startling in its vividness. His stomach knotted, his mouth went dry and his heart began pounding from the tiny injection of adrenaline this observation had triggered. He had a visitor, somebody who probably wanted him dead.

His first thought had been to get out of the building as quickly as possible. Then he realized there might be someone outside watching the entrance. If he left, that would tip them off, so he walked down to the apartment of the building attendant on the ground floor, explained that he had lost his key and asked to use the restroom. All he had been doing was stalling, trying to collect his thoughts. When he came out of the restroom, he knew that the time for decorum was past. He would never see this building attendant again. He smiled at the man, asked for a drink of water, turned and walked into the family kitchen, opened the window and jumped through it into the alley. He could still remember the look of bewilderment and fear on the man's face caused by the sudden realization that something was dreadfully wrong.

Zeki had gone to a pay phone and called in an anonymous tip to the security forces. According to protocol, he should have made a quick exit, immediately informed his superiors so that they could warn other operatives in the area, and made his way back to Ankara as best he could without doing further damage to his cover or contacting other field ops. Too new to understand the stakes, he failed to follow protocol. His desire to know what would happen, to know who was targeting him, to know that they were neutralized or brought to justice, blinded him. The rage that rose in his heart at the thought that somebody might actually be targeting him, and the fear he had felt standing in front of that door, prevented him from thinking clearly. If he had known then what he knew now, he would have realized that the price of knowledge can be a horrible price to pay.

Back then, there had been a rooftop teahouse at the end of the block on the opposite side of the street. He moved quickly, careful not to draw attention to himself. He had found a seat in the shade of the grape arbor near the edge of the flat roof and ordered tea. The entire city and the surrounding Anatolian plain lay before him, fuzzy because of the heat waves rising from the sunbaked buildings and farmland. It was a sweltering summer day. The heat-induced lethargy that seemed to hang over the city was a stark contrast to the apprehension and fear that gripped him. He reached for the glass of tea the waiter set on the table and realized his hands were shaking, so quickly set it back down in the saucer and turned to look down on the street.

Çevik Küvvet, the Turkish SWAT team, had arrived within minutes and immediately secured the entire block. Snipers were placed on the roofs of the buildings in front of and behind his apartment and then Hakan, Mustafa, Cengiz and Gökhan entered the building. He did not, of course, know their names until afterwards when his Commander forced him to read the autopsy report in Ankara. Several shots were fired, he heard shouting and then there was a deafening explosion. Two more teams immediately entered the building, but it was over. Another Kurdish Marxist infidel had chosen death over torture and had taken the lives of seven others, two of them children in the apartment next door. The report indicated that Gökhan suffered for a week in the hospital, but that the others had died instantly.

Zeki never found out how he had been compromised. The reports seemed to suggest that another operative in Hakkari was the lead domino because one of his informants turned out to be a PKK double-agent. Somehow, his sloppiness was to blame. He had been found dead in his apartment the next morning. The time of death had been several hours before the explosion in Şanlıurfa. One of their best men in Diyarbakır had also been shot on the street in broad daylight within an hour after the explosion, which had brought the death toll to nine—six officers and three civilians.

The whole thing had been a fiasco. Zeki received a minor reprimand from his boss that never even went into his record. The bureau chief was a man who recognized talent and knew it would ruin his career. Zeki understood, all too clearly, the mistakes he had made, and vowed never to repeat them. He could have just walked away from the safe-house, told his superiors he had been compromised and ask for a new assignment, depriving the nameless Kurdish terrorist of his moment of glory and leaving him to sit in that apartment until he ran out of food.

He could have let MIT deal with the problem in their own way though he wondered if they would have risked 'outing' an operative just to eliminate one Kurdish terrorist. He should have informed his superiors so that they could have dispersed their team, but the PKK moved immediately to eliminate his colleague, and both he and his superiors knew it might not have made a difference since the hits had obviously been planned as simultaneous actions. Still, it had been a breach of protocol and it ended his career as a field operative in the Southeast. He had been brought back to a desk job in Ankara for six months before getting his next field assignment in Cyprus.

Zeki stared blankly at the trash can. It slowly came back into focus as consciousness of his surroundings returned. He was in London now, far removed from the events that had taken place over two decades ago. *Was it fiasco or fate*, he wondered again for the umpteenth time. *Does my faith leave room for human error?*

He stood there at the door in the hotel room twenty years later wondering if Omar Khayyam's soul-searching analysis of theology might not have some validity.

The Moving Finger writes; and, having writ,
Moves on: nor all thy Piety nor Wit
Shall lure it back to cancel half a Line,
Nor all thy Tears wash out a Word of it.

He liked Fitzgerald's English rendition. The same stanza in Turkish was so very different, which was why he always had wanted to read it in Persian. In fact, one of his goals had been to learn the language just so that he could read the *Rubaiyat* in the original. After Diyarbakır, MIT never allowed him to work in their eastern theatre of operations again and so he never had the chance.

He glanced around to make sure there was no one in the hallway as he bent down and slipped the tiny piece of paper into the door jamb just under the hinge and slowly closed the door so that only about two millimeters were visible. Fate or no, he would stick with his training.

As he stood waiting for the elevator, he remembered the families of the four officers killed in the explosion. He had not been able to visit them officially, but he had learned the names and addresses of each one. Fortunately, only two of the officers had been married and only Gökhan had children, a four-year-old son named Orhan and a two-year-old daughter named Bengi. Zeki still carried their pictures in his wallet. He had been at Orhan's high school graduation ceremony and still made a deposit in their mother's bank account once every three months under a different name and from a different branch every time. The elevator door opened and he stepped back into the real world where stomachs growled at breakfast.

"Good morning, Mr. Öztürk. I had them put some white cheese, olives and tomatoes on the breakfast buffet this morning. I'm afraid the cheese and olives are Greek, but it was the best I could do in this neighborhood."

Advanced memory training for the Bedouin? he thought to himself. "That was very thoughtful of you."

"Don't thank me yet. I still don't have the tea you want. You will have to make do with English breakfast tea."

"I'm sure I could choke it down, but I think I'll have your coffee instead."

Now Mustafa's face lit up with a smile.

"There is nothing like a cup of Arabian coffee," Zeki said.

The human mind has an amazingly selective semantic filter and a tremendous weakness for flattery, so it made no difference to Mustafa that this sentence would have been just as true if it had been said of Kenyan coffee or that it could be an insult just as easily as it was a compliment.

After breakfast, Zeki sat out in the lobby waiting for his friend Haluk. They were supposed to meet at 8:30. Haluk was late again. He was the complete opposite of Zeki in every way, undisciplined, careless, not averse to partying, and a late sleeper. But they were in the same department at Istanbul University and the man had undeniable linguistic genius.

"*Günaydın*, Zeki *Bey*." Zeki turned to see the elevator door closing and Haluk coming towards him with his hair combed, but still slightly unruly.

"*Günaydın*, Haluk. How did you sleep?"

"Like a babe."

"Not with one?"

"Not yet."

"When did you arrive?"

"Last night around eight o'clock. I called your room, but no one answered."

"I was having dinner at that Indian place I told you about. Can't get curry like this in Istanbul, so I am taking advantage of every opportunity."

In a pretentious mocking tone, Haluk said,

"Indian? Is that a type of cuisine? I thought the only cuisines worthy of the name where Chinese, French and Turkish."

Zeki smiled at his friend's thinly-veiled criticism of the cultural myopia of Turkey.

"Yeah, well, I think our cultural understandings deserve to be revisited. If Indian curry isn't cuisine, then I'm not a son of the sultans. Anyway, after that, I went over to Russell Square and sat in a café for an hour or two. It helps me track with the new time zone if I don't hit the sack too early the first few days."

"Are you ready?"

"We can talk about it as we walk. I want to get a good seat for Dr. Herrin's lecture."

They stepped out of the hotel into the London drizzle and opened their umbrellas.

8

Ian walked into his office at 8:00 and called the department secretary located at the end of the hall.

"Good morning, Cathy."

"Good morning, sir."

"Is everything set?"

"Well, the coffee maker in the conference lobby isn't working, but I've brought over the espresso machine from Fine Arts."

"Good thinking. We'll still need to get that fixed. A whole week of espresso is probably more chemical stimulation than we need. Is there anything that needs my attention?"

"No sir. Everything is taken care of. The hospitality team is all set. There are conference programs available at the information points, and all of the AV equipment is ready in the break-out rooms."

"Superb. Can you get me the number for Dr. Brown in the Mediterranean Studies department?"

"Is that the same fellow who is doing the *History in Chaos* break-out session this afternoon?"

"It might be. Dr. Rittlin organized that part of the conference."

"Let me check on that."

"Thanks, Cathy."

He hung up the phone, opened his briefcase and removed a stiff cardboard folder. He had placed the document in a hard plastic binder for protection. He laid it down on the desk and busied himself tidying up the myriad of notes and papers that typically cluttered his desk. The phone beeped. It was Cathy.

"Dr. Brown is the one doing the break-out session this afternoon and I have him on the line if you would like to speak with him."

"Yes, I would. Thanks, Cathy."

She hung up and the phone clicked to indicate the handover was successful.

"Dr. Brown, this is Dr. O'Brien. I just learned that you are doing a break-out session on Tuesday afternoon. We appreciate your contribution."

"The pleasure is mine."

"I hope you have been made to feel welcome and are beginning to get settled in."

"Oh definitely. Everyone has been very helpful."

"I believe we have a mutual acquaintance in Dr. Peacock."

"Why yes, he was my committee chairman."

"Dr. Brown, I have an old document, which, I believe, is in Arabic. I wonder if you might be able to take a look at it."

"I would be happy to."

"It's a single page that probably dates back a couple of hundred years. I expect it is a letter of some kind. Where have they stuck you?"

"I'm on the third floor in B Block room 319."

"Well, then, we are neighbors. I am on the fourth floor in A Block. Would you mind if I dropped by for a moment?"

"Well, I'm putting the finishing touches on my break-out session, but if it's short I suppose I could take a quick look at."

"Thanks, I'll be right over."

In spite of the drizzle, Ian did not bother with his coat or umbrella. For an Irishman, a walk in the rain was almost as good as a visit to the pub. He crossed the yard and took the stairs. He never passed up an opportunity to exercise. Brushing the rain off his shoulders and sleeves, he moved down the hall until he came to Dr. Brown's office on the right. The door was open. The knock was courtesy.

"Dr. O'Brien?"

"Dr. Brown, I presume."

They shook hands and sat down. Dr. O'Brien extended the thick folder across the desk.

"Thank you for agreeing to look at this. I chanced upon it at a private sale, and it has piqued my curiosity."

Dr. Brown took the folder and opened it. Ian took a moment to study the man and his office. There were still stacks of books piled about the room so the process of getting settled in was obviously on-going. Dr. Brown appeared to be in his mid-thirties. He was a handsome man with an olive complexion and light brown eyes. His beard was short and neatly trimmed giving him the look of a Spanish conquistador. Most of the books on the shelves had titles written in a flowing script that looked identical to that on his mysterious document.

The Mediterranean Studies department had obviously chosen to expand its focus a bit. Classes had traditionally focused predominantly on the European cultures of the Mediterranean. Of course, the southern and eastern Mediterranean and all of Spain had been controlled by Muslim states beginning in the seventh century so it was natural that they should want to reinforce their faculty with an Arabic scholar. He turned his attention back to Dr. Brown. His brow was furrowed and he was shaking his head.

"I am afraid I won't be of much help. The script is Arabic, but not the language. Some of the vowel points are different. This is almost certainly Ottoman Turkish. I can pick out some of the Arabic loan words and think I recognize some borrowing from Persian as well, but the grammar is completely different."

"You're certain?"

"Absolutely."

"Strange. I suspect some sort of Morisco connection so I assumed it was Arabic."

"If you don't mind me hanging on to it, I have a friend who can probably help you."

"Actually there are several Ottoman scholars attending the conference, so I will see if one of them has time this week to look at it. If not, then after the conference I'll take you up on that offer."

He extended his hand to take the folder, but Dr. Brown appeared not to notice and continued staring at the document as if he were trying to work something out. Finally, he shook his head again and said,

"You will definitely need an Ottoman scholar for this. The orthography is very interesting. I would like to study this in more detail. The evolution of script has always fascinated me, and as you know, in Islam, calligraphy was the only form of art allowed under some rulers. Would you mind if I made a photocopy of it?"

"I would rather you took a flashless photograph. I am quite fussy when it comes to handling ancient manuscripts. If you don't have a digital camera here, I can have my secretary send you a high resolution digital copy."

"No, I don't have one here."

"No worries. I will have my secretary send you a digital copy."

Dr. Brown handed him the folder.

"Let me know if you have any luck with it."

"Once this conference is over, maybe we could have lunch together."

"I would like that."

Ian went back to A Block and walked down to the secretary's office. He asked Cathy to take a flashless high resolution digital photocopy, call Dr. Brown and ask for his university email address so it could be sent over to him right away. When he came back three minutes later, she handed him the folder and said,

"I put a copy of the digital image on a thumb drive for you too. It is in the

51

folder. Apparently our IT department hasn't assigned him an email address yet. He gave me his personal address to use instead."

"No matter, as long as he gets the file. Why don't you help our new colleague get his email set up by giving our IT department a call and expediting this process? It is a bit embarrassing that they have dropped the ball on this."

The secretary heard him muttering something under his breath about the curse of technology as he walked away.

✛══✛

As they approached the doors to the hall where the plenary lecture would be given, Zeki noted the security detail. It was inconspicuous yet efficient, consisting of a metal detector for bags and purses and two guards, one male and one female. After years of dealing with terrorist strikes from the IRA, it was only natural that the British would adapt rather quickly to the new reality of homegrown Islamic terror.

Haluk headed for the conference hall lobby to see if he could grab a cup of coffee. As usual, he had chosen an extra thirty minutes of sleep over breakfast and though it wasn't the strong Turkish coffee he would have preferred, right now he would take his caffeine in any form he could get it. Zeki went ahead to find a seat near the front of the conference hall. Ian was down front making last minute preparations with some of the staff. Zeki found a seat and sat down to wait for Haluk. Ian saw him and immediately his face broke into a smile. He raised his hand in greeting and began to make his way across the room.

"It's good to see you, *dostum*."

"Did you order the weather special for my arrival?"

Ian laughed. "You didn't expect sunshine in London, did you?"

"Well, at least the weather was nice this weekend." The smile faded and Zeki grew solemn. "Ian, I was deeply touched by the thoughtful gift you left with the hotel."

"Please don't mention it. We are still on for lunch after the first session, right?"

"Absolutely."

"Great, we can catch up a bit then. Listen, I have an old Ottoman document I want you to take a look at too, but right now I have to introduce Dr. Herrin. Let's meet at the conference hall entrance when we break for lunch."

52

9

Ian and Zeki had found a quiet corner in the dining hall. Lamb with mint sauce was a dish they both enjoyed, but today it was merely an excuse to catch up. After the customary inquiries about their health, family and conference gossip, Ian pushed his plate away and pulled a folder from his briefcase.

"This is the document that I mentioned this morning. I was told by one of our Arabic professors that it's probably Ottoman Turkish. It is a shame that I've never taken the time to learn the rudiments, but I am not an Orientalist. Take a look and tell me what you make of it?"

Zeki took the transparent folder and fished his glasses out of his shirt pocket. Ian watched Zeki's face as he scanned the document and noticed how his eyes narrowed when he reached the end.

"Where did you find this document? It appears to be quite old."

"Actually I found it in an old Byzantine history by Laonicus Chalcondyles that I picked up at private sale last week."

"That is odd. Doesn't seem to be the sort of thing you would find just tucked away in an old book."

"What's it about?"

"Well, that's difficult to say."

"You mean you are unable to decipher it?"

"My dear man, it is written in Ottoman Turkish and dates back several centuries. There are only a handful of men even in my country who can read it. Give me a moment."

Zeki took out a notebook. As his friend worked to decipher it, Ian nursed his wine and finished his salad. Zeki was writing in earnest now.

Ian ventured another question. "So, you are able to understand it, then?"

"Yes and no. What I mean is that it was not written to be understood," said Zeki matter-of-factly.

Zeki finished the sentence he was writing.

"Well, the letter begins with traditional flowery greetings and expressions of gratitude for services rendered and information provided, but once the pleasantries are over the real message gets very cryptic. From what I can tell, the important section is this part."

Zeki began reading from the translation he had just rendered.

> The council's decision to cancel son of prophet and erase every trace remains among our most solemn duties. It will be a red English sunset on Suri-Strend with a golden sunrise in Tunis when the bird which has flown is brought back to Südde-i Saadet. Walk in the snow, but leave no footprints. Assistance for the sendoff may be obtained from our ever faithful D. Hasten delivery.

"You see, unless you are already privy to the plot, it is almost impossible to understand it. It's like a poem written to your friend about a summer of adventures that only the two of you experienced, and in which you use your own pet names for the events and people."

Ian frowned and then probed further.

"But, it mentions the city of Tunis in North Africa so that is something and what is Südde-i Saadet and Suri-Strend?"

"Well, Südde-i Saadet means the 'threshold of happiness', but I am not familiar with the other name."

"And what of that phrase 'son of prophet'? Does that mean anything to you?"

"No, it is quite peculiar," Zeki admitted.

"Maybe it is personal correspondence as you suggest, and nothing really important at all. Still, I have my doubts."

"And why is that?"

"Well, it was not just lying loose in the book. It had been cleverly concealed by placing it between two pages and then gluing them together."

"Purposefully concealed?"

"Clearly. Is there a date on the letter?"

"Let me see. Yes. 13 *Jumaada al-awal* 1149 on the Islamic calendar, which begins with the Prophet's flight from Mecca to Medina."

"What does that correspond to on the Gregorian calendar?"

"I'm not exactly sure, but probably around 1730."

"Then it's not as old as I thought. The manuscript I found it in dates back to the fifteenth century. Is there anything else that might be significant?" asked Ian.

"There is one more thing," said Zeki. "The second part of the manuscript is written in a different hand and, though it uses the same script the language is not the same."

"You mean there are two parts?"

"That's right," replied Zeki. "I thought it was Arabic at first, and my knowledge of Medieval Arabic is admittedly poor, but I see now that it is definitely not Arabic or Persian."

Ian looked around to see if there was a waiter handy to fill his wine glass. Conference attendees were still streaming in and the staff was bustling about trying to keep everyone happy. He waited for a waiter to look his way, but finally gave up and turned back to Zeki, who was still scrutinizing the document.

"What do you think? Is it something worth pursuing?"

Zeki remained silent as if weighing several different possibilities. Finally, he looked up at Ian and smiled.

"My friend, make no mistake about it; this is an interesting piece of paper you have found."

"Well, let's begin with the obvious questions." Ian put his elbows on the table and leaned forward in earnest. "Is the sender or the recipient named? Is it an official letter or a personal one?"

"The answer to your first question is 'No', which is odd to say the least. As for your second question, I would say it is official except that we are unable to answer the first question in the affirmative. If it were official, the names of the sender and recipient would obviously be prominent."

"Then it must be a personal letter as you have already suggested. It's probably nothing. There could be any number of explanations for why it would be hidden. Still, I thought that there was a place at the bottom of the letter that looked like it might be a seal. What do you make of that?"

Zeki smiled. *Clever old man. How many people without any knowledge of Ottoman culture could have guessed that the fancy script was actually a sultan's tuğra?* "Well, that is exactly why I said that I would have called it official if there had been some identification. It is a seal of sorts."

"What about the little pictograph at the top of the page? Is that just Ottoman letterhead? Is it standard or something peculiar to this document?"

"Well, to tell you the truth, I don't know what it means. Would it be possible for me to get a copy of this?"

"Of course. Give my secretary a call and have her email it to you. She took a digital photograph of it this morning."

"That would be great. Okay, well, I think you should keep a close eye on this document of yours. Let me do a little research and see if I can find anything."

"Would you mind it if I kept that translation you just made?"

"Not at all."

Zeki tore the sheet of paper from his notebook and handed it to Ian. Then he looked down at his watch.

"It would be nice to check my email before the afternoon sessions start."

"The password for guest Internet usage was in the invitation everyone received via email."

"Right, I think I'll just sit out in the lobby and see if I can get a connection."

"If the rain has let up, I think I will take a stroll around the neighborhood to stretch my legs before the afternoon session begins."

⊹⊱⊰⊹

As soon as he stepped outside, Ian noticed that the clouds were breaking up and the gloomy atmosphere that had hung over the city early that morning was lifting. Soon the streets would be bustling with Londoners wanting to take advantage of the last rays of summer. Ian's mind was racing. *Tunis. That could be evidence of a Morisco connection, but the reference to an English sunset was perplexing, clearly a veiled reference of some sort. Walk in the snow and leave no footprints. Obviously, an assignment that required secrecy.*

Ian noticed he was heading to Hyde Park, but that would be a four kilometer walk and he didn't have that much time. Bloomsbury Square was close, but sure to be crowded, so he decided to go to Regent's Park instead. If he kept a brisk pace he could get there, wander around for a bit and still be back in thirty-five minutes.

His phone rang. He looked at the screen. It was Judith. It rang twice more. He stood there indecisive, a feeling he was not accustomed to. He finally answered on the fourth ring.

"Hello, Judith."

"On your lunch break?"

"Yes. I hope the weather is as nice in Brussels as it is here."

"Better, I'm sure. I invited the German and French committee members to a terrace cafe, and we are sipping champagne in the sun, or rather I am. They just left."

"How are your meetings?"

"The American delegation is applying more pressure than even I had hoped for. The Senator understands the importance of the initiative and has assured me that the Committee on Foreign Relations will lend its full support. In fact, he's personally introducing legislation next week that requires the Department of Education to mandate that interfaith dialogue be included in all state curriculums. I felt like there was rapport, so that gives me hope. How is the conference going?"

"The first day was a bit hectic."

"Any progress on the document?"

"To be honest, yes. It's an Ottoman document from the early eighteenth century.

"About what?"

"Don't know. It's short and a bit cryptic."

56

"You mean, like you're talking with me right now?"

Ian shook his head. She always came straight to the point.

"I'm just trying to put the pieces to together. That's all."

"Ian, you've been looking for Morisco documents ever since I met you. You could lecture experts on the subject, and it's not even your field."

"Well, that's what I get for taking a hobby too seriously."

"I know you're brewing up a hypothesis. What is it?"

"Well, it mentions Tunis, so it may well be linked to the Moriscos in some way. The peculiar thing is its reference to England."

"Really? In what context?"

"That's the problem. There is no context."

"Is there a date?"

"The date is given according to the Islamic calendar, and I haven't worked it out exactly on the Gregorian calendar, but it's around 1730."

"Hmm. Early eighteenth-century connection between England and North African Muslims. Nothing comes to mind. Anything else?"

Ian didn't respond. There was a longish silence. He heard her take a sip of champagne.

"Ian?"

"I'll be hornswoggled! I'm stupider than Jupiter. That has to be it!"

"Has to be what?"

"The letter referred to capturing '*the bird which has flown.*' That has to be a coded reference and the date is right."

"Right for what?" asked Judith in exasperation.

"I'll explain it all when I see you."

"Don't you dare!"

"Come on, Judith. Half the fun is having something to look forward to."

"You're so cruel, Ian O'Brien!"

"We'll make a date of it on Thursday."

He couldn't believe he had said it. She was the one who said things like that. She noticed too.

"Okay then, as long as it's a date."

———

Across campus, in a cool, underground room, the university server which constituted the backbone of the university's IT infrastructure was mindlessly implementing the commands of hundreds of minds around the world. Some requested documents, other Internet access, email, VoIP or some other form of cyber communication.

It wasn't as faceless and impersonal as it had been fifteen years ago. A myriad of social networking websites had changed all that, but there was still something about remoteness that stifled the human need to interact emotively. This fact explained why cyber communications became so vitriolic. People aggravated by a blog article that attacked their value paradigm were much more likely to make a response that violated normal rules of decency simply because their opponent was not physically present.

Cyberspace altered one's perception of reality, transforming the person at the computer on the other end of the optic cable into an ethereal demigod of sorts, who might exist, but whose existence affected reality only insofar as it gave them someone to lust after or curse. The Great Disconnect had started with television, the technological wonder of previous generations. It conditioned the populace with an endless stream of car wrecks, robberies, fights, murders and general mayhem. Today, it had moved to an entirely new level. Human relationships were virtual.

For centuries, philosophers debated the distinction between reality and perception, but this abstract discussion was mostly lost on the rank and file. Still, it was hard to think of any relationship in the Matrix as being quite as real as physical-presence relationships because the person-to-person encounter provided a myriad of reality clues that were missing in cyberspace—the smell of onion on the interlocutor's breath, facial expressions, posture, intonation, pupil dilation, etc. But the winds of change were blowing, and the prospect of a connection that would allow the human mind to be just another Internet portal, another data server, another CPU, was already being discussed.

The university mainframe was oblivious to the thoughts and commands of the sentient beings it processed with such admirable perfection. But, even if the server had been a sentient being endowed with some currently non-existent form of AI, it is doubtful that it would have raised a virtual eyebrow at the innocuous-looking email that zipped through its processor on its way to some binary address in cyberspace at a speed that made the synapses of human neural networks look like desert caravans of camels plodding across sand dunes. The message slipped past the filters of the intelligence community as well with a subject heading which read simply "Cool Quote":

> FOUND A REALLY COOL QUOTE I THINK YOU WILL LIKE.
> "A RED SUNSET IS PREFERABLE TO A RED DAWN".

A sentient being could hardly have been faulted for expecting to see the name of the author of this enigmatic saying, but they would have been disappointed. This was the sum of the message.

10

CAIRO, EGYPT   The horizon was rushing up to meet the sun as Cairo came to the end of another long summer day that had turned this city of seventeen million into a veritable blast furnace. The sunset, however, promised to be spectacular. There was a scattering of cirrostratus clouds in the west above the searing sands of the Sahara, so high above the earth that even in August they were composed mostly of ice crystals, which made them excellent spectral reflectors of the sun's rays. The result, of course, was brilliant hues of purple and orange that postcard photographers dreamed of.

From his office on the nineteenth story of the high-rise office building, he had an excellent view. Ahmet's job had plenty of perks consisting of more tangible worldly compensation, but the natural beauty he witnessed from his office was never lost on him. As the imperceptible movement of the earth produced the sensation that the sun was sinking, a thought flickered across the screen of his mind. The residents of the city would be thankful that *Ra* was going to bed for the night, giving them some respite from the heat. No one believed that the sun was a god anymore, but some probably cursed it as a devil, especially if they were not one of the privileged few who could afford air-conditioning. He said a brief prayer of thanks for the refreshing breeze that blew from the Korean Samsung air-conditioner, another privilege that came with the job and separated him from the fifteen million in the city who lived without it. Then the muezzin began to sound the *adhan*, calling the faithful to their prayers and he rose in mechanical obedience to the summons.

Ten minutes later, he rose from his prayer rug, and sat down at his desk, refreshed from the spiritual exercise. He closed his eyes and promised himself it would only be for five minutes. The first day of a crucial week had come to an end. The project was in the homestretch. All he had to do was push himself and everyone else to finish strong. If all went well, in three weeks, the UN would be announcing a new initiative promoting tolerance and understanding between people of different faiths. For almost five years, he had stealthily

59

applied the pressures necessary to get Islamic governments on board. The faith of the prophet was now viewed by outsiders as an ideology of fanaticism, violence and intolerance. It was time to repair the damage, which required an image make-over. A more obvious fact would have been difficult for him to imagine, but not everyone was convinced. Obstacles abounded, especially in the form of short-sighted traditionalists.

His phone beeped. He hit the intercom.

"Sir, it's the Minister of Foreign Affairs from Yemen."

"Put him through." Ahmet punched the speaker button and leaned back in his chair. "Mr. Secretary, how nice to hear from you. I hope you have good news for me."

"Mr. Karaman, the Minister of Culture and Religious Affairs refuses to sign off on the project."

"Mr. Secretary, this sounds unacceptably like our last conversation. I thought we had made it abundantly clear how crucial Yemen's support for this initiative is."

"Mr. Karaman, surely you know how much personal effort I have invested in this cause."

"Apparently, it has not been sufficient."

"The Republic of Yemen is a sovereign nation committed to sharia law. Our jurists are not convinced that your tolerance initiative complies with divine law and the will of Allah."

"Mr. Secretary, allow me to be blunt. The worldview of those who oppose this plan hearkens back to seventh-century Arabia. The world has changed."

"Allah has not."

"That is not being debated. However, I see your ministers driving cars instead of riding camels, which tells me they are able to adapt to changing conditions. They need a fresh interpretation of the Qur'an and, above all, a leader who can unite the *ummah* and repair Islam's tarnished image. Unfortunately, most of the opinion makers in the House of Islam lack the foresight Allah gave an ant. Even with their tiny brains, these insects have the sense to prepare for winter. We, on the other hand, have been engaged in an undeclared war with the West without making the necessary preparations. It is time to put the House of Islam in order. We have been chosen to accomplish this task."

Ahmet had no patience for the visionless leaders he worked with, but he feigned it well, and when that failed, he ruthlessly pursued other paths of persuasion. He was a doer, not a dallier.

"Mr. Karaman, it may take more than convincing arguments to persuade the minister."

"Well, you have come to the point at last."

"What about the other countries?"

"Sudan and Somalia are still giving us trouble, but the same pressure will be applied to them all."

"And what about support in the West?"

"Mr. Secretary, over the last twelve years I have personally orchestrated the establishment of centers for Islamic studies at nineteen of the best universities in Europe, North America and Australia, all funded by businessmen from Turkey, Jordan and Qatar as well as the governments of Saudi Arabia, the U.A.E. and Morocco. We have provided scholarships for thousands of students from the Middle East to study in the West, and placed hundreds of professors, instructors and post-doc students in the most prestigious schools. We have established non-profit organizations, and charter schools at the elementary, junior-high and high-school levels. We have won invaluable support among the Western elite."

"Mr. Karaman, you know that I agree with your vision. Believe me, I'm doing my best to convince the Minister that this compromise is a tactic of war."

"I'll give you ten days before I send in the bowstring. Don't disappoint us."

Ahmet reached for the off button. A frantic stream of pleas was cut off in mid-sentence. He heard a ding from his computer and opened his eyes just in time to catch the innocuous-looking subject heading "FW: Cool Quote" as it faded from the lower right corner of the screen. He quickly focused his mind and reached for the mouse. There was one thing that Ahmet never received and that was spam. Another perk that came with his job was that no email ever appeared on his screen unless the sender's digital signature was on a master list and the email's source had been contacted by his staff. In his office, this list was called the safe list. He had always thought that particularly ironic since it was anything but safe.

There was a short note from his top security analyst in Arabic that read, "So far it all checks out." He scanned down to read the one line message his analyst was forwarding to him. It was less cryptic than one might suppose. The quote was one of the organization's codes. To find out which operative sent the mail and what their mission encompassed, Ahmet entered the sender's ID— 3466-5725-9226. His database gave him the answer immediately. The sender was support and reconnaissance in academia.

Ahmet reached for the phone and told the switchboard to put him through to their London operative immediately and to route the call through any of several thousand innocuous local numbers. Since the 911 attacks, the eavesdropping capability, and more importantly, determination in the West had grown exponentially. His organization had learned the hard way that there is no such thing as a secure digital transmission.

The price of this knowledge had been high. They had lost some of their best and brightest sources. Everything was potentially traceable or decipherable and all of the crap in Hollywood movies about secure lines was just a smoke screen to keep the world believing that it could actually communicate incognito, making it easier for security forces around the world to learn what they wanted. Now his office routed all communications through a complex system that relied upon genuine local telephone lines or websites. Digital encryption was rarely used. It only drew attention, and attention was one thing they did not want. Transparent communications were tedious, but surprisingly effective.

The phone began to ring, and he clicked on the attached jpg file as he waited for the operative to pick up. What he saw almost took his breath away. A voice answered on the other end with the traditional Muslim greeting of peace.

"*As-salamu alaykum.*"

"*Wa Alaykum As-salam.*"

"Are you looking at the digital copy I sent?"

"I am," answered Ahmet. "I cannot read it, but it bears the Seal, which would suggest it was prepared by the Ottoman Bureau. Are you sure of its authenticity?"

"As the infidel says, 'Seeing is believing' and I have seen and touched it."

"What is the significance?"

"Let me just say that our connection with one of our largest disinformation and cultural subterfuge projects of all time is on the verge of discovery, and they have one of the original termination orders."

"Original?"

"Yes. From a man that has been under low-level surveillance for years."

"Which project is it?"

"Son of prophet."

"*Amanın!* You're sure?!"

"Sir, as you will see from a perusal of my file, this is my area of expertise."

"But, how can this be?! That was centuries ago?"

"That I do not know."

"Have you secured it?"

"It was impossible without arousing suspicion."

"Does the owner know what he is holding?"

"At present, he does not know enough to pose a threat, but he is an intelligent researcher. What's more, he has connections that could make this headline news. He is by nature slow and cautious, but it is essential that we move quickly. What are my instructions?"

"You will be contacted through one of the usual channels. We must recover the document and destroy any copies. Do you know if any have been made?"

"He only found it last week and his secretary took a digital photograph today. He is quite unaware of the document's importance, so I doubt he has made any other copies."

"Nevertheless, all of his storage devices, including his secretary's, must be wiped. No trace of this may remain. I will be back in touch with you in six hours. Begin your preparations."

"It will be done, *inshallah*."

"*Inshallah.*"

Ahmet turned off the phone and set it on his desk. He sat in quiet, but intense meditation for several minutes. The success of the son of prophet project was undeniable even if it had happened almost entirely by accident. Then again, he didn't believe in accidents. He knew that Allah had turned failure on its head and achieved a spectacular success with the fumbling efforts of his servants. They could not let it be exposed now.

He had been part of the brotherhood for nineteen years, much of it here, as a security analyst working under the auspices of the Islamic Bank of Egypt among the Arabs, but never had such an opportunity presented itself. If he could supervise a flawless execution, he felt certain this would win him the promotion that would return him to his beloved Istanbul.

The self-imposed exile, the difficulties of living and working in a foreign land were beginning to wear on him. He longed for the familiar, though the brotherhood strongly discouraged such bonds. Still, he missed the Bosphorus, the refreshing taste of *ayran*, and the redbuds in the spring.

The brotherhood rewarded cunning and shrewdness. Ahmet's rapid advance to Chief of Operations for Africa was proof of that. However, he had stagnated here in Cairo for almost ten years. Initially, his assignments had been thrilling as he took the brotherhood's fight to a corporate level. They were not above knocking off rivals in the middle of the night, but training and inserting key talent into positions of responsibility with financial institutions and government offices was where the battle would be won. Before long, his talent was recognized as too valuable to be wasted in the field, and he was elevated to more senior positions.

In two months, he would celebrate his nineteenth anniversary with the brotherhood, but he had only learned its secret last year. It all began right after his graduation from Istanbul Technical University where he had majored in finance. He landed a good job with one of Turkey's top investment banks where his talent attracted attention.

On that day almost nineteen years ago, the leader of his *tarikat* had invited him to his home alone. The *imam* explained to him that the total victory foreseen by the Prophet required the brightest and best Islam had to offer. He could still remember the old man's words:

"Yes, Ahmet, the sword won many victories in the early days of Islam, but even then, the pen that inscribed the Qur'an was what inspired the warriors. The pen is greater than the sword and the final victory of Islam will be won not with suicide bombers or the armies of sultans, but with the pen. It is not violence, but social pressure, the *dhimmi* status of the infidel under our rule, which has always provided the greatest enticement for conversion. Few are willing to pay extra taxes from their hard labor and suffer the indignity of being a second-class citizen just to continue in error, so they convert and gain wealth and prosperity in this world as well as heaven in the next. This is the power of the pen. Threaten them with swords and they may take some vain glory in dying for their cause. Yet the written word of the Qur'an has bled their idolatrous faith out of them in a way that even the sword could not.

"We are the Divine Light, Ahmet. Our esteemed leader, the Rightly Guided One, has received the divine strategy. We must circulate within the system without being noticed until we have infiltrated every position of influence. We believe that the *Nur* of Allah will enlighten the minds of the unbelievers. It is our duty to be its emissary. To excel at science and commerce so that our way becomes attractive to the outsiders. Still, the process needs prodding at times and we need devoted men like you to serve the cause."

It had only been after this speech that the guest in the side room was brought in. The imam had switched from Turkish to Arabic to introduce Ahmet to the dark-skinned newcomer. Like all Turks, Ahmet was deeply suspicious of all things Arab. He viewed the entire race as treacherous back-stabbers who had allied themselves with the British infidels in the dismantling of the Ottoman Empire during WWI. The imam sensed his hesitation and immediately switched back to Turkish saying, "Allah has given them oil and riches for the prophet's sake, but it is the destiny of the Turk to rule. Let us utilize their resources as a man milks a cow for his children."

This had been the beginning of his journey into the deep secrets of the brotherhood, a journey of discovery that would have shocked even the recruiting imam. One of the first things he had learned was that the book written to encourage Turkish contempt for Arabs was in fact a forgery. *Confessions of a British Spy* had been written by Turkish nationalists trying to forge a new identity for the republic and strengthen patriotic sentiment.

Like all politically astute Turks, he and his friends had taken at face value the book's claim to have been written in the 1700s by a former British spy named Hempher. The book detailed a British plan to overthrow Islam by encouraging immorality, addictions to wine and drugs and especially by fomenting dissension which would fragment the community of Islam with radical sectarianism. According to the book, the most remarkable success of the British was their creation of the radical cult of Wahhabi Islam born in Saudi Arabia.

A smile flitted across his face as he remembered how this story had fired the imaginations of young Turkish Muslims and, more importantly, how they had all accepted such an incredible fabrication without hesitation. He could still remember the raging anger, the intense hatred he and his friends had felt in university when they learned of the British designs on the holy faith of Allah as transmitted to the prophet. After he joined the brotherhood everything changed.

There had been a three-month orientation for beginners. One of the classes had been called 'Deceit as a Military Tactic'. He had sat dazed as the instructor explained that *Confessions of a British Spy* was a complete fabrication. The claim that the British had created Wahhabisim was every bit as fictitious as the claim that Neil Armstrong had heard the call to prayer on the moon or that Jacques Cousteau's scientific research had led to his conversion to Islam. His whole world had been turned upside down. All of these legends were part of the propaganda war. An ancient Ottoman proverb summed up the strategy, 'Sling the mud. Even if it doesn't stick, it will leave a stain.' Even now, he could vividly remember the shock and astonishment, the sick feeling in his stomach, and the anger at realizing they had been lied to. He had spent hours in counseling with the *imam* at the madrassa, trying to understand why it was all necessary.

The forgery had actually been aimed at keeping the Turks committed to nationalist Islam and explaining why the Arabs had sided with the British against them in WWI. The purpose was to cast a shadow of foreign intervention upon the Wahhabi sect because of the Arabs' opposition to Ottoman Turkish rule. It didn't matter that the book was taken seriously by no one outside of the country. The point had been to reinforce the Middle Eastern perception of Westerners as dangerous and irreverent meddlers.

Naturally, every Turk hated the Arabs for joining the infidel to fight against their own Muslim brothers. This act of betrayal was so unthinkable that any conspiracy, no matter how tenuous, would be preferable to the truth, so the book had legitimized Turkish contempt for the Arabs by claiming that they had sold out true Islam. The book even went so far as to claim that the house of Saud was of Jewish descent, provoking deep-seated religious anger against everything Western as the British were perceived to be the quintessential Christian nation of the time.

It was clearly an unmitigated success for the nationalists and a clear demonstration of how the conscience of an entire nation could be molded with a good story as long as it played on prejudices and values that were already present, and especially if it invoked religious sentiment. It was a shadowy world of lies and half-lies; success lay in subtlety and deceit. The stories about Armstrong and Cousteau had also been carefully crafted to give the impression that Islam was growing and attractive. Deception was a tactic of war specifically enjoined by the Prophet. It had to be something they excelled at.

After learning the truth, Ahmet had gradually overcome his Turkish aversion to the Arabs, and though he still considered the majority of them fickle and arrogant, there were cunning and devoted men among them who could still inspire the respect and fear that Hasan Sabbah's drug-induced assassins had centuries ago.

He snapped back from this nostalgic indulgence. There was much work to be done. He picked up the satellite phone, talked to the switchboard and seconds later a phone was ringing at the bank's London branch.

"*As-salamu alaykum.*"

"*Wa Alaykum As-salam.*"

"You have no doubt been put on alert"

"Yes, I just received word. The operation will be ready in the next forty-eight hours."

"Salih, I need you to give this job your personal oversight. Discovery of the brotherhood's involvement in this plot would be catastrophic."

"So, you are personally authorizing this?"

"I am. Use everything at your disposal. No cracks. No slips. No problems. Activate your mobile IT intercept group just to be sure things aren't moving faster than our man suspects. Schedule a grab for tomorrow night."

"Of course."

Ahmet hung up the phone with a smile. Salih was a good man. The interests of the Organization would be protected, and his promotion would deliver him from Cairo.

11

LONDON Salih opened the browser on his computer and typed in the URL for one of the countless trash blogs used by companies as link multipliers to increase their Google rating and drive traffic to their websites. He posted a comment under a prearranged pseudonym. For all intents and purposes, the comment looked like spam for a porn site with the appropriate link and nonsensical computer-generated text. The IT intercept team would be notified through an RSS feed of the new assignment and immediately put a trace on every possible avenue of communication Dr. O'Brien might use. He hit the "Submit" button and sighed with boredom. There was no challenge or sense of excitement in a hunt when the prey was so unsuspecting.

+——◆——+

CAIRO The Steward of the Council, a quiet man approaching forty, knocked on the door, poked his head in and said simply, "It is time."

Ahmet picked up his briefcase and followed the slender figure down the hall to where the video conference would take place. He noticed that the handle of the briefcase was wet from the sweat on his palms and his heart was racing. He began to analyze his fear. *What am I worried about? The fact that he can read people like the morning newspaper?* Was he afraid that the man would see his fear? His insecurities? His doubt? *Fear is counterproductive,* he told himself and recited the proverb his grandfather had ingrained in him as a child. *Fear of death will not delay it.*

The Steward punched in a code. When the steel door opened before him, Ahmet was still trying to get a grip on his nerves. They walked into the council chamber together. The carpet was a dark green. The walls were paneled with cherry and hung with the green and gold flag of the brotherhood. The chamber was used only for high level meetings by regional directors and lately, it had been in use almost constantly. The brotherhood's most ambitious project in years if not centuries was only weeks from its official launch. He sat his briefcase down on the elegant mahogany inlaid with mother-of-pearl forming a large *Rub el Hizb* star in the middle of the table.

67

He saw his place had already been chosen. There was a glass sitting on a leather coaster two chairs from the end of the table. He walked towards his seat and the Steward pulled back the chair for him to sit down. Then the Steward picked up the glass and filled it with water from an ornate silver pitcher sitting on a small stand beside the door and set it in front of him. The Steward pulled a remote control from underneath the folds of his flowing robe, pointed it at the giant plasma screen that hung on the wall and turned it on. For now, it was only a blue screen.

Turning to Ahmet and placing his right hand over his heart, he said, "Is there anything else, sir?"

Ahmet merely raised his eyebrows in the traditional Turkish sign of dismissal, and the man quietly closed the door behind him as he left the room. Ahmet could hear the numerous deadbolts slide into place and he visualized the Steward activating the electronic signal jammer with the keypad beside the door. In effect, it created a complete dead zone so that wireless signals of all kinds were scrambled and rendered useless. Nothing said in the council room, especially in a conversation with the spokesman for the Rightly Guided One, could leave the room.

Ahmet settled down into his chair and for some reason felt the need to look busy. He turned his mind back to the project. Internally, it was known as *Fethullah* and it had been almost a decade in the making, but it was already being discussed at the UN and other halls of power around the world as "Tolerance and Unity in a Multicultural World."

The name was innocuous. The objective was simple. Over the last thirty years, the oil-producing countries of the Middle East had amassed massive amounts of capital. Most of it had been invested in industry and finance, but the many debacles over the last few years, of which CitiBank was the latest example, had not only cost them billions of dollars, it had also taught the Arabs an important lesson. The world of finance was a complex game and the infidel was more crooked than a camel's neck. The doubters in the council had realized that the infidel must be won over or brought to heel. The infidel could never be an equal partner. Now, oil revenues would be funneled into more worthy projects and this was the most important of all. It was to be the final offensive, the last battle in the epic struggle to bring the world into submission to Islam.

Ahmet looked down at his watch. He had ninety seconds. This would be his first, and maybe only, chance to actually converse with the leader of the brotherhood. First impressions were everything. He closed his eyes for a moment and tried to imagine the secret abode of the Rightly Guided One. No one knew where he lived, but if rumors were to be believed, it could be in the Moroccan city of Tangier, or Saan'a in Yemen, or Islamabad in Pakistan. There was no end to the speculation, and no hard fact to base it on. He might live anywhere in the Muslim world. Some even postulated that he lived in Istanbul, but Ahmet found this hard to believe. His homeland was only recently starting to loosen the chokehold held for almost a century by a secular army enamored with the reforms of Atatürk and plagued with narrow-minded nationalism. The plasma screen on the wall flickered and Ahmet bowed his head to the screen in reverence.

"*As-salamu alaykum.*" The voice was rich and deep. What it conveyed to Ahmet was peace, wisdom and, most of all, power.

"*Wa alaykum as-salam,*" replied Ahmet. He looked up at the screen and his heart melted upon seeing the balding leader of the brotherhood, sitting cross-legged on richly embroidered pillows, dressed in brilliant white. The man's dark eyes were an ocean of peace, and he felt himself sinking into their warm embrace almost immediately.

"Allah smiles on those whose faith in His ultimate victory does not waiver. You know this, do you not?"

"Even if I were to forget, your sermons sow the seeds of truth in our hearts every Friday. May Allah be pleased with you."

"May Allah be pleased with all of us, Ahmet. We have not spoken before, but I have been following you for some time. I read your reports. My lieutenants are quite impressed with your performance. But, allow me to get right to the point. I am aware of the impatience that you are facing with our people in Egypt. I can sense in my spirit the grumblings and the earnest desire for jihad. It is on this point that I need your steady hand at the helm. A storm is brewing, Ahmet, a fierce storm, but our fleet is far from ready.

"Jihad is a state of mind, but not every day is the day of battle. When your enemy is stronger than you, it is essential to feign peace and cooperation. Fools like Bin Laden underestimate the resolve of the infidel to continue in error. Their impetuousness has cost us many years and thousands of lives. We must not fall into his error. Instead, we must prepare for war while pretending peace. Right now, the most crucial part of our mission is to win hearts and minds. We must create a fifth column and extend to the unbeliever an invitation to submit. We must have the patience of Job in affliction, and faith that our end will be as prosperous as his."

"What would you have me do?" said Ahmet quietly.

"It is the common man we must reach, Ahmet, the man on the street. We must preach patience and fortitude. Open conflict is foolhardy. Let this message be disseminated in all of our mosques. Send our people to speak with local clerics from every sect. We must squelch the warrior rhetoric and put on the face of peace even in the House of War. We must preach against the foolish Mahdi teachings of the Shiites. It is heresy found neither in the Qur'an nor in the reliable hadith. It causes the people to look for a heavenly savior, which does not instill diligence and preparation. We must not believe that Allah will fight our battles. It may sound like heresy, and yet I maintain, as I do in all of my sermons, that Allah cannot help those who will not help themselves. The deism of Benjamin Franklin did as much for America as anything. It made them self-reliant."

The man paused and took a sip of water from an ornate silver cup before continuing his prepared speech.

"The *ummah* is not yet prepared for holy war. We are not living in the days of the prophet, when the Byzantine and the Persian had essentially destroyed each other in a century-long war. Nor are we living in the days of Osman, when Europe was ravaged with plague and civil war. No, Ahmet. We contend with a civilization that surpassed us in innovation, discovery, and trade because our leaders were fools and ignored the wisdom of Allah. Our enemy is more formidable than any we have yet faced, and we are only now overcoming the age of colonialism and the fall of the house of Osman. We must be patient.

"Direct confrontation has brought only disaster. The rotten core of their social fabric will soon cause implosion. They forsake what little corrupted light is left to them in the words of the prophet Jesus. They have sold their soul to materialism and hired the entire Orient to make their goods. They consume, but they do not produce, so their accounts are drained while the Dragon grows ever more powerful. The days of the West are numbered, the end draws nigh; our message is patience. We must remain committed to this course.

"Unfortunately, there are still brothers who blindly preach nothing but jihad against the infidel and stubbornly refuse wise counsel. I have sent you a list of the names of clerics who have remained steadfastly opposed to our message. They must be persuaded. If their sermon on Friday does not indicate a change of heart, prepare the bowstrings. I will not have a single drop of their holy blood touch the earth. They are our brothers. But, if the Ottoman sultans could strangle dozens of their brothers upon ascension to the throne for the purpose of preventing civil war and dissension, we must be equally committed."

"Rest assured, my Master, it shall be done."

"*Inshallah.*"

"*Inshallah.*"

"One more thing, Ahmet. I was told just hours ago that there is a situation in London. Our ability to achieve our goals might be compromised if this is not contained. I would hate to see this become a news story when we have worked so hard to build trust. It is amazing that this document should come to light centuries later and at this particular time. The world is a testing place. This is but another trial, a chance to prove ourselves worthy and faithful. Allah is surely just in recompense. Use whatever means you have at your disposal to neutralize the threat."

"Servant of my Lord and His People, we are all keenly aware of how important this document is. Our team in London is moving as we speak."

"Excellent!"

"I commend you and your men to Allah."

"May He be pleased with you!"

"With all of us, Ahmet, with all of us..."

The connection was severed and Ahmet was left staring at the blue screen with the words of Fatih Gülben ringing in his ears...

12

LONDON   A man wearing a plastic surgeon's cap and latex gloves squatted beside the steel safe in Ian's closet. No one would have noticed, but he could tell his hands were starting to tremble ever so slightly. Sweat began to pop out of the skin on his forehead like worry beads. He had been working at the combination for fifteen minutes, which was ten minutes longer than it usually took. He turned the handle again, and to his relief this time it opened.

First, he made a mental snapshot of how the assorted documents were arranged inside and then he quickly sorted through the contents of the safe. His orders had been simple—general reconnaissance and a sweep for digital copies. He found a DVD with yesterday's date written on the front and stuck it into his bag. He closed the safe, walked over to the desk and turned on the computer. He took out a cell phone and sent a short text.

He adjusted the ID card that hung around the strap on his neck so that it could be easily seen as he left the building. Next, he drew a small bottle of penetrating oil from his bag. He looked through the peephole into the hall where he could see a cleaning lady sweeping the floor. He knocked from the inside of the door and she gave the All Clear sign, so he quickly opened the door and oiled the hinges before relocking it. They had squeaked terribly.

On the other side of the Thames, Salih's cell phone buzzed. The message was simple: NOTHING HERE. A cryptic message was immediately prepared and posted as a comment on three different blogs.

Ian arrived back at his house a little after eight-thirty that evening, plopped down in his comfortable leather chair and allowed himself a moment to just lean back and close his eyes. It had been an exhausting day of meetings in which he had had to be especially attentive to professional decorum, which always exhausted him. He loved his job as a lecturer and researcher. Political posturing, on the other hand, was a suffocating, but inescapable drudgery of academic life. It was more like jungle predation than civilization. The higher one moved up in the academic food chain, the more dangerous and cut-throat the predators became. The constant pretentiousness and self-aggrandizement occasionally bordered on buffoonery, and though he found it nauseating, it required careful navigation. His intuitive research genius and hard work gave him some degree of immunity from the political wrangling, but anyone who did not play had to pay. There was little doubt in his mind that he would have been selected to head the department long ago if he had viewed it more like the jungle it was. He was weary of it all.

He turned his computer on and logged into the university's online library. It was time to test his theory about the document. *First the date.* He looked for a calendar converter and plugged in the Islamic date Zeki had written down. *September 19th, 1736. That would be just two months before Sale's death. What about the seal?* Twenty minutes later, he poured himself a glass of wine and leaned back in his chair. *So, Zeki, you say it's a seal of sorts. Why didn't you just tell me it was a Sultan's seal?* He shook his head and smiled at Zeki's restraint. He had always been impressed by how the man handled himself, but for the first time he realized that what he most admired in the man could be summed up with a single word—caution.

He wasn't sure why, but suddenly Ian felt apprehensive. His intuition seemed to be paging his reason. Zeki had clearly withheld information. Why? He could think of no logical reason. Coupled with Zeki's low-key warning to keep the document close, it was like a needle pricking his subconscious. Had the bird been captured? Was that why the world was left with only half of the Spanish copy? Ian reread Zeki's translation, typed "SÜDDE-I SAADET" into the search field and clicked on the third link down. His eyes opened wide in wonder as he read. Zeki would have known Südde-i Saadet was just another name for Istanbul. He hid that from me too? Why? To hide the Turkish connection?

The doorbell rang and Ian looked at the clock. It was 9:35. He sighed, walked to the door and put his eye to the peephole.

"Mr. O'Brien, I wouldn't impose if it weren't important."

He opened the door.

"Good evening, Mrs. Askwith. How can I help you?"

The seventy-year-old widow stood there in a flannel nightgown with a tight-fitting white embroidered nightcap on her head.

"Mr. O'Brien, I meant to come over earlier, but I hit a snag on my cross-word puzzle, and it completely slipped my mind. I remembered just as I was turning in for the night."

"What is it, Mrs. Askwith?"

"I was at a neighborhood crime-stoppers meeting last week. Quite interesting. Have you ever attended one of those?"

"No, Mrs. Askwith, I haven't. My schedule leaves me precious little free time."

"That's no surprise with all the ladies calling at your door."

"Mrs. Askwith! I can only assume you are referring to Mrs. Herrin, so that would be a 'lady' not 'ladies'. Is that what you came to talk to me about?" he asked, trying to remain calm.

"Heaven sakes, no! Who you consort with is none of my business, although that dress she was wearing on Saturday looked more like black cellophane than fabric. You see, I simply adored Patricia. She will always have a special place in *my* heart even if she doesn't in yours."

"Mrs. Askwith, the woman is a colleague, nothing more. She is working with me on a research project. That's all."

"Well, that may be what it is *now*, but take it from me, Mr. O'Brien, that's not what the hussy wants. For Patricia's sake, and then God's, you'd do well to keep your guard up against floozies like that."

"Thank you, Mrs. Askwith, for the advice," said Ian with a sigh. "If that is all, I'd better get back to my work."

"Mr. O'Brien, you don't think I came over here to gossip about your love life, do you? I can do that with any of the other tenants. I told you about the crime-stoppers meeting."

"Yes, you did," Ian said, in a tone meant to convey his exasperation. "And, I told you I'm not able to attend."

"Who's asking you to? I came over here to tell you that they said suspicious activity should always be reported to the police, but I didn't know if it was suspicious enough."

"What, Mrs. Askwith? What was suspicious enough?"

"Well, the fellow from the telephone company who was in your apartment today."

"In my apartment?"

"Yes, I just happened to be looking out the peephole when he arrived. I would never do that, of course. Coincidence really. Anyway, I thought it was a service call until he came out with a surgical cap on his head and latex gloves on his hands."

"That wasn't suspicious enough for you?"

"I thought he might be compulsive-obsessive, suffering from pathophobia, amathophobia, or something like that. I called management after he left, and they said there were no scheduled service calls today. You know what was really weird though? He oiled the door hinges on his way out. Don't you think that was strange?"

Ian wasn't even listening anymore. He stood there like a bucket of cold water had just been dumped on his head. This confirmed everything he had just learned. More than that, it was proof that after three hundred years the game was still being played.

"Mr. O'Brien? Don't you think it strange?"

Ian said nothing. He merely stepped back, pulled the door almost to and then opened it again. The hinges turned as silently as a ghost moves through a wall.

"That is unusual. I'll have to check with the telephone company tomorrow. Thank you for letting me know."

"Not at all," she replied. "I did it for Patricia's memory anyway."

Ian watched as she went back down the hall to her own apartment, only closing his own door after he saw her go inside. He began walking through his home searching for any sign of intrusion. It was the same apartment he had sat in all night, and yet it felt different. A sense of personal violation hung heavy in the air, haunting him as he stepped through each doorway and opened every closet. Everything seemed to be exactly as he had left it, which meant only that it wasn't a common burglary.

It was another thirty minutes before Ian had convinced himself nothing was amiss. He looked at the clock. It was getting late. He would try to spend some time on *English sunset* and *Suri-Strend* tomorrow night. He shut down the computer and headed for the bedroom. When his head hit the pillow, it was with a silent, desperate prayer that Patricia would visit him again. Somebody heard.

┼━━━┼

The computer accepted the password and Windows began the two-minute process of installing start-up programs and connecting to cyberspace. He noticed there was an RSS feed from an art blog. He clicked on the link http://landscapeart19.blogspot.com. The browser opened to a photograph of a beautiful sunset, which he ignored entirely. He clicked on December 2010 and then the comments.

> FanofCairo says: Go red sunset! That is awesome! Did you take this yourself?

The man leaned back in his chair and took a deep breath. The operation was a go. He could feel his pulse quicken and knew that his sweat glands would be activated momentarily. It was strange how something as ethereal as a thought was capable of causing a physical chain reaction in the brain that affected the whole body. *No wonder Descartes had been a dualist.* It certainly seemed as if mind triggered the cascade of chemicals that put everything into motion and not vice-versa. He did not, however, have the luxury of time to engage the philosopher in an imaginary discussion of the metaphysical.

He had work to do and less than twenty-four hours to prepare. He went back to favorites and clicked on a different blog—http://art19travel.blogspot.com. He clicked on 2010 and left a comment under the red sunset.

> I am going to take one like that too. Yours turned out really good...

75

13

TUESDAY, LONDON   Ian slipped into consciousness as softly and effortlessly as a feather drifting on the wind. It was a strange feeling for him to find himself suddenly and completely awake without the normal sensation of sound. He hadn't heard a car drive by, a horn honk, a door slam, or anything else, much less an alarm clock. He had not even experienced the sensation of light gradually getting stronger as the sun rose...Then he began to swear softly. It was late morning. Golden light was streaming in the windows of his spacious apartment. He looked at the clock beside the bed and panicked. He had forgotten to set the alarm. It was 8:18 and the conference's first session would begin in just forty-two minutes.

His panic faded, and the memory of his dream came rushing back with such ardor and vividness that he fell back on his pillow in sheer delight. Patricia, his lovely wife, had been standing in a vast meadow of wildflowers that reached to the horizon, beckoning for him to join her. He wanted to cry. Not for sorrow at having lost her, but with the incredible joy of having been loved by such a beautiful soul. *No time for nostalgia.* Ten minutes later, Ian grabbed his coat, his bag and keys on his way out the door to meet the waiting taxi.

The crowded London streets slipped past in a blur that reminded him just how fast six decades of life had flown by, much of it filled with the drudgery of research in old libraries. Patricia had always been the spark that fired his passions when research turned into an academic grist mill. She had been a law student at SMU when they met. He was studying at the University of Dallas. She was the oldest daughter of a Protestant Scotch-Irish family that had left the Deep South after the Civil War. Sickened by the intrusion of carpetbaggers and their alliance with corrupt scalawags, her great-grandfather had packed up and headed west. She was a genuine Southern belle. Her family cherished the Southern charm and culture they had inherited. Ian's family, on the other hand, had emigrated from Ireland during the Great Famine and gradually moved west, stopping first in Tennessee, then moving to Missouri to join the abolitionist movement. His father, one of twelve children, had left the Ozarks for a farm in East Texas.

It had been a whirlwind romance. Graduate school had followed marriage with children making appearances in Notre Dame, London and then an early birth in Rome. With a PhD in Byzantine studies, the most promising career opportunities were all in Europe. So, O'Brien found himself pulled back to the continent his forefathers had left, and for twenty-five of the last thirty years, they had travelled the world, teaching, and conducting research at five different universities.

Patricia had always been gracious about their move. She possessed the charm, intellect and culture to enjoy every moment. She loved history and so Europe was a never-ending adventure of discovery for her. Yet, he had always felt guilty about taking her away from the simple life of pecan plantations, hay meadows, and cattle. It was a life the children never really understood. They had grown up in the urban centers of Europe, listening to Blondie, Dire Straits and Pink Floyd. He was afraid to even ask what his three grandchildren listened to. Now, from the backseat of a taxi, on his way to another conference, it all seemed like a lifetime ago—it almost was. He smiled at the prospect of seeing two of his three children later that afternoon. Patricia lived on in each one of them.

⊹┝═━┥⊹

Zeki could hear the first speaker of the morning session being introduced from the podium and he was tempted to curse fate. It was two minutes after nine o'clock. He carefully scanned every face as the late-comers hurriedly made their way up the sidewalk through the lobby doors and towards the conference hall. *Where is Ian?* The man was never late and this was not the time for him to be acting unpredictably. He spotted the tall, red-haired Irishman a few seconds later, cutting across the grass, obviously in a hurry. Zeki stood patiently in the hall waiting. The uneasiness on Ian's face flashed like a neon sign. The smile that had graced his face when he left his apartment had been replaced with a look of consternation as he mulled over the facts he had learned the previous night. Zeki could tell he had left home in a rush. His hair was disheveled and his tie was crooked.

He must have caught his reflection in the building's glass windows because he stopped before opening the door, took a comb from his pocket and started tidying his appearance. Once he was satisfied with his hair, he walked through the revolving doors, waved at the security guards and made straight for the main conference hall. That was when he noticed Zeki standing about mid-way down the hall. Zeki smiled and started towards him, but before they met, one of the conference room doors swung open and Ian found himself face-to-face with the department secretary.

77

"Dr. O'Brien, I have been looking everywhere for you."

"I'm sorry, Mrs. Davenport. I'm afraid I'm running a bit late this morning. Is everything quite alright?"

"Would I be looking for you if it were?" she said without the hint of a smile.

"Sometimes, I almost think your affection for me is purely self-interest," with the same expression she had just given him. She managed a weak smile.

"We sent the coffee machine out for repair yesterday. Well, the repair shop called and said the heating coil needs to be replaced and, on an old model like this one, the parts and labor will run about the same as a new machine. The copier has also broken down and several of the breakout session leaders are asking if they can run off some last minute handouts."

Ian sighed and waved her off. She could tell he was preoccupied, but she also knew that within fifteen minutes a solution for each of those problems would be set in motion.

"Good morning, Zeki."

"Good morning, Ian. You don't look so well. I hope everything is okay."

"Just running a bit late and we have a few logistical problems I need to deal with."

"I see. Well, I just wanted to talk to you about the document."

"If it is not urgent, maybe we could discuss it tomorrow."

"Of course, that is fine. I wanted to have a closer look at that seal. Shall we have breakfast together tomorrow?"

"Sure. How does seven o'clock sound?"

"If you can arrange feta cheese and olives, I would meet you at the crack of dawn."

Ian chuckled. Every Turk he had ever met felt the same about breakfast.

"You are my guest. After the lessons in hospitality you gave me in Turkey, I shall not fail you. I think you'll like this place."

"Okay. Tomorrow at seven o'clock then."

"Right."

Zeki turned and entered the conference hall and Ian stared at the closing door. Zeki's manner had been disarming. He had always felt there was a genuineness about the man, in spite of his guarded nature, and yet last night's revelation had changed everything.

―――

Dr. Brown walked into the department secretary's office on the fourth floor of A block. There was a copier humming in the back room, but no one was there and he sat down to wait. He was surprised five minutes later when Dr. O'Brien came through the door.

Ian nodded in greeting.

"Good morning, Dr. Brown. What a pleasant surprise. I would have thought you would be at the conference. Is there something that I can help you with?"

"Good morning, sir. I stopped by to ask if I might see that document again."

Ian set his briefcase down beside the secretary's desk and began to search for the office phone directory on her desk. Without looking up, he asked,

"Did you check your email? My secretary sent you a digital copy of that yesterday."

"That's curious. I checked my mail again not five minutes ago, and I still hadn't received it."

"Might have gotten hung up on a spam filter and sent to your junk mail folder. Did you check?"

"I did. No worries, though. I can catch her later, or leave a note asking her to resend it."

Brown made for the door and then stopped.

"You don't happen to have it with you, do you?"

"Dr. Brown, I would actually like nothing better than to sit down and go over that document with you again. I have done a bit of research myself and have a few questions of my own. However, right now, there are more pressing matters that I must deal with even if they are far more trivial. Why don't we talk about it over a cup of tea soon?"

"Of course. I understand. That sounds wonderful."

"Call me some time and we'll set up an appointment for next week, after the conference is over."

Ian found the directory and started flipping through the pages, looking for the number to the repair shop. He dialed the number and as he waited for someone to pick up, he wrote on a sticky note,

Please resend file to Dr. Brown. He didn't receive it.

"Hello. Yes, this is Dr. O'Brien from King's College, London…Fine, thanks…I believe you have a coffee machine of ours… Yes, that's right. Look, we really need that machine today if at all possible. If not, we'll need to borrow one until ours is fixed."

The secretary walked in as he hung up the phone. With some frustration in his voice, Ian asked, "What are we going to do about the copier? There will certainly be people wanting to make use of it and it won't do to have everyone coming over here."

"I just spoke with an aide in the library. She said that they have spare capacity during the summer break, and she is having one of the technicians move two of the library's copiers into the conference foyer."

"Wonderful." Ian looked at his watch and sighed. The first session was more than half-way finished and he wouldn't be able to attend even the first afternoon session if he was to be at the airport on time. Well, the least he could do was send Dr. Jones a text message and tell him that something had come up and apologize for not making the session. He flipped the phone open and cursed silently. The battery was dead.

14

CAIRO   The sun had almost certainly set in another blaze of glory on the horizon west of Cairo, but massive thunderheads blocked any view of it. It was late, but Ahmet had no intention of going home. He had hoped that word of their success would have reached him by now. He was a patient man though, and these operations were delicate. There was no need to risk making a mistake now. It had remained hidden for almost three hundred years, and Allah had seen fit to alert them of its presence as soon as it was rediscovered. His man had probably spent the day gathering intelligence and making preparations and would wait for the cover of darkness.

He had been reading and mulling over the case file for more than a day. They had been fortunate. No mistake about that. This document could have turned up anywhere. It would most likely have turned up in Tunisia or Morocco. Or, it could have surfaced in any of the Balkan republics and gone public before anyone was aware of it. It could have turned up in Australia as the incomplete Spanish copy it was meant to destroy had in the 1970s, almost two hundred and forty years after the fact. Instead, it had turned up right under their nose, in a place where they had abundant resources.

London was not only a bustling center of finance, but had also become one of the organization's most productive regional centers over the past thirty-five years. Oil could open any door. It had changed the face of the Middle East and ushered in a new era of influence that exceeded their wildest dreams. It had helped them amass incredible capital. After decades of being wasted by lecherous sheikhs, it was finally being funneled to wise men of faith who would advance the cause instead of being squandered.

He shifted his attention back to the screen. He should have at least had a scouting report back by now. His fingers began flying over the keyboard. He wanted an update. *Eternal vigilance is the price of power*, he reminded himself. The rationalist infidel, the American president, Thomas Jefferson, had said it was the price of freedom, but that could never be as gratifying, as exhilarating, and as addicting as power. *Let the Americans dream of freedom; it will do them no good when we have the power.* He hit return and leaned back in his chair to wait.

+)═══════<)+

LONDON   On the other side of the Thames, Salih's cell phone buzzed again. He flipped it open. NOT IN ATTENDANCE. The message was relayed immediately as a comment on three different blogs.

> NOT AT CONFERENCE. IT HAS MADE NO INTERCEPTS. PACKAGE PROBABLY ON HIS PERSON. F&F CONTACT DETAILS SECURED. ESTIMATED TIME OF RESOLUTION—8 HOURS.

Ahmet got his message. He didn't like it, but patience was the gift of Allah to the faithful.

15

Ian spotted them sitting at the back of the pub in their private corner. Gwyn called it 'face time'. She looked fresh and confident with her hair up in a bun. The tangerine sundress fit her personality—bright and sweet. Like her mother, she was cultured, demure and though she had an intelligence that bordered on genius, she did not aspire to make a name for herself. She was also the spitting image of her mother, with strawberry blond hair and blue-green eyes that sparkled like the sea one moment and shone like a cloudless day the next.

Like every father with young children, her brother Gilbert looked a bit ragged and tired. His red, white and blue Valentino Garavani tie hung loose around his neck. Ian looked instinctively at his son's lapel. A US flag in the shape of the Twin Towers was still there.

"Daddy, you look wonderful. I'm so glad we were able to do this."

Ian wrapped his arms around her neck. "You get prettier every time I see you, darling."

"Hi, Dad. Thanks for coming."

"Glad I could make it, son. I wouldn't have missed it for the world."

"Have we ordered?" Ian asked.

"No, of course not, Daddy. What are you hungry for?" asked Gwyn.

"I'll just have the usual fish and chips I guess."

"Vinegar not ketchup?"

"Of course."

"Gilbert, what do you want?"

"I'm really not that hungry to be honest."

"Come on, you can't just sit there and watch us eat. Daddy, what was that Turkish proverb we learned about that being bad luck or something?"

"I don't remember what you are talking about, dear."

"Daddy, you of all people should remember."

"I remember the trip. It was unforgettable. A fabulous six-day tour of

Topkapı palace, the Basilica Cistern, Hagia Sophia, the Blue Mosque, the Grand Bazaar, the Hippodrome..., but I don't remember any proverb."

"Remember when I was sick and we stopped for lunch at one of those places that serve...Oh, what was it called? Almost like pizza, but with a Turkish twist."

"*Pide.*"

"Oh, yes. *Pide.* Anyway, I was dreadfully sick to my stomach and didn't want to eat anything, but Zeki made a big to-do over it, and I finally ended up having a lemonade just to appease him."

"Well, I don't remember exactly, but it was something like 'All hell breaks loose if one eats and another watches.'"

It clearly hadn't changed Gilbert's feelings about dining with them.

"I know you mean well, Gwyn, but I think I may have an ulcer or something. I'd rather just have a cup of coffee so that I can finish my work on the plane." A look of mock horror came over Gwyn's face.

"An acidic cup of coffee is the worst thing you could have, Gilbert."

Her look was earnest, like her mother's, and he could tell there wasn't going to be any arguing.

"You don't feel well because you don't eat well. Ginger does her best, but you have to do yours. Now, you find something healthy on that menu, no matter how small and eat it. If you go to sleep on the plane, that will be because you need it. Besides, who knows when we will be together again? Can you imagine one of the disciples telling Jesus at the Last Supper that he didn't feel well, and passing on the bread and cup? Come on now. Let's make a memory here!"

Gilbert and her father looked at each other askance; the same thought going through both of their minds. *Where did that come from?* They didn't have to wait long to find out. After the waiter had taken their order, she cleared her throat and broke the news.

"I know this is going to sound crazy, and that you will try to talk me out of it. Please, don't waste your time. I'm moving back to the States. Uncle Henry is selling his blueberry farm. Aunt Bonny told me last week. She said it was killing him to see it leave the family. I found out how much it was going for, did some research and have decided to make a go of it. We're meeting this week to see if we can iron out the details. I'm going back to mother's farm. Doesn't that sound wonderful?"

Ian reached over and squeezed her hand. She loved nature and people.

"What about the start-up company you're involved in? I thought you liked Cardiff and your group of friends there?"

"I love Cardiff, Dad, and my friends are awesome, but the start-up is, well, it's started and we have already gotten an offer. I'm selling my stake in it to buy Uncle Henry's farm."

Ian sat trying to process it all. Henry was Patricia's brother. He had inherited the farm Patricia grew up on and every visit they made to the States was spent in their guest house.

"Ever since Mom passed away, I have wanted to go back and reconnect with family, slow down and explore my roots. More importantly, I want to breathe the air she did and find out what made her so special. I want to jump off the corporate ladder into a pond filled with catfish, work the earth, rediscover nature and maybe find some healing in the process…"

Her voice broke. No one spoke as she struggled to regain her composure.

"I really need this, Dad. I know Mom's passing has been hard for all of us. For some reason, though, the pain and the emptiness just aren't going away."

"I think that is a terrific idea, darling," interjected her father with the certainty that comes from knowing reason and logic would be unwelcome guests at this stage in the conversation.

"Work out the details and I'll be your first guest, but what about Uncle Henry and Aunt Bonny? What will they do?"

"Well, I'm hoping they'll stay on either in the guest house or the main house. They're getting too old to do all of the work and with no children…" Her voice began to break again. She sat there for a moment forcing the tears back. "I can't bear to see it leave the family. It is the most enduring memory I have of Mother and her roots. I would never forgive myself if I let them sell it."

Ian looked at Gilbert, who simply smiled and nodded in an attempt to be agreeable.

"Gwyn, my dear, that is an excellent idea, but I'm afraid you may find the company a bit more, shall I say, rustic than what you are used to in Cardiff."

The corners of her mouth upturned ever so briefly in acknowledgement of Gilbert's well-known contempt for rural Texas culture. He was enthralled with the corporate world, and in his mind, their relatives in East Texas were little more than country bumpkins. This air of superiority had always irritated Gwyn.

"You wouldn't know the difference between a human and a snake anyway," she said sarcastically.

"Sure I do. Snakes are the ones that bite in self-defense; humans strike for no reason at all."

Gwyn knew better than to let the discussion get side-tracked on this issue. Gilbert cared about investment schemes, productivity, maintaining America's super-power status and national security; the price he paid was the corporate carnage she knew surrounded him. The waiter arrived with their food. After he left, she turned back to her brother.

"You'd better eat up. Your plane will be boarding in fifty-five minutes, and I don't want to see anything left on that plate. It's too bad Gary couldn't be here with us."

There was silence. Gilbert pretended to take an interest in his food. She looked at her father. His face remained unchanged, his thoughts imperceptible.

"What's wrong with you guys?" The exasperation gave her voice a shrill quality. "He's still part of the family."

The silence continued as she looked from father to son, trying to detect some sign of compassion or feeling. Their faces were granite. A gray coldness settled over the table and she hung her head, grieved at and ashamed of their hardness. Gilbert finally broke the silence. She knew his impassive monotone was a mask meant to convey a sense of control and reason, yet his words lashed the air and stung not her ears, but her heart.

"A *family*, Gwyn, does what we are doing now. A *family* celebrates victory like they console each other in calamity. Desertion at a time of need, distance in sorrow, these are not what I understand family to mean. He is not part of the family right now. He has turned not only on us, but on our heritage, our culture and our values."

Ian sighed. "I love him, Gwyn. You know that. No one has suffered as much as I have when it comes to your brother. We can only hope that he comes to his senses. Let's talk about something else."

The finality in his tone of voice made it clear that now was not the time for dissent. So, the short time they had was spent catching up on Gilbert's kids and reminiscing about the fun times they had had with their mother travelling Europe and the Middle East. As always, it was too short.

"Dad, I have to go catch this plane. You and Gwyn stay here and keep talking."

They all got up and hugs went round the small circle. Gilbert grabbed his bags and they waved to him through the glass walls of the restaurant until he was out of sight. When Ian turned back to Gwyn, she was staring at him intently, then she dropped her eyes.

"Were you going to say something, Gwyn?"

"Well, yes and no. I mean I don't know. I want to, but..."

"Go ahead, dear. Is something bothering you?"

"That's not the right word really. I mean, it's just that I have been having these dreams of mother lately and...Well...I have been thinking of you a lot too. You were so busy with your career when we were teenagers and don't get me wrong, you were a great dad, but always so busy and now that Mom is gone..."

She dropped her head again visibly flustered and obviously trying to say something, but unable to form the words. Ian waited patiently.

"Daddy, I'm not going to be single forever and once I start my own family, there will be even less time."

She stopped again. Still, Ian waited. Then she blurted it out almost angrily.

"You could've retired last year. Why didn't you? Why are you still working? Gilbert and Gary and I are all splitting into different directions. Our family is splintering…Oh Daddy, why don't you retire and come back to Uncle Henry's farm with me? You can continue researching and writing there, teach as a visiting professor at SMU, participate in all of the international conferences, but I really need to reconnect. It's been years since we've really had much time together."

Ian sat there more shocked by this request than he had been by her abrupt decision to move back to her mother's home. He sat there wondering what to say. She came to his rescue.

"Don't give me an answer now. Just think about it, will you?"

16

Salih was getting apprehensive. The package had not been at the apartment or in Ian's office, but even more disturbing was the fact that Ian had been absent from the conference meetings all afternoon. He had instructed the IT intercept team to find his location from his cell phone signal, but that too had failed. *Was he on to them? Impossible. The old fool just found the document. Why did he turn his cell phone off? Why?* He knew Ahmet wouldn't sleep until he had received word that the mission had been accomplished, and if Ahmet was grumpy from lack of sleep, no one was going to get any.

◦──◦──◦

Just think about it, will you? That was all she had said and think he had. He had thought of nothing else all the way home. *Retirement?* He used to dream of retiring with Patricia in a small cottage with a garden surrounded by a rock wall and covered with begonias somewhere in the Mediterranean. Maybe Cyprus or Rhodes. The climate was perfect. It was relatively inexpensive, and it would put him just an hour away from Istanbul by plane. They would bask in the sun away from the cold, dreary climes of Northern Europe, spend lots of time playing Scrabble and reading books. There would be plenty of time to just enjoy one another, write poetry, take Gilbert's children for the summers, crisscross Anatolia from Ephesus to Artvin, studying its rich history.

For him, retirement had meant breathing the air of Homer and the Iliad, hiking in the mountains that Alexander the Great had traversed in his quest for world dominion, sitting in Hittite temples as the sun sank behind Mt. Nemrut. Maybe he could even poke around Antalya. If he could find a few more bilingual stones with Lycian script, he might even help scholars decipher one of the few remaining mystery languages. But the crowning jewel of retirement would have been spending weeks on end wandering through the streets of Istanbul with Patricia. He had spent his entire professional life studying the eastern capital of the Roman Empire, but there was so much more to be learned, and he would get to do it leisurely with his lovely Patricia at his side.

That had been the plan, but now she was gone and the dream had died. This thought snapped him out of his mental meanderings and forced him to think of the other thing Gwyn had mentioned—her dreams of her mother. Ian was not a superstitious man. Still, it seemed odd that they should both have had a string of dreams about her. Or was it so strange after all? He had lost his wife and love; Gwyn had lost her mother.

His taxi stopped in front of his apartment. He leaned over the seat to pay the Indian driver his fare. He liked the Indians and, because their taxis always smelled of curry, he had often joked with Patricia that they took an exotic, oriental chariot home each evening. He got out of the taxi. *The presentation tomorrow could be considered the crowning event of a lifetime of work. Maybe it would be fitting to retire after the conference.*

Two men watched Ian exit the taxi and ascend the steps to his apartment entrance. They were particularly focused on the briefcase in his hand.

⊹∺∺⊹

Salih was tired, and he still had a long night ahead of him. It was almost ten o'clock. London was still bustling. The city never went to sleep. *The wicked never rest*, he told himself. He had heard that Taipei and Tokyo were even more notorious for never sleeping. He had never been to the Far East, and, after those reports, he had no desire to go. He looked at his watch. It would still be several hours before they moved in. He leaned back in his chair and let his mind wander.

The Dragon in the East was rising. It had happened before. As always the *mu'min* were pressed from both east and west by the infidel. In the days of Genghis Khan and the Mongol hordes, the Muslim caliphs had grown lax in their application of jihad and the proclamation of freedom in Islam. They had become bloated with worldly pleasures derived from the taxes on non-Muslim minorities. They had forsaken *salat* and neglected *zakaat*. As a result, Allah had withheld his protection when the Mongol hordes swept out of Central Asia, sacked Baghdad and wreaked havoc in the Middle East for almost two hundred years. Yet, the Mongols had been the rod of discipline used to bring the faithful back to piety.

The Mongols had been an inexorable juggernaut. They had even taken Alamut, the impregnable fortress of Hassan Sabbah, the greatest assassin that the world had ever seen. The stories widely circulated in the West about Hassan Sabbah and his tactics were laughable. Marco Polo had said that young initiates to the secret Ismaili sect were drugged and then woke up in a beautiful garden with wine and virgins at their beck and call, after which they were drugged again and woke up in a dingy cell. They were then told that they had died and gone to Paradise, but had miraculously come back to life to complete one final mission. The story was obviously meant to help sell Marco Polo's new book and maybe help the feeble western mind understand why people would kill and risk death in order to attain Paradise.

They knew nothing of the power of *shahadah*—the confession of faith in the Creator of the Worlds. Allah had not deemed the infidel worthy of such magnificent faith. The Mongols had destroyed the Abbasid caliphate, but the chastened *mu'min* reformed their ways and eventually many of the invaders were won over. Genghis and the Mongols were great warriors. They were also fools led astray by Satan. They were not rightly guided and so did not understand the politics of religion. They had allowed religious freedom and equality for all their subjects. This had allowed Muslim missionaries to wield influence, thus ensuring their downfall, not on the battlefield, but where it mattered—in the hearts and minds of the people. Once they converted to Islam, there was no need for war.

Yes, the Dragon would rise again. He knew the East would be a formidable foe. Still, it was the spirit of the crusader that posed the greater threat right now with its secular atheism, immorality, and economic exploitation of Muslim peoples...Salih's blood boiled just thinking about it. Yet, like Genghis Khan, they allowed freedom and equality in religion and Muslim missionaries were pouring into every Western country, raising large families and winning their neighbors to Islam. The West was being led astray just as the Mongols had been. It was only a matter of time. Their ideologies would crumple in defeat before the onslaught of Mohammed's divine message.

They were not "rightly guided." Satan had deceived them with nonsense about equality and liberty. Arguments a five-year old could refute. Their delusion was powerful. They were incapable of understanding why humans could never be equal. The Qur'an and the *ulema* had decreed that there was freedom of religion for monotheistic belief systems, but equality? That was beyond absurd.

Under sharia, Christians and Jews were second-class citizens subject to onerous taxes, forced to wear special clothing, banned from striking a Muslim, bearing arms or even testifying in a court of law against a Muslim. This was, of course, the wisdom of Allah, a heavy burden in this life to persuade them to abandon the error of their ways and embrace the way of submission in Islam in order to attain eternal life. It had worked well for centuries. True, there were still pockets of Christians and Jews in the Middle East, but they were submitted minorities and inconsequential. A neutralized threat. They were nothing compared to the pockets of Muslims in the West. There were millions in Europe and America. He smiled to himself. The way of God would be victorious.

Salih looked back down at his watch. For all the fanfare about how important this job was, he was tempted to be unthankful. He had taken his second wife last week. It almost made him faint with desire to think that he could be with her instead of sitting here in the office. They were close to getting the British government to recognize their right to govern themselves by sharia law, but to avoid drawing attention to himself, the ceremony had been a clandestine one led by an imam at the local mosque. A small notification popped up in the lower right hand corner of the screen. He had mail.

THE SUN APPROACHES THE HORIZON.

Their man was back. Soon this would all be over.

⊢═══⊣

Ian read over his notes for tomorrow's presentation. Then he remembered his cell phone battery was dead, retrieved it from his coat pocket and plugged it into the charger. It lit up, and he turned it on to see if he had any messages. The screen read: 1 NEW VOICE MAIL. He would listen to it in the morning on his way to the university.

He felt too tired to even brush his teeth, but persevered anyway. Then he slipped into his pajamas, switched off the lamp and turned back the beautiful patchwork quilt that his wife had inherited from her grandmother. It was funny how some traditions outlasted the necessity which had birthed them. Her family had, by no means, been so poor that they needed to piece together tattered old rags to keep warm, but it was a tradition. Its true value lay in the fact that it was a labor of love with birthdays and anniversaries embroidered on every square. It was a true Southern masterpiece she had treasured and carried around the world for years.

Ian's head hit the pillow with the same prayer on his lips he had said every night for the past two years, except that tonight he asked for a repeat of last night's dream and it was answered.

17

WEDNESDAY   At 01:00 hours, the door to Ian's apartment swung open noise-lessly on freshly oiled hinges. Three masked figures clad completely in black slid through the door like shadows. Ian awoke with a hand over his mouth. He was secured before he was even fully awake. They left him lying on the bed gagged and bound hand and foot while they searched the house.

It had not been found in the search of the apartment, so the first place they looked was his briefcase. When that turned up empty, he was carried into the living room, roughly forced down into a chair and secured with a soft cotton rope around his waist. His hands were untied while one of the shadowy figures held him in a choke hold around the neck. In the darkness, he could sense their presence, but could not make them out. One of them walked up to the chair he was sitting in, leaned down to his ear and whispered,

"Old man, you may have no idea what we want from you, and then again you may know very well, but right now what you need to understand is how determined we are to get it back. What you found belongs to us. I have killed men for information not nearly as valuable, so save yourself and me the trouble of breaking you and tell us where the document is."

He thrust a notebook and pencil into his hand. Ian's mind was reeling. He took the pen and paper, but sat there motionless.

"Mr. O'Brien, I cannot risk allowing you to scream so please write down the location of the document. Once we have the document, we'll leave, and you can go back to bed."

Ian wrote slowly and deliberately, all the while trying to place the subtle, but distinct accent. He was fully awake now and desperately trying to buy time, so he could figure out what was happening. He held the notebook out for the man to read.

If you mean the letter I found, it's beyond your reach.

The man read what Ian had written and turned as if he was walking away.

Ian sensed movement. There was a blur as the shadow in front of him spun back around, and Ian doubled over in pain from a perfectly-placed blow to his solar plexus. The masked man stood for a minute looking down at the old professor gasping for air and then squatted in front of Ian.

"You old fool. A little cooperation would have gone a long way to resolving this."

Physical coercion in a crowded apartment building was out of the question. One of the men spoke in a foreign language and moments later the chair Ian was sitting in was lifted and carried to the kitchen table. The kitchen light was turned on, and for the first time Ian had a clear view of the intruders. Three masked figures dressed in black from head to toe, all of them wearing surgical gloves. Ian felt an arm wrap around his neck and tighten into a chokehold while another man stretched out his arm on the table. The third man pulled a loaded syringe from a small bag and removed the plastic sheath to reveal the needle.

"Mr. O'Brien, I am going to ask you one more time. Where is the document?"

Ian shook his head side to side, affirming his refusal to cooperate. The threat of psycho-narcotic torture was far more effective than the drug itself. The man wanted to allow time for fear to set in and have its full-effect.

"Mr. O'Brien, I do not understand you. You are an academician. This document is of no consequence to you or academia, but very dear to us, so dear, in fact, that I have been given explicit orders to use whatever means necessary to persuade you to talk. Once this drug is injected, you will be telling me everything I need to know, but it has unpleasant side effects."

Again, he paused for effect. Ian sat motionless. The man threw a large photograph down in front of him.

"This was one of my more interesting jobs."

When Ian refused to look down, the man thrust it in his face. Ian stared in horror at a grotesque frontal shot of a man's face with all of the skin removed from the left-side. From the look in the man's eye, he had still been alive when the picture was taken. Ian shut his eyes. His stomach did flip-flops. There was silence for a moment as the intruders waited for their private terror to take effect. The man looked at his watch.

"Mr. O'Brien, *I'm* not running out of time, but *you* are. What I *am* running out of is patience. Where is the document?"

Ian did not even open his eyes. He sat there in a daze while every clue he had pieced together over the last several days came into crystal clear focus. His captors waited silently for the gravity of the situation to sink in. They had seen it many times. Fear would squeeze every ounce of resistance out of him, the instinct of self-preservation would take over, and he would tell them whatever they wanted to know. Ian slowly raised his head. His eyes were bright and smiling. He said nothing. When the leader saw the look on Ian's face, he breathed a sigh, shook his head and said,

"Mr. O'Brien, we will finish this conversation elsewhere."

He immediately felt the grip on his arm and the hold around his neck tighten. This was followed by the prick of a needle.

Intelligence agencies around the world had searched for the holy grail of interrogation—a truth serum—since the 1930s. Billions of dollars later, the only real progress was a list of chemical concoctions that didn't work. There was no fool-proof way to slip past the firewall of the human conscious, take control of the mind and read data off of the cerebral hard drive. However, many useful things had been learned, and sodium thiopental was often used as an adjunct to interrogation.

The drug would not only make him groggy and easy to transport, it would also prepare him for questioning. Part of the effect was psychological; if the victim believed that he had been given a drug that would make him talk, then, when faced with physical torture, it was easier for him to rationalize capitulation as he was able to soothe his conscience with the idea that the drug had made it impossible for him to resist.

The men continued to comb the house, and scan electronic media for digital copies of the document. These were found on both the desktop and laptop computers, so they loaded a secure deletion program to overwrite the files. They also found a copy on the thumb drive in his briefcase. They checked his "Sent Items" He had apparently not sent the files to anyone. Still, to be on the safe side, their computer specialist intentionally corrupted Outlook's .pst file, and then did a recover to ensure that Ian had not executed a hard delete, which made normal recovery impossible while leaving the data in the .pst file. It was a long shot, but they had to take every precaution. Next, they recorded the professor's internet history and then performed a secure erase on the temporary Internet files, so that no one could delve into what he had been researching.

They were rummaging through the stack of papers on his desk when Ian started having difficulty breathing and slumped over, tipping the chair to the floor. One man rushed to remove the gag while the other two lifted him back into the chair. His breathing became more and more labored. They carried him to the couch. His breath was coming in gasps. They spoke among themselves in a foreign language. The panic in their voices was obvious.

Ian beckoned to the man doing most of the talking. The man realized the professor was trying to speak. He walked over to him and said, "You must be having a reaction to the drug."

Ian's mouth moved but the sound was practically inaudible. The leader knelt down and put his ear up to the professor's mouth.

"You have to speak up. I can't make out what you're saying."

The man's voice was less rough than it had been ten minutes earlier. Ian forced the words out, teeth clenched in a herculean effort to breath.

"Is this…how…George Sale…died?"

He paused, fighting for breath.

"Death…finds us…all. Take care…how…it finds you."

That was the last thing he was able to say. Five minutes later, the professor was dead. The man in charge began barking orders and raining curses down on the whole lot of them. If his curses had come to pass, the whole neighborhood would have been burnt with fire from heaven, swallowed up by the earth and erased forever. For another ten minutes, they looked around for the diary, but it was not there either. This revelation triggered another round of cursing as bad as the first. When Salih was informed of the situation, he said they were all bastard sons of a donkey and ordered them to leave without a single trace that they had ever been there.

18

Mrs. Davenport was irritated. By this time, she should have been on her second cup of coffee, but this morning she hadn't had a sip. When she arrived at the office, just after eight o'clock, Dr. O'Brien had still not picked up the disc she had left on her desk for him. It was the Power Point file he had requested for his presentation that morning. She had knocked on the door to his office. It had swung open, but he was not there. He had to be somewhere near if his door was open. Thinking that maybe he was in the restroom, she had gone back to her office and put the coffee on. When she returned a few minutes later, he was still not in.

She had called his cell phone. There was no answer. She had left a message. Her next call had been to the receptionist at the information desk in the conference hall. They scoured the building looking for him. He was nowhere to be found. *Maybe he was delayed in traffic? He would have called.* Besides, why was his office door open? She had to inform someone.

She scanned the faculty list looking for Dr. Jones' number. He was on the conference's organizing committee. Hopefully, he could make a last minute adjustment to the schedule. The phone began to ring, but before it was answered, Dr. Brown poked his head in the door.

"Have you seen Dr. O'Brien? I wanted to ask a question about how feedback from the breakout sessions was being collected."

"No, I am looking for him myself."

"No problem, I'll catch him after the presentation this morning."

Dr. Jones answered his cell phone.

"Good morning."

She smiled at Dr. Brown and pointed to the phone. He smiled that he understood and walked away.

"Hello, Dr. Jones. I'm afraid that Dr. O'Brien has not shown up yet today."

Dr. Jones did not take this news well.

"Pam, I'm standing on the platform in the conference hall getting ready to introduce his session!"

96

"I understand, sir. The disk with the Power Point presentation he planned to use is right here on my desk, but I can't find him. I have called his cell phone and his house and left messages in both places. He isn't answering."

"He wasn't at my session yesterday either, and he told me he was looking forward to it. Let me call my secretary and ask her to contact Dr. Bennet. She was going to present tomorrow morning. We'll have to ask her to switch places with Dr. O'Brien."

Mrs. Davenport hung up the phone and then bent down under her desk to turn the tower on, but stopped when her hand brushed the mouse and the computer screen came to life. *That's strange*, she thought, *I would have sworn I turned that off yesterday when I left.*

At precisely nine o'clock, Dr. Jones walked up to the podium and told the audience that, due to unforeseen and extraordinary circumstances, it would be necessary to change the program this morning. He asked that everyone be patient and assured them that the session would begin momentarily. For the first fifteen minutes, everyone in the conference hall had been quite content to chat over their coffee, but now he could see people casting curious looks around the conference hall as if attempting to actually see what was causing the delay. Dr. Jones was a model of composure. He minded the P's and Q's—Punctuality, professionalism, protocol. There was no Q, but he considered his list far superior to the Pints and Quarts of the English pubs in which the phrase had allegedly originated.

Inside, though, he was panicking. Ian's presentation was the result of years of research on the socio-religious factors surrounding the collapse of the Byzantine Empire. It was supposed to have been the highlight of the conference. *Where the hell is he?* Ian would never leave anyone in the lurch. He wanted to rush over to Ian's house and find out what in the world was going on. He was concerned and wanted to act on that. Instead, he found himself fretting over how this unprofessional glitch in the program was going to reflect on the university. He resented the fact that he had to stand before his colleagues apologizing for this disruption to the program. He could see that the hall full of researchers and professors had begun to get fidgety and impatient. *Where is Dr. Bennet?*

―――

CAIRO   Ahmet hadn't had breakfast and it was nearly time for his noon prayers. It was not quite ten o'clock in London, where the drama was unfolding. This was not turning out to be as smooth as they had hoped. The professor's last words and his temporary internet files were proof that he had figured out almost everything. According to Salih, their men had torn the place apart, only to come up empty handed. *What are we missing here?*

Somehow the package had slipped through their fingers. The IT intercept team said that Dr. O'Brien's phone had been off until he came home that night and that only one person had left a message during this time. The message was suspicious, but impossible to trace. The eyes of the man who had found the document would never open again. His sun had set last night, and now Ahmet regretted his sudden demise. Maybe the excitement and stress had caused a heart attack…

If he had been alive, he could have been persuaded to talk. Salih had seemed confident that the document was being carried in the man's briefcase. It had been a careless assumption. *Damn!* Ahmet closed his eyes, forced himself to shut out unproductive thoughts and get back on task. *Be methodical,* he told himself. *There has to be a break in the chain somewhere. Our man saw the physical document in Dr. O'Brien's hands on Monday. The operation was conducted less than forty-eight hours later. We know from his internet search history that he had probably figured it all out, and his dying words about George Sale confirmed it. Still, he couldn't have known he was in danger. It was impossible.*

But he knew that wasn't true. It was possible. It had happened. Ahmet's job was to find out how, and few could do it better. *Retrace every step, catalogue every conversation, every email, every…every everything.* He dialed Salih.

"*As-salamu alaykum.*"

"*Wa Alaykum As-salam.*"

"Do we have any leads yet on where the document is?"

"No, but Allah is all-seeing and aids those who keep faith. We are retracing his steps now. Our analysis should be finished within the hour."

"Salih, we know the professor was on the right track. I'm sure he already figured out almost everything. What we have to do is find where he would put something for safe-keeping. You said that there were irregularities in his routine yesterday. Did he not have a tail?"

"No, we deemed it unnecessary."

Ahmet knew that in Salih's place he wouldn't have put a tail on the man either. It was a difficult undertaking, and there had been no reason for O'Brien to be suspicious or for them to worry about evasive action. Still, hindsight was 20/20, and a tail might have prevented this undesirable situation.

"Find out where he banks, maybe he put it in a safe deposit box. Maybe he visited a trusted friend. Send everything that was recovered to PGP key *Hüdavendigar.*"

Salih replaced the phone on the receiver. The brotherhood refrained from using encryption on a regular basis because it drew unwanted attention. In fact, their American operations were forbidden from using it at all because it essentially meant extending an invitation to the FBI to install a trojan horse, Magic Lantern or whatever their latest key-logger was. American had already created the Big Brother society the populace feared, but it had all been done quietly, unobtrusively and in the name of national security.

Fortunately, the Internet had become such a garbage pile of information that it was possible to hide reams of information right in the open. The FBI was working hard on open source intelligence monitors to track the hundreds of thousands of blogs and junk websites. The fact that they publicized their efforts was proof their claims were bullshit. It was propaganda aimed at instilling fear and paranoia to prevent people from using it. *They might be able to search every website in the world and every blog for certain keywords, but what terrorist was going to use sensitive words in his communications?* It was ludicrous.

Ahmet had a dozen different encryption channels and just as many separate keys. Ahmet did nothing randomly, and Salih wondered what the choice of key signified. He was annoyed. It had only been fifteen hours since their team had tried to recover the document. They were working on it and had never failed a mission yet. *Why is Ahmet trying to micromanage this project?* If he had lived in Cairo as long as Ahmet had, he would have understood the man's desperation to get out.

+━━━+

Fifteen minutes into Dr. Bennet's presentation, Dr. Jones felt his cell phone go off in his breast pocket. It had been muted, but he hadn't wanted to turn it off in case Ian should call. He discreetly slipped into the aisle and walked through the doors to the side of the stage.

"Hello."

"Dr. Jones?"

"Speaking."

"Sir, I'm afraid there is a bit of a problem here. Dr. O'Brien's door is locked, and no one is answering. None of the neighbors saw him leave today. Shall I call the police, sir?"

"No, I will take care of it. Thanks for taking the time to stop by his place."

"Sorry I couldn't be of more help."

Dr. Jones hung up and dialed a friend. It was too soon to involve the police. *For heaven's sake, what would I tell them? That a professor had failed to show up for a lecture? If that were cause for concern, the police in London would never have a moment's rest.* Still, his friend, John McIntosh, might be able to offer some advice. He was now a chief superintendent at the Metropolitan Police Service. In spite of his new title, all his friends still called him Inspector McIntosh.

"This is Dr. Jones. I would like to speak with Chief Superintendent McIntosh."

"One moment sir, while I connect you." He looked down at his watch. It was just after ten o'clock.

"Dr. Jones, what a pleasant surprise. How can I help you?"

"Sorry to bother you, John, but I could use your assistance."

The professor quickly described how Ian had failed to show up for a most important lecture and related what he had learned.

"I can have a constable stop by and check it out. I'll call you as soon as I hear something."

"Thank you, John. I wouldn't normally bother you, but Professor O'Brien's presentation at this conference is essentially a summary of his life's work. I can't imagine what would have delayed him. It is so completely out of character for Ian not to let us know that he would be late. I'm afraid something must be wrong."

<hr/>

Zeki stepped up to the window at passport control and handed the female officer his passport.

"Good morning, Mr. uh... Sorry, I'm not sure I can pronounce this."

"It's Çölaşan."

"Mr. Murat Chorlashan"

"Couldn't have said it better myself."

She had the feeling he was only flattering her, but if she had just butchered his name, at least he was polite about it.

"Did you have a nice stay in London?"

"A bit on the wet side, but other than that, absolutely delightful."

He looked up at the clock on the wall. It was 16:00 hours. He would be safely out of the country in less than three hours. The officer stamped his passport and slid it back to him underneath the glass partition.

"Have a pleasant flight to Istanbul and do come back for a visit."

"Thank you."

Zeki put his sunglasses back on, kept his head down and made his way to the THY concourse. He picked up a Wall Street Journal on the way. Then he found a seat in the corner directly under a security camera, unfolded the paper and turned to page three.

<hr/>

Dr. Jones sat in his office drumming his fingers on the desk, looking blankly at the bookcase across from his desk and waiting for Cathy Davenport. He was more than a little peeved at the question mark hanging over the rest of conference program. *Ian's lecture will take the place of Dr. Bennet's, but if he is ill and can't make his presentation, then what?* He looked down at the list of contributors to see if any of the breakout session topics seemed worthy of a more prominent place at the conference, and he swore softly when he saw that at least two breakout sessions that very afternoon had been related to the research Ian was presenting and were supposed to have expanded on the theme.

Beads of sweat had formed on his brow in the last five minutes. It had turned into an exceptionally muggy day and with the extra pounds he was toting around, it would be late October before he could get through a day without drenching his undershirt. He loosened his tie.

Exercise was anathema to him, so, inevitably, every year he had grown a year older and a few pounds heavier. He had hoped there would be a note from McIntosh on his desk when the afternoon session was over. There wasn't, and now he was sitting at his desk, wondering what had happened. He had just started an internal debate as to whether or not he should go over to Ian's apartment when the phone rang. He had the receiver to his ear before the first ring ended.

"Hello."

"Dr. Jones?"

"Good afternoon, Superintendent."

"I don't know how to break the news to you, but I'm afraid Professor O'Brien is dead, sir."

"Dead?"

"I'm sorry. I have a team over there now with forensic experts. They are in the process of preparing their report, but the medic I talked to said he suspected a heart attack in his sleep. I don't have any further details. A full report should be ready first thing in the morning. I'm very sorry. We will need to notify next of kin. Can you help us with that?"

Dr. Jones stared blankly at the wall and struggled to control his voice.

"Yes, of course, the department should have contact information for next of kin. I'll have that sent to you right away."

He hung up the phone in disbelief.

19

Washington, DC, 12:30 PM   Gilbert pushed the door open and began undoing his trousers. The meeting had lasted three and a half hours without a single bathroom break and he was about to burst. He wished he could relieve his stress as easily as his body disposed of water. Before he boarded the plane last night, he had known that it was going to be serious, but this was way bigger than he had ever imagined. Jim Ross, Director of Operations, had picked him up from the airport and given him a foretaste of what was coming.

Select company directors and the technical team from McLean, Virginia had come in for the meeting at corporate headquarters in DC. Gilbert's company, Data Security International, provided security services to the world's largest firms, including law firms, banks and government institutions. DSI was an elite company. There had even been a rumor that the FBI was its largest shareholder, not directly, of course, but through intermediaries. So far, he had not been able to confirm the claim. He suspected it was true but in the shadowy world of intelligence, evidence was hard to come by. Maybe it was just a rumor started by the FBI as a decoy to provide cover for whatever other company it really did use.

The door opened, and Gilbert turned his head to see Mike Tate take his place at the next urinal. At six-foot-six and two hundred and sixty pounds, Mike was as physically daunting as he was intellectually intimidating. He was the company's most senior analyst, and resident pain in the ass.

"Hell of a deal, isn't it? The biggest blunder in the history of the company wrapped around Ross' neck like an albatross."

"He's going to blame it on software development for leaving a backdoor," answered Gilbert. "And the Director of Development will say the problem is the customer's failure to comply with the terms of the service contract to regularly implement upgrades and new releases."

"It's all bullshit. We don't even know how it happened."

"Well, Ross made it clear that he expects me to find out," said Gilbert, zipping his pants and walking to the sink. "Finch and Moreland's case before the International Court for the Settlement of Investment Disputes is worth 400 billion dollars. The investment consortium who brought the case against Libya is one of their biggest customers."

"With stakes that high, I think the company should have done a better job of protecting their data," replied Tate.

Gilbert sighed, "You would think the case is cut and dried. The Libyan government seized oil and gas wells, refining capacity and a pipeline network worth almost sixteen billion dollars."

"Nothing's cut and dried, O'Brien. How long do you think it'll be before they have a team of lawyers subpoenaing us for records?"

"That is what we are here to prevent, Mr. Tate. You're throwing in the towel a bit early, don't you think?"

He punched the silver knob on the hand-dryer and started rubbing his hands together. Mike had to raise his voice to be heard.

"They're going to want hard evidence about how and when this happened, a chain of discovery."

"Yeah, wanting it and getting it are two different things, but we'll do what we can."

"According to your report today, even after poring over system analysis reports for hours, no one knows how it happened. Your guys said there's no evidence that the client's security was breached. No spyware was detected and no files were erased. All of the traffic on every port has been reviewed and there's no sign of suspicious activity. Seems like Finch and Moreland have a mole."

"Or we do," remarked Gilbert dryly.

He knew Mike's assertion would be the angle DSI would take because it absolved them of all responsibility. Yes, they were responsible for background checks on employees. Yes, they monitored all of the employees' personal Internet activity. Yes, they provided the hard disk encryption for company computers, but at the end of the day, they could not be held responsible for a rogue employee. Mike zipped up and joined him at the adjacent dryer. Gilbert's dryer switched off, and he moved to the mirror.

"Do you believe their story?" asked Mike.

"Which part?" responded Gilbert, trying to sound matter-of-fact.

"The part about them discovering the leak because one of the lawyers on the opposing team left a disk in a folder of exhibits."

Gilbert kept looking at the mirror, brushing a stray hair or two back into place with his hand.

"Why shouldn't I?"

"Sounds like too much of a lucky break to me."

In the mirror, Gilbert could see Mike leaning against the wall at the door.

"Listen, Gilbert, I know you play your cards close, but you seemed to be hedging a bit with Ross in the meeting. Does your team have a lead?"

"To be honest, all the system analysis is clean. But, I found some curious stuff in my analysis of the metadata in some of our files that they had decrypted."

"Curious in what way?"

"I'd rather not say until I've finished the analysis."

Gilbert turned back to the door only to find Mike blocking it.

"Couldn't you at least tell me what your hunch is?"

Gilbert didn't like the look in his eye. Mike had worked his way up in the security business by staying one step ahead of his opponents, and he had a reputation for ruthlessness.

"I'm sure that Ross wants me to keep the circle tight on this."

Mike reached over and punched the knob to turn on both hand-dryers. He walked forward until he stood just inches from Gilbert's face and said in a voice so low he could barely make it out above the hot air blowing in the background.

"I know what you found. DoD decryption shadows in the metadata on those files. I already know what you suspect. The boys at the FBI were sloppy. Just let it go. DSI is in no danger, and we wouldn't want your part in Finch and Moreland's lucky break to become public knowledge, now would we? "

Gilbert couldn't believe his ears.

"I don't know what you're talking about."

"I'm sure you wish that were true. I'll admit that I had pegged you for a play-by-the-book type. Never thought you'd break the law. You're frugal too. I wouldn't have thought you could pull it off for a mere 29K."

"Tate, an Islamist government illegally seized the assets of private companies invited to invest in their infrastructure. That is a breach of international law. And we knew the French had evidence to prove it. They refused to hand over subpoenaed documents or produce the witnesses Finch and Moreland called. All they wanted was proof that the other side wasn't acting in good faith."

"So, you organized a third-party heist to steal their data. Not exactly legal though, was it? See, I didn't think you had that pragmatic the-end-justifies-the-means attitude. I took you for an idealist."

"And I didn't know you were moonlighting for the FBI. Are you telling me the US government has betrayed an American law firm to protect a corrupt state, ignoring the legitimate claims of investors?"

"I know this comes as a bit of a shock. Still, it shouldn't be too much of a surprise. You are quite the conspiracy theorist."

"I don't know what you're talking about."

"Oh, you think I don't know about your research into DSI shareholders and possible connections with the FBI? I know every lead you follow. You got that part wrong by the way, but you're too close to the truth for your own good. Curiosity has killed more than cats, Mr. O'Brien."

"So, it's the CIA that sold them out?"

"You already know more than it is safe to know. I like you, O'Brien. I'm providing this warning off the books and as a professional courtesy. Let's see a clean analysis from your team. What do you say?"

Gilbert took a deep breath and turned his head away to look at the reflection of the two men in the mirror. He had to make a decision.

"Fine," he said finally, "but I expect…"

"There are no conditions, Mr. O'Brien. "I'll see you around." And, with that, Tate turned abruptly and left the room.

Gilbert turned back to the mirror. He hardly recognized the face he saw there. His skin was pasty white. One question kept racing through his mind. *Is Tate a guardian angel or the angel of death?* He didn't know what to make of the warning, but the revelation that Tate knew about his part in procuring contractors to steal information from the French left him feeling naked. Ross had assured him it was a circle of two.

He felt the familiar vibration on his thigh as the Blackberry he had silenced for the meeting began to ring. He fished it out of his pocket and looked at the screen. It was a London number that he did not recognize. He waited for the caller ID to identify the number. He knew it would pop up on the screen before the second ring. The screen changed and his eyes narrowed as he read the words Metropolitan Police.

"Hello, Gilbert O'Brien speaking"

"Mr. O'Brien, John McIntosh with the Metropolitan Police Service. Do you have a moment?"

"I was just leaving for lunch with some of the company directors, but sure, how can I help you?"

"I'm afraid it's a serious matter. I need to ask you a few questions. You are the son of Ian O'Brien, aren't you?"

Gilbert answered with suspicion, "As a matter of fact I am. Why? Is something wrong?"

"Are you in London?"

"No, I am in Washington DC. I flew out of Paris yesterday, saw my father on my layover in London and arrived in DC last night."

"Mr. O'Brien, I am very sorry to inform you that your father has passed away."

Gilbert hardly skipped a beat.

"I'm quite sure there is a mistake. I saw him only last night. Are you sure you have the right O'Brien?"

The man on the other end of the phone cleared his throat.

"Yes, son. Ian O'Brien, Professor of Byzantine Studies at London University. Your father died in his sleep last night."

"You're serious?"

"Unfortunately, I am. I'm really very sorry. You were the first contact in the university file. I understand that Mr. O'Brien's wife, your mother, Patricia, passed on two years ago. If there are any other next of kin..."

Senselessness was the first feeling that welled up in Gilbert's heart, not grief or pain. There would be plenty of that later on. Right now, it just made no sense.

"No, no. Thank you. I'll contact my brother and sister."

"I understand. I suppose someone from the family will want to be here. I can have an officer meet you or a family member at the airport if you like."

"Very kind of you, but there is really no need."

"Very well. If there is anything else I can do for you, please let me know."

"I would like to know the cause of death, of course, but I suppose you won't share those details with me on the phone."

"I'm sorry, but that is correct, Mr. O'Brien. I am not at liberty and don't even have the report back myself. You can be sure there will be a thorough investigation. I have my best people working the case."

"Thank you, Mr....um..."

"McIntosh."

"Mr. McIntosh."

"Stop by my office when you arrive and I will be sure that you have every assistance."

Gilbert hung up the phone. Suddenly, he felt nauseous. He also felt alone. Then he remembered Gwyn and he felt even sicker. He couldn't break it to her on the phone. If he could catch her in Dallas, they could fly back to London together. That settled, he turned his attention to the matter at hand. His boss wasn't going to like it, not in the middle of this crisis, but Tate had already told him to make himself scarce. They'd just have to get along without him.

⬦

"Senator Giovanni's office."

"Hi Ashley. This is Tate."

She lowered her voice just a little and spun around in her leather swivel chair so that she faced the wall.

"Hello stranger. It's been so long, I'm not sure I'd recognize you."

"You know how it is."

"Let's say I don't."

"Listen, can we talk about this later?"

"Okay, how's seven o'clock at Altiramisu?"

106

"Can't do it tonight. I'll be boarding a flight for Paris then."

"Then, we can rendezvous at the airport."

"Tonight's not a good time, Ashley. Can I speak with the Senator?"

"I'm afraid the Senator is not in. Can I take a message?"

"Just tell him the Libyan problem is solved."

"I didn't know we had one."

"I just told you we don't."

"Maybe not with Libya, but with me you do."

"I'll make it up to you."

"I'm not sure you can."

"This trip to Paris will be a quickie. But, I'll have to go back for a trial in the first week of October. Maybe, you could arrange for some time off and join me."

"As long as you promise it's worth my while. No quickies."

"I promise."

+┣━┫+

DALLAS, TEXAS   Gwyn fished the ringing phone from her purse and looked at the screen.

"Hello, Gilbert?"

"Yes, it's me. You sound surprised. I hope you had a good flight."

"Lovely, until we hit customs, of course. I know this is going to sound awful, but a little profiling would speed things up there a bit. I've never seen it so bad here at DFW."

Gilbert managed a weak chuckle.

"Texas may suit you better than I thought."

"Oh brother, give me a break. You're in the security business. Tell me, how many of those messages intercepted by the FBI calling for terrorist attacks on innocent people were from narrow-minded, bible-belt, evangelicals and how many were from Middle Easterners of a certain religious persuasion?"

It was not the time to argue the fine points of civil liberty with her.

"So, are you driving out to Uncle Henry's?"

"If the truth be told, I spent the morning shopping at the Galleria. Now, there is culture for you. I have just sat down at La Madeline's to have a bowl of tomato-basil soup."

"Good. Look, I have to come to Dallas. In fact, I'm on the next plane. Why don't you pick me up at the airport?"

Gwyn fairly squealed with delight.

"That would be wonderful. We can go out to the farm together." She cut herself off mid-sentence. "But, you are coming on business, aren't you?"

"Sort of. I mean, I won't be able to visit the farm. I'll be on American Flight AA773. Don't make any plans, and bring your bags with you. Okay?"

107

"Will you tell me what's going on?"

"No."

"Okay, whatever you say."

"Alright then, talk to you soon, dear."

Gilbert felt like a hypocrite when he hung up the phone, but he had no time to wallow in guilt. He had a flight to book and a lost brother to find. Gwyn sat there puzzling as to why Gilbert had addressed her as "dear." He hadn't called her that in years.

20

CAIRO   The city was hosting another spectacular sunset, though few of the city's almost seven million residents could see the sky for the concrete labyrinth that suffocated them. Ahmet listened as the final call to prayer was sounded from hundreds of minarets across the city. The absence of emotion on his face was merely a testimony to the tremendous amount of self-control he had cultivated since his initiation into the brotherhood. His mind, however, was racing. The brain strain required to get through this day had brought him to the brink of mental exhaustion. He was extremely perturbed at the team in London. *How can such a simple job go so wrong?*

It didn't matter now. He tried not to think about the mistakes and focus instead on a way forward. He was a problem-solver, a mover, a man who made things happen, but he knew his limits. He had gone over the report again and again looking for clues, only to come up empty-handed. He opened a new email and began jotting notes for Salih.

They had no idea where Ian had been Tuesday afternoon or evening. He had made no phone calls. Indeed, his phone had apparently been turned off. *Had the professor been on to them? It seemed unlikely.* Their IT surveillance team had managed to get his phone records for the 24-hour period before his death. Only one was somewhat out of the ordinary. The caller had left a message, saying that he had information that would help Ian solve his puzzle. *Had the caller been referring to the document?* The problem was that the call had been made from a pre-paid SIM, purchased that same week, and had been paid for with cash, so it was impossible to identify the caller. Salih said he was working on a theory. The other callers were of no consequence, a few professors and conference participants.

A digital copy of the document had been found on both Ian's home computer and the secretary's computer. The one from the secretary might have turned into a lead except for the fact that the body of the message simply said, "Here it is," followed by the secretary's university signature. If she had addressed the recipient, it would have been simple, but even the fact that she didn't meant something. Obviously, she knew the recipient, and was therefore comfortable with a more casual style. Salih's team was working on the email address. Ahmet racked his brain for answers. They needed more data.

The digital files on Ian's computer and the secretary's computer had been inconspicuously and securely over-written with a secure delete protocol which exceeded that specified by US DoD 5220.22-M, so it was not going to be recovered. As far as they knew, there was only one digital copy unaccounted for, the one sent in the email from the secretary, and, of course, there was the original document.

A plan began to form. First of all, it was now imperative that the public announcement of Ian's death relate it as due to natural causes. Maybe the mysterious possessor of the digital copy would fail to draw any connection between Ian's death and the document. Discovering where Ian had been that afternoon was priority now. It would also be the most difficult piece of the puzzle. He would have a London operative with Scotland Yard hit the street with a picture of Ian and ask all the local cab drivers if they had picked up Ian and, if so, where they had taken him.

They would also need all the street video they could find. That would be easy since London boasted the most extensive system of security video cameras on the planet. There were hundreds of observation points around the city and security cameras installed at every major intersection. The tape that would need to be reviewed was less than twelve hours, but, multiplied by hundreds, it meant long hours in the London office. *That is the price the London team will have to pay for bungling this one.* He reviewed the notes he had been jotting down in the email. Satisfied, he hit the "send" button.

For the first time, his face registered emotion. He smiled. He had been so intent on solving the problem, and so perturbed at the mistakes, that he had forgotten that his earthly life was merely a test of his faith and submission to the will of Allah. He knew they would find the document like he knew that the trial he now faced was his destiny. He lifted his hands, palms up, and murmured a prayer of thanks for being considered worthy of the trial.

21

ISTANBUL, TURKEY   The avant-garde bookstore on Istiklal Avenue, the street the French were referring to when they spoke of Istanbul as "the Paris of the Orient", would have made the father of modern-day Turkey proud. Gary looked down on the crowds of people below. The energy was an invisible pulsation he could feel in his spirit. He wanted to be down there mixing with the crowds instead of proctoring an English grammar test. He looked at his watch. *Ten more minutes.* His eyes ran over the silent group of nine students with their heads bent in concentration on another practice TOEFL test, and then he went back to the window.

The avenue ran down from the lofty Taksim Square to Galata Tower. It was closed to traffic except for a single tram that ran every fifteen minutes for those pedestrians who didn't have the time or energy required to duck and dodge their way to the other end of the street, weaving through raucous groups of students, gawking tourists, amorous lovers and the occasional focused businessman. A favorite hangout for both locals and tourists, the avenue was a constant stream of humanity. It was the best place for people-watching in the whole country. One could sit in a Turkish coffeehouse surrounded by authentic Ottoman furnishings complete with the *nargile* water-pipes, or in a modern café like Gloria Jeans Coffee. Somewhere along the nearly three-kilometer avenue there was sure to be a gypsy musician playing a violin or harmonica and occasionally there was an *oud* as well.

It epitomized everything about the Republic Mustafa Kemal Atatürk had envisioned when he proclaimed the foundation of a secular state in 1923, thus ending over six-hundred years of Ottoman rule. It also left the Muslim world without a Caliph for the first time since the Prophet's first converts had stormed out of the Arabian furnace with fiery swords, carving out an empire for themselves and branding a crescent moon across the religious landscape of the Middle East. For this, Atatürk was, of course, reviled by pious Muslims. Many believed that every century a proto-type of the Anti-Christ or *Deccal* was born, and no small number believed that Atatürk was the twentieth-century version. He had liberated women and allowed them to study, encouraged science and the arts, and insisted that government authority not be based on religion. Some said that he was also a spiritual man, but so many myths had grown up around this legendary political and military leader that it was hard to separate fact from fiction. Spiritual or not, the man's fondness of spirits, particularly *raki*, was unquestioned.

The fruit of the revolution was everywhere on the street below. After being the de facto leader of the Islamic world for four hundred years, the Turkish people had set a new course, one that was diametrically opposed to that taken by their Ottoman forefathers. They had been the protectors of the faith and the holy sites of Mecca. They had led the jihad against the infidel for six hundred years and had come to the aid of Muslims from Spain to India. Now, they seemed to have been molded into a civil society with democratic elections, freedom of the press, co-ed universities, a rapidly growing industrial manufacturing base and telecommunications infrastructure, civil society organizations, free capital markets and even a pornographic film industry. In other words, Turkey had all the trappings of a modern society, all of which would have been unthinkable under the Islamic rule that existed a mere one hundred years ago.

Gary had devoted all of his spare time in the last six months to studying the history of these enigmatic people. Atatürk had somehow managed to transform the warrior Turks into a country which, at least superficially, resembled a secular democracy, and he had summarized the foreign policy of the new republic with his famous slogan *Yurtta Sulh Cihanda Sulh*, which was translated in the West as "Peace at home and peace in the world." His stellar leadership had not gone unnoticed and in Time magazine's "Man of the Century" competition, westerners were shocked to see Atatürk come in second after Winston Churchill. The surprise felt by ordinary western citizens confronted with this fact was only evidence of their ignorance and naivety. After all, his abolishment of the Caliphate, which had served to rally the armies of Muslims to the banner of Islam for centuries, was considered by many intellectuals in the Middle East to have truly been one of the great achievements of the twentieth century. After centuries of uninterrupted warfare, the Turks had gone almost eighty years without issuing a declaration of war or invading a neighboring country.

Well, almost...But then, the invasion of Northern Cyprus on July 20, 1974 could almost be forgiven, provoked as it was by a coup executed for the purpose of annexing the island to Greece and suppressing the Turkish minority. The resulting massacres and clashes between the Greek and Turkish populations on the island had to be stopped and the Turkish Armed Forces accomplished this quite surgically.

It was also difficult to view the operations of the Turkish Armed Forces against PKK guerillas as a declaration of war since they were directed at domestic insurgents. There were, however, several million Kurds who would take issue with this point of view. Three thousand Kurdish villages had been deserted, close to half a million people displaced and tens of thousands killed. The only other operation by the Turkish military in the twentieth century that could be defined as "war" was the Turkish participation in the multi-national United Nations force in the Korean War. Indeed, the Turkish units performed very well and their tenacity and courage were commended by many American officers. Just two years later, Turkey became the first and only Muslim country to join NATO. With the eighth largest army in the world, modern-day Turkey still evidenced the heart of a warrior. No slogan of Atatürk could ever erase that.

Atatürk would have been proud of the bookstore and what it represented. He would have been proud that the country was moving towards full membership in the EU, and the Turks were, as a whole, proud of him as well. But somewhere deep down in his soul, the Turk seemed to be conflicted. On the surface, there was convincing proof, like this bookstore, that a paradigm shift had been made, but the Turkish soul had an alter-ego and some said Mr. Hyde was starting to put in more regular appearances. Acts of violence against foreigners, the murder of Catholic priests, Armenians and Protestant missionaries, as well as the resurgence of Islamist political parties once every twenty years, were all positive proof of the conflicted soul, the alter-ego, the split personality of a culture torn between East and West.

The timer on Gary's watch beeped, eliciting groans of disapproval from the students.

"Okay, class. Test is over. Please pass your papers to the front."

He collected the papers and the students began gathering their books. The tallest boy in the class raised his hand.

"Yes, Murat?"

"Will we have the results tomorrow, *hocam*?"

"Yes, Murat."

"Thank you, *hocam*."

"Make sure you all do your homework. Tomorrow's lesson depends on it." He turned to go, but then stopped and said, "If any of you have Angela's number, give her a call. She's missed the last two lessons."

Murat turned to the attractive brunette standing beside him.

"Do you have her number, Esra?"

"Yes, I will call her for the *hocam*."

"Thanks, Esra. See you guys later."

Gary made his way to the small back office and knocked on the door. There was no answer. He turned the handle. It was locked. He put his head in his hand and sighed. Then he knocked again and waited. He heard what sounded like a book fall on the floor, then, a stifled moan.

"Eray. I need to get my stuff out of there. Let me know when you're finished."

He sat down at the nearest table with his back to the door. He was beginning to worry about Angela, and after their last conversation, he had reason to. Twice, they had gone out for tea after the lesson, and the last time she had really opened up. In some ways, they were like oil and water. A chemical engineering graduate from the University of Bucharest, she was five years his junior. She came from a poor family, and only managed to get an education through a competitive state scholarship based on university entrance exam scores. After graduation, she had landed a good job at a petrochemical factory making plastic.

Her older sister Bianca, however, had been less fortunate. After three attempts, she finally gave up on the university exam. Determined to help her younger brother get the education she had missed, Bianca had taken a job as an *au pair* in Istanbul three months ago. Her father had protested, but there was no work in Romania. She loved children and the salary was decent, so she had pestered her father until he consented, packed her bags and left. Except for a small note hastily scribbled on a postcard they received last month, they had heard nothing from her.

The note had been a call for help and her father had hopped the first bus to Istanbul in the hopes of finding her. Every night, he called home with no news. He said he had found a lot of girls trapped there, deceived by promises of employment and then forced into prostitution. Their lives were miserable, often seeing ten or more customers a day. Then, one night, he didn't call. Nor did he call the next day. It was a week before they heard from him. The phone call had been short. He simply said he was he was on a bus heading back home. What he didn't tell them was that he had been beaten to within an inch of his life for asking questions and passing out pictures of his daughter in the wrong part of town. They had broken both of his wrists, his nose and his collar bone, warning him never to come back. So Angela had quit her job and come to Istanbul to find her sister. Now, she hadn't shown up for class in two days.

He grabbed a copy of the *Turkish Daily News* someone had left lying there. His Turkish was decent, but reading the newspaper was still a time-consuming chore. So, he limited himself to news from the Internet or small English daily papers like this one. They were little more than propaganda for the outside world, as opposed to the Turkish papers, which were propaganda for the Turkish citizens. Either way, news in every country was what somebody wanted the public to know, not what it needed to know. He skimmed the headlines and tossed it back on the table. He folded both arms on the table and laid his head down exhausted. Almost six straight hours of lessons had left him exhausted.

The door behind him squeaked. He lifted his head and turned around to see Melike come out of the office. Her hair was a mess, but other than that she looked better than he had seen her after some of her other sessions with Eray. Gary headed for the office and found it messier than usual. Piles of paper and books had been pushed off into the floor. Eray was looking in the mirror that hung above a couch that stretched along an entire wall of the tiny office. The couch had seemed out of place when he had interviewed here. Now, it didn't. He walked across the room to retrieve his backpack.

"Sorry to cause you to wait, Gary. Melike had some trouble with her accounts, and so I had to go over with her the numbers."

Gary didn't doubt the veracity of the story for a minute. Melike was a drug addict. He had seen her take money from the cash register on several occasions. This was how they settled accounts.

"No problem. I just wanted to get my stuff. I have a few quizzes to grade for tomorrow."

"Well, I'm taking off. I promised my girlfriend I would meet her in front of Marmara Hotel at 9:30. Will you lock office when you go and tell Tuncay not to close before midnight?"

"Sure."

Eray grabbed the bouquet of flowers sitting in the corner and left the room. Gary watched the door close behind him in disbelief. Eray treated him decently. He had been managing this posh little bookstore on the busiest street between Rome and Karachi for almost two years. They struck up a conversation while Gary was browsing books one day. It had been his idea to let Gary use the room in the back for private lessons. He took a small cut, and Gary was able to make enough to live on. The owner of the store probably knew nothing about the arrangement, but he hadn't asked questions.

Gary decided to take advantage of having the office to himself. He put the backpack on the floor and sat down at the computer to check his email. Melike stuck her head through the door.

"Hi Gary. I put the tea on. Would you like me to bring you some?" She was a graduate of Boğaziçi University and her English was virtually flawless.

"No thanks."

"You drink tea with everyone but me. Why is that?"

She leaned against the door frame with her hand on her hip, clearly determined to receive an answer. Besides, the American boy was handsome, easy on the eyes. She figured him to be about 185 cm tall. His thick, dirty brown hair wasn't long enough for a pony tail, but long enough that his bangs dropped like a veil over his blue eyes. He was quiet and hard to reach. She had pegged him for a travelling hippie, but he had turned down all of her invitations to party.

"I'm just tired that's all. The caffeine keeps me from going to sleep."

"Why would you want to do that? You're dead when you're asleep. Listen, my roommate is gone tonight. Why don't you come over? I've got some ecstasy."

"I can't tonight."

"I want to be your friend. You're Irish and I love the IRA."

"I appreciate that. Tonight's just not a good time."

She walked over and stood in front of him. He looked up into her eyes.

"You think I'm a slut, don't you?"

"No, I don't."

"Yes, you do, and you're right. I am, and I hate myself for it. Are there any guys who can see past these?" she asked, pointing to her breasts, "and this?" pointing to her ass.

Gary dropped his head. The girl was drop-dead gorgeous. He couldn't figure out why a finance major from the Harvard of Turkey was working in a bookstore, especially when the Turkish banking sector was booming. There was talk of Istanbul becoming the new Beirut, the Switzerland of the Middle East. Banks were hiring. There was a tremendous influx of foreign money, especially from the Gulf. Goldman Sachs was involved in dozens of acquisitions. The demand for qualified English-speaking personnel was enormous, and yet this girl worked in a bookstore as a cashier.

"What are you doing here? Why don't you use your degree and apply to a bank or something?"

"It's bad enough I prostitute myself. I'm not going to be a slave to the banksters, pimping the country with their damn fiat currency!"

"Is that why you like the IRA?"

"Yeah, rage against the machine. Rand was right. They're all a bunch of parasitical bastards."

"You read Ayn Rand?"

"Don't worry. It's not catching here. These people wouldn't know an individual if they saw one staring at them in the mirror," she shrugged indifferently. "If you don't like tea, maybe you'd like something else? Cola?"

He kept his eyes fixed on the computer monitor.

"No, I'm going to take off as soon as I've checked my mail."

"Well, if you ever need anything, anything at all, you just have to ask."

She pulled the door to and Gary sighed in relief. She had never been so direct. He signed into his mail account and groaned when he saw over a hundred email messages. *What is wrong with the damn spam filter?* He started scanning down the list of messages and stopped about halfway down the first screen. It said simply:

GILBERT O'BRIEN NEED TO REACH YOU IMMEDIATELY

Gary clicked on the heading to open the email. True to form, Gilbert was short and to the point.

PLEASE SEND ME A TELEPHONE NUMBER WHERE I CAN CALL YOU.
IT IS URGENT. PLEASE RESPOND IMMEDIATELY.

Two "pleases" in one sentence. Must be awfully important. He clicked Reply, typed in 90 212 293-6968 and hit Send. He knew the phone would ring within five to ten minutes. If anybody was wired into the matrix, Gilbert was. Cyberspace was his playground. He started picking up the papers off of the floor. He hadn't finished when the phone rang.

"Hello."

"So, you're still in Istanbul, ey?"

"It's a nice place with good memories of Mom and Dad dragging us around on their academic adventures. Beats Bombay."

"Most places do."

"True."

"I need you on the first flight to London tomorrow."

"Can't make it. I have a regular teaching schedule here."

"Listen, there's a flight at 05:30. I would really like you to be on it."

"*You* aren't listening. I told you I have classes tomorrow."

"I'll cover the ticket."

"Are you going to tell me what this is all about?"

"I'd rather tell you in person."

Gary got a sick feeling in his stomach.

"Is Gwyn alright?"

"She's fine. I'm surprised you care."

Gary ignored the barb.

"Gilbert, I'm an adult now. You can tell me. If it's not Gwyn, then it's Dad. What's wrong with him?"

"He's had cancer for six months, Gary."

"You can't be serious."

"I'm not, but if he had, you wouldn't have known about it, now would you?"

Gary again held his tongue. The silence was deafening.

"Are you going to tell me what's wrong with Dad, or are you going to keep scolding me like a little kid?"

"There's nothing wrong with him, not anymore. It's just that...Well... He's..." Gary could feel Gilbert's emotional turmoil through the telephone receiver. Finally he was able to force the words out. "He's dead, Gary."

Now there was silence on the Istanbul end of the line. Gilbert gave his brother a minute to take it all in. Gary waited until he was sure his voice wouldn't crack. It was a long, uncomfortable silence.

"How did it happen?"

"Don't know. I just found out myself a couple of hours ago. I was in DC. The Metropolitan Police gave me the news. I'm flying to Dallas now to break the news to Gwyn and bring her back to London."

"She doesn't know yet?"

"No, I thought it best to tell her in person."

"Thank God, you'll be there to tell her. It would have been horrible if the police had called her. Okay then, I'll get a ticket booked for tomorrow."

"It's already done. I'm sending you the e-ticket now and I've reserved us a room at the Bonnington too. I'll call you when I arrive. Give me your cell phone number."

"Sorry."

"For the love of Mary, Gary, get yourself a freaking cell phone and join the twenty-first century. Damn it, a little more responsibility, a little more consideration, and a little more communication would be very much appreciated. I'm probably lucky you checked your email tonight."

The exasperation in his voice shot across the Atlantic like ocean water around a faulty hatch on a submarine at ten thousand psi. Gilbert continued, "My cell phone number will be in the next email."

"I'll see what I can do."

Gary sat there with the phone in his hand until he heard the click on the other end. *So, Dad is dead.* It was a hard thought to process. Ian O'Brien had been a good man, a man he loved and respected, but after everything he had gone through in the last two years, he felt that so many family ties had been severed it could never be the same. Certainly not with his father gone. *Gilbert won't make it easy either.* His brother was so predictable, so western, so much like a corporate junkie living off the high of position and power. Gary unzipped the front pocket on his backpack and pulled out his cell phone to make sure it was charged. Six thousand miles to the West at a height of thirty-three thousand feet, Gilbert stared out the window on a cloudless sky of severe clear, wondering what his brother had become.

22

Dallas, Texas   Gwyn's face lit up when she saw Gilbert walk through the doors. Gilbert gave her a big smile, but the guilt of hypocrisy promptly wiped it away. He sat his bag down and wrapped his arms around his sister. Gwyn knew immediately something was wrong. She couldn't remember when he had last given her such a warm and tender hug and when she let go, he didn't. It would have been awkward with a friend, and it was no less awkward with her brother. When he held her at arms-length and looked her in the eye, she could see tears welling up in his.

"Gilbert, what's wrong? This isn't for business, is it?"

Thoughts tumbled into her mind. *Is it his marriage? Has he been fired? Gary?*

"My dear Gwyn, I do have business and my business is you."

"Me? Well, I'm not such a hot commodity." she joked weakly.

"Let's find a quiet place to sit down so we can talk."

He picked up his bag, put his free arm around her shoulder and steered her towards a quiet corner. They sat down in an empty row of seats.

"Actually my business is in London, but I'm going to need you there with me, so I've come to pick you up. I don't think I can do it alone."

"Pick me up? But, I've only just arrived, Gilbert. Please speak plainly. What is going on here?"

He put his arm around her shoulder and pulled her close. He had spent almost the entire flight planning how he would break the news. He wanted to remind her of what a blessing it was that they had been given so many years with such a great man. He took a deep breath and leaned close to her ear.

"My dear sister, our chieftain has departed for the bright land of eternal sun, and I have come to escort his princess to the farewell party. He and Mom are together again, reunited at last. We should rejoice at their happiness."

She furrowed her brow, her eyes narrowed and then went wide in horror as her face began to contort. Gilbert did not stop.

"We are like wild flowers in the spring, Gwyn, all of us. We grow and bloom and then we are gathered up and planted by the river of life, where nothing withers or fades."

Gwyn broke down sobbing and threw her arms around Gilbert. He stroked her strawberry blonde hair and held her tight. He was glad he had come. She was sobbing uncontrollably. People were staring, but Gilbert was oblivious to everything except his grieving sister. It was several minutes before she finally pulled away. Her eyes were red and tears were still streaming down her face. Gwyn reached over and grabbed his hand. He looked into her blue-green eyes.

"We have lost them both now, haven't we? We are orphans."

"We have each other."

"As do the children in an orphanage... How did he die, Gilbert?"

"I don't know, Gwyn. I got a call from the Metropolitan Police at noon today. All they said was that he had been found in his apartment. The fellow who called me hadn't even received a police report yet."

There was silence. It was awkward. He didn't know what to say. She was the first to find words.

"Thank you for being here. You broke the news the way I needed to hear it. It's all so fleeting, isn't it? Our life, I mean. Oh, Gilbert, it was so thoughtful of you to fly down here and break the news to me like that."

She pulled some kleenex from her purse and wiped her eyes. Then, she quietly blew her nose. In spite of what he had said, Gilbert was overcome with grief. He regretted how busy he had been the last couple of years. Right now, this fact grieved him almost as much as his father's death. After all, death was something God ordained. He couldn't prevent his father's death, but he could have behaved differently while he was alive. Family had taken a back seat to his career and work for the company. Suddenly, he felt her hand clamp down on his knee. He looked up and found an expression of horror on her face.

"Gilbert, you don't suspect foul play, do you?"

Now it was Gilbert's turn to be surprised.

"Good God, Gwyn. What in the world are you talking about?! Our father would never harm a flea. He has no enemies. The police said nothing about anything suspicious..."

He stopped mid-sentence as Gwyn was clearly not listening. She was rummaging frantically through her bags.

"Gwyn, for heaven's sake, will you tell me what is going on?"

She finally found what she was looking for and pulled out a manila envelope.

"The night we met at the airport, did you think Father acted strangely?"

"No, not really. Why?"

"Well, maybe it is just me, but he spoke of Mother more than usual,

120

seemed very nostalgic and after you left, he gave me this. When I asked what it was, he said it was documents he had purchased recently, and which somebody seemed bent on obtaining. He asked me to put them in my safe deposit box. He said he had scanned them for himself, but wanted the original to be safe. It was all a bit strange."

"That was all he said?"

"I pressed him on it, but he would say no more. He was unusually somber though and it seemed serious."

"Do you think that his death could be related to this?"

"Oh, Gilbert, I don't know what to think. I am just telling you what he said."

Gilbert's face hardened. Gwyn handed the envelope to Gilbert, who promptly opened the silver metal clasp that held it shut, pulling out two transparent, vinyl sheet protectors. There was a sticky note on the cover of the first one scribbled in her father's hurried hand:

The original ass. order for G.S.?! G.O.B.?

Gilbert could see that the document was in a non-Roman script that looked like Arabic. He handed it to Gwyn so that he could look at the second sheet protector. As he did, a piece of paper fluttered to the ground. Gwyn picked it up. It was a hand-written note. At the top was a short sentence.

Translation of the pertinent section.

She didn't recognize the handwriting of the paragraph that followed.

The council's decision to cancel son of prophet and erase every trace remains among our most solemn duties. It will be a red English sunset on Suri-Strend with a golden sunrise in Tunis when the bird which has flown is brought back to Südde-i Saadet. Walk in the snow but leave no footprints. Assistance for the sendoff may be obtained from our ever faithful D. Hasten delivery.
13 Jumaada al-awal 1149

Gwyn looked up at her brother, who was staring a hole into the huge glass window looking out on the tarmac. She had seen this look of smoldering anger in his eyes many times as a child. When he spoke, it was low and measured.

"I intended to fly back to London with you. I booked two seats on a flight in an hour and a half because if we don't take this one, there won't be another flight until tomorrow afternoon, which would put us in London on Friday."

"So, that is why you asked me to bring my bags?"

"Yes, and it's a good thing you did, or you wouldn't have had the envelope. There may be something to all this, but let's not automatically assume that it's connected. Whatever the case, I'm going to ask you to stay here, Gwyn. I'll handle arrangements in London. Until we know what's going on, I want you to keep a low profile. I hate it, but I have to go or I'll miss this flight. You know what it's like getting through security these days. First, it was take off your shoes, then they banned liquids, and now they have every pervert in the country applying for a job as a groper."

Gwyn managed a weak smile at Gilbert's sarcasm.

"What about Gary? We need to send him an email."

"I've taken care of it," he said quietly. "He will be in London tomorrow morning."

"Really? How did you swing that?"

"Sent him an email and bought him a ticket."

She could tell from his terse manner he was in no mood for conversation, especially about Gary.

"Gilbert, thank you so much for coming. I will talk to the funeral home and start making preparations. I suppose you want me to keep this folder?"

"Yes, there is no reason for me to carry it. Besides, I'll have the digital copy on Dad's computer to work with if necessary."

Gilbert embraced his sister and she broke down sobbing again.

LONDON "Salih, you have to see this."

Salih looked up from the desk where he and a colleague had been poring over the Internet history and other files from Ian's computer, looking for clues. He had not left the office for almost thirty-six hours.

"What is it?"

"We have Ian on a security camera that afternoon. Time 14:10. He is in Paddington Station."

"What are the possible destinations?"

"We are cross-referencing that now."

Salih felt the fatigue begin to melt away. His energy level rose. The hunt had turned back into a chase. They had just had their first real break.

"Now that we have a time frame and starting point, this should be quick. Send the data stream to Abdullah and Aziz."

He began barking orders and the men sprang into action. In ten minutes, they had his destination—the airport. *Why the airport? Why would the professor visit the airport in the middle of the conference?* But, even as he asked these questions, a ball of worry and anxiety grew in his stomach. *Allah kahretsin!*

"Aziz, get us footage from the airport security cameras beginning at 15:30 hours. We have to find out who he met there."

122

Twenty minutes later, they were looking at the passenger lists for every flight that left that day. A search of surnames solved the mystery. His son had gone to Washington, his daughter to Dallas. *Could one of them have the package?* If he had been a gambling man, he would have wagered a considerable sum right now. One or both of them might have already been informed that their father was dead. He had to know if that had affected their plans.

Two hours later later an encrypted message went out on the PGP key Hüdavendigar.

O'BRIEN WENT TO THE AIRPORT THAT AFTERNOON. HE MET HIS SON AND DAUGHTER THERE. SON TRAVELLED TO WASHINGTON, DAUGHTER TO DALLAS. THEN, SON FOLLOWED TO DALLAS. PACKAGE PROBABLY WITH ONE OF THEM. COMMUNICATIONS INTERCEPT BEING INITIATED.

DALLAS, TEXAS Gilbert approached the security checkpoint at D Terminal and readied himself for the routine that had become automatic. The purple light on the passport, the scrutinizing look from his photograph to his face and back to the photograph. Then came the partial disrobement—off with the shoes, belt and watch, out with the cell phone, keys, change and wallet. He took his laptop out of the bag and put it in a separate container, and then approached the security agent for the physical pat down. The security guard asked him to spread his legs. He shook his head in frustration.

Because of a few radicals, every day millions of totally innocent people who would never contemplate harming another soul were subjected to time-consuming search procedures that bordered on indecent. *What were the chances that terrorists would continue to target air travel in the face of such stringent measures?* The terrorists had already achieved an important objective. They kept thousands of security personnel pre-occupied and forced their enemies to spend billions of dollars to stop an attack that would never come. The stupidity of government bureaucracy never ceased to amaze.

The guard directed him to step into the 'cabin'. There were two feet painted on the floor indicating where passengers were supposed to stand. Then, there was a computerized voice telling him that he would feel puffs of air and reminding him to stand still until the green light came on and the glass doors in front of him opened. This experience was like the glaucoma routine at the optometrist's office. You knew it was coming, and yet it was impossible not to jump back in surprise every time. The only difference was that in this security cabin the entire body was knifed with puffs of air that come from all angles.

Five hours later, Gilbert was standing in the narrow aisle of the 747, stretching his aching back. He had crossed more than twelve time zones in the last two days, and jet-lag and exhaustion had begun taking their toll. He wanted to sleep on this flight, but knew it would be impossible. He had tried melatonin, but had never noticed any benefit. A friend of his swore that a study in mice had shown Viagra to have a positive effect, and that it was being used as an off-label treatment, but he couldn't bring himself to try it. Popping Viagra for jetlag just seemed too weird.

23

Thursday, London   "Metropolitan Police, how may I direct your call?"

"Hello. This is Gilbert O'Brien. I was contacted by a Mr. McIntosh yesterday regarding the death of my father Ian O'Brien. He told me to call as soon as I arrived in London."

"Let me patch you through to his office. One moment, please."

Gilbert continued walking to the exit, rolling his carry-on behind him.

"Mr. O'Brien, this is Tom Jones. Allow me to offer my condolences on the loss of your father. The Superintendent is away from his desk, but should be back within thirty minutes if you want to come down to the station. I'll let him know you are coming."

"Actually I am picking up my brother and we are going straight to my father's house. I would appreciate it if he could meet us there."

"I'll let him know that you are coming. If his schedule allows, I'm sure he will do his best to be there."

"Thank you, Officer."

He closed the Blackberry and began scanning the crowd near the exit. Gary would be here somewhere. He looked out the huge plate glass windows on a perfect English summer day. A warm sun was shining out of a cloudless sky. The native Britons were dressed for a heat wave of 82° Fahrenheit, women in spaghetti straps and men in t-shirts and shorts. He couldn't remember the last time he had seen so much pasty white flesh.

He suddenly had a flashback of his father quoting Elizabeth Barrett Browning in a similar situation when their great uncle had died on a perfect spring day.

> But natural Beauty shuts her bosom to what the natural feelings tell!
> Albeit I sighed, the trees would blossom. Albeit I smiled the blossoms fell.

The whole realm of nature, with the exception of a few domesticated animals, paid absolutely no heed to the ebb and flow of human emotion. For all her motherly qualities, Mother Nature seemed strangely oblivious to the pain and anguish inflicted upon her children, and the joys and celebrations experienced due to human triumph seemed to be of no consequence to her either.

He felt a tap on his shoulder and turned to see his little brother with a sheepish look on his face.

"Good to see you, Gilbert. How long has it been?"

They both knew how long it had been.

"The last time we were in the same room was at Mom's funeral."

"Wow, it's been a long time."

"Or, maybe not long enough."

"What was that supposed to mean?"

"Have you forgotten English too?"

"Don't be a jackass."

Gilbert bristled.

"Don't act like one."

Gary sighed. "If you're done with the lecture, maybe we should go."

"You look like you've lost some weight."

"I picked up a bug in India. It took me a long time to shake it. A simple giardia infection, but this time it was resistant to the medication. I look good now. You should have seen me when I arrived in Istanbul."

"If you had arrived in London or Dallas, I might've."

"Listen, if sadism is your new drug of choice, by all means fire away. I'll indulge your habit."

"Damn it, Gary. You could've called."

"Thanks for the ticket," he said ignoring his brother. "I could've swung it, though."

"Well, I heard through the grapevine that freelance English positions in the developing world ranked somewhere between porters and those tea-guys, what did they call them?"

"*Chaiji.*"

"Right. Well, my job pays well and family has to pull together in hard times."

Gary could feel a sermon bubbling just under the surface of his brother's words.

"I didn't figure we needed two elder brothers in the house. Are we going straight to Dad's place?"

"Yes. The officer on the case asked me to come down to the station, but I asked him to meet us there instead. I want to see the apartment for myself. Are you ready?"

"Ready as I'll ever be."

They both grabbed their bags and headed for the curb to wave down a cab.

The phone rang. Salih looked up from the data he was reviewing and glared at the phone.

"*As-salamu alaykum.*"

"*Wa Alaykum As-salam.* Good work Salih. Now what is the plan?"

"We have no idea what his son and daughter know, what he told them when he passed off the file and, most importantly, if they've made a connection. We don't have the document, and at least one digital copy is also unaccounted for. We think we might know who received it, but haven't pinned it down for sure. Whatever we do, it has to be conclusive, no more loose ends, no mistakes, no unintended consequences."

Ahmet smiled on the other end of the phone. This was why he liked working with Salih. He understood the stakes.

"Are you sure the original is with Gwyn?"

"Positive. Our communication intercept is operational. During his flight to London, she sent him a text message asking whether or not she should put the document in their safe deposit box."

"He advised against it, *inshallah*."

"Correct. He said there was no need for such a move, but I wish he had said yes."

"Wouldn't that have made it more difficult to retrieve?"

"Not really. Safety deposit boxes have a specified location and I've never seen one that money couldn't open. What we have to be concerned with now is containment. Our job is to destroy these instructions. If it were in a safe deposit box, we would know exactly where it is, monitor it and ensure that it is not spreading or being copied."

Ahmet smiled again. "Bravo, Salih. Very good. What now?"

"Well, we grab the girl, make her talk, retrieve the original, find out if copies have been made, and then eliminate her."

"*Inshallah.* What is the closest team?"

Salih switched the phone to speaker so that he could pace as he talked.

"That's the problem, Ahmet. Putting together what I would call a clean, uncompromised team with the necessary training and expertise in America right now is difficult. As you have seen from the reports, operations are becoming increasingly difficult there. We've had two teams flushed out in the last six months and quietly sent to Cuba due to the FBI's new Internet monitoring capability. Besides, you know the orders are not to use sleeper cells for things like this. None of them are to be activated without specific instructions from the Rightly Guided One. I can put one together, but it will take two days for us to insert them."

"Ok, do it. Make sure the insertion is perfect. We cannot afford any more mistakes.

"Consider it done."

"*Inshallah.*"

Salih continued, "The police report is already calling it death due to natural causes. A routine autopsy won't be able to prove anything to the contrary."

"Right. Let's just make sure it is routine, and one more thing. Did you ever find anything on the email address on the secretary's computer?"

"That has proven to be a bit troubling. It's a gmail account. It didn't turn up on any of the initial scans conducted on email databases."

"Which can only mean that it's either a relatively new e-mail address, or one that is very infrequently used and sitting behind a good firewall."

24

There were two police cars sitting outside when they drove up. Gilbert paid the driver while Gary retrieved their bags from the trunk. As the taxi drove away, the two brothers exchanged glances before they ascended the steps. Gilbert began fumbling for the keys a few steps from the outside door that led into the apartment building, but the door opened before he could find the right one. A middle-aged man with a crew cut stuck out his hand.

"Chief Superintendent John McIntosh. Are you Gilbert O'Brien?"

"Yes, sir, and this is my brother, Gary," he said.

"I'm truly sorry for your loss, Gentlemen, and wish I could have made your acquaintance in different circumstances. I would have preferred to have met you at the office. It might have been easier for you in a place not so full of memory."

"Which is, of course, exactly why we had to meet here. This was his home, this was where he took care of Mom before she died, and this was where he lived, worked and breathed his last. No sir, we're very happy that you have honored our request by coming here. We also wanted to make sure his personal effects were secure. It would be almost impossible for your people to be absolutely sure there was nothing missing."

"Of course, you are right," McIntosh replied cordially.

They walked down the hall to the elevator, and Gilbert sent them up to the second floor. McIntosh let Gilbert open the door and noticed him grimace slightly as he swung the door open. It swung wide without a sound. Gilbert and Gary entered the apartment slowly and with reverence. It looked exactly like they remembered it. Gary sat down on the couch, turned to McIntosh and asked, without a trace of emotion, "What did your investigation find?"

"There were no signs of forced entry, though the locking mechanism isn't what I would call state-of-the-art, and the deadbolt was not drawn. Nothing appears to be missing, but you will be a better judge of whether this assessment is true. We took photographs of everything. His body had no apparent markings. He was lying supine on the bed. The first responders said it looked to them like a heart attack. They estimated that the time of death was between 01:00 and 03:00 on Wednesday."

Gary stood up and began walking through the rooms looking at the shelves. Gilbert headed for the office.

"Please continue, Superintendent."

He walked over to the computer with McIntosh in tow and pushed the power button.

"That is about it. I was just going to say that after the autopsy, we should be able to confirm death of natural causes."

"Who will be performing the autopsy?"

"Not quite sure, but I can find out. We actually had one of your father's colleagues from the university provide positive identification, but you are more than welcome to come down to the morgue with me."

The computer was prompting for a password and Gilbert typed in the passphrase that his dad had used for years. PsAlM2:2

"I may want to do that. However, if I could have a few minutes here in the apartment, I'd really appreciate it."

"Of course, I'll leave you gentlemen alone. If you need anything, I'll be outside."

"Thank you, sir."

Gary closed the door behind McIntosh and turned to find Gary standing in the door to the office holding a pearl and diamond necklace that had belonged to their mother.

"Nothing missing from the safe."

"Well, that's nice to know. It looks like Dad got around to oiling the hinges on that door too. The last few times I visited, it squeaked horribly."

"So, what are we going to do here, Gilbert? He said there was nothing amiss or suspicious. I've only taken a quick glance around, but everything seems to be the same as always."

Gilbert had been debating whether or not to tell Gary about what their father had given Gwyn, but again he decided against it.

"I just wanted to have a look at his computer and then we'll go."

Gary pulled up a chair beside his brother. *He is a computer geek, a security guru and one time hacker. Let him poke around,* he said to himself.

He watched as his brother conducted a search for a picture file created within the last five days. While he waited for the computer to scan the C drive, he opened the browser, looked at a few settings and hit Shift+Control+H to bring up the Internet search history.

"What are doing, Gilbert? I'm not sure you should be poking around on Dad's computer like this. Personally, I don't want to know what he did on the Internet and I don't think it is any of our business either."

"For crying out loud, Gary! What kind of person do you think I am?"

"How the hell should I know? Dad dies of a heart attack, and the first thing you do is look at his Internet history? It seems a bit weird. Are you going to tell me what is going on?"

Without saying a word, Gilbert turned back to the computer and scanned the list. There was no Internet history for the last ten days. *What's going on here?* He clicked back to the search window. It said simply, "No items match your search." Gilbert stared at the screen in disbelief and then, without a word, stood up and headed for the bag that he had left by the door.

"Gary, would you mind asking McIntosh to come back up here. He's going to want to see this."

"Damn it, Gilbert, stop playing games with me! What is going on?"

"You don't think it's strange that there's no history in his browser for the last ten days?"

"Maybe, but that doesn't explain what prompted you to go poking around on his computer. You know more than you are telling me. Stop treating me like your little brother and tell me what's driving this."

"To be honest, I don't know either. Gwyn and I met Dad at the airport Tuesday afternoon. I had a long layover on my flight to Washington DC, and Gwyn was on her way to Dallas, so she arranged for Dad to meet us for dinner at the airport."

"What night was this?"

"Tuesday."

"The night he died. Go on."

"Well, we had a nice meal together and I left to catch my plane. Gwyn stayed behind and chatted with Dad for several hours while she waited for her flight. He gave her a package before they parted. He said somebody was trying to obtain a document, and he wanted to give it to Gwyn for safekeeping. Gwyn told me about it yesterday in Dallas. We opened it together. It contained two folders. One was an old manuscript and the other contained several loose pages that looked like letters. There was also a piece of paper with a handwritten translation of a portion of the manuscript."

"And then he dies the same night and you are wondering if there is a connection."

"Exactly."

"And what about the file you were searching for?"

"He told Gwyn that he had a digital copy of the document."

"But that document is not on his computer?"

"Right, you have to admit that seems odd, and now we see that his Internet history has been deleted. Something weird is going on here, Gary."

"Are you suggesting foul play? Maybe this is all coincidence?"

"I had a biology professor in college who said life itself was a coincidence, but there is plenty of evidence that suggests otherwise. Too many things are wrong here. Dad sends a file with Gwyn to Texas, mentions that he has scanned a copy for himself, and yet, less than forty-eight hours later, it has mysteriously disappeared, and his Internet history has been erased."

"What are you going to tell McIntosh?"

"I want to run a data recovery program on Dad's hard drive. If something was erased, I'll be able to recover it. I just want McIntosh here to see the results."

Gilbert began rummaging through his bag looking for a thumb drive and Gary headed for the door. He reappeared with McIntosh a few minutes later. Gilbert had almost finished installing the data recovery program.

"What is it you want me to see about, Mr. O'Brien?"

"My father told my sister that there should be several scanned images on his computer. I did a search for them, but there are no picture files. There are a couple of other anomalies as well so I wanted to run a state-of-the-art forensics program our company developed to see if there has been any suspicious activity."

"I don't have the foggiest idea what you're talking about", McIntosh responded.

"My brother's a computer geek," replied Gary dryly. "The program he's going to run can recover files that have been deleted."

McIntosh seemed uncomfortable, but nodded in consent.

"Sure, go ahead."

Gilbert launched the program and leaned back in the high-backed leather chair to wait for the program to scan the hard disk. All three of them were staring at the progress bar on the screen, calculating how long they'd have to wait when the doorbell rang. Gary walked to the door and opened it.

"Mrs. Askwith. How do you do?"

"I saw you come up the stairs, but I had to freshen up before I came over. Allow me to offer my condolences for the loss of your father."

"Thank you, Mrs. Askwith. I trust you are in good health."

"As good as can be expected for an old woman flirting with the Grim Reaper."

Gary smiled. Mrs. Askwith had a flair for the dramatic.

"I know you two are busy," she continued. "So, I won't keep you. Your father gave me this book on Tuesday night, and I wanted to return it before I forgot."

She handed Gary a worn leather journal, gave him a hug and began shuffling back to her apartment.

When Gary returned, the scan was finished. Gilbert was scrolling through the list of recovered files sector by sector. It all seemed so surreal. He had only just begun to recover from the grief and loss of his mother's vicious battle with breast cancer. Now, he was overcome with feelings of intense guilt for neglecting his father over the last few years, and something else gnawed at him.

He replayed in his mind the last night he had spent in Istanbul. After leaving the bookstore, he had walked down to Şahkulu Mosque at the head of Galipdere Street, where Istiklal Boulevard dead ends at Galata Tower Square. He had desperately hoped Yusuf would be there, although the lateness of the hour all but guaranteed that he would not. He was surprised to find the old man sitting beside the door as if expecting him.

The imam had risen to his feet, clasped Gary's hand and kissed him once on each cheek in the traditional greeting. Then he gently held Gary at arm's length and stared through the windows of his soul right down into his heart until he was sure he had read it right. He said, "Your grief is deep. I feel your pain. A black noose of evil is tightening around you and your family, but do not be afraid, for you know as well as I that darkness will never overcome the light."

Gary had stood there in shock. He spoke like a fortune-teller or maybe even like a prophet of old. Gary had been debating whether or not to tell him about the strange dream he'd had the night before. There was nothing to lose, so he had proceeded to tell his elderly friend that he had just received news of his father's death and then related his strange dream…

Several choice expletives brought Gary back to the little apartment in London. He looked down to find Gilbert rapidly scrolling through screen after screen and muttering to himself before finally slumping back in his chair. Gary and McIntosh looked at the screen, but all they saw was a page filled from top to bottom with lines of the letter 'a' in small caps.

"What is it Mr. O'Brien?"

Gilbert put his head in his hands and took a deep breath, but made no response. He was obviously processing it all. The silence began to be uncomfortable.

"Mr. O'Brien?"

"I'm sorry, sir. I'm trying to put it all together. Can you get a cyber-forensics team down here?"

"Of course."

"I think it would be a good idea to have them document this."

"Document what?"

"A totally secure deletion of information from my father's computer that exceeds DoD 5220.22M protocol."

"What exactly do you think is going on, Mr. O'Brien?"

"Sir, someone has performed a secure wipe on my father's computer, overwriting select files multiple times with random data so that it could not be recovered. We might've missed this if it had been a single file, but they also wiped all of the Temporary Internet files so that no one would know what my father was researching. We can't recover the data, but the program can also identify sectors that contain random data and flag them as having been wiped. Over a hundred thousand files have been deleted in this fashion. There is no way to know what they were, but clearly they were sensitive enough to warrant special attention. I would bet that they oiled the hinges on the door as well, so that their intrusion would be totally silent. I don't know if my dad woke up to find intruders in the house and died of a heart attack or if he was killed, but I certainly mean to find out."

"You think your father may have been murdered? I think that is a bit hasty."

"He gave my sister some documents he said someone was trying to obtain. If my father was murdered, it may be connected to these documents."

"And just what are they related to?"

Gilbert pulled out his Blackberry and scrolled through his directory.

"I don't know, sir. I don't know, but I sure as hell intend to find out."

Gilbert put the Blackberry on speaker and sat it down on the desk by the computer. He took a thumb drive out of his bag and started transferring the results of the scan to the USB memory device. A woman answered on the second ring.

"Good morning, Gilbert. I got a message from Tracy this morning saying that you would be out of the office for a few days. I hope everything is okay."

"Hi Kiyomi, I'm in London taking care of personal business."

"London? I thought you flew into DC yesterday."

"It's a long story. My dad passed away here in London."

"Oh dear. I'm sorry to hear that."

"Listen. I need you to find out if we have anyone here in London that we use for medical forensics on legal briefs. I need the best man available and I need him ASAP."

"I'll get on it right away."

"Great. Hang on a sec, will you?"

He turned to McIntosh and asked, "What morgue is my father's body being kept at? Our company works with some of the best forensic specialists in the world and, if you don't mind, I would like to request that one of our people be allowed to act as an observer and consultant on this case."

"Mr. O'Brien, that really won't be necessary. The Hornsey Public Mortuary has excellent facilities and personnel."

"I'm sure they do, but, all the same, two minds are better than one and I would certainly feel better about it. Anything we can learn would be helpful and if the conclusion is that my father died of natural causes, I will feel better knowing that two experts concurred."

"Mr. O'Brien, this is highly unusual. I'm not sure that we can accommodate this request."

Gilbert turned back to the phone and said, "Kiyomi, sorry to keep you waiting. If he could just meet us at the Hornsey Public Mortuary, that would be great."

"I'll do my best."

Gilbert set the Blackberry in his pocket and turned back to the Superintendent.

"Do you mean to tell me that English law does not permit independent verification of an autopsy report? I find that difficult to believe. Listen, I'm not trying to be difficult. I know that you want to help us, but if you have a problem with this, then I am sure I can have a lawyer at your office tomorrow morning and that would be unpleasant for both of us."

The Superintendent's face hardened. He was clearly not a man who was accustomed to having his authority challenged. He liked Americans in general, but their impetuous nature and lack of decorum had always been something that ruffled his feathers. He rubbed his chin. *Do these bloody Americans have to respond to everything with an M1 Abrams tank?*

"Mr. O'Brien, until a few minutes ago, everything about your father's death seemed natural. This sudden turn of events has certainly given us reason to explore the possibility of foul play. Let me see what I can do, but in the meantime I expect you to tell me everything you know."

"If you can give me and my brother a ride down to the morgue, I will tell you everything that..."

The doorbell rang before Gilbert could finish.

"...everything we know," he said walking across the room to get the door. "We want to get to the bottom of this too."

He turned the handle and expected to see a policeman, but found himself staring at Judith Herrin.

"How can I help you?"

"Sorry, if I'm interrupting something. Is Professor O'Brien here? If I'd known he had guests, I wouldn't have stopped by."

"I'm Professor O'Brien's son."

"Oh, nice to meet you," she said extending her hand. "I'm Judith Herrin, a friend and colleague of your father's." He shook her hand. "If you'll just tell the Professor I stopped by."

Gilbert studied her more carefully. Her long black hair was pulled up in a ponytail. She wore a blouse that invited the eyes downward, but a string of pearls formed a safety net that held one's gaze from descending further. Her lips shone from a fresh application of lipstick. Gilbert subconsciously began employing security protocols.

"Come in," he said quietly, stepping aside to allow her to enter. "How long have you known my father?"

"We taught together at the university before I left for a position with the UN. We still do some research together."

"So, you're a historian?"

"Not compared to your father, but, yes, history is my passion as well."

He saw her demeanor change when Gary and McIntosh walked in. A shadow of puzzled consternation moved across her face at the sight of a policeman. He paused for a moment to see how she would react. She said nothing. He waited until the pause bordered on rudeness before continuing.

"Then, I'm sure you'll be sorry to hear that my father has passed away."

Her smile vanished and the lower lip began to quiver. He could see her confidence melt. Tears welled up in her eyes. She blinked several times in an attempt to keep them back. It was useless. They fell anyway. The burst of uncontrolled emotion lasted only seconds. The grief-stricken look of shock hardened into ice.

"I just spoke with him on Tuesday…" she said to no one in particular. "I'm so sorry. Please accept my condolences. This is such a shock. We had just begun working on a new project together." She started to turn away.

"Please, sit down," said Gilbert. "He clearly meant something to you."

"No, I should go. How did it happen?"

"We think it was a heart attack," said Gilbert repeating the initial summation of the medical team.

"When will the funeral be?"

"We just arrived ourselves. Nothing has been set."

She pulled a card from her purse. "I should very much like to be there." Gary took the card.

"I'll be sure you receive the details."

"Thank you," she said quietly, turning to go. Gilbert stopped her.

"What was the project you were working on with my father?"

Judith turned back and stared at the ground, wondering how to answer.

"Last Saturday, he and I found a document hidden in a book he purchased in Amsterdam. It was in Arabic, so I don't know what it said. He was going to have it translated. I had to leave for meetings in Brussels and only just returned today. On Monday, I talked to him about it on the phone. Apparently, he had found some clues and was obviously working on a hunch, but refused to share that on the phone. He said we could talk about it on Thursday, and he seemed pretty excited. That's why I stopped by."

"Ms. Herrin, we're on our way to the morgue right now. I might want to talk to you about this document later. Would it be alright if I called later in the week?"

"Of course. I know this is not the time, but I'd very much like to continue the project. Maybe, after the funeral, you would allow me to copy some of his notes."

"I'm sure that won't be a problem."

25

Salih leaned back in his chair and re-read the plan he had put together. He had decided to only send two men to take the girl. There would be three technical intercept personnel assigned to the job, but only one needed to be in the States and he was already in place, an electrical engineering student at the University of Texas at Arlington. He would be completely isolated from the details of the plan. His job was merely to provide technical support if necessary to run GPS-cell phone triangulation. The two men assigned to take the girl out and recover the document were the best he had. Most volunteers were Arabs as there was no shortage of unemployed 25-year-olds bursting with testosterone and boiling in the cauldron of hate the Middle East had become. But their performance was not always stellar, so this time he had chosen two Turkish brothers.

One of them had gained his experience fighting the infidel in Chechnya, Afghanistan, Iraq and Somalia. The other had worked in the Turkish intelligence agency, MIT, for years as an inside contact for the brotherhood in their struggle against secularism. Salih had complete confidence in both of them. He breathed deeply and moved his mouse to the "send" button, closed his eyes and muttered a fervent prayer for success before pressing the button. This had to be perfect, or Ahmet would see to it that he was assigned to some particularly hellish place like Peshawar, Somalia or Saudi Arabia. It would be difficult enough for him after having the comforts of London for the last fifteen years, but it would be sheer torture for his new, British-born bride.

ISTANBUL   The travel agent one street off of Taksim Square took the passport Zeki held out to her.

"It is too bad that you need to leave right away. If you can wait until tomorrow, I can get you a better flight—shorter and cheaper."

"I'm afraid I really must leave as soon as possible. There has been a death in the family and I must get there quickly."

"Well, Mr. Çölaşan, in that case we can give you a refund for a portion of the ticket if you present a certified copy of the death certificate when you return. However, for now I have to charge the full amount."

"I understand."

She turned back to the screen. With the advent of e-ticketing, it had become extremely unusual for them to have walk-in customers for simple transactions like this. His age was the only explanation she could think of. He probably didn't use a computer or the Internet. Otherwise, he would have booked the ticket online. The young people were all cyber freaks, but older people were slow to change.

Zeki watched her as she scanned the screen, looking for the flight which would suit him best. He already knew that Madrid was the option she would give him. She was an attractive girl. With unemployment among young people at twenty-seven percent in the big cities, a pleasing appearance was an important asset when it came to getting a job that involved interaction with customers.

"Mr. Çölaşan, the only flight I have is Turkish Airlines to Madrid and then American Airlines non-stop to Dallas. The layover is short, so you will only have one hour to get from terminal 1 to terminal 4, the new facility that handles most of the trans-Atlantic traffic."

"Will that present a problem?"

"No, of course, not, but you won't have any time to spare. Have one of our agents at the gate point you to the right shuttle and when you arrive at terminal 4, be sure to ask for directions. I am told that the new concourse is a bit confusing."

"That's fine."

"Now, if I can have your credit card, I will go ahead and issue the ticket."

"I'll be paying in cash."

"Cash?"

"That's right."

"I see. Well, the total is 4,573 TL."

Zeki reached for his bag, unzipped it and took out a large wad of cash. The travel agent watched him put a bundle of Euro and another of dollars back in the bag before he began counting out forty-five 100 TL banknotes. Then, he took out his wallet to find the smaller bills, after which he handed the whole stack to the girl behind the counter. She counted the bills once more and then went to the printer to retrieve the ticket.

"Your flight leaves at 6:55 AM and you arrive in Dallas at 14:05 PM." She folded the itinerary and slipped it into a shiny THY envelope along with the ticket. She handed it to him and said,

"Have a safe trip."

"Thanks."

TIRA, TEXAS   Gwyn lay staring at the ceiling fan spinning gently above the bed, wondering if life really was just an unending circle of birth, pain and death. It was 4:30 in the morning. She had been up for half an hour, fighting back the tears. It was no use though, she could not go back to sleep because her body was on a different time zone and if she kept lying there in bed, she knew she would spend the whole day crying, which was not what she wanted to do.

A rooster crowed outside and Gwyn smiled to herself as she waited for the other testosterone-charged members of the flock to take up the challenge. In seconds, every other male member joined the chorus. It lasted less than thirty seconds, and they would crow intermittently right up until sunrise. *What was the instinct that drove them to compete?* She heard footsteps in the kitchen. She started to panic and then remembered Aunt Bonny had told her last night that she would be over with fresh ground coffee. Gwyn rolled out of bed and walked into the kitchen in her night gown.

"Good morning, Aunt Bonny. I didn't expect you so early."

"I knew jetlag would have you up early, so I wanted to bring over the coffee grinder and some fresh eggs. They're in the paper sack on the table. Besides, those roosters won't let anyone sleep in anyway."

"Oh yes, the roosters. I love to hear them crow."

"Now, don't you go getting sentimental on me, young lady. Nothing nice about a rooster unless he's in a pot of dumplings."

"Well, that is a lesson we learned right here."

"It's too bad you didn't visit more when you were kids. Your uncle and I loved watching you and your two brothers running around. You never came inside, always fishing in the pond, gathering crawdads, climbing trees, swimming in the lake, feeding the animals and picking blackberries. It sure felt like family then."

"We all have very fond memories of those visits, Aunt Bonny."

"All but Gilbert, you mean?"

Gilbert's disdain for country life was well-known.

"Can you blame him after his scrape with the rooster?" Gwyn laughed.

Aunt Bonny smiled. "Well, that's what he gets for mocking them."

"He was just crowing along with them, Aunt Bonny, being a kid. How was he to know they would take it personal?"

Gwyn could see it now. The flock's alpha male had set to crowing while they were gathering eggs. Gilbert echoed the call, and the next thing they heard was the sound of flapping wings and Gilbert screaming in pain. She and Gary came out of the henhouse to find an eight-pound rooster attacking a boy weighing over hundreds pounds, flying up at his face and raking him with the spurs on the back of his feet. His fury was shocking.

Fortunately, Gilbert had instinctively covered his face with his hands, but the rooster had scored several times and blood was oozing from superficial scratches on his arms. He was clearly determined to drive this invader out of his harem. As soon as Gilbert recovered from the initial shock, he had sent the rooster flying through the air like a football with one well-placed kick, but he never crowed at the rooster again and the kids never forgot the experience.

"Gwyn, if you'll excuse me, I'm gonna run down to Walmart before the sun comes up and turns the asphalt into blackstrap molasses. Stop in for lunch. Henry promised to make us some iced tea with fresh mint and lemon."

"My favorite. I'll be there."

She watched her aunt walk out the door and down the steps on the porch, but she was still thinking about the rooster. She had thought about it years earlier in college too when reading a convincing treatise which claimed to demonstrate that all human behavior was connected to the survival instinct and consequently to sexual desire. This, the author claimed, was the determining factor in relations of all kinds. It had taken several months before the jury of Gwyn's heart returned a verdict. The thesis clashed with everything her parent's had taught her. And, yet the idea that sexual desire was the foundation of human relation seemed to play a dominant role in animal behavior. *Especially male behavior*, she had thought wryly. *No wonder a male rooster has become synonymous with the male organ.*

Gwyn had more suitors than a bloodhound has fleas. "Unlucky in love" was what all her friends said, but she had learned that her star-crossed love life, or lack of one, had nothing to do with destiny or fate, but rather her refusal to give it up early in a relationship. Consequently, none of the suitors persisted for long. Dozens of guys had come and gone. All handsome, some rich, some talented and some funny, but none of them shared her values and none of them had been willing to keep the relationship going once they found out that she was not just being coy, but that she really was not going to allow them to score.

She had read Pinker's book right after a particularly promising relationship came to a heartbreaking end. The book had been such a blow to her worldview that she decided she had to sit down and talk with her mother about it. It was hard for her at twenty-four to bring up the "birds and the bees" with a mother battling cancer and suffering the agonies of chemotherapy, but she knew she had to do it before she was gone. She would never have the chance again.

That four-hour talk with her mom had probably been the most important event in her adult life. Her mother had always been fairly prim and proper, so Gwyn was very hesitant to even bring it up. She did not know how her mother would respond. After all, her mother had not been particularly open about sex in Gwyn's teenage years, though she had dutifully given Gwyn "the talk". However, when Gwyn told her about the book, the doubts it had generated and how her experience with men and the thesis of the book had combined to deal her lofty ideals a "below the belt" blow, her mother was unexpectedly candid.

The first thing she had done was ask Gwyn a simple question. 'Does your dad love me?' It was an easy question. Her dad had been devastated by the cancer diagnosis, but over the last year and half, his love for Patricia was the light that lit the darkness for all of them. He was more romantic, gentle, supportive, encouraging and positive than anyone she had ever seen. He brought her mother fresh flowers every week. In between her chemo treatments, he took her to Jamaica to relive their honeymoon, to Rome to celebrate their anniversary, and then to Dublin to work on their family tree.

He saw to it that she didn't have to deal with the mundane affairs of life. No housework, no bills, no errands. She spent her time reading poetry or books that she had never found the time for while raising three children. Her friends took her to the museums in London when she was well enough, or came and drank coffee with her when she was too weak to leave the house. Ian taught his classes, and when he came home, he was at Patricia's side for as long as her mother was awake. When she went to sleep, he stayed up late doing the dishes, paying bills and cleaning house. No, there was no question, her dad loved her mother.

Then her mother proceeded to describe how her dad had demonstrated from the first day of their relationship that he was interested in her as a person and not as a concubine. Maybe it was the chemo, maybe it was her approaching death, and an awareness that she would not be there for her daughter when she got married and began her own adventure, but whatever the case, her mom had shared openly about the sexual intimacy she had enjoyed with her husband.

At first, Gwyn had listened to her mother in absolute shock, but the more she talked, the more she realized the depth of the passion in her parent's marriage. Gwyn had determined right then and there that she wanted the same experience and would not settle for anything less. For her, the jury had rendered its verdict, but life had a way of continuing to plant seeds of suspicion and there were certainly moments when she still wondered why God had allowed Pinker to be right about so many things.

Her mother had not stopped there, though. Gwyn had never talked with her dad about sex. He had left that to her mother, but her mother went on to tell Gwyn what he had taught the boys and her respect for him was bumped up a few more notches, which actually took it completely off the scale. She had viewed him as a superhero before; now he was elevated to angel status. According to her mother, Gilbert had received his first talk several years after the scrap with the rooster, when it was obvious that the hormones of puberty were coursing through his veins.

It had been during their vacation at the farm. Dad had made a pitcher of lemonade and taken Gilbert out to the chicken pen. They sat down in the shade of the big oak tree and sipped their lemonade. After ten minutes of chitchat, Dad gave Gilbert a small notepad and pen and told him he had an assignment. He was to watch the cock for the next two hours and note everything he did.

When Dad returned two hours later, he asked a pointed question: "How many hens did the rooster have sex with?" Gilbert's cheeks flushed, but he answered directly, "Eight." Dad's response was straight and to the point. "That is why we call them animals, Gilbert. Don't forget it." The lesson had stuck too. Gwyn was proud of how her brothers treated women. *Why can't I find someone like that?*

She reached for her iPhone and checked her email, but there was nothing from Gilbert. She reached for her laptop and turned it on. It was time to do a little research on this document.

26

A morgue attendant led Gilbert and Gary though swinging stain-less steel doors into a room that was clearly several degrees cooler than the hallway had been.

"Are you sure you want to do this?" he asked.

Gilbert nodded in the affirmative. The attendant turned to Gary,

"And what about you?"

"Yep, let's get it over with."

"This is harder than most people realize," he responded. He knew there was a fifty percent chance that both of these men would be bawling like babies in the next sixty seconds. *At least the chap wasn't smashed in a car accident. That at least makes it easier.* He opened the door and pulled the slab out of its reposi-tory, unzipping the black body bag to reveal the man's face and looked up at the two brothers. Their faces were almost as cold as the body in front of them.

Gary moved closer and Gilbert stood there fixed on the face of the father who had instilled him with character and values. Grief. Loss. Regret. The emo-tions welled up inside too fast for him to even name. Just a few days ago, life had twinkled in those eyes and laughter had rolled from his mouth. He could feel his eyes start to water and then the hot tears coursing down his cheeks. Gary, on the other hand, was intent on the body and without looking up addressed the attendant.

"If you don't mind, we'd like you to unzip it all the way."

"But, he is naked, sir. We don't..."

"I'm well aware of the fact that he is unclothed."

Gilbert studied his brother's face. It was grim, expressionless and cold. The attendant unzipped the bag and Gary picked up his father's hand. Rigor mortis was fully developed so the entire arm was raised with it. It was unnatural, and Gary set the hand back down, sorry that he had even picked it up. He did not, however, move his own hand. From the corner of his eye he saw the stainless steel doors at the other end of the room swing open.

143

"Is Gilbert O'Brien here?"

They turned to see a slightly balding, but well-built man in his mid-50s in a white lab coat walking towards them.

"That would be me," said Gilbert.

"Allow me to offer my condolences. I'm Dr. Timothy White. The chairman of the board of directors called me himself. He told me that I'd find you here. What's going on?"

Gilbert pointed to Gary and said, "This is my younger brother."

"Pleased to meet you."

"Thanks."

Gilbert cleared his throat and struggled to get his emotions under control so that his voice didn't crack.

"Look, Doctor, we really appreciate you coming."

"Don't mention it. As you know, this company is like family. We have to be there for one another. I assume that there is some doubt as to the cause of death, or you wouldn't have called for me."

"That's right, sir. I don't want to go into the details here, but my father's death is surrounded by a number of suspicious events. The police initially said it was a heart attack, but we think there may be more to it."

"So, if I understand correctly, my purpose in being here is to provide a second opinion of the autopsy."

"Exactly, I want to be absolutely sure about this."

"Well, to be as thorough as possible, it would help to have his complete medical history from your family physician and any prescription drugs he might have been taking."

"We can manage that easily enough. How soon can we have the results?"

"If the chaps here at the Hornsey Public Mortuary can get started soon, then I can have the results for you tomorrow."

"Excellent. My brother and I will be staying at the Bonnington Hotel until the police finish their work at my dad's place."

"I will call you as soon as I know something."

CAIRO   Ahmet looked down at Nafrit's beautiful body stretched out on the bed among the tangled sheets. She was light-skinned, but had long, beautiful, kinky hair that belied the Negro blood coursing in her veins. Her charms were more than magical, they were bewitching and had kept him from sleeping more than a couple of hours the whole night. He was late for work and she was the reason. He couldn't think of a better one.

Ahmet was the paragon of a perfectionist. Everything he touched turned to gold, every endeavor was a success, everything that was, but love. He had been with Nafrit for almost two and half years, which was about the average length of a marriage for him. She was the eighth girl he had married since leaving Istanbul almost nineteen years ago, and she was seventeen years younger than he was.

He never got married with any intention of getting a divorce. He enjoyed female companionship too much for that, but something always seemed to snuff out that initial spark. The truth was he had no patience for petty, insubordinate or manipulative women, and that is where the relationship always seemed to end, so they ended up on the street and he ended up shopping around for someone new.

It wasn't difficult. In the poverty of the Middle East, his paycheck made finding a beautiful girl almost as easy as hailing a cab. In fact, he was amazed at how many women would surrender themselves for the opportunity to live in comfort. It bothered him too. His approach to everything was unapologetically pragmatic, and still he entertained the most unabashedly romantic notions when it came to love. What was even stranger was that the contradiction didn't trouble him in the least.

He bent down and gave her a kiss on the cheek. She rolled in the lush satin sheets, grabbed his shirt, and said, "Don't go, Ahmet."

She pouted with a luscious lower lip hanging like fruit from a pomegranate tree.

"What could there possibly be at the office that could be as much fun as staying here with me?"

He smiled and removed her hand. She stood up in the bed pulling the sheet with her to cover one half of her naked body and beckoned seductively with her finger.

"You know I would gladly stay, but we are in the middle of an important project. Do you have any plans today?"

She let the sheet drop back to the bed. Yearning stirred deep down, and he remembered the hadith of the Prophet 'The woman comes and retires in the shape of a devil.' *Is there anything else that could drive a man to do the things a woman could? I look upon the devil himself and am driven mad with desire. How mysterious are the ways of Allah.* Life was a test and no one believed that more than he did.

Nafrit stepped off the bed and headed for the bathroom to perform, for the third time, the ritual washing required after intimacy.

"I feel like just having a lazy day here at the house. It's far too hot to be outside."

"Okay, well, let me know if you need to go out, and I'll send a car."

She turned and gave him another full frontal and a huge smile

"You are sooo sweet." She blew him a kiss. "I'll be waiting for you tonight. Will you be working late again?"

"I hope not, but it is possible. I'll call and let you know. I need to run."

"Bye, darling."

She closed the bathroom door. He grabbed his bag and headed out of the room.

The porter standing at the end of the marble hall pushed the button to call the elevator as soon as he saw Ahmet's door open.

"Good morning, Jamil."

"A blessed morning to you too, sir."

"Did you tell me that your cousin was looking for work?" asked Ahmet.

"Yes, sir. He's a very bright kid. Good with computers. He has a degree from Al-Azhar."

"Can he use a digital camera?"

"Of course, I told you he is very good with technology."

The elevator doors opened. Ahmet stepped in, turned to face the porter, and pushed the button to keep the door open.

"Tell him I want him outside this apartment in one hour with a camera. If Nafrit leaves, he is to follow her and take pictures of where she goes."

He handed the man one hundred Egyptian pounds. The porter took the money with a slight bow.

"That is for taxis."

The elevator doors closed, and less than twenty seconds later Ahmet stepped out of the elevator into the underground parking garage. His chauffeur was waiting at the elevator to take his bag when he stepped out.

"To the office, sir?"

"Yes, and hurry."

He walked briskly to the black Mercedes CL. The chauffeur opened the door and he sank into the leather seats. As always, his driver had already started the car and turned on the air-conditioner. Ahmet hated to sweat unless it was in bed. He grabbed the phone installed in the back seat and called the office.

"Good morning, Jabbar."

"Good morning, sir."

"Any news?"

"Nothing good."

"Okay. I'll be there in a few minutes."

He terminated the call, placed the phone back in its charger and looked out the window. They were crawling.

"What's the problem?" he asked the chauffeur.

"There's an accident in the other lane and every mother's son has to stop and see who has been killed."

Ahmet sighed. He hated waiting. He began to think about his objectives for the day and a few minutes later traffic started to flow again. Five minutes later, the car stopped at the security check-point in front of Baraka Bank while two guards carrying HK G36s searched the trunk and the bottom of the car for bombs before waving them on to the parking garage underneath the bank. The car stopped in front of the elevators and a security guard opened his door.

"Good morning, sir."

"Good morning."

He placed his computer bag on the belt in front of the X-ray machine, walked through the metal detector and picked up his bag on the other side. Another security guard had already called the elevator and was holding the door for him. His ID card said that he worked at the bank as a security analyst, and though he was sure these men had no idea what he really did, they knew he was no security analyst and treated him accordingly. The elevator doors closed, and he began his uninterrupted ascent to the nineteenth floor. He didn't even have to push a button to indicate the floor. The elevator only had buttons for floors 1-18. When the doors opened, he walked into his a high-tech command post.

27

"Okay, sleepy head. Wake up!" Gary looked over at his sleeping brother. He didn't even stir. Gary set his book down on the table, walked over to the bed and looked down at his brother. *He probably hasn't slept in forty-eight hours.* He would have gladly let him continue sleeping even though he knew that he would never hear the end of it if he did.

"Gilbert."

He shook his arm gently.

"It's time to wake up."

Gilbert only groaned and rolled over. Gary walked to the window and pulled back the curtains, flooding the room with light. Gilbert pulled the covers over his head. Gary decided to appeal to his brother's over-developed sense of discipline.

"Hey, it's almost nine o'clock. Imagine what Dad would say if he heard you were sleeping in this late. You sleep any longer and you'll miss lunch like you did breakfast."

It had the desired effect. Gilbert sat upright in bed, rubbing his eyes and then squinted in the bright light.

"Don't you think you should have gotten me up for an earlier start today?"

"I've been up since 7:30, had breakfast, read the paper and finished half a novel while you were in La-La land. But we can't do anything until the autopsy is completed. Besides, you needed the rest."

"Fair enough."

He jumped out of bed and headed for the shower. Gary returned to his book. Hardly, a minute had gone by before the Blackberry beside Gilbert's bed began to ring. Gary ignored it, but it didn't stop. Finally, it stopped and switched over to voicemail. But thirty seconds later it rang again. It might be urgent. He set down the book and walked over to the bed.

"Hello."

"Hello, Gilbert. This is Dr. Timothy White."

"Doctor, this is Gilbert's brother, Gary. He is in the shower right now. I can have him call you back as soon as he gets out."

"No need. Just tell him that his suspicions were justified. If we could meet down at the police station around eleven thirty, the Superintendent would like to be there when we go over the autopsy."

"You mean my father was killed?"

"Well, it was probably unintentional, but yes."

"Wait a minute. What the hell does "unintentional" mean?"

"I think it would be better if I explain it to you and your brother in person."

"Of course. We'll be down there as soon as possible."

Gary turned off the Blackberry and sat staring out the window. *Unintentionally killed? Was this the evil the Turkish imam was talking about? How does a 65-year-old man get killed accidentally in his own apartment?*

A few minutes later, Gilbert walked out of the bathroom with a towel around his waist. He didn't look any better than he had ten minutes ago. He hadn't shaved, and his eyes were still swollen. He walked to his suitcase and pulled out his shaving kit.

"No time for that now, man. We need to get moving. The doctor called while you were in the shower."

He paused.

"And…?"

"He wants to see us at the police station in thirty minutes. It's not good."

"What did they find?"

"He wouldn't give any particulars on the phone. He just said that Dad was accidently killed."

Gilbert's eyes narrowed and his face hardened.

"Alright, let's get down there and find out what happened."

Gilbert dropped the towel and walked butt-naked over to the suitcase and started rummaging, pulling out socks, underwear, a t-shirt and jeans.

"You said the document was old, right?"

"It looked old to me."

"What kind of document do people kill for, Gilbert? Could it be some rare and priceless collector's item? It's all a bit weird, don't you think?"

"I have no idea what it is, but as soon as this meeting with the Doctor is over, that is what we need to focus on. Say, do you think one of us should be with Gwyn? Could she be in any danger?"

"I don't see how."

"Gary, what if Dad was killed for the document that she has now?"

"Hmm. I see your point, but could anyone know that she has it or where she is?"

Gilbert shook his head and scowled before saying with an I-know-more-about-this-than-you tone of voice, "It is not hard to find this information if you have the connections and the money they will want for it. Believe me, we deal with cases like this all the time. Information is the gold of the modern age, and there are plenty of miners out there. Let's just hope that isn't the type of people we're dealing with."

+━━+

Salih was fit to be tied. "You told me the autopsy would be a formality, that the cause of death would be a heart attack, and that no suspicion would be aroused. That doesn't seem to be the case"

The man in the chair on the other side of the desk was wearing the uniform of the Metropolitan police, but he was clearly not the authority figure in this conversation.

"Apparently Gilbert O'Brien had a doctor retained by his company to provide a second opinion on the autopsy. There was nothing we could do without attracting attention."

Allah kahretsin. Gilbert was on to something. What was it? Had the professor left an explanation? Salih could not know for sure, but his gut feeling was not good; even worse, it didn't matter now. There was no way to speed up the plan. The feeling that catastrophe was lurking around some inscrutable corner had been haunting him all day. This new development only intensified the feeling. He had handled delicate jobs before. This was the first time he had experienced such anxiety. It was almost like a panic attack. He told himself to relax. It didn't work.

The operation was hours away and all the preparations had been made. There was no sense sitting here allowing himself to get more and more wound up. It would be a long night anyway. His decision was instant.

"Mahmut."

"Yes, sir?"

"I'm going to have lunch at home today. Escort our friend out by the freight elevator. I'll be back in an hour and a half. If anything unexpected happens, let me know immediately."

"Yes, sir."

He picked up his bag and headed for the door.

"One more thing. If Ahmet calls, just patch him through on my cell. There is no need to tell him I am out for lunch."

"Of course."

+━━+

The taxi slowed down and pulled up to the curb. He looked at them in the rearview mirror and said with a thick Jamaican accent,

"This is the police station."

150

Gilbert looked down at the meter, pulled out a fifty pound note and said, "Keep the change."

Superintendent McIntosh was there to meet them at the door. He led them down a long hallway with tiny offices teeming with detectives. Gary could see the doctor in an office at the end of the hall through the large glass wall. The Superintendent held the door for them and they walked in and shook the doctor's hand.

"Thank you for meeting with us, Doctor," Gilbert said.

McIntosh moved between them to his chair behind the desk and motioned for them to all sit down.

"Boys, I know the doctor has already told you the bad news. I'm very saddened by this sudden twist in the investigation. The autopsy report was a surprise to us all. Your father's apartment is still being treated as a crime scene. I'm afraid you may not have access for a couple of days."

Gilbert cleared his throat.

"Has your team found anything else at the apartment?"

"No, nothing. And that is troubling. There were no fingerprints and nothing suspicious. The cyber-forensics team agrees. Definitely, a secure deletion of selected files. If we learn anything, you'll be the first to know."

He turned to the doctor, who cleared his throat.

"First of all, I want to say that we are lucky to have found anything at all. We ordered an expanded set of blood tests because of Gilbert's suspicion of possible foul play. As bizarre as this may sound, I believe your father was unintentionally killed. He had high levels of sodium thiopental in his blood."

"You mean sodium pentothal?" asked Gary.

"Well, that is a common brand name, but not its technical name."

"I thought that was used for anesthesia."

"It's a barbiturate, a common anesthetic agent although not preferred these days."

"Every spook flick I've ever seen shows it being used for interrogations."

"Yes, it has been used for interrogation, though its efficacy is mostly psychological. It's not the truth serum TV makes it out to be. It does have a calming effect though, making people less inhibited and easier to handle."

"Who would do this?" asked Gary tersely.

"I'm afraid the motive for the crime is outside of my area of expertise."

"So, he was killed by an injection of sodium thiopental?"

"Yes and no. Given in a large enough dose, it is fatal, as are most drugs, but your father was not given a lethal dose. Whoever did this definitely did not intend to kill your father."

"But, he's still dead."

"Yes, and that is because your father was taking a prescription drug that

151

contained pentoxifylline. You probably know he suffered from intermittent claudication."

"You mean the pain in his legs whenever he exerted himself too much?"

"Well, yes, that is a symptom, but it is a bit more complicated than that. Your father took at least a double dose of his medicine. I can't be exactly sure how much because I don't know exactly when he took it, and so I cannot accurately calculate the amount of metabolic elimination. Unfortunately, pentoxifylline and sodium thiopental are a dangerous mix that can result in pulmonary edema, which is what actually killed your father."

"So, whoever gave him this injection was not expecting him to die?"

"That's right. They were probably totally surprised when he started having trouble breathing."

"I'm sorry, Doctor, but what exactly is pulmonary edema?" asked Gilbert.

"It is a build-up of fluid in the lungs, which makes it difficult to breathe, inhibiting the transfer of oxygen to the blood, so the exact cause of death is hypoxia, a fancy word for a lack of oxygen."

"So, he drowned in his apartment?"

"You could say that. After we realized that he had been given this drug, we looked more closely and found a large number of miniscule cotton fibers on his tongue. He had apparently been gagged with some sort of cloth. There is also bruising on his wrists, but so slight it could easily have been overlooked as well. We can deduce from this that he was also tied up, but apparently for a very short time."

The doctor reached down and pulled a folder out of his bag and handed it to Gary, who was sitting next to him.

"Here is the full report if you are interested in reading it."

Gilbert watched his brother begin to open the folder and immediately stood up.

"Dr. White, I cannot tell you how much it means to me that you agreed to get involved. We want to get to the bottom of this and your help has been invaluable."

Gary closed the folder and stood up as well. Gilbert breathed a sigh of relief inside. He had read dozens of autopsies. They were not pleasant reading, and he knew that in his current frame of mind, Gary would not want to know how much his dad's brain weighed, what color the liver was or what the contents of his stomach were.

The doctor grabbed his bag and stood up.

"If you have any questions later, feel free to call me anytime."

"Thank you, Doctor."

The doctor left, and Gary turned back to the Inspector. He was visibly shaken.

"So, what is going to happen now? Do we have any leads? Who would do this?"

McIntosh looked down at his desk as he replied.

"Well, the case is now an official homicide. Right now the only thing we have to go on is that document you say your father gave to your sister. I really need to get a copy of that. How soon could you have that for me?"

"I'll call my sister and ask her to get that for you as soon as possible."

"Thanks. I wish we were able to tell you more, but at this point, we don't have many leads. In fact, without you, this might have been missed altogether. Our men will be looking at this from every angle. But if you know more or learn something new, anything, please share it with us. We don't have much to work with."

"Believe me, Inspector, if we find out anything, you'll be the first to know."

"One more thing, if this was related to that document, and it appears to have been, then you might be in danger here in London, so I am assigning a team to protect you for as long as you are in the city, or until this is solved. It is a team of six working in two-man shifts around the clock."

"Are you sure that's necessary?"

"No, I'm not sure of anything, except that whoever did this is extremely professional and therefore dangerous. That's why I am sending these men to protect you. They will do their best to stay out of your way."

"We appreciate the gesture," Gary said, "Can we ask you to inform us the moment you have any leads or developments in the case?"

"You have my word."

<hr/>

Salih walked up to the door, slipped the key into the door and turned the lock gently. He wanted this to be a surprise. His first wife lived in the flat next door. He rented two, so that his new bride had her own home. It was better that way. Less fighting and jealousy. He opened the door, stepped softly into the entryway and removed his shoes. He could hear the television in the bedroom, so he tiptoed in that direction. The door was ajar. Alicia was lying on the bed watching a reality show, still in her pajamas. She was definitely spoiled, but that had been part of what attracted Salih to her in the first place.

Salih glided into the room and ran his hand along her back, which elicited a loud scream.

"Damn it, Salih. You scared me to death. Why aren't you at work?"

"Sorry darling," he smiled at her. "I thought I would come home for lunch today and you could help me unwind a bit."

She knew what that meant and smiled eagerly,

"Whatever you want, darling. What would you like for lunch?"

"We can worry about that later," he said nibbling her neck and inhaling the fragrance of her perfume in deep breaths. She rolled over and gave him a long, passionate kiss. Then he directed his attention to her beautiful neck. He had just begun moving down when his cell phone rang on the nightstand. He grabbed it quickly and looked at the number. It was from the office, probably Ahmet.

"Sorry darling, I have to take this."

But before he could stop her, she grabbed the phone out of his hand and began running away from him through the house, laughing and playful.

"Alicia, bring that back. This is a really important deal I've been working on."

"We don't need more money, honey. Ignore it. You can call him back in twenty minutes."

He cornered her in the kitchen. She was still laughing and holding the ringing phone above her head, then behind her back, trying to keep it out of his reach. To her, it was a game. Salih hated this part of marriage. Still, he knew it would come to this sooner and later, and this was clearly the time. Without another word, he stopped and looked into her eyes for about three seconds. She was still smiling and laughing when his hand came out of nowhere and slapped her across the face.

"Alicia, I am your husband and I said give me the phone. This is no game."

It was hard for Salih. He was not by nature a violent man, but this was the hard truth of marriage. Even his first wife, a girl raised in a good Muslim family, had needed a few beating to bring her to heel. It was an unfortunate reality of the gender divide. Alicia dropped the phone and ran back towards the bedroom crying. He waited until he heard the door slam before answering the phone. She would get over it. They always did.

"Hello."

"Salih, this is Ahmet. Is there a problem? The phone must have rang ten times."

"No, I was just in the middle of something."

"Good, I was worried there for a moment. Look, I heard the news. This is not good."

Salih grimaced. "You are referring to the autopsy. No, it was not what we had arranged, but there is still no way to trace anything back to us."

"Maybe not, but they will almost certainly connect his death with the document."

"Yes, and we will retrieve that tonight. Another death will just give them more to clean up. We are safe."

"And, what if they have made copies?"

"Well, there is nothing we can do about that. I'm sure the girl will tell us what we need to know, and we will deal with that if it is an issue. However, without the original, our people can always claim that the digital copies were actually created out of thin air. We must keep faith."

"And your plan B is ready?"

"Of course. May Allah make it unnecessary."

"*Amin.* A thousand times over. Still, I have reviewed it. Not bad, but lacking in imagination. I have a bold addition to make, one that gives us even more leverage, one that creates the chaos we have always thrived on. I will send you a rough draft within thirty minutes. Please advise me about teams we could use to execute it, and provide an operational analysis and a risk assessment before tomorrow morning."

"Will do."

Salih hung up the phone and looked towards the bedroom door in frustration. He would have to go back in there and get his shirt so he could go to work.

28

TIRA, TEXAS   Gwyn turned over to look at the clock on the bed-side table. It was 4:45, which meant it was almost eleven o'clock in London. She picked up her iPhone to check her e-mail and messages. She was hoping to hear something from Gilbert. Nothing. As soon as she finished her run, she would give him a call. She stood up, pulled off her nightgown and started feeling around on the chair for the jogging shorts, athletic bra and the shirt she had laid out the night before. Then she stuck her iPhone in her pocket just in case Gilbert decided to call.

She detested jogging but needed the release. It was still almost an hour before sunrise and yet outside it was a muggy 79 degrees. Early morning was the only time to run in August and still it would be miserable enough to make her question her decision to leave Wales. She went to the kitchen and rummaged through several of the drawers, looking for a headlamp. It was in the second drawer from the top. She adjusted the strap and put it on her head.

When she opened the door, the breeze she had hoped would greet her was absent. It was dead calm. She stepped out onto the porch and closed the door softly behind her. The moon was close to full, bright enough to illuminate her surroundings very well. She had barely crossed the yard when she heard her Uncle's geese start honking. *O bother, I hope that doesn't wake anyone.* Her uncle had kept geese as long as she could remember. He called them his watch dogs and every time they visited he had told her and her brothers how the geese had saved Rome in the early days from a siege by their Celtic ancestors. He would always smile and say 'Learn from your enemy.' Uncle Henry swore that geese were more attentive than any dog and the noise always set the dog to barking as well.

It was too dark and dangerous to run on the county road without any reflective running gear, so she headed for the dirt road that meandered for about three miles through pastures and woods on Uncle Henry's farm. She switched on her light and forced her legs to move fast enough to call it jogging.

In the city, she listened to pod-casts while she ran. Out here, she wanted to enjoy the sounds of nature. It was so peaceful, but the first mile was torture.

She realized just how out of shape she was as her body protested the sudden rigorous activity. The two raccoons and three deer she saw in the first mile helped her take her mind off of it. At the halfway point, however, she decided that pushing herself the entire distance was too much and had just slowed to a walk when her iPhone vibrated against her leg. She almost jumped out of her skin. She glanced at the screen before answering.

"Hello, Gilbert. Thanks for calling."

"Good morning, Gwyn. You sound like you're out of breath."

"Yeah, well I decided to take a jog this morning, and it's really kicking my tail."

"Good for you. How are Uncle Henry and Aunt Bonny?"

"Well, they certainly look frailer. They were devastated to hear that Dad had passed away. Uncle Henry is going to help me with funeral arrangements today. Is Gary there yet?"

"Look, I asked Brittany to stop by and check in on you around nine o'clock."

It was not lost on Gwyn that he had ignored her question.

"What for?"

"I thought you could use the support."

"That was thoughtful, Gil. How are you holding up?"

"As well as can be expected under the circumstances. Is there anything I can do for you?"

"Don't worry about me, Gilbert. I'm fine. I'm glad I'm here."

"Can you scan a copy of that document and send it to me? The Metropolitan Police want to have a look at it."

"Well, there isn't a scanner here. Is it urgent? I was planning on going to town tomorrow."

"It can wait until tomorrow. Listen, we're going over to the university now to start taking care of dad's personal belongings and then we'll go back to the morgue to make final arrangements. I'll call later."

"Okay. Take care."

Gwyn hung up and continued jogging. She had wanted to ask what he had learned about the document. It would have to wait. What concerned her now was the relationship between her brothers. *I just hope Gilbert isn't too hard on him.*

She worried about her little brother. They all worried about him. It had happened without any real warning about a year after their mother was diagnosed with cancer. He had been in a serious relationship, but soon after his mother started chemo, something happened and it all blew up. He never spoke of it. He seemed to just withdraw into a shell. No one pressed him, but when they asked how he was doing, the answer was always a cynical comeback. Then, about a month before he left home, he had told the family that he would be making an important announcement at their Easter get-together.

He was conspicuously absent at the Easter morning service, and arrived about thirty minutes late for dinner. They had tried to guess what it was he wanted to tell them. Gilbert thought he might have a secret girlfriend and was going to announce that he was getting married. Gwyn and her dad had agreed that he had probably found a job and was moving off somewhere. Their mother had only said, "I just hope it's something positive. For months now, a dark cloud has doused the light I used to see in his eyes."

Throughout the meal, they all waited for him to make his announcement, but he was very quiet. At one point, Ian had said, "Son, we missed you in church today."

He never looked up. He stared at the lamb and mint sauce on his plate for a moment and then he raised his head and glanced around the table. He stared into each of their eyes and held their gaze for just a moment before moving to the next one. Then, very softly, almost as if he were making an apology, he said, "It's all a chasing after the wind. I don't want to believe it, but I think he was right. I've been reading it now for months. 'A grievous evil' is what he calls this life we live under the sun. In another place, it says, 'I am like a mute who cannot open his mouth or offer a reply.' Life has taken the wind out of my sails. I need to find the wind again."

Then, he had put his head back down and finished the meal in silence. After the table was cleared, they had all gathered back in the living room. It was Gilbert who asked the question.

"Alright, lover boy, we are all bursting with curiosity. What is this announcement you have for us?"

His answer still rang in her ears.

"I made it at the dinner table," he said quietly.

That day was the last time they had been together as a family. Gary began travelling and, at times, seemed to drop off the face of the earth. First, it was the Far East and India, most recently he had been in Damascus and Istanbul. It was strange. He wasn't angry and privately conveyed this to all of them. He had dropped in for Christmas the year before Mom died, but Gilbert hadn't been able to make it. He had been at the funeral. Gwyn had gone back and read Ecclesiastes a dozen times. She had tried to talk to him, but he was too angry, too pessimistic, too dark…All he would say to her attempts at encouragement was, "This too is meaninglessness, a chasing after the wind…"

Gwyn looked in the mirror. Her eyes were still red from crying. She had jumped in the shower after her run and simply melted, sobbing uncontrollably as the water coursed over her body. The pain she felt seemed as fresh as the moment Gilbert had broken the news to her at the airport. She took some comfort in that. The grief made her feel more alive, more human. The feelings of loss and heartache seemed to give existence meaning. It was proof of just how meaningful the relationship with her father had been. It was the positive side of pain and she felt a pang of sorrow for anyone whose relationships were too shallow to experience the blessing of grief.

She got out of the shower and looked at the clock. It was almost 8:20. Brittany was supposed to be here before noon, and Gwyn wanted to do some more research before she showed up. She dressed in a hurry and then gulped down a breakfast of yogurt and muesli. She settled down in front of the computer nursing a cup of Costa Rican coffee brewed from the Fair Trade beans she had purchased at the Galleria on Wednesday. When she heard a knock at the door sometime later, she looked at the clock and was shocked to see that it was already 11:00 AM. She heard the screen door swing shut and turned around to see her childhood friend and companion from every summer vacation.

"Gwyndolyn O'Brien!"

"Brittany Kirkpatrick, it's so nice of you to stop by."

"What are friends for?"

It was a long hug and Gwyn felt like it infused her with energy.

"I'm sorry to hear about your father. He was a great man."

"He was. Thanks. Now, he is reunited with Mom. As long as I remember that, I do pretty well."

Brittany pointed to the computer. "Working remotely?"

"No, I'm actually doing some research on a document that, strangely enough, might be connected with Dad's death."

"Get out. You've got to be kidding."

Gwyn told Brittany what her father had given her and what they had found when they opened it after his death. She let out a low whistle.

"Wow! Imagine that, a bona fide mystery right here in our own backyard. What have you learned so far?"

"I spent most of the day yesterday working on it and to be honest, I learned far less than I had hoped."

She motioned for Brittany to sit down. "You majored in anthropology. Maybe you can help me."

"Actually it was a double major in anthropology and international studies, which I have to admit is a strange route to take back to one's hometown. What have you learned?"

Gwyn handed Brittany the document.

"First, I researched that symbol at the top. There is no exact replica of it anywhere. It seems to be composed of two different symbols. In the middle is the Ouroboros, the snake swallowing its own tail. It is a very ancient symbol used by the Chinese and Egyptians thousands of years before Christ, but also by the Greeks, Gnostics, and Masons, as well as in Kundalini teaching, Theosophy, Norse mythology and West African belief systems like that of the Yoruba."

159

"Well, I'm glad to see you've narrowed it down."

"Right. The only thing those groups seem to have in common is a genetic code that makes them homo sapiens."

"Now, that is what I call international studies. As far as I'm concerned, every snake is evil. It's been that way since the Garden of Eden."

Gwyn smiled. Her Texas relatives had taught her how to identify and kill cotton-mouths, copper-heads and rattlesnakes almost as soon as she could walk. Still, most people could not be bothered to identify them. They simply grabbed a .410 and played it safe. The cartridge was cheaper than a ride to the emergency room.

"What is that funny star?"

"Well, that proved to be much simpler. This eight-point star is really just two squares one on top of the other with a 45-degree twist. It is called *Rub el-Hizb* if I'm pronouncing it right."

"That sounds like Arabic."

"It is. From what I can tell, it means something like 'lord sustainer of the party or sect.' Think about it. El-Hizb."

"What's it supposed to make me think of?"

"I thought of Hizbullah."

"Goodness sakes, girl. You don't mean those people launching rockets at Israel?"

"Yeah, but I don't know what the connection is."

"What else did you learn?"

"Take a look at this," she said, handing her the hand-written note. "This is a translation of the important part of the document."

The council's decision to cancel son of prophet and erase every trace remains among our most solemn duties. It will be a red English sunset on Suri-Strend with a golden sunrise in Tunis when the bird which has flown is brought back to Südde-i Saadet. Walk in the snow but leave no footprints. Assistance for the sendoff may be obtained from our ever faithful D. Hasten delivery.

13 Jumaada al-awal 1149

Brittany sat looking the document for a minute.

"Well, Tunis is in Tunisia, but that is about the only thing that makes sense to me."

"I have learned that *Südde-i Saadet* was one of the nicknames given to Istanbul during the Ottoman Empire. It apparently meant something like 'threshold of felicity', a reference to the happiness of entering the capital of the Islamic realm."

"What are the numbers at the bottom?"

"That is a date using the Muslim calendar. It is September 19, 1736 on the Gregorian calendar."

Brittany looked down at the document and murmured to herself.

"So, you have a document that refers to Istanbul and a city in North Africa prominently featuring a virtually universal self-consuming snake called Ouroboros combined with a Muslim symbol, and it was written during the 18th century when the Ottoman Empire was in full-blown decline. Interesting…"

"Interesting. Yes, but Dad must have found something here, something important. Why does someone want to steal this document?" *How can I ever hope to make the connections or have the insights he did?*

She checked the despair she felt rising up in her. There was no time for it. She had to find out what it was her dad had suspected.

"What about 'son of prophet'? Any idea what that is referring to?" asked Brittany.

"I researched that all day yesterday. Obviously, it is the key point of the text, what the author wanted to get rid of. A search on the Internet returns plenty of Old Testament verses and Islamic sites. I waded through them for hours, looking for clues and hoping the answer would jump off of the screen. It didn't."

"Well, I took the day off. What do you say we tackle it together? Let me get my laptop out of the car. You keep looking at that angle and I'll research some others."

One pot of coffee and several hours later, Gwyn pushed back from the desk in frustration.

"We're no closer than when we started. I've searched 'son of prophet' with every combination of Tunis, Istanbul, *Südde-i Saadet*, sunrise, English, council and everything else only to find nothing. I'm beginning to think that maybe Google isn't the omniscient Prime Mover of cyber space after all."

Her phone rang. She looked at the screen. It was a 214 number, but there was no name. She looked at the clock. It was already almost three o'clock in the afternoon. They had been so absorbed in their research they had lost track of time and forgotten lunch.

"Hello."

"Hello, may I speak with Gwyndolyn O'Brien please?"

The voice sounded familiar.

"Speaking, and who, may I ask, are you?"

"It has been a long time, so I am not surprised that you don't recognize me. This is Dr. Zeki Öztürk."

"Dr. Öztürk? Oh my gosh. I am sorry I didn't recognize your voice. Are you in Dallas?"

"Yes, I am. I have business here this week. Gwyndolyn, a friend of mine at the conference in London this week phoned to tell me about your father's death. I wanted to call and convey my condolences. I am truly sorry. Your father was a great scholar, and a great man."

"That is very kind of you. I appreciate it very much."

"I am free tomorrow morning and wondered if I could stop by? I have a few old manuscripts I had planned on giving to your father, and I would still like to pass them on to you."

"That's very thoughtful. I don't know what to say."

"I would like to know that they are included in the works he spent his life putting together. It would mean a great deal to me if they were in his collection, whatever library it ends up in. If it is not convenient, I can mail them, but it would be nice to see you again."

"No, that's fine. Come on out. Do you have a car?"

"I'm renting one for the week. If you give me the address, I'm sure the GPS can get me there."

"Okay, it is 1900 FM 1536, Tira. That is past Greenville and just north of Sulphur Springs, so you'll take I-30 most of the way."

"That should be easy. What time is convenient for you?"

"Anytime is fine. I'll be here all day."

"Then I will try to be there between 10:00 and 11:00 in the morning."

"Great, I look forward to seeing you."

"Me too. Take care."

"Bye, now."

"Bye."

Gwyn hung up the phone.

"Who was that?"

"Just a colleague of my father's. Let's grab something to eat," she said heading for the kitchen. "I'm starving."

"I'd love to stay, but I promised Mom I'd stop by this afternoon and I still have to go shopping. But I can come back tomorrow."

They hugged again at the door. Gwyn watched as her childhood friend climbed into a white Ford dually. It was a different world out here. When she was gone, she turned back inside and went to the kitchen. As she opened the refrigerator, she stopped and stood there for a minute, puzzling over how Zeki had gotten her telephone number.

DALLAS, TEXAS Zeki hung up the payphone and looked out over the airport. He had studied the layout as an exercise in breaking airport security towards the end of his career with MIT. It was the world's third largest airport and boasted the largest number of non-intersecting runways. North Texas was the quintessential land of big sky. The second floor of the concourse made him feel like he was on top of a small mountain. It redefined flat. From the VIP lounge, he had a 360 degree view and visibility was unlimited by anything except the curvature of the earth.

When he walked out of customs into the waiting area of terminal D, he found himself surrounded by members of the USO greeting several hundred soldiers returning from duty in the Middle East. He had often been in such close proximity with the forces of empire. He had never gotten used to it. These men were being hailed as returning heroes after killing who knew how many innocent Muslim women and children. It was wrong that they should live in peace and security while freedom fighters around the Muslim world were afraid to even use a cell phone for fear that their house would be hit by a cruise missile or a smart bomb from an unmanned drone.

Part of him knew that these men were merely unwitting slaves projecting the power of the global elite and that his anger should not be directed at them. Yet, without them the global elite had no teeth. *How can they be so blind!* The ruling powers legitimized their actions by paying off or acquiring the "free press". As a result, the sacrifices of life and limb were borne bravely and with honor. It was a charade, and the superman costume donned by western democracies had grown threadbare, no longer able to conceal its corpulence, its festering sores, its moral depravity. No matter, these so-called empires were nothing more than a morning vapor. This one would be no different. *They inevitably collapse under the weight of their own corruption and hubris.*

He picked up his bag and walked along the row of windows towards the Avis kiosk. A stubby white woman greeted him with a smile. She was young, apparently too young to realize that no amount of foundation could hide her blotchy red skin or the chicken-pox pattern of pimples that covered her face. Five minutes later, the paperwork was finished, and he was asked to take a seat. His car would arrive shortly. It was another ten minutes before the Avis desk manager, overweight and sweating, walked through the door to his left. The smile on his face had melted from the heat.

"Mister, huh, I'm not sure I can pronounce your last name."

"Çölaşan."

"Mr. Chorlashen, your car is just outside. Here are the keys and a copy of the rental agreement. Can I help you with your bag?"

"No, thank you. It is quite light. What's the temperature outside?"

"It's supposed to hit 107° today, but it seems hotter than that already. Are you here on business or pleasure?"

"Hopefully both," replied Zeki with a smile as he took the keys.

"Very well, then. I hope you enjoy your stay in Dallas."

"I intend to."

Zeki walked outside into a veritable blast furnace. A lidless nuclear blaze streamed unhindered through a cloudless blue sky, turning the concrete into a gray charcoal that furnished heat for the Texas sauna. The heat waves rising off the concrete made anything over fifty yards away look blurry. The lady had assured him that the air-conditioner was ice-cold. He quickly threw his bag into the passenger seat and cranked the car. Then he turned on the Magellan GPS and typed in 1900 FM 1536, Tira, Texas. Technology made everything so much easier.

Now, all he had to do was obtain a weapon, which, in Texas, would be as easy as finding a Qur'an in Saudi Arabia. America's obsession with weapons was no secret. It was part of the national psychology—something that had been passed down from the pioneers and was now an intrinsic part of the national conscience. He remembered how an intelligence officer had told his class during training years ago that private citizens in America owned more than two hundred and fifty million firearms. They had all been appalled. The officer's words still rang in his head. 'It's called a standing army, boys. Now, you know why they can afford to have an all-volunteer army. The enlisted men run the big toys—fly the planes, launch the missiles, sail the fleet. The infantry is the citizenry.' In Turkey, a rifled barrel was prohibited, and gun-control laws were strict. The Americans might be a hornet's nest if stirred, but they certainly made his job much easier.

Three hours later another Turk, named Hasan, travelling on a passport issued to Tuğrul, would arrive on a flight from Munich to join his teammate already in the country. The mission was simple, so simple, in fact, that he felt it quite beneath his training. A single woman on a farm in the country, untrained, unsuspecting and unarmed. There was no risk. His partner was one of the best. The orders had been simple too. 'Don't screw it up. Use any means or force necessary to retrieve the document and all copies. Subject the woman to forceful interrogation and then dispose of her discreetly.'

29

No one noticed the light blue Ford driving up and down FM 1536. Nor did anyone notice that it was left parked in front of the community center in the Texas village of Tira, or that the driver emerged in Army camos carrying a black bag. It was too hot to notice things like that. People didn't go outside in this heat. They didn't even sit by the window. It was too depressing.

It had taken Zeki a little over two hours to reach the address Gwyn had provided. He scouted the area for another thirty minutes in the car and used Google Earth to memorize several different aerial profiles—a one-square-mile layout complete with terrain, fence-rows, nearby houses and bodies of water, a five-square-mile aerial with every single county road and highway, and then a fifty-square-mile satellite picture to plan alternate escape routes.

The heat was beyond stifling. A gentle breeze from the south blew in enough Gulf moisture to raise the heat index several degrees. He was drenched in sweat by the time he reached the outskirts of the farm. When he was three hundred and fifty yards from the house, he compared the Google aerial image he had memorized with the landscape that lay before him, looking for the large tree he had identified. He needed a place that would provide cover and a clear line of sight to the main house and the cottage.

The only place that offered both was this tree, which, to his eye, was bizarre. It was covered with lime-green fruit the size of a grapefruit and the branches bowed practically to the ground. It was not ideal, but it was the only cover available. Who would dare to move in this heat anyway? The tree was located on a small knoll about fifty yards from the pond. Once he reached the tree, it would be a straight, unobstructed shot across the pond to the house and cottage. The only problem was that the tree was out in the open, which meant a belly crawl to get there. He had no time to waste. It was over a hundred yards away, and he knew that meant at least an hour's worth of tedious snaking through the knee-high grass on his belly.

Fifteen minutes later, he was sweating so profusely and the heat was so oppressive he was sure his sweat was leaving a muddy trail behind him. An image of the barren tree-less landscape of Şanlıurfa flashed into his mind. It had been hot there too, but he had been much younger. About ten yards away from the tree, he suddenly felt a burning pain on his right wrist. It felt like an insect bite. He tried to ignore it. Impossible. Suddenly, his whole arm was engulfed in flame. He looked down to find he was on top of an ant hill the likes of which he had never seen. There were hundreds, if not thousands, of tiny red ants crawling all over his sleeve. He began beating his right arm in an attempt to kill the ants, but he quickly realized that this was futile. There were too many, and the pain was excruciating. He knew he had to get that shirt off as fast as possible. He gritted his teeth and finished the last few yards on his belly at lightning speed.

As soon as he was behind the trunk and hidden by the leaves, he stood up and stripped to his waist. The pain induced by this miniscule creature was extraordinary. His arm was swollen. His chest and neck were with covered in red bumps. He rummaged through the bag until he found a syringe and needle containing antihistamine. He hoped it would provide some relief. Fifteen minutes later, he was still trying to convince himself that it had.

Meanwhile, he removed his hardware from the bag and laid it out on the ground in front of him. He assembled the AR-15 in less than three minutes. This would be his first time to use the weapon, but he knew it by heart. It had a Trijicon scope, which would afford plenty of light. The forecast was for clear skies and the moon was full. He also had three thirty-round magazines with seventy-five grain hollow-point bullets. It was far more ammo than he would need, but if there was one thing you could never have too much of, it was ammunition.

Of course, there were Geneva Convention rules against soldiers using anything but the more 'humane' full metal jacket bullets. These rules meant nothing to him. All that mattered was maximum kill power. A knife and a .45 caliber Colt were strapped to his belt. There had been a wide range of handguns to choose from at the pawnshop, but the idea of "hunting" in the Lone Star state with a cowboy sidearm gave him peculiar satisfaction.

His preparations were painstaking. Several hours later, he pulled out a tube of paint and began blackening his face. The sun was getting lower in the sky, and he could tell the temperature had dropped ever so slightly. He slapped a mosquito on his neck and then another on his arm. Within minutes, he found himself enveloped in a cloud of the pesky blood-suckers. He grabbed another camo shirt from the bag and pulled it over his head, all the while wishing that he had brought insect repellant. *Why did Allah create such bothersome creatures?* He knew the answer. Like everything else, they were a test. The whole world was a test, a giant classroom, to see whether or not man would grumble and complain about his fate or patiently endure his trials as proof of his faith.

It was still more than an hour until sundown, and he knew from experience that when the sun went down, the number of mosquitoes would swell exponentially. He was going to have to cover every inch of skin or end up looking like a human pin cushion. It would be a trying wait, but there was no way an insect weighing less than two and half grams would distract him from this crucial mission.

30

SATURDAY, LONDON   Gary woke up and just lay there staring at the ceiling. More dreams, the same dreams, strange disturbing dreams. *Where were they coming from?* He rolled over to see if his brother was up yet. The bed beside his was a mess of tangled sheets. His brother was not there, but the sound of running water could be heard in the bathroom. He glanced at the clock. It was 6:49. Gilbert was back to his old disciplined self. He walked over to the window beside the desk. His brother's laptop was open to an online version of a British newspaper. There was a picture of his father and a caption that read, 'Byzantine scholar found dead in apartment.'

Gilbert's Blackberry rang. Gary walked over and grabbed it off the nightstand between their beds. He looked at the number but didn't recognize it. He decided to play secretary.

"Hello."

"Hello. Is this Gilbert O'Brien?"

"This is his brother Gary."

"This is McIntosh. I hate to call so early, but I promised Gilbert that I would let you guys know immediately if there were any developments."

"Of course. Have you found a lead?"

"No. I'm afraid I have more bad news. We don't know yet how it relates to this case. I'm hoping that maybe you or your brother can help us. Apparently, another professor has been killed."

"From the same university?" asked Gary incredulously.

"Not exactly, but it was a professor attending the conference at King's College. Yesterday afternoon, when the coroner confirmed that your father's death was suspicious. I put out an internal memo, requesting any information that might be connected. It was flagged by someone who noticed that another professor was found dead less than six hours after your father's homicide. His death was ruled a heart attack as well, but I asked Dr. White to take part in a second autopsy to collaborate that. It was determined that he had also been given sodium thiopental, a non-lethal dose. He was apparently suffocated with a pillow. Obviously, we are exploring the possibility that the two deaths are related. The man was apparently found on Wednesday morning by the hotel maid who came to clean his room. He is a Turkish citizen."

"What is his name?" asked Gary.

He could hear the inspector rustling through papers on his desk. Gilbert walked out of the bathroom with the towel around his waist. Gary covered the phone with his hand and whispered, "It's McIntosh. He just told me that another professor attending the conference at King's College has been found dead."

McIntosh came back on the line.

"The name is Haluk Bayram. Do you know him?"

"Nope, but let me ask my brother. He just stepped out of the shower. Hey Gil, do you know a Turkish professor by the name of Haluk Bayram?"

"No, the only Turkish professor I know is that fellow Dad used to work with. What was his name? Zeki something. I can't remember."

"Öztürk," Gary responded.

"Yeah, that's right. Dr. Zeki Öztürk."

Gary quickly put the phone on speaker and sat it down on the nightstand, so his brother could hear the conversation.

"No, Mr. McIntosh. Gilbert doesn't know Dr. Bayram. The only Turkish professor we are acquainted with is Dr. Zeki Öztürk."

"Did you say 'Öztürk'?"

"Yes. Why?"

"Mr. O'Brien, Dr. Zeki Öztürk was also at the conference, and he is currently missing. He hasn't been back to his hotel room, and he hasn't left the country. We ran a check on all foreign nationals leaving the country since Monday. His passport hasn't been scanned."

Gilbert was pacing the room, processing this new information.

"Do you think he may have been killed too?"

"Well, anything is possible, but in the absence of a corpse, we're not assuming that he's been murdered. We're keeping all of our options open."

"I don't understand. What options?"

"I simply mean that we do not know if Dr. Öztürk is involved in this incident in any way at all."

Gilbert stopped his pacing and strode quickly over to the bed where he sat down and spoke towards the phone.

"Inspector McIntosh, I am very sorry, but I just realized that my father had a portion of the document translated. I don't know who did this for him, but it could have been Zeki. He and my father have known each other for years; in fact, they were close friends."

"Mr. O'Brien, I don't know how to say this tactfully, so I am just going to be direct. We do have reason to suspect, especially in light of what you have just told me, that Prof. Öztürk might have been involved in your father's murder."

"I find that impossible to believe."

"We've obtained messages and telephone calls placed to your father in the week prior to his death. He received a voice mail from someone the night he died, and we believe it could have been Zeki."

"What do you mean, 'Could have been Zeki'? Can't you trace the number?"

"We've had a team working on this all night, Mr. O'Brien. It seems Prof. Öztürk has quite a colorful history."

"Meaning?"

"Did you know he was a former member of the Turkish intelligence agency, MIT?"

"No, I did not, but then, he was friends with my father, not with me."

"Of course, I understand."

"What does that have to do with the voice mail?"

"The number of the cellphone that sent the voice mail was a brand new SIM card, bought only last week, paid for with cash and registered to Bobby Jones. However, all of the information given for Bobby Jones is fictitious. The voice mail contained the word *dostum*. I had a friend with the Foreign Service take it to their translation department. Apparently, it is Turkish for 'my friend.'"

"I find it very difficult to believe that Professor Öztürk would kill my father for an old document."

"Your father's death was an accident. Maybe Zeki didn't mean to kill him. He only wanted this manuscript."

"He wouldn't betray my father. They were quite close. He has stayed in our home many times."

"Isn't closeness a requirement for betrayal? Anyway, the message was peculiar too. It said, 'Dear *Dostum*, I really must see you as soon as possible about the document. It's urgent. Please get back with me as soon as you can.'"

"Did my father ever return his call?"

"Well, that is another strange thing. Apparently, your father never retrieved this voice mail, and so he never received the message. Does your father have any other Turkish acquaintances who might have sent him a message like this?"

"Not that I am aware of."

"Until we find out where Prof. Öztürk is, I am afraid that he is the only person of interest in this case. We have notified the university, but so far no one remembers seeing him after Wednesday. If he should happen to contact you, please let us know immediately."

"Can't you use the cell phone number to track his whereabouts?"

"We have already tried that. The SIM card has not been plugged into a cell phone in the UK or any EU country since Wednesday. All of this is circumstantial, of course, but it is not doing much to ease our suspicions. I'm sure that I do not need to say this, but if Prof. Öztürk is involved, then I would say that there is a certain amount of risk to you and your families. He is obviously a highly-trained individual. He may still be active for all we know, and if he was the one who made the call, then his purchase of the pre-paid SIM card suggests a level of caution you don't see in ordinary citizens. I'm glad we assigned protection to you and your brother, but you might alert your sister to the situation and your own wife and children as well."

"I don't know what to say, sir. Thank you for keeping us in the loop."

"We will get to the bottom of this, Mr. O'Brien."

"Thank you. I'm sure you will."

"One more thing, you were going to get a copy of that document for me. Our investigators are anxious to see it. It might yield some clues."

"I will have that for you today."

"Excellent. We'll be in touch."

"Of course."

The two brothers sat there in silence for a moment. Then Gary picked up the phone and thrust it towards his brother.

"You need to call Gwyn right now, Gilbert."

"It's the middle of the night there."

"I don't care. I have a bad feeling about this. I'll explain later, but right now I want you to make this call. You need to call your wife, too."

Gilbert was surprised at the intensity he saw in Gary's eyes. He really did not want to frighten Gwyn by waking her in the middle of the night with news like this.

"Ginger and the kids are in Italy with Shelly, one of her girlfriends. Shelly's mom and dad own a villa in Otranto, a small town down in the heel. They've been gone for three weeks and won't be back for another two. No one could possibly know where they are, so I don't want to upset her by dragging them into this right now. Gwyn, of course, is a different story. Let's wait until she wakes up. It's only a couple of hours from now, alright?"

"No. It's not alright."

He grabbed the phone from Gilbert and began flicking through recent calls to find Gwyn's number.

"I'm telling you. I have a bad feeling about this."

"It can wait a couple of hours."

"No, it can't, damn it!"

Gilbert knew the look he now saw in his brother's eyes. The same one he had gotten as a child when he or Gwyn teased him too much, a look that said emphatically, 'I'll take the fun out of your world if you mess with me.' There was no talking to him when he got like this.

"Hi Gwyn. This is Gary. Sorry to wake you."

He put the phone on speaker and laid it on the bed. Her voice was groggy.

"Gary, is everything alright. What time is it?"

"I know it is the middle of the night, but I'm afraid we have some bad news, sis."

"I'm really not in the mood for more bad news."

"The autopsy has concluded that there was foul play involved in Dad's death."

Gwyn gasped on the other end of the phone.

"You mean Dad was murdered?"

She sat up in bed, reached over and switched on the bedside lamp.

"Actually it isn't quite that simple, but yes, in a way. Someone broke into his apartment. They erased the copy of the document on his PC and his Internet search history. If it hadn't been for Gilbert, we might not have even realized anything was wrong. The autopsy determined that he had been given an injection of sodium thiopental which resulted in an adverse reaction with the medicine he was taking for the pain in his legs."

"Oh my God…"

Gary could hear his sister's voice cracking.

"I know this is hard to hear, Gwyn. The police are doing everything they can to find who is behind this, but, unfortunately, it gets worse. A Turkish professor has also been found dead with the same drug in his body. The police are certain that the two deaths are related. We don't know much, but I am calling in the middle of the night because I believe you could be in danger too."

"What are you talking about? I am half-way around the world."

There was a racket in the background that Gary found strangely familiar but could not place.

"What is that noise I hear, Gwyn?"

"Oh, it's just that flock of geese they keep here on the farm. Something must have spooked them. Let me shut the window."

They could both hear her walking across the creaky wooden floors of the old farm house. Gwyn struggled with the window. Humidity had swollen the wooden frame and it was stuck. She sat the phone down so she could use both hands to close it. The geese were making a terrible clamor. *Probably a raccoon,* she thought. She bent down to put what little weight her wispy frame could offer into closing the window, and it suddenly gave way, closing with a loud bang, shutting out the noise of the geese and plunging the room back into silence. She picked the phone back up and put it to her ear.

"Gary, you haven't answered my question. How can I be in danger here?"

"I don't know for sure, but I have a really bad feeling about this. You need to go the police right away."

"In the middle of the night? Are you crazy?"

"I just want to know that you're safe."

"Safe from who?"

"We don't know."

"Who could have had anything against Dad?"

"Gwyn, what I am about to say is going to be hard to hear, and the police are not certain, so we shouldn't rush to judgment, but they think that Dad's friend from Turkey, Dr. Zeki Öztürk, may be involved."

Both of the brothers jumped at the stifled scream that came from the Blackberry lying on the bed. Gary grabbed it, and said in a voice that was both intense and dead calm at the same time.

"Gwyn, I need you to get a hold of yourself." He could hear her starting to hyperventilate. "This is no time for hysteria. What's wrong?"

A feeling of dread began to swirl and swell like a black cloud in Gary's mind. *What had the old man at the mosque said, 'A black noose of evil is tightening around you...'* That was exactly what it felt like. It was like being suffocated by blackness. Finally, the words began to claw their way out of Gwyn's mouth.

"He called me...He called earlier...He's coming here..."

"Who called?" Gilbert shouted, but Gary knew.

"Dr. Öztürk?"

"Yes, he said he had heard about Father's death. He offered his condolences. He said we had lost a father and he had lost a dear friend. He said he was in Dallas and had a few old manuscripts he wanted to donate to Dad's collection...Oh my God, Gary, what am I going to do? I gave him my address and he said he was coming out tomorrow morning."

"Gwyn, Dr. Öztürk was in London this week at the conference. No one has seen him since Wednesday. The police think he's still somewhere here in Britain because his passport has not been scanned. I don't know how in the hell he left the country without his passport, and I sure as hell don't know how he got your phone number. Do you?"

"I don't know, Gary. I don't know, but I'm scared."

"Gwyn, you need to leave right now, make sure Uncle Henry and Aunt Bonny leave with you."

"They left this morning for Austin to visit friends," she replied.

"Good. Take the document and go to the police. I'll have the Metropolitan Police call the Sulphur Springs chief of police and explain everything. Stay with the police until we..."

He never got a chance to finish the sentence. The Blackberry he was holding in his hand virtually exploded with sound. There was the noise of breaking glass, gunshots and Gwyn screaming.

"Gwyn, what is going on? Gwyn, can you hear me? Tell me what is happening!" Gary was shouting into the phone. The screaming continued for several more seconds before it stopped abruptly and the phone went dead.

31

Gilbert swung into action.

"Get on my computer and find me the number for the Hopkins County Sheriff and then the FBI's field office in Dallas. I'm calling Ginger."

Gilbert's voice had the cool, steady quality of a professional who had compartmentalized his emotions to maintain objectivity. He hit speed dial, and a cell phone rang on a beach in Italy.

"Hi, Ginger."

"Hi, darling. How are you doing?"

"Not so well. We found out that Dad didn't die of natural causes. There was foul play."

"Oh my gosh. You can't be serious."

"Deadly so."

"Do they have any leads?"

"They're following up a few possibilities. Listen, Ginger, I want you and the kids to join me in London. We think you may be in danger."

"What do you mean by danger?" she asked hesitantly.

"I don't have time to explain. This is serious, Ginger. I want you on the next plane to London, and I want you to be careful."

"Gilbert, the kids are having a wonderful time. They're going to be devastated if I cut this vacation short. Are you sure it's necessary? We both know that your job as a security analyst can make you bit paranoid."

Gilbert took a deep breath. He had hoped to avoid this.

"Darling, I was on the phone with Gwyn a moment ago. She's in Dallas. There were gunshots and then we were cut-off. Someone just attacked her at Uncle Henry's farm. I don't know what happened, if she's dead or captured, and I have no clue who is doing this or why. Right now, I need to call the authorities, and you need to get on a plane. Understood?"

"Understood."

"I love you."

As he hung up the phone, he could picture the panic that was erupting, her yelling at the kids to get their beach paraphernalia together so they could get back to the hotel, pack their bags and leave for the airport to get on standby. She was a strong person in her own way, but she didn't handle stress well.

Gary read a number off the computer without looking up from the screen. "The Sheriff's Office is 903 438-4040."

Gilbert punched it in, set the phone on the desk and turned on the speaker. "Hopkins County Sheriff's Office."

"Hello, I'm calling to report gunshots at 1900 FM 1536 in Tira. Can you send a deputy immediately?"

"Are you at that location?"

"No. I'm in London, but I was just on the phone with my sister, who is staying at that address. We heard gunshots, her screaming and then the phone went dead. I'll be calling back in fifteen minutes to find out what you've learned."

"Can I have your name, the time of the call and who might be on site?"

"Damn it. This is no time for an interrogation. You get a deputy out there, and I'll call back to answer your questions in fifteen minutes."

He hung up and nodded at Gary, who responded with another number. "972 559-5000"

"You have reached the Dallas office of the Federal Bureau of Investigation. If this is an emergency, please press nine."

He did.

"Agent Johnson. What is the nature of your emergency?"

"My name is Gilbert O'Brien. I'm calling you from London to report a possible armed assault on my sister in Tira, Texas, north of Sulphur Springs less than ten minutes ago."

"What is the basis of your report?"

"I was on the phone with her when I heard gunfire and she started screaming. Then the phone went dead. My father was killed in London this week and the Metropolitan Police here in London believe that a Turkish national named Zeki Öztürk may have been involved. This same man called my sister yesterday from Dallas."

"Have local authorities been notified?"

"Yes, I just got off the phone with the sheriff's dispatch. A deputy is on his way to the scene now."

After a barrage of questions from the FBI agent, Gilbert finally hung up and dialed McIntosh's office.

"McIntosh speaking"

"Sir, this is Gilbert O'Brien. I think we may have found Zeki."

"May have?"

He quickly explained what had just happened.

"You have notified the local authorities, I presume."

"Yes sir, but it's a rural area, and the closest deputy is fifteen minutes out."

"Keep me posted. I'll see what we can do from our side with this new information. He obviously left the country with a different passport. We'll start by reviewing security footage at every gate that had a flight from London to Dallas since Wednesday and widen it from there."

"I've already contacted the Dallas office of the FBI. Can I ask you to call Agent Johnson?"

"I'll have an inspector call him right away."

"Is there anything else we can do, sir?"

"I think the best thing you can do now is pray, son."

Gilbert closed the Blackberry and stood there with his jaw clenched, staring a hole in the wall for a minute. He turned to find Gary doubled over on his knees.

"Are you okay?" he said. "What are you doing?"

"Exactly what he said to do."

<hr>

TIRA, TEXAS   A late model, white GMC truck belonging to the Hopkins County Sheriff's Department turned onto the long quarter-mile drive that led from the road to Uncle Henry's house. The gate was closed and the deputy on the passenger side got out to open it. Then he climbed back into the truck and began working a powerful spotlight, looking for any sign of movement in the trees and bushes that dotted the pasture on either side of the road. The sirens were off, but the lights were flashing. The truck stopped about fifty yards from the house while the spotlight combed every inch of the place. There were no lights on, not even a porch light. The deputy working the spotlight turned to the driver and said, "Well, what do we do now?"

"What kind of question is that? We're going to have a look around; that's what we're going to do."

"Shouldn't we wait for backup?"

"It doesn't look like there is anybody home, Leroy. For all we know, the dispatch could've taken a prank call. Just walk up and knock on the door. I've got your back."

"You're the boss, Darrel."

The deputy got out of the truck, walked into the yard and called out, "Anybody home?"

He waited a few seconds, but there was no answer. Then he called out again. "Anybody home?"

He had only been on duty for two weeks, and this was the first time that he had responded to a call involving firearms. He was apprehensive. As he walked towards the porch, shining the light in the windows and listening intently for movement, he realized they didn't pay him enough. He also regretted the fact that he had not filled out the cheap life insurance policy that had come in the mail two weeks ago.

He walked up to the main house and rang the bell.

"This is the Hopkins County Sheriff's department. Is there anybody home?"

He waited about thirty seconds. No lights came on inside, so he began walking around the house shining his flashlight in the windows.

"Doesn't look like there is anyone home."

"Go look at the guest house."

When he got to the porch, he immediately drew his sidearm and started backing away, yelling to his partner,

"Somebody's been shot. There's blood on the porch and empty cartridges."

"Oh, shit!"

He heard his partner throw the truck into reverse and back up to face the guest house. In twenty seconds, the headlights of the truck and the powerful spotlight had the old farm house lit up like high noon at the OK corral. Darrel and Leroy took positions on the opposite ends of the porch and began moving up to the house. Now they were shouting in earnest.

"If you have a firearm, slide it out the front door and come out with your hands up!"

Again, there was only silence. Darrel had made it to the porch and could see a puddle of blood on the porch. There was some smearing but very little. He had expected to see a trail of blood leading back into the house, but there was no trail at all. He motioned for Leroy to cover him and pushed on the front door. It swung open effortlessly and without a sound. He went in low, expecting at any minute to see a body or a bleeding victim, but three minutes later they had swept the house and found nothing at all. No body, no gun and no sign of burglary. When he came back outside, he could hear the sirens of the ambulance in the distance. Darrel just shrugged his shoulders.

"Somebody needs one, that's for sure, either that or a hearse, but that somebody isn't here anymore."

When the ambulance came roaring up the drive, they found Darrel on the radio reporting back to headquarters, and Leroy examining the bullet holes in the front door and walls.

"Who needs medical care here? We got a report of gunshot wounds."

"There is a gunshot wound. We just can't locate the owner," Darrel said dryly.

He knew that his answer would come off as callous, but eighteen years of domestic disputes, drug traffickers and petty thieves had left him more than jaded.

"What the hell are you talking about?"

"He means that there is a puddle of blood here, but nobody home. That's all," Leroy volunteered, pointing down to the porch.

The medic walked up to the porch, took one look at the blood and said, "Well, they can't be far. Unless they get medical attention quick, the person with this wound will bleed out in a hurry. Have you guys looked in the woods?"

"We've shown the spotlight around the entire house. The problem is there's no blood trail, so we have no idea what direction to start looking in."

"No blood trail? Are you sure? There's no way someone could bleed that bad and not leave a blood trail, even if it were faint. It ought to be pretty easy to pick up with everything so dried up and yellow."

"Well, if you can find one, we'll gladly follow it," said Leroy to no one in particular.

"You don't suppose someone could have backed a car right up to the porch and thrown the body in the trunk, do you?"

Darrel began shining his light on the grass in the yard looking for tire tracks. He didn't see any, but the ground was so hard and dry and the grass in the yard mowed so short that he wasn't sure a car would even leave tracks.

"I suppose the only thing to do is widen our circle a bit. Let's work in pairs. Backup is on the way. Until they arrive, Leroy, keep your wits about you and your gun at the ready. If there is a wounded person here, we need to find them quick."

———✠———

LONDON   Gary could hear Gilbert's voice fading and felt a wave of nausea rising in the pit of his stomach. He raised his head. There was movement in his peripheral vision, but his brain was no longer processing the signals transmitted by the optic nerve. He was falling headlong, racing through layers of emotion deposited throughout his life.

His mind was a blur of color-coded feeling devoid of rational thought - the anguish of rejection, the disappointment of unfulfilled dreams, the desperation of hopelessness, the security of loving moments with his mom, the pleasure of success tinged with an empty feeling of meaningless vanity, the camaraderie of friends and the pain of their loss. Personalities from the past flashed before his mind. Neighborhood kids from his childhood, cousins, bullies from school, teachers, colleagues, friends, strangers he had seen in airports, orphans and beggars he had seen on the streets in Asia... Each image was a burning brand on his mind, and he saw how the event had marked or scarred his life. All the while, he kept falling.

A newsreel began to play in his mind. A political rally in India turning into a bloody riot, a US naval fleet engaging the Chinese in the Indian ocean, the streets of Tehran filled with invading Pakistani and Turkish soldiers, a mushroom cloud over Damascus and Cairo, worldwide famine and economic collapse, and he was still plummeting downwards.

Suddenly, everything went completely dark, a black cloud of malice deprived his mind's eye of light, and yet he could sense movement. A twisting torrent of evil assailed his consciousness and bombarded his mind with a harsh, discordant melee of sound. The dream he'd had the night before receiving news of his father's death was replayed in vivid detail. It began as a jumble of dissonant noise, like a crowded marketplace or a bazaar, but gradually he was able to identify some of the sounds. There were cathedral bells, Buddhist gongs, the Muslim call to prayer, a Jewish shofar, the chanting of Sioux medicine men, moans and groans from entranced Zulu witch doctors, Hindu hymns of praise to Shiva. All religious, all evil.

The cacophony continued, but the black haze over his mind lifted. What he saw was his father's body in the morgue. The picture was high-definition. He saw the laugh lines under his eyes. The cold, blue lips... Gradually, this audio vision began to fade, and inexplicably he realized that the sensation of falling was also gone. He could not tell how long all of this lasted, but when the flood of sensation had passed, he felt like a diver fighting to regain the surface, clawing his way back to the top for air after being plunged into a sea of subconsciousness. When he finally broke through, back into the real world, into his own consciousness, he was looking at the ceiling, and Gilbert was talking on the phone in the background.

"...What do you mean there was no one there? I'm telling you I was talking with her on the phone when the guns were fired less than half an hour ago."

Gary motioned for him to put it on speaker.

"I understand your frustration, Mr. O'Brien. I'm just relating what the deputy on the scene told me. We are doing everything we can to find your sister."

"Thank you, officer."

Gilbert hung up and turned to Gary.

"Are you alright? You stood up from praying and passed out. I laid you on the bed and propped you up with pillows."

"I feel better now. I think that all of this has just left me emotionally exhausted. Sorry, if I scared you. What did the deputy say?" asked Gary.

"Gwyn is not there. They found blood on the porch. There were no bodies and no blood trail."

Gary put his head between his hands.

"Now what?"

"All we can do is wait and hope those local yokels do their job right."

"I think it may be a little bigger than that."

"Meaning?"

"You wouldn't believe me if I told you."

"Try me."

Gary took a deep breath. He could guess what Gilbert would say about his dream in Istanbul, and the vision he had just experienced. His brother didn't buy into metaphysical mumbo jumbo. He hadn't either until recently...

32

SATURDAY, NORTHEAST TEXAS   Zeki pulled into the parking lot of the public boat ramp and began looking for the most strategic place to park the car. They were almost a mile from the Farm to Market road. He needed to change out of his blood-stained clothes and review his exit plan before the sun came up. He had always thought that fluorescent street lights seemed a bit eerie. Tonight, the effect was compounded by the circumstances. A chill ran up his spine. After what had just happened, the resources of the world's most powerful country would be mobilized for the express purpose of hunting him down. The best minds in law enforcement and intelligence would be tracking him day and night, and he knew it had already been set in motion.

The small parking lot was surrounded by woods. There were two trucks with empty boat trailers, obviously late night fishermen, but no lights anywhere. He stopped the car, turned it off and without looking at his passenger said, "I need to change out of these bloody clothes. I have an extra set in the trunk. It doesn't look like there is a bathroom, so I'll walk into the woods over there. We are going to have to work together as a team to get through this."

He stopped talking and continued staring straight ahead, waiting for a response that didn't come.

"Are you listening to me?"

His voice was gentle, but there was urgency in it too. He understood the psychological trauma, and knew it would evoke a reaction of some kind. He just didn't know what it would be like. He was about to find out.

"Am I listening? Yeah, I'm listening, but you'll have to forgive me if I have some trouble comprehending it all. I was just attacked by two masked gunmen in the middle of the night. Then, an old friend of my recently murdered father, who just happens to be waiting outside my house ten hours before he said he would be there, comes out of nowhere, dressed like Rambo, guns blazing, and drops one of these two would-be assassins with the efficiency of a special ops team and proceeds to torture the other one for information. When the man

180

won't talk, Rambo blows his brains out. Then, this fifty-something man I knew as a professor very calmly gives me instructions while he carries, not drags, mind you, but carries their bodies and throws them into a well. Yeah, I am listening, but I can't believe what I have seen with my own eyes. How do you expect me to believe anything you have to say?"

"Gwyn, I told you we have to keep their deaths a secret as long as possible."

"For God's sake, Mr. Öztürk, who are we keeping it a secret from?"

"I'm not sure."

"Then, I suppose you will have to forgive me for being a bit reluctant to swallow this whole thing hook line and sinker."

"That must be a local expression. I'm afraid it's not one I am familiar with. All I know is that the people who sent them must believe they are alive as long as possible. By wrapping them in a coat and carrying them to the well, we were able to avoid leaving a blood trail. That buys us time."

"Dr. Öztürk, I graduated from university with honors. Simple things like that are not difficult to comprehend. What I am having trouble understanding is how, after killing two men, you have the presence of mind to rattle off those instructions, much less the strength to carry two men weighing almost two-hundred pounds apiece fifty yards by yourself."

"Gwyn, there is much you do not know about me. Much of it you wouldn't want to know. Let me just say this. I worked in Turkey's National Intelligence Organization for years and may have a skill set unlike any you've ever seen before. What you need to understand though is that you are as precious to me as my own daughter would be. Your father was a dear friend. For most of us Turks, friendship is sacred. There is nothing I wouldn't do for your father and the fact that he was recently killed by men from my country is not only a source of great shame for me, but it also makes me doubly responsible for your safety. Your people cannot protect you like I can because they do not under-stand their enemy."

"So, you are not really a professor at all?"

"Teaching is my second career," he replied softly.

"Second career? I suppose your first career was 007. You have a lot of explaining to do."

Zeki had no time for this, but he knew that Gwyn would need some time to process everything and that he needed her cooperation.

Gwyn continued, "When you shot the man on the porch, I was talking to my brother. He said that you were at the conference in London. He said the UK police considered you a person of interest and were looking for you. The police told my brother they knew you were still in Britain because your passport hadn't been scanned. But somehow, you show up in a small town outside of Dallas two days later carrying an assault rifle. Why don't you explain that for starters?"

Zeki sighed and reached his arm to put it on her shoulder. She shoved it away and shouted, "Damn it, I have a right to know what the hell is going on."

"Of course, you do, but don't expect to understand it all in the next five minutes. I don't even know exactly what is going on myself."

He looked down at his watch. It was 02:30 local time. He wanted to be in Dallas before the sun came up, which meant they had one and a half hours before they needed to be on the road. His intelligence training told him that every minute they sat there increased their risk. If the authorities were smart, road blocks would already be springing up to take advantage of the fact that there should be virtually no traffic at this time of night. But he melted when he looked into the eyes of the young lady sitting across from him, a beautiful creature who had just lost her father and had almost been killed herself. She deserved something.

He rewound the tape in his mind to Wednesday morning at the hotel in London and that terrifying moment of *déjà vu*. After his prayers, he had gone to an early breakfast and then gone out for a brisk walk to get some exercise. He had taken the elevator up to his floor, and as he walked towards the door, images of the trap set for him by a terrorist in Şanlıurfa years ago froze him in his tracks. The tiny piece of paper he had placed under the hinge of the door was lying on the ground. The sound of Gwyn clearing her throat brought him back to the present.

"I'm sorry," he said, "It hasn't been easy for me either. I'll spare you the details, but on Wednesday morning, which was just hours after your father was killed, I returned to my room after an early breakfast only to realize that someone had been there while I was out. It was obviously too early to be house-keeping, so I went down to the lobby and called my friend's room."

"Your friend?"

"Another Turkish professor who was attending the conference with me."

Gwyn gasped and put her hand to her mouth.

"I already know," Zeki said. "I learned of his death the next day."

"I'm so sorry, Zeki," Gwyn said softly.

"Me too. Anyway, when he didn't answer, I was suspicious. He's not an early riser. I called your dad and when he didn't answer, I went to reception, told them that the TV in my room wasn't working and asked to move to the room across the hall if it was empty. They apologized profusely and said housekeeping would move my belongings for me when they cleaned the room. They gave me a new key card. I slipped into the room and put out the 'Do not disturb' sign.

"For the next two hours, I watched my own room through the peephole to see what was going on. Finally, housekeeping came and sixty seconds after the maid went into my room, I saw a man in his mid-thirties come walking out the door."

"You mean someone was waiting there to kill you?" asked Gwyn in shock.

"I didn't know that then, of course, but I knew it spelled trouble.

"Do you have any idea who they are?"

"The document gave me several clues, so yes, I have some sort of idea. They obviously have a powerful network in London."

Gwyn sat there for a minute, wondering how to ask the next question. She had heard her father talk about Zeki being a devout Muslim. It made her uncomfortable, but she finally blurted it out.

"Is this some Islamic fundamentalist group?"

"Why do you ask?" probed Zeki.

"Well, I've been researching the document myself for several days. Some of the symbolism on the document and what I gleaned from the translation seem to suggest a connection with Islam."

"Let's talk about that later when we have more time."

"Fair enough. How did you get out of the country?"

"Well, I had to assume that these people did not have my best interests at heart, so I decided to warn your father. I went back to the conference where I learned that he hadn't shown up for his presentation. I knew that if they were on to me, they might have already gotten to your father. I called a friend in London and told him to get someone over to your father's place immediately. Fifteen minutes later, he told me that your father was dead. At that time, the local police didn't even know."

"This friend of yours is a Turkish spy in the UK?"

"I'll have to leave that question unanswered."

"But you still haven't told me how you got out of the country."

"As anyone in intelligence will tell you, a second passport is more valuable than a gun."

"But with the computer tracking they use today, they would know instantly if you are a real person who has actually entered the country. You can't leave on a fake passport or one that has not already entered the country. The tracking is too sophisticated."

"True, and I suppose someone is going to be in for a surprise at the border when they try to leave Britain because the records will show that they have already left. But, as you Americans are fond of saying, 'Desperate times call for desperate measures.'"

"Wow!" she said in a breathy and awe-struck tone. "That's impressive."

"Not hard, really. As security gets more sophisticated so do efforts to circumvent it. I flew to Istanbul and then drove to a friend's house so I could lay low. The first thing I did was ask my friends in London to help me get in touch with my friend, Dr. Haluk Bayram. Several hours later, I was told that he too had been found dead."

183

Gwyn just sat there staring out the window at the moonlight reflecting off the lake. It was a beautiful clear night, peaceful and quiet. The only sound was the buzzing of cicadas and the croaking of frogs. It was serene, but her heart was numb to it all. In less than a week, her father and a Turkish professor had been killed. Someone had tried to kill Zeki and then tried to kill her half-way around the world in a small Texas town.

"How did you know they were coming for me?"

"I didn't know for sure. But your father was killed sometime Tuesday night or early Wednesday morning. If these people had found what they wanted, they wouldn't have come after me and certainly not after Haluk. He doesn't even know your father. His death made no sense. Why Haluk? Then, I remembered that I had left your father a voicemail about the document and used the Turkish word for friend. If they were intercepting his telephone calls, one of the first things they would have done is search for Turkish professors at the university and the conference. Haluk and I were the only Turks as far as I know."

"That doesn't explain what brought you here."

"Well, your dad told me at lunch on Monday that he was going to meet you at the airport the next day, so I took a chance. You have to believe me when I say that your father was very dear to me. He was an honorable man. Like you, I am still grieving his passing. I didn't know you had it, but I figured this group might think you did, and I could never live with myself if something were to happen to you too."

"Did you know your behavior was one of the reasons my father was suspicious and passed the document on to me?"

"Your father was a brilliant man. I am not surprised that he picked up on that. The fact that he gave it to you makes me think that he may have figured out more about the document than even I know. I wish I had warned him directly, but I didn't know it was this dangerous either. I didn't want to seem paranoid. Please, believe me."

"Mr. Öztürk…"

"Please, just call me Zeki if you prefer."

"Fine. I do believe you, actually. After all, you just saved my life. In fact, I don't think I have properly thanked you for that. You went to a lot of trouble and put yourself in harm's way. Thank you!"

"I'm glad I got here in time."

"You said earlier that it was people from your country who did this. How do you know?"

"Well, I don't know who all of the actors are, but the men who were killed tonight spoke Turkish to one another as they made their approach to the house. Listen, I'm going to wash up in the lake and change clothes. We can continue this conversation later. The last thing I want right now is a run-in with Texas

184

Rangers hoping to bag a Muslim terrorist. We need to get moving, and we have to warn Gilbert."

Gwyn immediately became agitated. "Oh goodness, yes. If you have a cell phone, I'll give him a call."

"I'm afraid we can't do that," he said.

The tone of her response betrayed the suspicion she still harbored.

"What are you talking about? Obviously, I have to warn my brothers. They could be in as much danger as I am."

Zeki sighed, but, with the air of an intelligence instructor, patiently explained, "Think about it for a minute, Gwyn. How did they know where you were? How did they know that you, and not your brother, had the document?"

Her eyes widened even as she asked the question.

"You think they were listening to our telephone conversations?"

"Unless you think they have psychic powers? I'd be delighted to hear a different explanation."

Gwyn leaned her head back on the headrest, revealing a beautiful white neck. Then, without lifting her head, she turned to him and said, "So, until you called me, they did not know for certain that you were involved at all, did they? You blew your own anonymity for me."

"In all things, there comes a time to throw caution to the wind. That time had come. From now on, you cannot call friends or family."

Gwyn turned back to stare at the ceiling of the car. Zeki stared at her intently. She was just as beautiful as her mother. He hadn't seen Patricia after she was diagnosed with cancer, of that he was glad. Suddenly, Gwyn sat upright in her seat and turned earnestly to Zeki.

"Who are these people? How can they tap telephone conversations? I mean even the FBI has to get court orders to force service providers to divulge this kind of information."

Zeki's face became grim.

"The FBI is supposed to stay within the boundaries of the legal system it seeks to uphold, and in the end, it is collecting information for a criminal trial before a judge and jury. However, if you are not hampered by such constraints, then it is not technically difficult to monitor telephone calls, especially cell phone calls. All you need is money. That will get you the two necessary things: equipment, and access, which can be easily obtained by placing qualified and loyal individuals in key positions. Once you have compromised the system with a silent tracker—essentially a virus program installed as an add-on to any legitimate system software, you're set. The tracker can be activated remotely. Or, better yet, put a man on the inside. Then it is fairly simple to move within the arteries of the system without being detected."

"So, how are we going to get in touch with Gilbert?" asked Gwyn.

"I have a plan, but we need to get to Dallas first."

"You know that the authorities are going to be looking for you. We should just go straight to the police. I'll explain everything, and then there won't be a problem."

"Gwyn, I know that the American and British authorities would be able to corroborate our story, so there is nothing to fear from them, but I'm not sure your government or any government, for that matter, can protect us from the people who have targeted us."

Gwyn was incredulous.

"You can't be serious. You believe that this group is more powerful than the United States government?"

Zeki managed a weak smile. "Gwyn, I hate to burst your bubble. I have seen the innocence of the average citizen around the world, so I know how naïve people are about their own country. Believe me, I've discovered many shocking things about my own country over the years. You speak of the US government as if it were a monolithic entity with a single guiding purpose. That is the myth of government, one that has been particularly well ingrained here in America. To quote a famous poem, there are 'gods behind the gods'. Democracy and liberty are the ideals used to forge national unity because they are widely accepted aspirations here in the West, but the 'halls of power', so to speak, care for liberty or democracy only as it serves to expand their power base.

"Do you think that large banks which think nothing of intervening in the affairs of foreign governments, banks that are willing to gamble and squander the pensions of millions of working class families on risky investments, banks that collude with the government to fix monetary policy, orchestrating economic crises for their own personal gain, care about democracy and liberty? Do you know that in every economic bust, every recession, and every downturn, the number of millionaires and billionaires increases? If capitalism is a system where the rich put their money at risk, how can it be that economic pain is mostly felt by the lower and middle class? I could go on, but suffice it to say that "government" is not always a force for good, even for its own citizens, and that corruption is not the exclusive domain of banana republics. In the grand scheme of things, all governments are pawns of the real power brokers. In other words, we are not necessarily safe in their custody."

Gwyn shrugged. "You obviously have more experience in this than I do. It's your call."

Zeki opened his door and reached down to pull the lever that popped the trunk. With the dome light on, she realized for the first time that his neck was swollen.

"What happened to your neck?"

186

He chuckled. "These ants you have in Texas are apparently incapable of distinguishing friend from foe."

Gwyn laughed.

"Fire ants have no friends. Don't take it personal."

"Strange name," he said, "I can't imagine where they came up with it."

Gwyn smiled at his sense of humor. Their family had always had fun with him.

"Give me a couple of minutes to change clothes," he said. "I won't be long."

She watched him walk towards the lake until he disappeared in the woods and marveled at how the events of the last two hours had turned her world upside down for the second time in less than a week. She said a silent prayer of thanks for the honorable life of her father. It had clearly brought them a family friend worth having around.

33

ANKARA   Yusuf had barely turned on his computer when his secretary walked in with tea, a *simit* and a folder full of papers for him to sign.

"Hello, Captain."

"Hi, Selda. What are you doing here on a beautiful Saturday afternoon?"

"So much paperwork piled up this week in connection with the processing of those foreign women rescued on the Black Sea that I didn't want to put it off until Monday."

"That doesn't explain the *simit*. How did you know that I would be in today?"

"Just a hunch, sir"

He shook his head and smiled. Selda was the future of Turkey. A recent honors graduate from the police academy, she was bright, respectful, hard-working and conscientious in her duties. Her job was to lighten his load, and she took it seriously in every detail.

"Anything pressing?"

"No sir, I mean not really. Interpol issued a green notice for a Turkish national this morning."

"Anybody on our list?"

"No, sir."

"Then, it doesn't concern us."

"Of course not. Still, I pulled this person's file just to have a look."

"Pulled his file? Why would we have a file here if he is not on our list?"

"Sir, we have files on all active and decommissioned MIT members."

"He's ex-MIT?"

"Apparently. Retired several years back though. He's a professor named Zeki Öztürk."

It was barely perceptible, but she saw his eyes narrow and his jaw harden.

"What's he supposed to have done?"

"He is a person of interest in a double-murder in London. The authorities think he's in the United States, but his passport was never scanned in Britain, so they know he left the country on another passport. That's all the notice said. Obviously, they are asking all international law enforcement agencies to cooperate and share information about the man."

"Should we tell them to stop wasting their time?" he asked quietly.

"Excuse me?"

"They'll never catch him," he said matter-of-factly.

"Do you know him?" she asked.

Yusuf knew that if she had pulled the file there was a good chance she already knew that they had finished their military service in the same unit, so there was no sense pretending.

"He's a good friend of mine, and I can assure you he's not a criminal."

"I understand your personal loyalty, sir," she said sympathetically.

"My assessment," he said with conviction, "has nothing to do with personal loyalty. It is a totally professional judgment. I know the man. He would not murder an innocent person."

Selda hesitated before saying, "You know we are bound by treaty to cooperate with Interpol."

"I haven't seen Zeki in several years, so there's nothing I can do to help them," replied Yusuf. "Keep me posted if there are any developments."

"Yes, sir."

Yusuf turned back to his computer. Selda stood at the door making no move to leave. He could feel her staring at him. The office was empty and it made him uncomfortable. Without looking up, he asked,

"Is there anything else?"

"Just one thing, sir."

"What is it?"

"Murat told me about what happened in Akçakoca, how you stood up for those women, that you filed a criminal complaint against the local chief of police..."

She stopped, unsure of how to continue. He pulled his eyes away from the computer screen.

"And?"

"Well, I just wanted to say thanks. That's all."

"For what?"

"For giving us hope."

"Hope? You're not making sense, Selda. What kind of hope are you talking about?"

"The hope that we can do our duty, stand for human dignity and preserve the Republic without being crushed. We all know that our position is rapidly falling out of favor, but you give us hope that right can make might."

"I haven't done anything that you or anyone on our team wouldn't do given the same chance."

"Maybe, but you are the one who shows us what it means to take the chance. Thanks!"

She turned and left the office, closing the door behind her. Yusuf just stared at the door. Selda's praise made him cringe inside. If only everything were as clean-cut as the situation with the prostitutes had been. Providing Interpol with information about anyone sought with a notice was his job.

Zeki had called him just three days ago in the middle of the night to tell him that he was in Istanbul and would need some help. He had refused to go into detail on the phone. He just said, 'The shadow of Allah's shadow is moving.' It was a cryptic statement, but Yusuf knew exactly what it meant. The Shadow of Allah was a title given to the Ottoman sultans when they were the Caliph of the Islamic world. The shadow of Allah's shadow was the power behind the throne.

He had expected Zeki to get in touch with him, but three days had passed and now an Interpol green notice had been issued. He logged on to the Interpol site to read the bulletin. It contained little that Selda hadn't already told him. Zeki would be in touch if he needed help, but what worried Yusuf was whether or not he would be able to provide it. To do that, he needed to know what had happened in London.

The phone rang. He picked it up.

"Hello."

"Captain, your wife is on the line for you."

"Thanks, Selda. Can you bring me what you have so far on the identity of Turks killed or injured in the attacks in Europe?"

"Sure."

He heard the line click and switched the phone to speaker,

"Hello, love."

"Hello, darling. I just called to remind you that we are supposed to go see Hamid and Ebru this afternoon. I bought a gold piece to pin on their new baby."

"I'm sure he'll love that. Probably melt it down and mint an Ottoman *akçe* from it. Honey, can't you do this without me? I'm really busy."

"Yusuf, don't be like this. I know you don't like his politics, but Ebru is my niece."

"Yeah, well, she has clearly forgotten her roots. I can't stand to see her wearing the head covering and being stepped on by that jackass."

"Yusuf, I am surprised at you. It's their life. She seems happy."

"Yeah, that is the problem. How can she be happy with a person attempting to live by a seventh century moral code from Arabia?"

"Listen to yourself. He's a handsome, charismatic young man with a bright

190

future. Just because he belongs to the AKP, doesn't mean he's backward. Their family is merely going back to their roots."

"Darling, the key phrase there is 'going back'. The struggle for individual liberties and the rule of law in this country has been hard fought, and now they want to 'go back' to sharia law."

"I don't need to remind you that his uncle is assistant to the Minister of Interior and could be your boss someday."

"Don't remind me."

"Ok darling, I'll pick you up at three o'clock."

"Call first. Who knows, maybe something will come up. In fact, that is something even I can pray for."

"I know God is not going to answer a prayer that would help you avoid blessing this child. They need our example."

"A man who rejects the example of Atatürk is not going to look to me for guidance."

"Ok, I don't want to talk about it anymore. They're family and that's enough for me."

"Well, when they took over in Iran, being family was not enough to spare relatives from the sword. Remember what Burak said about his mother and father."

"Stop it Yusuf. That's morbid."

"I didn't say it," he retorted. "He should know his own mother."

"I don't believe that he would be the first person his father and mother would hand over to an executioner if sharia law were restored."

"No, but he does. Allah before mother, father, sister, brother. Isn't that what they say? I'll see you a little before three."

"Great."

Yusuf hung up the phone and called Selda.

"I need you to get me any information you can about the incidents in London involving Zeki. The more I know about the situation, the more assistance I will be able to lend the authorities trying to find him."

"I'll see what I can find, sir. I just sent you everything we had on the Turks killed in the neo-Nazi attacks in Germany."

"Was there anything that stood out?" asked Yusuf.

"Not really, the only thing noticeable was the fact that in both places, the victims were all immigrants from the same region of Turkey. Those in Berlin were mostly from Sivas and the ones in Cologne were from Tünceli."

"That's odd," said Yusuf thoughtfully. "Is there any way you can find out if they were Alevis or not?"

"Excuse me? Their birth certificates will only indicate whether or not they were Muslim, not what sect of Islam they subscribed to," ventured Selda cautiously. "I'm not sure I understand where you're going with that."

Yusuf found himself shaking his head. *Poor girl.* He knew from her file that she was an Alevi. This was a sensitive issue with her. He had to proceed with caution.

"Listen, Selda, I know your family background, and I hired you anyway. You should also know me well enough by now to understand that I am not sectarian or racist. I don't care if you are a fire-worshipper, a Christian, a Greek or a Kurd. For me, everyone is equal before the law. I know your people have suffered persecution for centuries, and that you try to keep your family history a secret. But can we put that behind us for a moment and just follow every possible lead? If there is a connection between the skin-head attacks and Bekir's sudden re-appearance, if he is planning retaliation, then I have to stop it."

"I understand, sir," replied Selda calmly. "But, I don't see what the identities of the victims have to do with Bekir. And besides, to be honest, if they all turn out to be Alevis and this information becomes public, I'm not sure the ruling party will put as much pressure on Germany to bring the perpetrators to justice." The bitterness in her voice was palpable. "After all, a few less Alevis is not something they are really going to be concerned about."

"I just want to find out what's going on here. There's no agenda. We can sit on the information if that seems more prudent. But you have to admit that Alevis make up the majority of the population in Sivas and Tünceli, and if it is more than just a coincidence, I would like to know. Obviously, German skin-heads know very little about Turkey's internal matters, but they probably would not intentionally target the most secular group in Turkey if they were trying to make an anti-Islamic statement, now would they?" asked Yusuf.

"I don't suppose they would," she said.

"Nor," he continued, "Would Bekir be very willing to avenge them by planning a retaliatory strike. So, every piece of information helps us figure out whether or not he's connected to any of this."

"I'll find out everything I can about the victims, and whether or not they're from Alevi villages."

Yusuf didn't have the heart to tell her that the security directorate had a database that could be searched to find out not only the religious views of every citizen, but their political affiliations going back three generations. He would have Murat do the research for him. He didn't want to spoil her innocence and she was far too touchy about it.

✦

CAIRO   "I expected to hear something from you a couple of hours ago, Salih. Has the document been recovered? What have we learned from the girl?"

Salih had been racking his brain for hours wondering how he was going to answer these questions.

"I didn't want to bother you at home on a Saturday, sir."

"Do you honestly think I'm at home with everything we have going on? The launch of the UN initiative is just around the corner."

"Unfortunately, we have not been in contact with the team since they made contact with the girl."

Ahmet's silence on the other end was uncomfortable. When he did speak, his tone raised the hair on the back of Salih's neck.

"Salih, is there a problem?" Salih gritted his teeth and swore deep down.

"Sir, we don't know for sure what has happened. We had a live audio feed on the operation. The last update we had from them was that they were less than fifty yards from the house and were moving in. Less than a minute later, we heard gunfire and the girl screaming. One of our men said, 'I'm hit,' and within ninety seconds both of our live feeds were down."

There was another pause, more uncomfortable than the first.

"You mean we were ambushed?" Ahmet's voice was cold and icy.

Salih said nothing. There was nothing to say.

"I see from your report," continued Ahmet, "that Zeki Öztürk made contact with the girl yesterday from Dallas."

"That is correct," answered Salih, "He told her that he would be there around noon local time. Our operation would be finished long before he showed up. Our plan was to then wait for his arrival, keeping the girl alive just in case he called and we needed her to say something on the phone with the encouragement of a 9 mm pointed at her head."

"Salih, you disappoint me. You assumed that he was the professor he appears to be, assumed that what he said on the phone was true."

There was a third pause. Salih could feel his palms sweating on the phone and caught himself biting his lip.

"We don't make assumptions, Salih," said Ahmet. "This is not going to look good in your file. I am not even going to ask what you intend to do to fix this. I'm taking charge. You will immediately begin implementing the back-up plans I drew up."

Salih took a deep breath. Ahmet's plan was a dramatic escalation, one that he was uncomfortable with. He knew the safest course of action was to go on the record with his objections.

"An Interpol bulletin has been put out for Zeki. We're monitoring all security channels. They may locate him faster than we can. We'll have to improvise as new information becomes available. If they're taken into custody, we have enough resources on the inside to make the evidence 'disappear' and to silence them as well."

Salih paused. The door to Ahmet's room opened and a senior Lieutenant walked straight to his desk, handed him a note and walked back out. Ahmet's eyes narrowed as he read it and then turned back to Salih.

"What you say seems reasonable, but unlike your first two operations, which failed miserably, this situation now involves variables totally beyond our control. On the first two operations, we had reason to believe that the element of surprise was on our side, that the targets were unsuspecting. This is no longer the case. The brotherhood may have connections with many high-level authorities and may be able to bring its influence to bear in grand matters of state, but we do not have anyone in a local sheriff's department, especially in Texas!"

Ahmet's voice had been growing steadily louder, and by now, he was fairly shouting. Salih prepared himself stoically for the tongue-lashing he suspected was coming. He also noted with some dissatisfaction how Ahmet had referred to the failures as 'your operations'. Ahmet continued, "Your operation was critical, Salih. You have exposed us to grave danger. Secrets kept for hundreds of years, 'truths' carefully cultivated to shepherd the *ummah* away from danger are on the verge of discovery. Do you realize what this could mean?"

Salih's answer was textbook. "Sir, I accept all responsibility for the failure and will do everything within my power and with Allah's help to resolve the problem I have created for the brotherhood."

Ahmet's response was clinical. "I expect nothing less. I see from the detailed operations plan that you have not implemented open source intelligence monitoring. This must be done immediately. You need an exhaustive list of anything Zeki or Gwyn would search for in an attempt to find out what the document is about. This could help us to pinpoint their location. Make sure this includes not only topics related to the document, but the names of all the people involved. As for the back-up plan I outlined, how long until you can put it into place?"

"The grab is easy. We can do it as soon as you give the order. The theft you mention is more intricate. It'll take at least several days to put the whole thing together. We've begun to source potential assets, but the papers, the reservations, and the travel will take time to arrange. You cannot just waltz into the Augustinerlesesaal and request to see any ancient manuscript they have. The security is relatively light. If it was a simple theft you wanted, it would be a piece of cake. It becomes a bit more involved when you want us to frame the Vatican for it. This whole affair will be subjected to incredible scrutiny."

Ahmet turned to the computer screen, located the report and pushed the send button.

"I am aware of the intricacies, Salih. I drew up the plan." He paused for effect. "The theft is pre-emptive. When a renowned Muslim scholar discovers its absence, and the theft is traced back to the Vatican, the release of their little document can easily be spun to look like they are attempting a cover-up for the theft."

"But," said Salih, "If the kidnapping plan works, we won't need to remove the manuscript from the library in Vienna."

"Need to? No. We won't need to, but we'll do it anyway. Just imagine the mileage we will get out of this in terms of public relations. The Vatican embroiled in yet another scandal, and this time, it won't be pedophilic priests. I think the West has gotten bored with that anyway, don't you? This time the scandal will be a plan to destroy and cover-up what the Muslim world has claimed for centuries is the most accurate copy of their beloved Gospel. No, Salih, this plan will be implemented whether we get the document back or not, and if, for some reason, we fail to recover the document, we can say that it's a forgery. Remember 'sling the mud, even if it doesn't stick, the stain will remain.' You should have received an e-mail from me just now. Read it."

He tried to imagine Salih's face as he scanned the email.

"Son of a jackass! May Allah damn his cursed soul. I am going to crap in his mouth! Why didn't you tell me this earlier?"

"Because *you* were supposed to be running the operation, not *me*! I only found out two minutes ago, less than an hour after I decided to take over operations. How could you be so damned clumsy, Salih? Our asses are on the line and you cannot be bothered to find out that Zeki is ex-MIT? He's not only a field operative but a counter-intelligence agent as well! If you had known this, you wouldn't have lost two good men and the document. In fact, he would've never left the country. Pull your head out man and get your mind off of that blonde concubine of yours! You've got to focus, damn it!"

"Why in the hell is Zeki helping these guys?"

"Again, if you had done your homework, you would know that Zeki and Ian's friendship goes way back. Ian visited Turkey on numerous occasions to conduct research on Byzantine history and invariably stayed in Zeki's home. Listen, you're still going to do logistics, but I need you to assure me there will be no more mistakes."

"You have my word."

There was a click on the other end and Salih turned off the phone. His chances for advancement were all but gone. He knew that. The brotherhood would not easily forgive two failed operations. But this was the least of his concerns. Right now, he knew, as did Ahmet, that his neck, not his career, was what was on the line and a successful recovery was the only way to save it.

34

SATURDAY MORNING, DALLAS   Zeki had been watching the silhouette of the
Dallas sky-line grow closer for the last twenty minutes. In his rear-view mirror,
he saw that the spinning globe was about to turn its unveiled face once again
towards the sun as a cloudless Texas day threatened record heat. He felt more
exposed than he had ever been before. For the first time in his life, he was
engaged in a game of hide-and-seek with the world's most powerful country
and no backup. Their first priority was to ditch the car. He veered out of the
middle lane to take the exit for 635 North. The plan was simple. They'd leave
the car in a parking garage and arrange for lodging at different places. He
would stay at Hotel Indigo since he could use one of his many IDs without fear
of being caught. She would look for a bed and breakfast reasonably close that
didn't require a driver's license.

Traffic was not bad, not yet anyway. He looked over at Gwyn. She had been
sleeping for over an hour. His heart broke for this young woman robbed of her
parents before she had even married or given them grandkids. He had seen the
gambit of human depravity in his line of work. *More senseless violence, more senseless bloodshed.* His assessment was subjective and he knew it. 'Senseless' was not
how the perpetrators would characterize it. He had learned long ago that 'sense',
whatever it meant, was not something people held in common. As far as he could
tell, there was no evil the human heart was incapable of. The clerics did not teach
the depravity of man, but he knew it to be true. He saw the DART mass transit
station Gwyn had told him about and started looking for a good place to ditch
the car. They had a lot to do and not much time to do it.

Two and a half hours later Zeki was standing at 1515 Young Street waiting for Gwyn in front of the Central Library. He had checked into his hotel,
grabbed a light breakfast in the hotel restaurant and then placed a call to London. He didn't really like using a public library for their research. He knew
that the people who had come after Gwyn had intercepted Gwyn and Gilbert's

phone calls, that they had been able to triangulate her cell phone signal to find her location in a rural part of East Texas, and that they would have learned by now that he had taken out two of their men. He saw Gwyn walking down the street. She was wearing a wide-brimmed hat and sunglasses like he had suggested.

"Hello, Zeki."

"Hello, Gwyn. The hat is very becoming on you, but I'm afraid even in Texas, it makes you stand out a bit."

Her voice carried the slightest hint of offense when she answered, "You said to wear a hat that would hide our faces from traffic and security cameras. This is the best I could do. The only thing bigger is a sombrero, and that would have stood out."

He smiled at the irony of the situation. Everyone in the Middle East viewed cowboys as the oppressors of the Native American Indians. They were the symbol of European imperialism. Yet, here he was in the middle of Dallas, Texas helping a "cowgirl" escape Muslim assassins.

Gwyn looked impatient. "Shouldn't we get moving?"

Zeki turned and began walking towards the library. "Yes, we should be receiving an email very soon. In the meantime, I suppose we have some research to do."

⊹━┉━⊹

SATURDAY AFTERNOON, LONDON   There was a knock at the door. Gary looked through the peephole and saw a man in uniform standing outside.

"Who is it?" asked Gilbert.

"Looks like a policeman, but he's not one that I recognize from the team McIntosh assigned to us."

He opened the door.

"Good afternoon, sir."

"Good afternoon. Are you Mr. O'Brien?"

The man was of medium-build with dark hair and a generic, clean-shaven face. It was hard to tell if he had olive skin or a good tan. He had a backpack hung on his shoulder. Then Gary noticed the envelope the man held in his right hand.

"I do hope you have some information about our sister."

The man's face was expressionless, but he stuck the envelope towards Gary and said, "I was told to deliver this to Mr. O'Brien."

"Which one?" responded Gary.

"To Gary or Gilbert O'Brien."

"Well, I am Gary O'Brien and this is my brother Gilbert," he said, opening the door to invite the man inside. The policeman held up his hand in a gesture of refusal.

197

"I must be on my way. Please, take this," he said, offering the envelope to Gary.

"Did McIntosh send this?" asked Gilbert.

"Sir, I'm just a messenger. My job is to convey this message to one of you in person."

Gilbert noted that his question had gone unanswered.

"But, you haven't asked for our ID," continued Gilbert.

"I was shown a photograph of you both."

Gary took the envelope hesitantly. It was unsealed. He opened it and pulled out a small slip of paper. It said,

I AM SAFE, AT LEAST FOR NOW. DO NOT BELIEVE WHAT THE POLICE TELL YOU ABOUT Z. HE SAVED MY LIFE. HE'S EX-MIT. SAYS STOP USING ALL COMMUNICATION THAT IS PERSONALLY IDENTIFYING IMMEDIATELY. ALL BEING TRACED. EMAIL ADDRESS FOR COMMUNICATION IS: G109B@ HOTMAIL.COM. PSWD HIZB19. I WILL CONTACT YOU FROM G901B@ HOTMAIL.COM. IN OUR COMMUNICATION, DO NOT USE OUR NAMES OR THE NAMES OF ANYONE INVOLVED.

IS THIS REAL? REMEMBER THE ROOSTER ATTACK ON THE FARM WHEN WE WERE KIDS. THE LESSON WITH DAD AND THE LEMONADE. THE SCAR IN THE LEFT CORNER OF YOUR LIP FROM A FIGHT IN THE LOCKER ROOM...

G.

Gary looked back up at the man only to find that he was already walking into the elevator. Gilbert impatiently grabbed the slip of paper from Gary's hand.

"For God's sake man, what does it say?"

Gilbert read the note quickly and Gary closed the door. Gilbert immediately began verbalizing what they were both thinking.

"How do we know this is authentic? Everything points to Zeki being involved in the murders. Gwyn gets a call from Zeki, who is supposed to be in Britain, saying that he is in Dallas and wants to visit her. In the middle of the night, Gwyn disappears amid a hail of gunfire. The police find a pool of blood on the porch, but can't find our sister. Now, just few hours later, we get a typed note here in London purporting to be from Gwyn, telling us that Zeki has saved her life. This hardly seems likely."

He turned to look at his brother and gauge his reaction. Gary's face was ashen.

"Gilbert," he said, "If there is a one in a million chance that your mother will develop breast cancer and then she does, 'unlikely' becomes a fairly irrelevant concept. Nothing could be further removed from reality than probability.

There are billions of possible and millions of probable outcomes, but there is only one reality. Something tells me that this is real."

The look on Gilbert's face remained skeptical.

"Maybe it's some sort of trap."

"Look, only Gwyn could've known those things. She could've been coerced or tricked into giving some details about our childhood, but what would the motive be? If Gwyn is dead and they have the mystery document, why would we get a letter at all? If it's true though and Gwyn is alive, then I'm afraid reality has just gotten more complicated."

Gilbert ran his hands through his thick, dirty blonde hair.

"Did you notice how the man left our question about whether or not McIntosh sent him unanswered?"

Suddenly, the color began to drain from Gilbert's face.

"Oh my God, if this note is real, the call I just made to Ginger a couple of hours ago might have been intercepted."

This realization struck them both very hard. Instinctively, Gilbert reached for his Blackberry to warn his family. Gary quickly grabbed his hand.

"We can't do it like that. If this is real, we have to get in touch with her another way."

"Damn it, Gary, this is bullshit. This note is implying that the people who killed Dad are capable of tracking cell phone calls. My job is security, remember! That's not something a common criminal could pull off."

"Yeah? Well, who said we're dealing with common criminals? Tell me this. How did they find Gwyn? How did they know she had the document and not you? Can you explain that? We don't know what the document says. We don't know who is after it. Obviously, we are dealing with state actors or worse."

Gilbert was silent for a moment, his mind racing down a dozen paths at once.

"The US consulate nearest Otranto is in Naples. I'll contact someone at my office and see if they can get in touch with my family. Then, we'll alert both the local authorities and the US consulate."

He grabbed his bag, threw it on the bed and started shoving his clothes into it.

"Get your stuff together," he said with urgency and more raw emotion than Gary had ever seen. "I'm going to use the computer down in the lobby to check that email address. I'll ask one of those chaps that McIntosh assigned to us if we can use his phone."

"Where are we going?"

"That I don't know. What I do know is that we aren't staying here with Ginger and Gwyn in danger."

Gary didn't move a muscle. His eyes were closed. There was a look of intense concentration on his face. Gilbert finished scouring the room, and then unplugged his cell phone charger and laptop adapter from the wall and started putting them in his computer bag. Gary finally spoke.

"Gilbert, leave your stuff here."

"What?"

"This doesn't add up. None of it adds up."

"Are you talking to yourself or do you think that statement is a novel thought? None of this has made sense from the beginning. We have a one-thousand-piece puzzle in front of us, and we can't even find the corner pieces."

"We have to start where we are," said Gary pacing back and forth across the room.

"Listen, a policeman just delivered a note saying that Zeki is not the bad guy. I'll bet you McIntosh didn't send him and knows nothing about it. If he did, then he would've had one of the chaps downstairs come up and tell us that Gwyn was safe, and they were mistaken about Zeki. McIntosh wouldn't send a typed note. That means the guy who delivered the note was not a policeman, but had to look like one, so we'd trust him. He had to deliver a typed note because that is the only form of communication that wouldn't be intercepted. Whatever the case, it's easy to test."

He walked briskly over to the phone and rang reception.

"Hello, this is Gary O'Brien. Have you seen a uniformed policeman walk through the lobby in the last fifteen minutes? No one?" Without pausing Gary continued, "Can I speak with the plain clothes officer in the lobby please?" He covered the phone with his hand and whispered to Gilbert. "You saw the backpack. Another change of clothes, maybe?"

"Hello Sergeant. I just wanted to know if you have received any word about my sister. No? Okay, thank you, Sergeant." He hung up the phone. "They haven't seen a uniformed policeman enter the building."

"This doesn't sound like Gwyn," said Gilbert doubtfully. "She's not that paranoid and calculating. Besides, who would she know in London who has a police uniform hanging in their closet?"

"If she's alive, then she has just narrowly escaped death. That could make her a bit paranoid, but I agree with you. This isn't Gwyn. It has to be Zeki. Let's do a little intel-gathering of our own."

"Whoa. Slow down man," Gilbert protested. "Why don't we just call McIntosh and tell him what has happened?"

"If Gwyn is alive, she could've called the police herself. If she's chosen not to, there might be a good reason. Let's operate on the assumption that the note is genuine and eliminate doubt systematically. Remember, McIntosh said Zeki was a suspect in the murder of our father and the note says Zeki saved Gwyn. Both of these ideas cannot be right."

"You don't think we can trust McIntosh?"

"I don't trust anyone," Gary said flatly. It was a simple statement pregnant with meaning. "Does your laptop have an internal webcam?" he continued.

"Yes, why?"

"Perfect. We need to leave, but we cannot take anything because we want to give McIntosh's men the slip and use this room as bait. That will only work if they think we're still here. There are only two men on duty at a time. One is in the lobby and the other is at the service entrance in the back. They aren't expecting us to try and loose a tail so that part should be easy. You run interference for me in the lobby and then tell him you're going to grab a bite to eat. The kitchen has an exit on the side street that no one will be watching. Where is a good place to meet around here?"

"Remember the Internet café on Rupert Street in Soho?" asked Gilbert.

"Yeah, vaguely. You took me there back when you were a hacker."

"It's easy to find. Everyone knows the place. Just ask when you get there. Use the tube. The nearest station is at Russell Square. Take a left on Boswell when you leave the hotel. Then, turn right on Theobald's Road and right again on Southampton. You will run right into it. Take the Piccadilly line and get off at Leicester Square. I'll meet you there."

"Fine. The first thing we need to do is call someone who can get in touch with Ginger."

Gilbert clenched his jaw. "I'll make that call from the lobby phone before I leave."

"Good. Then, we can check the email address in the note from Gwyn. I assume someone in your line of work has their hard disk encrypted with something as good or better than PGP and that you have a VPN set up with a secure tunnel so that we can access your computer remotely?"

"Of course, but I still don't understand what you are doing. And, how in the hell, would you know anything about a VPN and an anonymizer, Mr. I-don't-even-have-a-cell phone?"

"Remember what Dad used to say, 'You're minimum wage from the neck down, son. Never forget that.' Well, I never did. Do you also have a recent back-up of your data? We'll probably lose the computer."

"No problem. All they will get from this computer is a dead hard-drive."

"Put an encrypted folder of several megabytes on a thumb drive and insert it into the USB port. Make sure the encryption is fairly weak. Do you have a worm?"

Gilbert's fingers were flying over the keyboard. "What kind of worm?"

"Well, preferably one that can duplicate itself across a secure network."

"You have to be kidding. Hell, the FBI can't even do that. Any sophisticated security program can detect that sort of propagation. About the best I can do is a simple key-logger that captures keystrokes and sends the data to a remote location. Our company developed one for industrial espionage. Of course, I am bound to deny that should any accusation ever be leveled against me. It's damn good too. As far as we know, nothing can detect it."

"We'll have to make it work. I assume you can attach it to Word as a macro or something. Oh, and I need you to leave your Blackberry here on the table in front of your computer. Make sure it is charged and make sure the laptop is plugged in and left on."

Gilbert listened in amazement as his brother continued to explain his on-the-spot improvisation. It was simple, yet ingenious. Five minutes later, they were walking out of the elevator on the ground floor.

"Hey, what's the book?" asked Gilbert pointing to the leather bound volume Gary was carrying.

"Oh yeah, I forgot to mention this. Remember Thursday when Mrs. Askwith stopped by? Well, she said that on Tuesday night dad asked her to hold on to this. I didn't think anything of it until now. But maybe he forgot to give it to Gwyn, and so he gave it to Mrs. Askwith for safekeeping. It's a diary written in the 1730s belonging to George Sale." Gary stopped and pretended to admire a fabulous painting of a desert caravan. "We'll talk about it later."

Gilbert nodded and kept walking. He crossed the lobby and went straight up to the Sergeant.

"Good afternoon, Sergeant."

"Good afternoon, Mr. O'Brien"

Gilbert moved toward the window overlooking the street, forcing the Sergeant to turn his back on the lobby.

"I'm really sorry you have to sit down here reading magazines all day just for us. It must be awfully boring. I appreciate your chief's gesture though I'm not sure it is necessary."

"With all due respect sir, if the Superintendent thinks there's reason to be cautious, then we mustn't let down our guard. Besides, if I weren't reading a newspaper here, I'd be pushing a pencil in the office or staking out suspected radicals in Newham or Tower Hamlets."

"Aren't those predominately Muslim neighborhoods?"

"Yeah, and it gets a little hairy in there sometimes."

Gilbert paused for a moment sensing a bit of irritation in the man's voice.

"Well," Gilbert said, "I think I'll grab a bite to eat and then head back up to the room and check on my brother, but first I need to make a phone call. The battery on my cell phone has run down and I forgot to pack the charger." The sergeant nodded towards a small alcove near the front door.

"There is a lobby phone over there. You can have it charged to your room."

"Thanks Sergeant."

By the time this conversation was over, Gary was already making the first right turn on Theobald. Gilbert walked over to the lobby phone and dialed the number for his assistant.

"Hi Kiyomi. Listen, I hate to call you on a Saturday, but I need you to do me a favor."

"No problem. What do you need?"

Her voice betrayed the fact that he had woken her up.

"Can you call Ginger for me and have her call me back at the hotel. I'm in the lobby so I'll just take the call on the lobby phone. Do you have a pen and paper to take this number down?"

"Yeah, just a sec."

He heard the sound of a drawer opening and Kiyomi rummaging around for a pen.

"Go ahead. I'm ready."

"020 7242 2829."

She repeated the number back to him and then asked, "I'm happy to do this for you Gilbert, but would you mind telling me why you don't just call her yourself?"

"It's complicated and I really don't have time to explain. Just tell her that she needs to call me back right away."

She could feel the tension in his voice. She had never seen him rattled before.

"Anything else?"

"If you can't reach her, call me back at the lobby right away."

"Got it."

There was a click on the other end. Gilbert walked over and sat on the couch wondering who would be on the other end of the phone when it rang. He felt helpless, hamstringed and harried. He was a doer. His job and the company he worked for were about making things happen and keeping clients happy with stellar results. He had a whole department full of the best resources in the world that, normally, he could call in on any problem, and here he was trying to figure out if he could even use his phone. He was not a patient man, but in less than ninety seconds, the lobby phone rang. He leapt to answer it.

"Hello, Ginger?"

"No, it's me, Kiyomi. Ginger must have her cell phone off. It went straight to voicemail."

There was only silence on the other end of the phone.

"Gilbert? Are you there? Is something wrong?"

"Yeah. I'm here and right now nothing seems right. Listen, can I ask for another favor?"

"Sure."

"First, I need you to write down this email address—gob901@hotmail. com. I may be contacting you from address, and you need to set up an email that is gob109@hotmail.com. Do you have that?"

"Yeah, but..."

"Second, I want you to call my Blackberry in exactly one hour and leave a message. Jot this down, so you don't forget. The message I want you to leave for me should say simply, 'Gwyn wants you to go through the files on the thumb drive from your father. It has a copy of the document and the names of two people you should give it to. She said she will meet you in Seattle at Tim's house.' Did you get all of that, or do I need to repeat it?"

Now there was silence on the other end of the line. Gilbert waited, assuming that she was writing the message down. Finally, Kiyomi spoke and her voice had a knife-like sharpness, "Look, Gilbert, you don't have to tell me what's going on, but at this stage in my life and career, the last thing I need is to be mixed up in something of questionable legality."

Gilbert took a deep breath. Kiyomi was bright, which was why he had hired her. She was already processing the different reasons he would want her to leave a message on his own phone.

"I'll explain it all later. Everything is above board. Don't worry and please keep calling Ginger's number. I will be in touch soon."

35

DALLAS "So, what do you make of it," whispered Gwyn, pointing to the letter carefully spread out before them. Zeki had been looking at it for almost five minutes without saying a word. She had watched the pensive concentration oozing from his fingertips and drumming a beat on the table. Once, he picked up the document and held it up to the light, looking for a watermark that might indicate where the paper was manufactured. Finally, he condescended to quench her curiosity.

"I certainly see it in a somewhat different light after the events of the last week. I suspected from the start that this was no ordinary piece of paper. Everything about it is wrong."

"What do you mean?"

He pointed to the seal.

"Well, first of all, the sultan's seal is always affixed to the top of the document. Here, however, we have it at the bottom of the letter. But, this is nothing compared to what we see in the seal itself. The writer used the seal of a sultan who had been dead for more than three  hundred and fifty years when this letter was written. This *tuğra* belongs to Murad I, a sultan who lived in the late fourteenth century."

"Is there anything exceptional about Murad that could help us?"

"Is there anything exceptional about Murad?" Zeki repeated the question, and a sad smile lit upon his lips. "What wasn't exceptional about the man? He's the one who formed the house of Osman into an Empire. He took a small burgeoning fiefdom and put it firmly on the road to Empire and eventually super-power status. He was the first ruler of the dynasty to use the title of sultan. He personally led his armies from victory to victory, shrinking the once-mighty Byzantine state to a tiny island within the walls of Constantinople. He expanded Turkish rule throughout the Balkans of southeast Europe and so hastened the end of the Eastern Roman Empire's thousand-year reign from the Pearl of the East on the banks of the Bosphorus.

"His armies shattered the pride and strength of the Serbian nation, forcing them into submission and making them vassals for the next three and a half centuries. Had it not been for Murad, the Ottomans might never have become the rulers of the Mediterranean and Black Seas, the Caliph of Islam, the Defender of the Faith and the Terror of the East. Ironically, he was also the only sultan ever killed in battle. It was at the Battle of Kosovo against the Serbs. His death gave rise to the reprehensible practice of fratricide, which continued for three centuries as each sultan who ascended the throne eliminated all of his father's male heirs by strangling them with a silken bow string.

"The awe which he inspired in his contemporaries is clearly expressed by his nickname—*Hüdavendigar*, which means the God-like one. So, the short answer to your question is that Murad was the medieval personification of *exceptional* though I have no idea how that relates to this letter."

"Wow!" exclaimed Gwyn. "Sounds like Napoleon on steroids. So, besides using the seal of a sultan long dead, what other peculiar features do you see?"

"*Rub el Hizb* has been used as a symbol in Islam for centuries. However, I don't know why it is combined with that other symbol, what did you call it?"

"Ouroboros," answered Gwyn,

"Right. Why a self-devouring snake would replace the traditional circle is more than puzzling. It's bizarre in the extreme, but oddly enough, I've seen it once before."

"You have? Where?"

"About five years ago, I was doing some research in the Ottoman archives in Istanbul. You've been there."

"You mean the building across from the Hagia Sophia? The one with the marble fountains on either side, and the beautiful calligraphy above the massive red doors? I was there with my father. I always thought it looked very exotic."

"Yes, that's the place," Zeki said with a smile. "Your memory is excellent. It is called *Bab-ı Ali*, which means the 'grand gate'. The archives are written, like our document here, with the Arabic script in Ottoman Turkish. I had requested a certain series of documents regarding the reign of Murad II. These were histories compiled during the reign of his son, Fatih Sultan Mehmet, and among them was a document, obviously misplaced, which had the *Rub el-Hizb* with the Ouroboros in the middle. Because my time was limited, I didn't read it, but I pointed it out to the clerk when I returned the documents and said that I would like to examine it in greater detail on another visit. When I returned a week later, the document could not be found, the clerk I had spoken to was absent, and I was told in no uncertain terms that there were no documents in the archives that fit this description."

"Sounds strange."

"Strange indeed. I thought little of it until I saw the same symbol on the document your father showed me. It was the first red flag. Have you researched that symbol at all?"

"Yes, I have," she replied. "Ouroboros is an esoteric symbol of unquestionable antiquity, predating both Christianity and Islam. It has been found in the pyramids and is referred to by Plato as the first living thing in the universe. In the west, it seems to have approximated the Taoist concept of Yin-Yang—the eternal act of creating and destroying. It was used by Gnostics, alchemists, Masons, the Unitarian church and others, but it's not limited to the West. It pops up in cultures all over the world."

"So," Zeki continued, "We have an Islamic symbol, which incidentally has been adopted by the most powerful political party in modern Turkey, used together with a very un-Islamic symbol on a document dating back to 1736. I find all this very peculiar indeed."

"What is the *Rub el Hizb*?" asked Gwyn.

"It's used to mark sections of the Qur'an. But, from what I have read, the symbol itself dates back to Tartessos in ancient Andalusia."

"Excuse me, but you lost me there."

"Andalusia is the Anglicized pronunciation of the Arabic *al-Andalus*, which is the name for Spain in the Islamic world. Tartessos is the name of a civilization that thrived in this region before the Roman Empire. Some even say it is the Tarshish of the Old Testament because it is an area rich in metals."

"Old Testament?" Gwyn looked surprised.

"You haven't read it?" asked Zeki, seeming just as flabbergasted.

"Well, yes, I have, but I am surprised that you would be so knowledgeable about it."

"And, why is that? Because I am a Turkish Muslim?"

"Well, yes, to be honest, I did not expect you to have studied the Old Testament since it is not your religion."

"Not my religion? Each statement of yours is stranger than the last. My faith is in the God of Abraham. Is there another more complete record of Abraham's faith than that in the Old Testament?"

"I guess it's just not what I expected."

"You mean not what you've been conditioned to believe. If I knew your father, he probably taught his daughter to expect the unexpected, to question every assumption and look for truth behind reality's mask. I suggest you start applying those lessons. I suspect our path may be illuminated by surprises over the next few days."

Zeki had turned his attention to the second paragraph of the document. It was written with the Arabic script, but the words were completely unintelligible. It wasn't Ottoman, Persian or Arabic. After a few minutes, Gwyn suggested that he transliterate the Arabic letters into the Roman alphabet so she could help. This was trickier than it sounded because the letters in Arabic did not always have a direct correspondence in the Latin script. He read through the lines again, made a couple of small changes and pushed it across the table to Gwyn.

"Looks like Spanish or Portuguese to me," he said.

La decisión del consejo de cancelar al hijo del profeta y borrar todo rastro dél sigue entre nuestros deberes más solemnes. Una carmesí puesta de sol inglesa en Suri-Strend habrá, y también un dorado amanecer en Tunez, cuando el pájaro que volose sea devuelto a Südde-i Saadet. Caminad sobre la nieve, pero no dejéis huellas. Nuestro siempre fiel D. os proporcionará la ayuda necesaria para el envío. Que la entrega sea rápida.

Gwyn scanned the quickly scribbled lines.

"Probably Spanish, but let's get a dictionary." She pushed back from the table. "I'll be back in just a sec."

She walked towards the library reference section. In two minutes, she reappeared carrying a bulky Spanish dictionary, which she plopped down on the table.

"I'm certain that the language is Spanish. I mean I don't speak it, but I have seen enough of it written to recognize grammatical structures like *de, del, una,* etc., I thought we could look up a few of the words to see what it's about."

Three minutes later Gwyn was satisfied all of the words in the first line were equivalent to words in the first line of the English translation. She turned to Zeki.

"So, we have a letter in Ottoman Turkish with a Spanish translation using Arabic characters. This just keeps getting more and more bizarre."

"Let's start with the obvious," replied Zeki. "Tunis is a city in Tunisia, south of Spain across the Mediterranean. It's an Arabic-speaking Muslim country so the use of the Arabic script is not so strange. Obviously, there was some doubt as to whether the person or persons who would be reading it could understand Ottoman Turkish so it was provided in Spanish as well. The Arabic script is strange, I admit, but there is certainly a geopolitical conjuncture that seems plausible."

Gwyn interrupted. "Do you know when the Spanish finally succeeded in defeating the Muslim rulers of Spain?"

"Every Muslim knows the answer to that," he replied. "It's remembered every year throughout the world of Islam as the Lament for Andalusia, but I've read that American children memorize the same date as 'In 1492 Columbus sailed the ocean blue.'"

"Then this letter was written two hundred and thirty years after the conquest," Gwyn responded doubtfully.

"Yes, but the Moors did not leave Spain in 1492. I don't remember the exact date of their deportation, but I know that it was much later."

Gwyn typed MUSLIM, ARABIC, MOORS, SPANISH, DEPORTED in the search engine and hit return. She began scanning the results and then without taking her eyes off the screen, she asked,

"Who are the Moriscos? That name occurs in several places."

"The Moriscos," replied Zeki, "were the Muslim inhabitants of Spain who were given an ultimatum by the Spanish Crown in 1501 to convert to Catholicism or be deported. It is a long and sad story. You may add it to the list of topics to research. I suppose they retained some veneration for the Arabic script, but after several generations under Spanish rule, I'm sure most spoke Spanish as their native language."

"So, why did they write in Arabic?" asked Gwyn.

"Muslims believe that as the language of the Qur'an Arabic is divine, almost magical."

"So, why did the Turks abandon the Arabic script after the Republic was established?"

"There were several reasons I suppose. First, there was the practical issue of literacy, which, at the time, was below five percent because Ottoman Turkish was amazingly complex, with many Persian and Arabic loan words. Atatürk knew that a simplified alphabet would help the nation achieve greater literacy. Secondly, he was determined to make Turkey part of the modern world, and, in 1928, that meant moving towards the West, as it championed objective scientific inquiry. They used the Latin alphabet and I suppose he figured this would help Turkey integrate with Europe. More importantly, however, he wanted a new beginning, unfettered by the traditions of Empire, the Caliphate and the dogma of religion. So, by introducing a new alphabet, he insured that the next generation would be unable to read the vast amount of material produced by the Ottomans. When he outlawed the Arabic script, literacy literally fell to zero in a single day, but by 1935, literacy was at thirty-five percent. Today, only experts can read documents written before 1928."

"So, it was a tool of social reform?"

"Of course, societies are shaped by what they read, and how they express themselves. Obviously, the Moriscos felt the same way."

†═══†

LONDON   Gilbert spotted Gary in the far corner of the café and began weaving his way through the rows of computers. The room was very dim with black ceilings and walls. The layout was unique too. In some places, there were islands of computer screens arranged in circles or ovals for the most avid gamers who circled around the tables like Neanderthals around a fire in a cave. The walls were dotted with modern-day cave paintings consisting mostly of Salvador Dali prints. The clientele was practically unchanged. There might be a few more girls now, but it was still a testosterone-charged atmosphere of young men and boys between the ages of twelve and nineteen. They were video game junkies who spent hours every day honing their neural synapses to develop some of the best hand-eye coordination on the planet, extremely refined skills that would produce absolutely nothing in the real world.

Gilbert appreciated the fact that the human brain longed for stimulation, longed for excitement, the thrill of the chase, the lust for blood, victory and renown. In fact, the mind almost seemed hard-wired for war and violence. These kids plugged their instincts into a virtual world, killing, conquering, creating, and wrecking mayhem in a fantasy universe where no one actually suffered. They got their names on the leader board, which gave them the feeling of accomplishment and identity, becoming in essence the chief of their virtual tribe. After venting all of this pent up destiny, they would go out for ice-cream and then back to the computers in their bedrooms to view things just as primitive but more private. Now, he thought about how different it felt in real life, the hunt, the chase, the carnage.

He remembered the hours he had spent with his friends either playing games or trying to hack any computer they could find. Once, he had actually narrowly missed being arrested in this very room. He had hacked an account at a London bank and transferred a modest amount to an NGO providing water pumps operated by foot to poor Indian farmers. He had left the connection up, planning to come back and make a few more "anonymous" donations. Another kid had taken his spot and when the police raided the café, Gilbert was just coming out of the bathroom, so he simply made for the exit.

It had been a close call, and he had never come close to being caught again. He had followed the case, willing to turn himself in if it looked like the kid would be convicted, but the boy had passed every lie-detector test and stuck to his story, saying that he had only just sat down at the computer and that he hadn't even loaded his game when the officers grabbed him. In the end, the authorities let him go. Gilbert looked around the room. Things weren't the same anymore though. The games were different, and so was hacking.

Gary had chosen a discreet spot. Their backs were against a wall, so no one would be looking over their shoulders. Gary handed him a pair of headphones.

"Put these on," he said softly.

"Did you check the email account?" asked Gilbert.

"Yep." He reached over and clicked the browser. Gilbert noted that the URL was anonymized. The email opened on the screen. It was a single line.

"Have you already responded?"

"I did right before you walked in."

"What did you say?"

"I said that I once knew a five-year-old girl who filled the pockets of a white dress with bubble gum and candy at a church picnic in the middle of the summer and ended up wearing her brother's shorts. I also asked her what she found on the walls of Troy."

"No response yet?"

"Nope. When is Kiyomi making the call?"

Gilbert glanced down at his watch. "She should be making it in two minutes."

"Then let's get this thing set up."

He watched as Gilbert first logged into the VPN and then accessed his computer remotely. He opened the webcam and suddenly an image of the hotel room flashed onto the screen. The trap was set. Hopefully, Kiyomi was baiting it right now.

⊹═══⊹

CAIRO "What is our status?" Ahmet asked curtly.

Jabbar, his chief intelligence officer, responded without lifting his eyes from the screen, "You already know about the phone call to his wife."

Jabbar was a tall Circassian whose family had moved to Damascus in the late nineteenth century before migrating on to Jordan, where his clan had formed the elite palace guard for the Hashemite Kingdom in its early days after World War II. Ahmet trusted him implicitly.

"But, that is not all. We've also just had a call to Gilbert's cell phone from a DC number. He didn't answer, but the caller left a message that you'll want to hear."

"Play it."

Jabbar clicked the play button and they heard Kiyomi's message. 'Hey Gilbert. Gwyn just called and told me that you need to check the thumb drive your father left with the package. It has a copy of some document he says is important and the names and contact information of the two people you need to send it to. She'll meet you at Tim's in Seattle two days from now.'

"That was it?" asked Ahmet.

"Yes sir."

"Who does the number belong to?"

"Kiyomi Saito. Japanese father, American mother. Graduated from Cornell and works as Gilbert's personal assistant."

"What's Gilbert's location?"

Jabbar checked his computer screen again. "His cell phone is in the hotel and most likely in his room. When I checked with our team five minutes ago, they said the two undercover police were still on site, one in the lobby and one at the back service entrance."

"I want that thumb drive. Send in our Johnny right now. Make sure he is armed. This information is priority number one. Then, put together a list of every flight out of Texas or a contiguous state with Seattle as the final destination. Next, find every Tim in Seattle and see if we can find any connection with the O'Brien family. This may be our lucky break. Do we have anyone in Seattle?"

"No sir, but we can have someone there in four hours out of Chicago."

36

Gilbert nudged Gary and pointed his chin at the screen. The door to their hotel room was opening. They both held their breath. This confirmed it. Gwyn was right. Somebody with incredible resources was tracking them and desperately wanted what they had falsely claimed to have on the thumb drive. They had intercepted the message and responded with unbelievable speed. Gilbert pushed the record button on the screen to capture everything via the webcam.

A policeman wearing gloves opened the door and immediately drew his weapon. He said something into a shoulder mike, but he was too far away for the computer's internal microphone to pick it up. He closed the door with his foot and started towards the bathroom, still aiming down the barrel of the pistol. He disappeared from the screen only to reappear a few seconds later with his gun holstered, walked to the door and drew the deadbolt. Again, he spoke into the mike. Again, he was too far away for them to make out what he was saying.

He began searching the suitcase beside the door, methodically taking everything out and laying it on the bed. When the suitcase was empty, he did the same with Gary's bag. He was a white male with a ruddy complexion, very tall and slightly over-weight. He looked to be between thirty and forty years of age. Gilbert felt his pulse quicken and wondered if Gary was feeling the same seething anger he felt burning his cheeks right now. *Who the hell are these people and what do they want with us?* Anger wasn't the only emotion he felt though. Icicles of fear pierced his heart as he thought about his wife and sister.

When the man was finished looking through both bags, he began looking around the room. He checked the drawers in the nightstands and saw the Blackberry. He grabbed it and stuck it in his pocket. Then, he headed for the computer sitting on the table in front of the window. Gary and Gilbert watched as the man walked straight towards them. It was an eerie feeling to see a man who might very well want them dead starting to fill the screen in front of them. He sat down at the computer. They could only see his face. He was probably moving his finger over the mouse-pad to get rid of the screensaver.

He would be disappointed when he was greeted with the login screen. Then, he touched the shoulder mike again.

"I found it. It's in the port on his computer. His Blackberry is here as well. Shall I take it?"

They saw the man pull out a ruggedized PDA and stick the thumb drive into it. He had clearly been ordered to send the data somewhere. Then, he took Gilbert's Blackberry and hooked an adaptor to the port and connected it to his PDA. Gary turned to Gilbert.

"What will he be able to get off your phone?"

"Only phone numbers. All the email is encrypted. Listen, we have to inform McIntosh and have him send men up to the room."

"Are you sure we want to tip them off about the trap. If the police take this guy in, or out, as the case may be, they will know that we are on to them. It could be easier for us if we keep them on the goose chase with the bogus names and the meeting in Seattle."

"They are about to find out anyway," said Gilbert grimly.

"What do you mean?"

"I was sloppy. I forgot to change the creation date on the Word file I made. If they see it was created two hours ago, they will realize it was a trap."

"Then I guess you better make the call. Will the key-logger still work?"

"It should install itself as soon as the file is opened and will remain even if they delete the file. It's the best that corporate espionage has to offer. I'm not aware of anything that can detect and delete it. The corporate world is every bit as secure as the CIA if not more so."

"I thought corporate world was synonymous with government."

"We'll argue your politics later."

"How will we know if it worked?"

Gilbert brought the browser window to the foreground and typed a URL into the window. A small screen that reminded Gary of DOS appeared in the upper left hand corner of the screen.

"If the program loads successfully, we will see information begin to arrive on this screen."

Gilbert clicked on the Skype window. Gary had already signed into his account. It had no identifying information. His location was shown as Celestial City in the US Virgin Islands. He had only $1.87 worth of credit left, but since it only cost three cents per minute that was sixty-two minutes. He punched McIntosh's direct number in using the onscreen keypad and waited for him to pick up.

"McIntosh."

"This is Gilbert O'Brien. I need you to get someone up to our room right away. Make sure they're armed and ready for trouble."

"What are you talking about?"

"There is no time to explain. All you need to know is that there is an armed man in our room right now and he's connected with the murder of our father. If you want to find the perpetrators, then you need to apprehend this man."

"You aren't in the hotel? I don't understand"...

"Sir, you don't have much time. The deadbolt is drawn. You will have to blow the door. We'll be in touch."

He clicked the red dot to disconnect the call. They turned their attention back to the screen. The man was now tidying the room and repacking their belongings. Gary prodded Gilbert and pointed to the small window in the upper left corner of the screen. Characters were popping up on the screen.

GOOD. GOT IT. DON'T FORGET TO LEAVE THE COMPUTER AT THE DROP. DOSYAYI ALDIK. ŞIMDI GÖNDERIYORUM SIZE. BIRI ŞIFRELI. KIRMA IŞLEMINE BAŞLIYORUZ.

Gary gave his brother the thumbs up. It had worked. Thirty seconds later, another stream of characters began to appear in a second column.

"What is that, Gilbert?" asked Gary.

"That, my friend, is the key-logger installed on a second computer."

PACKAGE AT SEA YET?. CONFIRM AND SEND ETA.

Back in the first column, they read.

AUGUSTINERLESESAAL RESERVASYONU TAMAMDIR. RAHIP LUIGI FRANCHINI ADINA. 4 GÜN SONRA.

Gary quickly translated the Turkish for Gilbert.

"So, they're going to try and break the code. Good. I didn't get the part about the priest though."

"Yeah, I don't understand it either. A reservation has been made in the name of Father Luigi Franchini four days from now at Augustinerlesessal, whatever that is."

Now, both columns were beginning to fill up with data. They turned their attention back to the webcam in the hotel room. The man was sitting on the bed, obviously waiting for further instructions. Several minutes passed without any change. Then, Gary pointed to the inbox icon, which showed that there was one new message. It was from the email address Gwyn said she was using. He clicked on it.

A TEN LIRA COIN MINTED IN 1982. ☺ OK. Z. SAYS CHAT IS FINE BUT AVOID KYWRDS BECAUSE OF OPEN-SOURCE MONITORING. OPEN THE CHAT WHENEVER YOU ARE READY.

They looked back to the webcam window. The phone the man held in his hand rang. He answered it, but again he was too far away for them to make out what he was saying. Suddenly, he turned and stared at the computer, said something to the person on the phone and started walking towards them. His body had just filled the screen when they heard the explosion. The webcam resolution and connection speed were too slow to follow the action. Everything was a blur. The room was filled with smoke and dust. There was shouting and then two gunshots.

CAIRO   Jabbar had been uneasy from the moment their man had reported the room empty. It made no sense with the Blackberry in the room. Something wasn't right, but he hadn't been able to put his finger on it. Now, he sat looking at the screen in horror. It was so simple. How had they missed it?

"Ahmet!" he shouted. "Get our man out of there. These files were created just a few hours ago. They can't be from Ian. This is a trap."

Ahmet dialed the number on his desk phone to contact the man in the field directly. Normally, he would have asked Salih's team to do it, but there was no time.

"Hello."

"The code is St. George," said Ahmet. "Listen, you need to get out of there. We think this could be a trap. The files you sent were created today. They're not what the message said they were."

Ahmet was just about to say there was no need to worry about the computer when the explosion happened. Ahmet couldn't believe what he was hearing. There were voices shouting, "Down! Get down!" Then, there were two gunshots. He kept the line open, hoping that his man would come back on and tell him that the threat was eliminated. Instead, he heard scuffling, groans and then another man shouting, "Where did you get this uniform, you son of a bitch?" That was enough for Ahmet. He disconnected the phone and turned back to his team.

"The police just took out our man in the hotel room. Find out what happened in there and how we were compromised. I want a full report in one hour and keep me apprised of any pertinent information in real time. Cancel the Seattle operation. That's a diversion. Jabbar, can I see you in my office?"

Ahmet turned and walked to the glass door that separated his office from the long, rectangular operations room. The shades were open so that he could see everything that was going on. Jabbar closed the door behind him. Ahmet was pacing the room.

"What is your assessment?"

"You want the truth?"

"Of course, I do," he said with conviction, but he could tell from the apprehensive look on Jabbar's face and the tone of his voice, he wasn't going to like it.

"If he weren't your friend, I would say Salih needed to be relieved of his duties. It may sound ironic, but we are talking about criminal negligence here. I've been following standard protocol since you put our team on the case. The gaps are appalling. Why didn't we at least spot check his threat assessments? You should've had someone here double-check the backgrounds he was working up on these people. He took too much at face value, assuming Ian was a simple professor and his sons were normal, working-class peons. I've looked at his record. This is very out of character. Is he under some pressure?"

"I suppose you could say he was trying to release some pressure."

"I'm sorry. I don't understand."

"Forget it. What do you have?"

"Well, Ian was probably just a professor, but it would be wrong to call him a simple professor. He was a genius and his sons are even smarter."

"What are you driving at?" Ahmet asked impatiently.

"First of all, Gary had scholarship offers from just about every Ivy League school in the States. He actually accepted a scholarship to Georgetown but never enrolled. He has travelled extensively and has connections with several clandestine, albeit peaceful organizations whose mission is to alleviate poverty and oppression. He was in Istanbul teaching English when he got the news that his father had died. He doesn't seem to have been involved with anyone in Turkey, but in India, he worked for several years with a group of social radicals educating the poor and teaching them to reject exploitive jobs, pool their labor and beat the system by creating their own.

"He organized a charity network that not only provided micro-loans with money donated by a wide variety of philanthropic groups, but he also had dozens of educational books translated into local languages. He worked on a variety of radical projects, including a translation of the *Injil*. This upset the local elite, and he had to go underground. For over two years, he received death threats and was constantly on the run. Finally, he realized there was no choice but death or flight. That was when he came to Istanbul."

"How did you find all this?" asked Ahmet curiously.

"I did the research Salih should have done," said Jabbar dryly. "Once I knew he had been in India, I contacted our resources there. Salih would have known he was in India just from his passport records."

"What about the eldest brother?"

"The only thing Salih said in his workup was that he was employed by a security company. That is hardly a fitting description. The man was the valedictorian of his class. And upon graduation, he was immediately hired by DSI. He rose quickly and now runs a corporate intelligence unit. He's an expert on cyber security systems and technology. You know the Libyan case before the ICSID?"

"Of course, our branch in France is handling the suit. What about it?"

"His company provides security for the American law firm representing the private consortium whose investments were seized. I had our DC liaison call Mike Tate. Apparently, Gilbert organized the team that infiltrated the French law firm representing the new Libyan government."

"Isn't Tate a consultant with the same company?"

"Yes, he is. In fact, he is the one who has been handling our interests. He thinks he's doing it all for Senator Giovanni, of course."

"Well, I take it as a compliment that Allah has given us worthy opponents, but if we had known that all of this, especially our connection through Tate, we wouldn't be in this predicament."

Jabbar shook his head. "I suspect that Gilbert and Gary put this ruse together themselves. They are certainly capable of it. I don't know what would have prompted them to do it. The attempt on their sister's life would have been sufficient I am sure. Whatever the case, they will be very difficult to find now."

"Which means, of course, that informing them of our demands is going to be a problem."

"It's hard to deliver a message to someone you can't find, sir."

"So, what else did they hope to learn or gain from this?"

"Sir, they confirmed that someone is intercepting their phone calls."

"Is that all they would have gotten out of it?"

"Well, from what I gather, the police now have one of our men in custody."

Ahmet cracked a wry smile. "That will not do them much good. He will never talk and the British police will never try to break him. Fortunately for him, it is a very civilized country."

There was a knock at the door. A member of the cyber-surveillance team poked his head through the door.

"Sir, Gilbert's credit card was just swiped. He purchased two Chunnel tickets for tonight at 7:00 PM somewhere close to Russell Square."

"For himself and his brother?"

"That's what it looks like. He also took out several large cash advances on the same card."

"Okay, I want someone on that train," said Ahmet. "Tell Salih to get someone to Folkestone ASAP. And find out the status of our package."

"Sir, they just confirmed ETA in fifteen minutes. The oldest boy gave them a lot of trouble, but apparently he is a quick learner and is more cooperative now."

Jabbar smiled as he pictured the lesson Gilbert's son had just received.

37

LONDON   Gary and Gilbert watched the scene being captured by the laptop web-cam for another fifteen minutes while they monitored the stream of data intercepted by the key-logger. Hotel personnel arrived almost immediately, followed by a hotel doctor. The medics were not far behind, accompanied by swarms of uniformed policemen who began treating the area like a crime scene in an attempt to protect it from further contamination. Apparently, one of the agents assigned to protect them had been hit in the shoulder. He was taken out on a stretcher first. The uniformed police-pretender had been shot in the knee. He screamed incessantly. No one but the hotel doctor paid him any mind. He was handcuffed and lying on his stomach. When the doctor tried to move him to a more comfortable position, one of the officers who had just arrived intervened and told him in no uncertain terms to leave him where he was. Finally, a medic was told to sedate him.

Gary prodded his brother again and pointed at the key-logger stream. Most of it had been in the foreign language, but now there was an English stream.

> WILL HE LIVE? I SEE. WELL THAT IS TOO BAD. NO, THERE IS NO
> NEED TO ELIMINATE HIM. TOO RISKY. BESIDES, HE'S COMPLETELY
> INSULATED. IF HE TALKS, WE'LL HANDLE IT. CAN YOU SECURE THE
> COMPUTER? OH WELL, IT WOULD HAVE BEEN NICE.

"What the hell!" exclaimed Gilbert.

> I NEED A REPORT BY 19:00 HOURS GMT.
> EVERYTHING ON THE O'BRIEN CASE.

Gilbert ripped his headphones off. Gary just brought his hands together, index fingers extended to form a pistol and put the barrel over his lips pushing up against his nose as he continued staring at the screen.

"Do you see this?" whispered Gilbert furiously, air hissing through his teeth. "Am I losing my mind or do these guys have somebody on the inside feeding them information?"

"That's what it looks like," responded Gary calmly. "Makes you feel like a small fish in a big ocean teeming with sharks, doesn't it?" Gilbert said nothing.

"We need to call Gwyn."

"Right. Remember, no names."

Gary opened the chat window. The email address she had provided said she was online. He hit the 'call' button and waited for her to pick up.

"Hello."

"Sis? This is your little brother. Your older brother is sitting right here beside me. Can you hear me?"

"Yes, we can hear you fine."

"I can't tell you how good it is to hear your voice. We're so glad to hear you are safe. We thought...." His voice cracked, and he stopped for a moment to regain composure. "Is Z. there with you?"

Zeki's deep baritone filled their headphones. "Yes, I'm here too. Please accept my sincerest condolences for the loss of your father."

Gilbert cut in. "Thank you for your sentiments, but we owe you a tremendous debt of gratitude for saving my sister's life."

"God was gracious to us and allowed me to get there in time," said Zeki solemnly. "I'm glad you received the note from my friend."

"Your friend? He works for the police force?"

"I'm afraid I can't say more than that."

"I understand. Listen, we don't have much time. What are the most urgent things we need to talk about?"

Zeki responded very earnestly. "First, let me remind you to use no names in our conversation. These people may be able to track more than cell phone calls. Anything you do on the Internet might be intercepted. They probably have the capability to monitor every search conducted on the Internet and unless you are using an anonymizer to hide your IP address, searching for specific words would lead them right to your physical location."

"Don't worry," said Gilbert, "we're using an anonymizer. Would you mind telling me who *they* are? Do you have any idea why they believe this document is worth killing people to get?"

Zeki grunted. "My friend, *they* are the people who want to kill you. Is that not enough? Will giving them a name change that? They have no name, and yet they have many. *They* might be *Hizb ut Tahrir*, *they* might be *Hizbullah*. *They* are clearly people you do not want to cross, and yet unintentionally we have managed to put ourselves squarely in their cross-hairs. To be quite frank, I am amazed that any of us are alive. It is Providence pure and simple. Nothing else can explain my good fortune in arriving in time to protect Gwyn. *They* are the 'shadow of God's shadow,' or what some people call the 'deep state.'"

"I'm not sure I follow you," said Gilbert.

Gary decided to clarify. "He is referring to the power behind the Ottoman throne. The Ottoman sultan, who served as the Caliph, the supreme spiritual leader of Islam, was known as the 'shadow of Allah.'"

"Bravo, that's right," continued Zeki clearly impressed, "But, just like today, he was often a puppet whose strings were pulled by others. That's why I said these people are the 'shadow behind the shadow of God.' The real power is wielded by others. I don't know who they are for sure, nor can I give their organization a name. What I do know is that the tentacles of this monster stretch across the centuries, and now they have slithered into our lives. Our situation is grave indeed."

"But, you know who they are?" asked Gilbert, pushing the issue.

"No, I know what they do, and I know how they operate, but I don't know who they are. They are an idea with many faces. Let's not waste more time on this. Tell us what you've learned."

Gilbert started by filling them in on events in London—the autopsy results, the Interpol notice against Zeki, their simple but effective counter-surveillance at the hotel, how they had planted the key-logger and how they had warned Gilbert's wife and children to cut their vacation short and come home. Zeki immediately cut him off.

"Gilbert, you must consider the possibility that they might try to abduct your family. It would be nothing for them. They certainly have the resources. Maybe the information you have gathered from the key-logger can help us."

Gilbert and Gary both fell silent. Finally, Gwyn broke in.

"What's wrong? Do you guys know something you're not telling us?"

Gilbert interjected, "I've tried to call my wife several times, but there is no answer. We think the key-logger information indicates they've already been abducted. Several messages refer to a 'package,' 'ETA' and 'a boy giving them trouble.'"

Gwyn drew in a sharp breath. "Oh my God!"

Zeki cut in. "We have to find out why this document is so valuable to them. It is the only way we can understand what they are after. Is all the data you're getting from the key-logger in English?"

"No, it's not," said Gary. "More than half of it is in Turkish, but I'd like you to look at them. My Turkish is still a bit shaky."

"Since when do you speak Turkish?" asked Zeki puzzled.

"I've been living in Istanbul for a while now."

He didn't volunteer anything else and Zeki didn't ask. He only said, "The guys that came for your sister spoke Turkish as well. Send me those logs and I'll have a look if you can do it securely."

"I was just about to suggest that. I can upload it to a secure ftp over an encrypted connection and give you the login, but you will have to supply a secure connection on your side. This chat is certainly not safe."

"No problem. Make the password something your sister will know."

221

"Okay, I'll make it the name of my sister's first dog. You'll see the ftp info in your chat window." He hit return, sending the ftp address zipping through cyberspace.

Zeki spoke again. His voice was grave.

"If they have your family, they will use them as leverage to acquire the document. You will have no choice but to comply with their demands. They would think nothing of killing your family or something far worse. I wish I could say that it will come out right in the end, but this is a different league from any you have ever played in before. They play for keeps."

"We'll see who keeps what," responded Gilbert angrily.

"What have you guys learned?" asked Gary.

"The document found by your esteemed father, Professor O'Brien, may God grant that he rest in peace, was written in Ottoman Turkish in 1736. It's not an official state document. I suspect that it was probably an order issued by a secret society. It seems to be an order for a covert operation in England. There is a Spanish translation of the order at the bottom of the page, but it's in *aljamiado*, which is essentially Spanish written with the Arabic alphabet. That means it must have gone through North Africa."

"You guys keep talking about a document I haven't seen," said Gary.

"Sorry," said Gwyn. "Let me read it for you.

> *'The council's decision to cancel son of prophet and erase every trace*
> *remains among our most solemn duties. It will be a red English sunset*
> *on Suri-Strend with a golden sunrise in Tunis when the bird which*
> *has flown is brought back to Südde-i Saadet. Walk in the snow, but*
> *leave no footprints. Assistance for the sendoff may be obtained from*
> *our ever faithful D. Hasten delivery.'"*

"Do you have any idea how this could be related to George Sale?" asked Gary.

"I have no idea who that even is," replied Gwyn. "Why do you ask?"

"Dad gave Mrs. Askwith George Sale's diary the night he was killed. I'm wondering if maybe it was something he meant to give to you but forgot, and so when he got home, he took it to her house."

"Wait a minute. George Sale. G.S."

"G.S.?" asked Gary.

"His initials are G.S. There was a sticky note on the folder that said, 'THE ORIGINAL ASS. ORDER FOR G.S.?! G.O.B.?

"Dad had circled three passages at the end of the diary." They could hear Gary flipping through the pages. "Listen to these three entries:

> *July 5th 1736, My meeting in Amsterdam with the Morisco printer was*
> *peculiar in the extreme. His lavish hospitality and overanxious manner*

made me apprehensive. When I inquired about his business and family, he was elusive. After some pleasantries, he quickly came to the point, offering me ten thousand guineas for my copy of the Spanish translation. It is impossible for me to conceive what purpose would warrant such an exorbitant sum. I asked for a few days to consider his offer, at which point he became very agitated and insistent. When I refused to budge, he dismissed me out of hand, saying I was a fool to even consider rejecting such a magnanimous offer. Needless to say, it is incumbent upon me to ascertain what his true purpose is. A friend recommended I contact an acquaintance of Eugene of Savoy, which I intend to do on my next visit to Amsterdam.

September 3rd 1736, It is now two weeks since I sent the printer a letter informing him of my unwillingness to part with the Spanish translation in my possession. Now, for the last three days, I have been shadowed on the street by two men. I could swear one of them was present at my meeting in Amsterdam.

September 29th 1736, I saw the two shadows again today in the market. This evening, Mr. Callamy informed me that several foreigners have been making discreet inquiries about me. I am more convinced than ever that this is a matter of State. It is imperative that I find out more. In the meantime, I must take measures to protect it."

"Spanish translation of what?" asked Gwyn.

"I don't know," said Gary closing the diary, "but I researched the man and jotted down a few things while I was waiting for Gil. Sale was a lawyer and an Orientalist educated at King's College. He edited an Arabic version of the New Testament, but is best known for a highly appraised translation of the Qur'an into English. He owned an extensive collection of Arabic, Turkish and Persian documents. He died in 1736 at his home on Surrey-Strand at the age of thirty-nine just two months after the date on the document."

"Surrey-Strand?" asked Gwyn incredulously.

"Yes. Why?"

"The document refers to a 'red English sunset on Suri-Strend.' That has to be a misspelling of the street name."

"Do you think this document could have been an order to assassinate Sale? For refusing to sell them a book?" asked Gary.

"Well, it was obviously important to them. That was an enormous sum of money," replied Gilbert, "Maybe, when he refused to sell it, they decided to take matters into their own hands."

"But, what kind of book do you kill someone for?" insisted Gary.

"I don't know," said Gwyn "And I don't want to know. I don't care about their book. I just want them to leave us alone."

"But we need to know why it's so important to *them*. Was there anything else in the document that could help us?"

"Well, if it's an assassination order for George Sale, then I think we understand everything in the document except for the key phrase."

"And what is that?" asked Gilbert

"It's the phrase 'son of prophet', which is clearly the object of the letter. It says that every trace of 'son of prophet' must be erased. We have researched it as thoroughly as we can, but have no idea what it means."

"Barnabas," said Gary quietly.

"What did you say?" asked Gwyn. "I couldn't make that out."

"It means Barnabas," he repeated just as softly. "The term 'son of prophet' is the literal translation of *barnabya*. *Bar* means 'son of' and *nabya* means prophet. The Greek form was 'Barnabas'. He was also called the 'son of encouragement' because of a reference in the book of Corinthians to prophets being encouragers. His name literally means 'son of the prophet'. You should have paid more attention in Sunday school."

Gilbert shook his head. Somehow he doubted Gary had learned that in Sunday school even though he had always taken faith more seriously than his siblings. Zeki was silent. Gwyn looked at his face. His brow was furrowed. His eyes didn't seem to be focused on anything in particular. He was obviously processing this new revelation. Gilbert spoke first.

"Well, whatever it means, I doubt it is going to help us find my family. Don't you think..."

Zeki gently cut him off. "Excuse me, but if we can just wrap up the Barnabas issue first. The sticky note your dad left included the initials G.O.B. I think this could be referring to the Gospel of Barnabas."

"What is that?" replied Gwyn. "I've never even heard of it."

Zeki was silent for a moment. Everyone waited for him to continue.

"Among Muslims, the Gospel of Barnabas is widely believed to be the truest extant copy of the message of Jesus. This would certainly explain why they think this is so important."

"Wait a minute, if 'son of prophet' is the Gospel of Barnabas, and if it is so revered in Islam, why would someone connected to the Ottoman Empire be trying to 'erase every trace'. That makes no sense," said Gary.

"I don't know the answer to that question," responded Zeki. "But Gilbert's right, we can research that later. Right now, we have to find Gilbert's family. Give us half an hour to look at the transcripts from the key-logger. Maybe I can learn something from them."

"Right," said Gilbert. "I am going to make a phone call, and then we are moving to a new café. Talk to you in half an hour."

He terminated the call and redialed Superintendent McIntosh.

"McIntosh."

"Hello, sir."

"Gilbert, thank God you're okay."

"We're fine. I just wanted to check on your men. Looks like one of them might have been shot."

"A flesh wound. He's stable. How did you know?"

"We watched the whole thing. Please convey our sympathies and thank them for their service."

He quickly explained what had happened, leaving out for now the part about a key-logger and their physical location.

"Listen," McIntosh said. "Why don't you and Gary come in? We can provide protection."

He seemed genuinely concerned.

"I wish I believed that."

"You don't?"

"With all due respect sir, these people intercepted cell phone calls between my sister and I. They had a team of assassins try to take her out in a small rural Texas town just a few days later."

"Try? Do you mean she is alive? Have you been in contact with her?"

He obviously had the Inspector's attention.

"Yeah, she is alive and Zeki is the one who saved her." He paused for effect.

"Zeki?" McIntosh was incredulous.

"That's right. Zeki. He didn't kill my father and doesn't know who did. I would like you to revoke any Interpol notice against Zeki. Can you do that?"

"I can try, but he will still be wanted for questioning. He has violated immigration laws by using false documents."

"Oh, I suppose he could have used his own passport and taken his place next to my father in the mortuary! Come on, he's been one step ahead of us the whole time. You can do better than that."

"I'll try."

"Inspector, I am afraid there is more bad news, but I don't trust the security of your line enough to tell you. The man you captured in our hotel room might have information I need."

"Mr. O'Brien, excuse my bluntness, but the paranoia you are exhibiting is very normal with people who have experienced serious emotional trauma. We need to sit down and talk, so you can tell me everything you have learned."

"I'm a little busy right now. Don't worry. I'll be in touch. Let my assistant in DC know if there is anything important. Do you have a pen?"

"Sure."

He gave him the number and was about to hang up when McIntosh said,

225

"You were going to get me a copy of the document. Can you at least send me that?"

"Sir, have you ever heard of the mental condition known as AGP?"

"No, I can't say that I have."

"Well, I have just come down with a severe case of it."

"I don't understand."

"You will though. Do you have any cheese for a trap?"

"Mr. O'Brien, why the riddles?"

"I am sure you will soon find out. In the meantime, Mr. McIntosh, try not to get yourself killed. I'll do the same."

Gilbert terminated the call and turned to Gary.

"Do we have the video recorded?"

"Yep."

"Then let's go, Gary. This place may not be safe anymore."

McIntosh opened his browser and did a search for 'AGP' and 'illness'. He didn't have to look far. It was the second result from the top. AGP IS A RECENTLY DIAGNOSED MENTAL CONDITION. ANTI-GOVERNMENT PHOBIA. He picked up the phone.

"Bob, get everyone working on the O'Brien case down to the situation room in fifteen minutes. Have we heard anything back from the local police in Texas?"

"Yes, sir. They've found two bodies in a nearby well. One was shot in the head with a hollow-point. Perfect shot, surgical entry, messy exit, immediate death. They didn't find the bullet. The second man was shot four times—once in the right elbow, once in the left hand, and once in the left knee. One bullet recovered. It was a .223 caliber weapon. The second man did not, however, die from these wounds. He was killed with a bullet to the back of the head, .45 caliber at close range. Their weapons were in the well too, HK 91, semi-automatic versions of the Koch G3 assault rifles. Their magazines were full. Neither of them even got off a shot."

"Sounds like Zeki does good work."

"Excuse me, sir?"

"Zeki saved the girl from these two men. Or, at least that's what his brothers just told me."

"So, does that mean he isn't our man?"

McIntosh made no attempt to hide his irritation.

"No, it means he has the girl and killed two other men. That's what it means."

"Well, if he's clean, then I'm sure Gwyn will be contacting the police or her brothers very soon."

"I doubt it. I don't think the O'Brien brothers are coming in. Send a bulletin to airport security. We may not be able to detain them, but, if they leave the country, we can find out where they're going, which might help the FBI find Zeki. I have a feeling they will be joining him shortly."

McIntosh almost mentioned Gilbert's comment about 'cheese,' but decided against it. If there was a rat, he wanted to move with caution.

+)======(+

Zeki spent the next ten minutes reading over the logs Gilbert had uploaded to the ftp site. It was uglier than he thought. Most of the exchanges were in Turkish although some sections were in English. These were the sections that bothered him most. They were clearly being written to someone in London, someone on the inside at the Metropolitan Police Service.

For a while, he read over the data stoically, saying nothing to Gwyn, who continued downloading every file she could find on the Gospel of Barnabas and the Moriscos. *How much do I tell her? Will they even believe me if I tell them what they are up against?* He had no choice, so he took a deep breath and plunged in.

"Gwyn, these people have kidnapped your sister-in-law, her children and another woman. They are going to be used to ransom the document and are currently en route to Istanbul. But that is not all. They are planning to steal something from Augustinerlesesaal. We need to find out what that is."

He spelled out the words for Gwyn as she typed them into the search engine.

38

Gary followed Gilbert out of the café and back to the underground. The Internet café they were going to was in Covent Gardens, just a short ride back towards Russell Square on the tube. The walk to the station through the Soho streets was bizarre for Gary. He had been so removed from the opulence and excess of western youth for so long that he had almost forgotten what it was like. The local young people were ready to enjoy the last few days of summer heat. The streets were pulsating with the beat of dance music. Weekend clubbers were preparing for a long night of physical exertion on the dance floor. Gary could only wonder if any of them had Pict ancestors. If so, their forefathers would surely have been proud of the tattoos, the wild hairdos, and clothing that left little room for imagination, and probably downright jealous of their extensive body piercing.

When they got off the tube a few minutes later, Gilbert led him to another internet café on a side street. It was not nearly as chic as the one in Soho had been, but the clientele was the same. They found a computer in the corner and put on their headphones. Gary logged in and opened the chat window. It began ringing instantly. Gwyn had been waiting for them.

"Can you hear me?" asked Gwyn.

"Clear as a bell," he responded.

"Z. has read everything from the key-logger you managed to install." Her voice was trembling. The emotional roller coaster ride was taking its toll. "I'll let him tell you about it."

"I'm afraid I have bad news," began Zeki. "They have your family and one other woman. It looks to me like they were put on a boat heading to Vlore, Albania."

He paused for a moment to let that sink in.

"Albania?" said Gilbert. "That would make sense. Fairly unstable political environment with plenty of organized crime. How far is it across the Adriatic there?"

"We were just looking at that. It's about one hundred kilometers, so a speed boat could do it in less than two hours if the weather is nice. The final destination, however, seems to be Istanbul, which means that if they go overland, they will have to pass through at least two border checkpoints. That would be our best chance for intercepting them and recovering your family, which is why they will probably choose to travel by boat instead. Still, you should alert the US consulate in Italy and tell them what you know. The US government will have to make a special request for Interpol to issue a yellow notice for missing children. This should be expedited to all of the countries on their potential route to Istanbul—Albania, Macedonia, Bulgaria and Greece. We should inform the Greek coastguard as well."

"I'll make sure that the appropriate contacts are made," responded Gilbert solemnly. "Is there anything else?"

Gwyn couldn't believe how detached her brother sounded, and it bothered her. A volcano that was constantly flowing was not nearly as dangerous as one that released all of its pressure in a single blast. She knew her brother, and when his anger fell silent, it meant the pressure was building.

"I know this is hard," she said gently. "But Z. says they're probably not in any grave danger right now because they plan on using them to ransom the document."

"I know," said Gilbert, "And you know, that doesn't make it any easier."

Zeki continued, "It looks like they plan to contact you with ransom demands through your secretary although I am pretty sure we all know what those will be."

"So, it's going to be the document in exchange for my family? I don't like how lopsided everything is. Given all that these people have managed to do, how high up do you think their connections go?"

"To the very top," responded Zeki without hesitation.

"Then, who can we trust?"

"No one. At least not because they wear a uniform and have sworn to uphold justice and public safety. As you know and the key-logger confirms, they have someone on the inside at the Metropolitan Police. Your sister tells me you work in security so you must know that even your own FBI is…"

"I know," interrupted Gilbert, "there to preserve social order and the status quo."

"That wasn't what I was going to say," said Zeki. "But I guess the result is the same. In my opinion, the four of us should plan to meet in Istanbul as soon as you can get there. If you give me two hours, I can have new identities for both of you to travel on. Obviously, you cannot go anywhere as Gilbert and Gary O'Brien."

"You seem almost as well-connected as the people who are hunting us," said Gilbert dryly, a hint of skepticism seeping through.

"I have a few favors I can call in, but believe me when I say that I am rapidly depleting what little capital I accumulated in over twenty years with the Agency. These are all personal friends who will ask no questions and have proven their loyalty to me many times. If you don't want their assistance, I'm sure they have other things they could be doing."

His voice conveyed no irritation, which only served to heighten the sting everyone felt from the man who had just saved Gwyn's life.

"I'm sorry," said Gilbert quickly. "It's hard not to be skeptical and cautious in the face of so much coincidence."

"I think you meant to say 'Providence,'" replied Zeki softly. "Besides, coincidence or no, the facts speak for themselves."

"Fine, but I have a personal friend I would like to involve if you don't mind," said Gilbert. "He has a wealth of experience in international politics, so maybe he could help us unravel this mess. He was with the State Department for…"

Gwyn interrupted emphatically. "Absolutely not. I do not want you bringing Matt Connor into this."

"Do you know anyone else we can trust? Anyone else who would want to stick their neck out on our behalf? Anyone else who could bring something to the table?" He paused. She remained silent, so he continued, "He was with the State Department for six years, a rising star in the diplomatic corps, but he resigned two years ago."

"I didn't know that," said Gwyn. "Why didn't you tell me?"

"Probably because you told me never to mention his name again, or had you forgotten that?"

"No, of course I hadn't, but…well…that is a pretty significant development. You could have let me know without using his name."

The two brothers looked knowingly at each other. It was obvious she still had feelings for him.

"He and I have stayed in touch. Don't worry. I'm sure he's over you by now. It's been three years. Anyway, as I was saying, he is able to maneuver comfortably in the world of diplomatic relations."

Zeki interrupted and the urgency and rapid-fire manner in which he gave instructions surprised them all.

"I think we are finished here. If you think you can trust him, and if he is as connected as you say, then any addition would be welcomed. We will contact you in Istanbul via this email address to arrange a rendezvous point. Don't contact your secretary by any usual channel. They will definitely be monitoring her communications. That will buy us time. They won't do anything until they deliver their demands. Your sister has downloaded a significant amount of information we think is related to G.O.B. and a group called the Moriscos. It will take us twenty hours to get to Istanbul, so we should have plenty of time to brush up on our history. She will upload everything about Barnabas to your ftp site. We'll take the Moriscos. If we can find out why they are so desperate to recover this document, we might be able to use that to our advantage."

Gwyn interjected, "I'm expecting you two cerebral superstars to be ready for a thesis defense on the Gospel of Barnabas by the time we meet. We'll compare notes in Istanbul. Any questions?"

"Where will we meet your friend to get new ID?"

"He'll meet you at Paddington station in two hours. Bring your current passports and allow at least one hour for him to prepare new ones."

Gilbert sighed deeply. "Well, I guess we'll see you in Istanbul, then."

"Bon voyage," said Gary.

"*İyi yolculuklar*," responded Zeki.

⊹⊱⋅⊰⊹

Gilbert opened his bag and removed a thick stack of one hundred Euro bills, counted out seven and handed them to Gary.

"If I had known security paid that well, I might have followed in your footsteps. Do you always carry that much cash?"

Gilbert was too preoccupied to make a witty comeback.

"I knew the credit card would be traceable, so I made a cash withdrawal at several ATM's near the hotel before I went to Soho. Then, I saw a young couple, probably university students, standing in line for Chunnel tickets. I told them that as my daily random act of kindness I would like to pay their fare."

Gary let out his breath in a low whistle.

"Not exactly what I would call a 'random' act of kindness. Clever though. So, now these assassins are going to be looking for us in Folkestone or on the French side at Coquelles?"

"That will be only the beginning of their chase," said Gilbert, without taking his eyes off of the screen, his fingers flying over the keyboard

"What do you mean?"

"You'll see soon enough. Right now, I need you to get us a laptop so that we can read these files from Gwyn on the plane. I'll download them from the ftp site, try to contact Connor, arrange transportation and meet you at Paddington station in one hour."

Gary stood up to leave, and Gilbert grabbed his arm.

"Hey man, it's good to see you again." His eyes were watery.

"It's good to be back. Don't worry about Ginger and the kids. If all they want is the document, we give it to them. It's as simple as that."

"I wish I were half that confident. Those ruthless bastards have my wife and kids. We know what they did to Dad, to the other Turkish professor, what they intended to do to Gwyn. I can't even leave the country safely without help from a member of Turkish intelligence. Why does he want to help? How did he just happen to show up?"

"I think in English we call it a god-send, Gilbert. Stop worrying and make your call. I'll see you at Paddington."

231

Gary turned and started weaving his way through the banks of computer towards the door. Gilbert turned back to the computer screen and punched in Connor's number. On the third ring, Connor picked up.

"Hey Matt. This is Gilbert O'Brien."

"Great to hear your voice, man. It's been awhile."

"Yeah, listen, do you have a minute?"

"Sure, what's up?"

Gilbert quickly told him about his father's murder, Gwyn's narrow escape and the kidnapping. Connor listened without interruption until he finished.

"I'm so sorry, Gilbert. Your father was a great man. He treated me like a son."

"Probably because he wanted you as a son-in-law," replied Gilbert.

"You know I would have assumed that title quite happily..."

"I know," said Gilbert. "The whole family took it pretty hard when you and Gwyn broke up."

"She was right to break it off, you know." Matt's voice was soft and serious. "She saw more clearly than anyone that I was already married to myself and my work. It has taken that long for me to see that everything she said was right. I'm only just now starting to put things back together. So, what are you going to do about getting Ginger and the kids back? You know I'll do whatever I can."

"I was hoping you would say that," replied Gilbert. "I need you to pull any strings you have to get a yellow notice issued for the kids. We need to intercept them before they get to Istanbul."

"That should be easy."

"We know they had help on the inside in London and have to suspect they may have people in America. It was amazing how fast they put that strike team together. Do you have anyone who could make some discreet inquiries?"

"Absolutely."

"There is just one more thing."

"What's that?"

"I'd really like it if you could be with us in Istanbul."

"I was hoping you'd ask. Bounty hunting can be lonely. It would be great to catch up with you."

"Don't tell me you find this new line of work boring."

"No, not boring, but local mafia bosses, pimps, brothels and corrupt police are a far cry from the glamour of the diplomatic core. The mafia in three different countries – Moldova, Ukraine and Albania – put a price on my head after I brought in those two ring-leaders in May. Tit for tat you might say. Legitimate governments, if you believe in that sort of thing, offer a bounty for the capture of criminals, and the underground government offers a bounty for me."

"Matt, I want these S.O.B's to pay."

"Get your family back, Gil, and let it go, or you're going to end up in a body bag. Trust me on this one."

"When can you be in Istanbul?"

"I'm in Iaşi now. We just had a week-long training session with border police at the University."

"Iaşi?" asked Gilbert.

"Sorry, eastern Romania. It's a large university town that serves as a place to recruit and transfer girls being trafficked to the expensive markets of Western Europe. I can be there tomorrow night, if you need me to be."

"I do," said Gilbert. "I'll call you when I get there. We'll plan on meeting Monday morning. Gwyn's coming too. I hope that's okay."

"If she's okay with it, I am."

"She'll be fine," said Gilbert coolly. Right now, whether or not these two were over their relational pain was taking a backseat to getting his wife and kids back safely. "Do you think you could bring one of those canisters carried by the mules running stuff for the mafia?" he continued.

"Sure. You'll be on the European side?" asked Matt.

"Yeah, probably somewhere near Taksim. Gary knows the area well."

"I thought he was in India."

"He was," replied Gilbert.

"The last time I talked to Gwyn about him, she was worried sick. Of course, that was three years ago."

"He's changed. You'll see that yourself."

Gilbert clicked on the red button to terminate the call and did a quick search on the Internet for flights to Istanbul. He didn't want a direct flight. He suspected that McIntosh might be looking for their next move. With a new ID, it would make his job harder, but, if they were picked up on security cameras at Heathrow, he at least wanted to make them think he was traveling somewhere on the continent and not to Istanbul. He picked a flight through Zurich with a long layover that put them in Istanbul at six AM the next morning. Then, he checked seat availability. There were still fifteen seats left. All he could do was hope that they didn't sell out. It was impossible to reserve a seat without ID.

He grabbed his bag and left the Internet café, turning right as he left the door. He walked two blocks, took another right and crossed the street. The express parcel delivery office was smaller than he expected. The lady at the counter greeted him without looking up from her computer.

"How can I help you?"

"I need to send a letter to DC. Can you guarantee delivery of the letter on Monday?"

"That's why we're called 'express' delivery."

39

DALLAS   Gwyn stared at the passport Zeki had just thrown in front of her.

"You've got to be kidding me," she said incredulously. "You want me to travel on a man's passport?"

"Unless you've got a better idea. I don't have friends here like I do in London. We're going to have to make do with what we've got. We'll replace my picture with one of you in short hair, no make-up and some more masculine attire. It's not difficult really."

"And what about these?" she said, indicating her breasts. "Aren't these sort of a dead giveaway?"

"Hmm, I hadn't thought of that," said Zeki. "I don't suppose wearing a heavy jacket in August would work, would it."

"Well, if you want to attract attention, it would work fine." She thought for a moment. "I could wear a running bra to flatten my chest as much as possible and claim to be in the middle of a sex change if it causes a problem," she suggested with the hint of a smile.

"Not a bad idea. ID engineering is not my specialty, and I don't have the equipment to do something from scratch."

Gwyn picked up the passport and looked at it more closely. It was Ukrainian with the typical royal blue cover.

"I don't know a word of Russian. If you had a French passport, I could probably be convincing to a Turk."

"I do have a French passport, and an Italian one, and…" Zeki stopped. "I suppose your strawberry blonde hair, white skin and pretty green eyes would raise some eyebrows on an Iranian passport." His eyes were twinkling and a broad smile lit up his face. "But unless you want to be pulled aside by a customs officer for travelling on a fake passport, you had better use the Ukrainian one. The others are biometric, you see."

"Oh right," said Gwyn, looking slightly embarrassed. "I forgot that all of the EU countries have chips with your picture and fingerprints conveyed electronically to the passport reader before you even get to passport control."

"A Ukrainian passport is best. The security features are not quite as technologically advanced so it is easier for me to change the picture with simple equipment and the biometric feature is not yet mandatory."

Gwyn turned to the mirror and looked down at the scissors Zeki held in his hand. With a sigh of resignation, she sat down in the chair he had brought into the bathroom.

"Snip away," she said. "But leave it as long as you think we can get away with. It took me three years to grow it out like I wanted it."

"I'll do my best," replied Zeki, "But, this isn't going to be a work of art."

"That's what I was afraid of," she said dejectedly.

He continued, "If we want to catch the flight tomorrow, we have a lot to do. We still have to find a place to get your picture taken and then doctor your passport."

+≻━━━≺+

LONDON   Gary stood in front of the mirror in the men's room at Paddington station, watching his brother behind him pacing back and forth in front of the stalls, checking his watch every ninety seconds. Zeki's friend had taken their pictures, set up his equipment in the middle stall and asked them to keep watch while he produced their ID. There had been no introductions. He knew who they were and they didn't expect him to volunteer his identity. Gary had half-expected that the man would search them, but he didn't. Apparently, the fact that Zeki had vouched for them was good enough.

For half an hour, they had pretended to be combing their hair or washing their hands every time someone walked in, and Gilbert was starting to get nervous. He was worried that the security cameras might be monitored and that someone would grow suspicious if they saw the two of them loitering in the bathrooms.

Gary knew that wasn't what was really eating him though. He knew his brother was revisiting every event over the last week, blaming himself for not taking this or that precaution. Now that his wife and children had been turned into collateral in a cruel twist of fate, they were all swept up in a dark and mysterious game where the only rule was staying alive, and Gil was a poor loser. Gary finally broke the silence in an effort to take his brother's mind off of it.

"So, were you able to get in touch with Matt?"

"Yeah, he said he would meet us there tomorrow."

"You said he resigned from State. That's a shocker, Especially with his connections and talent. You didn't say what he's doing now."

"I didn't want to upset Gwyn. After they split up, he went into a tailspin. Apparently, some of the things she said made him take a second look at where his life was headed. A year later, he told me that he had resigned and was going to start working with a charity organization, an NGO focused on stopping the sexual exploitation of women. I was surprised, of course, but tried to be supportive. The weird part was he asked me to help him get some training in security protocols and weapons handling with one of our clients. Basically, he has turned into a bounty hunter in a crusade against human trafficking."

"Now that's what I call a career-killing move," exclaimed Gary. "Are you saying that he's gone from candidate for exploiter-in-chief as a rising star in the State Department to a gun-toting Mother Theresa?"

"Something like that," said Gilbert.

The stall door opened, and Zeki's friend walked out with his metal equipment case in one hand and two US passports in the other. Gilbert looked skeptical as he flipped through the blue passport and tilted it back and forth, looking for the hologram security features, examining the quality of the paper and the glaze over the picture page.

"The Lewis brothers? Dan and Duane?"

"Given your physical similarities, I thought it would be appropriate to give you the same surname."

"You didn't take our fingerprints. I thought the electronic passports contained digital fingerprints in addition to the digital picture. The last thing I want to do is get stopped at passport control and thrown in jail for falsifying my ID."

The man's faced remained completely expressionless.

"The US biometric chips do not contain fingerprints," he replied.

Gilbert flushed, slightly embarrassed for not knowing this.

"What about the authentication codes?" he asked.

The only thing required by the American passport is Passive Authentication. The contactless smart chip that I installed meets ICAO requirements."

Gary interrupted to head off what he sensed was an interrogation coming from Gilbert.

"Listen, we really appreciate your help. What do we owe you?"

The man looked offended. "I wouldn't do this for any amount of money, only for *hatır*."

"For what?" ventured Gilbert quizzically.

"I'm not sure you westerners have the concept," the man replied dryly.

And with that, he made for the door. Gilbert started to say something, but Gary stopped him with a firm squeeze on the arm. After the door shut, he turned to his brother and asked, "Have you no concept of honor?"

Gilbert did not like the reproachful tone in his brother's voice.

"Excuse me?"

"This man has risked his cover and maybe much more to help two total strangers because of his *hatır* for Zeki." Gary was clearly exasperated. "The man is a professional, and here you are second-guessing his work and expertise."

"I was just trying to…"

"I know," interrupted Gary. "You were just trying to put your own fears to rest with no regard for his honor or sacrifice. Get rid of your freaking attitude. Foreigners are not slightly inferior resources to be used; they are human beings. The Turks ruled southeastern Europe, the Caucasus, the Middle East and North Africa. They turned the Mediterranean and the Black Sea into Muslim lakes for three hundred years. The decline of their Empire lasted over two hundred and fifty years, longer than America has even existed as a nation, and at their absolute lowest and weakest point in the early twentieth century, they still had the strength to defeat Britain, the world's only super-power, forcing the British to retreat with terrible losses at Gallipoli. They deserve your respect, and if Dad were here he would tell you the same thing."

His final words stung and Gilbert recoiled visibly at the verbal lashing. Gary knew the rebuke would hurt, but he knew Gilbert needed to have something to think about. It worked. Without a word, Gilbert stuck his passport in the side pocket of his bag, slung it over his shoulder and headed for the door. Gary followed, hoping that this little exchange wouldn't sour their flight.

<hr />

DALLAS   Gwyn had a window seat two rows in front of and diagonal to Zeki, who was stuck between a massive basketball player and a young mother with a two-year-old infant. She could imagine Zeki's frustration. The man hadn't had a decent night's sleep in who knew when, but every time she looked back, he was entertaining the toddler whose mother had gone to sleep.

All the way to the airport, Zeki had drilled Gwyn on how to control her emotions in case there was trouble at security. He did not want her to get flustered or raise suspicion. He had explained to her the signs security personnel were trained to look for: avoiding eye contact, sweating in an air-conditioned room, enlarged pupils, being over-talkative, being defensive instead of asserting her rights if challenged, excessive touching of the face…The list was longer than she could remember. The more time she spent with him, the more exposed she felt. He had mastered the art of reading people.

She had been deathly afraid of blowing her cover going through passport control, but she also felt guilty for lying about her identity. Somehow, he had picked up on that too and said, 'Remember the Hebrew midwives and it will be easier for you.' He was right. It did make it easier. *How had he known it would?* She was beginning to understand her father's appreciation for this complex man.

Gwyn was eager to start reading the material she had downloaded on the Moriscos. She needed the distraction. She didn't see how anything they learned could help them in their dilemma, but she had to find out what it was that drove these people to be so ruthless.

No electronic devices were allowed until they reached cruising altitude or from their stationary position in a line of 747s waiting to get airborne, so it did not look like that would happen anytime soon. The pilot had been assuring them for the last hour that they would be taking off momentarily, but finally he conceded that they might have to wait another half an hour. Everyone on the plane groaned. The air-conditioning was not keeping up with the summer heat augmented by the calories being burned by two hundred irate passengers.

Gwyn grabbed the airline magazine out of the seat pocket in front of her. No one with their own reading material ever cracked the cover of these magazines. They were advertising space masquerading as culture and entertainment. She felt like a proletarian anytime she read the drivel and knew that her father would have disapproved, but she had to occupy her mind with something. Otherwise, she felt like the emotions of the last few days would come flooding in and leave her sobbing uncontrollably.

Her eyes landed on an advertisement for a dating service for professionals. The tagline resonated with her, and she hated herself for it.

HELPING YOU FIND THE NEEDLE IN THE HAYSTACK—FOR PEOPLE LONG ON CHOICES AND SHORT ON TIME.

She skimmed the article. Directed at wealthy young professionals, too busy with their careers and the demands of the corporate elite to find time for meaningful relationships, it promised a comprehensive personality profile recommended by leading psychologists who praised it as the surest route to compatibility and happiness in relationships. The company guaranteed a match of interests, temperament and worldview. She continued reading up until the phrase "women join for free." She shook her head in disgust and closed the magazine. *So, the men have to pay, just like in the slave markets, and the women are still auctioned off like commodities, except that now we put ourselves on the block willingly.* It made her sick. It also made her think of Matt Connor, and the hole he had left in her heart.

They'd had everything in common, well almost...They were both easygoing, fun-loving people with an appetite for adventure. They both enjoyed sports and the outdoors. They were voracious readers who appreciated poetry, especially Dickinson, as well as history and the classics. The only passion she didn't share was his obsession with military history and action cinema. It was a guy thing, so it wasn't a problem.

There had been a problem though. She closed her eyes and played it back again for the umpteenth time. "What exactly is the matter?" he had asked. "I don't get it." After patiently listening to her pour out her heart, he had said,

"Metaphysics? You are breaking this off because of a philosophical difference?" What he called 'metaphysics' was what she called atheism, a train wreck waiting to happen, and the real reason she left the man everyone said was the catch of a lifetime. He probably was, but not in her lifetime. The bitterness of their separation had left her jaded. She still longed for a healthy, fulfilling relationship, but it was a longing she had lost all hope of fulfilling.

Everyone said her standards were too high, that no one was perfect, and that she was being unrealistic. *Are they? Of course not*, she told herself once again. *This is love. If it can't be the fairytale variety, what is the point anyway?* For her, it could never be a reproductive hook-up or a financial arrangement. She wanted a real, authentic soul-mate. Nothing else. That was what she had been taught about marriage. Somehow knowing that her mom and dad would agree didn't make the loneliness any easier to bear.

FOLKESTONE, ENGLAND   None of the passengers coming in and out of the Chunnel Station paid any attention to the burly man wearing jeans and a sleeveless sweatshirt at the entrance, or to the wispy, dark-skinned fellow on the platform, dressed like a businessmen and talking non-stop on his cell phone.

In his London office seventy miles away, Salih sat with his headphones on, listening intently for any indication from their man in Folkestone that the two brothers had shown up.

"We've been here at the Chunnel station for over half an hour. There's no way they could have gotten here before us. They haven't entered the building" said the smaller dark-skinned man.

"How long until the train leaves?" asked Salih. He already knew the answer.

"Six minutes."

"Have Mohammed check each of the cars again. I want to be absolutely sure there's no mistake."

"Yes sir."

"If they don't show, text Ahmet and tell him that his prey is a goose and his is the chase."

"But,…." The man started to say something and Salih's voice silenced the thought before it could be formed into words and leave his lips.

"Just do as you're told."

ZURICH, SWITZERLAND   What Gilbert loved about airports was the fact that they never sleep, not even at two o'clock in the morning. He had been watching a group of Africans across from the La Carbeille café and bar against the window overlooking the tarmac. Their country of origin was still a mystery to him. They wore colorful tribal robes, and their speech had an exotic singsong

239

lilt. A tall, beautiful black woman directly across from him lay stretched out on two chairs, resting on a pillow she had clearly pilfered from an Egypt Air flight. Beside her sat a lady reading a French newspaper in a pair of shimmering silver pants so tight and a top so low it she looked like she belonged on the front of a mechanics magazine.

The woman occasionally stood to stretch her legs and then sat back down. He would have guessed her to be about forty-five, and she was clearly trying to cope with the effects of a biological clock that was winding down, doing everything within her power to wind it back up again. She had the body of an athletic twenty-one-year-old, sported a pair of classy Bvlgari designer eyeglasses and wore dark burgundy lipstick that accentuated their fullness as well as complementing the color of her glasses. Her efforts had paid off.

It was really just a diversion, his people-watching. He was merely trying to keep from thinking about the storm brewing in his soul. It was a feeble attempt at keeping the pain at bay. He had tried to read the materials from Gwyn on the flight from London, but it all seemed so surreal. He had never even heard of this 400-year-old book and could hardly believe there was any connection to the death of his father and the kidnapping of his family. It was like a Phoenix that had risen from the ashes with the power to kill centuries after the fact. He looked down at his watch. Their plane was scheduled to take off in an hour. He tapped Gary on the shoulder.

"Let's go to the gate."

Gary nodded and closed the laptop. Gate A-86 was at the very end of the concourse, so it was a long walk. As they passed the high-end shops, Gilbert remembered all the times he had stopped in at the Swiss chocolate legend Lindt or one of the fashion shops to pick something up for Ginger, and even this harmless memory was too painful to entertain. He plodded past mountains of duty free whiskey. As he looked at the amber bottles neatly stacked in mounds down the center walkway, he thought of people who sought solace in the bottle, and for the first time, his own pain gave him an inkling of the desperation that drove people to drown their sorrows in the golden liquid that seemed to hold out the promise of forgetfulness.

It was a ten-minute walk to the gate after the first security check and when they arrived, there was yet another, more thorough than the first. Still, Gilbert noticed how discreet the Swiss were compared to their American counterparts. They had a partitioned area with a curtain just past the metal detector anytime a physical pat-down was required and he thought they were doing a better job of guarding human dignity against terrorists than his own country.

40

MONDAY, UKRAINE Situated in the midst of well-kept spacious grounds that boasted a dozen varieties of rose as well as cherry and apple trees, the white-washed villa on the outskirts of Odessa was protected from prying eyes by a twelve foot wall. In the daytime, only the steep, red tile roof could be seen from outside; at night nothing at all. Though it was still almost two hours until sunrise, the entire house had been awake and dining on a spread that included soup, olives as big as walnuts, a smorgasbord of cheeses both hard and soft, fresh bread topped with sesame seeds, a huge tray of meat pastries, *halal* sausage, tomatoes, cucumbers, fruits, butter, honey, omelets and tea.

Breakfast was winding down and the men began moving to a large sitting room to recite the Qur'an and perform their ritual prayers while the women retired to their bedrooms to do the same. The sexes were not allowed to mix, even at meals, because non-blood relatives were always present. Once it became light enough outside to distinguish a white thread from a black one, total abstinence from worldly pleasure would commence until sundown, which meant forgoing the mundane pleasures of eating and drinking. Even swallowing one's saliva was forbidden, as were the more obvious carnal cravings. The holy month of fasting had begun, allowing the faithful to express their contempt for this world and their devotion to Allah by abstaining from food. They hoped that their sacrifice would win Allah's favor and that He would forgive at least some of their sins.

His prayers finished, Bekir summoned two of his companions out to the balcony. A few trucks could be heard on the highway a little over a mile to the south. The noise of traffic was the only thing Bekir regretted about purchasing the villa. At the time, however, he had not been focused on the fact that the largest bazaar in the world was located just a few miles south of his new house. Traffic never stopped on Highway T1604 on its way to the Seventh Kilometer Market. A more uninspired name could hardly be imagined, but a visit to the site never failed to impress. It was over one hundred and seventy acres of raw jungle capitalism, bursting with cheap Asian goods unloaded at the port of Odessa for distribution throughout Eastern Europe. This market had it all, including the electronics they needed to build their communication devices and explosives. There was even an underground arms dealer there. Allah always provided.

The market was an economy unto itself with its own rules and rulers, consisting mostly of a homegrown mafia Bekir considered insufferably pig-headed. In spite of his instructions to keep a low profile, on several occasions, his men had come close to getting crossways with the locals. He had no intention of muscling in on their territory. All he wanted was a safe haven for his four wives, two concubines and nineteen children. In the end, he managed to recruit the local ruffians. They helped him transport girls to Istanbul and points further south. Bekir had a particular genius for manipulating events and people, regardless of their moral persuasions, to serve his own ends. He believed it was inherited from his father, who had used it to make millions; he used it to spend these millions and win favor with Allah.

Without turning his head, he spoke into the night sky.

"Five hundred years ago, our brothers, the Tartars, raided throughout these lands every year, gathering slaves for the Mediterranean markets. The harvest of the steppe. Every Ottoman family of consequence owned several of these slaves either for labor or pleasure. The harems of the Sultans were filled with flaxen-haired maidens. As they say, 'to the victor go the spoils.'"

Abdullah, his second in command, grunted. "Yet, I find it distasteful that we, the warriors of the faith, must peddle flesh to finance jihad."

Bekir only smiled, "It is the way of war. Do you imagine it was any different for the ghazis of old?"

"Of course it was. They took more than slaves. They took cities, land, gold and more importantly they instituted *jizye*, which made the entire non-Muslim population of the subjugated country part of jihad. Yes, it was different. They had a huge base of labor and materials with which to finance never-ending war against the infidel. Millions of Christians in Southeast Europe were turned into vassals, tools used in our victories against their brothers. Today, we have no such resources. Yet, Allah has decreed that we must submit to Him and the world to us. It is our destiny to reign as Sultan of the world. The Turk is the crown on the Sultan's head.

"When we were conquering and leveraging the intellectual and physical assets of the infidel, the jihad was unstoppable, but when we lost our zeal for spreading the glory of Allah, it gave our adversary, the devil, time to hone the shrewdness and cunning of the infidel and the armies of Islam were put to flight."

Bekir knew what Abdullah thought. He was a true intellectual, a student of history, especially the history of conquest. Few could equal his knowledge

242

and still fewer his passion for a return to true Islam, where Muslims were rulers and not subjects. Most leaders would have viewed him as a threat, but Abdullah lacked the spiritual charisma necessary to lead, and he knew that, which is why he had attached himself to Bekir. They made a perfect team.

"These days," continued Abdullah, "a wealthy businessman from the Middle East has to make do with housemaid concubines from among the infidels of Cambodia, North Korea or Thailand. Only the sheikhs can afford the beautiful Slavic women we provide."

"Did you know," asked Bekir, "that the word *slav* is actually derived from the word slave?"

Abdullah nodded. *Of course Abdullah knew. He knew everything.*

"Yet, today," Bekir continued, "It is impossible to imagine a Muslim power in any of these lands. The infidel drove us out of Hungary, Romania, Ukraine, Bulgaria, the Balkans, Greece, the Crimea and the Caucasus. The Reconquista overthrew us in Spain. The realms of the Mongol rulers of India were shrunk to less than half their former size. Our forefathers failed because they grew soft and broke faith with the principle of jihad. We must not let our zeal wane."

He turned to face both of his companions and asked quietly.

"Is everything ready?"

"It's ready. They are merely waiting for us to give the go-ahead."

"What about the response?" he asked again quietly.

"Everything is in place. Vienna confirmed yesterday."

"Are you satisfied with the plan for Vienna?" Bekir asked pointedly. Abdullah knew how much this part of the plan meant to him.

"Yes, I have reviewed everything: building layout, the resources, the drop-off point and the escape route. It is flawless as far as I am concerned."

"When," continued Bekir, "will we have the banner?"

"We should have it two days after it is retrieved. It will cross the border into Hungary hidden on a recycling truck. The Bosnians will take it to the Adriatic through Croatia. We want to avoid all of the border checkpoints on an overland route to Istanbul."

"Excellent. Make the call and set everything in motion."

His voice was beaming with enthusiasm and fierce joy. Abdullah's face was grave. He had to make one last appeal.

"Bekir, you know that I've been your most constant companion against the enemies of Islam. I led your guerilla war against the Russians in a hopeless bid for Chechnya's independence. You know how we were slaughtered down to the last man and only I escaped. You know I believe in the cause and have proven it, but do you think that the *ummah* is ready? Will they rise up in arms? Will their strength be sufficient? This will change the political landscape forever. We must be certain."

Bekir spun around in anger. "If we wait for another generation, do you think there will be any Muslims left? We can barely find enough fighters as it is. The insidious inroads of the infidel threaten to turn our people into selfish individualists with no stomach for jihad and no faith in the command of the Prophet to subdue the infidel! How long will we wait? Now is the time to sound the call to arms, to invite one and a half billion Muslims to come back to faith, back to jihad, back to power! Allah has guided us to this point and opened every door. It is for us to walk through them."

"I just want to be sure the timing is right, that's all. If this is to be the match that lights the fire, we must be sure the wood is dry enough to catch. If it is wet, it will only smolder for a while and then go out. Are you sure the time is now? In twenty years, our numbers will be far greater, all the while their population declines. Their cynicism and unbelief will bleed their hearts of courage. In the past, they too rallied around their religion and their Church, but that has become virtually irrelevant. In twenty years, it will probably cease to exist altogether. Sometimes, victory requires patience."

Bekir's voice began to tremble.

"Three years of planning, and over five million Euro in research, equipment and man-power backed by the hopes and prayers of thousands. We are poised to strike these cursed dogs of unbelief. Now is the time. Now! May Allah kindle the fire of jihad in the hearts of every true Muslim and remember us with favor on judgment day. Make the call. I want a full day's worth of news from this. I want every infidel to hear it over their cornflakes and every Muslim to begin their day of fasting with thanksgiving. I pray their joy makes them forget their pangs of hunger today."

Bekir said nothing about the narrow escapes they'd had over the last three years, nothing about the fact that both governments and other Muslim groups had put a price on his head. Everyone understood that concern for his own safety and his fear of not completing his mission also guided his decision to move forward immediately. Any morning now, he expected to wake up and find himself dead.

⊹══╍══⊹

ANKARA, TURKEY Yusuf pawed the nightstand beside his bed trying to silence the ringing phone. It was no use. He had left it on the chair just out of reach. He rolled out of bed, picked up the phone and forced his eyes to open and read the number. It was Selda. He looked at the clock. It was 05:59. His alarm would have gone off in one minute anyway. He flipped the phone open.

"Good morning, Selda. I assume there is a good reason for robbing me of my last minute of sleep."

"Good morning, Captain. You need to turn on CNNTürk right now. We have no details yet, but I knew you would want to know."

244

"Okay, thanks. See you in a couple of hours," he said.

"I doubt it will be that long," was all she said in reply.

He hung up, grabbed the clothes his wife had ironed the night before from behind the door and then closed it gently behind him. He walked across their small apartment. It was furnished a bit nicer than most of his colleagues could probably have afforded. Fortunately for him, his wife's family had enough money to satisfy her tastes. His salary never would have. He grabbed the remote off the couch and turned on the flat-screen plasma TV, completely unprepared for what he was about to see. The images on the screen were horrific. There was no reporter holding a microphone in front of a camera. It was just raw footage with an unseen male voice providing a running commentary on the images being broadcast all over the country. A news flash scrolled across the bottom of the screen.

TWIN TERRORIST ATTACKS ON TURKEY'S MEDITERRANEAN COAST. RESORT HOTEL IN ANTALYA LEVELED BY BOMB BLAST. GERMAN APARTMENT COMPLEX SET ON FIRE IN ALANYA.

Yusuf sat down to watch the broadcast sensationalized by an off-camera reporter. The hotel was flattened. He couldn't image anyone surviving. It looked like a professional demolition job. The whole building had collapsed in on itself, which could only mean that the concrete columns supporting the structure had been sheared off with explosives.

The apartment complex in Alanya was still burning. The entire building had obviously been engulfed in flame, but the fire department had managed to extinguish the blaze at one end of the long rectangular structure. Orange flames still shot up at least twenty feet higher than the top floor at the other end of the three-storey apartment building. Yusuf guessed the building had a minimum of thirty flats. The absence of stretchers and ambulances was conspicuous. When the images began to be replayed, he grabbed his cell-phone and called Murat.

"Good morning, Murat. Have you seen the news this morning?"

"Yeah…Clearly retaliation for the skin-head attacks in Germany seven weeks ago."

"Most likely. Do we have casualty figures?"

"Nothing official, of course, but I heard a reporter ask a manager from a nearby hotel what occupancy was. He said all the hotels were booked solid. This is the height of the tourist season, and that this was a 400-bed hotel, one of the largest on the Mediterranean. It had extensive connections to travel agencies in Russia. Because it happened so early in the morning, we can be fairly certain that the death toll will be almost one hundred percent of the guests."

"Has anyone claimed responsibility?" asked Yusuf?

"I just got off the phone with media relations. He said all three of the conservative newspapers—*Zaman, Vakit* and *Vatan*—received anonymous phone calls five minutes after the explosion claiming that Hizbullah was behind the attacks. Apparently, the last thing they said on each call was the same, 'Islam will rise on the wings of Jihad.' All three were made from recently purchased pre-paid cell phones in Istanbul. But something seems strange about it all."

"What?" asked Yusuf.

"Two things. First, it's strange that the Turkish Hizbullah would hit non-political public targets. That isn't how they work. They were created by the state to neutralize the leftists and separatist Kurds. As you know, most of the attacks like this in Turkey have been organized by the PKK, leftist splinter groups or Islamic groups like IBDA-C and Al Qaeda."

"True, but once a monster is created, you cannot control how it develops or what it will feed off of. We have to assume there may be more attacks planned. Remember the last time this happened there were a string of attacks that hit two Jewish synagogues in Istanbul, and two British targets: a bank and the British consulate."

"Right. The second thing I find odd is that Bekir and his group would strike targets in Turkey and not in Europe. Weren't you sort of working on the assumption that he was leaving Turkey to organize something in Europe?" asked Murat.

"Yes, and I still think that's the case, but right now, we need to find out what is happening here in our own backyard."

"Well, they pulled this one off completely under the radar, so unless we get a break, I don't see us making any headway any time soon."

"Tell your wife not to make any elaborate dinner plans. Neither of us may be home for a couple of days."

41

ISTANBUL, TURKEY   A bearded man in his early twenties wearing a worn leather jacket sat on a park bench across from the statue of dancing girls in the Levent Square. None of the passersby paid him any mind. He stared up at a beautiful golden sculpture of five Turkish girls wearing knee-length dresses doing a folk dance in a circle. Their arms were joined, each had a foot thrust into the middle of the circle and they were leaning back with their long, beautiful locks flowing backwards in a stream of frozen bronze. What scandalized the young man was how they pushed their breasts up towards the sky. The statue twirled on top of a nine-foot chrome pillar, accentuating the sense of movement the sculptor had captured so well. It was a symbol of Atatürk's Turkey. Yet, the young man considered it the work of the infidel because, like everything from the West, it was immodest and suggestive. Many of the young girls passing through the square on their way to work or school could have easily passed for the beautiful maidens twirling atop the pillar.

Over the last half hour, a constant parade of uncovered women and girls flaunting their hair and more besides had passed by in high heels, skirts or tight pants. He saw a long-haired girl with snow white skin walking towards the bank across the street. She reminded him of the Romanian prostitute he had been with a couple of weeks ago. The girl had obviously been crying as her face was red and streaked with tears. This made her look even more like the girl he had been with. The prostitute had cried most of the time.

His group leader understood the needs of young men, and made sure they were taken care of at least once a week. The brothel run by their organization was a small building in the Fatih neighborhood. All of the girls were forced to wear the head-covering though none of them were Muslims. For the last year and half, he had been assigned Monday night. Last week, however, he had been given permission to visit any time. His sheikh told him it would whet his appetite for paradise.

The man surveyed the square. It did not look like a very strategic target. It was small, only about fifty yards wide and one hundred and twenty-five yards long. None of the surrounding buildings were more than two stories tall. The landscaping was quite recent as well, part of the Istanbul municipalities' push for more green space. The red oaks planted by the city were no more than fifteen feet tall. But the square had been chosen for a reason. There were more than a dozen banks represented around the square and all of them had adopted the infidel's practice of charging interest.

Some were foreign; some were domestic, but all were oppressors, perverters of justice who had abandoned the path of righteousness. More importantly, this conglomeration of banks was located directly behind the massive HSBC building bombed by their sister organization IBDA-C in 2003 during a meeting between that devil George Bush and the English imp, Tony Blair. It was the perfect place to repeat the message. He knew every detail by heart. Planning for the operation had been going on for six months. Fourteen banks would be completely destroyed within the hour. Every major holding in Turkey had an interest in one of these banks. All of them would hear the message loud and clear.

He looked across at the bakery. People stood in line to grab some breakfast on their way to work. Others stopped at one of the carts pushed by street vendors selling *simit*. It was Ramadan, the holy month of fasting. None of them should have been eating. They too had abandoned faith and even the pretense of Islam. Like the attacks in 2003, no attempt was being made to spare Turks. The message had to be explicit. The infidel within was every bit as bad, if not worse, than the infidel without. This was not about xenophobia or bigotry. It was about faith, and this area had been chosen because of its peculiar lack of the same.

He looked down at his watch, still fifteen minutes to go. He closed his eyes and began repeating the names of God, hoping it would calm his nerves. It didn't. Then, he heard the flutter of wings and opened his eyes to find pigeons flocking around him. An old lady approached the bench. In her hand, she held a large cup full of wheat. She was pouring small amounts into her hand and scattering it on the sidewalk as she approached. The pigeons continued to come and within thirty seconds there were hundreds hopping around, fluttering up and down, fighting for a kernel of grain.

Even this infuriated him. There were Muslim children in Palestine who went to bed hungry every night, and yet here was an old woman, who, judging from her clothes, was clearly well-to-do, feeding pigeons. He could not hold his tongue.

"Why, old woman, do you feed the birds of the air food fit for humans when so many of our brothers are starving?"

The lady's face registered surprise at being addressed so directly and in such a hostile manner, but she looked straight ahead and said nothing. The wheat was cheap, no more than fifty cents, but it was food and if half of his country's seventy-three million people were to send just one dollar a day to Palestine, they could feed the whole country. They could give the Palestinians the strength and dignity they needed to resist the accursed and murderous Jews.

He remembered the sermon from last night. The sheikh was a Sunni and no lover of Shiites, but he had begrudgingly acknowledged Shiite success in Lebanon. He had even held them up as an example to shame his congregation into action. The Shiites fed the people, provided basic services, brought electricity and schools, assured security and in two decades they would be the majority. They elevated women to the status of warrior-maker. Every son was another sword in the hand of the Righteous one. After the sermon, he had joined the night of *zikir,* where he spent hours with his brothers chanting the name of Allah until they attained a state of spiritual ecstasy. Afterwards, the sheikh praised their spiritual energy and fervor, saying it was what made Europe and the world theirs for the taking. It was destined to be so. Islam would rule the world and the Turks would rule Islam.

For decades, Muslims had immigrated to Europe in search of work, being exploited for cheap labor while they strengthened the hand of their oppressors. But, now just as many went as missionaries. They proclaimed the truth of Islam and invited the infidel to submit. Yet, the results were disheartening. For over three years, he had sent fifty dollars a month to help support a young missionary, his cousin, who was studying in Paris. Not one person had submitted to the way of Allah in three years. He turned back to the lady and asked again, "Why do you feed the birds instead of caring for the poor? Do you think that Allah will not feed the birds?"

The old woman continued looking straight ahead. Then, she smiled and replied.

"He *is* feeding the birds. I did not make the wheat."

Her answer irritated him.

"Allah gave them wings. Let them fly to the fields and eat the wheat that has fallen from the combine," he retorted.

"And God gave you a heart to love, but you have let it shrivel and die," she said, as she threw another handful of wheat amongst the swarming pigeons.

"Only Allah is eternal. Everything else is mortal," he rejoined.

"Which, of course, is why you don't believe in eternal life? Because only God will live forever?"

He could feel his blood pressure rising.

"Of course, I do. I believe in eternal bliss for the faithful and eternal damnation for the infidel," he said with conviction.

"You are right, my son, God is immortal and He is love. Do you hope to see paradise without it?"

He looked down at his watch. It was 8:57. The time had arrived. He stood up, grabbed his backpack off the bench and then turned to the old woman and said,

"I wish that today we might both stand before Him."

"I am an old woman and would welcome the opportunity, but you are a young man with a heart full of hate. Today would not be a good day for you. You have your whole life in front of you. Live it well."

He turned and walked away, muttering under his breath, "I intend to end it well."

He stomped off through the pigeons, causing them to scatter in every direction. As soon as he passed, they flocked back to the old woman. He saw that the first truck had pulled up and parked on the northwest corner of the square beside Garanti Bank. He had to hurry and make sure the others were in place. There was to be a truck on each end of the square and two in the middle. He could see the MNG courier delivery truck pulling up at the other end of the square. It drove twenty meters past the TEB Bank and parked. The driver of each truck would attach a wheel lock and leave. They were both right on time.

He quickened his pace and looked down the side street. Another courier truck was parked in front of HSBC. There was just one truck missing. The Turkish security forces, the lapdogs of Atatürk's secular regime, had developed one of the world's top anti-terrorism forces. They had decades of experience fighting an amazing variety of anti-government forces. They were good, too good. They had stopped hundreds of plots and infiltrated dozens of networks over the years, resulting in thousands of arrests. For this reason, all of the trucks had been prepared in isolation from the others in remote locations.

Istanbul traffic was unpredictable, but the fact that school had not yet started and that the fast had begun should mean traffic would be light. He looked down at his watch again. It was 9:01. He could wait another four minutes, but then his instructions were to move ahead regardless. He breathed a silent prayer. Three trucks would be enough, of course. He knew from their calculations that it might still kill everyone in the square, but he didn't want a single glitch in his grand finale. He looked back at the other three trucks. The drivers were gone. He turned for one final look down the side street and smiled. The DHL truck was just now turning off the main highway. He breathed another prayer of thanksgiving and headed for the HSBC branch.

Their choice of a bank had not been random. The security cameras at this one had a live feed to an offsite server. They had a message to deliver, and it wasn't just the obliteration of a city block. The offsite server ensured the message would be heard. He went back to the bench so that he could arm the device sitting down. The old woman was gone. He pulled a small box out of

250

his jacket and attached the battery. They had tested the wireless signal extensively. It had a range of over three hundred yards, more than twice what they needed. The LED light on the box lit up, flickered red and then went to green. He was a go. He felt under his left sleeve for the trigger. It was a small button connected to the box via wires taped to his arm. He put the button in the palm of his left hand and slid his right arm under the jacket to feel for the 9mm Zigana holstered under his left arm. He was ready.

The security guard at the door smiled as he opened the door

"Good morning." The guard pointed to the X-ray machine, "Please place your bag on the belt."

Those were the last words he ever said. The young man pulled the backpack off his left shoulder and held it in front of his torso just long enough to conceal his right arm retrieving the pistol. The backpack dropped to the floor and two 9mm rounds slammed into the security guard's chest.

A personal banker stood up from his desk and two more hollow-point rounds sent him tripping backwards over his chair and crashing onto the floor. The bank manager came out of her office, hands in the air.

"Listen, whatever you want, we'll cooperate. There is no need to kill anyone."

She was scared, but consciously implementing her training.

"I want all of you lying prostrate on the floor. Now!"

He sent four more shots into the ceiling and made a mental note that he had seven left in that clip. Everyone started scrambling out from behind counters and desks to comply with his demand. He rushed over and grabbed the manager by the hair, yanking her head back and shoving the muzzle of the pistol under her chin.

"I know there are four bank officers upstairs," he screamed. "I want them down here now, or this woman dies."

Ten seconds later, he heard footsteps on the stairs and three men and one woman took their place beside their colleagues prostrate on the red carpet. He shoved the woman away and motioned with his gun for her to get on the floor.

"Keep your head on the ground. You raise it, I blow it off."

He kept his gun at the ready as he backed towards the front door. He took the keys off the dead security guard's belt and locked the front door. Then, he walked back towards the middle of the room and faced the security camera. He knew one of the employees would have probably already pushed an alarm button, which gave him less than ninety seconds to deliver his message.

42

ANKARA   "Captain, I'm sorry to interrupt," said Selda through the cracked door. "There has been another bombing in Istanbul."

"Damn it! And, I suppose my best source of information is CNNTürk again?

"No sir, NTV has a reporter on the scene. No one else has arrived yet."

Murat grabbed the remote, changed channels and turned up the sound. The phone on the desk rang. Yusuf sighed. He was already wishing this day would end, and it had only just begun.

"Counter-Terrorism, Yusuf."

"Captain, this is Bülent from Istanbul."

"What do you have, Bülent?"

"A few minutes ago, fourteen banks in Levent were obliterated. HSBC was one of them."

"The whole square?"

"That's what it sounds like."

"The bastards!"

"To deliver their message, the terrorists used the live security feed at that bank, the only one that streamed data to an offsite location and the only one with audio."

"Meticulous planning," observed Yusuf.

"I just saw the tape. You need to see it right away."

"It can't wait? We are swamped here with the bombings on the Mediterranean.

"I know, but the message has a personal reference to you. I wanted to give you a heads up."

"To me?" asked Yusuf incredulously.

"It's unusual. That's why I wanted you to see it immediately. It's on its way now."

"Okay. Thanks."

He replaced the receiver, turned to his computer and hit Send and Receive. He saw the mail from Bülent and the fifteen MB attachment. He double clicked the file and turned to Murat.

"Mute the TV for a moment. We have video of the suicide bomber in Istanbul."

Murat muted the TV and walked around behind Yusuf's desk. The screen showed a bearded man in a leather jacket pointing a gun at nine bank personnel prostrate on the floor. They immediately noted that he had no mask on. He approached the camera and spoke very clearly.

"Today, the world has seen how people of faith respond to the oppression of the infidel. You cannot attack Allah's beloved slaves in Europe without consequence. You cannot continue to prop up corrupt Middle Eastern regimes that oppress their people while you siphon off their petroleum. You cannot continue to turn a blind eye to Zionist terrorism and the Palestinian genocide. Allah has made us their protectors. We will drive the unbeliever from the lands of Islam. They leverage the labor of honest Muslims to fill their banks, and then with this money, grant us IMF loans to keep us in poverty and slavery. For over a century, our leaders have collaborated with the infidel in commerce. But the winds of change are blowing. Today marks the beginning of the end of this relationship. Every company who maintains this unholy alliance will be destroyed."

The man paused for a moment. Obviously, all of this had been memorized. He pointed to the group of people on the floor and continued,

"This is the posture of a true Muslim before Allah. Hopefully, theirs is sincere. Salvation is found only in Islam."

He stopped again as if for effect, took two steps towards the camera and in a low voice said,

"Yusuf has the clothes that cover Pharaoh's nakedness. We want them back, Captain. The waters of the Red Sea shall part for the people of faith and Pharaoh shall be swallowed alive. *Allahüekber!*" The screen went black.

Murat let out a low whistle followed by a string of swear words. Yusuf reached for his phone to call his wife.

"Hi darling, I need you to come up to the office," said Yusuf, without any greeting

"To the office? Whatever for?" She could hear the tension in his voice.

"You could be in danger. Hüseyin will pick you up in five minutes. Bring a bag with a few things. I'll explain when you get here. Bye."

Murat had turned the volume back up on the TV and was viewing the carnage. The entire block had been leveled by the blast. First responders were everywhere. The square had been the site of a fruit and vegetable market, fourteen banks, several small restaurants and shops. Now, it was a heap of rubble.

253

The cameraman zoomed in on a bloody arm ripped off at the shoulder lying on the street.

"Well, the message clearly states that it is retaliation for the attacks on Turks in Europe," said Murat.

"Yes, it does," said Yusuf thoughtfully. "And if so, it might be the first time in history that a radical Sunni group has avenged the deaths of Alevis…"

He said it to no one in particular. Then, he swung into action.

"Murat, the end of that message was about the tapes we found in Akçakoca during the raid. Obviously, he wants to use them to compromise key officials. The threat to me was obvious. They will try to contact us soon."

"Sir, you need to immediately take this to the Minister of Internal Affairs. They will put you in a witness protection program."

"Would you go into a witness protection program under this government if you were facing the same threat?"

The look on Murat's face gave him the answer.

Yusuf continued. "Find out if we are intercepting any communication between radical groups and how they are viewing today's events. This could inspire other cells to carry out their own acts of violence. Also, make sure all of the country's political leaders are advised to change their schedules for the next several weeks. I think Pharaoh could be a veiled threat to heads of state and it is certainly credible."

They were about to see *credible* muscle its way into reality.

+⊨━━┥+

PRAGUE, CZECHOSLOVAKIA   The air in the hotel conference hall was jovial. After two years of wrangling over delays and budget concerns, the partners of the international natural gas consortium had finally resolved their differences. A pipeline project that would carry gas from the Caucasus, Kurdistan and Central Asia to the energy-hungry markets of Europe was finally back on track. Delegates, including the ministers of finance from every country on the pipeline route, were here to sign the agreement and to celebrate this important breakthrough. The biggest challenge had been persuading the Turks, who were demanding twenty percent of the gas in addition to transit fees. The Turkish government was only dissuaded from this highway robbery when Romania threatened to use a Russian pipeline planned for the north shore of the Black Sea. News of the bombings in Turkey had not, for the most part, dampened the mood here at the signing of a nine-billion-dollar project. Except for the fact that the Turkish delegation arrived with an extra security detail, no one seemed in the least concerned.

Several blocks away, a man sat in front of a window on the fourth storey of an apartment building behind a curtain. The window was open and the muzzle of the barrel just barely visible. It was an eight hundred and thirty-seven meter shot. There was no wind to speak of, and since the .50 caliber AS50 sniper rifle had an effective range of over two kilometers, this was not even considered a long-range shot.

He kept the scope trained on the front door of the hotel just over the top of the black limousine waiting outside to pick up the minister. He fully expected the man to be shielded by security guards wearing bullet-proof jackets and might even have one on himself. It didn't matter. There was no body armor in the world that could stop a .50 caliber bullet with a steel core. It could penetrate a brick wall two-feet thick or one inch of steel plate. The energy released on impact was enough to cause certain death through blunt force trauma. There were five rounds in the clip, one for the minister and four for whoever else happened to be standing there.

Sunlight flashed off of the hotel doors as they opened. There were two security guards blocking his view. He squeezed the trigger. The first bullet ripped through the bodyguard's neck like it was tissue paper and hit the minister in the chest, sending him to the ground. The next four bullets took out three security guards and the driver.

CAIRO   "Damn it, Jabbar. How in the hell did this slip past our nets?" said Ahmet, pointing at the television. "And, in Turkey no less. We have over a thousand people in the field and a budget of five billion dollars a year aimed at keeping these guys under our thumb, and yet we can't stop them from blowing up hundreds of foreign citizens on Muslim soil and assassinating a key member of our group placed strategically in the Ministry of Energy and Natural Resources. Have we found out who is behind this?"

"The Turkish Hizbullah claimed responsibility," replied Jabbar.

"I know that. What I meant is who executed it?"

"No one knows. I'm sure the general assumption is that this is the work of Bekir Kaya," Jabbar answered.

Ahmet shook his head slowly.

"He's directly challenging us, isn't he? Overzealous fool! What good will his jihad do? Escalating armed conflict with the West is suicide. It's just too bad he won't rot in hell for his folly. All they want is their moment of glory, the title of Martyr and the rewards that go with it. They are small minds whose brains would fit in the tip of their libido."

Jabbar noted the Freudian slip. Ahmet's was nothing to sneeze at.

"What do we know about Gilbert? Has he contacted his secretary again?" asked Ahmet.

"Nothing and no. We don't know where he is, and he hasn't emailed or phoned the secretary. Did you still want to call her with a ransom message today?" Jabbar asked.

"Yes. He's smart enough to guess what we're after, and that his secretary is likely our only point of contact. If he wants his family back, then he'll call her." He exhaled a long sigh. "Jabbar, this document has suddenly become a major distraction and a serious liability. I want to end this thing quickly. Call our liaison in DC. Have him contact Mike Tate. We need an international search warrant from the FBI for Gilbert O'Brien on charges of corporate espionage. Have it forwarded to Interpol immediately. Make sure our DC team informs the Senator's office of the situation as well. I would have just sat on this information, but now we need the document, and Interpol can help us find Gilbert. Besides, this revelation of illegality might be enough to turn the tribunal against Finch and Moreland so that our assets can be unfrozen."

"I'm on it."

"Is everything set for the exchange when we do get in contact with Gilbert?"

"Yes, the two women and children are being held at a container terminal on the Anatolian side of the Sea of Marmara. Somebody has informed the authorities of the kidnapping because a yellow Interpol notice was issued for the kids."

"Where did that come from?"

"Washington DC."

"His secretary?"

"No sir, the report was called in from a number at the US State Department."

"Shit! The last thing we need is someone running interference and blocking our search warrant. See if you can find out who it was. What is the plan once we contact the O'Brien's?"

"They'll be told to go to Istanbul, but no details will be provided until they contact us from there with the document. Since the document is in the States with Gwyn, it'll probably take two days to get the document to Istanbul after we inform them of our ransom demands."

"Call O'Brien's secretary and have it routed through London. Tell her to get a number for Gilbert where we can reach him and to do it immediately if he ever wants to see his children alive."

"Will do. The FBI is still looking for Zeki. So far, no luck. But, he can't go far with the girl."

⊢⊶⊣

ISTANBUL   Ginger could hear the crunch of boots on gravel clearly through the walls of the steel shipping container which had been their prison ever since they got off the boat. Their captors were probably bringing them food. It had been steadily growing warmer for the last hour, so she guessed it was mid-morning. Shelly gripped Ginger's arm. The poor girl was a total wreck. The daughter of a stockbroker who had made millions on the dot.com craze and multiplied his winnings during the collapse, Shelly was a tall and slender brunette without a care in the world. She had never experienced deprivation of any kind or worked a day in her life. In the West Texas farm community Ginger grew up in, they would have said that Shelly had more money than she had sense.

For two days now, they had been kept in the pitch black container. The only time they had any light was when the door opened and someone shoved trays of food and bottled water through the door. The menu never changed—two loaves of French bread, a large block of salty feta cheese, and a pile of fresh tomatoes and cucumbers. For toilets, they had been given two five-gallon buckets, and using them in the pitch black was a challenge. There was no toilet paper and Ginger had been making do with scrap packaging material strewn about the floor. The container wasn't ventilated and the stench was becoming unbearable. There were five people using the toilet several times a day. She found herself profoundly aware of something she had never given much thought to before—the blessings of a sewer system.

For Shelly, the ordeal might as well have been a torture chamber. Two years ago, she had married a young broker who worked with her father. They had a yacht, a home in the Caribbean and a villa in Italy, their European base. For Shelly, hardship meant a New Year's celebration without Dom Perignon White Gold Jeroboam. Ginger had met her two years ago on a tour with Gilbert. Later, they learned that they lived only a couple of miles from each other. Shelly had latched on to Ginger like the older sister she had never had. Ginger liked to believe that she was a good influence on the young woman.

Ginger could hear the men talking outside and tried to determine how many there were. *Three? Four?* She couldn't be sure, of this or anything. Suddenly, one of them burst out laughing, and the emotion she had experienced so little of in her life sunk its icy claws into her soul once again. Fear. Something she had known nothing about until now. It was a debilitating paralysis. She had never experienced fear on this level. Since the first day, Ginger had tried to keep the children preoccupied with stories from her childhood. When she ran out of these, she started telling them about every hero she could remember from Moses to Martin Luther. But, the story the children kept asking for in the cavernous darkness of the container was the story of Daniel's deliverance from the lion's den. It was in the telling of the stories that she found the antidote to fear. It was faith.

The kids were all fast-asleep, fatigued from the stress. Ginger gently pried Shelly's hand off of her arm and stood up carefully. First, she felt for the wall and then began shuffling her feet slowly forward.

"What are you doing?" asked Shelly, her voice trembling.

"If they open that door, I'm going to ask them to change out these buckets."

"Please do. I feel like I'm going to puke with every breath."

257

"Do you believe the stuff you were telling the kids last night?" asked Shelly, trying to sound nonchalant, but failing horribly at hiding her earnestness.

Ginger didn't answer right away. She continued inching down the wall towards the buckets, wondering to herself, *Do I believe these stories? Do angels really shut up the mouths of lions? Is it only prophets like Daniel that get special attention? Where were the angels when the Romans were feeding the followers of Christ to lions in the coliseum?* Yes, she had been asking herself these same questions as she told the story to her children. Her foot bumped against the plastic bucket.

"Yes," replied Ginger, "I do believe, now more than ever."

"I thought you did," replied Shelly. "I wish I could say the same thing. You've been so strong. I could never have faced down a man who did to me what they did to you."

The memory struck Ginger like a whip. Unconsciously, she felt down the front of her shirt to make sure the twine was still in place. It was. It had taken her and Shelly almost two hours working in the pitch black with a small nail they found on the floor of the container to make tears in the cloth where the buttons had been and then run a length of twine through the holes to keep her shirt closed.

It had happened on the boat. Her oldest son Garret had fought the men twice after being put on board. She was proud of the eleven-year-old boy. He was a fighter, a boy who shared his father's passion for justice and honor, but he had paid dearly for it. On the boat, he had rushed one of the men, jumped on his back and tried to choke him. It had taken two men to peel him away. The man he had tried to choke had spun around in a rage and slapped Garret across the face so hard it knocked the boy to the ground. Then, he kicked him several times in the ribs before the other men pulled him away. In less than an hour, Garret's eye had swollen shut.

One of the men, a tall fellow with dark hair and striking looks, spoke English. So well, in fact, that Ginger had a hard time believing he could be a foreigner. There was no discernible accent. His sentences were perfectly formed. The other men deferred to him and spoke only English with him, but among themselves, they spoke another language she did not recognize. He seemed to be the leader. He warned Garret that he would not tolerate any more misbehavior. Ginger tried to calm the boy down, but the harsh treatment had enraged him.

Later, Garret apparently found a screwdriver under the seat he was sitting on. He said nothing to any of them, but when he saw they were slowing down and approaching land, he attacked the man who had hit him earlier. A warning shout from one of the other men at the last second was the only thing that stopped Garret from burying the screwdriver in the middle of the man's back. He still managed to connect with the man's shoulder, giving him a nasty puncture wound. The man removed the screwdriver, whipped out a switchblade and lunged for Garret, who raised his arms to block the man's attack and received a deep cut to his forearm.

Again, the other men kept their companion from doing further harm to Garret, and the tall, dark-haired fellow grabbed Garret by the waist and started pulling the boy away. Garret kicked and flailed his arms like a mad man. He finally managed to twist Garret's arm behind his back and seemed about to say something, when suddenly he just let him go. He turned to Ginger, grabbed her by the hair and ripped her shirt open to reveal a black lace bra.

"Now," he had said to the boy, "I will not tell you again. Any more trouble from you and your mother and I will be going out on the deck." In response, Ginger had slapped the man in the face as hard as she could. The man had responded with a right hook to her jaw, which cut her chin to the bone. Still, she put herself between him and her son, blood streaming off her perfect chin onto the floor and glared at him defiantly. The man only spat on the floor and walked out.

Garret had been broken from that moment on. He had hardly said a word since. Just once, after they were put into the container, when his brother and sister were asleep, he had begun sobbing on his mother's shoulder and said over and over again, "I'm so sorry. I'm so sorry."

The sound of someone fumbling with the lock on the door brought Ginger back to reality and away from the painful memory. Ten seconds later, bright, strong sunlight was streaming through the crack in the door. She shielded her eyes with her hand as her retina screamed in pain at the sudden overstimulation.

43

OREGON Fatih Gülben stood on the shore gazing over the heads of ten bearded men dressed in white robes and watching the moon set on the lake. They had eaten the pre-dawn meal together, and then he had taken them down to the water for a teaching on the peace of God. It was a beautiful cloudless sky with the moon just past full. The stillness was eerie. It was almost as if Allah wanted to drive the point of the morning devotion home. Peace was something one had to cultivate and experience in their soul, but the environment certainly helped. It was time to wrap up his discussion.

"Sometimes I am astounded by the fact that Allah did not allow our fathers to discover the New World and instead let the blood-thirsty Spanish and the cold-hearted English imperialists settle this continent. In my childhood, I grieved over the darkness that had engulfed this continent for centuries. Yet, now I have lived to see the faithful sowing the seeds of freedom in every corner of this great land. Allah has given to us the honor of conquest. It is our generation, the chosen generation, which is building the mosques that will sound the call to prayer from sea to shining sea over purple mountains' majesty. And that is indeed a great honor. Our generation is the second beginning. The *hadith* makes it clear that in the last days a chosen generation will accomplish the same feats as the Prophet and His esteemed companions. You are that generation!

"Remember brothers, final victory is assured. This is not in question. It is not a matter of *if* but *when*. Allah *will* make us prosper. It is ours to submit and keep faith, the sign of which is our abiding inner peace. Peace in the struggle for our faith, peace in the face of persecution and opposition, peace in setbacks and seeming defeat. Peace is the testimony of our faith, and it will ensure our victory. Islam will cover the earth like water blankets the depths of the sea. Let's spend the rest of the day reciting the holy Qur'an and preparing ourselves to be ambassadors of the kingdom of Allah. It will overwhelm this continent from both coasts like a tsunami. We will meet again at sunset to break the fast."

He watched as this hand-picked group of young men born in America to successful Muslim families began to wander off in different directions, looking for a spot of solitude on the three hundred beautifully forested acres of his ranch. He began walking back to the mansion. Oregon reminded him of his home on the Black Sea. The facilities here were perfect for his ambassador program which sponsored young men interested in business or politics. Here, they were thoroughly grounded in the Qur'an, their loyalty was cultivated and they were taught the principles of community-building and organization.

Generous support from Muslim businessmen had enabled him to take these young men and form a network of non-profit organizations and charter schools in over twenty states. Once trained, these ambassadors would transform the network into an effective tool for recruiting and evangelism. The short-term goal was to make these seemingly disconnected groups a powerful voice for Muslim rights here in America. The intermediate goal was to secure the right for American Muslims to live accordingly to sharia law. It was an uphill battle, especially when it came to provisions regarding the family, but family values in America were in free fall. It was only a matter of time. Men would eventually realize that the provision for multiple wives was better than the serial polygamy currently being practiced.

Fatih looked down at his watch and then up towards the mansion sitting on a knoll overlooking the lake. His assistant was standing on the porch to make sure he didn't forget about the early morning teleconference, which was scheduled to begin in less than five minutes. He quickened his pace. When he stepped onto the porch, he saw that his assistant was holding a folded piece of paper.

"I thought you might want to see this before the conference call."

"Who is it from?" asked Fatih.

"It was dictated to me less than an hour ago by our liaison in DC."

Fatih unfolded the note and read it with a furrowed brow.

INITIATIVE ON TRACK. US PRESSURING EUROPE. ICSID CASE AGAINST LIBYA LIKELY RESOLVED DUE TO NSC PRESSURE ON FINCH AND MORELAND. ASSET FREEZE MAY BE LIFTED AS EARLY AS NEXT MONTH.

"How much would that free up?" asked Fatih.

"About ten billion dollars, sir."

"When was the last time we talked to the Senator from Minnesota?"

"At the banquet hosted by the Association for the Advancement of American Muslims last week. It was well-attended by members of Congress who support a multicultural society unfettered by the chains of Western civilization."

Fatih wondered how the man managed to say that without a smile.

"The upcoming vote on implementation of the Tolerance and Unity in a Multicultural World initiative is a crucial first step in securing more broad-based support here in the US," said Fatih. "It will give us a platform with global recognition. Did Tom indicate how much headway he has made with the US Permanent Resident to the United Nations?"

His assistant cleared his throat and said, "Your excellent reputation in interfaith dialogue has convinced the committee to give our Association for the Advancement of American Muslims in Atlanta a leading role in the project. Let's talk about it on the way to the teleconference room. We don't want to be late for the call from Cairo."

He opened the massive white French doors for his master, and once they were inside, he continued, "At the AAAM meeting, Tom was very positive about US support for the initiative. The American government has made repairing its image in the Middle East a top priority. He sees American support for this initiative as a chance to communicate American sensitivities."

Fatih smiled. "If that is Tom's report, then it shouldn't be hard for them to get results from the Brits and Germans."

His assistant looked uncomfortable.

"There have been some unforeseen developments, sir. This morning, there were three separate terrorist attacks in Turkey, all targeting foreigners or banks who do business with foreigners. The loss of life was extremely high, but this is not what concerns us most. Casualty reports are just numbers to most people. It is the visual impact that worries us. The international press is beaming images of the carnage around the globe—buildings full of innocent civilians all brought down by powerful explosives. These grim pictures will only add fuel to the fire of anti-Muslim sentiment and provoke greater ground roots opposition to Muslim integration in Europe. Policy-makers have been able to squelch most of the disquiet by appealing to tolerance, but this latest incident in Turkey will make their job extremely difficult. The initiative could be in danger."

Fatih glanced down at his watch. The conference call would begin in less than two minutes.

"We'll discuss this later. In the meantime, get our people praying…"

He moved quickly down a corridor and into his private study, where his assistant locked the door behind them. This was his sanctuary, a place to renew his faith and regain strength, a bunker where he could distance himself from the toil and strife of an evil world, a world where jihad was an unfortunate necessity. The walls were paneled with the finest cocobolo wood, and he sat in a chair made of zitan, an antique from China's imperial era. His assistant turned a spotlight on to illuminate the green crescent banner behind his Master. He heard the familiar ring of the VoIP call, and his assistant clicked a button to answer. The flat screen TV hanging on the wall flickered, and he was looking at Ahmet sitting in the council chamber in Cairo.

"*As-salamu alaykum*, Ahmet"

"*Wa alaykum as-salam*, Servant of my Lord."

"This is bad news," said Fatih slowly. "The *ummah* is weak and divided. We need peace in order to attain the prosperity required for Islam's expansion. These amateur distractions by sincere but misguided zealots seeking to secure their own place in Paradise have crossed the line."

"A point I have been making for a long time, sir."

"Your views on this issue have been noted yet again, Ahmet. I can assure you that all of us are doing everything we can. What I want to discuss today is your plan for managing this disaster with the religious leaders and the press."

"The press," replied Ahmet, "is easy. We simply ignore it, bury it and direct their attention elsewhere like we have done with all such acts of violence for the last fifteen years."

"Easier said than done."

"Sir, suppression of the news regarding the attack at Fort Hood several years back was practically one hundred percent in the Middle East. This will be more difficult for obvious reasons, but our office here has been working around the clock to prepare a ten-day news cycle. We have over one hundred columnists throughout the Middle East ready to bombard the public with articles condemning the violence while blaming the West for inflaming tensions with the attacks on Turks in Germany.

"The angle we are taking is to focus on how natural the desire for vengeance is, while at the same time, reminding the faithful that we are the ones who desire peace and that it is the infidel in the House of War that is constantly stirring up strife. I am very confident that our control of the media will be able to prevent this from radicalizing more of the population."

Ahmet noticed that the corners of his Master's mouth turned slightly upwards and this put him at ease.

"And what about the religious leaders?"

A dark shadow flickered on Ahmet's face.

"In our last conversation, you asked us to identify the hotheads and warn them. We have done so, but already we hear that three of them have ignored us and redoubled their efforts. This attack in Turkey will only embolden them more."

"You've never failed us," said Fatih, "But I think it is time to give you more free rein. As you know, my policy has always been that we do no harm to a Muslim, even the radicals. They are our brothers, and we cannot know how Allah is using even them in the grand scheme. Yet, even they may cross a line. Prepare the bowstrings. Do not let a drop of their holy blood touch the ground, but send a message. I'll leave the details to you."

"I know this must pain you deeply, and yet it is the course of righteous wisdom, a necessary sacrifice."

"Sometimes, people must take the place of sheep as the sacrifice, Ahmet. Now, about the initiative, I hear that heads of state in Sudan and Yemen are starting to grumble. It is very important, especially in light of these terrorist attacks, that the world of Islam present a unified front that calls for peace."

"Servant of my Lord, we have approached the Sudanese through our contacts in Egypt. They are demanding more funds and they want certain officials cleared of genocide charges related to their war with the Christians in the South."

"How much are we talking about?"

"They are demanding five hundred million dollars for infrastructure development, but we all know that sixty million put into the right hands will suffice."

"I'll have the money transferred today. Confirm receipt, but do not deliver until the concerned officials have signed an official protocol stating their support for the initiative. Half of the money now and half of it after the initiative is implemented. What about Yemen?"

"The Yemeni government is being cowed by radicals, but they have such a limited international presence that we're not concerned about their impact. The leaders are weak and will not chart their own course in the face of a united front. They want funds as well and concessions from Saudi Arabia, but I do not think we should give in to their demands. They will cave, and just to make sure they do, I've arranged a small surprise for them. Two days from now, a Chinese delegation will visit the government and tell them that support for the initiative is a condition for renewing their petroleum contract."

"Good work, Ahmet. Our steadfastness and resolution will certainly inspire and shame the West into further cooperation and support for the initiative. With the entire Muslim world calling for an alliance of civilizations, they dare not refuse."

"Thank you, sir."

"Now for developments on the Iranian front," said Fatih. "Our people have ensured that new sanctions will be voted on by the UN Security Council next week. The latest polls continue to show that Westerners increasingly identify radicalism with Iran."

"Then we should focus on the fact that the terrorist attacks in Turkey were carried out by Hizbullah. The American people will immediately associate it with the Iranian Hezbollah in Lebanon. We'll even spell it the same way. No one will know the difference."

Fatih rubbed his chin.

"Yes, good idea. We'll continue to emphasize Shiite obsession with the Mahdi too. Elites in the West already think apocalyptic beliefs like the second coming of Christ are ignorant religious superstition, so they'll continue to look at Shiites in the same way."

"Exactly. Our think tank strategy is also working well."

"You mean *your* think tank strategy. I'm well-aware of the fact that you were the person who outlined the strategy conference in Dubai three years ago."

Ahmet bowed his head ever so slightly in acknowledgement of the compliment. Now, he understood why he had been given direct access to the Rightly Guided One. His work was being rewarded. Fatih continued, "The strategy you presented has been implemented meticulously. The upper echelon of the intelligence community has hired at least a dozen of our people to assist in their war on terror. Of course, they all come from organizations with no direct ties to us. They will ensure that American intelligence agencies continue to focus on Iran. In other words, your strategy is paying off. These agencies are cultivating relationships with us to counter Iran, just as you predicted. In fact, one of our enterprising businessmen has run with your idea for t-shirts targeting American conservatives. It has a picture of the Ayatollah with the words 'Shiite for brains' printed underneath. They're selling like palm dates during Ramadan. You will be rewarded in due course."

"Knowing that I have helped crush the Shia heresy will be reward enough. All we need now is for Washington to realize once and for all that good relations with Muslims means good relations with Sunnis. The only future they have in the Middle East is siding with us against Iran..."

Fatih raised his hand to cut him off. He knew how much Ahmet hated Shiites, Alevis and other non-conformist sects, but he didn't have time right now.

"There is just one last thing, Ahmet. Has the 'son of prophet' situation been taken care of?"

"We have the leverage we need to resolve the problem, but we have not yet been able to contact the person holding the document. London's initial handling was a bit sloppy and that caused some problems, but I'm handling it personally now. There is nothing to worry about. I suspect it will be concluded soon."

"Make it soon, Ahmet, and make it perfect. This would be a huge blow."

Fatih terminated the call, turned to his assistant and said, "It will be almost 10:00 AM in Washington. Call Senator Giovanni's office. It's time I made direct contact. Arrange for the Senator to call me today if he has time. I want to thank him for the generous federal support our charter schools have received and his assistance with not only the Libyan affair but also the UN initiative. Once the freeze on those assets is lifted, make sure he has a nice holiday somewhere in Europe, or Thailand, if that's the sort of thing he likes.

44

ISTANBUL   Matt hung up the phone and turned to look at the two brothers sitting on the bed across from him in their room at the Grand Seigneur hotel. The look on his face was a mixture of disbelief, pity and fear.

"What's wrong, Matt?"

"That was a friend at State, the same guy who issued the yellow notice for your kids yesterday. He said a red notice and a green notice have just been issued by the FBI for Gilbert O'Brien. Apparently, you are being wanted for corporate espionage in a case before the ICSID. Tell me this is bogus."

Gary turned to his brother.

"Gil?"

His brother's jaw was clenched and his eyes were slits. But, he said nothing.

"Gil, talk to us. What is this about?"

"It's about corruption, Gary. Fighting fire with fire and how you can get burned. Matt, I need to know where this originated from. Can you find out?"

"You're going to have to tell me more than that if you want me going to bat for you. I'm ready to believe you, but I need some details."

Gilbert spent the next five minutes explaining how files and evidence had been stolen from a French law firm, why he had agreed to find a team that would execute the job, and how somebody within the US government had perpetrated the same crime against Finch and Moreland to help the French. When he was done, Matt just shook his head.

"That's why I left State. The whole damn thing is too crooked to fix."

Gary opened his backpack and pulled out a notebook and pencil. He had taken over twenty pages of notes in the last ten hours as he poured over the material Gwyn sent. Gilbert didn't understand what his brother found so fascinating but was happy to let him research it so that he had more time to spend looking at the files sent by the key-logger.

"If you told Tate you would sit on what you learned, why would he turn you in?" Matt continued.

"I don't know. It doesn't make any sense. If your friend can find out where this all originated, and what role Mike Tate played in it, I'd appreciate it."

"I'll do my best."

Gary pointed at the laptop sitting on the nightstand beside Gilbert.

"Hey bro, would you mind handing me that computer? There are a couple of things I want to look up on the internet."

Gilbert didn't seem to hear. Matt hopped up from his chair, retrieved the laptop, and handed it to Gary. He looked around the room. He was restless and wanted something to do.

"When will Gwyn be here?" Matt asked, trying to sound casual.

"Zeki said he'd call us when they arrived."

"Whoa. Zeki's with her? You didn't tell me that."

"You didn't ask."

"You said he was ex-MIT."

"That's right."

"Do you have any idea why he would get mixed up in this?"

"Look," said Gilbert, "the man was a good friend of my father's. I believe he's sincerely trying to help."

"No offense, Gil," continued Matt, "but there's no such thing as sincerity in the world of intelligence. And, Turkish intelligence is renowned for its disinformation campaigns, its false flag attacks, and its psychological warfare. Their perception management strategies are byzantine in the extreme though I'm sure they would bristle at the adjective. You know that I've captured two of the Muslim ring leaders involved in human trafficking and spent a fair bit of time among them trying to get leads. I'm afraid I've developed a serious aversion to their attitude."

"I don't follow," said Gary.

"For starters, I'm sick of the American imperialism bullshit. Don't get me wrong. I'm not so keen on American intervention in the Middle East, but these guys are borderline lunatics. They claim that America caused the 1999 earthquake in Izmit to destroy Turkey's industrial capacity. They say that the tsunami in the South Pacific was our doing, as if we could shake the earth's crust at will."

"Well," said Gary, "That's the world they live in. That's the paradigm ingrained in them since birth."

"Yeah, ingrained in them as part of the psychological warfare and perception management waged by their intelligence community. Well, in twenty years, when there are Chinese soldiers keeping the peace in the Middle East instead of American ones, we'll see if they don't pine for the good ol' days. Anyway, back to this friend of your father's, what do you know about his connections and activities?"

"Nothing. Where are you going with this?" asked Gary.

"How much do you know about operation Gladio?" asked Matt.

"Never heard of it," said Gilbert.

"I know about it," replied Gary, taking a deep breath. "It is supposed to have been a stay-behind clandestine paramilitary structure in NATO countries after WWII. The goal was to prevent the spread of communism. The modus operandi was 'strategy of tension', which is basically governing through fragmentation and chaos, creating an environment that makes it easier for governments to manipulate and control their citizens."

Gilbert's surprise was unfeigned.

"Did you pick up a degree in political science during your travels?"

"I do a little reading in my spare time."

Gilbert shook his head in unbelief. "Well, I do a bit of reading myself, and I have never heard of it."

"I guess we haven't been reading the same stuff," said Gary indifferently.

Matt put his head back and stared at the ceiling.

"Let me see if I can give you two a primer in how these things work. In the end, this crap is the reason I decided I had to resign from State. You probably don't know that Turkey is generally regarded as the most active member of the Gladio network, which, by the way, was officially condemned by the EU on November 22, 1990. Even though a number of generals and intelligence officials have confirmed its existence, the CIA has responded to FOIA requests with its classic Glomar bullshit. 'We can neither confirm nor deny the existence or non-existence of records responsive to your request.' In Turkey, right-wing groups, such as the fascist Grey Wolves, were trained and financed to stop communism and to implement the 'strategy of tension.' Do you remember the assassination attempt on Pope John Paul II in 1981 by Mehmet Ali Ağca, the Turkish operative?"

"Are you suggesting there is a connection with our document?" responded Gilbert dubiously.

"Not directly, no. I am just using this as an example of rule number one: 'Nothing is what it appears to be'. Never forget that. Do you remember how the attempted assassination was portrayed?"

"Yeah, it was a supposed to be a KGB plot to stop the Pope's support for Solidarity in Poland."

"We'll see if you still believe that in ten minutes."

"Fire away."

"The assassin, Ağca, was a member of the Grey Wolves, a right-wing ultra-nationalist group. He was personally responsible for the killing of Abdi İpekçi, a left-wing journalist, after which he was apprehended, convicted and placed in a military prison. A few months later, he miraculously escapes with the help of Abdullah Çatlı, another Grey Wolves Counter Guerilla. Then, Ağca shoots the Pope four times, is arrested and sentenced to life in prison.

"The investigation showed that he had travelled to several countries on the Mediterranean in an alleged attempt to hide his point of origin, which was Bulgaria. After the failed assassination attempt, Ağca said he did it because 'the Pope is the incarnation of all that is capitalism.' Later, several sources claimed the assassination attempt was the work of the KGB. It seemed plausible given Ağca's stated motive, the fact that John Paul was a staunch anti-Communist and the fact that he was linked to operatives in Bulgaria, which, at the time, was a communist country."

"Wait a minute, why would a right-wing operative like Ağca target an outspoken opponent of communism like Pope John Paul?" asked Gilbert.

"Aha, you are asking the right questions."

"Nothing is what it appears to be," said Gary.

"Exactly," continued Matt. "Would a NATO-controlled Gladio operative, an avowed right-wing fascist who had murdered a left-wing reporter in cold blood suddenly turn into a dedicated communist? No, he was a right-wing operative, so why would he try to assassinate an anti-Communist pope at the height of the Cold War?"

"He wouldn't," replied Gilbert.

"But, he did try, and the reason is as convoluted as it is simple. The shooting of the Pope aroused nationalist sympathies in Italy and other European countries with significant Catholic populations, many of which had developed strong leftist movements that sympathized with the Soviet Union. Pinning the foiled assassination plot on the KGB turned the sentiments of the people against the communists, obviously a key objective of the western elite. If you remember, John Paul II supported the Solidarity strikes taking place in Poland at the time, and this plot only served to strengthen the resolve of the staunchly Catholic Polish population against their communist leaders as a show of support for the first Polish Pope."

"So, Ağca's comments and the Bulgarian connection were carefully crafted to make it look like the KGB was involved," remarked Gilbert.

"Exactly," said Matt.

"Maybe," continued Gilbert, "He was just a hired gun ready to work for the highest bidder."

Matt was ready for this logical possibility.

"It's possible. Anything is. But does anyone think that the Soviets really believed killing the Catholic pontiff would demoralize Solidarity and the Polish opposition? The 'martyr effect' is a well-known psychological phenomenon. The Soviets would never have been so stupid, and that's who the alleged employer would have been."

"Of course, you're right," said Gary, "Heightened religious devotion is almost invariably the response to persecution."

"Plus, the fact that the assassin was a Muslim added even more intrigue, raising the specter of religious conflict. At first, Ağca claimed to be working for the Marxist-leaning Popular Front for the Liberation of Palestine. But his story changed constantly, which, I'm sure, was a tactical decision. It was an attempt to create confusion through complexity. I am simplifying it, but you get the idea. In short, the incident created a chaotic situation and uncertainty, offering endless possibilities for exploitation. In fact, I believe that chaos or the appearance of chaos is a critical strategy in the control of democratic societies."

"So, was his escape from the military prison in Turkey arranged with help from the government?" asked Gary.

"That is one of the most amazing aspects of the whole story. He was connected with a man named Abdullah Çatlı, who allegedly broke him out of prison. Çatlı was also a member of the Counter Guerilla Grey Wolves, and MIT was rumored to have paid the man in heroin. He was arrested in Paris on October 24th 1984 for drug trafficking. He spent seven years in a French prison, which, to be honest, doesn't sound too bad, and was then transferred to Switzerland in 1988 to serve a sentence on drug charges there as well. In March 1990, however, he inexplicably escaped and was subsequently recruited by security forces in Turkey. His death in a car accident in November 1996 rocked the establishment in Turkey because he was traveling with a member of parliament and a well-known police officer. To make matters worse, he had diplomatic credentials issued by the Turkish government, a weapons permit, a stash of US dollars, narcotics and a fake passport issued to Mehmet Özbay, the same alias Ağca was known to have used."

Gilbert whistled lowly. "So, numerous state or supra-state actors were clearly involved in all of this."

"Absolutely," said Connor, "My point is that Turkey employed considerable counter-guerilla resources. Their intelligence agencies have supported or conducted more strategy of tension operations than you can imagine. The goal? Chaos. Fear. Suspicion. Turkish national psychology has been shaped by a distrust so deeply ingrained that it is a proverb, 'The Turk has no friend but the Turk.' There is nothing as valuable to a government as having an enemy."

"Then the Turkish government is sitting on the mother lode," said Gary.

Gilbert interjected, "How is it that you know so much about all of this?"

Matt merely shrugged. "One of my political science professors said he believed Turkey would rise to lead the Muslim world. Turkey has ethnic connections to almost all of the oil-rich Central Asian republics, and it's also the most industrially developed and politically stable Muslim country. Historically, it has maintained very close ties both in terms of trade and finance with Europe. More importantly, the Ottoman sultan was also the last Caliph of Islam."

"But that's a thing of the past."

"For us, yes. For them, bringing back the Caliph is the only way forward. If it were revived, the Turks would naturally be a leading candidate for the position. I think it is difficult for westerners to understand this part of the Muslim psyche, but just imagine the Catholic Church being without a Pope since 1923."

"I see your point. Every Catholic would be clamoring for the office to be filled."

"Anyway," continued Matt, "This professor convinced me to do my master's thesis on what is known as the 'deep state' in Turkey."

"Wait a minute," said Gilbert excitedly. "Didn't Zeki refer to that in our conversation with him?"

"Yes, he did," replied Gary. "He said that the people we were dealing with were the deep state. I don't know how he knew that. He referred to them as the shadow of Allah's shadow, the same thing, except that it refers to one of the Ottoman Sultan's titles, the Shadow of Allah."

Matt closed his eyes and tried to get his mind around it all.

"You know," he said finally, "The Islamic state is reemerging in Turkey. NATO has been in denial for a decade. In Turkey, that power is now wearing a turban inwardly if not outwardly. There's a power behind the throne in every country, and all the talk about justice is a façade. It's a power struggle and the only rule is to win. It doesn't matter who pays, or how many promises you break. There are no friends or allies, just business partners looking for a way to shaft each other. That's why I left State. There are no statesmen anymore.

"Of course, I knew most of this before I got in. I decided that I would be willing to play by a different set of rules too, if it was in the best interests of the country. But, after a few years, I started to realize that the game we were playing wasn't Axis and Allies but Monopoly. I realized it was all about money. Sure, it was always spun as national security or the balance of power, but it's all a smokescreen for increasing profit margins via access to cheaper labor and cheaper raw materials or restricting the access of your rivals to the same.

"To make it worse, the whole thing is based on value-neutral multiculturalism. The cardinal sin in national building is to destroy the sense of national unity. If a nation's identity becomes fragmented, it doesn't survive. The West is ignoring this fundamental rule. I lost faith in the system and my ability to change it. Besides, I couldn't stomach the corruption. Anyway, enough of this. When do you expect Gwyn and Zeki to arrive and how will they contact you?"

Gilbert pointed to the laptop on the dresser. The chat window was open.

"They are supposed to contact us when they arrive. If they were able to catch the afternoon flight out of Dallas, I expect them to arrive within the next couple of hours. Maybe you could show me how this canister works."

Matt pulled a dull silver tube from his bag. It had ornate floral decorations

271

etched into the sides. One end looked like the base. It was flat and slightly larger. The other end had a hollow in the end.

"The canister is made of stainless steel. It is twenty-one inches long and four inches in diameter. It is meant to fit inside a normal travel bag or suitcase and is used by smugglers moving high value materials via a mule."

"A mule?" asked Gilbert

"The courier. They're usually freelancers, so they cannot always be trusted with valuable articles."

He laid the canister on its side and pointed to a row of barely discernible letters underneath the cap. The cap had several lines of varying lengths, also very faint, along the rim pointing down to the symbols. "Remember the little arrow that marked the stopping point on your school locker?"

"Are you kidding? I still remember the combination – sixteen clockwise thirty-one counter-clockwise and nine clockwise," said Gilbert.

"Well, this canister has no arrow. Only one of these lines serves as the arrow. In this case, it is the shortest one. Each canister is custom-made, and only the owners know which of the lines to use as the marker. There is no clicking, so very few people even suspect it is a container. In fact, it is usually called a candlestick if anyone should ask."

He pointed to the hollow at the narrow end.

"Candles fit perfectly in this hollow. The end with the cap serves as a base. This one has a rare added security feature. The hinge on the lid turns a series of small gears so that the combination changes each time the canister is opened. In other words, it is a rotating combination. This one is a 1-2-3 sequence on a letter combination. In other words, right now the combination is A E H. That means the next time it is opened the first letter moves forward one, the second letter two and the third three, so that the combination will change to B G K. You must know the sequence not just the combination."

"So what do we want with it?" asked Gary, clearly confused about its purpose.

"Ask your brother," replied Matt.

Gilbert continued staring at the canister almost as if he hadn't heard.

"Gil, what's your plan?"

"I'm not just going to hand this document back to those sorry bastards. They killed our father, kidnapped my family and tried to kill our sister. I want a guarantee that my family will be set free."

"You've lost your mind. You're going to get them killed. Don't try to screw these guys, Gil."

"Listen gypsy boy, family may not mean much to you, but my wife and children are somewhere in this city of fifteen million. For all I know, they could be gagged and tied up in the room next door. Do you have any idea what that is like? Any idea what kind of hell I have been going through, wondering how they are being treated?"

Gary averted his gaze.

"No, I probably don't. It's your call."

Gilbert picked up the canister and spun the cap.

"Tell me how the tracking system works."

"It's equipped with a GPS device. The signal has a range of five miles and uses cellular networks to relay coordinates. The battery will last about six days. It's all state of the art. The tracking software is integrated with Google Earth. I can have it set up in fifteen minutes."

"Great," said Gilbert. "Let's do a test run. Gary wants to look in on a friend anyway. He can carry the canister, and we'll stay here to wait for Gwyn's call while we track his movements."

Gary walked over and grabbed his bag off the bed. He realized just a split second too late that he had forgotten to zip it up, and the contents spilled all over the floor. Gilbert bent over and started picking the stuff off the floor and then froze. Gary looked up at his brother, saw what was in his hand, and took a deep breath.

"I thought you said you didn't have a cell phone," Gilbert said slowly.

"You wouldn't understand."

"You're right. I don't understand why you lied to me!"

"I didn't lie to you."

"You said you didn't have a cell phone, but you do. I call that lying."

"No, you asked if I had a cell phone and I said, 'Sorry.' Sorry doesn't mean 'I don't have a cell phone', so it wasn't a lie."

"But you led me to believe you didn't have a cell phone," said Gilbert, as he began thumbing through the menus.

"I led you to believe nothing. You believe whatever you want to. Now, give me my phone."

"So, why wouldn't you give me the number?" he asked without looking up from the screen.

"I have my reasons."

"Reasons you won't share?"

"That's right. Now, I need my phone."

Gilbert began reading the names from the cell phone directory out loud, "Ardavan, Armeen, Atash, Babak, Bahar, Bahram, Darya…"

Matt interrupted, "Those sound like Iranian names."

Matt's tone was icy. "Gary, what the hell is going on here?"

Gary stared at the floor.

"Gary?"

"Listen, Gil, you don't tell me about your job, do you. I don't have to share details about mine with you either."

"Job? What kind of job? Your clients are Iranians?"

"Listen, I have to go or I'm going to be late."

Gilbert, looked at him for a minute and then said,

"Fine. Have it your way. Keep us all at arm's length. We're used to it," he said, handing the phone back to his brother.

Gary turned to Matt.

"Gil told me about your new line of work. Angela, the girl I'm going to meet, is here looking for her sister Bianca. She has good reason to believe the girl has been forced into prostitution. I was wondering if you had any contacts here in Turkey that might be able to help her."

"I could make a few calls if you give me a photograph."

"Thanks."

45

Gary left the hotel and took a right. *Maybe Matt will be able to help.* He thought about his last conversation with Angela and how horrible it must be to have a sister abducted and forced into prostitution. It had seemed so distant then, the grief of this Romanian family, but now it struck much closer to home. Against his will, images of Ginger falling prey to a similar criminal network and being humiliated in the same way flooded his mind. As he started trudging up the steep hill, he felt for a moment that he was going to be physically sick.

That morning he had received an email saying that Angela had been trying to get in touch with him for three days. She had sent a message every day, each more desperate than the last. He picked his way along the narrow sidewalk heading for their rendezvous point at Galata Tower. He had been up and down the street dozens of times on his way to visit the old imam at the Şahkulu mosque and knew it well. Like many Turkish cities, certain artisans congregated in a certain area. He knew it was because the country and infrastructure were so much older that it was easier for shoppers if they knew they could go to one place and find a selection of a certain product from different vendors. This particular street was lined with shops selling musical instruments.

The few cars were parked helter-skelter wherever they could find a spot. This neighborhood was a Genoese city six hundred years before Henry Ford. Parking was a challenge that had not yet been accommodated. A street vendor blocked the sidewalk with a cardboard stand offering a selection of best-selling authors, all pirated. He stepped out into the street to get around the stand and noticed that Hitler's *Mein Kampf* was among the books being sold. One of his students had said that the ultra-nationalists had financed a new printing of the Turkish translation. It seemed hard to believe, but there it was right in front of him - Aryan Supremacy in a land whose forefathers hailed back to the steppes of Central Asia. He shook his head in disbelief. *How absurd can it get? People Hitler would have viewed as second-class or worse reading his book. What gives?*

He stopped in front of another dingy-looking shop that sold sketches of the Istanbul skyline and Ottoman motifs. He had browsed through the shop several times, but always left empty-handed. He noted that the window display had not changed in the week since he had been gone. Then, he passed a tiny shop that had literally been a hole in the old castle walls. Now, it sold world-famous Zildjian cymbals and drumsticks. The contrast of bright, state-of-the-art musical instruments was striking in a shop so old it had probably seen Fatih Sultan Mehmet storm the walls of Constantinople.

Another fifteen meters and he was at the end of the street, standing on the southern edge of Galata Tower square, scanning the crowd for Angela. The enormous tower blocked at least a third of the small square from view, so he began walking in a circle to the right and soon spied her reading the informational plaque on the northeast side of the square at the tower's base.

Dressed in a pair of old jeans, threadbare at the knees, she had her dark hair pulled up in a ponytail to keep it off her neck in the humid August weather. She was wearing a non-descript, light-green t-shirt with writing that had long since faded away. He liked that about her. She didn't try to draw attention to herself. Yet, her pure natural beauty always stood out in a crowd.

She was five years younger than he was but in some ways seemed older, more mature. The post-communist Romania of her childhood had not been an easy place to grow up. The fall of Ceausescu and the collapse of Communist rule may have brought some measure of freedom and openness to the outside world, but it could not make up for decades of neglect to infrastructure and trade. She was a rare combination of beauty, intelligence and toughness and right now it was the latter that was most evident. He could still read the same determination on her face and in her posture that he had seen the night she told him her sister had been abducted and forced into prostitution.

"Hey, Angela," he called out.

She looked up quickly and her face softened into a smile when she saw Gary walking towards her.

"Hey. Thanks for coming."

"No problem, I'm sorry if I kept you waiting."

"No, I just arrived about ten minutes ago. I hopped on the Istiklal tram so I wouldn't have to shoulder my way through the crowd."

"Where shall we go?" asked Gary.

"What about the café at the top of the tower, unless of course, you have been there before and would rather go somewhere else?"

"No, that sounds fine."

They both walked back around to the entrance on the south side and climbed the steps leading to the door. Once inside, Gary pulled a few Turkish lira notes out of his wallet to pay the admission fee, and they walked over to the elevators. He was surprised at how empty the place was. They entered the elevator and hit the button for the top floor.

"So, have you seen the news today?" she asked.

"No, but given my fluency in Turkish, or rather lack thereof, I doubt I would have benefited from the experience."

"Well, it's international news, so every English station or website is carrying the story," she replied. "This morning, there were two separate bombings on the Turkish Mediterranean coast targeting foreigners. I never heard how many were killed, but the footage was gruesome. Then, the same group blew up the Levent market, a small square north of Beşiktaş known as a banking complex in the commercial district. The whole country is on high alert."

"Holy smoke. That explains the empty streets and solemn faces," he said

"No, it just explains the empty streets. A smile is a rarity in this city at any time."

There was no arguing with that observation, one he had made himself on several occasions. Outside of the tourist centers, Turks were quiet and somber in public. The elevator stopped, and the doors opened. He had expected to step out into the restaurant, but saw only a sign pointing up another flight of stairs. They began ascending the stairs.

"Has anyone claimed responsibility?" he asked.

"Apparently, it was a radical Muslim group called Hizbullah, not the one in Lebanon but a separate Turkish group. The newscasts gave very little information. It was mostly images of buildings reduced to rubble with first responders looking for survivors. CNN was speculating that it was retaliation for some skin-head attacks in Germany almost two months ago."

"I remember reading about that," he said.

They had arrived at the door to the restaurant. A waiter greeted them at the door. Except for a group of what looked like tourists from Northern Europe, the place was empty. Gary pointed to the empty side of the room and the waiter took them to a table beside one of the small arched windows. He handed them each a menu and left them to look it over.

"What a view," exclaimed Angela, looking out the window.

It was a beautiful, cloudless day. The sea looked like brilliant diamonds had been strewn on the surface. Across the water, they could see the magnificent Blue Mosque, the Hagia Sophia and then the Sea of Marmara beyond that.

"Wow! This is magnificent. No wonder emperors and sultans chose this piece of real estate as the capital of government. Are you hungry? A friend told me that the kebab and the *kokoreç* were both very good."

"*Kokoreç*? What is that?" she asked.

"It probably doesn't sound appetizing, but it is surprisingly good. It's roasted sheep intestines."

"I'll have the kebab," she replied, wrinkling her nose, "with maybe one of those yogurt drinks."

"*Ayran?*" he asked.

"Yeah, *ayran.*"

He waved for the waiter. "We'd like two of the lamb kebabs, a salad and two *ayrans.*"

The waiter took the menus, and Gary looked across the table at Angela.

"Have you learned anything about your sister?"

She closed her eyes and took a deep breath. When she opened them again, they were steely with resolve and smoldering with anger.

"Yes, I won't bore you with all of the details. I found a hotel, don't ask me how, filled with women from Eastern Europe and a couple of Romanians. I showed them the picture of my sister and asked if they had seen her. They hadn't. However, when I told them the story of how she had come to Istanbul in response to an Internet ad for a nanny with a Turkish family, one of the ladies, who looked to be about thirty-five, though for all I know and everything she's gone through, might be twenty-five, said this was one of the most common ways to get fresh girls.

"She said she knew the man who ran the outfit. I asked if she could take me to him and she looked at me like I was out of my mind. You won't believe what she told me. She said, 'If you don't want to end up working with your sister, you better get on the next flight out of this country. If they even hear that you are asking around, they'll come after you. Consider her dead. You'll never find her and even if you do, she'll never recover from the shame.' And then with the saddest, most cynical, most broken look I've ever seen, she said, 'Take it from someone with experience. She doesn't even want to be found anymore.' I told her I would go to the police. She burst out laughing like I had just told the funniest joke in the world."

Angela's eyes became teary. She fought to keep her emotions in check.

"I'm not giving up, Gary. I don't care if they kill me. I'm not going to give up on my sister."

Now the tears were streaming down her face. She turned to the window in an attempt to hide them. Gary sat there for a minute, unsure of how to proceed and overwhelmed by the sense of tragedy. *Is that what life is, one long complicated tragedy with a few moments of comic relief thrown in to keep it from getting too monotonous?* He had just gone through a time in his own life when he had thought the same. He was over it now, but it didn't mean there weren't moments that made him think that maybe Job had been justified in wishing that he had been stillborn. *But, it's not just pain,* he thought. *Many have experienced pain and borne it gladly. No, this is the voice of senseless pain. A pain that has no apparent purpose, this is what drives people to despair.*

"Angela, I've got a friend who may be able to help you," said Gary.

"I did manage to get the man's name from the lady. I just don't know what to do now. I'm determined to find her, but…" Her voice trailed off.

"Give me the name and a picture of your sister. I'll see what I can do," said Gary reassuringly.

"Sure," she said rummaging in her purse. "The man's name is Elvir Zubak. That's all I know. Here is a picture of Bianca and I taken a year before she disappeared. She is a natural brunette but had her hair dyed blonde in this picture."

Gary took it from her hand and looked it at carefully. Except for the hair, she looked exactly like Angela. They could have been twins.

"So, where have you been since we talked last? You didn't answer my messages for days. Esra says you haven't showed up for class. You just disappeared."

"It's a long story, and I'm not sure how much of it I can share right now. Can we talk about it later?"

"Sure," she shrugged her shoulders. "I was just curious. I didn't mean to pry."

Gary saw the waiter coming with the food and smiled at him. They both sat in silence while the kebab, salad and drinks were set before them.

"Is there anything else I can do for you, sir?" asked the waiter.

"No, this looks great, thanks," said Gilbert.

For the first couple of minutes neither of them talked. The smell of roasted tomatoes, peppers, eggplant and lamb was mouth-watering. The salad was his favorite. Plain and simple, it was made of minced green onion, fresh diced tomatoes and cucumbers, parsley, olive oil and lemon juice. He noticed that Angela seemed to have quite a healthy appetite and wondered if she were running out of money. She was the one that broke the silence.

"Did you know that Isaac Rousseau, Jean Jacques Rousseau's father, worked for the Ottoman Sultan Ahmed III as a watchmaker from 1705 to 1711?"

"Nope, I had no idea,"

"He actually lived in this very tower," she continued. "It's sort of scary to think that the sperm donor who brought the advent of Socialism and eventually Communism into the world, worked here in a Muslim country as a watchmaker for the sultan."

Gary almost coughed on his food.

"Sperm donor?" he asked. "Is that how you view fathers?"

"Not generally, but the man abandoned his son. That's what I call a sperm donor. It probably explains why Jean Jacques did the same thing to all of his children, but from birth. Anyway, Rousseau came because he was a Protestant and the Ottomans were more tolerant of Protestants than the Catholics were. What can explain this?"

Gary was a bit taken aback by the turn the conversation had taken.

"I'm not sure what you mean or where this is going."

"I don't know where it will take us either," replied Angela with a smile. "Why don't we find out?"

Gary loved her playful attitude and intellectual curiosity. It had made their English lessons more interesting too.

"Very well," he said. "We shall take this path you have proposed, but first you must answer me a question. Your English is already excellent. Why did you sign up for private lessons with our group?"

"I just wanted the social interaction, I guess. I figured the practice would keep me from forgetting what I worked so hard to learn. Plus, I saw that the teacher was a native English speaker. We had very few of those in Romania."

"I see," replied Gary. "I'm not sure I know the answer to your question, but I'll take a stab at it."

"Excuse me?" she said with that quizzical look and tone he had come to realize from their English class meant she didn't understand something.

"Sorry. That's an idiom. It means 'I'll give it a try.'"

"But, I thought 'try' was a verb. How can you 'give a try'? That sounds ungrammatical," she protested.

Gary chuckled. "Yeah, I see what you mean, but 'give it a try' is a colloquial term that simply means 'try'. It might imply some uncertainty on the speaker's part about the likelihood of success. It must be tough learning English with all these idioms and stuff."

"Why is that?"

"Well, they say it's the richest language in the world."

She shook her head and rolled her eyes.

"You Americans are all alike. You think other languages cannot match English for richness? That is absurd. I speak fluent Russian and French, decent English and, of course, Romanian. Every language is an ocean of culture and meaning onto itself. They are all complex and profound enough to keep you learning a lifetime."

"Listen, I ..."

She raised her hand to cut him off.

"No, you listen to me for a second. In my first year of high school, I was given a scholarship to go to a university prep school. It was supposed to be very strong in the sciences. We were poor, so my father encouraged me to attend. The science instructors were very good, and the people were very kind. Still, it didn't take long for me to realize that it was a school of indoctrination. I did some research and found out that the organization behind the schools was a Turkish Muslim missionary enterprise. At the time, I think they had four schools in Romania. They wooed poor students with scholarships, won their hearts with kindness and then brainwashed them with Arab imperialism. They said we had to pray in Arabic, as if God couldn't understand my perfect Romanian.

"To be quite honest, it scared me. I finished that year and then went back to the Romanian school. My father's an atheist, but, at that time, I was beginning to explore the idea that maybe there was an intelligent being with creativity and emotions that made the rest of us intelligent and emotional as well. It made sense to me. In fact, it still does. But, all of their religious mumbo jumbo about Arabic being the most perfect human language nauseated me. It was no different than the Catholic Church insisting that mass be said in Latin."

"Look, I wasn't trying to say English was absolutely the hardest or richest language."

"But," she teased, "That is what you said. To plagiarize and adapt a phrase from the man you call the Bard, 'a rose by any other name will smell as sweet, but no one will know what the hell you are talking about.' If you had said, 'it must be tough learning another language,' then I wouldn't have thought you were a cultural imperialist, an exceptionalist who held the view that English was difficult to learn because it was richer than other languages."

"*Touché.* My sincerest apologies," said Gary feigning obeisance. "I am no cultural imperialist. One day, you will see that, I hope."

"Make sure I do," she rejoined with a smile. "Now, if you will get back to the original question."

"What was it?"

"Why the Ottoman Turks were more tolerant of Protestants."

"Hmmm," said Gary, trying to gather his thoughts, "I suppose the Ottomans did not view Protestants as a threat because they comprised less than one percent of the population of the empire. Besides, the Protestants were at odds with the Catholics, and since the armies that marched against the Turks were almost always Catholic, they probably figured that the enemy of their enemy was their friend."

"That's a fair assessment."

"What does it have to do with Rousseau's father having lived in this tower?" asked Gary.

"Well, as I said, I went through a phase when I explored religion. One of the things I read was Rousseau. You know he's viewed by many as the father of socialist thought even though he was a fairly religious man. In today's world that would be a contradiction of sorts. Do you know anything about his religious views?"

"Didn't he say, 'A State has never been founded without religion serving as its base'?"

Angela sat back with a look of mock astonishment on her face.

"I'd heard you Americans were so busy making money and policing the world that you had no time for philosophy. This is a pleasant surprise. Do you think Rousseau was right?"

"You could be asking me two questions here," replied Gary carefully. "The first one would be whether or not that statement is an accurate reflection of history, in which case I would say that up until the modern era it has been true by and large. In antiquity, every nation has had its own official religion, from the Egyptian and Sumerian pantheons, to those of the Romans and Greeks. In Athens, it was forbidden to introduce strange gods. Socrates was condemned to death for essentially doing just this. Strange religions were frowned upon and those who adhered to them were persecuted and viewed as traitors. Many nations of antiquity proclaimed their kings and emperors to be demi-gods that demanded worship. Religion pays serious political dividends. A fact I'm sure you're aware of."

"Rousseau apparently agreed," she said, chasing the kebab around her plate with her knife. "And, until the modern era, this view was practically universal. Rousseau understood the purpose of the Spanish Inquisition. It was to prevent religious division, not because that was bad in and of itself but because it invariably caused the dissenters to seek a new state where they were in power. The Spanish had just concluded a 700-year war to reclaim their country from the Muslims. When the Muslims refused to assimilate, they were forced to convert to Catholicism, but the priests were never confident the conversions were genuine. And, why should they be? Faith cannot be coerced. So, to resolve the dilemma of their own making, they instituted the Inquisition to smoke out the heretics. That is just pious, or rather impious, politics, not religion. Anyway... What is the second interpretation of the question?" she asked.

Gary took a sip of *ayran*.

"Whether or not Rousseau's statement is *true*. It may be reality, but that does not make it truth. Just because it has always been that way does not mean that it should be."

Angela cocked her head to the side and screwed up her face.

"That is stating the obvious if I ever heard it."

"True again. But, if it's so obvious, how have so many people been duped by it for so long?" he rejoined.

"Simple," she said. "Classic misdirection. The rulers never actually say that religion and politics are related, they constantly pretend that their religious zeal is sacred and sincere, and hence they are duty-bound to squash dissent."

"That is an empirical fact," said Gary, "But, it only happened because these societies violated Rousseau's principle prohibiting theological intolerance. He said that intolerance of different faiths turned the king into the priest's executioner, and so all faiths must be tolerated."

Angela shook her head sadly.

"Yes, but in his view religion is neither true nor false; it is merely functional. A religion's moral code keeps peace in the community and makes good citizens to line the pockets of their oppressors. It is no wonder Marx embraced atheism and rejected religion."

"Rousseau was a pragmatist," offered Gary. "Every religion makes different claims about religious truth. Muslims say Mohammed is the last prophet and Catholics say the Pope is infallible. These details were irrelevant to Rousseau because the important thing was a moral code to provide the cement which holds society together. It is there to ensure a certain kind of behavior, behavior that makes it easier for a ruler to maintain peace and control his subjects. Rousseau spoke quite highly of Islam. He said that combining the office of priest and politician was more efficient because it avoided the complicated relationship the kings of Europe always had with the Church."

Gary took another bite of kebab.

"I've concluded that Rousseau is right," said Angela wearily. "So, I've given up on god."

She tore off a piece of bread and wrapped a chunk of lamb in it.

"I've been where you are, but I eventually reached a different conclusion."

"How could your conclusion be any different? The facts are the same. Religion is a sham. You have articulated the reasons yourself," she retorted.

"Yes. But that is assuming God and religion are synonymous. What if they are diametrically opposed to each other?"

"Every priest is on his way to hell," she said with a smile.

"And maybe they are," Gary sighed. "Maybe they are."

"That's it?"

"That's what?"

"You say you've reached a different conclusion. I want to know why."

"Have you ever read the New Testament?" he asked

"Yes," she replied. "It was a few years back, but I read it through a couple of times."

Gary sat up straighter in his chair, took a deep breath and in the most solemn and somber voice he could muster, said,

"Then, like Socrates of old, allow me to introduce to your Athenian mind a 'new god.' And, prepare the hemlock."

"That would be much too humane for your crime," she said with a mischievous twinkle in her eyes.

"Let's do it through a series of questions then, just like Socrates. Do you remember what Jesus did when the crowd tried to make him king?"

"Yes, he refused."

"Exactly. Do you remember what he said to Pilate when he was asked whether or not he was King of the Jews?"

"Something like 'my kingdom is not of the earth.'"

"Right again. Do you remember the people he was most angry with?"

"Wasn't it the religious people?"

"You're three for three."

"You're asking questions any junior high student might know."

"Now, for the last and final question, how did he summarize the entire moral code?"

She thought for a moment. "You mean the golden rule?"

"Not exactly. I was actually thinking of something else he said, a quote from the Old Testament. 'Love God and love your neighbor as yourself. All the Law and the Prophets hang on these two commandments.'"

"Right. I remember that," she answered.

"So with these statements as a backdrop, tell me, can we conclude that the kingdom of God he described was apolitical, other-worldly and characterized by love?"

"Well, as a student of history, that is not the picture I get from the pogroms, inquisitions, crusades, jihads, persecutions, witch-hunts, massacres, conquests and cultural imperialism practiced in the name of religion.

"That's my point," continued Gary. "Rousseau's theological tolerance is a pipe dream because, unlike their rulers, the masses must actually believe their religion is true if it is going to work its magic. But, actually believing you are right and everyone else is evil breeds intolerance of the 'damned' heathen who won't accept your dogma."

"Which, of course," she said triumphantly, "is why later socialists rejected religion altogether as unnecessary for society. After all, it's not true. It's only functional. It leads to intolerance and we can accomplish the same function without it."

"Really?" Gary replied, "You think there is any ideology that does not end up being the double-edged sword? Ideology only works if people believe it is true and once they do, all other ideologies are wrong and worthy of persecution. Communism was a religion too, and you know how many millions died for it."

His voice trailed off. They were both silent for a moment. Finally, Gary finished his thought.

"Most ideologues are as dogmatic as any crusader or jihadist ever was. They are often willing to kill if it will further their faith."

"So, what is your new god Socrates?" she asked sarcastically.

"You may pour the hemlock on the ground, Athenian. I bring you no new god. I only ask that you consider the faith of Abraham, a faith that predates Judaism, Christianity and Islam. In the Middle East, it might be called *hanif.* What if our ideology, our religion, were to love our neighbors as ourselves, to love our enemies, to pray for them and not curse them? What if religion, as it is generally expressed, has nothing to do with God at all? Jesus doesn't seem to preach it and God doesn't need it. We have only ourselves to blame if we allow God to be used as 'social cement.'"

The cell phone in his pocket rang.

46

ANKARA   Yusuf breathed a sigh of relief as he watched his wife Leyla approaching the office. Murat saw her coming too and ushered the junior officers towards the door. She was standing there when he opened it.

"It's good to see you, Leyla. We were just leaving."

Leyla stepped inside, followed by a security guard who had been carrying her bags. Yusuf nodded his thanks, and the man shut the door as he left. Yusuf kissed Leyla on both cheeks, took her by the arm and led her to a chair in front of his desk.

"Yusuf, are you going to tell me what is going on?"

Yusuf had been working on how to break the news to her for the last hour, but had found no way to soften the blow.

"Darling, I think you could be in danger. You know about the bombings. What you don't know is that the suicide bomber in the Istanbul blast left a message regarding some evidence we found in the Akçakoca raid last week when Bekir Kaya escaped. His group has claimed responsibility, and they have delivered a thinly veiled message demanding this evidence be returned. We were afraid that they might do something rash."

"You mean kidnap or kill me to pressure you," she stated flatly. She was direct and to the point as always.

"We're just taking precautions, darling. We have no indication they're planning something like that."

She closed her eyes and without opening them asked, "Did you have any idea these terrorist attacks were being planned?"

"No, we didn't"

"That's comforting," she responded wryly. "What's the evidence he wants returned?"

"It's blackmail material, videos of politicians with prostitutes."

"Then give it back to them with instructions on how to get the maximum mileage out of the damned things. What do you care if these politicians get sacked and these images get splashed on the front pages?" She was clearly getting angry now. "Serves them right."

285

"That's the problem," replied Yusuf. "They'll never make it to the newspaper. The politicians will sell out to protect their reputation, and our government will be even more compromised than it already is."

The phone on his desk beeped. It was Selda. He pushed the button to put her on speaker.

"I'm sorry to interrupt," she said, "but Murat says you need to take this call. The man asked for you by name and said you would want to speak with him."

"Who is it?" asked Yusuf. The fatigue in his voice was obvious. Leyla could tell the stress from his job was wearing him down.

"He said he was Pharaoh's tailor."

Yusuf's eyes opened wide.

"Patch him through and trace this call." He put his hand on the phone. "Sorry, darling, but I have to take this." He picked up the receiver. "This is Yusuf Demir. Who am I speaking with?"

The voice on the other end was a deep baritone, smooth as honey. He sounded like a DJ.

"Captain Demir. Thank you for taking my call. I understand you are having a busy day, so I'll get right to the point."

"Please do."

"Your wife looked a bit frazzled when she arrived at the police station eight minutes ago. I'm surprised her security detail consisted of only two men with no more than thirty rounds of ammunition. I hope you have this on speaker and she's listening. She's a very pretty lady. I would hate for anything to happen to her."

"Listen," said Yusuf calmly, "I don't respond very well to threats. My psychiatrist says it is an overdeveloped alpha-male syndrome. In fact, I have stopped seeing the sorry bastard because he wants to have me committed every time I go in. He says the perverse pleasure I derive from watching low-life scum like you in the interrogation chair spitting teeth on the floor is abnormal."

"Captain Demir, that's hardly the sort of tactful diplomacy I was expecting from you. I was expecting you to say something like, 'Thank you for making this phone call before taking out my wife. What can I do for you?' But, no, you have started believing your own macho bullshit. That's very dangerous, Captain."

"What do you want?" said Yusuf curtly, cutting him off.

"You know what we want. In fact, we both want the same thing, but we have different ways of going about it. You hate corruption and smartass politicians pimping the country out to the highest bidder. You want the whores out of office and so do we. You want honorable leadership. That is what we want. So I guess you were happy to hear about the little accident in Czechoslovakia earlier today."

"No one has claimed responsibility for that assassination yet."

"Well, consider this our official announcement then. It's been a busy day for us too. We probably overlooked the press release for that one. I want the tapes you took out of the tunnel, a careless oversight by one of my lieutenants."

"Bekir? Am I speaking with Bekir Kaya?"

"My dear Captain, excuse my breach of etiquette. I thought that after all these years of cat-and-mouse, a formal introduction would be superfluous, maybe even insulting."

Leyla could see the veins in her husband's neck bulging.

Bekir continued, "Captain, have one of your men drop the tapes off at the location I am about to relay. Please get a pen and paper. I'm only going to give these directions once."

Yusuf scrambled to find a pen among the jumble of papers on his desk. His wife opened her purse and handed him a pen before he could locate one.

"Okay, shoot."

"How appropriate. I appreciate that coming from a policeman. Have your man take highway E90 towards Polatlı. He should take the exit for Macun Village. Exactly four miles from the exit, he will see a white sedan. Have him put the tapes in the backseat. No tracking devices. No tricks. No choppers either unless you want to see them shot down. If I don't have those tapes exactly when the sun goes down, you will not live to see the New Year, and I couldn't even speculate about what might happen to Leyla. She's definitely too pretty to kill, but I'm sure someone would find her useful."

"You son of a bitch, you better hope…" Yusuf stopped. The line was dead.

Yusuf looked over at Leyla. She spoke first.

"Don't give the bastard anything."

Yusuf only swore under his breath. He expected this from her. After all, it was her spirit and character that had attracted him to her in the first place. She was a fighter. He closed his eyes in concentration, thinking about the practical consequences of what he was facing.

"Darling, I think you should go down to the cafeteria while Murat and I decide what to do here."

"If you want to go to the cafeteria, go ahead. I'm not going anywhere. If this S.O.B. wants to use me as leverage against you, I'm damned sure going to be here to make sure he fails."

Yusuf saw through the glass window that Murat was standing outside the office door and waved him on in.

"Did we get a trace on the call?" he asked.

Murat shook his head. "No, I'm afraid not. It looks like he was using VoIP. If it had been a satphone, we could have gotten pretty close."

"He made it sound like he saw Leyla walk into the police station," snorted Yusuf. "If he is in this city… Damn it, Murat. How did we let this guy get away?"

287

"Intimidation, sir. He probably had a lackey standing outside the station somewhere who called or messaged when Leyla arrived, and then he just said that stuff to scare us."

"Maybe so," said Yusuf wearily. "He certainly picked a hell of a spot for a drop. That area is about as barren as it gets. There isn't a tree for miles. You can bet he has his people in place already, so there is no way we could get an intercept team in there to set up an ambush."

"Sir, what good would it do? If he doesn't get those tapes, then he's going to put his plan in motion, and he has all the time in the world. There is no way the department could protect you. We could get the boys over in intelligence to lend us some satellite capacity and track the car after the drop-off, but again, what would be the point?"

Yusuf felt just like he had in Akçakoca a little over a week earlier. Trapped. Outmaneuvered. Powerless.

"How did this deranged, jinn-struck bastard find out that I was leading the raid in Akçakoca anyway? I know he didn't send the message based on a guess. He has somebody on the inside."

"Captain, we have been battling these Islamists since the Republic was founded. One variety is currently in power. Of course, they have people on the inside. The reports we file pass through several offices."

"Do we have copies of the tapes made?" asked Yusuf shaking his head in resignation.

"I don't think so," replied Murat.

"Do it now. Don't let anyone know, not even Selda," ordered Yusuf.

"Wait just a minute," exclaimed Leyla, jumping up from her chair. "You are not seriously considering giving these tapes back to this terrorist, are you?"

"No, I'm not considering it. I'm doing it. I'm not going to put your life in danger. These guys play rough. I'm not taking chances where you are concerned."

"I'd gladly die to see this man and his organization destroyed. You know that," she said vehemently. "Did Atatürk beat the English, the French, the Italians, the Greeks, and set up a modern republic replacing sharia law with a constitution just so these self-proclaimed saviors could systematically dismantle it? I am not going to let you compromise your principles out of fear and a desire to protect me."

Yusuf walked over to Leyla and tried to give her a hug. She pushed him away.

"Don't do this, Yusuf. You'll never forgive yourself. It's the slippery slope you always talk about. No one ever claws their way back to the moral high ground. Don't give it up!"

"Darling, life requires compromise. This is one of those times, but this is not the kind of compromise you think it is, so stop worrying. Two can play this sick game. You were right when you said earlier that every single one of these politicians needs to be sacked. But, it doesn't have to be by breaking a news story. I'm going to give Bekir his little private collection of pornography back. He'll have no reason to come after us. Then, I'm going to use the tapes to discreetly force every single one of these sleazy parasites to resign. Since they aren't honorable enough to commit *hara-kiri*, we'll force their hand. Then, Bekir's tapes will no longer pose a danger to the political process. Those politicians will be doing something else for a living, no doubt just as dishonorable, but we'll deal with that later. I'll out them through a proxy, so we are not directly connected. Maybe by the time he realizes we've gotten the jump on him, his sins will have caught up with him, preferably in the form of a lead bullet."

Murat smiled. "Damn it, Chief. I love working with you."

ISTANBUL   Zeki stopped in front of a locker in the bus-station and fished a key from his pocket. He was still wearing the funny, wide-brimmed hat he had bought in Dallas to hide his face from security cameras. He looked more like a Japanese tourist than a Turk. He opened the steel door, removed a small bag and dumped the contents onto his suitcase. Six smart phones tumbled out – three red and three black. He put the three red ones in his pocket and replaced the others. Then, he took the phone he had used in England out of his suitcase and put it in the bag as well. He was sure to need it again.

Next, he removed a small metal box from the back of the locker, inserted the key and laid his jacket over the top of it so no one could see the contents as he opened the lid. He pulled out a Zigana 9 mm and two fifteen-round clips, wrapped them in the jacket and then closed the lid and returned the box to the locker.

He turned to look for Gwyn. She was sitting on a bench about fifty yards away in the cavernous bus station. He walked over and sat down beside her.

"Are you ready? I'm sorry for having to drag you on this detour for a phone."

"I understand," she replied. "What will we do now?"

He didn't even look up from his Blackberry.

"I'm sending Gilbert a message, telling him we've arrived. Then, I need to make a couple of phone calls. One is a friend of mine in the government. Not that our government always inspires a lot of trust, but this man is as good as gold. I don't know what your brother has in mind, but help from a reliable person in uniform may come in handy. Besides, I want to find out about the bombings that happened today."

Gwyn just nodded and watched him finish typing the message to her brother.

289

Gilbert heard the electronic blip that said he had a new email. The message was short and to the point.

> WE'RE HERE. WE'LL MEET YOU AT THE HOUSE CAFÉ ON ISTIKLAL BOULEVARD IN ONE HOUR AND STAY IN A FLAT NEARBY. BRING ALL YOUR STUFF.

He reached for the phone and called Gary.

"Hey, Gwyn is here. Zeki said to meet at the House Café on Istiklal Boulevard in one hour. You're going to have to tell me how to get there."

"Are you able to track the canister?"

"Yeah, we've got you on Matt's Blackberry. It says you're in Galata Tower."

"Well, I'm glad it's working. That means you should be able to find the House Café easy enough. I'll be there with the canister."

"Yeah, but give me directions anyway. I could still get lost."

"It's easy. I mean the streets are crooked as a barrel of snakes, but if you say *Istiklal* to anyone, they'll point you in the right direction. Then, stay on Istiklal Boulevard and have someone point you towards Taksim. You'll know you're on the right street if you see the Galatasaray High School. You can't miss it. On your right, you'll see a piece of modern art that looks like either a battery of mortars or the pipes of a church organ. I'll let you be the judge. The House Café will be on your right. I'm just a ten-minute walk from there myself. You can make it in forty minutes from the hotel. "

"Great. We'll bring your bag."

✦

ANKARA Murat had finished copying the CDs and was putting the originals in a black bag.

"I'll have unmarked cars no more than three miles from you in any direction. If there is any indication of trouble at all, you call immediately and abort. We'll be all over these guys."

Murat just shrugged. "We both know that's not going to happen. They want the CDs. They don't care about the messenger."

"I hope you're right," replied Yusuf, "You know that I wouldn't normally send you at all, but I don't want this getting out. If our plan to quietly out these low-life bastards is going to work, secrecy is crucial."

Murat smiled as he opened the door to leave. "Don't worry about me," he said over his shoulder. "I'll be fine."

Yusuf's cell phone rang as the door closed.

"Hello."

"Hello, friend."

Yusuf recognized Zeki's voice immediately.

"I was wondering when you were going to call."

"I told you I'd call as soon as I had a chance. Sounds like the natives are restless, and you have your hands full."

"That would be an understatement," sighed Yusuf wearily.

"I figure you'll be needed at the scene of the crime in Istanbul. Pretty messy down there. You should pick up some reading material for Leyla while you are in town. I hear there is a new book out about Atatürk that she would enjoy."

"I'll be sure to look for it," replied Yusuf.

"What time does the fast end tonight?" asked Zeki.

"Sunset is at 7:48," he replied.

Zeki cleared his throat. "Look, I don't want to keep you. I know things are crazy right now. Give my love to Leyla and don't forget to duck when you hear shooting,"

"Like that would do any good," replied Yusuf dryly.

"Well, if you hear the shot, you know they missed. The next one may not."

The line went dead. He was always like that. Short and sweet. No wasted words. *So, Zeki is back and wants to meet at the Atatürk Library in Istanbul. He knows how frantic our department is right now so this must be big.*

47

İSTANBUL   Gilbert walked along the left side of Istiklal Boulevard so he could see the shops on the right side of the street. He saw Gwyn, Zeki and Gary before he saw the House Café sign. Gwyn was the first to spot him. She waved excitedly, but her enthusiasm became more subdued when she saw Matt walking behind him.

"Gil, I can't tell you how good it is to see you."

She wrapped her arms around his neck and wouldn't let go. He could feel the tension in her body.

"It's great to see you too. But what in the world did you do to your hair?"

She grimaced. "I had to travel as a man. Zeki only carries men's passports. Logical, given his gender, but not so convenient when a female decides to tag along."

"Well, I think it looks fine," said Gilbert. "It's weird to be here in Istanbul. All I can think about is Dad dragging us to every old Byzantine monument he could find, through the underground cisterns, to the hippodrome, the old churches and constantly lamenting that so little had been preserved."

"Yeah, I remember." Gwyn turned to Matt and stuck out her hand. "Thanks for coming. We all appreciate it."

Matt gently took the hand she offered and squeezed it slightly. He felt awkward and wondered if it showed. She was so beautiful, so elegant, so feminine. Seeing her again was more painful that he had thought it would be.

"You know I would do anything to help the O'Brien clan. It's nice to see you again."

Zeki interrupted. "I hate to cut reunions short. It is very un-Turkish, but we have a lot to talk about, and I have another meeting tonight."

He led the way and everyone followed. Gwyn walked beside him. She felt safe there. He felt like an uncle. Zeki took them down several narrow streets with buildings towering up on either side. It was clearly an older part of town. Gilbert was careful to note the route. A right, a left, another right and then two lefts. Ten minutes later, they were climbing the stairs in a building that didn't

292

have an elevator. *The place needs a lot more than a paint job*, thought Gwyn, *but that wouldn't be a bad place to start.* They climbed to the third floor, Zeki removed a key from his pocket, opened the door and ushered everyone in, reminding them to take off their shoes.

Gwyn looked around the flat. It wasn't impressive. The place was clearly unoccupied. It smelled musty and needed airing out. She walked over and opened the curtains to let in some light. Sunlight streamed into the room, transforming the cloud of dust into a golden mist in the middle of the room. The windows hadn't been washed in ages either. Not that there was anything to see. Only another drab building across the street. Zeki immediately crossed the room and closed the curtains.

"Sorry," he said, "But, I think it's best if we keep those closed." Then, he walked back to the door and locked it. Gwyn introduced Zeki to Matt, and then he proceeded to show them around the place.

"First, let me say I'm sorry that I couldn't arrange better accommodations. This belongs to a good friend. There are three bedrooms and some of you can sleep here in the living room if necessary. There is only one toilet and it is the old Turkish style, so I hope you're comfortable squatting. My friend said there's no hot water. Hopefully, you all had showers at your hotel. I promise it'll be ready in the morning.

"Now, if no one minds, I'd like to get down to business right away. There is a wireless connection here. The password is 73311337. I'll have to leave about thirty minutes before the sun sets."

Everyone nodded in agreement and he pointed towards the living room. It was furnished with elegant, though somewhat dated, Ottoman style divans.

"If you don't mind," said Zeki. "I'll just put some tea on," and with that he disappeared into the kitchen.

Everyone sat down. Gary opened his bag, took out his laptop and started looking for a place to plug it in. Matt purposefully avoided eye contact with Gwyn and everyone could feel the tension in the room. Gwyn broke the silence.

"Gil, have you heard anything about Ginger and the kids?"

"In fact, I have," he replied. "I got an email from Kiyomi right before you called. On her morning run, she received a call on her cell. The caller said she needed to contact me and have me provide a phone number where they could reach me if I wanted to ever see my family again. They said they would call back in two hours. That was an hour ago."

He stopped not sure if his voice was going to crack or not.

"Oh my gosh," exclaimed Gwyn. "What are you going to do?"

"Nothing," said Zeki, walking through the door with a tray filled with teacups, sugar and spoons. "At least, that is my recommendation. What did Kiyomi tell them?"

Gilbert took a deep breath. "She told them that she didn't know where I was and that I wasn't answering my cell phone."

"Well, they know that's true," said Gary.

"Until they've spoken with you, I'm sure your family will be safe," said Zeki reassuringly as he sat the tray down on the long coffee table in the middle of the room.

"Sooner or later, we are going to have to give them a number though," said Gwyn. The frustration in her voice was intense.

"I know," said Gilbert. "I'm working on it. I'm not sure we want them to know that we are in Istanbul right now, which means setting up a proxy call of some kind."

"Have you thought about the exchange?" asked Zeki.

"Yes, I have, but you know that they're going to set the terms. They'll pick the spot. There is not much we can do in the way of preparation, and I will not endanger my family by involving the authorities."

"Of course not. I suspect they might have people on the inside anyway."

"What!" exclaimed Gwyn, "Are you guys out of your mind? We have to help Ginger now! I can't believe she has been in the hands of these terrorists for three days already!" Her voice was trembling. "Who knows what they are going through? Let's give them this document and get this over with."

Everyone in the room lowered their eyes. She looked around the room in desperation.

"What are we waiting for?"

It was Gary who summoned the courage to speak first.

"Gwyn, that thought is torturing us as much as it is you. But it may not be that easy."

"What do you mean?" she asked.

Zeki leaned forward in his chair.

"I think everyone is concerned about there being a trap of some kind. We know that this document is very important to them. They've been ruthless in their pursuit of it. They killed your father. They killed Haluk Bayram. They tried to kill you and were waiting for me in my room. I can think of no reason why they would allow you and your family to live after they have obtained it. For all they know, you have copies, which may not be as damning as an original, but again there's just no reason to let you walk away. We need some leverage."

Gilbert's jaw hardened again. "That is the elephant in the room, Gwyn. There is no reason to dance around it when it's staring us in the face. We will avoid contacting them and try to get something we can use against them. None of us want to be sitting here having an academic discussion about old books, secret societies or 16th century European history, but the more we know, the better equipped we'll be."

294

"Right." said Zeki. "Let's get down to business. You and your brother were going to go over everything Gwyn found about the G.O.B."

"We did, but I should let Gary tell you about it. I think he understands it better, strangely enough."

Gwyn looked at her older brother as if to say, *What was that supposed to mean?*

Gary turned to Zeki.

"I want to say once again that we owe you a tremendous debt. I know our father thought highly of you. The last thing I would ever want to do is offend you. Ten lifetimes would not be enough to repay you for saving Gwyn."

He paused, unsure how to continue. Zeki came to his rescue.

"Son, don't worry about offending me. You may find it more difficult than you imagine."

"Let me be frank. I know you are a Muslim and, well, most of what we learned about the Gospel of Barnabas, strangely enough, seems to be related to Islam and I..."

"Truth is what takes the chains off of our minds. It's not something to be feared. Please, just tell us what you learned," prompted Zeki.

Gary turned to Matt.

"We are working on two assumptions. The first is that the letter is related to an effort to destroy every trace of the Gospel of Barnabas. The second is that it ordered the assassination of George Sale. Zeki and Gwyn realized that the document my father found was in two parts. The order was written in Otto-man Turkish. Underneath that is a Spanish translation written with Arabic characters and that makes the case for Morisco involvement practically water-tight. I think for that reason Zeki and Gwyn should tell us what they learned about the Moriscos. It might confirm some of my own conclusions. Besides, Zeki has an appointment tonight, so why don't you guys start?"

Zeki was struck by the young man's desire to show him honor and defer-ence.

"Very well," replied Zeki. "The Spanish completed the *Reconquesta* in 1492 when they conquered Granada, the last Muslim stronghold on the Iberian Pen-insula. They signed a treaty with the Muslims promising them the same free-dom of religion and culture Muslims in other parts of Spain had enjoyed up until that time. However, the Spanish violated the terms of the agreement on several occasions and, just seven years later, the Muslims of Granada rebelled. They didn't stand a chance against the rising super-power of Europe, so when Granada was subdued again in 1501, the Spanish issued an ultimatum to the residents of this province: convert or leave. By 1526, this was applied to every Muslim living anywhere in Spain. Deportation in an agricultural society based on land ownership was essentially the same as condemning them to poverty and slavery somewhere else. Most pretended to convert, but secretly continued to practice their Islamic faith.

"I don't want to bore you with the details. Spanish tolerance wavered over the years with Muslims enjoying greater or less freedom under different rulers and in different parts of the country, but in 1567, Phillip II prohibited Muslim names, Muslim dress, the speaking of Arabic and decreed that the children would be educated by priests. This led to a second rebellion in the Alpujarras Mountains, which was only put down with much difficulty two years later. Eventually, the Spanish decided in 1609 to implement their own 'Final Solution', which was to deport roughly three hundred thousand Moriscos. The authorities believed they would never assimilate because in their words, 'Moriscos were shifty and unreliable, refused to integrate into Spanish society and given to treason.'"

"So much for loving your enemy," said Gary dryly.

"You mean, so much for the multi-cultural society," retorted Matt. "I have studied this period as well. I may be a bit fuzzy on the details, but you have to remember that the Spanish fought a seven-hundred-year war to reclaim their country. The Moriscos not only took up arms in open rebellion, they also conspired with the Dutch, the Turks and even the French Huguenots. All of these groups opposed the Catholic Hapsburgs ruling from Spain. In fact, there was even intrigue between the Moriscos and the English under Elizabeth.

"Queen Elizabeth ignored a Papal ban on commerce with the Muslims, sold lead and tin to the Turks for cannons and carried on a brisk trade with Morocco. She also courted the idea of assisting the Moriscos if they rebelled against the Spanish Crown. None of these plans for a general uprising with foreign support ever materialized, but you can hardly blame the Spanish for regarding the Moriscos as a dangerous 'fifth column,' ripe for exploitation by foreign powers. The Ottomans were still a dominant world power, and the Moriscos were petitioning them for help. Sounds like a national security threat to me."

Matt suddenly realized that everyone in the room was looking at Zeki. Matt stopped, obviously assessing the politics in the room.

"My intention is not to offend," he said. "Nor is it to defend the Catholics."

"No, what you say is all fact." replied Zeki. "But, you are right. It is generally truth that offends, not lies."

Matt continued, "I have a pragmatic view on all of this. It's simply *realpolitik*. Government is about power and nothing is more powerful than an idea, which is why governments are always afraid of them."

"If you think this is normal," Gwyn said, wanting to make Zeki feel more comfortable. "Explain Ottoman tolerance of different faiths in their Empire. They welcomed the Jews who were expelled from Spain in 1492. Many of their citizens were Orthodox or Catholic Christians."

"That works as long as the minority isn't viewed as a threat," replied Matt. He turned to Zeki. "Correct me if I'm wrong here, but the Ottoman Empire in the 15th, 16th and 17th centuries was to Europe what America is to the world today. Nobody picked a fight with them. They were the superpower of the Western world. Until the 18th century, they never even graced a foreign court with their presence, insisting instead that everyone pay them homage in Istanbul."

"It's true," replied Zeki. "The Ottoman armies were practically invincible."

"For example," continued Matt, "In 1571, all of the Christian nations of Europe joined forces to break the stranglehold Islam had on the Mediterranean. At Lepanto, they inflicted a crushing defeat on the Ottoman fleet. It was a time of tremendous celebration. But, when the Sultan asked how long it would take to recover, he was told that the treasury was so rich a better fleet could be built from scratch before the next campaigning season, and it was. In other words, they shrugged off a loss that had required all of the combined forces of Europe to inflict. Yeah, it's easy to be the bigger guy and show tolerance when you actually are the bigger guy. Spain had not yet developed that same confidence.

"And look what happened to all of that religious tolerance when the Empire went into decline. They had their own 'Final Solution' for the Armenian, Greek and Assyrian Christians. Over two million of them were liquidated. Those that weren't massacred or didn't die in forced labor camps were often sent on a death march out of the Empire with few surviving. The International Association of Genocide Scholars passed a resolution in 2007 acknowledging the crimes of the Ottoman Empire before and during WWI as genocide. Is this the tolerant Ottoman Empire you were referring to?"

Matt's tone was steady, almost scholarly, but everyone sensed the underlying aggression.

"It is sad, but true," replied Zeki. "Tolerance is a function of strength, not philosophy or religion. European powers intervened in the politics of the Middle East for centuries, claiming to protect the Christian populations there. When the European countries became more powerful, they squeezed concessions from the Ottomans. The Turks realized that, in their weakness, a multicultural, multi-ethnic society was a liability, just as the Spanish had realized centuries earlier. In the end, a program of homogenization was implemented. This was the primary motivation for the cleansing of the Empire. Before WWI, one in every five citizens of the Empire was a Christian. Compare that with today, when less than one percent of the Turkish population is Christian."

As Zeki spoke, Gwyn could see astonishment spread across Matt's face like ripples across a pond.

"Tolerance is not the message of institutional religion. Their approach is to preach peace, while preparing for war. I can give you an even more recent example." Zeki turned to Gwyn. "Did your father ever talk about the ethnic pogrom in Istanbul in 1955?"

"No, I don't remember anything like that."

"It began when the house where Atatürk had been born was bombed in Greece. But, the bombing was a false flag terrorist act. The next day the perpetrator, a Turk, was arrested and confessed to the crime. This fact was conveniently never reported in the Turkish newspapers. As a result, mobs incited by the government burned and ransacked almost every single Greek business and church in Istanbul, raped women and forcibly circumcised men. The Greek population of Istanbul has fallen from sixty-five thousand in 1955, to less than four thousand today."

Matt could hide his astonishment no longer.

"I can't believe you are saying this."

"Do you imagine, son, that my nationality or religion prevents me from seeing the truth?" He made no attempt to hide his irritation.

"To be honest, I thought that politics and religion were synonymous in Islam."

Matt did not look at Gwyn, but he could practically feel the daggers she was almost certainly staring at him. Gary pursed his lips, hung his head to the side and narrowed his eyes like he was thinking of joining the fray, but apparently decided against it as he simply leaned back on the couch. Matt looked at Gilbert. He was drumming his fingers nervously on his knee and staring off blankly into space. *Is he even listening or is he so worried about his family that he had tuned them out?*

"I am not bound by the mistakes of others," replied Zeki. "In my mind, institutionalized religion serves, not God, but the institution. Why more people haven't seen that is beyond me. In the West, you had your Luther, your Wycliffe, your John Huss. You had the Anabaptists, the Waldenses, the Moravians, the Cathars, the Huguenots. They all opposed the institutionalization of religion, so the Church hunted them down, persecuted them and killed them, but their ideas survived to change the face of Europe and then the Western world. Your Reformation was bloody and some of your reformers, like Calvin, turned out to be almost as cruel as their oppressors, but they prevailed ,and finally, in some limited sense, the words of Jesus, 'Render to Caesar what is Caesar's and to God what is God's' were actually put into practice. We, on the other hand, killed our Luthers, we destroyed our Anabaptists, and so we have not yet had our Reformation. But, please don't be so naive as to think that all of us accept politicized religion."

The rebuke stung. Matt backpedaled but didn't back off.

"I apologize for making the assumption. Yet, the lessons of history are indisputable. You mentioned the Cathars, so you might know about the Albigensian Crusade. You probably know that for over twenty years the Catholics systematically massacred the entire sect. At the siege of Beziers they asked the Commander, an abbot, a 'man of God', how they were to distinguish the heretic Cathars from the Catholics in the city? He said, 'Kill them all, the Lord will recognize His own.' That, sir, is where religion takes a person!"

He looked back at Gwyn, but she was looking at Zeki not him. He could tell that she had developed an emotional bond with her father's friend, and she was worried about how Zeki would take this. Gary tried to lighten the mood.

"And I thought that idea originated with the Marines. Just goes to show that there is nothing new under the sun."

"I understand you, son" replied Zeki calmly. "Really, I do." He looked at Matt for a moment without speaking and then said, "You have a keen mind; it is a shame you don't use it."

There wasn't the slightest hint of condescension. It was spoken with compassion, but this was lost on Matt.

"Excuse me?" he asked, struggling to maintain his composure.

"You don't believe in God, do you?" he asked.

This was getting too personal for comfort. Gwyn squirmed in her seat and tried to catch Matt's eye. She desperately wanted him to just let this go, but she knew he wouldn't. He never backed down.

"No, I don't suppose I do," replied Matt.

"And the reason you don't believe in God," continued Zeki, "is because of *men* who you *know* do not represent Him. Now, that is bizarre logic, but let's not banter words. We're not here to save your soul but Gilbert's family."

There was finality in Zeki's tone of voice. The room breathed a collective sigh of relief and Zeki turned to Gwyn,

"Your friend is quite right about Ottoman tolerance of the infidel. They called the non-Muslims *rayah*, which translated literally means 'flock'. Why were they called the flock? Because they were for fleecing, that's why. The Spanish had a similar view of the Moors. It even became a proverb, 'Whoever has a Moor has gold.' The conquered Moors in Spain were literally serfs working the land of Spanish nobles. This is *realpolitik*. We Turks like to think of the Ottomans as tolerant, and compared with the Spanish they definitely were, but even at the height of their power, under Süleyman the Magnificent, when they had the least to fear, they did not tolerate ideas that upset the status quo."

"But there was nothing like the Inquisition in Turkish history, was there?" asked Gwyn.

"Well not exactly. It was a different system. But let me give you an example. During the reign of Süleyman the Magnificent, there was an Islamic scholar named Molla Kabız. We know very little about him. We will never hear his side of the story, but those who sat in judgment on him have given us their version, and from this we can glean certain facts. Apparently, he became convinced that Jesus was spiritually superior to Mohammed, and, surprisingly, he claimed to have reached this conclusion from the Qur'an itself. This idea was obviously unpopular with the ruling Sunni Muslims, especially given that many of their subjects were Christians. The Ottomans claimed that their right to rule was based on the fact that they submitted to the will of Allah as revealed by Mohammed. Anything that undermined this claim was sure to have unpleasant consequences.

"When Kabız was brought before two of the highest ranking local magistrates, he left them speechless with proofs for his position, both from the Qur'an and the hadith, and they were unable to refute his arguments. This, of course, infuriated them. The fact that they had been unable to silence this nutcase, a man who overturned everything the ruling class believed, was embarrassing to say the least, so they did what governments generally do. They called for his immediate execution. However, the governor who was observing the trial realized that the two magistrates were only venting their anger, and trying to cover *their* shame with *his* blood. Therefore, the governor stopped them from carrying out the sentence and Kabız was set free."

"So, at least cooler heads prevailed, and the man was spared," said Gwyn.

Zeki sighed. "I wish that was the end of the story, but it isn't. The Sultan was furious when he heard that the man had been let go. He summoned the *Sheikh ul Islam*, the highest religious authority and a new trial was held in which the authorities claimed to have refuted what Molla Kabız said about Jesus."

"Did they?" asked Gary.

"I wasn't there," smiled Zeki. "And the record does not tell us what they said, but Molla Kabız must not have been convinced, because in spite of their appeals to forsake his so-called heresy, he refused to recant and was executed."

"That's horrible," exclaimed Gwyn.

"No, as your friend here pointed out, that is *realpolitik*."

"But, how can you punish someone for an idea?" Gwyn protested. "How can an idea be a crime?"

"Simple," replied Matt. "Make a law against it."

Zeki put his hand up. "I think we should get back to the Moriscos." Everyone nodded in agreement. "I've given you the general background to what is obviously a long and miserable story. I don't see how the details of their suffering and the political intrigue help us much, but there were some strange discoveries in Granada after the second rebellion that I think might be relevant. Gwyn is the one who stumbled upon this, so I'll let her tell you about it. The tea should be ready. Let me get it."

48

"Mrs. Davenport?"

"Yes, how can I help you?" Cathy said, turning away from the computer screen to find herself looking at two MPS officers. He could tell from the way her face fell that she had already guessed why they were there.

"I'm Chief Superintendent McIntosh. If you have a moment, I'd like to ask you a few questions about the O'Brien case."

"Of course." She pushed her chair back from the desk, stood up and walked around to where they were standing.

"Won't you have a seat?" she said, pointing to the chairs against the wall.

"I spend too much time atrophying those muscles already, Mrs. Davenport. I'll stand if you don't mind."

She shrugged and leaned against the edge of her own desk. McIntosh was trying to take in everything about the room. Her desk was neat as a pin, decorated with a bouquet of fresh flowers in a beautiful glass vase he would have bet was crystal. Judging by the wrinkles and gray hair, he guessed her to be around fifty, although if he had just gone by her physique, she could have easily passed for a forty-year-old. She wore a flowing black dress that was tight at the hips and flared out from there to her ankles. He wondered if it was just a favorite color, or if it was a sign of private mourning for the passing of Dr. O'Brien.

"I understand that you are the department secretary and have worked with Mr. O'Brien for a long time."

"That's right," she said. "I took the position the year Dr. O'Brien was hired."

"And that was how many years ago?"

"Twelve, this month," she replied. "But, then you don't need to ask me questions you already know the answer to, do you?"

McIntosh smiled. He liked women with spirit.

"Right," he responded with a smile. "Let me come right to the point then. I know you already spoke with someone from the department last week, but there has been a new development. We believe that Dr. O'Brien's death may

301

have been connected to a document he had in his possession. That document is missing, and we have not yet been able to receive a copy of it."

"Yes, Dr. O'Brien asked me to take a digital photograph of an old document. In fact, it was a week ago today, last Monday."

"Do you have the digital copy?"

"Of course. It's on my computer," she replied, walking back around the desk. "He asked me to send it to Dr. Brown."

"Dr. Brown?" McIntosh looked at his colleague who was taking notes. "Jack, did Pete talk with Dr. Brown last week?"

"No sir."

"Mrs. Davenport," continued McIntosh.

"Please call me Cathy," she inserted quickly.

"Very well. Cathy, would you mind calling Dr. Brown for me? If he's available, we'd like to speak with him."

"Classes haven't started yet, so if he is on campus, I'm sure he would be more than happy to speak with you. But I doubt it will do much good. He's new here and didn't even know Dr. O'Brien."

"Didn't know him," asked McIntosh. "Why would Dr. O'Brien want you to send a document to a professor he doesn't know?"

"I'm not sure. I suppose it was related to Dr. Brown's area of expertise."

"Which is?" prodded McIntosh.

"His specialty is Arab history. Would you like to see the document first, or shall I call Dr. Brown?"

"Please, call Dr. Brown. We can look at the document while we wait for him."

While she made the call, he stared out the window on a damp, drizzly day. So far, everything pointed to a document he still hadn't seen. It was the only lead they had that could shed light on a motive. Two professors were dead. O'Brien's daughter had been attacked by professional assassins whose fingerprints were not contained in any criminal database. *What made the professor give the document to his daughter? Why and how did Zeki show up on the scene? Who wants it? We won't get anywhere until we answer these questions.* The secretary's voice brought him back.

"Dr. Brown is in today and said he'd be right over."

"Excellent."

She sat down at her computer and moved the mouse to bring the screen back to life. She clicked through a couple of folders, scanned down the list of files and began muttering to herself.

"Is something wrong, Mrs. Davenport?" asked McIntosh.

"I'm quite sure I saved it to a folder that I have reserved for Dr. O'Brien, but it's not there."

"Try a search by date or name if you can remember what you called the file."

She began typing into the search window and hit enter. From across the room, McIntosh could see that her search did not return any results. He remembered what they had found at Ian's apartment and had a sinking feeling of *déjà vu*. The secretary tried another couple of searches before turning back to McIntosh.

"I don't understand this at all," she said, clearly flustered. "I know that it was here. This is inexplicable."

"Inexplicable? I'm not sure that's the right word," McIntosh said staidly. "You see, on the force we operate on the assumption that nothing is inexplicable. Our job is to explain why things happen and bring those responsible to justice. If it isn't there, the explanation is that someone erased it. You said you sent the document to Dr. Brown. Maybe you could check your sent items," he suggested.

She turned back to the screen, opened her email program, double-clicked on the Sent Items folder and scrolled down the list to last Monday, but once again, what she expected to find was to her mind inexplicably absent. Her email to Dr. Brown and Dr. Öztürk were both missing.

"This is weird," she said. "Those emails are also missing. I sent a copy to Dr. Brown and Dr. Öztürk on…"

McIntosh cut her off. "You sent one to Dr. Öztürk?"

"Yes, Ian asked me to on Monday afternoon."

"We'll have someone from computer forensics take a look at your computer and see if the file can be recovered. But, right now, I need you to tell me anything you know about the document. How did Dr. O'Brien obtain it? How long had it been in his possession? How many people knew about it? Anything you can tell us might prove to be helpful."

Cathy continued to stare at the screen for a moment and then turned back to McIntosh.

"I know nothing about the document other than what I have told you. I don't know what it was, where he got it, or how long he had been in possession of it. He asked me to take a flashless digital photograph of it and send it to Dr. Brown. In fact, the next day, he left me a note asking me to send it again because Dr. Brown hadn't received the first email. I also sent a copy to Dr. Öztürk. Dr. O'Brien had asked him to do some more research on his behalf. That's all I know. But seeing these files missing just reminded me of something else. When I arrived in the office on Wednesday morning, my computer was on. I remember being surprised because I never leave it on. I figured I had just forgotten to turn it off."

"And you think someone was here?" he asked.

"Well, I can't see how. The computer has a password. How could anyone else have turned it on?"

There was a knock at the door. McIntosh turned to see a man in his mid-thirties standing at the door.

"Dr. Brown?"

"Yes. Mrs. Davenport said you wanted to ask me some questions about Dr. O'Brien."

"Thank you for coming, Dr. Brown. I'm Chief Superintendent McIntosh. I know you're busy, so I'll try to keep this short."

"If there is anything I can do, I'm glad to help."

"Cathy tells us that Dr. O'Brien shared a document with you on Monday of last week."

"That's right."

"Would you mind providing us with a copy of the document?"

"I'm afraid I don't have a copy," said Dr. Brown.

McIntosh didn't have to feign surprise. It was genuine.

"You don't have a copy of the document that Dr. O'Brien gave you?"

"Well, he didn't actually give me a copy. He came to my office with the document and asked me to translate it. Unfortunately, it was not written in Arabic, so I was unable to help him."

"So, why did he ask his secretary to send you a copy?" asked McIntosh.

"Superintendent, I am a professor of Arab history and one of my interests is the development of calligraphy as an art form in Islam. The language was not Arabic, but the script was. I asked Dr. O'Brien if I could have a copy of it because the style was unique. He said that Mrs. Davenport would send me a digital photograph, but I never received it."

"You never received it?"

"No, sir."

"But, she sent it twice."

"Then, I didn't receive it twice," said Dr. Brown with a slight bit of irritation. "Besides," he continued, "I'm not sure that I understand the purpose of your questions. Are you suggesting that Dr. O'Brien's death was in some way related to the document?"

"We have reason to believe that it was, but the document is missing, so we're trying to find out what it contained."

"Like I said, it wasn't Arabic. I told him that it might be Ottoman Turkish or maybe Persian."

"I'm sure you're also aware of the death of Haluk Bayram, a renowned Ottoman scholar who was attending the conference."

"Yes, his passing was announced at the conference."

"Would you be surprised to know that the two deaths are connected?"

"As much or as little as the next man, I suppose. I didn't know either of the men."

"Of course. Back to the document. Was there anything unusual about it?" asked McIntosh.

"No, nothing remarkable at all. It was a single page document. Obviously quite old, but I couldn't hazard a guess at its age."

"Did he tell you where he found it, or why he was interested in it?"

"No. Our conversation was very short. He said that he had obtained it only recently. After I told him that it might be Ottoman Turkish, he said that he knew a couple of scholars at the conference who might be able to help."

McIntosh rubbed his chin and found a rough spot he had apparently missed that morning. To no one in particular, he said, "It's odd, even counter-intuitive, but apparently Ottoman and Byzantine scholarship have unexpected occupational hazards. One may be thankful to have chosen Arab history after a week like this."

Then, turning to Dr. Brown, "I don't suppose you have any idea why the secretary's email never reached you?"

"I don't," he replied. "I was quite keen to see it and stopped by again on Tuesday. Mrs. Davenport was out, but Prof. O'Brien was here. He said that he would remind her. I figured it had just been overlooked in all of the hustle and bustle surrounding the conference."

"That's right," said Cathy. "Dr. O'Brien left me a note, asking me to resend it to Dr. Brown."

"I see," said McIntosh. "I guess those are my only questions for now. Thank you, Dr. Brown, for your time."

"I was looking forward to working with Dr. O'Brien. He had quite a reputation in his field."

He stood up and headed for the door. When it closed, McIntosh turned to Jack.

"Make a note to subpoena the university's server records going back at least three weeks."

"If you're wondering if a copy of the document is on the server, it won't be under Dr. Brown's university account," she volunteered. "It hadn't been issued yet. He gave me his personal account."

"Can we have that please?"

"It's not in my sent mail anymore, but it was too simple to forget. dbrown19 @gmail.com"

"I don't suppose you keep curricula vitae for professors in the department?"

"Yes, I do."

"Would you mind sharing a copy of those with me?" asked McIntosh.

"Sir, I cannot provide those without the express written permission of the professors."

"Or a court order," said McIntosh, as if finishing her sentence. "I'll make sure you have one in the morning. I shall not have the least amount of trouble in obtaining it. This is a murder case, Mrs. Davenport, and it is quite clear to me that Monday was the first day that Dr. O'Brien showed the document to anyone with expertise. Dr. O'Brien apparently didn't even know what he had. In fact, he thought it was an Arabic document, which explains why he contacted Dr. Brown. But now one of the Turkish professors attending your conference is dead, another is missing and a respected Byzantine scholar from your university has been killed. Crucial evidence is no longer on your computer, and Dr. Brown says he never received the email. Mrs. Davenport, this all started right here last Monday, and I mean to get to the bottom of it."

49

ISTANBUL   Gwyn pulled a small notebook from her bag and started flipping through the pages.

"Bear with me. I've got these notes all over the place."

Matt pulled out a legal pad and pen.

"Gilbert said you split the research, so none of you have seen both sides, and I haven't seen any of it. We all need to concentrate here and look for connections."

Zeki walked into the room holding the traditional double teapot used by the Turks. "If two minds are better than one, imagine what we might do with five. Does anyone want their tea particularly weak?"

"Yes, please," said Gwyn.

The rest of them shook their heads. Zeki poured dark, strong tea from the top and then diluted it with boiling water from the bottom. Gwyn looked at Matt. She could see that he was trying to refocus and put the rebuke from Zeki behind him.

"Alright," said Gwyn, "I found it interesting that several of the references on the Moriscos mentioned something called the Lead Books of Sacromonte. On the flight over, I read almost two hundred pages of research, and oddly enough, it turns out that most modern scholars believe there is at least an ideological link, if not a physical one, with the Gospel of Barnabas. Remember the situation in Spain at the time. Arabic was completely and totally banned in 1567. The Inquisition was being used to squelch all religious dissent. People who had lived in Spain for seven hundred years as Muslims were being forced to abandon their entire culture.

"Then, in 1588, when the minaret of the Grand Mosque in Granada was being torn down, a lead box was discovered. It contained a parchment written in Latin, Arabic and Spanish, and claimed to date back to the Emperor Nero. It included a prophecy from St. John predicting the rise of Islam and the coming of Martin Luther. There was also a piece of cloth that the Virgin Mary supposedly used to dry her tears at the crucifixion, and a bone that was said to belong to the martyr St. Stephen."

Matt jumped in. "Even if you did believe in prophecy, Spanish did not exist as a language until several hundred years after the fall of Rome, and Arabic wouldn't have arrived in Iberia until the conquest of Spain in the seventh century. It's obviously a forgery."

"It's obvious to you because you live in the information age," said Zeki slowly, weighing his words. "But this was the late 1500s. Most people were illiterate. Many never travelled more than fifty miles from their place of birth. Besides, people tend to believe what they hope to be true. From what I understand of Catholicism, the status of a church was greatly enhanced by its possession of relics. In their eyes, these artifacts authenticated their connection to the apostles. They would have wanted it to be true."

"Right," said Gwyn. "Actually there were a few people who voiced their doubts, but the mania that surrounded the discovery prevailed for years. Christians in Granada greeted the finds euphorically because they confirmed the city as a bishopric. It gets much better though. Seven years later, starting in 1595 and continuing until 1599, a series of books called the Lead Books of Sacromonte were discovered in caves on a mountain outside the city of Granada. These lead books claimed that the relics found in the tower belonged to Arab Christians who had come to Granada with St. James, who, it just so happens, is the Patron Saint of Spain. These Arab Christians were supposedly martyred there. In the caves, they discovered bones thought to be human remains."

Gwyn noted how intently Matt was listening and taking notes. His intellect and inquisitiveness had always been one of the things she liked most about him.

"Clever," said Gary. "Faking a fifteen-hundred-year-old parchment would be a serious challenge. Iron, copper, and silver would have corroded excessively over fifteen centuries. Gold is too expensive, so lead is the perfect choice. It would have been difficult to prove its age."

Gwyn nodded her head in agreement and continued.

"They were written in an angular Arabic script without diacritics..."

"Diacritics?" asked Matt.

"The vowel points in Arabic," responded Zeki. "Hebrew and Arabic were not originally written with vowels because the words could generally be understood from the structure of the sentence."

"In other words," said Gwyn, "the forgers had done their homework. The angular script and lack of vowel points were meant to make it look ancient. Anyway...There were tons of these booklets, but probably the most important one was where the Virgin Mary speaks to Saint Peter. I wrote the quote somewhere. Here it is. 'I testify to you that the Arabs are one of the good nations and their tongue one of the good tongues. It was chosen by God to exalt his holy law and his sacred gospel and his holy church at the end of Time ...'"

Zeki crossed his legs and took a deep breath.

"The Virgin Mary is held in high esteem by Muslims but venerated by

Catholics. The fact that she is calling the Arabs a good nation and Arabic a good language would have carried much weight with the Spanish, especially her claim that they had been in Spain since the days of Christ."

"Here we go again, manipulating religions for political ends. Whoever wrote this was looking for a way to save Arab language and culture, so they pulled out all the stops and resurrected Mary to have her deliver their message."

"That's probably right," continued Gwyn. "The text also mentions the Virgin Mary commissioning St. James to go and evangelize the Arabs of Spain."

"Wait a minute," objected Gary, "There were no Arabs in Spain during the first century."

"We know that," replied Matt, smiling at Zeki, "But, back then, only serious historians would have known it. The Arabs had been in Granada for seven hundred years. No one could remember a time when they didn't live there. It seems to me that the Moriscos were trying to convince the Spanish that Arabs had been inhabitants of Spain since the time of Christ. They also wanted to show that they could be genuine Christians in order to alleviate the pressure put on them by the Inquisition."

"Exactly," replied Gwyn, "As I said before, there were a few people who immediately called the discoveries a forgery, but the local church was so enamored with its newfound status that it swept all these objections under the rug. In fact, they refused to send the lead books to Rome for several decades, probably because they knew the truth would come out. In the end, Rome condemned the books as heresy, but strangely enough, did not indicate that the relics were not genuine, so they are still venerated to this day."

"I still don't see a connection with the Gospel of Barnabas though," said Matt.

"The connection is primarily theological," replied Gwyn. "The Lead Books of Sacromonte present a theology that Zeki says is manifestly Islamic. For example, they contain the phrase, 'There is no god but God and Jesus is the Spirit of God', which is very similar to the affirmation of Islam, 'There is no god but God and Mohammed is His prophet.' Plus, the title of Jesus as the 'Spirit of God' is one found in the Qur'an. Strangely enough, the books also contain a thinly-veiled reference to the post-Reformation doctrine of the Immaculate Conception."

"Another anachronous appeal to the intended Catholic audience," groaned Matt.

"Right. The Virgin Mary says, '…in the end times the 'King of the Arabs, who is not himself an Arab, will hold a Great Council in Cyprus revealing the True Gospel.'"

"That is almost certainly a reference to the Ottoman Sultan, a Turk ruling over the Arabs," said Zeki. "The conquest of Cyprus happened just a few years before these books were discovered."

"Talk about faking prophecy...These guys had it down to an art form. Write about the past as if it were the future, back-date your text and presto! You've got yourself a bonafide prophet. They were even clever enough to avoid the words 'Ottoman' or 'Turk' since those were unknown in the first century. "

Gwyn flipped through several more pages. "Somewhere I wrote down a prayer that Mary commands everyone to pray in preparation for the Council that will be held in Cyprus. Listen to this, 'O Allah, my Lord, watch protectively over the humblest of Thy creatures, over him who interprets the Truth of the Blessed Gospel in the Great Council. Smooth the way for him and make me believe in the Truth contained in it that he will expound...'"

"Wow," said Matt. "The Ottoman Sultan will call a Council to expound the Truth of the Gospel on the island of Cyprus. That is a pretty specific prophecy. I don't remember anything like that ever happening though."

"It never did," said Zeki quietly. "But, we can list a number of Islamic elements in the texts. They emphasize the unity of God, as opposed to the Trinity, while prohibiting the cult of images, which Muslims consider sacrilegious, and downplaying the role of wine in the Eucharist because alcohol is proscribed by Islam."

"Classic politics," said Matt, "Using religion, no, even worse, blatantly making it up."

"It does sound horrible, but they were just trying to encourage a more tolerant attitude towards their language and culture," rejoined Gwyn.

"Seems to have failed," remarked Gary, "Didn't you say they were kicked out in 1609?"

"That's right," replied Zeki.

"What's the point of inventing a religion?" snorted Matt in disbelief. "It's like bowing down to a creation of your own hands."

Zeki took a deep breath. "You can be sure that no one ever invented a religion for themselves; it is always for someone else. The forgers may have been attempting to make the Moriscos more comfortable with their conversion to Christianity by removing certain thorny theological issues, or they may have been encouraging the Spanish to respect Morisco culture and language. We should not judge them too harshly. Desperate times call for desperate measures. Their children were being taken away and brought up in a foreign religion. They faced the horrors of the Inquisition..."

He stopped. Gwyn reached up for a strand of hair to twirl around her finger, but found none. She smacked her lips in disgust. It was her favorite thing to do while she was thinking. Gary cleared his throat and tapped his watch.

"Are you done, Gwyn?"

She nodded, "That's it in a nutshell. What did you find out about the Gospel of Barnabas?"

50

"I read everything that Gwyn sent," said Gary. "Then I spent all morning reading stuff on the Internet. I'm more convinced than ever that the Gospel of Barnabas and the document my father found are connected with this whole Morisco affair. For example, the first reference to the Gospel of Barnabas which can be clearly connected to the extant version is in a Morisco text written by Ibrahim al-Taybili. Today, the text is known as BNM ms 9653 and it was probably written in 1634 in Tunisia."

"Were the Moriscos sent there?" asked Matt.

"Yes," replied Zeki, "Many were sent to Tunis, and this same city is also mentioned in the letter Prof. O'Brien found. Others ended up in Morocco or Istanbul. Some actually settled in European countries, but very few."

"1634 would be roughly twenty years after the last Moriscos left Spain," noted Gwyn.

"That's right," continued Gary. "The reference in this Morisco text is only a single line. The G.O.B. does not appear to be referenced in any other Morisco literature. In fact, as far as I can tell, it isn't mentioned again in any document for two generations."

"That is odd," said Gwyn, screwing up her face. "From what I read, there are supposed to be hundreds of extant Morisco documents. If they wrote it, surely it would be quoted often."

"Yes, it *is* odd. Extremely odd, unless there was an attempt to destroy it, which is exactly what the document Dad found seems to suggest."

"You mean a cover-up?" asked Matt.

"Let's not get ahead of ourselves. First, in the context of the Bible allegedly predicting the coming of Mohammed, MS 9653 says, 'the Gospel of Saint Barnabas where one can find the light.' The Gospel of Barnabas is a tome, as long as the canonical four Gospels combined. As a forgery, this would've been a massive undertaking. It would have required serious financial backing and scholarly support."

"Wait a minute," said Zeki. "Did I miss something? Are we jumping to the conclusion that it is a forgery? How do we know that? I grant you the Moriscos certainly forged documents and tried to influence policy through religion. But, just because a Morisco document refers to the Gospel of Barnabas as the truth doesn't mean they wrote it or that it is a forgery. That is guilt by association. The Gospel of Barnabas is regarded throughout the Muslim world as the truest copy of the message of Jesus. We have been told that it was suppressed by a corrupt clergy intent on retaining power because it validated the message of the Qur'an. There was even a movie of the life of Jesus produced somewhere in the Middle East a few years ago based on the Gospel of Barnabas. I didn't see the movie and haven't read this Gospel, but I'd like to hear some evidence before we jump to a conclusion that flies in the face of everything I know."

Gary took a deep breath. The last thing he wanted to do was offend his father's friend.

"Well, the truth is a difficult thing to fabricate, sir. The Gospel of Barnabas contains so many geographical and historical errors that it couldn't have possibly been written by someone who lived and walked in Palestine."

"For example?" asked Zeki.

"For example," said Gary, looking back down at his computer and scrolling through his notes. "It has Jesus saying that the year of Jubilee comes every one hundred years, but throughout the Old Testament and church history, it was celebrated every fifty years. There was only one time in history when it was celebrated every hundred years and that was when Pope Boniface changed it in the thirteenth century. It was later changed back to fifty years by Pope Clement VI."

"That could be a subconscious scribal error," offered Gwyn.

Gary shook his head, "Which would, at the very least, prove that the extant copy was written in the thirteenth century or later, but there are much more serious problems." He continued reading off the screen. "First, the Gospel of Barnabas also says that Jesus was born when Pilate was governor. Pilate did not become governor of Judea until 26 AD. Second, the G.O.B. says that wine was kept in casks, but this technology was developed much later. In the Palestine of Jesus' day, wine was kept in wine-skins or amphorae. Third, it has Jesus saying that a golden *denarius* can be exchanged for sixty *minuti*. But, *minuti* were Spanish coins used by the pre-Muslim Visigoth rulers hundreds of years after Jesus and never in Palestine. "

"I don't see how those can be scribal errors," said Matt. "Looks like the author simply used the oldest monetary unit he was aware of. That's a solid Spanish connection then."

"Combined with a reference in a Morisco document, I would say it is a reasonable conclusion," continued Gary. "Anyway, there are dozens of examples like these. Let me give you two more. In one place, Jesus comes by ship to Nazareth and then departs by ship for Jerusalem. Nazareth is located at an elevation of two thousand feet and Jerusalem at two thousand five hundred feet and neither of them are close to any body of water."

Matt laughed out loud. "Travelling by boat to Jerusalem would have been a greater miracle than walking on the water or parting the Red Sea. Palestine is a small area. No one acquainted with it could make this mistake."

"And," continued Gary, "The author, who claims to be Barnabas and would have spoken Greek and Hebrew, refers to Jesus as 'Christ', but throughout the Gospel which Barnabas allegedly wrote, Jesus repeatedly rejects the title of Messiah. He says instead that the one who would come after him would be the Messiah and that he was not worthy to untie the Messiah sandals."

"I don't understand," said Gwyn.

"It's simple, really," replied Gary. "The writer didn't know that these two words meant the same thing. Most likely, he knew Greek and not Hebrew, but maybe he knew neither. He apparently thought that Christ was Jesus' surname and Messiah was a title."

Matt laughed again. "How did they expect anyone to take this seriously?"

"You laugh," said Gary, "And it does contain numerous errors, but suppose a pagan Irish king in the eighth century wanted to give legitimacy to his Druid religion and hired you to write a gospel claiming that St. Patrick was a disciple of Jesus and that Jesus was actually a Druid."

The smile disappeared from Matt's face. "Hmmm, I see your point. That would be a tough assignment with no internet and no encyclopedia. Still, I don't understand the motive with the Gospel of Barnabas. With the Moriscos, the evidence and the motive are clear. But you said this book is not even referred to until twenty years after the Moriscos had been expelled from Spain?"

"The fact that there is no written record before then can hardly be taken as proof that it did not exist," replied Gary, "especially if there was some attempt to 'erase every trace' as it says in the document Dad found. The project had to have been completed earlier than this for Ibrahim al-Taybili to mention it. The overriding purpose of the G.O.B. is, like the Lead Books of Sacromonte, to recast the message of Jesus in a way that reflects Islamic values. I found an English copy online and read about sixty pages of it. I have an example here."

He brought the document up on his screen and began scrolling down to the portions he had highlighted.

"Listen, this is Jesus speaking.

'As God liveth, in whose presence my soul standeth, I am not the Messiah whom all the tribes of the earth expect, even as God promised to our father Abraham, saying: 'In

313

THY SEED WILL I BLESS ALL THE TRIBES OF THE EARTH.' BUT WHEN GOD SHALL TAKE ME AWAY FROM THE WORLD, SATAN WILL PRAISE AGAIN THIS ACCURSED SEDITION, BY MAKING THE IMPIOUS BELIEVE THAT I AM GOD AND SON OF GOD, WHENCE MY WORDS AND MY DOCTRINE SHALL BE CONTAMINATED, INSOMUCH THAT SCARCELY SHALL THERE REMAIN THIRTY FAITHFUL ONES: WHEREUPON GOD WILL HAVE MERCY UPON THE WORLD, AND WILL SEND HIS MESSENGER FOR WHOM HE HATH MADE ALL THINGS; WHO SHALL COME FROM THE SOUTH WITH POWER, AND SHALL DESTROY THE IDOLS WITH THE IDOLATERS; WHO SHALL TAKE AWAY THE DOMINION FROM SATAN WHICH HE HATH OVER MEN. HE SHALL BRING WITH HIM THE MERCY OF GOD FOR SALVATION OF THEM THAT SHALL BELIEVE IN HIM, AND BLESSED IS HE WHO SHALL BELIEVE HIS WORDS.'"

Gary looked at Zeki. Everyone else was silent. Finally, Zeki spoke.

"That's very close to what a Muslim might say about Jesus. 'The one from the south' is obviously a reference to the Prophet Mohammed."

Gary continued. "I think you're right. In fact, in other parts of the G.O.B., Mohammed is referred to by name. The book also claims that the Messiah will come though the seed of Abraham through Ishmael, not through Isaac."

"Again, this mirrors Muslim belief," replied Zeki. "However, to be perfectly honest, the issue of Ishmael and Isaac is not really addressed in the Qur'an. It was only raised much later when the two religions began to develop a polemic. For example, I know that the Old Testament says Abraham was going to sacrifice Isaac and Muslims say it was Ishmael, but the Qur'an only says 'his son' without referring to which one it was."

"Finally," continued Gary. "The central Christian teaching of the crucifixion—the death, burial and resurrection of Christ—is denied. The G.O.B. says that it was Judas, not Jesus, who was crucified."

"Another teaching of Islam," admitted Zeki.

"Yes, but this teaching originated with the Gnostics. The Muslims simply borrowed it," explained Gary.

Gwyn lowered one eyebrow and raised the other, but held her tongue. Gary continued.

"Most scholars seem to agree that the G.O.B. is an attempt to render the Gospel in a manner that defends Muslim positions on a number of issues. John the Baptist, who was the forerunner of Messiah tasked with preparing the Jews for the Messiah's arrival, is completely absent from the Gospel of Barnabas. In every passage that refers to John the Baptist in the canonical New Testament, he has been replaced with Jesus, who is portrayed as heralding the coming of Mohammed."

He looked at Zeki, his tone apologetic, "Even though the book is highly regarded in the Muslim world, there have also been several Muslim scholars who acknowledge that the text cannot be genuine. I'm just trying to make sense of it all."

Zeki smiled back at him. "My faith is in the God of Abraham, the Lord of the Worlds. I do not worship a book."

The room was silent. Matt poured himself another glass of tea.

"There is one thing that is still bothering me," said Gwyn. "Why would they go to all the trouble and never use it?"

"I agree it seems odd," said Gary. "It was a total rewrite of the Gospel, an ambitious project, requiring years if not decades of research. There are only two existing copies of the Gospel of Barnabas in the world. A fact I find equally as strange. One is an Italian version, which is kept in the Austrian National Library. I will come back to that later. There is also an incomplete Spanish copy which was found in 1974 in Sydney, Australia, and I believe it is more important given the Morisco connection."

"Australia?" said Gwyn, screwing up her face. "What in the world does Australia have to do with it?"

"Now, that is a tale worth telling. Remember, the entries in Sale's diary referring to a Spanish translation?" said Gary, turning back to the screen and reading from his notes. "I think he could be referring to the G.O.B. You see, Sale had the Spanish copy of the G.O.B. in his possession. He referred to it in his introduction to the English translation of the Qur'an in 1734. Sale had borrowed it from Dr. Holme, Rector of Hedley. We don't know where Holme acquired it. From there, the book went to Dr. Thomas Monkhouse, Fellow of Queen's College. But, Sale's reference in 1734 was the last time anyone referred to the Spanish copy until 1974 when the incomplete copy was found in Australia. Interestingly enough, this copy has a note in it.

> Transcribed from MS in possession of Revd Mr. Edm.
> Callamy who bought it at the Decease of Mr. George Sale
> 17.. and now gave me at the Decease of Mr. John Nickolls
> 1745 (signed) "N. Hone".

"Wait just a minute," protested Gwyn. "Who were those people, what did they do, why were they involved?"

"Forget the names," replied Gary. "Except for George Sale, all we know about any of them is that each had, at one time, been in possession of a copy of the document."

"So, either Sale bought the copy from Monkhouse, or he made a copy himself," said Matt. "And, the incomplete manuscript in Australia was copied from the one Callamy acquired when Sale died. What happened to the complete version Callamy got from Sale, and why is the copy from Australia incomplete?"

"Lots of questions with no answers," replied Gary. "The copy that Callamy acquired from Sale has never been found nor has any other copy. The trail is simply lost. The complete Spanish copy Sale referred to as a Muslim forgery in his introduction to the Qur'an is gone. Numerous efforts have been made to find it in the libraries and museums of Europe, all to no avail. So, there is no full Spanish version today as far as we know."

"But," interrupted Zeki, pointing to the document on the table. "That shouldn't come as a surprise. After all, the letter your father found was an order to destroy the G.O.B. We also know from Sale's diary that someone tried to purchase it. When he refused to sell out, maybe they had him killed and stole it."

"But, they couldn't have stolen it," protested Gwyn. "The copy found in Australia says it was transcribed from the copy Sale had."

Zeki nodded his agreement.

"Right," said Gary. "His diary says he wanted to keep it safe. So, maybe they killed him but failed to retrieve the manuscript. Maybe Nickolls obtained it, started copying it, and before he finished, someone either bought or stole the original from him. We'll never know. What we do know though, is that according to Sale the introduction to the Spanish version claimed to be a translation from the Italian copy, which first surfaced in the Netherlands in 1709, so let's look at that."

"The Netherlands? Very interesting," said Gwyn. "Especially given that the Netherlands had been engaged in a war of independence with Spain. They had even collaborated to some extent with the Moriscos."

"Nor should we forget," added Matt, "that the Protestant Huguenots also conspired to join forces with the Moriscos to defeat their common enemy, the Catholic Hapsburgs. When the Huguenots finally realized it was a lost cause, many of them fled to Holland. The connection could have been through France as well."

With a mischievous smile, Zeki said, "Should I also point out that the Sultan had promised help to the Dutch Protestants against the Catholics, and the man who wanted to buy it from Sale was in Amsterdam."

"Do all roads lead to Holland?" asked Gwyn.

"We may never know how the Italian version of the Gospel of Barnabas arrived in Holland," said Gary, "But, it was eventually given to Prince Eugene of Savoy, who, apparently, was quite a connoisseur of rare books and the arts."

Zeki chuckled. "Prince Eugene of Savoy, a 'connoisseur of rare books?' I've never heard a less fitting description."

"I know nothing of the man except for the one reference to him purchasing the book and being a patron of the arts," said Gary innocently. "He apparently had large holdings. With his extensive revenues, he supported writers and artists, as well as acquiring a brilliant collection of paintings and an extensive library."

"Did you know he was a general?" asked Zeki.

"No, but I'm not sure how that is relevant to the G.O.B."

"Well, I'm not either," snorted Zeki. "But, saying that he was a patron of the arts is like saying Newton was a theologian, which may be true, but Newton was pre-eminently a physicist. In the same way, Savoy should be rightly characterized as a general, not a patron of the arts. No, not *a* general. He was *the* general. The general who turned the tide against the Turks. The commander who decisively stopped Ottoman expansion in Europe. In 1683, as a mere boy of nineteen, he fought at the Battle of Vienna, when Kara Mustafa Pasha with almost 150,000 men was routed by the Polish general, Sobieski, leading a multinational force of Germans, Austrians and Poles. Then, in 1697, he led the Austrian force that defeated the Turks at Zenta, making the first significant dent in Ottoman controlled territory and forcing the Ottoman Empire to sign the Treaty of Karlowitz, which ended one hundred and fifty years of Ottoman rule over Hungary. It is strange indeed that with all of the scholars in Europe he should come to have this book. Very peculiar. Why? Why should a general be given this book?"

"That's an impressive impromptu summary of an Austrian general's life," said Matt, making no attempt to hide his surprise.

"My dear fellow," said Zeki, "If there is one thing Turks know it is war, and if there is anything a soldier studies, it is the history of war, especially one's own wars and those of one's enemies."

Gary continued, "As to why the general received the book, apparently Cramer, the man who acquired the Gospel of Barnabas in Holland and presented it to Prince Eugene of Savoy, may have exchanged it for a sum of money because he had fallen on hard times. After all, the Prince was a man of means and probably paid him handsomely."

Zeki ran his fingers through his hair. "Not convincing. I'm quite sure the Vatican had deeper pockets. I find it hard to believe that this book just happens to end up with the top general of the Austrian Empire, the man who not only routed the Turks but also put down the Hungarian Protestant revolt. There must have been hundreds of monasteries, dozens of museums, and any number of religious scholars who would have been interested in the book and willing to pay a tidy sum for it. Why should it end up with a general? Anyway, no time for speculation now. What happened after that?"

"Well, Savoy died in 1736. His library was purchased by the Emperor. The book eventually went into the National Library of Austria and was not heard from again until 1907, when it was translated into English by Laura and Lonsdale Ragg."

Zeki stood up and began pacing the room like a court prosecutor.

"We have to think like the conspirators, get into their minds. Do you know if there are any obvious Catholic elements in the Gospel like there were in the Lead Books of Sacromonte?"

Gary shrugged. "I haven't come across any reference to particularly Catholic elements."

"What about the paper it is written on?" continued Zeki.

"There was something about that…" Gary's fingers flew over the keyboard and then he waited for the search results. "Yes, there is a watermark," replied Gary. "The paper is Italian, and interestingly enough, the watermark on Morisco document 9653 is the same."

"Interesting" continued Zeki, still pacing the room. "The Ottomans imported most of their paper since their own attempts to produce it were not very successful."

"It was bound in Turkish leather with a simple floral design on the cover," said Gary.

This elicited only a grunt from Zeki. "Is there an introduction to the book that might help us determine its origin?" he asked.

"In the Italian version? No. But…" Gary turned back to his computer and did a quick search. "The Spanish version has an introduction. Give me a second." He scanned the search results for the link he was looking for. "Here it is. There is a note in the introduction to the Spanish version that says it was translated from Italian by a Spanish Muslim named Mostafa de Aranda in Istanbul. There is also a preface that relates the story of its discovery in the Vatican."

"The Vatican?" asked Matt dubiously. "If the book is a forgery, and I think we have proven that it is, then we can discount any information provided in the preface."

"Misdirection," agreed Zeki. "Pure and simple."

Gary continued reading, "A certain Fra Marino had, for years, wondered if the four gospels accepted by the Church fathers were the originals. One day, he chanced upon the writings of Irenaeus, an early church father, who condemned the doctrines of Paul and quoted as his source the Gospel of Barnabas. He goes on to tell how he was with Pope Sixtus V in his library, and that when the Pope fell asleep, he began perusing the shelves to pass the time. He took a book off the shelf and much to his surprise found he was holding the Gospel of Barnabas, which he hid in the folds of his cloak and smuggled out of the library."

"Likely story…" retorted Matt sarcastically.

Gary interrupted. "There are problems with it. First of all, there are no known works of Irenaeus that criticize Paul."

"Is there anything else?" asked Zeki.

"There is a short prologue in the Italian. Hang on. I'll find it." Gary began reading from the screen.

'BARNABAS, APOSTLE OF JESUS THE NAZARENE, CALLED CHRIST,
TO ALL THEM THAT DWELL UPON THE EARTH, DESIRES PEACE AND
CONSOLATION.

DEARLY BELOVED, THE GREAT AND WONDERFUL GOD HAS DURING
THESE PAST DAYS VISITED US BY HIS PROPHET JESUS CHRIST IN
GREAT MERCY OF TEACHING AND MIRACLES, FOR WHICH REASON
MANY, BEING DECEIVED OF SATAN, UNDER PRETENSE OF PIETY,
ARE PREACHING MOST IMPIOUS DOCTRINE, CALLING JESUS SON OF
GOD, REPUDIATING THE CIRCUMCISION ORDAINED OF GOD FOR
EVER, AND PERMITTING EVERY UNCLEAN MEAT: AMONG WHOM ALSO
PAUL HAS BEEN DECEIVED, WHEREOF I SPEAK NOT WITHOUT GRIEF.
IT IS BECAUSE OF THIS THAT I AM WRITING THAT TRUTH WHICH I
HAVE SEEN AND HEARD, IN THE DISCOURSE THAT I HAVE HAD WITH
JESUS, IN ORDER THAT YOU MAY BE SAVED, AND NOT BE DECEIVED
OF SATAN AND PERISH IN THE JUDGMENT OF GOD. THEREFORE,
BEWARE OF EVERY ONE THAT PREACHES NEW DOCTRINE TO YOU
CONTRARY TO THAT WHICH I WRITE, THAT YOU MAY BE SAVED
ETERNALLY. THE GREAT GOD BE WITH YOU AND GUARD YOU FROM
SATAN AND FROM EVERY EVIL. AMEN.'

"Wait a minute," said Gwyn, "I don't remember Barnabas being one of the
twelve disciples."

"As far as the canonical New Testament goes, he wasn't," replied Gary.
"He isn't mentioned in any of the Gospels, only in Acts, but in the G.O.B.,
Barnabas replaces Thomas. Hang on. I highlighted that somewhere. Here it is:

THEIR NAMES ARE: ANDREW AND PETER HIS BROTHER, BARNABAS,
WHO WROTE THIS WITH MATTHEW THE PUBLICAN, WHO SAT AT
THE RECEIPT OF CUSTOM; JOHN AND JAMES, SONS OF ZEBEDEE;
THADDAEUS AND JUDAS; BARTHOLOMEW AND PHILIP, JAMES, AND
JUDAS ISCARIOT THE TRAITOR.

"So why did the forger or forgers choose Barnabas as the author?" asked
Gwyn.

"I think it is quite apparent," ventured Zeki. "Everyone who has read the
New Testament knows that Paul and Barnabas had a disagreement, and they
went their separate ways. Barnabas went back to Cyprus. Paul continued his
missionary journey."

"So?" said Gwyn, with a perplexed look on her face.

Gary saw where Zeki was going and countered quickly, "But Acts says that
the disagreement was about personnel, a man named John Mark, who had
deserted them earlier, not about doctrine."

"Yes," returned Zeki, "That is what the New Testament says, but for centuries, Muslims have blamed Paul for corrupting the message of Jesus, since he wrote much of the New Testament…"

"So, this would allow them to claim that the split was actually over doctrine?" asked Gwyn incredulously.

"Sounds like a clever plan to me," said Zeki. "They could say that the account in Acts was cleansed to cover up what the disagreement was about, that Barnabas recorded the true Gospel, and that this was suppressed by the Church."

"Actually, there might more to it than that," said Gary.

"Then enlighten us," said Zeki, cheerfully.

The change in his manner over the last few moments was lost on none of them. He seemed to know where he was going and was now enjoying the ride.

"Well, two things," said Gary. "First, there is the Gelasian Decree, which dates back to 492 AD and lists ten apocryphal works rejected by the Church. Most of them are named after one of the disciples, and one of them is called the Gospel of Barnabas. The problem with the list is that the supposed Gospel of Barnabas in the list would have been written in Greek, but the only copies we are aware of are in Spanish and Italian. The Gospel of Barnabas referred to in the Gelasian Decree has never been identified, it is not quoted by any church fathers. Except for this list of heretical books and a similar one like it, there is no mention of it, either before AD 492 or after, until this Italian or Spanish version was brought to light in the early 1700s."

"Bingo," said Zeki. "There it is. They needed an ancient witness and they found it in the Gelasian Decree. They chose the only work for which there were no copies, so they were not in any danger of being found out."

"Hmmm," said Matt thoughtfully. "That's a nice angle. It also means an incredible amount of research and preparation must have gone into this work. What was the other thing, Gary?"

"In 478 AD, the Bishop of Cyprus claimed to have received a vision of Barnabas in which the saint said, 'You will find a coffin in a cave where my whole body has been preserved, and there is a Gospel written in my own hand, which I received from the Holy Apostle and Evangelist Matthew.' Many Muslims claim that the G.O.B. is the gospel referred to in this legend."

"But the vision said that it was the Gospel of Matthew, copied down by Barnabas," Matt protested.

"You're not putting stock in visions now, are you?" Gary asked wryly.

"No, just pointing out an inconsistency, that's all."

"You're right, of course. But, there was a connection," said Gary, "Hang on. In the list of disciples given in the G.O.B., it said something similar. Listen:

…BARNABAS, WHO WROTE THIS WITH MATTHEW THE PUBLICAN…

"Nice," said Matt with a low whistle. The forger had clearly begun to gain his respect. "Clearly, the forger needed to make Barnabas appear to be one of the twelve, so the forger adds Barnabas to the list. He also connects him with Matthew, which is especially clever in light of the vision received by the Bishop of Cyprus."

"And can you tell us why the good bishop invented the story?" Zeki asked Gary with a twinkle in his eyes.

"I hadn't thought about it," replied Gary.

Zeki turned to Matt.

"How about you, Matt?" he asked, clearly enjoying himself. "I'm sorry. We already know you don't believe it, but tell us why."

Matt caught the quick look from Gwyn, warning him to be tactful.

"Well, first of all I don't believe the spirits of people who have been dead more than four hundred years can visit us in our dreams. Secondly, I would guess that once again this is a case of religious shenanigans, a church looking for relics that would increase their standing in the Christendom and give them revenues from pilgrims visiting a holy site. Bury an old man in a cave, let him get good and dry, claim that you received a vision and *voilà*, your church suddenly has a direct line to the first Christians, bones to prove it and a Gospel to boot."

"Exactly," said Zeki. "See, we do agree on some things, maybe more than you realize." He turned back to Gary and asked, "Is there more?"

"Wait a minute," interrupted Gwyn, scanning her own notes. "Remember, the Morisco forgeries in Spain referred to Cyprus as well. It said, 'the King of the Arabs, who is not himself an Arab, will hold a Great Council in Cyprus revealing the True Gospel.' Why Cyprus?" she asked. "What's the connection?"

"The patron saint of Cyprus is Barnabas," said Zeki matter-of-factly.

Matt looked at him dubiously.

"I was stationed in Cyprus as a new field agent," he said with a shrug of his shoulders.

"There is no end to the surprises with you, sir," said Matt, shaking his head. "But let's bring this closer to home. Is it possible that the Gospel of Barnabas was a Morisco-Ottoman plot? Maybe the relics in Granada and the Lead Books of Sacromonte were the opening performance, and the True Gospel, I mean the politically correct version in the Muslim world, the Gospel of Barnabas, was the final act. Was the plan to introduce it with some fanfare at a Council in Cyprus? The religious leaders of Cyprus might be easily convinced to go along as the Gospel would have been written by Barnabas, their patron saint, and the Ottoman Turks would obviously prefer a Gospel that helped the Christian population accept Islam."

Matt slapped his leg and stood up, whirling to face Gary.

"Damn, that *would* be good! Too good!"

"Cyprus wasn't an important religious or cultural center. It was the backwaters of the Mediterranean, which, at the time, was practically a Muslim lake. There is no reason for the Lead Books of Sacromonte to say that the Ottoman Sultan would hold a Council in Cyprus."

"Unless," said Zeki, "the Gospel of Barnabas project was covertly supported by elements within the Ottoman government. Then the so-called prophecy in the Lead Books of Sacromonte makes perfect sense."

"And the document found by my father is proof positive that the Ottoman Empire was involved," added Gary.

"I knew this was going to be big, but I never imagined it could be this big," said Zeki. "The Turks took Cyprus in 1571, not long before the Morisco writings. If a pseudo-gospel were being prepared in the name of Barnabas for the purpose of slanting the New Testament towards Islam, then it would be ingenious to have the Virgin Mary 'prophecy' a council on Cyprus, hosted by a non-Arab king of the Arabs. The fulfillment of this prophecy and the unveiling of the Gospel of Barnabas on the island that recognizes him as their patron saint would be powerful, especially since church tradition says that the body of Barnabas was found in a cave on the island clasping a copy of the Gospel."

Matt let out a low whistle. "Talk about the public relations project of the millennium. Just think of it, a brand new religion melding Islam and Christianity and ending the conflict between them."

Gwyn began flipping through the pages in her notebook. Everybody waited.

"This dovetails perfectly with something else in the Lead Books of Sacromonte. The Virgin Mary claims to have received a copy of the Gospel from the 'hand of power' and commands St. James to bury it in Sacromonte, where it will be discovered when 'the earth is rent by heresy and dissent about Jesus and the Gospel'. She says the discovery of this book will lead to a revival of faith led by the Arabs."

"Impressive," said Matt, folding his arms. "They were definitely taking the long view on social change here, carefully setting it up and laying a foundation for introducing the G.O.B. that would give it the authority of prophecy. Was there anything else, Gary?"

Gary went back to his notes.

"The Italian manuscript was clearly being prepared for printing, but the headings for the different chapters are only provided up until page twenty-two. After that, they're all blank, so it was obviously never finished. There are, however, notes in the margins on almost every page that suggest different headings or a better text, usually so that it will conform better to Muslim theology. For example, Mohammed is called the 'messenger of God' but the notes over and over again suggest that this be changed to 'Apostle of God'.

"Of course," said Zeki. "Apostle has a much higher status than messenger."

"One change suggested by the editor," continued Gary, "is even a quote from the Qur'an, which obviously dates the work after Mohammed. The notes are all written in Arabic, and…"

"Wait a minute, I thought our conclusion was that the Ottoman Turks not the Arabs were behind this," said Matt grimacing. "This is starting to give me a headache."

"Well, it's not quite that simple," cautioned Gary. "Language experts say that the Arabic is quite poor. We don't know who wrote the notes."

Zeki raised his hand, as if asking for quiet, while he paced across the room. After several trips back and forth he stopped.

"First of all," he said, "there are many dialects of spoken Arabic, some mutually unintelligible to the others, and the written language is a difficult one to master. Second, a Morisco could easily have been less than proficient in Arabic if he had been brought up in Catholic Spain where Arabic was prohibited, so that might explain why the Arabic is bad. What else do we have to consider, Gary?"

He began to pace the room again while Gary scrolled down through his notes. Gwyn stood up and headed to the kitchen, shaking her head as if the whole thing were just too astonishing. Matt walked over and sat down beside Gilbert, who hadn't said a word in the last half hour. He picked up his notes. Gary continued.

"There are a lot of tiny details, nothing really important. For example, the first three occurrences of God, which is, of course, *Dio* in Italian, are crossed out and the word Allah is written over it in Arabic."

"So," said Matt, look down at his own notes. "Is it fair to say that that this pseudo-Gospel was probably prepared with some Morisco involvement and Ottoman support, that the purpose was to present a version of the Gospel that confirmed the truth of Islam to Christians by resurrecting a respected early church figure like Barnabas and still retain enough Christianity to encourage some sort of common ground between the two?"

Everyone nodded in agreement.

"But, we still haven't answered the crucial question," continued Matt. "Who would go to this much trouble, create a work this involved, and then just drop it? It makes no sense. In Muslim literature before 1906, we have no trace of it until 1634 and then only a single reference in a Morisco document that does not even quote a single passage from the book. Then, we have a few references by Western scholars in the early 1700s and nothing else until it is translated into English in 1907."

Zeki smiled again. "We may never know the answer to that. What we do know is that whoever was behind the project decided to cancel it. It's as simple as that. The first line of the order Prof. O'Brien found is clear: 'The council's decision to cancel son of prophet and erase every trace remains among our most solemn duties.' They almost succeeded, too. The Spanish copy or copies, which were all either in Holland or England, are gone except for one half-finished version that turned up in Australia forty years ago. The single Italian version in Vienna is the only other copy. Gwyn, can you read the translation of the order again?"

She turned to the front of the notebook.

"The council's decision to cancel son of prophet and erase every trace remains among our most solemn duties. It will be a red English sunset on Suri-Strand with a golden sunrise in Tunis when the bird which has flown is brought back to Südde-i Saadet. Walk in the snow, but leave no footprints. Assistance for the sendoff may be obtained from our ever faithful D. Hasten delivery."

"Now, you were saying the English connection was Sale, right?" asked Matt.

"That's right."

"What do we know about him?"

"Sale," said Gwyn, "Was the editor of the Arabic New Testament, probably not a popular project in the Muslim world. More importantly, he translated the Qur'an into English. I read the introduction this morning where he mentions the Gospel of Barnabas. He died at his home on Surrey-Strand in England, allegedly of a fever…"

"So, 'the bird which has flown' is the G.O.B.," said Zeki confidently and to no one in particular. "Sale had it and they wanted it back. Maybe he did come down with an illness and die prematurely, maybe he was killed. Whatever the case, we know that they were after the Spanish version of the G.O.B."

"And yet," continued Gary, "The Italian version somehow escaped."

"Let me ask a question," ventured Zeki. "If you had the Italian version and knew how it was meant to be used by the enemy, who would you give it to for safe-keeping?"

No one spoke. Gwyn simply shrugged. Gary crossed his arms and tilted his head back in a thinking posture. It was Matt who spoke first.

"The General?" he asked.

"Precisely!" said Zeki. The pieces were coming together in his mind. "A man who had fought the enemy, a soldier whose honor would prevent him from ever being tempted to sell it, a place where it would be safe from Morisco assassins like the one who carried this letter."

324

"How do we know the assassin was Morisco?" asked Gwyn.

"The *Aljamiado* translation at the bottom only makes sense if they were Moriscos," replied Zeki. "And, they were to be paid handsomely with a 'golden sunset' back in the city of Tunis."

"It says that assistance can be obtained from 'D'. Any idea what that is talking about?" asked Gary.

"Maybe, it is the Dutch?" ventured Gwyn.

"It's possible, but it's not critical to understanding the message," replied Zeki.

"But, why did they abandon it?" asked Matt again.

Zeki sighed. "All we can do is speculate. Maybe they had hoped to use it to make Christians in their own realm accept Islam, but finally decided it might backfire. Maybe the plan was to retake Spain or use it in Hungary, but the political tailwinds turned to headwinds. Maybe there was internal division about how to implement the project or maybe there were theological disputes. Who knows? It could have been anything. What is clear is that they didn't want anyone to know of the existence of such a plot."

"Why not?" asked Gary.

"Why not?" repeated Matt, "I'll tell you why. How do you think this news would have played out in the West? Just imagine the headlines. 'Ottoman Empire rewrites Gospel to attract Europeans to Islam.' By the 17th century, the Industrial Revolution was cranking out a military machine the Ottomans could not have matched if the Europeans joined forces. And, religious sentiment was still strong enough to make this happen. We already know that the only thing which did bring the Europeans together was the Crusades, a common enemy, a common threat."

"Exactly," said Zeki.

"Tell me this," said Matt, turning to Gary. "If, as Zeki says, many Muslims today believe the G.O.B. is the real gospel, how did that happen if the whole project was canceled?"

"Except for the 1634 Morisco document, there is no mention of it in the Muslim world. Their erasure, if you will, was quite thorough. If the Italian version had not been preserved by Prince Eugene, modern-day Muslims would be totally ignorant of its existence along with the rest of the world. However, it was translated into English by Raggs in 1907. No sooner had it been printed in English than an Arabic translation from the English was executed in Egypt. From there, it spread like wildfire through the Muslim world. Of course, the translators left out the introduction by Raggs, which detailed all of the reasons to believe it was a fraud, and the next thing you know, the front pages of Pakistani newspapers are publishing whole chapters of it. It spread over the entire Muslim world."

"Like we said," remarked Matt dryly, "if it says what people already believe is true, then it's an easy sell. Regardless of what the original project aimed to accomplish, now the news is out and everyone believes it. Ironic, isn't it. They tried to destroy it in the 17th century. Yet now, they're trying to protect it by hiding their involvement. You wouldn't want to upset what people believe with the document Prof. O'Brien found."

"I understand that," said Gwyn, "But there is already plenty of internal evidence, everything points to a forgery. Why would the document my father found make any difference?"

"Oh, it would be quite damning," responded Zeki, "I'm also convinced now that the book is a forgery. We have used inductive reasoning to arrive at this conclusion and the evidence is persuasive, but until your father discovered this document, there was no direct evidence outside of the text of the G.O.B. itself. A document written in Ottoman Turkish that relates a secret plot to destroy evidence of the forgery. Now that is explosive. It couldn't be good for interfaith relations, especially now with tensions between Islam and the West rivaling that of the Middle Ages."

"Can you imagine," asked Matt, "how this would fuel the fires in anti-Muslim sentiment in the Bible Belt? With mosques being built all over the country and Muslims having a much higher profile in the government, I can definitely see why this would make waves. I doubt even the US government would be happy for a thing like this to come out."

"Wait a minute," exclaimed Gilbert, startling everyone by breaking his silence so suddenly. "There is some UN project... Oh, what was it called... It will be unveiled next month with a bunch of fanfare in New York. Our company is providing security for the event. 'Tolerance and Unity in a Multicultural World.' It's a global pact of some sort. The UN is billing it as a move towards interfaith dialogue built on the foundations laid by the Prime Ministers of Turkey and Spain after 911. Muslims are playing a prominent role."

"You mean, preach peace and prepare for war," said Matt grimly. Gilbert had obviously touched a nerve. "I don't believe the Muslim world wants dialogue. I was in the State Department. I know how this game is played. I'll believe they want dialogue when Saudi Arabia allows Buddhist temples or Christian churches. No offense to our friend here," he said, pointing to Zeki, "But all this stuff about tolerance is B.S. pure and simple. There is not a single gesture on their part to show tolerance. Millions of petro-dollars from the Saudi government are funneled into building mosques in the States, and yet you can't even carry a Bible, much less build a church in their country. Ninety-five percent of the terrorist acts in the world, maybe more, are committed by Muslims. They expect freedom of religion when they are in the West, but won't give a square inch of land to ensure others enjoy the same freedom in their own country. I don't know what their Prophet says about that, but I'm pretty sure Jesus would call it hypocrisy."

"Whatever," said Gilbert, trying to ease the tension. "Maybe the reason they are so desperate to keep this from coming to light is because of what it would do to the launch of this initiative."

"I'll research it when we're done here," said Gary, scribbling on a notepad. Gilbert fell silent again.

51

Zeki cleared his throat when it was evident that no one else was going to talk. "I must beg your indulgence. I've been holding back two pieces of information waiting to see where all of this was going. Now that we have gained some clarity, it is time to give the tale a Turkish twist. I remembered something related to G.O.B. back in the mid-80s in Turkey, so I did a little research on the plane to find the details. In 1986, the Turkish military claimed that a Syriac copy of the Gospel of Barnabas had been found near Hakkari."

Gwyn raised an eyebrow and bit her lip as she twirled a pencil between her fingers, "That's odd. I didn't see that in my research."

"I'm sure you didn't," continued Zeki. "The reason is because this extraordinary claim was later retracted when it became clear that the manuscript they found was merely the canonical Bible. However, the retraction didn't make headline news like the discovery did."

"Typical disinformation tactic," observed Matt.

"If you had conducted your search in Turkish," continued Zeki. "You would have found dozens of websites still claiming that this Syriac bible is the real Gospel of Barnabas. The book is supposedly held by the military."

"The military?" asked a perplexed Gwyn. "Why would they be holding a religious document?"

"Because the military was the 'shadow of Atatürk'. The fact that the military is still holding it and won't release it is a huge controversy, fodder for more conspiracy actually. Some say the military is being pressured to keep it silent by this or that group—NATO, the Vatican, the Masons, or whatever group you want to demonize. In the end though, it doesn't matter what the facts are. Truth is created in people's minds. Have you ever heard of repetition-induced belief?" he asked.

"Yeah, it's a well-documented psychological phenomenon," replied Gary. "People have to use an information filter to make sense of all the competing truth claims they encounter, for example, whether Nokia or Samsung phones are better. As a result, subconsciously, they tend to believe the things they hear repeated. They figure that if multiple sources report the same thing as true then its chances of being true are much higher."

"Exactly. Now let me ask you a question. Do you believe that Neil Armstrong is a Muslim?"

Zeki waited a minute for a reaction. No one said anything although he could tell from the grimace on Matt's face that he was tempted.

"You don't believe that, do you?"

"This is the first time I have heard it," said Gwyn.

"My point exactly," said Zeki. "But, if you were to ask people on the street in Turkey, nine out of ten would say, 'Yes, he's a Muslim. He converted when he heard the call to prayer on the moon.'"

"He did?" asked Gwyn, with a puzzled look of disbelief on her face.

"You don't believe it because it doesn't fit your understanding of the facts and because you are hearing it for the first time from me, a Turkish Muslim. But, imagine you were a Turk and had heard this from your local imam, had seen it in print, had heard it discussed on TV programs and your neighbors and friends had relayed the story."

"I see your point," said Gwyn. "Of course, I would want to believe that God had confirmed his message miraculously to an infidel on the moon and that he had responded in faith."

"No one cares that Armstrong wrote letters disavowing it because they've never heard of those letters. What they *have* heard, again and again, is that Armstrong converted to Islam, and since this is what they want to believe, the standard of proof is much lower than it would normally be."

Zeki continued pacing back and forth, speaking rapidly and with great confidence.

"I really don't think that Turkey's secular army invented this claim to have found the G.O.B. because they have some desire to see radical Islam rise in Turkey. They are the guardians of the secular state. But, in the mid-eighties, when this 'discovery' happened, Turkey had just come back from the brink of a leftist revolt and revolution was in the air. The people were tired of the elected elite fleecing them like sheep and many were turning to socialism and communism. I think that the claim made in 1986 was an attempt to stir up religious sentiment. We know that the rise of communism was viewed as a threat by both Islam and capitalism, making Muslim countries junior partners, if you will, in the crusade against atheism. European elites opposed communism too, but the common man in Europe was much more sympathetic."

Zeki paused to let it all sink in. Matt turned to Gary and picked up where Zeki had left off.

"This was only a couple of years after the attempted assassination of the Pope, so you'll remember the context. At the time, the State Department actively courted Muslim countries to form an alliance with Islam. It was the perfect flanking maneuver, as it ensured that Russia would not have access to warm sea ports. Turkey was the cornerstone of the Islamic alliance, not only because it bordered Russia but because it was the only NATO member country that was predominately Muslim. Hell, we even kept tactical nuclear weapons at the Incirlik Air Base in southern Turkey. But, if a socialist revolution had taken place in Turkey, this entire strategy would have been jeopardized. Zeki is saying that the elites used religion to turn the ideological tide against communism and atheism by resurrecting proof that God, or Allah, or whatever you want to call him, had affirmed the truth of their faith. Maybe the supposed discovery of a Syriac Gospel of Barnabas was a shot in the arm, a morale booster, if you will, an event staged to put the G.O.B. back in the headlines."

"There is something else," Zeki said, "I have saved it for now. I hope you'll agree that I made the right decision. Remember how I said that the key logger Gilbert managed to install indicated this group was trying to steal something from Augustinerlesesaal?"

"I do," said Gary, "But I forgot to research it."

"Augustinerlesesaal," said Zeki, "Is the reading room of the Austrian National Library."

Gary's eyes widened.

"And, what are they planning on stealing?" asked Matt.

"Oh my God!" exclaimed Gary. "That is where the Italian version of the G.O.B. is kept."

"Exactly." replied Zeki.

"They want to steal it?" asked Matt.

"Yes, and you are going to tell me why," replied Zeki, "In the Turkish portion of the key-logger data from Gilbert, they said that an appointment had been made at the Augustinerlesesaal in four days and that the appointment was made in the name of a priest—Luigi Franchini."

"A priest!" said Matt incredulously. Everyone could see the wheels turning in his mind. When the light came on, it was accompanied by a string of curses. "The low-life bastards!"

"I don't get it," said Gwyn. "Why would they steal it in the name of a priest?"

"Because they want it to look like a priest did it," replied Zeki, shaking his head in disgust.

"Oh my gosh," said Gwyn suddenly. "They mean to pin the blame on the Vatican…"

"That's what it looks like to me," he said. "If they were to steal the only complete surviving copy of the G.O.B. and frame a Vatican priest for it, then it would look like the Vatican was trying to hide something. The western media would have no qualms about broadcasting it, and it would confirm the suspicions of Muslims around the world that Christians have forever suppressed the true message of Jesus. I assure you it would be a much bigger story than our little document."

"Wow," said Gary, turning to Matt. "Now, when these guys want to upstage somebody, they do it on a grand scale."

"But why," asked Matt, looking up at the ceiling "are *you* telling us this?"

Gwyn shot him a quick look. She knew from the tone in his voice that he had just drawn his sword. She wanted to tell him to back off, but Matt turned to Zeki, suspicion and distrust written all over his face, and asked again. "Why are you telling us this?"

"Why shouldn't I?" said Zeki coolly.

"Look, let's stop playing games here," Matt replied. "You are a Muslim. I also know from Gilbert that you are ex-MIT, and for all I know, maybe you still are. Why are you helping us uncover this? This is huge. You could have kept this information to yourself."

Zeki grinned, "But, I didn't, and still you don't trust me."

Matt was ready with his disclaimer. "I don't know what your motivations are. This is not personal. For me, rule number one is 'nothing is what it appears to be.' You said so yourself. Aren't the people who tried to kill Gwyn Muslims like you?"

"Like me?" repeated Zeki, returning Matt's stare with a look that might have been a lightning bolt it was so intense. "If they were like me, they'd be here discussing the history of this forgery, not holding innocent children as ransom. Or, to put it conversely, if I were like them, I would have already slit your throat for your insolence and unbelief and taken the document and Gwyn as the spoils of war."

Matt stood up indignantly. Zeki looked at him, his face a strange mixture of contempt and compassion.

"Sit down, son. You are a smart man. Stop letting doubt, suspicion and extraneous facts cloud your judgment."

"Matt," said Gwyn. "Zeki saved my life. I can't believe that is not proof enough."

She walked over and stood beside Zeki.

"He's been right about everything so far," Gary pronounced in a somber voice.

There was a long silence. Matt was clearly uncomfortable with everyone lining up against him. Finally, he looked at Gilbert, who was still strangely silent.

"It's your family. I'm just here for the ride. I'm going out for some fresh air."

With that, he walked out of the room. Zeki waited until he heard the outside door shut.

"Now," said Zeki, "What are we going to do?"

"It's simple," said Gary. "We inform the library and have them arrest the man when he comes in and presents his fake ID."

Zeki shook his head and smiled. "I don't think so."

"Why not?" protested Gwyn.

Gilbert slammed his hand down on the table. Gwyn jump back a step in fright.

"For goodness sake, Gil. What is wrong with you? You scared me to death."

Gilbert stood up in the middle of the room, talking to everyone and no one in particular.

"You know, right now, I don't really give a rat's ass about some 17th-century group of religious perverts trying to sell their own damned twisted version of history or whether or not Father Franchini starts a jihad aimed at the Vatican. I want my family back. Does anyone see how any of this shit is going to help us?"

Gary stood up and walked over to his brother. "Gil, calm down, man. Get a hold of yourself."

"Get a hold of myself? Get a hold of myself? What I want to do is get a hold of these criminals. That's what I want." His voice was getting louder and louder. "I want to make these sorry bastards pay and I want my family back."

Gwyn jumped up and got right in his face.

"Stop it Gilbert! Right now! Stop it! When has your anger ever solved a problem, huh? In this condition, you are like a city whose walls have been broken down."

The proverb their mother had drilled in their heads combined with the visual image of a young lady who was the spitting image of her jolted him back to reality. He sat down and put his head in his hands. No one wanted to speak, but the silence was worse. Gary looked at Zeki. The man had walked over to the window and was staring at the curtains as if they were glass and he could see the people on the street outside. Gary walked over, kneeled beside his brother and put his hand on his knee.

"Gil, are you okay, man?" His question went unanswered and he waited another minute. "Hey bro, talk to us. What are you thinking?"

More silence. Gary was about to give up when Gilbert said quietly,

"I'm not thinking. I'm praying."

"So am I," said Gary.

He looked at Gwyn, who immediately said, "Me too, Gil."

From the other side of the room came Zeki's deep baritone, "Me too, son. God is great. He is bigger than any challenge we face."

A strange peace seemed to wash over the room, and Gwyn felt the knot in her throat slowly dissolve. She couldn't help wishing Matt had been here for this moment, and for the first time in almost a year she breathed a quick prayer for him as well.

52

İSTANBUL   Zeki asked to be excused and slipped out of the room. Gwyn refilled their tea glasses. Gary immediately turned to his brother and said in a voice just barely above a whisper.

"I thought you were going to talk to Matt and tell him to keep a lid on it!"

"Cut him some slack," said Gilbert, picking up a glass of tea. "If you had spent the last year rescuing victims of human trafficking, many kidnapped and sold in the Middle East, you might have an attitude too."

Gary sighed. "Well, his attitude is straining our relationship with the only friend we have in this city."

Gwyn cocked her head and looked askance at her brother.

"What are you talking about, Gilbert?"

"I'm talking about Matt," he said.

"Not the Matt who was just in this room?" She lowered her voice.

"One and the same," he said. "A lot has changed since you guys broke up."

"He works with prostitutes?" she asked.

"Gwyn, please! You sound like a jealous schoolgirl. He helps rescue victims of sexual exploitation. You should be proud of him."

"Oh, I don't have a problem with that. I was just surprised; that's all," said Gwyn, reaching up again for locks that were no longer there and then nervously folding her hands in her lap.

"I can't believe he left State," she continued. "He always talked about climbing the ladder, winning an appointment as an ambassador and then maybe running for Congress. Why would he leave a career in foreign affairs? That was his dream."

"Dreams have a funny way of working their way to new endings and sometimes turning into nightmares," replied Gilbert.

"So, what department or agency does he work with now?" she asked.

"He isn't with a department," replied Gilbert.

"Well, who does he work for?" she insisted.

"Look, Gwyn, I think that is something you should ask him yourself."

"Why can't you tell me?" She shot back.

From the corridor came the sound of a door closing. Gilbert just smiled at his sister and turned towards the door as Matt walked into the room.

"Is anybody getting hungry?" asked Gilbert. "I bet Gary knows a reputable place somewhere close that serves up some good kebab."

"I'm starved," said Matt.

"Sure, I can pick something up and bring it back here. Let's wait for Zeki and see if he wants something too."

"I don't know how long Muslim prayers last," said Matt. "But you'll have to wait for him to finish. The door to the bedroom at the end of the hall by the bathroom was left in a crack. I peeked in and found him prostrate on the floor. I'm pretty sure that's what he is doing."

Gilbert looked at his sister sitting on the couch and shook his head. He knew that look, that icy stare. Her reaction came faster than he thought.

"So, Matt, what have you been doing with yourself since you left State?" Her voice had a steely and sterile tone.

Matt didn't know her as well as her brother did, but he could still sense the hardness in her voice. He had a split-second debate with himself about how much to share and immediately decided that a vague answer was safest.

"I work with an NGO that focuses on social reform, mostly in Eastern Europe. It has been a tough transition, but I think I'm starting to find a groove. In fact, if I were perfectly honest, it has been therapy of sorts. Helping hurting people rebuild their lives has helped *me* do something I don't think I've done in a long time, at least not while I was at the State Department with all of the political maneuvering and career ambition."

He stopped. Gwyn waited until his silence outlasted her patience.

"And what was that?" she asked.

"I got my eyes off of myself long enough to see the world around me," he said quietly.

The answer confused her. Her face screwed up funny for a second and then she continued.

"And just what is your position at this NGO?"

"Well, I'm not really on staff. Our relationship is focused more on collaboration not employment."

"I see. So, who are you working for?"

He understood now where she was going and that she wasn't going to be satisfied until she got an answer. There was no sense playing cat and mouse with her.

"I'm self-employed, Gwyn. I work outside of the system to apprehend criminals and bring them back into the justice system."

"Outside the system? What is that supposed to mean?" she asked.

He sighed and looked her straight in the eye. The intensity she saw in his eyes made her uncomfortable, but she held his gaze.

"What it means? Are you sure you want to know?"

"Why wouldn't I?"

"I think it would be better if you let some things lie. But you can't do that, can you? It's always total and complete transparency, isn't it? So, if you must know, I'm a bounty hunter," Matt said flatly.

"A bounty hunter," she repeated the words in disbelief and then fell silent, trying to keep her face expressionless. *Why did it matter anyway? He can do whatever he wants.* Inside, however, she knew she still cared. There was no way she could process all of this right now.

Zeki entered the room. The atmosphere was pensive, and he wondered what had transpired while he was out. He made his way towards his chair trying to read their faces.

"Where is Gary?" he asked.

"I think he stepped out to go to the restroom," replied Gilbert. "He'll be right back."

Zeki moved towards the table in the middle of the room to fill his tea glass. Gary appeared at the door before the two sugar cubes he had put in the glass could dissolve. Zeki sat down in his chair and looked at the glass as he stirred the piping hot tea with a small spoon. The small white grains of sugar were spinning in the warm brown liquid. In seconds, they would disappear from sight entirely, still present, only invisible, a perfect picture of human life. *We are born into this whirlpool called the world, where the dizzying spin addles our mind and confounds our reason. We struggle to maintain our shape, our individuality. In the end, we disappear entirely, but we leave our taste in the tea.* He felt like he was standing on the edge of a huge glass, wondering why he was willing to throw himself in, but just as certain that he would. He drew himself up straight, took a drink of his tea and plunged in just as Gary walked in.

"I have a proposal for keeping the G.O.B. from being stolen that I think you might be interested in," announced Zeki

"We're all ears," said Gilbert.

"We steal it ourselves," he said simply.

Matt chuckled to himself and shook his head. Gwyn's face remained expressionless. Gary sat down on the couch and leaned back in a sign he was ready to hear more.

"That will certainly stop them from getting it, but I'm not sure what you think makes it important enough to take the risk," asked Matt.

"I have been considering the idea ever since I realized what they were up to, and the more I think about it, the more confident I feel that this is the right course of action. Not only will we thwart their plan, but we might be able to turn it into a situation that gives us an advantage. Something that could help us make sure the exchange goes well and that Gilbert's family gets returned safely. Besides, I want to see whoever murdered Prof. O'Brien pay for their crime."

Gary, Gilbert and Matt exchanged glances as they turned the idea over in their minds. Gary was the first to speak.

"Zeki, we all want to see these people punished, but avenging our father's death is not going to help us save the lives of his grandchildren."

"Son, revenge is not something I believe in either. I do believe in justice though, and I'm not under the illusion that corrupt governments instituted by men are the only way justice can be served."

"Vigilantism is not our way," replied Gary.

"Listen, you'll have your hands full here in Istanbul with the exchange," continued Zeki. "I don't expect you to do anything. I'll handle the entire thing."

"Stealing this manuscript is not an operation you can throw together in just a few days." said Matt. "What is your plan?"

"To beat them at their own game, to frame them for the theft they want to pin on the Vatican. I am beginning to suspect a certain organization might be behind this, so if I can take the book before they do and set it up so that when the loss is noticed, it looks like they are responsible, we will be holding the aces. Then, I can confront the man masquerading as Father Luigi Franchini at Augustinerlesesaal.

"I will convince him that we have the upper hand, and that we will return the original of the document discreetly in exchange for the safe return of Gilbert's family. I think they will want to stay out of the papers. After all, the reason they are pursuing this so ruthlessly is because they do not want their involvement to become public. If the man refuses to cooperate when I meet him in the library, I have friends who can tail him after he leaves so that we can arrange another meeting under less cordial circumstances."

"What friends?" asked Gwyn innocently.

"Good ones," said Zeki with a smile. "The kind you need in times like these."

Gilbert's face lit up at the thought of getting a break.

"Zeki," he said eagerly, "This is the first thing anybody's mentioned that might help us, but..." he stopped and rubbed his forehead. He didn't want to say it.

"But what?" asked Zeki

"I think you've put yourself in harm's way enough already."

"Nonsense! You're never in harm's way when you're doing the right thing. Being killed in the line of duty would be an honor, not a shame, and you have no idea what a tremendous debt I owe your father. I'm sure he never told you about my own bout with cancer five years before your mother's."

Gwyn looked at her two brothers. They both shook their heads.

"I figured as much," continued Zeki. "He had a funny thing about 'the right hand not knowing what the left was doing.' It was his way, I suppose. The long and short of it is that I had colon cancer. He arranged for me to have the best treatment in the world at a US hospital, and used his contacts in academia to get me in. More importantly, he took care of the entire bill. He said he raised the money from friends and charitable organizations, but as you can imagine in my line of work, I have a few money-sniffing friends of my own. They found out that your father transferred almost twenty thousand dollars from his retirement account to the hospital. That was money he could have left to you or used in retirement. When I told him this he simply said, 'I must do what good I can today. None of us knows what the future holds. You, my friend, need this today. Who knows what I will need tomorrow.'"

Zeki stopped. Gwyn thought his eyes were a bit more sparkly than they had been just a moment ago.

"I want to do this," he continued. "It is, in your father's words, 'the good thing that I can do today.'"

Gwyn closed her eyes. It could not stop the flood of tears that came rushing down her face. She jumped up and ran out of the room, sobs racking her body. Gary followed.

Gilbert cleared his throat.

"You are a man of surprises, Zeki. We would be honored to have your help."

"According to the messages captured by your key-logger, the theft is scheduled for Wednesday. That means I have to be in Vienna tomorrow morning, and there is a lot to do before then."

"But, won't you need a reservation? I'm sure that you can't just walk in and ask to see the manuscript," asked Gilbert.

"I made that phone call from the airplane over Holland. Sort of ironic, isn't it?" he said with a smile. "Anyway, I have it reserved for tomorrow. Apparently, it's not a book people are lining up to read. I asked for Wednesday too, but that was already taken, and we know who has it reserved."

He looked down at his watch.

"Listen, I have to meet an old friend in half an hour. Hopefully, he will be able to help. I probably won't see you again before I leave for Vienna." He reached into his shirt pocket, pulled out a slip of paper and handed it to Gary, "This is the name of my friend I'm meeting and his phone number. If you need anything, just let him know. Remember his phone will almost certainly be monitored by Police Intelligence so, to protect him, say that you are a mutual friend. When he asks who, say 'Şanlıurfa 1986'. I'm sorry that my hospitality has not been better. I hope when this is over I will have the honor of hosting you properly."

53

Ten minutes later, Zeki had crossed Taksim Square and was walking through the park towards the corner of the expansive grounds at the Ceylan Interconti-nental. He began angling off to the right when he saw the security wall around the imposing twenty-storey hotel. He stopped in front of the building to wait for a break in the traffic. Everyone was rushing to be home to break the fast. In ten minutes, there would be almost no traffic.

He could see a fifty-meter gap in the approaching traffic, and shook his head in disgust at the difference between drivers in Dallas and Istanbul. In Dallas, traffic stopped for pedestrians in crosswalks. Here, the drivers actually sped up. It took several minutes and two false starts, before he made it to the other side and turned down a narrower street. There was no sign of Yusuf. He walked another seventy-five meters before he noticed a white sedan with tinted windows parked ahead on the right, flashing its lights. He walked over to the car, opened the door and sat down beside his friend.

"*Selam dostum.* Thanks for coming. I know it wasn't easy."

"*Aleyküm selam*, Zeki. It's good to see you in one piece. Any chance that you are being followed? You know, Interpol is looking for you."

"I suspect they're still looking for me in Dallas, don't you?"

"I wouldn't doubt it," said Yusuf with a smile. "Where are we going?"

"Is Kopyaji still in business?" Zeki asked.

"As far as I know."

"Then, let's pay him a visit. But, take a scenic route."

Yusuf started the car and pulled out into the street. Neither man spoke for several minutes. It was Zeki who broke the silence.

"The news report I saw at the airport said Bekir Kaya claimed responsibil-ity for the bombings. Is this true or is somebody massaging the facts?'

"It's true."

"Any idea where he's at?" asked Zeki.

"We believe he's in one of the countries north of the Black Sea. Probably

Ukraine or Romania, but we have no concrete leads. I doubt he's in Russia. It's too risky there. Bekir sent a personal message too."

Yusuf quickly explained the blackmail tapes they had found during the raid and how they had returned the originals. Zeki's only response was a deep sigh. Yusuf turned left onto Dolmabahçe Boulevard, and they drove by the palace in silence. Again, he waited for Zeki to continue.

"I would love to help you with Bekir, but I'm sure you don't need me, and I have a certain debt to repay. I suppose you know about the murders in London."

"Yes, I read the Interpol report."

"O'Brien was a friend of mine and whoever was behind this also killed Haluk Bayram, the professor I worked with at the university. They tried to kill me and then O'Brien's daughter in Texas. When that failed, they kidnapped his son's wife and children from Italy and brought them here to Istanbul. They have somebody on the inside with the Metropolitan Police Service. We know they can intercept cell phone calls, and who knows what else. I'm not sure who's involved, but Turks were part of it."

"How do you know?" asked Yusuf

"Because I heard the two men they sent to Dallas to kill O'Brien's daughter speaking Turkish on their approach to the house. Besides, they're too technically sophisticated, too organized and too well-equipped for me to believe that they are Arabs."

Yusuf grinned at Zeki's expression of a common cultural contempt for the Arabs. "What are they after?"

"A document that ties the Ottomans directly to a plot to hijack Christianity in the 16th century by forging a gospel. Have you ever heard of the Gospel of Barnabas?"

Yusuf kept his eyes on the road and shook his head in disbelief.

"Even an atheist like me has heard of the Gospel of Barnabas. Didn't the TAF find a copy of that in 1986 somewhere down by Mardin?"

"That was what the military claimed initially, but it wasn't true."

They heard a cannon go off marking the setting of the sun and the end of the fast.

"If you like we can stop and eat something," said Yusuf.

He had never understood Zeki's faith. In fact, he generally had nothing but disdain for anyone who believed in God. To his mind, they were backward, uneducated or blindly traditional. Zeki was different though. Different in a way that he couldn't explain.

"No need," responded Zeki. "I'm not fasting."

Yusuf didn't know how to respond. He was so surprised that before he could think better of it, he blurted out,

"You haven't given up your faith, have you?"

Zeki continued staring out the window at the blue waters of the Bosphorus and thought of all the Ottoman sultans who had lived and died in the palace along this coveted stretch of water, spending their entire lives in the service of Islam, leading the armies of the Crescent into battle with the infidel, enslaving the subjugated populations. He thought about all the pain and suffering inflicted on both sides. He remembered how the Asian side of the Bosphorus, the Muslim hinterland across the water, had not only supplied the men and raw materials for the never-ending jihad, but how they had also chaffed at the ruling aristocracy. For centuries, the most serious threat to Ottoman power had been from its own oppressed Muslim populations. He remembered sheikh Bedreddin and the dozens of insurrections, the uprisings aimed at throwing off the yoke of the throne. Yusuf's great grandfather had fought in the war of independence. His entire family had heartily embraced the secular republic and the abolishment of the Caliphate. He couldn't blame them.

Yusuf cleared his throat. The long silence made him uncomfortable and he worried that he had offended Zeki.

"No, my friend," said Zeki slowly, "I have only concluded that abstaining from food for the daylight hours will not earn me points with the Creator. It would also impair my ability to think clearly in this crisis. But you shall never convince me that creation is the product of time and chance."

"Well, that is the most sensible thing I have heard you say on the subject," said Yusuf with a sigh of relief. "I'll consider it progress."

"And you aren't calling me an ignorant jackass like you did when we were in the military. I'd say that is progress too. Listen, I need to know if there has been an uptick in activity in Gülben's group over the last week."

Yusuf shook his head and said, "Not that I know of. I'll look into it, but Turkey is changing. Sometimes I think there are more of them in the government than there are of us."

"I know. The danger to the Republic seems to grow graver every day. Do we have anybody in London, somebody from the old team, who could research this for us? I know MIT has identified suspected radical groups overseas that might work for regime change here in Turkey. Is there a Gülben group in London that we have under surveillance, or better yet, one we have penetrated? I suspect these guys will be close to banking, commerce and technology. I know one thing. They didn't make this much money selling *halal* meat, like Bekir's group did. They would require an excellent cover for the technology I've seen them use in the last few days. I tell you it is a miracle that girl is alive, or any of us for that matter."

"I'll see what I can find out. Call me in the morning."

"Great. I knew I could count on you. Now, do you know if Baba is still in business?"

"Are you kidding? The Turkish movie industry is going gangbusters, so he's always got work."

"I hear they are exporting films with an anti-Western slant throughout the Middle East."

"Yep, a bit strange for a NATO-member country still on the road to membership in the EU, don't you think? But, the dream of resurrecting the Ottoman Empire and restoring the glory of Islam is alive and well. Economic initiatives and overtures to poor countries in the Balkans, major industrial investments in the region, a film industry that targets the Arabs, and a resurgence in diplomacy with states hostile to the Atlantic alliance certainly seems like a change in strategy. What do you want with Baba?"

"I need a facelift."

"It won't be cheap," replied Yusuf.

"How much?" asked Zeki with a grimace.

"Five thousand dollars."

"What? That's ridiculous!"

"Inflation…"

"Well, I need it done tonight."

"Tonight? You've got to be joking."

"I also need a passport, biometric if someone can do it," continued Zeki. "It'll be a Turkish passport."

"You don't want much, do you? I suppose you'll want Marilyn Monroe for an escort."

"No, too much of a distraction."

"You need to see Kopyaji," said Yusuf dryly. "He's the only one who might, and I stress the word *might,* be able to help you."

"Does he still have database access?" asked Zeki.

"Would he be in business if he didn't?" replied Yusuf. "But, I hope you are carrying some serious cash because this isn't going to be cheap."

"Now that you mention it, I *am* having a bit of a cash flow problem. You don't suppose I could borrow about twenty thousand dollars, do you? I'm going to have a few other expenses as well."

Yusuf didn't answer. He didn't know what to say.

"Look," continued Zeki. His tone was apologetic. "I've got a summer house in Bodrum. I'll sell it as soon as this is over to pay you back. I know I'm putting you on the spot, but…"

"Even if I had it, I couldn't get it for you tonight, and these guys are a cash-only operation," explained Yusuf.

"I know, but if you come with me, and promise to send the money tomorrow or the next day, we might be able to squeeze a bit of work out of them. After all, you carry a big government stick, and we've got enough evidence between us to arrest them both and send them to the boy's room if you had to."

He was serious, but there was a twinkle in his eye.

"You're an adrenaline junkie, you know that?" said Yusuf finally, shaking his head. "This is not a one-man show. They run a syndicate, and we don't even know who all the members are. Locking up a couple of guys at the top is just asking for trouble."

"Of course, but we won't actually do that. I'm just talking about a little persuasion, a little reminder that the law sometimes needs help too. It might go a long way tonight. This is urgent. I'm not going to stiff them. I just need an installment plan. That's all."

Yusuf shook his head and sighed.

"Okay, but I can't be out more than a couple of hours. Which one are we going to visit first?"

"Baba. It'll take him a good twelve hours to get the mask ready. In fact, call him now. Tell him we've got an urgent job, and he's going to need a couple of assistants to meet the deadline, but they have to be his most trustworthy people. If this gets out, we're both dead."

"Who do you need to be?"

"Fatih Gülben."

Yusuf gripped the steering wheel tighter and swore.

"Damn it, Zeki! How do I let you talk me into this shit? You're going to get us both killed!"

"All in good time, *and* at the right time, *and* not a minute before," he replied solemnly. "Remember, 'Fear of death will not delay it.'"

Yusuf put on his left turn signal, pulled out his cell phone, and hit the speed dial for Baba. His studio was close by. They would be there in half an hour.

"Baba, this is Yusuf. Zeki sends his greetings...Thanks, it's been a stressful day. Listen, something's come up and we need a piece done tonight...No, it can't wait...We'll be there in half an hour...I think you're going to need some help with this one...Yeah, you could say a particular person...No, we don't have a picture, but finding one on the Internet won't be hard... Who is it? I'd prefer to tell you in person, but if you can start right away...It's Fatih Gülben."

Yusuf held the phone away from his face and grimaced at the cursing the name elicited. Zeki could hear the string of expletives as well. The profanity-laced tirade even included some novel variations he had never heard before.

"Listen, I don't like this either," continued Yusuf at the first break in the swearing. "But, for a friend, a man could do anything, even eat raw chicken, right? We'll be there in half an hour."

He closed the phone and turned back to Zeki.

"He's going to be happy to see you."

54

WASHINGTON, D.C.   Kiyomi felt weird handing the cashier at Starbucks Gilbert's credit card. It had been delivered to her that morning via courier with a short handwritten note that explained nothing and said only,

'Please, use this to make a few small purchases on Monday. All your meals are on me today ☺.'

There was no explanation; none was needed. Gilbert wanted somebody, a very powerful somebody, somebody who could access credit records, to believe that he was in D.C., and she couldn't believe she was doing this for him. The last twenty-four hours had been nerve-wracking. The same London number called almost every hour. She ignored it every time. She had nothing to tell them.

"The cranberry cheesecake muffins are delightful. Would you like one with your latte?"

The cashier's voice startled her.

"No, thanks. I'm trying to cut down on the carbs. It's just more calories I have to burn off in the gym."

She said it without thinking and then realized that the cashier was at least sixty-five pounds overweight and probably had Starbucks desserts to thank for it. She felt like a heel.

"Besides, I'm in a hurry. They look delicious though. Maybe next time."

She had argued with herself for the last hour. In the end, she did it out of pity for Gilbert's predicament. She also had a healthy dose of confidence that her boss was a decent fellow and wouldn't do anything to put her in danger. So, instead of going down to the cafeteria for lunch, she had walked out the back exit onto 11th Street NW to the trendy coffee house cattycorner to her office. She chose Starbucks because she was a regular and hoped they wouldn't ask for ID. Still, she had an answer prepared just in case. Gilbert wouldn't have approved, but she couldn't think of anything to say except that she had mistakenly pulled out her boyfriend's card.

CAIRO   "When did this happen?" asked Ahmet

"Just about five minutes ago," replied Jabbar. "But, I have a hard time believing that Gilbert would use his credit card to stop in at Starbucks after what happened at the Chunnel."

"Salih may have been right about that being a goose chase," replied Ahmet, "but what if he bought the tickets and then changed his plans? Maybe he decided to go back to Washington D.C."

"It's possible, I guess," said Jabbar scratching his chin thoughtfully. "But I've already checked with our people, and they say his passport never scanned in London or the US, so if he is in D.C., that means he's travelling on a different passport, and if he's that gun-shy and has those kinds of contacts, then he wouldn't be using his credit card."

"Sometimes even smart people do the dumbest things. Salih made a bunch of assumptions too, which is why we are in this predicament. We can't afford not to follow up every lead."

"Or, maybe he was mugged in DC, killed by a common thug, stuffed in a dumpster and some piece of street trash is using his credit card. That would put a kink in our kidnapping plan," replied Jabbar with a smirk.

Ahmet smiled at his friend's sense of irony.

"See if you can get one of our guys to pose as a policeman and get a look at the Starbucks security tape on the pretense of credit card fraud. That would tell us who is using the card. We might get a lucky break. No word from the guys staking out his apartment?"

"Nothing, and the girl went to work. She refuses to answer our phone calls. Either she's scared and she's ignoring us, or she hasn't contacted Gilbert and does not know what to say when we call. As far as we can tell, she hasn't received any communication from him," answered Jabbar.

"We need to get in contact with this guy." Ahmet muttered a string of curses. "Salih really screwed this up. If Gilbert's as clever as you think he is, then he's going to be hard to find. Call Salih and find out how many men he has reviewing security tapes. Surely the two brothers have walked in front of a British security camera in the last two days. I need some results."

"Yes, sir."

"What are we hearing from our friend in the FBI?"

"Nothing yet. They've brought Homeland Security in on the case. Zeki has been classified as a potential terrorist. It is just a matter of time. They'll find him and when they do, we'll have O'Brien's daughter and the document. Of course, destroying it or retrieving it may be a bit more challenging in the US. We don't have as many people on the inside of the Agency as we do in London."

"One thing at a time. Listen, I need to take care of some wire transfers.

344

Keep me posted if there's anything unusual, and next time let's use a different number to call the girl. I want to talk to her."

He walked back into his office and closed the door. Jabbar started writing a short message for posting on craigslist. It would go out as an RSS feed to everyone who subscribed to the keyword. The internet made open communication easy, and there was no encryption to draw unwanted attention.

DO ANY FRIENDS OF CAIRO WANT TO MEET FOR COFFEE AT STARBUCKS AT THE CORNER OF 11TH ST. NW AND E ST. NW AFTER MY SHIFT AS SECURITY GUARD ENDS? I'LL HAVE TO LOOK AT THE SECURITY CAMERA TAPE AT 12:28 PM BEFORE I CAN GO.

LONDON   Salih flipped through the TV channels while Fatma prepared the *iftar* meal to break the fast. After work, he had come back to his first wife's apartment for three reasons. First, sexual intimacy was not allowed until after the fast was broken and the temptation would be too much if he went to Alicia's apartment. The second reason was that Fatma cooked the kind of food he liked. After fasting all day, he didn't want English food. And, finally, he was in a sour mood and didn't feel like answering Alicia's incessant questions. Ahmet had taken over operations and cut the London team completely out of the loop. What made it even worse was that Jabbar, not Ahmet, had informed him. In fact, it made Salih nervous. He looked at the clock. It was still ten minutes until sunset and his stomach was rumbling.

He grabbed the remote and flipped to another news channel. A pretty blonde was telling the same story he had already heard on three different stations. The news was all the same; massive, well-coordinated attacks in Turkey followed by Muslim demonstrations in Cologne and Berlin, both of which had clearly been organized weeks earlier to protest the Neo-Nazi attacks in Germany. The demonstrations in Cologne had turned ugly with many Muslim youth setting fire to cars. This had become a hallmark expression of Muslim frustration in France, but the Germans had responded with overwhelming force.

The TV showed thousands of police in full riot gear facing an angry mob of almost 100,000 Muslims who had descended on the city from all across Europe. The tipping point came when the protesters tried to erect a green banner with a verse from the Qur'an on a thirty-foot pole in the middle of Heumarket. The German police were given orders to seize it. Before it was over, the whole square was transformed into a war zone with officers brutally beating hundreds of young Muslims, many of whom were trying to keep the police officers from stepping on the banner as it was trampled on the ground. This was followed by scenes of three hooded men attacking a police officer and slitting his throat on the opposite side of town in retaliation for the desecration of the Qur'an at the protest. It had come to light several hours later and was captured by a traffic camera. He closed his eyes and let the announcer drone on.

"Appeals for calm from politicians and community leaders on both sides have fallen on deaf ears, and Muslims organizers are vowing to take to the streets again tomorrow. The European Commission will meet in emergency session tonight and has invited delegates from Turkey, Algeria, Tunisia, Morocco and Egypt. The Commission is expected to pressure these governments to address the European Muslim community in an attempt to calm tensions..."

He imagined Ahmet in the Cairo office. The man had probably been spitting bullets of molten lead all day. Ahmet had been warning the organization for years about the danger posed by radicals and had recommended actively supporting western security forces to eliminate the threat. He had also argued that by assisting the West in eliminating radical Muslims they would win the trust of the western intelligence community, making their own operations much easier. However, until recently, the Rightly Guided One had refused to even consider such action. He had said that the tactics used by radicals might be different from their own, but the objective was the same. Their leader insisted that everyone who joined the group adhere to his policy: 'Do no harm to a fellow Muslim.'

Apparently, there had been a reversal, and he had been persuaded to make certain exceptions to his policy. Salih figured Ahmet had a hand in bringing this policy reversal about. Salih had read the action plan for Friday prayers. He approved, but the news that certain radical clerics would be rounded up by security forces only reminded him of his own precarious position. Tonight, he was praying for two things: the recovery of the document, not a difficult thing for Allah, and for Ahmet to forgive his missteps in the operation. Allah was forgiving; Ahmet was not.

+)=====(+

UKRAINE Bekir leaned back on a pillow holding a tiny blue and white ceramic cup encircled with verses from the Qur'an in beautiful flowing calligraphy. He took a sip of the strong Turkish coffee. It had been the perfect *iftar* meal, and after today's triumphs, it felt more like a victory feast. *Perfect execution. Powerful impact. Over one thousand dead and hundreds more wounded.* This alone would have been enough. It was certainly more than he had dared to hope for, but the protests in Europe had been successful as well. He motioned to his friend.

"Change the channel to Al-Jazeera. I want to see how our people are responding to the violence of the German police."

The flat screen TV flickered and Arabic flooded the room. Everyone fell silent. A huge crowd of Muslims chanting slogans marched on a grassy lawn

346

carrying a green banner. The name *Allah* and a verse from the Qur'an were embroidered in gold. Then, a flag pole was shown being passed through the crowd. The banner was attached to it and hoisted above the crowd. The vantage point of the camera shifted and the same footage they had seen on CNN was broadcast to the almost four hundred million Arabic speakers around the world. Police in riot gear were beating protesters, many of them covered women. His happiness was etched on his face with a grin that would have made the Joker jealous.

"It's working, my brothers," he said to the fifteen *mujahedeen* gathered in the room. "This struggle will be the longest, most costly, and most desperate war the West has ever fought. Today, the awakening begins."

Bekir looked at Abdullah. He was the only one in the room not smiling. He knew his friend was cautious, not entirely supportive of his latest decisions, but his lack of enthusiasm perturbed Bekir.

"Abdullah, why is there no smile on your face? Are you not happy with the victory of Allah?"

"Me? Not happy? How silly! I am merely contemplating the enemy's next step. Isn't that what you pay me for?"

"Yes. Yes, it is," replied Bekir slowly, "But, there is a time to work and there is a time to rejoice in your accomplishments."

Abdullah faked a smile.

"As always, you are right. It is even better than we dreamed it could be."

Bekir was glad to see his chief strategist warming up.

"You have always said that this is a war of attrition. For now, it's an economic war. You are the one who convinced me of this, of the incalculable costs incurred by the infidel for security on every flight, the expense of x-raying millions of shipping containers unloaded in dozens of ports, the security precautions taken at every special event, all of the millions of man-hours spent keeping the electrical grid, nuclear power stations, water supplies, and the internet safe from attack and the vast network of intelligence agents they have built in a vain attempt to counteract us. Yes, we have imposed the greatest security burden in the history of the world on the West, and yet it costs us almost nothing. A few suicide bombers a year. All the while, they spend billions of dollars trying to stay safe. All we have to do is keep the fear fresh. The cost in lost productivity alone will bankrupt them. They cannot go on forever."

"No, they cannot, and that is part of the reason I worry," replied Abdullah. "A crumbling empire does not go meekly to the grave."

Bekir smiled again. His whole demeanor exuded confidence.

"Let me do the worrying for a while. Allah has decreed that we should enjoy the fruits of our labor. It's like the fast. We abstain from food all day and our enjoyment of it is heightened when we break the fast. In the same way, we have laid our plans, taken risks, and finally struck at the opportune time. It is Allah's will that we enjoy the jihad just as it is our destiny to wage it against the infidel. It would be a pity if we did not bask in the pleasures of the task and our moment of glory. The next stage is about to begin. Is everything ready in Vienna?"

"Yes, everything is ready."

"Excellent! The banner that led the armies of Islam to victory has lain too long in the museum of the infidel. It is time we reclaimed the honor lost at the gates of Vienna. It is time we reversed the retreat of Islam that began on that fateful day. It is time to hoist the banner of the Prophet. We will raise the standard, and Muslims from around the world will rally to us, rally to the reestablishment of the Caliphate."

Abdullah willed a smile back to his face. Bekir's charisma was contagious. He remembered how he had been swept up in it during their first years together.

"Yes," said Abdullah. "Your success today will only make them redouble their efforts, bringing us one step closer to our goal."

He didn't express his true fear. He was nervously trying to calculate how long it would be before the redoubled efforts of their enemy had them running for their lives.

<hr />

WASHINGTON, D.C.   "What can I get for you today?" asked the server behind the Starbucks counter.

"Your manager, I suppose. I'm following up on a case of credit card fraud, and I need to view your security tapes. We think the card may have been used here within the last hour."

"I'm sorry, but the manager is out for lunch."

"Does anyone else here have access to the security camera tapes?"

"Oh sure. Danny, the assistant manager, can help you."

She turned and stuck her head through a door and yelled, "Hey Danny, there's a cop here that needs to talk to you."

55

Istanbul   Gary was happy to see that Matt was impressed with the food he had ordered. It had improved his mood considerably as well. He seemed to relish every bite of his *iskender*, carefully wiping the buttery tomato sauce off his plate with a piece of bread. Gwyn merely toyed with her food.

"Don't you like it?" asked Gary.

"The eggplant kebab is wonderful, but I'm stuffed," she replied.

"There are starving children in Africa," said Matt playfully. "It would be a shame for it to go to waste."

She pushed her plate towards him with a smile.

"I'm not sure how it will help them if you eat it, but go ahead."

Gilbert had hardly touched his food, nor had he joined the conversation unless asked a direct question.

"You've probably got an ulcer," Gwyn said to Gilbert. "Not eating will just make it worse."

"I don't have an ulcer. I just don't have an appetite," he replied.

"Do you mind if I try some of your *iskender*?" asked Matt, with an impish grin. "Maybe it is different from the one I had."

"No, go right ahead," said Gilbert. "But, I don't know where you'll find an antacid for the heartburn you're giving yourself."

"You worry about your ulcer, and I'll deal with my heartburn."

"You know," said Gwyn, "With Zeki gone, I don't feel nearly as secure here."

Everyone was thinking the same thing. They were alone in a city of fifteen million. Except for Gary, none of them could speak a word of the language.

"There's no reason to worry," said Gilbert finally. "That is something mother would disapprove of. What did she always say? 'Worry wouldn't cure a wart, and our problems are much bigger.' I'm going to spend some time with the logs if you'll excuse me."

He got up from the table, and walked into the living room to get his laptop. In minutes, he was immersed in a world that gave him a sense of control, but didn't stop him from worrying about his family. Gwyn started clearing the table and gathering up the styrofoam boxes the food had been delivered in. Gary leaned back in his chair and addressed Matt,

"Were you able to contact your friend here in Istanbul, the one who might be able to find Angela's sister Bianca?"

"In fact, I did. He gave me the name of a captain in Ankara with the Counter-Terrorism Bureau. Apparently, there was a big operation a little over a week ago on the Black Sea. The target was a terrorist who uses the white slave trade to finance his activities. They didn't capture the terrorist, but dozens of girls were rescued. He said this Captain was now heading the investigation to bring down the whole network."

"Do you think we could call him now?"

"Sure, let me find the number. I wrote it on the back of an envelope from the hotel."

Matt rummaged through his backpack.

"Here it is. Yusuf Demir is his name. The number is 312 221 1212."

Gary got a queer look on his face and reached into his pocket for the slip of paper Zeki had given him.

"Yusuf Demir?"

"I'm probably pronouncing it wrong, but that's what it looks like."

"No, I'm sure that's right, but the card from Zeki has the same name, different telephone number. This one is a cell phone."

"You think it's the same person?"

"I don't know. We could call and find out."

"Did this girl Angela tell you anything else today?"

"Have you ever heard the name Elvir Zubak?"

The fork stopped halfway to Matt's mouth.

"I should hope so. He's the fifth most wanted human trafficker in the Middle East. Bosnian by birth, the man is a veritable shadow. We don't even have a good picture of the guy. Are you telling me he's in Istanbul?"

"I don't know where he is or who he is," replied Gary. "That was just the name a prostitute gave Angela, along with a warning to forget she had ever heard it and leave the country. She said there's no hope for the girl."

Matt dropped his fork.

"I'll be hornswoggled!"

Startled to hear one of her father's favorite phrases, Gwyn felt the corners of her mouth rise in a smile. Matt and her father had gotten along so well.

"This Yusuf guy, we've got to give him a call. He's our man," continued Matt, suddenly very excited. "I've been trying to find Elvir for six months. He runs a drug and human trafficking ring to finance a terrorist named Bekir Kaya. Turkish Counter-Terrorism must have been hunting Bekir and stumbled on a stash of their girls. If that's true, then the captain is the best person to contact about Elvir. The government of Romania has a bounty for one hundred and fifty thousand dollars on Elvir's head because he or his organization killed five border guards almost ten years ago at a routine car inspection. There are smaller bounties offered by other Eastern European countries too."

"So, you do it for the money?"

Gwyn said it with a nip in her voice, not because she thought it was true but because she could not filter the pain out of her voice.

Matt was stung by the question. His instinct was to lash back. Instead, he sat there arguing with himself, trying to control the raw emotions he felt boiling up. He failed.

"Yeah, Gwyn, I do it for the money. But, I also do it because I'm a warped person who receives some debauched pleasure from bringing perverts to justice. You see, I came to the conclusion that pushing pencils at the State Department so that we can sell fighter jets and T-bills to the Saudis, or facilitating back-door deals with third-world countries so that multinational corporations can exploit cheap labor and raise their profit margins on MP3 players while putting Americans out of work is not nearly as satisfying as playing some small role in stamping out the exploitation of little girls. Forgive me, but I thought someone with your moral compass might be able to understand that."

He got up without saying another word and walked out of the room. Gary looked at his sister. He could see that she was struggling with old emotions, but there were more pressing matters at hand.

"Geez, Gwyn. Did you have to do that? Can we just focus on getting Ginger and the kids back safely?"

She started to say something and thought better of it. Gary looked at Gilbert. He gave no sign that he had even heard the conversation; he was too absorbed in his computer.

The phone Zeki had left with them vibrated on the table. Gary picked it up. "Hello."

"This is Zeki. I'm afraid I won't be able to come back tonight, and I've got an early flight out in the morning. My friend Yusuf will be in touch with you tomorrow."

"Say, would this Yusuf be with the Counter-Terrorism Unit in Ankara?"

"As a matter of fact, yes. Why do you ask?"

"Matt is looking into a case of human trafficking and his contact in Istanbul gave him Yusuf Demir's name."

"Then your friend Matt has very good contacts."

"Okay, thanks for confirming and for all your help. *İyi yolculuklar ve başarılar.*"

"Your Turkish is good."

"I've picked up a bit in the last couple of months, enough to get me in trouble," said Gary.

"No trouble comes from wishing people well, my son."

✦

"I don't know what you plan to do with this, but it damn sure better not come back to me. Can you guarantee that?" The skinny man with a stylish goatee ran his fingers nervously through his long hair and looked to Yusuf and Zeki for assurance.

"Do you really have to ask that question, Baba?" said Zeki quietly.

"You want me to help you impersonate the Anti-Christ and wonder that I am a bit antsy?"

"He's not the Anti-Christ, Baba. He's just a popular religious teacher."

"I thought that 'being a popular religious teacher' was a prerequisite for being the Anti-Christ," retorted the wispy man fiercely. "Do you know how many people there are in this country who want him to be the Caliph? Anyway, what about the money? Will it be here tomorrow?"

"Or Wednesday at the latest," replied Yusuf.

Baba clearly didn't like the arrangement. He ran a cash business. There was no line of credit. But Zeki's opening speech about past jobs and his client portfolio had worked its magic. If there was one thing Baba knew besides masks, it was seeing past them to read people. He knew a veiled threat when he heard one.

"Am I going to read about this in the newspapers?"

"Not a chance. Totally risk-free, absolutely benign," said Zeki confidently.

"Well, don't just stand there then. We have to get started if you are going to make your flight tomorrow. When I'm done with you, you could fool the man's wife until she got your clothes off."

"That good?"

"Isn't that why you came to me?" he said with a grin. "You're going to look good bald too."

He pointed to what looked like a barber's chair surrounded on three sides by mirrors and bright lights.

"Bald?" asked Zeki, sitting down in the swivel chair.

"As a pumpkin," Baba said as he walked away.

The inside of this dilapidated building looked like a swanky, state-of-the-art technology mall and a Hollywood set rolled into one. From the outside, one would have said it was a candidate for demolition. Zeki sat down and looked at himself in the mirror. It seemed strange to be back in the game after so many years working in academia. Yusuf had been right. He was an adrenaline junkie, and for the first time in the week-long whirlwind of events, he was seriously wondering if this was the right thing to do.

352

The decision to protect Gwyn had been simple. This felt different. For the first time in a long time, he was having trouble sorting through his own motives. *Am I doing this to repay a debt to a departed friend? Am I doing this for revenge? Is it because I am trying to show the O'Briens that not everyone in the Middle East sides with terrorists? Do I really think this man posing as a priest can be persuaded to talk? Or, is this just a desire to be back in the game and experience the adrenaline rush?* He didn't know the answer. It didn't matter either. He had given his word.

One of Baba's assistants approached with the clippers and immediately began removing his thick salt and pepper hair in huge clumps. Another started dabbing splotches of skin tone paint on Zeki's forehead until he found a perfect color match. Then, he began applying something that looked like petroleum jelly to protect his face from the chemicals that would be used to shape the mask. Zeki looked in the mirror to see Yusuf was still standing behind him in the shadows. Yusuf looked at his watch and then walked up to Zeki.

"In ten minutes, your face is going to be covered in straps of gelatinous plaster. There is something I should tell you."

"I'm all ears," replied Zeki.

"It's curious that you are going to Vienna. Something is going on in that city. Two of the cells we have under surveillance there have disappeared, vanished without a trace."

"So?"

"What would you say if I told you that all of the Turks killed in the Nazi attacks in Germany were Alevis?" asked Yusuf.

"I would say that is quite a coincidence except that even atheists like you know Allah allows no coincidences."

"Exactly!" replied Yusuf.

Baba's assistant had finished smearing the protective cream on Zeki's face and was now dipping thin strips of gauze in a chemical solution.

"But, if you wanted to justify an attack on foreigners in Turkey, then posing as skinheads and killing Alevis would be framing one enemy while disposing of another."

Zeki was silent.

"I think that the attacks on Turks in Germany, which served as the pretext for today's bombings, were actually committed by the same people. That would mean Bekir is behind them both. It's logical. My gut tells me it's true, but we have no proof. Right now, I'm more worried about guessing his next move than anything else. I think something is being planned for Vienna. I think that the disappearance of the cells we had under surveillance proves something is going down. The same thing happened in Cologne and Berlin before the alleged skinhead attacks. I think a pattern may be emerging. But that's not all, I learned today that two cells have disappeared in France, one in Germany and another in Italy."

The mask-maker placed a wet strip of gauze across Zeki's forehead. The pungent smell of the chemicals was almost unbearable. As the man positioned a second strip parallel to the first, he said, "You need to wrap this conversation up or finish it later. In a couple of minutes, Zeki will have to stop moving the muscles in his face until this solution sets. It will only take ten minutes, but he will have to stop talking."

Zeki answered quickly,

"Well, after such a huge success here in Turkey today, maybe they are just playing it safe and laying low to avoid being rounded up as part of a general crackdown to disrupt their activities."

"Maybe you are right, and then maybe the protests organized today in Europe were meant to coincide with the bombings here to provoke the German police and create a new pretext for more attacks in Europe."

"Any corroborating evidence?" asked Zeki.

"The imam who organized the protests is known to have connections with Bekir. At six o'clock this morning, our Ministry of Foreign Affairs asked him to call off or postpone the protests due to the bombing in Antalya. He refused. That, in and of itself, is strange. Very few clerics would oppose a Ministry request. The protests could have waited another few days. The deaths of the Turks in Germany happened almost two months ago. I think his insensitivity indicates that the plan is to provoke the Europeans."

"You could be on to something," replied Zeki. "Call me in Vienna if something turns up and you need another set of legs on the ground. Are you going to be able to stop and see Kopyaji for me?"

"Yes, I'll make sure one of his men meets you at the airport tomorrow morning with your passport."

"One last thing," said Zeki. "I need the schematics for the electrical grid in that quarter by tomorrow at ten o'clock in the morning. Would you give Josef a call? Tell him it's for me and I need this one done on the house."

"I'll see what I can do. Expect a text from him if he agrees, but are you sure this is a good idea?"

"What do you mean?"

"Well, it sounds to me like you are calling in a lot of favors on the front-end. Your real problems will begin when this is all over."

56

The phone had rung five times. Washington D.C. was seven hours behind Cairo, which made it one o'clock in the morning there. Ahmet was watching a live feed on his computer screen as he waited for someone to pick up. Finally, a sleepy female voice on the other end answered.

"Hello, Gilbert?"

"Hello, Kiyomi."

"Who is this?" she asked.

"Gilbert does not seem to be taking the message you passed on to him very seriously."

Kiyomi recognized the voice and immediately went from groggy to fully alert. She checked the number. It was Gilbert's. *Damn! They're calling on Gilbert's phone or replicating the number to get me to answer.*

"I'm afraid I haven't been able to deliver your message," she said hesitantly. "He hasn't contacted me."

"I thought I made it very clear how grave the situation is. Surely someone as communications-savvy as Gilbert would make sure his assistant could get in touch with him."

"You're right. It's strange, but I assume there are extenuating circumstances."

This guy was creepy. She stood up and turned on the light. This was not a conversation she wanted to have in the dark.

"That is strange. How did he give you his credit card then?"

Kiyomi was unprepared for the question and stammered

"Uh, I'm not sure exactly what you are referring to."

"You're a smart girl. I appreciate that, but that's not a reason to treat me like an idiot. You used Gilbert's card yesterday at Starbucks."

"Excuse me?"

She was smart, and in nanoseconds alarm bells started going off in her head as her mind raced to understand the implications of what she had just heard.

355

"I wish I could help you more, but I'm not sure what else I can do," she continued, trying to buy herself more time.

"On your lunch break, at 12:28 on 11th St. NW, you used Gilbert's card to buy a latte. Does that jog your memory?"

The security camera… She said to herself. *That's the only way they could know who used the card.* She was trapped.

"So, Gilbert has given his personal assistant a credit card. Is that such a surprise?" she asked, trying to sound sarcastic.

She couldn't believe what was coming out of her mouth, but the script she had prepared for the cashier the day before started outlining a scenario in her subconscious. She just followed its lead. Ahmet looked down at his screen.

"I warned you to quit playing games with me," he said coolly. "That's a nice pink nightie you're wearing. I suggest you stay away from the windows though."

He needed psychological leverage. Nothing worked better than fear. Kiyomi looked at the window beside her bed, saw the open blinds and gasped. She slid into the adjoining study away from the window.

"You don't really think that moving into another room is going to help, do you? The sheetrock wall between you and the window is like a piece of paper for a fifty-caliber sniper rifle, but if I had wanted to kill you, we wouldn't be having this conversation, would we?"

She could feel her heart pounding from fear. She decided to go for broke. The words tumbled out.

"Listen here, asshole," she said in the most cynical tone she could muster. "I don't know who you bastards are, but you would be doing me a big favor if you got rid of his prissy wife and the kids too. I can't reach Gilbert and don't know where he is, but if you tell me what you want, maybe both of us can get what we want."

Ahmet's voice was icy.

"The only way you can help me or save Gilbert is to convey my message. You may be his mistress, you may hate his wife. I don't know. What I do know is that you talked to Gilbert on Saturday and followed specific instructions to leave a certain message on his cell phone so you've obviously been in touch."

She couldn't tell from his voice whether he was convinced and whether her ruse was working or not.

"Yes, I did talk to Gilbert on Saturday, but that is the last time. I don't know why he asked me to leave the message. He was in London at the time. Believe me, I'd love to help and I'll do whatever I can, but I'm telling you the truth. I don't know where he is. If he calls, I'll relay your message. I promise."

"Make sure you do," said Ahmet. "Oh, and I do like your taste in lingerie. A little tight for comfortable sleeping, but maybe that's not what you got it for."

She started to call him a vulgar jerk, but the line went dead.

Ahmet turned to Jabbar.

"Call her every three hours tomorrow. Tell our man to maintain a constant tail. She's still the only reasonable chance we have of getting in contact with Gilbert.

—┼═══┼—

VIENNA   Zeki turned off the main boulevard lined with shops and restaurants and took the first left. He was only one block off Mariahilfer Straße, but it felt almost like he had entered a ghetto. The buildings were old and several of the doors were boarded up. On the wall of the building across the street there were vulgar works of graffiti spray-painted on the walls. The subject matter may have been sleazy, but the proportion and life that the Austrian vandals had imparted to their creation showed real potential. There was no doubt that Vienna was a capital of art and culture.

The street was deserted except for an old man shuffling towards him on the opposite sidewalk. He spotted the sign for Pension Quisisana, and crossed to the other side of the street. As he walked past the wizened old man, he couldn't help wondering what the end of his own life would be like. Would he be able to walk anywhere without fear after what he was about to do today? He remembered what Ian had said about being careful in the choice of one's enemies. *Make sure they are the common enemy of mankind, and you can't go wrong.*

He stopped underneath the sign and grimaced. It wasn't the Hilton. It was just a place to sleep for the night. He pushed on the heavy iron door. It was locked. He looked around for a bell. After about five minutes of pushing on it intermittently, a rough woman opened it.

"*Guten Morgen, Wie kann ich Ihnen helfen?*" She was a bottle blonde who looked to be around thirty.

"*Guten Morgen,*" replied Zeki, and immediately switched to English. "My German is quite poor. Do you know English?"

The expression on her face told him that there would be a fair amount of gesturing and pointing with this woman.

"A bit I can speak English," said the lady with a smile. Her accent told him she was not Austrian either, probably Eastern European.

"I have a reservation for one night."

"Name?"

Zeki drew a blank for a minute. The jetlag caused by hopping time zones for the last week was taking its toll. He sat his bag down and reached for the Turkish ID card he had at least thought to put in his shirt pocket on the metro from the airport. Kopyaji had charged him eight hundred dollars for it and another twenty-five hundred for Fatih Gülben's passport.

"Hasan Kaya," he said, as he handed her his ID.

She took the identification, verified his reservation on the screen and handed back his ID.

357

"I see you no use credit card. How you pay?"

Zeki pulled out a fifty Euro note and handed it to her with a smile.

"Do you take cash?"

She smiled back and took the money.

"We have no change. I make note, and you take when you check out."

Then, she turned to a board on the wall and found his room number.

"Follow me."

She led him through a door at the back of the office, and he found himself looking at a black steel cage and an open elevator shaft that ascended in the circular space created by majestic spiral stairs. The elevator had obviously been added long after the building was built. She pushed M for mezzanine. When the elevator stopped, she looked at the luggage, put her hand out palm down and motioned for him to leave them there. She stepped out onto the mezzanine floor and pointed down the hall.

"Bath," she said, hooking her hand to the right to indicate which side of the hall it was on. Then, she motioned for him to get back in the elevator. The elevator cables creaked as the pulleys turned, raising the metal cage one more floor. When it stopped, she motioned for him to bring his luggage. The structure was simply an old apartment building that had been converted into a cheap hotel.

She pointed down the hall again.

"Toilet."

Then, she walked to the door directly across from the elevator, opened it and moved aside so he could enter.

"Breakfast six to ten. Check out 11:00 in the morning," she said.

He nodded that he understood.

"Are you travelling alone?" she asked.

"Yes."

"I can have friend for you tonight. You like?" she asked with a smile.

He didn't return it.

"That won't be necessary," he said, and closed the door.

He looked at his accommodations. It was worse than he had feared. It was little more than an oversized closet. There was a single bed, no TV, a sink, and a tiny dresser that doubled as a table and looked so rickety that he would be afraid to set his laptop on it. The only other piece of furniture was a cheap press-board wardrobe so thin he knew without looking that the bars would run perpendicular to the door so that a suit could hang parallel to the wall. Otherwise, the door would not close. He wondered for a moment if maybe the building was an old monastery and this was a monk's cell. There was a shared toilet down the hall and a bath on a different floor. Thirty-two Euro had seemed cheap, but after seeing the room, he felt like he had been mugged.

He set the bag on the bed, pulled out his phone and a small notebook and punched in a telephone number.

"Good morning. I'm here. Is everything ready?"

"Just waiting for a photograph of the cover."

"I will have that for you in about an hour. Are you sure about the dimensions and the content?"

"I found the dimensions in the description by Ragg. For content, I took what few facsimile images are available on the internet and simply made enough copies to fill the book. Obviously, this would not stand two minutes of serious scrutiny by a G.O.B. expert, but the receptionists are not experts. They probably don't know Italian and will take only a cursory glance, if they even crack the cover, when you return it."

"Is Josef providing the schematics?" asked Zeki.

"He sends his greetings, but is not happy that this is going to involve every major museum in Vienna."

"It's only ten minutes."

"He's nervous. There are priceless pieces of art being protected by electronic security in that district."

"Yeah, well most of it, including Augustinerlesesaal, is on a back-up generator that will take over in less than sixty seconds. Just remind him that he owes me and tell him to pray I don't need more time than that."

"Okay, I'll meet you at the statue in front of Hofburg Palace."

"I'll be there."

Zeki terminated the call and looked at himself in the mirror. The mask Baba and his team had worked almost all night to make was truly a masterpiece. The silicone was far thinner than he had thought possible. Fatih Gülben was a balding man in his sixties. He wore a short mustache that was mostly grey. His face was fuller than Zeki's, and the silicone mask had been made thicker in the cheeks to achieve the same effect. It was the hair that had taken the longest for Baba's team to get right, but in the morning light Zeki could see it was as close to perfect as could be hoped for. Baba had earned his five thousand dollars. It had taken a team of three more than four hours to fit the mask and seal the eyes, nose and mouth so that speaking and blinking were natural. Baba had also warned Zeki to avoid laughing or any sign of extreme emotion because the mask simply could not convey the necessary facial expressions. He zipped the bag. It was time to go.

Five minutes later, Zeki was in a taxi on his way to Augustinerlesesaal. He had gone over every detail of the mission in his mind. He knew that if he gave his mind a break, it would improve his mental acuity when the pressure began to build. So, he allowed himself a few minutes to enjoy the magnificent museums they were driving past.

The architecture and grandeur of the capital of the Hapsburgs had always impressed him. Empire was etched into every stone, every building exuded the hubris of the ruling class, an elegant, refined arrogance reflected in the European gods and goddess that graced almost every corner of the capital. It had been built of course, not by its owners, but by the serfs and slaves who served them under pain of death. It was a cruel reality that the most extraordinary structures in the world were built with slave labor: the Colossus of Rhodes, the Hanging Gardens of Babylon, the Parthenon and the Great Wall of China, aptly called the longest cemetery in the world. He wondered how many of the gawking tourists that flocked to these sights ever reflected on the misery endured by those who labored to erect them.

In spite of its grandeur, Vienna was in decline, the rollercoaster ride of Empire. What went up inevitably came down. Riches provoke jealousy, which creates challengers. Power leads to pride, pride to pomp and pomp to decay. Sooner or later, new challengers displace those in power. Yet, somehow they never fail to perpetuate the same cycle of exploitation. There was nothing new under the sun. The rivers run into the sea, and yet the sea is never full.

These thoughts were a pattern and an unpleasant one, so he turned his mind instead to his recently deceased friend. Great cultural distance had separated them. Ian was a child of the West, shaped by a fusion of Greek and Roman philosophy, the teachings of Christ, the Enlightenment, the industrial revolution, religious war and colonization. It was so different from what had shaped his own life. He was a product of Islam and the Middle East, with cultural values stretching back three millennia, encompassing the Hittites, the Persians, the Assyrians, the Arabs and the Turks. Anatolia was the melting pot of the Middle East where the terror of Nebuchadnezzar, the pride of Xerxes, the cruelty of Kublai Khan and the faith of Abraham, Moses and Mohammed had been the furnace that forged the nomadic Turk into the ruler of the world. That empire had also come to an end.

Somehow, the two of them had still found common ground in their humanity and in their ability to circumvent the narrow cultural confines imposed on them by the circumstances of their birth. They discovered their visceral connection one day when Zeki told Ian stories of the Anatolian rebellions, when common men proclaimed equality before the Creator and freedom of conscience. Ian reciprocated with stories of the tumultuous Irish and Scottish struggle to rid themselves of English shackles. This was where they had connected, in the belief that man was created by God in His image, that every person could become a bearer of the divine spark. They had differed on the details for sure, but their dialogue had opened new horizons for Zeki.

"That is the imperial palace ahead on the right. Now, it serves as the National Library," said the taxi driver as he drove under the arches that had been the gates in the wall that protected the castle.

Zeki gazed upon the expansive royal grounds known as the *Volksgarten*. It was filled with residents walking dogs, flying kites and enjoying the summer sun. The walls of the castle had been torn down, but the towering arches with the massive, wooden gates had been preserved and now functioned as separate lanes in the road.

Zeki looked to his right to see the massive bronze sculpture of Prince Eugene of Savoy on a rearing charger. A smile teased his lips. *How appropriate.* It was fitting that Eugene of Savoy should be honored in front of the Austrian palace instead of an Emperor. After all, it was the general who had protected the Empire from its enemies. And, the most dangerous of these enemies might not have been an army but the devious deception housed just a stone's throw from this monument to the man who had been entrusted with keeping the book safe. Time had bestowed a turquoise hue to the bronze masterpiece, giving it an otherworldly feeling.

"Yes, but I am going to the reading room. You can drop me off at Michael Plaza," Zeki replied.

He thought of the Ottoman army that had laid siege to the city in 1683 and how they might have marched through those same gates had they been victorious. Now, Turks moved freely throughout Europe as one of the largest sources of immigrant labor. Some people said time healed all wounds. He wasn't so sure that this one wasn't still festering.

On the other side of the *Volksgarten,* they passed a row of horse-drawn carriages waiting for tourists who wanted to visit the grandiose palace complex in royal style. Then the taxi passed through another set of arches into Michael Plaza and pulled over in front of an ornate fountain of Neptune to let him out. Zeki handed the man a ten-Euro note, stepped out of the taxi and shouldered his bag. He looked around the square and shook his head in wonder at the magnificent statues. Above the entrance to St. Michael's Church was an enormous stone rendering of Raphael's famous painting where the archangel Michael is depicted vanquishing Satan.

He turned around and looked at the passageway the taxi had just driven under. On either side of the arches were colossal depictions of Hercules slaying Cerberus and lifting Antaeus off the ground to deprive him of contact with his mother the earth, the source of his power. They were awe-inspiring. Islam had deprived its people of such fantastic visual arts, works he was sure had inspired many. It was the blindness so peculiar to religion.

Zeki completed his 360-degree visual tour of the square, allowing himself to bask in the artistic and architectural grandeur for just a moment. Then he took off his jacket, stuffed it inside his bag and refocused his mind on the job ahead. He started down Herrengasse, a narrow street that led past the Spanish Riding School. Fifty paces further on, he walked past the Stables of the

Lipizzaners on his left. Several beautiful white mares were being groomed in the courtyard. He wanted to stop. He wanted to spend a month drinking in the sights and sounds of these streets, but the reading room had already been open for thirty minutes. His deadline was unforgiving. He quickened his steps and walked under another arch and into the open cobblestone square of Josef-splatz.

The square was surrounded on three sides by a three-storey complex of white buildings executed in quintessential baroque with black iron bars across the windows. In the middle of the square was another equestrian bronze of the Holy Roman Emperor Joseph II. On his left was the Augustiner Church. The entrance to Augustinerlesesaal was in the far left corner of the square. At one time, it had been part of the monastery for the imperial house of worship. He walked diagonally across the square, past the bronze sculpture, staring at the artwork on the parapet. There was statue of Atlas straining to lift a globe covered with gold leaf and behind him rose a red-tile roof steep enough to shed the heavy winter snowfall.

At the corner of the square, he found himself standing in front of two massive doors that were easily twelve feet tall. The doors were open and an attendant stood at the entrance.

"Good morning," said Zeki

"*Guten Morgen*," answered the attendant, but looked flustered at himself for answering in German instead of English.

"Do you have an appointment in ze reading room?" he continued.

"Yes, I do," answered Zeki.

"Zen you vill turn left, tru zose doors," he said, pointing to another set of doors inside, "ant it iz on ze first landing."

"Thank you," said Zeki.

He had spent the four hours on the plane reading about the palace library. He entered the building, and walked through a door under the words Biblio-theca Palatine. He found himself looking at a staircase so broad he was sure five men could have walked side by side without difficulty. At the base of the stairs was a statue of a woman holding a wreath aloft in one hand while the other hand rested on a long rectangular shield. *Athena? No, the shield would have been round, and she would be wearing a helmet.*

He looked up. The walls and ceilings were painted snow-white and high above him were ten busts protruding from the walls all around the U-shaped stairwell, four on each of the side walls and two on the narrow wall opposite him. A gigantic wrought-iron street lamp hung from the ceiling, no doubt dating back to a time when candles lit the staircase instead of electricity.

He rehearsed the whole plan as he ascended the stairs, but he was not prepared for what he saw at the top. On the second-floor landing, there stood a museum attendant beside beautiful wooden doors made of rich reddish-brown oak and beyond that was a lavishly furnished halls. He recognized the room from pictures he had seen. None of them did it justice. This was *Prunksaal*, literally the "Hall of Pomp". Designed by Johann Bernhard Fischer von Erlach, one of the most prolific Baroque architects of the day, it was intended to be a reflection of the Empire's glory.

The hall was a veritable feast for the eyes. Copious amounts of fine marble polished to a beautiful sheen, liberal applications of gold leaf and stunning stucco work were combined with frescos executed in vibrant colors, elaborate wood decorations and elegant chandeliers to create an impression of opulence and regality he had never experienced. Zeki wondered how anyone could read sitting in the midst of such beauty. He wouldn't have been able to take his eyes off the ceiling to look at a book. *So, this is the library founded with the private collection of books Eugene of Savoy had donated to the crown.* It was an exquisite masterpiece of Austrian art and culture. Eighty meters long, it was the largest Baroque library in the world and held two hundred thousand volumes.

The man at the door cleared his throat, forcing Zeki to pry his eyes away from the magnificence.

"Do you have a ticket?" the man asked. "If not, they can be purchased on the ground floor."

"Ticket? I made a reservation yesterday."

"You mean for the Augustinerlesesaal?"

"Yes."

The man bowed ever so slightly and raised his hand with the palm up and pointed to the door on the left. Zeki nodded his head in thanks, turned and walked towards the small anteroom, vowing to return and spend an entire day in the Prunksaal at his first opportunity.

The anteroom was paneled with wood up to about eight feet and there was a heavy plexiglass security door set in the left wall. He saw a small rectangular metal panel left of the door, put his finger on the button and pushed. A few seconds later, there was a buzz and click. He pulled the door and it opened.

He walked into a small room filled with what looked like modern lockers made of a blonde wood and accented with trim in primary colors of red, yellow and blue. He thought the style more suited to a kindergarten classroom than an imperial palace museum. On the other side of the room were four steps leading through an open door.

He climbed the steps and walked through double doors into a surgically white, brightly lit, long rectangular reception room with three large windows on each side. At the other end of the room was another pair of matching doors. *This is it. Game time.*

He noticed the security camera above the second window across from the receptionist desk. *They didn't think that one through very well. They are videoing the backs of the visitors and the face of the attendants.* There were also small cameras mounted on the book cases across from the reception room and pointed down at the study tables. The absence of a metal detector surprised him. In Turkey, even shopping malls had a metal detector.

All of the furniture and even the fishbone parquet flooring were the same straw-colored wood, a striking post-modern contrast with the dark oak used in the original doors and window frames. Obviously, the room had been redecorated in the not-too-distant past. Behind the counter on the right were three librarians.

57

"Guten Morgen."

A pleasant looking young lady with short black hair had addressed him. He noticed immediately that she had a lazy eye, a physical defect that had no effect on her smile.

"Guten Morgen," replied Zeki. "My German is not so good. Do you speak English?"

"Yes, of course," she answered. "How can I help you?"

"My name is Fatih Gülben. I believe you are the lady I spoke with yesterday on the phone. I called about reserving Codex 2662, THEOL. 62 and N.B. 215."

"Oh yes. Now I recognize your voice."

Zeki noted the comment. Tomorrow, when he showed up with his real face, he would need a new voice to go with it.

"I really appreciate you allowing me to see the manuscript on such short notice."

"It's no problem. In fact, we had already requested it from the archives for another researcher from the Vatican tomorrow, so it was already here and the other two volumes are used very infrequently. I'll need to see your ID."

He handed her Fatih Gülben's passport. She looked at it carefully and then compared it with his face. She scanned a digital copy for the library records and set it down on the counter to copy the passport number into the library checkout register along with the titles he had reserved. When she was finished, she put the passport in a cubbyhole.

"I'll also need you to sign this," she said as she spun the thick, black binder around on the counter so that it faced him. She pointed to the column for his signature and then handed him the pen.

"Right there, please."

Zeki took the pen and carefully executed the signature he had practiced for hours on the flight from Istanbul. It had to be perfect. When he lifted the pen from the paper, he was pleased.

"Thank you," she said, taking a deep breath in preparation for what was obviously a memorized spiel regarding library rules.

"I must ask that you leave your computer bag in one of the lockers you passed at the entrance as no bags are allowed in the reading room. There is a key in each locker. You deposit a two-Euro coin and the key can be removed. When you retrieve your belongings, the deposit will be returned. Photographs are not allowed in the reading room. You must use a pencil for any notes you want to take. We can provide one if necessary. Pens with permanent ink are strictly forbidden. You may use the book for the entire day, but as I told you on the phone, another researcher has it reserved for tomorrow."

Zeki grimaced.

"I'm not sure I have any Euro coins on me. I just arrived this morning, you see. I rushed to the hotel, left my belongings and came straight here."

He checked his pockets, feigning a genuine attempt to find what he already knew was not there.

The girl attempted to come to his aid.

"I can give you change for a five or ten-Euro note."

He feigned another ruffle through his wallet and with an oh-boy-I-hope-you-can-help-me look he pulled out a 100-Euro banknote and said, "I don't suppose you have change for this?"

She smiled and shook her head.

"I'm afraid not."

Zeki's face dropped, and he faked a cough.

"Excuse me, I think I may be coming down with a cold. Well, I suppose I shall have to go back out for change."

He could see from her face that the girl felt compassion for him.

"There is no need for that, Mr. Gülben. I will give you a two-Euro coin. You can return it when you leave."

She opened a drawer, picked up a two-Euro coin and handed it to him.

"That is very kind of you," he said.

"Not at all."

Zeki headed out of the room back towards the lockers and made sure to cough a couple of more times. He inserted the coin she had given him and opened the locker. He removed a yellow legal pad and a pencil from his bag before placing it in the locker, closing the door and removing the key. When he returned to the counter, the short-haired girl was gone, but his manuscript—codex 2662—was sitting on the counter between two black, foam pads.

A tall fellow with a 72-hour beard noticed that Zeki had returned and dutifully shuffled towards him. The man wore a thick sweater even though it was summer time. His back was slightly hunched and his shoulders drooped unnaturally. His head looked like it was permanently tilted forward because when he came up to Zeki he raised his eyes to look over the top of his glasses but did not lift his head. The lethargy one would expect from a caretaker of dusty old forgotten books in an old monastery oozed from his gait and posture. One couldn't have cast for the part and found someone so perfectly suited for the role.

He handed Zeki a rectangular cube of transparent plastic about five-inches long with the letters Ö.N.B. inscribed in yellow and a number on one end.

Zeki took it and coughed again.

"That is your seat number and this is to hold the book open," he said handing Zeki what looked like a short piece of velvet rope.

Zeki took it and was surprised at the weight.

"What's inside this?" he asked out of a desire to appear harmless and curious.

"It's filled with round, lead balls encased in plastic."

The attendant picked up the two foam pads and put them side by side with the narrow edges touching in the middle and the thicker edges on the outside.

"This is for holding the book as you read. It keeps the cover of the book from lying completely flat, which, of course, prevents unnecessary strain on the binding."

"I see," replied Zeki.

Without a word the man shuffled away. Zeki picked up the manuscript and the other two volumes, took a deep breath and turned so that he was squarely facing the security camera. He didn't want it to look like a mug-shot. He gave it a sense of naturalness by patting his pockets, pretending to look for his cell phone. Now, Austria border police had Fatih Gülben entering the country and there was a clear video record of Fatih Gülben checking out the G.O.B.

He turned to his right and headed for the Augustinerlesesaal. As he stepped out of the bright, sterile atmosphere of the reception area into the reading room, he was struck by its beauty. It was nowhere near as opulent as Prunksaal. It had a simpler elegance. Zeki could tell his adrenaline levels were rising and his mental processing power with it. Every detail was etched into his mind on the off-chance that it would be important. *This is it,* he told himself. *The slightest mistake could mean failure.*

He stopped at the entrance and scanned the room, all of which stretched away to his left. Immediately on his right was a beautiful wooden banister, behind which were two computers for library personnel. He turned left and looked down the length of the long rectangular room. He noticed that the banister actually encircled the entire chamber on both sides, restricting access to the shelves of books that hugged the walls. Behind the banister on either side were tall wooden ladders on wheels allowing library personnel to reach books on the top shelves. A red carpet stretched between two rows of study tables, each of which had two chairs on either side, and two reading lights with pale, green lampshades. There were fourteen tables, seven on each side of the room. Five tall, narrow windows allowed slivers of sunlight into the otherwise dimly lit interior, and five video cameras mounted on the shelves glared down on visitors to ensure the security of the libraries priceless holdings.

Zeki began to make his way to his assigned seat looking at the numbered brass plates. The walls were painted in soft, malachite green. At first glance, they appeared to be supported by plaster columns and topped with crown molding. It was a visual trick; they had merely been painted to create a three dimensional effect. A beautiful fresco of blue sky and white fluffy clouds surrounded by noble human figures made the ceiling look like a portal to heaven.

He stopped at his table more than halfway down on the right and sat down facing the far end of the room where another attendant sat at a computer on his left. The other end of the room was elevated above the rest, almost like a small stage accessed by four steps. The librarian sitting at the desk in front of a flat panel computer screen looked to be about fifty years old. She had jet black hair, dyed of course. Her turquoise shirt seemed out of place, a bit too loud for a library; her nails had been painted to match.

The security camera directly above him was the next thing he noticed. He set the books on his left and put the notebook on his right. He arranged the foam pads like the man had shown him and placed the package containing the Gospel of Barnabas in front of him. Thick, gray card stock protected the manuscript. The only marking on the outside was a label in the upper right corner with the words *Österreichische Nationalbibliothek Cod. 2662.*

He took a deep breath and released it as a prayer. *Show the world Your Kingdom is not of this world.* Now that the book was sitting in front of him, the question that had consumed every idle thought over the last week came flooding into his mind. *Who was this secret group? Who was behind Gülben? Who had given the order to take Ian? Who had planned and sponsored the G.O.B. in the first place?* The question he did not ask was why. He had long since answered the why of religion, though he normally framed the question as, Why not? Why shouldn't rulers take advantage of mankind's profound yet inexplicable yearning for eternity? Why not exploit the ineffable yet inexorable certainty that evil existed and, consequently, so did virtue? The answer was simple. There was no reason not to.

The only why question raised by the G.O.B. was why such a major undertaking had been shelved? It made no sense. *Why not use it? Why had the perpetrators tried to hide it?* He opened the gray card stock to reveal the original protective box the manuscript was kept in. It was black and shaped like a book with intricate gold leaf borders and fake gold leaf for the pages. The spine was ribbed, and on the front, it said,

L'EVANGELIO DI GIESU CHRISTO DAS BARNABAS

Zeki opened this box and saw a red compartment, like a cloistered crypt where the manuscript lay hidden from the world. A strip of paper had been placed underneath it and stuck out on either side. He held the two ends between his thumb and forefinger and gently pulled the manuscript out of the close fitting coffin where it had been entombed. Once it was free, he picked it up and turned it over in his hands.

It was approximately two inches thick, bound in dark olive-green leather without text or title on the front or spine. The only marking was an oval-shaped floral pattern embossed on the cover with the same pattern on the back. It certainly resembled the artistic style of Islam, which prohibited the depiction of anything except plants. He continued to examine the binding. The centuries had creased the leather ever so slightly. Now, numerous tiny fissures ran the length of the spine.

Zeki opened the manuscript and began to leaf through it. The light tan paper was supple and remarkably well-preserved. The handwriting was clear and legible. Pages three to seventeen were blank except for margins outlined with a hand-drawn red square, probably intended for an introduction that somebody never wrote. The same red ink had drawn narrow, horizontal rectangles in the middle of the text for subheadings, which he quickly realized had only been filled in up until page twenty-nine. *So, the manuscript was never finished.*

The text of the manuscript was written in black ink inside large hand-drawn red squares located in approximately the middle of every page. These red lines were meant to form a margin. On the first page, he saw that the first three instances of the word *Dio*, which was always written in red ink, had been crossed out. The word Allah was written over it in Arabic. What caught his attention more than anything were the abundant Arabic notes written in the margins with red ink.

His telephone vibrated in his pocket, announcing the arrival of a text message. He pulled it out.

SCHEMATICS READY. WHERE AND WHEN?

There would be no time for a detailed examination of the text this time. He closed the book, slid it under the reading light so that the picture he snapped would be clear and began writing his answer.

STATUE OF EUGENE OF SAVOY IN HALF AN HOUR.

He hit the send button, but continued to move his fingers back and forth as if writing a text message. In fact, he switched the cell phone to camera mode and began taking pictures of the book. When he was finished, he coughed again loudly, got up from his seat, walked over to the lady in the turquoise shirt and in a whisper said, "I don't suppose the air-conditioner could be turned down. I have a bit of a cold and have forgotten my jacket."

"I'm sorry, but the temperature and humidity is centrally controlled. I'm afraid I can't change the settings."

"I understand," replied Zeki. "Can I leave my things on the table while I run back for a jacket?"

"No, sir. You must return them to the reception area and pick them back up when you return."

"That's fine. I understand."

Ten minutes later, a white Fiat pulled up in front of the statue of Eugene of Savoy. Zeki opened the door and said, "Do you have room for a passenger, Patrick?"

A man in his mid-fifties with blonde hair and a red beard looked at him in surprise.

"You didn't say you were going to be in costume. If I hadn't recognized your voice, I might have shot you. Who are you supposed to be?"

"Need to know only," replied Zeki.

"I see. Well, it's good to see you. I thought you and MIT had parted ways, and you were out of the spook game."

"I am."

"So, this is a private contract?"

"Not private. Personal."

"Personal?"

"That's the only thing that makes it worth the risk."

"Makes more sense too. I never figured an idealist like you would stoop to mercenary work. Still, personal makes it sound pretty damn serious. You're the last person I would want holding something personal against me."

"I'm glad to hear it. Let's just make sure this is clean and tight. I've walked into the lion's den; make sure you don't get dragged in with me. Keep your distance. Who are you working for these days?"

It was Patrick's turn to smile.

"You know I can't answer that, but suffice it to say the whole world seems to be outsourcing intelligence and security, so business has never been better. Even the Cold War didn't have this kind of turnover."

"Working iron doesn't rust. I suppose it keeps you on top of your game."

Patrick took the first right and pulled over to the side of the road.

"Are you using your phone for time?" he asked Zeki.

"Yes."

Patrick took the phone and checked it with his own to make sure they were both retrieving time data from the same server. They were.

"Alright, you want this to happen at 2:19?"

"Unless I give you an alternate time before then. How much warning would you need?"

"Five minutes. This is a simple job. We did one just like it two weeks ago in the business district for a corporation that needed a trading office to be offline for ninety seconds so they could create a flash crash in a particular stock. We took out the in-house generator first. Too bad that's not possible here. If you'd have given me another day's notice, I could have arranged it."

"Did you get the pictures?" asked Zeki.

"Yep, Sally confirmed receipt of your email just before I picked you up. She is working on the cover right now. Should be ready by one o'clock."

"How is she doing? I heard what happened."

The smile vanished from Patrick's face.

"She's better now."

"I'm glad to hear it," replied Zeki. "Are you going to be able to help with the tail tomorrow?"

"Yep, we'll be there. Sally's coming to."

Zeki looked surprised.

"She doesn't need to."

"She wants to."

Zeki grabbed his bag, opened the door and said,

"I'll see you in front of Albertina Museum at 1:00."

"No, you'll see Sally. She's bringing the book."

58

Ginger and the kids had finished their lunch of cheese, bread, black olives and tomatoes. It was the same every day. The white bread and cheese were starting to give her youngest son constipation, so this morning he was restricted to tomatoes. The constipation wasn't just caused by the cheese and bread though. The container was unbearably hot. The poor kid wasn't drinking enough water to keep up with the sweat pouring out of his body.

She couldn't help thinking of the reports she had seen on TV about illegal immigrants in Arizona and Texas being found dead in semi-trailers, and now she knew why. It was like living in a sauna. The stench of soured sweat combined with the odors coming from the five-gallon bucket they used as a toilet was beyond insufferable. There was one positive outcome though. She felt like the guard was becoming more and more disgusted at their appearance every time the door opened. This was a relief because when they first arrived, he had looked at her with such hungry eyes that she had feared sexual assault. This morning he didn't have that look in his eyes. Apparently, even body odor had a positive side.

This morning when the guard opened the door, she could tell it was going to be another hot day, so she had insisted that the guard go back and get them more water, twice as much as they were normally given. He was clearly unhappy about it, but seemed to understand their plight and was clearly charged with keeping them alive, not killing them. She asked him to leave the door open so that she could see to wash the cut on Garret's forearm. It was caked with dried blood and oozing a clear, watery fluid, but there was no pus, so she didn't think it was infected.

When the guard came back with more water, she forced each of the kids to drink as much as they could, and then she sat in the corner and sang songs to them. When she grew tired of the singing, she asked Shelly to play twenty questions with them and felt her way down the wall of the container to the make-shift toilet on the other end. She didn't know which was worse—the pain of a bursting bladder or lifting the board that covered the five-gallon bucket.

She had gotten through the last five days by praying constantly. She had poured out her heart to God. She had begged him to spare her children, rescue them from their troubles and protect them from wicked men. But, now, strangely enough, she didn't feel like praying at all. God knew where they were and what they needed. Her babbling on and on about it wasn't going to change anything. She reminded herself over and over that He was in control and that He was good. In the end, this was what made the difference. Their situation didn't change, but she did.

Over the last three short days, she had put her life under the microscope like never before. One minute they were enjoying a European vacation; the next minute they were being held hostage in a shipping container only God knew where. It was doing something to her, something good. She couldn't remember who said it, but she knew she was the one prayer was changing, not God.

She thought of Gilbert. She missed his strength, his confidence, his intelligence. The last two years had been difficult for them both. It seemed like he was always away on business, always under considerable stress. She had felt neglected and had taken her frustration out on him in a hundred ways. In fact, her trip to Italy was meant to punish him and get away from all the bickering. Looking back on the last year from inside this dark container put everything in a new light. She realized she had not been supportive. Instead, she had been selfish and justified it by focusing on her own needs. Gilbert deserved better. She knew that now, but all she had been able to see was her own narrow world of constantly changing wants and whims. She had intentionally frustrated his attempts to do what was good for all of them. Prayer had opened her eyes to all of this and this realization grieved her as much as anything.

Ginger sat there in the darkness, wondering how he was coping, and discovered this too was a new perspective. It had been ages since she had taken the time to consider anything from his point of view. She knew this ordeal would be sheer torture for him. His sense of honor and virtue would only make the pain more excruciating for him. She didn't know anyone more responsible, more hardworking and more devoted to his family. In fact, she was happy that she was the one taken hostage. The feeling of helplessness, the uncertainty and the separation he had to be experiencing now would have driven her crazy. She knew he would pull himself together, think clearly and do everything within his power to get them back. If anybody could, he could. She also knew that three days in a dark container had filled her soul with more light than a week on a sunny Italian beach had.

⊬⊶⊷⊣

Matt looked across the low table into Gwyn's eyes. She hadn't said a word during their five-minute walk from the apartment to the tea house on Istiklal. Her face was hard. He could feel anger emanating from her, forming a force field capable of blocking whatever overture he made.

"Look, I really appreciate you coming," said Matt. "I know it isn't easy for you and believe me, it's not easy for me either."

She remained silent. Matt didn't know how to begin either. The silence became more and more uncomfortable. The waiter provided some relief when he arrived with two small plates of baklava and tea. When he was gone, Matt took a deep breath and plunged into the lines he had been rehearsing all night.

"First, I owe you an apology. It was wrong of me to just cut you off after you told me that a romantic relationship was not in the cards. I was so disappointed in how things ended that I couldn't face you. Still, I know you were hurt by what I did. It wasn't right."

"Wrong?" she said sarcastically. "I didn't think you believed in that sort of stuff. You couldn't score with me, so like the male of every species, you went looking for another female in heat. What's wrong with that?"

Matt closed his eyes and bowed his head. This was not going to be easy.

"Well, first of all, that's not true. I haven't had a girlfriend since we broke up."

"Not having a girlfriend is not the same as not having a girl."

"I haven't had a girl either."

She put on a look of mock surprise.

"Are we having performance problems?" she asked with feigned concern.

"Knock it off, Gwyn. I'm trying to tell you that I was wrong and apologize. Psychological revenge isn't going to get us anywhere."

"I see you're still trying to get somewhere."

"Yeah, I'm trying to get back to the place I was with you, a place where we enjoyed one another as unique and gifted individuals capable of making life beautiful. I miss that."

"Sounds a bit too metaphysical for someone like you."

"I'm not the same person, Gwyn. Your pain prevents you from seeing it, but it's true. I've changed."

"Well, that's a story I probably need to hear," she said, picking up her tea and leaning back against the cushioned back. "You can start by telling me why you've thrown away a career in the diplomatic core to work with hookers."

Matt picked up the small dessert fork and knife. This was a side of Gwyn he had only seen once. It was when her father had been passed over for a promotion in favor of a well-connected intellectual pygmy, but borderline schizophrenic professor. She had been angry about it for weeks. He had seen her biting sarcastic genius come out in heated conversations with her dad.

"Have you ever heard of Babek Reza?" he asked, cutting a slice of baklava in half and putting it in his mouth.

"No, I don't think I have," she replied.

"And you probably never will," continued Matt. "He was a nuclear physics professor from Tabriz in the north of Iran. He was also a political dissident who worked for the overthrow of the regime. Normally, he would have wound up in prison or in a garbage dump, but the government needed him, so for years he was forced to work on their nuclear development program. He was tortured when he failed to produce results. He was only allowed to see his wife and children once every two months and that was if certain progress objectives were satisfied.

"To make a long story shorter than it should be, he managed to get a message to the US State Department indicating that he wanted asylum and would cooperate with the International Atomic Energy Agency to prevent Iran from getting the bomb if we would help him get out of the country. At the end of a clandestine two-year operation, a plan was put into motion to extract him while he was on vacation in his hometown near the Caspian Sea. A team of Navy Seals was sent in to make the grab. Two hours later, a friend of mine in the CIA called and told me that the Seals had been ambushed and were fighting for their life.

"A rescue operation would have created an international incident. It might even have led to war with Iran, and so the men who had risked their lives to save an Iranian dissident were sacrificed. To this day, we have no idea how it happened. Maybe the original message passed to the State Department was actually handled by someone inside the Iranian government trying to bait us. We'll never know."

"That was the world that you loved though," said Gwyn. "I know you didn't quit because one operation went bad. You weren't even directly involved."

"Of course we weren't, but it was the State Department who had to clean up the mess, and at the time, I was on a special task force responsible for improving the image of America in the Middle East."

"So, they gave you mission impossible," Gwyn said, with a roll of her eyes. "I'd rather be Leonidas facing a million Persian soldiers at Thermopylae than work with a bunch of bureaucrats on a job like that."

"That makes two of us. Anyway, when the whole thing went south, we had a meeting with the spooks. Everyone in the room was split into two camps— those concerned with nothing more than saving their own asses and avoiding political embarrassment, and those who wanted to do what was right. Pardon my Spanish, but the ones without the *huevos* to stand up and tell the world the truth are the ones who carried the day. If we aren't proud of what we do, why in the hell are we doing it?"

He found he was getting too worked up, so he cut another square of baklava and took a sip of tea. Gwyn waited for him to continue.

"Even worse in my mind was the fact that they didn't give a damn about honoring the men who gave their lives. They couldn't just hold a press conference and say, 'We were contacted by an Iranian dissident being held against his will and forced by an oppressive regime to develop nuclear weapons. He asked to be extracted, and we did our best to help him. We failed, but honorable men gave their lives in a brave attempt to do what was right for humanity and for the world. We are not ashamed of what we have done and will gladly do it again.' Can you imagine how that would have boosted morale in the military and the public at large? After that, I realized I didn't want a career as a professional bull-shitter."

"So they sacrificed the Seals," interrupted Gwyn. "Isn't that what you call *realpolitik*?"

"If your audience is the UN, then maybe it is. Bu, I was under the misguided notion that we were supposed to do what was best for the United States of America. Letting our allies know that ideals guide our actions, that we still have a soul, and that we stand behind our friends seems politically expedient to me. If they want to improve their image, they're going to have to change who they are. You can't bamboozle the whole world in the information age."

"So, you just walked away from it? Why not stay and change it?" asked Gwyn. Some of the iciness had left her voice.

A sardonic smile flashed across Matt's face.

"Let me ask you a question? What do you call a leader with no followers?"

Gwyn paused for just a second.

"Delusional? I don't know. What are you driving at?"

"A leader without followers might be a revolutionary, he might be a prophet, he might be a dissident, but he isn't a leader. The truth is you can't lead people who won't follow, which is why this pipedream we call democracy will only work if citizens are noble enough to follow noble leaders. I'm not sure that is true anymore. When the only people the citizens will vote for are sweet-talking villains drowning in corruption, the end of the republic is near. The kind of man we need is feared and hounded by the establishment, Gwyn. A perfect example is John. He learned that the cost of confrontation was first incarceration and then decapitation."

"John?" she asked quizzically.

"John the Baptist," he replied.

"Right," she said, cocking her head sideways and staring at him with a look of disbelief on her face. He didn't notice her surprise.

"Anyway," he continued, "That's the problem. We say we want leaders with character and integrity, men and women who will put the good of their country ahead of everything else, people who will stand up for our values and stand behind actions that reflect those values. But, we get a never-ending stream of self-serving, disingenuous low-life trash masquerading as statesmen and intent only on maintaining the status quo of the new American aristocracy.

"And, who is to blame? The followers, of course. After all, in a democracy, it is followers who make and mold leaders, not the other way around. We need leaders who will give us our medicine, not leaders who give the dying cancer patient a clean bill of health. We are sick."

Gwyn took another bite of her baklava and stared out the window at a group of Turkish students in white and blue uniforms streaming out of the schoolyard across the street on their lunch break. Matt's honesty was softening the anger she felt.

"Listen, Matt," she said, "I think you made a mistake in leaving. Politics, especially foreign relations, is what you were cut out to do. I'm sorry you left."

Matt thought he was going to choke on his baklava.

"You hated the thought of me going into politics. Surely you haven't forgotten all the grief you gave me?"

She held the tea glass by the rim between her thumb and forefinger. It looked a bit like an hour glass or maybe a perfect 34-26-34 woman.

"You want the truth?" she asked quietly, swirling the tea in the glass and staring at it blankly.

It was a rhetorical question. He didn't respond. Without looking at him, she continued, "My reasons were totally selfish, Matt. I couldn't see myself married to a diplomat or a politician and for some bizarre reason I thought you and I were made for each other. That is why I tried so hard to dissuade you."

Matt had always known this to be true. He sat there looking at her until their eyes met. He wanted to stare into those beautiful eyes of ocean blue and green forever. He held her gaze, and she let him. He felt it, and knew that she did too. That barely perceptible transfer of energy released when two souls connected. His heart began to race.

"But, you were right," he said at last. "You said that statesmanship and honor had been wrung out of the fabric of society and that politics would leave me disillusioned. You were right. Look at me now."

"Disillusionment is not sufficient grounds for quitting," she replied quietly.

"I'm not so sure our leaders have the heart to win. We damn sure can't win if we lose our honor. We can't defeat our enemies by pretending to be their friends either, or worse, getting in bed with them."

"How do you define our enemy?" asked Gwyn. "You surely don't mean that we are at war with Islam?"

"I'm sure you want me to qualify it by saying radical Islamic terrorists or some other media-inspired claptrap. You haven't lived in the Middle East like I have. Those people see us as the enemy. This is a direct result of their faith. I have seen how they play in the Middle East. They say Islam is a religion of peace, and if you say anything to the contrary, they want to kill you! The Pope apologizes for the Crusades, which, by the way, were only Christianity's answer to jihad. But, where are the clerics speaking out against killing in the name of Allah? Why do we constantly catch Middle Eastern governments funding terrorist groups or providing them with intel? You haven't seen the reports."

"I haven't, of course, but you are making sweeping accusations."

"Gwyn, it is a totally different paradigm. How many times have you seen the American flag desecrated in the Middle East or one of our presidents being burned in effigy?"

"I don't know. Maybe a dozen times. Maybe more."

"And how many times have you seen Americans doing the same thing to their flag or leaders?" he asked.

"I don't remember ever seeing that."

"My point exactly. America is arguably the most multi-cultural place in the world and I suppose it is something to be proud of, but we have allowed it to blind us to cultural reality. All cultures do not have equal value. Why don't we stand on our record and our values? I am sick of the mandatory cultural sensitivity training telling us that jihad is a legitimate tenet of Islam, and that there is a lot we could learn from them. How about Muslims try learning a little from us?"

"Zeki is a Muslim, and he's not like that."

Matt noticed that Gwyn was looking around the room to see if anyone was listening. She wasn't comfortable having this discussion in an Istanbul café.

"The actions of one honorable man trying to repay a debt to your father cannot negate the dozens, if not hundreds, of terrorist attacks carried out every year in the name of Islam."

"Listen, I disagree, but this is hardly the time to debate it. If Islam is the problem, apply for a transfer to the Far East, Europe or South America. You don't have to work in the Middle East."

"I thought about it, but the challenge of our generation is the Middle East. If I were to get reassigned somewhere else, all I'd be doing is negotiating favorable trade terms for American products. The State Department turns you into a damn salesman hawking American wares and negotiating favorable trade agreements. It's corporatism plain and simple. Sometimes I wonder if the corporate elite are the ones who write the directives we receive. The State Department greases the wheels for the big boys, who make a killing, and then shuffle the money through offshore accounts using the Irish Double or the Dutch Sandwich to avoid paying taxes to the free market society which gave them birth."

"You lost me."

"Many of the largest global conglomerates are American companies, but they pay a fraction of the taxes a typical American company is forced to pay because they have the infrastructure to move the profits offshore. It's absolute bullshit, and that is what I would be doing if I were out of the Middle East. That or negotiating condom distribution programs to prevent the spread of AIDS in Africa."

"I understand your frustration, but I think you should reconsider," she said.

"And I think you should try some baklava. You haven't even touched yours," he rejoined. "Besides, that is enough about me. Tell me what you've been doing."

59

VIENNA   Zeki stood in front of the Albertina Museum, looking at an extravagant marble depiction of Zeus and Hera beneath a bronze of one of the Austrian emperors. He scanned the pedestrians on the street, hoping to see Sally's signature red hair. She was nowhere in sight. He did, however, see another street security camera, and casually walked thirty meters to his right so that it had a clear frontal shot of him. Together with all of the cameras he had passed in airport security and on the streets this morning, there would be plenty of collaborating evidence that Gülben had been in the city. He moved out of the camera's line of sight and looked down at his watch. It was 12:59. Patrick had said thirteen hundred hours, and they were never late.

For years, she had been a freelance field operative. As a team, Sally and Patrick were among the best in the field. Zeki had even used them for a job in Greece years back. But, they ran into trouble on a job in Mexico. Patrick wouldn't say who the employer was, but he suspected it was the US. Something had gone wrong, and Sally was caught leaving the country. The government had turned her over to the cartel, and they were nasty. The grief drove Patrick crazy. He spent half of their life savings, almost two million dollars, to get her back. Then, he called in a bunch of favors and spent the rest of their savings setting things straight. For the next eighteen months, members of the cartel dropped like flies. Sally was never the same though. Now, she ran the document side of their "security services" business.

He felt someone touch his elbow and spun around.

"Hi Zeki."

It was Sally. Her red hair was gone, and so was the sparkle in her eye.

"Patrick said you were going in as a bald fellow. There were two of you, but the other guy walked off three minutes ago, so I knew you had to be the one still standing here."

"Sally, it's good to see you."

"Here's your book." She handed him a white and red Swiss chocolate shopping bag.

He held out an envelope.

"It's not much, but it's all I can afford."

"Keep it," she said, pushing his hand away. "Patrick told me it was personal. We don't charge for personal stuff, you see. If it's personal, it's on the house."

He pulled the book out and turned it over in his hand. The cover was exact and the dimensions looked right too. He opened it and thumbed through a few pages.

"It looks great. Good work as always."

"We're professionals. Besides, it was for a friend."

He smiled, but the mask felt funny, and he resolved not to do that again. Her face remained grave.

"You and Patrick need to visit me sometime."

"Yeah, I'd like to see your real face again."

<hr>

Zeki looked around the reading room. It was getting full. There had only been a handful of people that morning, but now there were over a dozen. He glanced at the clock on his cell phone. It was 2:15. He had four minutes. He closed the Gospel of Barnabas and moved it to his left elbow. He wanted all of the motion to be as close to his body as possible, and it would be easier to reach across his body with his right hand. He had rehearsed it in his mind a thousand times. He knew when the lights went off it would take him less than five seconds, and the generator would take twenty to forty seconds to kick in, so he had plenty of time. He opened N.B. 215

Then it happened. The only thing that could have gone wrong did. He had always known it was a possibility, and now an obese woman moved out of the ethereal realm of potentiality and plopped smack dab in the middle of his reality. She laid a book down on the opposite corner of the table, pulled out the chair and lowered her bulk down gingerly as if she half-expected the chair to break beneath her. There was no way he could swap the books with someone sitting directly across from him. He could text Patrick and tell him to wait, but this lady might be here until closing time, waiting might gain him nothing. He was already warm from the jacket he had brought in on the pretext of having a summer cold. His face began sweating underneath the mask. He had hoped this job would go off without hitting a snag. Now, he was going to have to improvise.

He quickly scanned the room. There were no empty tables or zones except for the area right in front of the reading room librarian. He grabbed his pencil and legal pad, placed the G.O.B. under it and felt in his jacket for the substitute Sally had given him. He looked down at the clock and waited for it to hit 2:18. It was no more than fifteen steps to the elevated platform where the librarian sat. When the clock hit 2:18, he stood up and walked over to the librarian.

"Good afternoon," he said.

"Good afternoon. How can I help you?"

"I know that pictures are not allowed in the Augustinerlesesaal, but I was wondering if I could make a rough sketch of that fresco," he said, pointing to the ceiling in the empty alcove on the other side of her desk.

"Why, certainly. Go right ahead."

"Thank you."

He took a few steps into the alcove and began sketching on the legal pad. There was a security camera here too. Then the lights went down, and only the natural light from the windows lit the reading room. He feigned surprise and turned to face the room as soon as they went down. The librarian stood up and broke the silence that had dominated the room for hours.

"There is a generator. It will come on momentarily."

Zeki returned to the fresco on the ceiling so that his back was to the entire room and quickly switched the books. Fifteen seconds later the lights were back on. Zeki remained in the alcove for another couple of minutes, finishing the sketch, and as he passed the librarian's desk, he nodded again.

"Does the library have stock photos of this room or maybe postcards?"

"I believe they do, but you should ask at the reception area."

"Okay, thank you."

He returned to his seat, picked up his cell phone and sent Gilbert a text.

Switch successful.

Then, he picked up N.B. 215 and continued reading. He hoped to finish it before he left. He wanted to stay until closing when the rush of people returning materials would make it even less likely that anyone would give his substitute more than a cursory glance. The only thing left to do was have the receptionist take a photograph of him with the book.

60

Wednesday, Vienna   Zeki had finished his continental breakfast and was nursing a cup of coffee as he waited for the sun to rise and the waitress to take his plate. His room was too dreary and cramped to be enjoyable. Besides, the wireless was spotty on that floor, and he had work to do. The waitress came to take away his plate, and as he pulled out his laptop, he thought for the umpteenth time that 'continental' must be a synonym for 'sparse' in some European language. Their breakfast made Turkish fare seem like a feast. Still, the coffee lived up to the Vienna's reputation for the finest and he savored every drop as well as the irony. The Austrians' first experience with coffee had been at the Battle of Vienna when the combined forces of the Holy League led by the great Polish general and King John Sobieski routed Kara Mustapha Pasha, stopping forever the Turkish advance into Europe. This was undoubtedly the chief advantage for Austria, but coffee beans from Yemen had been found in the supplies the Turks were forced to leave behind when they were routed. It was to mark the beginning of a delectable addiction to caffeine.

He felt his face. It was still tender and a bit blotchy from wearing the mask for almost twenty-four hours the day before. This morning he had used almost half a bottle of aftershave trying to get his skin to perk up a bit. Today, for the first time in a week, he would be using his real name. It already felt weird, but there was no sense hiding anymore.

He thought about his meeting with the man posing as a priest today. At last, he would be in the presence of someone from the group responsible for Ian's death. He had arranged for Patrick to have the man followed after he left the reading room, just in case he didn't get the results he wanted. It was only a precaution. Physical coercion probably wouldn't do much good either, but one never knew until one tried. He at least needed the man's real identity.

He looked down at the screen. Gilbert had sent him Turkish data from the key-logger. Until Augustinerlesesaal opened, he would go over these files. He hadn't looked at them since Dallas. There had been no time. He was anxious to see just how far Gülben's network spread. Ten minutes later, Zeki could feel the butterflies in his stomach pushing out of their cocoons one after another until it began to make him nauseous. He stared at the screen, paralyzed by fear and wishing he had never read the file. Terrorists didn't scare him. They were outlaws preying on the margins of society. They would never win. What scared him were legitimate organizations with public support and sinister motives. Governments were far more frightening than terrorist cells.

⊢━━━⊣

ISTANBUL   Gwyn was awakened by the sound of plates clattering in the small kitchen. She lay there trying to remember where she was. The sound of a boy in the street below, yelling in a foreign tongue, brought the realization crashing in on her consciousness. She was in Istanbul. She pulled the covers up over her face.

Gary had slipped out at seven o'clock that morning and bought some Turkish pastries filled with meat called *taş böreği* and sesame-covered pretzel-like things called *simit*. He had set the table and was busy washing the tea glasses from the night before. He yelled into the living room.

"Gil, wake up Gwyn. She said she didn't want to sleep past eight o'clock."

Gilbert was busy looking up words in an online Turkish dictionary and gave no indication that he had even heard his brother. He had been up before any of them, going over the massive amount of key-logger data that had piled up, looking for anything that might help them. Most of it was in Turkish though.

"I'll knock on her door," offered Matt.

"Thanks."

A couple of minutes later Gwyn came into the room in a pair of sweats.

"Alright, everybody to the table. I'm up," she said.

"You guys go ahead," said Gilbert. "I'll just have some tea."

"You need to eat," protested Gwyn.

"I'm not hungry," he said flatly.

The other three sat down. Gary filled four tea glasses. He set one of them on the end table beside Gilbert. Matt, Gwyn and Gary sat around the table eating in silence and wondering about what no one wanted to talk about—would Zeki's meeting provide them with any leverage? Without looking up from his computer, Gilbert addressed Matt.

"Was your friend able to learn anything about who was behind the complaint filed with the FBI that resulted in an Interpol bulletin being issued for me?"

Matt cocked his head to the side and set his tea glass down.

"Actually, I phoned him last night after he got off work to see what he had learned. Because of the time difference, we didn't talk until about midnight local time, and you were already asleep. The complaint was filed by a French law firm

384

named Girard, Babin and Broussard, which is a connected with the A.L.S. Mediterranean Legal Group, the firm representing the Libyan government."

"I figured as much. I guess we'll just have to face the music when this is all over."

"Unfortunately, there is more."

"More?"

"Yes, my friend spoke with the agent handling the case and he said that he had received three calls from the office of Minnesota Senator Giovanni asking for updates on the status of the search."

"That's strange. Why would a Senator be concerned?"

"Either he is getting a kickback of some sort from the Libyan government if they win this case against private equity, or he has a stake in a certain French law firm. The intrigue may be layered to look complicated, but all you have to do is follow the money."

"Alright, I'll do some research when I'm done with these logs. You finish your breakfast."

"Speaking of research," Matt said, turning to Gwyn and Gary. "Last night, I also did a bit of snooping on George Sale and read about fifty pages of his translation of the Qur'an. Did either of you know that this is the same translation of the Qur'an that was used to swear in the first Muslim member of the US congress?"

"Once a diplomat always a diplomat," replied Gwyn with a sigh. "I didn't even know a Muslim had been elected to Congress."

Her voice sounded dull and indifferent.

"It was the very same book that President Thomas Jefferson bought when he was preparing a military response to the Barbary pirates in the Mediterranean. These Muslim pirates were capturing American ships and ransoming off the crews for handsome sums. Apparently, he wanted to understand his enemy. In the end, he decided appeasement was the wrong strategy and sent the Marines to the 'shores of Tripoli', which is, of course, commemorated in the Marine Hymn to this day."

Gilbert interrupted.

"Gary, have a look at this."

Gary walked over and looked at the section of the screen Gilbert was pointing at. He had highlighted several words.

Baraka AH748TEM, Uzy7!9d3 *Erguvan* c66GyT7

"Looks like passwords to me," Gary said. "When did this happen?"

"It's from Monday. I've reviewed everything with English in it, so I thought I'd just look through some of the Turkish. I sent these files to Zeki, but I'm sure he's probably too busy to spend much time on it. Besides, there are two hundred pages of data. He could never get through it all."

"Is there anything in the surrounding text that would indicate what it is related to?"

"That's all there is in this time segment."

"Can you search the log to see if this occurs anywhere else?"

"I already did. This is the only occurrence. Do you know what the words mean?"

"The first one is Arabic for 'blessing' or 'fruitfulness'. That's all I know. I think we should call Zeki."

Gilbert reached for the phone, hit the speed dial number, put it on speaker and laid it beside his computer. It started ringing.

"Hello."

"Hello, Zeki. This is Gilbert. How was the flight yesterday?"

"A bit of trouble getting through customs though I don't suppose that is unusual for someone carrying a Turkish passport after what happened on Monday. I think the fact that the ticket was purchased the same day made them nervous too. You received my text?"

"Yes."

"I'm almost to the reading room. I expect the man to be there as soon as the doors are open."

"That's great. Do you think it will work?"

Zeki didn't respond immediately. When he did, he sounded tired.

"I think they will see things our way in the short term. Start preparing for the exchange. I will insist it happen as soon as possible."

Gwyn could see her brother blinking back the tears.

"Look," said Gilbert, "I found something on the key-logger that looks like a username and two separate passwords. Unfortunately, I don't know where they were being used. There are only two words in the same time segment."

"The first is B-A-R-A-K-A, which occurs before the username. Can you tell me what that means?"

Zeki sighed. "It's Arabic and means something like 'blessing', but if you found it together with a password, it might be referring to the Islamic bank. *Baraka* may have been typed in to activate the auto-complete on a browser and open the web page. Are you at your computer?"

"Yep."

"Type in this URL."

He began coding it out. w-w-w.b-a-r-a-k-a-b-a-n-k-a-s-i.c-o-m. That is the website of an international Islamic bank. You could try the password there."

"What about the second word? It is E-R-G-U-V-A-N, and occurs after the username and password, if that is what they are."

"That is the name of a famous tree in Istanbul that has beautiful blossoms in the spring. I forget what the English equivalent is, and I have no idea how that could be connected."

"Okay, I'll try this and call you back in five minutes."

Gilbert hung up the phone and returned to the computer screen. He looked at the screen for a minute and tried to orient himself. Security was his field, his specialty, and his mind was churning through the possibilities. The first thing he had to do was choose between 'Personal Accounts' and 'Corporate Accounts'. He took a chance and clicked on 'corporate'. His screen switched to the login page. He typed in the username and the first password, held his breath and clicked OK.

There was a ten-second lull as the information was sent and processed. The screen flickered, and he found himself on another page with a single question.

WILL YOU USE THIS COMPUTER FREQUENTLY TO LOGIN?

He clicked the 'Yes' button and then 'Next' while shaking his head. He knew what was coming. There would be a security question that he didn't know the answer to. It was even worse than that. The question was in Turkish.

ISTANBUL'DA EN ÇOK ÖZLEDIĞIM ŞEY

"Can you read this, Gary?"

"I could pick out the words, but I might not be able to sort out the grammar. You should ask Zeki."

He hit redial again and prayed Zeki would pick up. There was probably a 120-second security time-out on this webpage.

"Hello."

"Zeki. The password worked, but it's asking me a personalized security question that is in Turkish. I can't even pronounce the words, but Gary will give it a try."

Gary repeated the words on the screen. They were both surprised to hear Zeki laugh out loud.

"That explains the second word. The security question is, 'What do I miss most about Istanbul?' And, the answer is the second word—*erguvan*—that beautiful flowering tree prized so highly by the Byzantines and Ottomans."

"Wow. Did we ever get lucky!" exclaimed Matt.

Gilbert typed in the answer to the security question and clicked 'Continue'.

He couldn't believe it when the account detail screen opened up in front of him. Gary slapped him on the back.

"Way to go, man. Whose account are we looking it?"

Gilbert scanned the screen and then addressed Zeki.

"Have you ever heard of a company called Waqf International Trading, Ltd?"

"No."

Gilbert scanned the page for other information and then drew in a quick breath and pointed at the account balance. Sixty-two million USD.

"Zeki, this account has a balance of sixty-two million US dollars." He clicked on the account transaction history. "And, fifty million dollars arrived yesterday."

"If the account login you have managed to acquire has the necessary authorization," said Zeki, "you might be able to transfer money out of that account."

"But why would we risk tipping them off to our spying?" asked Gilbert.

"When I confront their so-called priest this morning, it won't take them long to figure out they've been compromised. Besides, all of you are going to need some cash for your life in exile."

Gilbert had been trying not to even think about what would happen after the exchange. Zeki was forcing him to. Gwyn spoke first.

"What do you mean by 'exile', Zeki? Once the exchange is over and they have the document, everything will be okay, right?"

"I'm sorry, Gwyn," responded Zeki, with the tone of a father breaking bad news to a child. "This problem isn't going to just go away. They are using Gilbert's family to get the document back, but we already know too much. In fact, through the key-logger, we have gathered an amazing amount of information about their operations, information that, to be quite honest, scares me. This morning I read the data Gilbert sent me. This is way bigger than I ever dreamed. International organizations, local and federal governments, security forces, intelligence agencies, investment funds, the UN…"

His voice trailed off. A look of horror dawned on Gwyn's face as she began to think of the implications. Everyone else waited for him to continue.

"Once they know that their communications have been intercepted by us, and they *will* find out, the price tag on our heads rockets into the stratosphere. Sixty million? That is small change for these guys. They control the natural resources of many nations. It's time to face the fact that your lives, however long or short, will never be the same. You will never be able to go back to the way things were. They aren't going to stop until we've all been silenced."

Zeki stopped. He was finished. Gilbert could feel the darkness of despair settling down over the room. He could not let that happen. He made his decision.

"I don't have an account that would be beyond their reach. In fact, my bank in America would almost certainly reject any such transaction on suspicion of money-laundering. Can you help us?"

"I have a bank account in Switzerland that I have used for years, but you should route it through another account of mine in Bermuda first. That will make it difficult to track and even harder for them to retrieve. If you are able to send it to Bermuda, I'll immediately take it out and move it to Switzerland and then to London. I can have it physically removed from that account within the hour.

"All of this depends, of course, on whether the login you captured belongs to an officer in the company with the authority to make such a transfer. If it works, let me know right away. You can be sure they will be on to you very quickly. Even if you are using an anonymizer to hide your IP address, I'd say the police will be there in half an hour. Are you sure this is what you want to do?"

"Well, you've made it clear that we've nothing to lose and everything to gain," replied Gilbert.

"I'll send you the Bermuda account details in a text right now," replied Zeki.

"And, I'll let you know if the password works."

"One more thing, do you remember the name of the officer on your father's case?"

"Yeah, McIntosh. John McIntosh. Why?"

"It may come in handy. That's all."

Gilbert hung up the phone, and now Matt was pacing the room.

"Gil," he said, "Are you sure you want to steal sixty-two million dollars from these guys? You are about to really piss them off."

Gilbert didn't even answer. He focused his attention on the account information in front of him. His mind was spinning. He had to be sure he was covering everything. He had used the anonymizer to connect, so the bank shouldn't be able to retrieve his location. Still, he knew that nothing was one hundred percent safe. *How long will it be before they miss it?* He was certain they would be notified of the transaction electronically. That would be practically instantaneous. The only question was whether or not someone would be in front of their computer to read the email.

The phone buzzed. Zeki's text message had arrived. Gilbert began searching the screen for the wire transfer tab. He found it, and Gary began reading off the information in the text from Zeki for Gilbert to enter on the screen—account number, beneficiary name, and SWIFT code. Then, he typed 62,000,480.00 into the field for the transfer amount, leaving exactly 190 dollars in the account. There was another field for a description of the transfer. He thought for a second and then typed:

FIRST INSTALLMENT ON LIFE INSURANCE PAYMENT FOR THE LATE PROF. IAN O'BRIEN.

He moved the mouse over the 'Continue' button and Matt repeated his question, looking at Gwyn.

"Are you sure about this? An old document is one thing. Sixty million dollars is another. You could be signing Ginger's death certificate."

"I don't think so," replied Gilbert coldly. "I've given this a lot of thought. This piece of paper is not just any old document. I spent several hours last night researching what has been done with the G.O.B. in the last century. They've bamboozled millions of people with it. I don't think they want to risk having their deceit uncovered. You've seen what they're capable of!"

"Which is exactly why you need to let this go!"

"No, it's exactly why we can't. The best chance we have at tilting the odds in our favor is to play according to their values and not ours. Ginger is not nearly as valuable to them as the document...and our silence."

The finality in the word 'silence' was sobering. Matt didn't give up though.

"You're going to ruin whatever small chance there is left for your family to live a normal life. You aren't the only one affected by this decision. I've got friends. I can help you."

Again, he glanced at Gwyn, who had her head in her hands.

"I'm not so sure about that, Matt. The world has changed. I'm starting to see that now," he continued, looking straight into Matt's eyes. "In fact, I think it's time for *you* to go home. Right now, they don't know you're involved. If they find out you're with us, we'll be sharing the same bleak future."

Matt looked at Gilbert like he had lost his mind.

"I'm *not* leaving my friends in need. You asked me to come, Gilbert!"

"We don't need you anymore, Matt. It was great to have you here helping wade through it all. Besides, without you, I wouldn't have known about the FBI search warrant or who was behind it. The canister may still come in handy, but there is no reason for you to risk your life any further. It's too dangerous."

Matt wasn't even looking at him anymore. He was staring at Gwyn. Finally, he tore his eyes away and looked back at Gilbert.

"You're right, of course, but I'd rather throw my lot in with you guys right here, right now, no matter what the consequences are."

"I have no doubt you would do that for us, Matt. But, I'm going to ask you to do something else. Right now, my father is lying in a British morgue waiting to be escorted to his final resting place beside our mother. None of us are going to be able to go back. I wonder if you would honor us by taking care of these final arrangements. Dad liked you a lot, and it would mean the world to us."

Gilbert looked at his brother and sister. Gary's face was impossible to read. Gwyn was already fighting back the tears as she walked up to Matt and took both of his hands in hers.

"Gil is right, you know. This *is* the best thing to do. You're a fighter, so it's not what you would normally do, but I'm going to ask you to do it for me. Will you?"

Matt looked stunned. He looked away to avoid her eyes. His face was hard, but he slowly nodded his head.

"Yes. Yes, I will, and gladly if that is what you want."

"It is," she replied.

Gilbert didn't like the emotionally charged atmosphere. The room was heavy with it and he wanted to move on.

"It's all settled then. Get a power of attorney from Uncle Henry. I'd give you one, but that would only tie you directly to me. Now, let's see if we have the winning lottery ticket."

He looked back down at the computer screen, clicked 'continue' and waited for the system to ask for the second password. He felt sure it was used to confirm transactions in the system. He was right. A new screen asked him to confirm the transaction. He typed it in slowly, double-checking each character and then hit ENTER. Time stopped. Everyone held their breath though unconscious of the act. The seconds seemed like minutes. The same thought going through all of their minds. *Did the account have the authorization necessary for a transfer of this size?*

61

Ginger woke with a start. Someone was unlocking the door to the container. She was surprised that she was not awake before they brought breakfast. The door at the other end of the container opened and she realized it was just now growing light outside. It was the guard with the hungry look in his eye, the one that made her feel so nervous. He was carrying something in his hands. She stood up.

"Good morning," he said with a heavy accent.

"Good morning."

"You want bath?" he asked in very broken and stumbling English.

Ginger could see that he was carrying towels and a bar of soap.

"I bring water. You clean."

Her oldest son Garret stirred. She took the towel he handed her.

"For you and other lady."

He turned and walked out of the container. A few minutes later he returned carrying a large bucket of water and a large metal bowl to use as a washbasin.

"Thank you," she said.

"Children sleep. It is good. Now, you and lady clean."

He leaned against the wall of the container and stared at them. Ginger looked at him suspiciously.

"Okay, you can go now," she motioned with her hand for him to leave.

He only smiled and made a circular motion with his index finger extended as if to say, 'Hurry up'. That was when Ginger understood what was going on.

"Oh my God," whispered Shelly in terror. "Is he thinking what I think he is thinking?"

Ginger whispered back.

"I think so."

"Well, I'm not taking my clothes off and bathing in front of him."

Ginger acted like she hadn't heard. She took the bucket of water and poured some of the warm water into the metal bowl. She walked over to her sleeping children, dipped the towel in the water and began unbuttoning Garth's shirt. This brought the man charging towards her.

"Not for children. For you!" he said, pointing first to Shelly and then to her. "You smell bad."

"So do the children," replied Ginger. "They must bathe first. Then we will bathe."

"No!" he said angrily. "You bathe now."

Looking straight in the man's eyes, she addressed Shelly. "You took French, right?"

The man thought he was talking to her and he was trying to understand what she had said.

"What?" he asked.

Ginger repeated the question, hoping that Shelly was getting her message. The man screwed up his face and said, "Why you ask me that?"

"I did," said Shelly in response to Ginger's question.

Ginger continued looking at the man and to create more confusion she said in a soft voice, "*La porte est ouverte. Exécuter ou d'être violée.*"

Shelly looked at Ginger in disbelief.

"Now," whispered Ginger. The man was still staring at them with a confused look on his face. Ginger gripped the washbasin tightly, waiting for Shelly to make her move.

The man started to say something. From the corner of her eye, Ginger saw Shelly start to run, and she threw the washbasin full of water straight at his head. He exploded in anger and started towards her, but then realized Shelly was already at the door and turned in hot pursuit, yelling something in his own language. Gabriella woke up screaming. Garth jumped up and ran to his mother.

"What's going on? Are you okay? Where's Shelly?"

Ginger ran over to the water bucket and dumped it on the ground. Then, she grabbed the towels and soap and raced towards the five-gallon buckets they used for toilets at the other end of the container.

"Comfort your sister, Garth. Keep her quiet."

She kicked the board off with her foot. A horrid stench engulfed her, and a cloud of flies flew up in her face. She held her breath as she stuffed the towel and soap into the bucket and replaced the lid. *If they want me clean, they are going to have to provide more towels.* Then, she walked to the open door and looked out. The sun had only just come up. It was the first time she had seen the sky in days. She surveyed her surroundings. They were surrounded by containers and she noticed a crane unloading a ship about five hundred yards to her right. Then, she saw the man with the broken English round a corner, dragging Shelly back towards the container. She turned to her left and saw two more men with radios sprinting towards the container.

This was not going to be good. She took the kids back inside the container and marched them over to the makeshift toilet.

"Listen, this is going to be gross, but you have to trust Mommy."

She quickly removed the board that covered the five-gallon bucket. Stoically, she stuck her hand to the bottom, withdrew it and wiped it in her hair. She repeated the action three times, starting with Gabriella. It was a desperate attempt to keep her captors from perpetrating even greater horrors. Then, she grabbed the bucket, waved the kids to the back of the container and waited for them to bring Shelly back. The same question kept running through her mind. *All this will do is buy time and ill will. Time for what?* She still hadn't answered the question when Shelly was shoved through the door. Ginger didn't hesitate. She dumped the rest of the bucket on her head. Shelly looked at her friend in shock and immediately began to gag. The man stormed in behind her and found Shelly bent over double vomiting.

"This how you repay my being nice?" he said in a rage.

The stench hit him even before he had finished the sentence. He saw the bucket of water had been knocked over on the floor. He looked up at Ginger and the kids and saw the excrement in their hair.

"*Allah kahretsin!* You are disgusting, filthy animals, but no matter. There is more water. This time you clean her too," he yelled, pointing at Gabriella, and with that, he left and the heavy iron door clanged shut.

<hr>

For ten minutes, Gwyn had been looking at the phone lying on the table, dying to know what Zeki was doing in Vienna. Gilbert had been sitting at the laptop, monitoring the key-logger data ever since the transfer. There were still three columns, one for each of the computers that had opened the file. Most of it was in Turkish, occasionally it was English or just gibberish, which he figured was probably due to a non-Roman language like Arabic or Urdu. The data had been a fairly steady stream all morning in two columns and one had just picked up about fifteen minutes ago. *Obviously someone arriving late for work.*

The phone vibrated on the table, indicating the arrival of another message. Gwyn picked it up and read it out loud.

FUNDS RECEIVED. TRANSFERRED TO GENEVA. NEXT TIME I RING, CONTACT YOUR SECRETARY.

Gilbert ran his hand through his hair. He wanted to smile. It was the biggest break they could have asked for, but his mind was on Ginger and the kids, and so the smile wouldn't come. He looked at everyone and said,

"Are we ready?"

394

62

VIENNA Zeki scanned the reception room as he walked in. The only one behind the desk was the girl with short, black hair. Being careful to alter his voice, he greeted her with a smile.

"Good morning. I have reserved two books—THEOL. 62 and N.B. 215."

"What is the name?" she asked.

"Zeki Öztürk," he said with a smile, using his real name for the first time in his travels over the last week. "I suppose you want to see some identification."

"Yes, of course."

He handed her his passport. She opened it to the picture page and then looked back up at him quizzically.

"I know," he said. "I had more hair then."

She smiled.

"I think the bald look is very becoming on you."

"You're very polite, Ms ..."

"Elizabeth," she responded, with another beaming and authentic smile.

She took him through the same procedure he had performed yesterday and gave him the same spiel. When she handed him the plastic cube that indicated his table number, he screwed up his face and pointed to the two tables in front of the check-in desk.

"Would it be alright if I sat at one of these tables instead of in the reading room? When I was here last summer, it was so cold in there I could hardly focus."

"Of course, but it's not a quiet zone. I hope the talking won't bother you."

"No, not at all."

As he handed the plastic cube back to her, his cell phone rang. He smiled apologetically.

"It's okay," she reassured him. "This is not a quiet zone, remember."

He acknowledged her with a nod and looked down at the screen. It was Yusuf.

"Hello."

"Zeki, I hope this is a good time."

"Not exactly, but go ahead."

Yusuf spoke rapidly.

"I told you I had a suspicion that Bekir was doing something in Vienna. Now, I'm sure of it. All of the cells we were monitoring in Vienna have gone dark. No cell phone calls, no internet drops, no blog posts, empty apartments, failure to report for work or class...In retrospect, this is the same pattern we saw before. Did you hear what happened this morning at the Vienna mosque?"

"No, I haven't seen a paper today," replied Zeki.

"We just found out ourselves," continued Yusuf. "There was an all-night vigil at the mosque to commemorate the Night of Power and as they were leaving, the worshippers were attacked by a group of masked men. No one was hurt badly, but it is all over the news here, and we have also just learned that the imam with connections to Bekir has called for a demonstration at noon. The protesters say they are going to march through the Museum Quarter and through the *Volksgarten*. We think they are hoping for more exposure via tourists."

"I am less than two hundred meters from there," said Zeki.

"I wanted to let you know, so that you could avoid the area. I've got a bad feeling about this."

"Listen, Yusuf. You need to watch your back."

"What do you mean?"

"I saw data today that proves that the Cairo cell of the organization we're dealing with has close ties with our Ministry of Internal Affairs Intelligence Bureau Headquarters."

"So what? We both know the fundamentalists have been infiltrating agencies for years."

"Just watch your back."

"Thanks for the warning."

Zeki hung up, walked over to the table closest to the check-in desk and sat down with his back to the wall. He didn't know whether the man posing as Father Franchini would be wearing his collar or not, so he wanted to be able to hear him ask for the reference number. He opened one of the books and began to wait. He didn't have to wait long.

Ten minutes later, he saw a man dressed as a Catholic priest step through the door. Zeki guessed he was in his mid-fifties. A pair of wire-rimmed glasses perched precariously on a Roman nose. At least, that is what it would have been called in the West, but his nose was also quintessential Ottoman Sultan. The marriage history of the Ottoman Sultans flashed through his mind. With only one exception, the mother of every sultan had been a foreigner, sometimes Greek, sometimes Slav, yet a man would have to be ignorant of Mendel's law to think that after five generations there was much Turkish blood left in the line at all. Maybe it was a Roman or Greek nose after all. He had obviously been chosen as the person who looked the most like the real Father Franchini and a low-resolution security camera might never be able to tell the difference. He was well-built and obviously very fit. He wore a loose fitting black jacket. Zeki knew it had to hold some book meant to replace the gospel of Barnabas.

Though he felt certain this was his man, Zeki only made his move when he heard him ask the attendant for Codex 2662. This was his man. Zeki punched the speed dial for Gilbert's number and terminated the call after the first ring. Then, he stood up and called out to the man before the attendant could return with the manuscript he had requested.

"Good morning, Father Franchini."

The man turned around with a dumbstruck look on his face, but he quickly erased the surprise from his face.

"Good morning."

Zeki beckoned with his hand and pointed to the empty chair across from him. The man approached the table slowly and suspiciously.

"Do I know you?"

"You probably don't remember me, but I was in a class you taught at the seminary," continued Zeki. "I almost didn't recognize you. It's been fifteen years. Please sit down."

He extended his hand across the table. The man took it and stammered...

"Uh, forgive me, I'm not that good with names, or faces for that matter. What class were you in?"

"It was a course on the History of Islam."

"I remember the class, but I'm afraid there were too many students for me to remember them all," he lied.

"I understand. It's impossible to remember everyone. Your classes were so popular. Our class must have had over one hundred students. Anyway, I just wanted to thank you. Your description of Molla Kabız as the Luther that Islam never had, and the light you shed on Sheikh Bedreddin literally changed my life. Were it not for that class, I'm sure I would have ever been another mindless Muslim zombie. You released me from the chains of civil religion. You awakened my mind to how it preys on man's search for the eternal, turning it into a mechanism of social control and political gain. You saved my soul, sir. I will be forever indebted to you."

He could tell the man was struggling to maintain his composure. Zeki wondered if the man had ever heard of Molla Kabız and how long he would try to keep up the pretense of being Father Franchini.

"Well, I'm glad to know that my teaching did not fall entirely on deaf ears."

"What brings you to Augustinerlesesaal?" asked Zeki.

The man pointed back to the check-out counter behind him.

"I'm here to check out a rare manuscript for some research I'm doing with the Vatican."

"Which one?"

"The Gospel of Barnabas."

"Surely there is a copy at the Vatican you could have worked with," replied Zeki.

"Actually, the earliest extant copy is the one here in the National Library of Austria," the man replied.

"You mean the *only* extant manuscript," Zeki said casually. "I mean, we can hardly count the Spanish version found in Australia since it only contains half of the text."

Zeki could see panic slowly starting to rise in the man's eyes.

"Original research?" continued Zeki.

"Yes, you could say that."

"Something has always puzzled me about the Gospel of Barnabas," said Zeki.

"What is that?"

"The authorship," replied Zeki. "Who do you think wrote it?"

The man cleared his throat.

"Well, I don't think we can say with certainty," he replied.

"Really?" asked Zeki leaning back in his chair and feigning utter astonishment. "I find that mind-boggling, coming from a man of your training and background."

"And why is that?"

"Because you know it isn't true."

The man looked offended.

"Excuse me, Mr... What did you say your name was?

"Zeki," he replied. "In fact, I'm surprised you don't remember me. I must have been one of the few Turkish students studying at the Vatican."

The man's eyes became furtive.

"I'm sorry, but I'm afraid I still don't remember you. I don't mean to appear impolite, but I really do need to return to my studies."

Zeki's voice hardened.

"Let's stop the pretending. You are no more a priest than I am a student of theology."

He took off his tinted glasses and continued.

"Look at me again and imagine me with hair. My name is Öztürk. Zeki Öztürk. Do you know me now?"

An I'll-be-damned look that signaled recognition spread across his face. He had found another piece to the puzzle.

"I thought you might have seen a picture of me in your briefings over the last week."

Zeki pulled out his cell phone and extended it towards the man.

"The original you came to steal was apparently taken by your beloved leader Fatih Gülben. This is a picture of him taken yesterday standing in this very room."

The man's eyes narrowed as he studied the photo and he looked around the room to see if it really had been taken there. He immediately recognized the shelf and window directly in front of him. Zeki continued.

"You probably didn't know he was in town. I'm sure they kept it very quiet. What I don't understand though is why they sent you to steal the G.O.B. today. You see, he was the last person to check it out, just yesterday in fact. Now, I can walk over there with you and we can 'discover' this fraud together, and your beloved leader will get the public blame for the theft. Or, I can tell them that you are only posing as Father Franchini and give them the real man's telephone number to confirm it while you wait here for the police, and your beloved leader *still* gets blamed for the theft while you go to jail for using false ID."

"How do I know anything you say is true? And, how do I know that you have framed us for this?"

Zeki pointed back to the desk where a line had begun to form.

"Put your cell phone on the table, get in line, and go ask to see the sign-in registry. Look at yesterday's entries. It's all there."

The man sat for a moment, processing this sudden turn of events. Zeki put his elbow on the table and placed his chin on the heel of his hand, staring intently into the man's eyes.

"Don't even think of leaving the building. If you walk out before my friends receive the 'all-clear' signal from me, you're a dead man."

The man hesitated.

"I'm not asking you," Zeki said softly. "I'm telling you. Now, go."

The man placed his phone on the table, got up and walked over to the check-out desk. Zeki guessed he was thinking of a credible reason for asking the library attendants to let him see the registry. Five minutes later, he sat back down across from Zeki.

"What do you want?"

"I want to kill you," said Zeki gravely. "But, I'm not going to, at least not yet."

The man slowly moved one hand under the table.

"You're not thinking clearly," said Zeki calmly. "Remember what I said about leaving this building. Now, there is one option I haven't mentioned. You give me the name of the person who organized this little ruse, put him on the phone right now, and I will make sure the world never finds out that Fatih Gülben, the self-proclaimed preacher of tolerance and interfaith dialogue, stole the Gospel of Barnabas from the National Library of Austria."

"I don't know who the architect is. I'm only following instructions."

"Okay, have it your way." Zeki began to stand up.

"No, wait," the man whispered.

"Are you out of London?" asked Zeki.

"Yes." Zeki could hear the resignation in his voice.

"Who runs the office there?"

The man leaned forward and whispered through his teeth.

"You know I can't tell you that. They'd kill me. You might as well tell your men outside to knock me off when I leave the building."

Zeki sighed and shook his head.

"You know, I'm not sure you have the ingenuity and intellect required for this job. It is hardly your fault that I'm here today. Your operations were compromised much higher up. I'm sure you'll figure out how to put the right spin on everything."

Zeki paused to let the man think it over. They always needed a minute to think it over, no matter how obvious the choices were. Again, it was Zeki who broke the silence.

"I can see the headlines tomorrow. 'Leading Islamic Scholar Steals Controversial Gospel.' And to think that you could have prevented that bad press. I wonder what your boss will say when he learns you didn't."

"What do you want to know?"

The game had begun. Now, he could use the information from the keylogger.

"Does Salih run the London office?"

"Yes."

"But, he's not the architect?"

"No."

"His last name?"

"I don't know. Everything is first name basis only. And that might not even be his real name."

"How is DC connected to Waqf International Trading Ltd.?"

"I don't know."

"Who gives London its orders?" asked Zeki.

"I don't know."

"Bullshit!" said Zeki. "I want to know who is at the top."

The man just shook his head and looked straight into Zeki's eyes.

"I don't know."

"Is it Ahmet? In Cairo?"

The man's pupils immediately dilated. The telltale sign of fear and adrenaline.

"I don't know any Ahmet."

Zeki sat there processing the man's body language. By looking into Zeki's eyes, he was trying to communicate honesty to cover for the lie. The clenched jaw told Zeki the man was digging in. Working with amateurs was so tiresome.

"You're stone-walling me. I'm sitting here with all the cards and you're stone-walling me. You're gambling with your life here. Start talking or I'm walking."

"I'm telling you the truth. The different teams are isolated for protection."

Zeki slid the man's phone over to him.

"Then you need to start making some phone calls. If I don't speak with the man who had Gilbert O'Brien's family kidnapped, I walk away and you deal with the fallout."

63

ISTANBUL   The phone on the table rang. Gilbert looked at the screen. It was Zeki. He waited for the second ring. It never came.

"That's our signal," was all he said.

He punched in Kiyomi's number. It was 3:30 in the morning there. It rang six times and then went to voice mail.

"Hi Kiyomi, this is Gilbert. Tell them to call me at 90 535 222 5482."

"So, what do we do now?" asked Gwyn

"We wait. It won't be long and when they call, we'll need to be moving, so gather your things."

The phone rang again. He looked at the number. It was Kiyomi. He was sure the call would be monitored. It was time for him to return some favors.

"Hello, Kiyomi…I'm fine, thanks. I just need you to give them this number, so they can contact me…No, I can't tell you what this is about…Do you know where I am…Good. Do you know what I'm doing?…Good. Do you know who is trying to get in touch with me?…Good. Kiyomi, I'm sorry you had to be involved at all, but for your own safety, I had to keep you completely out of the loop. If you know nothing, then you will be safe…The FBI?…So, they've involved the office, have they? Well, for your own piece of mind, I did nothing wrong…No, I won't be calling you again. In fact, I need to go. So long, Kiyomi. You were the best…"

He hung up the phone and looked around the room.

"All of us need to go. They will be calling me any minute, or maybe they'll try to triangulate my location. You guys go back to the hotel. I'll stay mobile and in crowded areas until they call. Don't use this phone. Use the other one if you have to reach me."

⊢═╾═╼═⊣

CAIRO   Jabbar watched Ahmet walk into the office. He was late again and the look on his face made everyone who saw him avert their eyes. He was clearly in a foul mood, but Jabbar's news couldn't wait. He walked up to his boss and said,

402

"*As-salamu alaykum.* I trust you slept well."

He obviously hadn't as he didn't even return the customary greeting.

"Is it important?" asked Ahmet flatly.

"It's our contact in the Sudanese Ministry of Internal Affairs, sir. He has called twice this morning asking when the transfer will take place."

"Has he signed and returned the memorandum of understanding?"

"He says it should arrive today by private courier."

"What about the guarantees we demanded?"

"The bonds will be delivered with the memorandum."

"When we receive and confirm the authenticity of the signatures and the bonds, then we will transfer the money and not a minute sooner. Have the call to Gilbert's secretary ready to go in thirty minutes."

Ahmet continued towards his office and Jabbar heard him swear under his breath. "The brazen, blackmailing bastards! Fifty million dollars for *us* to improve *their* image with the world. They should be paying us a reputation consultancy fee."

Ahmet sat down at his desk, turned on his computer and took a sip from the glass of piping hot tea that was always sitting on his desk when he arrived. The computer's login screen came up. He pulled the first knuckle of his ring finger across the fingerprint scanner, grabbed the TV remote and turned on Al-Jazeera. The lead story was still the bombings in Turkey the day before. He watched for a couple of minutes and then flicked it off, satisfied with what he saw. The spin on the story was exactly what his team had crafted the previous day.

He turned to his email. There were only two messages in his inbox. One was from Gülben's assistant. He opened it and skimmed the short paragraph, which was merely a request for a status report on their contacts in Sudan and Yemen. He typed out a short summary and hit send. The other was from the bank. He clicked on the email and reached for his tea. But his arm froze with the glass halfway to his mouth as he read the content of the email. It was an electronic notice of transfer on an account belonging to Waqf International Trading Ltd., one of their many holding companies. This particular company had neither employees nor non-cash assets. None of this was strange. He received a notice every time he made a transfer. The problem was he hadn't made a transfer and certainly not one for sixty-two million dollars. But that is what had just happened. Sixty-two million dollars had been sent to an account in Bermuda just over an hour ago.

A surge of emotions—fear, incredulity, anger and suspicion—flooded his mind, accompanied by a cascade of chemicals that made his heart race even though he was sitting down. He could feel his hand beginning to shake. He set the tea glass down on his desk and took a deep breath. The note said it all.

In his mind, it all fell rapidly into place. The elaborate trap set for their man in London. The bogus file that they had retrieved from Gilbert's computer. Gilbert's disappearance in London and his failure to get in touch with them. They were being played. Gilbert had hacked their communications. He sprang from his chair, raced out of his office to the T3 internet connection and jerked it out of the wall. He turned to see everyone in the open office staring at him.

"Jabbar, shut down the LAN," he barked. "Keep Hamdi, Remzi and Abu here; send everyone else to our back-up location on Al Dokka. No one is to use anything but satellite phones until told otherwise. I want our two best IT men running diagnostics on the entire system. We've been hacked with some sort of spyware, probably a key-logger. Find out if it is replicating itself across the network and how compromised we are. I want a status report in half an hour."

He walked back to his office, picked up the phone and called the bank president seven floors down.

"Nazim, we have an emergency here. This morning, a transfer for sixty-two million dollars and change was made from one of our holding companies, Waqf International Trading Ltd., to a Bermudan account. I need you to file a fraudulent wire report, cancel that transfer and retrieve the funds."

"For the love of Allah, what are you talking about?" asked the president.

"I don't have time to explain. Just file the fraudulent wire report, call the bank in Bermuda and get back to me in five minutes."

He hung up the phone. Five minutes was asking for the impossible, but that is what he expected of people and the president knew that. Next, he picked up the secure satellite phone to call Salih, but set it back down when he looked through his office window and saw Jabbar running towards him. He burst through the door.

"Sir, ten minutes ago, Gilbert left a message on Kiyomi's phone. She called him back. I just sent the audio recording to your phone."

Ahmet took out his phone, found the file, opened it and listened intently. When it was over, he simply said.

"He's in Istanbul, isn't he?"

Jabbar merely nodded.

"Damn it! We've been tearing the UK apart trying to find the son of a donkey, and he's been right under our noses. Zeki is either with them or orchestrating it from the States. The man is bound to have a network of friends from his days with the agency. I know the brothers are smart, but there is no way they could have managed the fake identification papers so quickly on their own."

He reached for his satellite phone and punched in Salih's number. While he was waiting for it to ring, he turned to Jabbar and began rattling off orders. Jabbar listened with most of his brain, but in a remote corner of his cerebrum, he contemplated with astonishment the man's intellect. This was why Ahmet ran the office and not someone else.

"Get Istanbul on this. I want the man's approximate location in the next five minutes. This bastard just transferred sixty-two million dollars out of one of our accounts. Set up a secure line. We'll need to talk to O'Brien. Call Vienna and cancel the op. We have to assume it's compromised. Put a rush on the deal with Sudan. Someone might try to sabotage that. Also, you need to personally verify that protocol was rigorously followed in all communications with our hostage team. Otherwise, their location may be compromised."

"Yes, sir!"

Jabbar turned to go.

Ahmet called out behind him, "For now, you and I are the only ones who need to know about the stolen money."

"Yes, of course."

Ahmet spun around in his chair to face the wall. It helped him concentrate. London picked up.

"Salih, our office is down for the next twelve to twenty-four hours. I'm going to have to ask you to assume the lead on this operation until we are up again."

There was no traditional greeting of peace, and Salih could feel the tension in Ahmet's voice.

"What do you mean 'down'? What happened?"

Ahmet could feel searing, red hot anger rising in his belly.

"Remember the file that you retrieved from Gilbert's hotel room?"

"Of course."

"Did you run any diagnostics on it before you sent it to us?"

Salih didn't like the tone Ahmet was using.

"The IT intercept team handled that. I would have to ask them."

"You shouldn't have to ask them. It should be protocol, or does the team you lead know what protocol is?"

Salih wanted to remind Ahmet that every office was responsible for its own security due diligence, and so the team in Cairo should have checked the file as well, but he knew it would only make things worse. Ahmet continued.

"The file you sent us installed spyware of some sort and we don't even know how badly compromised we are yet."

"That means we are compromised too," responded Salih, panic beginning to set in.

"Yes, it does, but we can't afford to be down without any ears or eyes, so you'll have to keep operating until our office here is up and running. Make sure there is absolutely no sensitive information sent out and that the IT-intercept team continues monitoring high priority targets. Do not, I repeat, do not allow any other outgoing communication via the computer network. Call me on the satellite phone if there are any developments."

He terminated the call and looked up to find Jabbar. The man was already weaving through the desks, heading back to Ahmet's office. His face was grim.

"First, the good news. The hostage team is not compromised. There were a few text messages sent, but they contained no identifying information except for the name of the city. The Sudanese courier with the bonds and the MOU is waiting downstairs."

"Good. What about O'Brien?"

"We have the Intelligence Bureau Station in Istanbul tracking him, but he's obviously in a car, maybe a taxi, driving erratically around the city. He's too smart for us to catch this way. He'll probably be changing taxis at random intervals or even walking through crowded shopping areas. If we don't call soon, he will suspect we are trying to pinpoint his location, and he'll leave the phone under the seat in a taxi sending us on a wild goose chase. The call is set up and ready whenever you are."

"And Vienna?"

"The line was busy. He didn't answer."

64

Istanbul   Ginger and Shelly sat in the darkness fighting back their fear, hoping against hope that the door at the other end of the container would stay shut. To pass the time, Ginger was telling the kids how Horatius had single-handedly held the bridge against the Etruscans. A story of victory against all odds was what she needed to hear. She knew it was as much for her as it was for the kids. Shelly listened until she finished and then put her hand on Ginger's shoulder.

"Come over here," whispered Shelly. "I want to tell you something."

Ginger turned towards the children she could not see in the pitch black and said,

"I'll be right back. Shelly and I need to talk for a minute."

Shelly took Ginger's hand, and they both felt their way along the wall. Ginger could feel Shelly's hand shaking violently. When they had gone almost the length of the container, Shelly whispered in a halting voice, "Listen, I'm not going to let them do this to you in front of your children. When they come, I'll tell them to take me outside. That is the best thing to do."

"Are you out of your mind?" said Ginger in a hoarse whisper. "How can you even suggest such a thing? Besides, they probably won't even come back after what we've done to ourselves."

"But, if they do?" insisted Shelly.

"That was an empty threat. Just intimidation," Ginger replied, wondering if she even believed her own words. "We are going to stick together, and they are not going to touch us. God will protect us."

"And if they come back and He doesn't protect us?" asked Shelly.

"If they come back, we stick together. I'm not going to listen to you talk like this."

Ginger started to pull away, but Shelly grabbed her arm.

"Listen, I've lived in a dream world for much of my life, Ginger. You've helped me see that. You've been strong for us these last few days. You've shown

407

me the meaning of faith. You've kept our spirits and our chins up, but you're not facing the facts. If it weren't dark, I'd tell you to look at your little girl. You wouldn't be talking like this if you were looking at her face. Do you want them to touch her? Would you have your sons watch them violate you?"

"Will you just shut up!" said Ginger angrily.

"Yes, I will," replied Shelly softly. "Because there's nothing left to say. You know I'm right and the only reason I'm telling you now is so that when they come you won't interfere."

Ginger shuddered at the thought. Shelly was right. She was refusing to face this very real possibility.

"But, what if they come back and humiliate me and my daughter anyway? What difference will it have made?"

"We will have tried," replied Shelly.

"It's not going to come to that," Ginger said again, unable to even consider what Shelly was proposing.

"Remember the stories about the coliseum you told the kids a couple of days ago? Well, sometimes the lions are allowed to roar even if only for a short time. It's not how we die but how we live that matters, and this is my decision. Besides, if our positions were reversed, I know you would do exactly the same thing. In fact, that is how I realized what I must do, by asking myself what you would do."

She grabbed Ginger's hand and started to lead her back towards the children. This time she wasn't shaking at all.

They had just sat down when she heard the familiar crunch of boots on gravel. Seconds later, the creaking of the container door as it swung open and drove the darkness out with an evil light confirmed their worst fear. The man stepped inside carrying a bucket of water and two towels.

✦

When the phone rang, Gilbert was crossing the Golden Horn toward Topkapı Palace. He looked at the number. Caller ID was blocked. He took a deep breath. *This is it.*

"Hello."

"Is this Gilbert O'Brien?"

"Yes, it is. With whom am I speaking?"

"Let's just say that I am a collector of rare documents," said the man on the other end.

Gilbert had been thinking about how this conversation would go for days.

"Listen, I just want my family back safe and sound."

"And, I wanted a particular document, but now I'll need sixty-two million dollars to go with it. Your theft has only complicated things."

"I'm afraid I can't return a life insurance policy unless, of course, you can bring my father back from the dead."

408

There was silence on the other end of the phone. Gilbert hoped this was a good sign.

"Mr. O'Brien, I have your family. You have a document and money that belongs to my organization. There is no reason for us to make things more difficult than they need to be. I think this ordeal has been hard enough already. We are going to have to trust each other if we are to resolve this satisfactorily."

The man's voice was smooth, deep and disarming. For a moment, Gilbert imagined that the man was actually sorry for what had happened.

"Killing my father, attempting to kill my sister and then kidnapping my wife and children didn't exactly inspire a lot of confidence in your good faith."

There was another silence.

"For what it is worth, your father's death was an accident."

"Which still leaves him dead, now doesn't it? So, it's not worth shit. If you want your sixty million dollars back, my wife and children must be delivered safe and unharmed. In fact, I want to speak with them."

"You're not in a position to bargain, Mr. O'Brien. I think your family is worth more to you than the money is to me. If I were willing to walk away from this and say, 'You keep the money and I'll keep your little girl,' that would not make you happy, now would it?"

Gilbert fought to keep his anger in check. He was going to have to show some of his cards and hope the bluff would work.

"Listen, you'll never find the key-logger, which means reformatting or maybe even replacing every hard disk in your operation. That'll cost you thousands of man-hours. Plus, you'll never know which of your operations have been jeopardized by the information I've gathered. What's worse, before you're even finished erasing the sensitive stuff, I can have the Cairo police swarming all over you. How would your boss feel about that?

The voice on the other end chuckled.

"Mr. O'Brien, we are the police in Cairo. Surely, you are not that naïve."

Gilbert didn't know what to say.

"I'm only trying to clean up a mess made by our people in London. Your father's death really was an accident. Our people should have talked with you about it. I would have done that if I had been in charge then."

"All we have to talk about now is when you are going to return my family."

"In exchange for the document and the money."

"No, the money is the price you pay for my father's death."

"Mr. O'Brien, I'm sure your father already had life insurance. You can collect that."

"We'll have to assume he didn't."

"I could return your family, and then have all of you killed within forty-eight hours."

409

"Of course you could," Gilbert said sarcastically. "But, you still haven't found me, even with the FBI's help. Not very convincing."

The man ignored him. "Do you have the document?"

"Maybe."

"Let's not play games, Mr. O'Brien. I want the money and the document, in return for which I will give you your family. Do you have it?"

"Yes, but if I return it, how do I know my family will be safe?"

"You don't." The man's voice was absolutely frosty.

"No deal," said Gilbert abruptly. "My agent will be in touch shortly."

He terminated the call, extended a twenty lira note to the driver and asked to be let out. As soon as the taxi was out of sight, he hailed another cab going in the opposite direction. He hoped Zeki was ready.

⊹⊱⊰⊹

VIENNA "Put it on speaker," Zeki said softly.

On the third ring, a man with a British accent answered.

"Hello, Ismail. Is it done?"

"Salih, we've got a problem," the man replied looking nervously at Zeki. "I need to speak with the Cairo office."

"Cairo? What in the world for?"

"The operation's been compromised."

"You know I can't do that."

"You're going to have to make an exception."

"There are no exceptions, Ismail."

Zeki picked up the phone.

"There are always exceptions, Salih. Exceptions are what prove the rule. It's nice to finally meet you. I was getting bored with the cryptic first name references in the logs."

"Who is this?"

"The man you've been looking for but cannot find."

He paused for just a second to let that sink in.

"O'Brien?"

"No, his friend."

"Zeki?"

"Bingo. It's an interesting game by the way. Do you know it?"

"Never played."

"Really? I can believe that coming from you. You see, in Bingo, it's about getting all your ducks in a row. Apparently, you're not very good at that."

"*Geberteceğim seni.*"

"I don't think so. Anyway, I'm here to turn in my winning Bingo card. If you don't release O'Brien's family tonight, the whole world is going to know that Fatih Gülben stole the Gospel of Barnabas from the Augustinerlesesaal

410

and tried to frame the Vatican for it. I wonder what that will do for his reputation and your UN initiative."

"You could never pull it off."

"I already have. Why don't you confirm it with Father Franchini?" said Zeki, giving the phone to Ismail.

"It's true, Salih. I've seen the proof."

Zeki took the phone back.

"Now, I want Ahmet, the one in Cairo, to call me back within the next five minutes."

"I may not be able to…"

Zeki closed the phone and set it back down on the table. Ismail looked at him with disgust and virtually spat his question through clenched teeth.

"How could you do this?"

"Do what?"

"Betray your own people."

"Was Molla Kabız a traitor?"

"Who was Molla Kabız?"

"The only thing worse than trying to have a conversation with a fool is trying to have one with an ignorant fool. If there is a traitor here, it is you. *You* have betrayed everything decent. *You* have chosen to deal in lies and deceit."

"Deception is permitted in the way of jihad."

"Does that ring true to you? In your heart?"

"That is the teaching of Islam."

"That's not what I asked you." said Zeki, quietly but firmly. "But you have obviously never tested your religion to see if it violates your conscience."

"We are slaves of Allah. We do not question His wisdom."

"Right, of course. But, did it never occur to you to question the wisdom of man?"

The phone on the table vibrated. This would be Cairo.

"*As-salamu alaykum.*"

"*Wa Alaykum As-salam.* Mr. Öztürk, I presume."

"At your service."

"If you were on the right side in all of this, I would certainly avail myself of your services."

"But, I am on the right side."

"The right side is my side. I don't suppose you're calling to tell me you're coming to work for us."

"Not exactly, nor do I intend to discuss with you the philosophy of religion. Salih has told you about your predicament?"

"Yes."

"Then we have a deal?"

"We'll return O'Brien's family safely if he gives us the document and the money, and you agree to return the G.O.B. without implicating the Rightly Guided One."

"I'll make sure the G.O.B. is returned within a week."

"Forty-eight hours."

"Ten days, and I make no guarantees about the money. You'll have to talk to Mr. O'Brien about that. In fact, you'll need to call him within half an hour and let him speak with his family."

Ahmet stopped. He knew he was beaten.

"Fine, ten days then. Are we done here?"

"No, we're not done."

"What else do you want?"

"To give you a message."

Zeki left the sentence hanging.

"So, what's the message?" asked Ahmet impatiently.

"Your days are numbered."

"True for us all, isn't it?"

"Yes, but in your case, I'm the one doing the counting. You will wake up one day soon to see me standing over you, and I won't be carrying a bowstring either."

Zeki hung up the phone and turned to Ismail.

"You can go now, but leave the fake copy of the G.O.B. you prepared on the table. I'll keep your phone too and let my friends outside know you're free to go."

The man stood up indecisively, pulled a book from underneath his jacket, turned abruptly and walked slowly towards the exit. Zeki pulled out his own phone and hit speed dial when the man was out of earshot.

"He's on his way out. Let him go but keep a tail on him. Make sure I don't pick one up as I leave either. I'll sit in the church for fifteen minutes after I leave as we planned. Did you contact the real Father Franchini?"

"Yes," answered Patrick. "He is with the Italian police now and since the swap didn't take place, I'm sure that if their plan was to kill him, they will be calling that off now anyway. Did you get what you wanted?"

"Everything and more. I'll be walking down the stairs in two minutes. I owe you, Patrick. Look after Sally."

Five minutes later, he walked out of Augustinerlesesaal, across the cobblestone square to the entrance of the Augustiner church. Instinctively, he bent down to remove his shoes, and then remembered that in the West, they didn't do this when entering a place of worship. It felt sacrilegious somehow, so he took them off anyway and held them in his hand. As he passed into the sanctuary, his eyes were automatically drawn heavenwards by the vast expanse and the sheer height of the ceiling. Rows of empty pews stretched down towards an ornate altar.

About halfway down the aisle, he chose a pew on the right side, sat down, pulled out the man's cell phone and began scanning the list of recent calls. The phone had no directory. It had probably been purchased within the last week. There were numbers from Italy, Turkey, Egypt, Albania and the UK. He would have time to examine the phone numbers later.

As he sat there considering his next move, an awareness that he was not alone popped suddenly to the surface of his consciousness like a pool ball held underwater. Without moving, he tried to pinpoint the source of this presence. Then, he heard the sound of soft shoes shuffling across the stone floor. Half afraid of what he would see, he swiveled in the smooth, wooden pew and looked behind him to find that it was only a monk on the balcony. Ten seconds later, the church organ took a deep breath and came to life. The beautiful notes of a hymn being rehearsed for Sunday mass filled the sanctuary like incense.

The majesty and dignity of the music was augmented and refined by the setting and its acoustics. It was magical. Zeki looked around the empty room and imagined the pews filled with parishioners lifting their voices in praise to God. He knew it would have been an impressive sight. He could imagine only too well the power, the grandeur, the pride that people would have felt worshipping in a place as beautiful as this. It was enchanting.

These were not conscious thoughts as much as they were projections of his subconscious triggered by his surroundings and then flashed onto his mental viewer. Almost instantaneously, they created a sense of mystical serenity. This was, however, promptly shattered by another thought. *This is the pride of a nation, not the glory of God. Does the One for whom the heavens are a throne and the earth a mere footstool need a building to dwell in?* It was absurd in the extreme.

It was not for God that kings built temples, churches and mosques, but for themselves. They were the ultimate public relations tool, like today's corporate social responsibility projects, but on a grander scale. They galvanized sentiments of national and religious pride, reinforcing a sense of identity that made people willing servants. Their strength lay in the heavy spell cast on the people by their awe-inspiring dimensions and the aura of spirituality created by liturgy, hymns, vestments, ritual and tradition.

Suddenly, he felt a dark shadow cross his mind and a wave of nausea washed over him, tying his stomach in knots. It was overpowering. It was frightening. And, it was not the first time he had felt it. His lips began to move in silent prayer as his mind went back ten years to the beginning of his spiritual life.

The first time it had happened was on the Night of Power during the month of Ramadan. He had gone to the Sultan Ahmet Mosque for the *teravih* prayers. This splendid mosque had evoked in him an even greater sense of majesty and pride than the church he sat in now. That night he had recited his prayers with as much fervor and faith as he had at any time in his life. The experience was nothing short of magical and everything required to induce the spell was present—the rhythmic chanting of the Holy Qur'an, a vast multitude of worshippers bowing in reverence towards Mecca, the beautiful blue interior of the mosque with its exquisitely decorated tile, and an awareness that millions of the faithful had performed their religious duties before him in this magnificent mosque.

He had kneeled there for almost two hours praying and meditating. When it was over, he had simply sat there basking in the afterglow of this sublime experience. That was when the 'prodding' began. He knew of no other way to describe the steady stream of questions, prickly, disturbing questions. Questions that demanded honesty. Questions that made his heart quiver with fear. Questions that sent him spinning headlong into a whirlpool of doubt.

Where the questions came from was an enigma. At the time, he thought maybe a wicked *jinni* had whispered them in his ear. They were not new questions. They were the same issues raised by Sufi mystics for centuries. He had spent the entire night wrestling with them just like Jacob had wrestled with the angel. And, when morning came, he was the one crying uncle. He had no choice. It was submit or die. He submitted.

Yet, for all of the disturbing questions of the night and the spiritual turmoil they caused, his eyes were opened. No sooner had he accepted the truth than he was plunged into a different, more sinister encounter. Up until that time, he had never experienced what could be described as tangible evil, but when he rose from his knees, an overwhelming sense that he was in the presence of a malevolent being washed over him. He had a keen sense of malice, ill-will and hatred directed at him. This feel of spiritual animosity was completely foreign to him. It was then that he realized he had somehow switched sides.

65

İSTANBUL   Gilbert looked down at his watch. It had been twenty-five minutes since the last call. He was standing across from the famous Blue Mosque. He had told the taxi driver to wait. As soon as the call came, he wanted to be mobile. It was a beautiful, sunny day, and the weather had brought the tourists out in droves.

The phone rang. He turned and got back into the taxi.

"Okay," he said. "Let's go."

As the taxi pulled away from the curb, he answered the phone.

"Hello."

"Listen to me carefully. You will do exactly as I say or tomorrow your wife and children will be dead. Return the money by electronic funds transfer to the same account by sunset tonight, and you can pick up your family at 10:00 pm on the beach outside of the village of Kısırkaya in exchange for the document."

Gilbert was ready for the pressure.

"You need to work on your listening skills," he said quietly.

"Excuse me?" said the voice on the other end of the line.

"All this stress has muddled your tiny little brain. My family will be returned at sunset in exchange for the document and our promise to return the G.O.B. The money is not part of the deal."

"Who the..."

"Hell do I think I am?" said Gilbert, cutting him off and finishing the sentence. "I'm obviously not the idiot you thought I was. Or, maybe I am, but your IQ is just so much lower than mine that you let a moron like me make off with sixty-two million dollars. I'll let you decide which of these propositions is correct. However, in view of the possibility that number two is true, I'll make this real simple and use as many single-syllable words as possible so you'll understand."

He had given this a lot of thought. It was a gamble on cultural values and he hoped it was going to pay off.

"We're both men, and men, like us, we like women. I'm young, and as you know, I've just come into a fair bit of money, which makes it easy to get another wife and start over. In fact, I might get a couple of wives and start my own little harem, so stop jacking with me. The money is not part of the bargain."

"Impossible, you give me no guarantee whatsoever!" protested Ahmet.

"None at all," replied Gilbert calmly. "But then you said earlier today that you could have me assassinated within a week, so if I don't return the money, you shouldn't have any problem finding me."

"Your demands are too great."

"If you hadn't killed my father, I would never have known the true value of this piece of paper. Now that I do, you'll have to pay for your mistakes."

There was silence. Ahmet thought about what Kiyomi had said about her affair with Gilbert. Maybe the American really didn't care. It was a risk he couldn't take.

"And if I refuse," Ahmet said finally.

The tone of his voice told Gilbert that his threat was hitting home. He was using the man's own cultural values as a shield, deflecting his demands and refusing to be held hostage to his own values. It was working.

"Then, you go back and tell your boss that he's been framed, I turn over all of the information I have to the CIA, disappear with your money and start a new family while you waste precious resources trying to track me down. Even if you end up killing me, it's a lose-lose proposition, and at best, it's a win-lose proposition with me in the winning column. I'm offering you a win-win solution, but this is my last offer. I'm not going to let you jerk my chain. Give me a 'yes' or I terminate this call and throw the cell-phone in the nearest trash can."

Again there was silence.

"Now, I want to speak to Ginger."

The silence continued.

"Okay," said Gilbert. "Have a nice life…"

"Wait!" said the voice quickly. "Just a minute."

There was more silence, but he heard static on the line for several seconds and then Ginger's shaky voice.

"Gilbert? Are you there?"

Gilbert could feel a lump beginning to form in his throat. This was no time to appear weak though.

"Yes, I'm here. Are you okay?"

"I've been better, but your timing couldn't have been."

"Have they hurt you?"

"Not yet, but I'm afraid they were about to. One of these animals tried…."

Her voice broke and she began sobbing uncontrollably.

"Tried what? Listen, it doesn't matter. This is about to end. You just hang in there and nobody is going to get hurt. Isn't that right?" he asked, clearly addressing the man on the other end of the line.

The line clicked again, and the man's voice returned.

"Now, you are satisfied that your wife is safe?"

"Satisfied she's alive, which is not the same as safe, you bastard. And, if I talk to her and you've touched her or any of the kids, and I mean in any way, the deal is off," replied Gilbert.

"Fine. Tonight, be at the beach east of the village of Kısırkaya on the Black Sea north of Istanbul fifteen minutes before sundown. Bring the document. No document, no deal. Come alone and don't involve the authorities. If you return the Gospel of Barnabas as promised, you will have nothing to fear from us. If you cross me, I will not leave a single member of your family alive. That is my promise."

"Can you give me directions?" asked Gilbert. "I don't know my way around. At least spell the village name for me."

"Mr. O'Brien, someone in your line of work should be able to use something as simple as Google Earth."

"Not if I can't spell it."

"K-i-s-i-r-k-a-y-a."

"We still haven't been properly introduced," continued Gilbert. "You know my name. What is yours?"

His answer was a dead line.

Gilbert opened the phone and removed the battery. Then he turned to the taxi driver.

"Take me back to Taksim."

"But, you want tour of history district, no?"

"Change of plans. I need to go back to Taksim."

He sat in the back seat, turning the conversation over in his mind. *Where is Kısırkaya village? Why did they choose it?* He pulled another phone from his pocket and dialed Gary.

"Hey Gary, the other phone is gone. Use this one now. The transfer is on."

"When?"

"I'll give you the details when I get to the hotel. Look, we're going to need a second car. We need to arrange a rendezvous point where we can switch cars quickly without being seen, a shopping mall with a multi-storey parking garage would work best. I know they are going to track us until the original G.O.B. is returned. We have to assume they mean to kill us when it is, so we have to make sure we ditch any tail and find any tracking device they may have planted. Have Gwyn get a new set of clothes and shoes for everyone since that would be the most likely place to put one, and we won't have time to look for it."

Gilbert terminated the call. The taxi turned right and began driving along the sea towards the first bridge. Out the window was a massive complex of mosques and religious schools dating back to the Ottoman era. Further ahead was the famous Spice Market. A vast crowd, mostly tourists, covered the sidewalks, and colorfully dressed men in traditional garb carried big vats on their backs, offering passersby plastic cups of sour cherry juice. He could still remember the taste from his childhood when the whole family had visited the city on one of his dad's research trips. It was like liquid cherry pie and the whole family had fallen in love with it. In fact, Zeki had even sent them a crate of it for Christmas one year.

As they neared the bridge, he could see a line of street vendors with an appetizing assortment of tomatoes, peppers and parsley lining the front of their carts and a selection of kebabs on a grill in the back. He remembered all of the fond times he had enjoyed here in this city. It had been a magical month in his childhood. Everything had seemed so exotic and everyone was so friendly. *Have they changed or am I just seeing a different side to them? Or is this whole thing just a fluke, a cosmic coincidence with no meaningful correspondence to reality?*

The taxi driver turned left onto the bridge and Gilbert began rolling down the window. The smell of the sea and the sharp cry of gulls were refreshing. There was a walkway on the side of the bridge and a few fishermen wetting hooks. He started looking for a gap in the line of pedestrians so he could make a clean throw. About sixty-five yards from the end of the bridge, he saw his chance and flung the phone he had used to set up the transfer into the choppy blue waters of the Golden Horn.

<hr/>

CAIRO   Jabbar sat looking across the conference table at Ahmet. Ahmet stared blankly at the wall. All of the technical personnel had left the room when the call ended.

"I'm sorry," said Jabbar. "The man was obviously in a moving vehicle. There was no way to pinpoint his location. The only thing we were able to tell was that he was somewhere south of the Golden Horn. Now, the signal is gone completely. He bought the phone two days ago at the Atatürk Airport."

Ahmet made no reply. In fact, there was no indication he had even heard. His face was expressionless. All of his emotions were focused in his eyes, which bored into the opposite wall like laser beams. So intense was his glare that Jabbar would not have been surprised to see a black spot materialize in the paint and begin to smolder and spread. Jabbar knew better than to push Ahmet when he was under so much pressure. He just sat there patiently waiting for the explosion. But, when Ahmet finally spoke, he was dead calm.

"If they have the document in Istanbul, the sister may be there with her

418

brothers as well. Damn it! Zeki has been helping them the whole time! Why, Jabbar? Why is he helping them? I need an answer to that question, and I want this man found. Find out who can help us in Austria. Meanwhile, I want you to build a web of all of Zeki's relationships. Who did he work with at MIT? Who did he do his military service with? Family, friends, colleagues, everyone. He couldn't have pulled this off on his own. This is priority one. Inform all our people—at the Turkish Security Directorate, MIT, the Gendarmerie, the Police Intelligence Bureau Headquarters, Counter-Terrorism, everyone… And, send one of our boys from the Ministry of Internal Affairs to Istanbul. I want him onsite when this goes down."

He closed his eyes. Silence pervaded the room. Jabbar thought he could see Ahmet's lips moving almost imperceptibly.

"Prepare the bowstring," he said at last. "When our operations are back online and Salih's office is taken down for disinfecting, make sure he shares the fate of Mustapha Pasha after the Battle of Vienna. See to it that not a drop of his blood touches the ground. His failure does not make him an infidel. Have the body delivered to his family and make sure his entire family, even that British hussy, is returned to his father's house. If any refuse to go, then they shall share the fate of Mustapha's concubine."

Jabbar's face registered his shock.

"But, I…What about Fatih's rule?" asked Jabbar, careful to remain calm and dispassionate so as not to inflame the situation. "He won't even let us take out Bekir, much less someone in our own organization."

"The society has rules Fatih is not aware of. He is the tail, Jabbar, not the dog. He provides a face and a voice, yet he is but a mask, not the reality. You would do well to remember that in the future."

"Sir, I'm not sure I understand your meaning?"

Ahmet's fist slammed down on the table.

"I don't give a damn if you understand! That is not a prerequisite to following orders, is it?"

"No, sir. Of course not, sir."

"Now, are all of the teams ready for the exchange?" asked Ahmet, regaining his composure.

"They have been rehearsing every day, sir."

"And you're confident the device will work?"

"Gilbert has proven extremely competent. If I know him, he has already destroyed the cell phone we called him on. The tracking device cannot be put in their shoes or clothes. A rectal or oral application will not work for more than two days at the most. The best thing is to use a surgical implant."

"But, they will see the incision."

"I've thought of that already. We'll have one of the guards provoke the oldest boy. That should be easy enough. That'll be their excuse for giving him a good beating with plenty of different cuts and bruises. Then, knock him out with halothane, and insert the capsule in one of the wounds."

"Are you confident that it will be sufficient?"

"If you want them dead in a month, we have plenty of time. The device is modeled after one used to track migratory birds except it is far more sensitive and operates for sixty days. It only transmits when there is a GSM network available. As long as he is within range of a GSM network, we will be able to pinpoint his location. Think of it as a silent cell phone."

"Okay, do it then," replied Ahmet.

"Tell the team to release the hostages in exchange for the document. We'll track them electronically until the G.O.B. is returned. Then, I want the entire family taken out at their earliest opportunity. Have the bodies buried in concrete at a construction site somewhere."

"I understand. What about tonight?"

"I want a full team on hand. We'll monitor the whole thing live. I want every asset we have on stand-by. Have the Istanbul office make preparations, but Cairo will have operational control. Make sure they understand that. If anything goes wrong at or before the exchange, have them kill his youngest child, and get out with the rest of his family. We need them alive until this is resolved."

"What about our other operations?" asked Jabbar. "Shouldn't we suspend everything in case they are compromised?"

"A blanket suspension would be too costly. There is nothing that can't wait a couple of hours. Let's give our technical people until noon to see if they can learn anything about the scope of the damage and how badly compromised we are. But, if we haven't found out something by noon, begin suspending sensitive operations."

Ahmet stood to leave and Jabbar rose to his feet as well.

"Yes, sir."

"I have some business to take care of. Call me after you've talked to our people in the Security Directorate in Ankara and Istanbul. I need confirmation that Gilbert hasn't spoken with local authorities."

Half an hour later, Ahmet's black Mercedes pulled up beside a mosque. It stuck out in the poor neighborhood and was drawing more attention than he wanted. He hated waiting, but he was early so it was his fault and this only irritated him more. He was scanning the crowded street on the passenger side looking for Jamil's cousin when a sharp knock on the window behind him caused him to jump. His man was here. He opened the door and slid over to make room for him.

"*As-salamu alaykum.*"

"*Wa Alaykum As-salam.* Tell me what you have."

"Each time she left the apartment, I followed her. She went to her father's house every time. While she was there, no other guests arrived and after a couple of hours, she went back to your apartment."

"She made no stops at all?"

"No sir, straight to her family and straight home."

Ahmet could feel some of the tension melting away. With everything else that was going on, the last thing he needed to deal with was a cheating wife. Two of his wives, the last two, had played the harlot on him. Both times, he had realized what was happening and caught them in the act. Islamic law gave him the right to demand their execution, but that would have been an act of mercy, a concept Ahmet was not familiar with. No, he had wanted them to live. He did not believe that any cruelty would equal the suffering and shame they had subjected him to. He had provided them with everything, and they had shamed him, so he had branded the word *fahişe* right above their pubic bones and cut the tips of their noses off.

"I appreciate your doing this for me," he said as he opened his wallet and began looking for the right bills.

"I'm glad to be of assistance, sir."

Ahmet folded several bills and pressed them into his hand.

"I want you to keep following her for another week. Let me know if there is anything suspicious."

"There was one peculiar thing, sir."

"What?" asked Ahmet sharply. He was surprised at how quickly all of the tension snapped back into place.

"Well, both times she came out wearing different clothes. It looked to me like her hair was wet."

Ahmet forced a smile.

"This has been one of the hottest Augusts on record and her family has no air-conditioning. I'll see you next week."

He opened the door to let the man out and nodded to the driver. The black Mercedes drove away with a hundred pairs of eyes following it, and Ahmet wondering if Nafrit had taken a bath both times. The car phone rang. He looked at the number. It was Jabbar.

"*As-salamu alaykum.*"

"*Wa Alaykum As-salam.* Neither Ankara nor Istanbul has picked up anything that would suggest Gilbert has contacted local authorities. There is no record of him entering the country, but I've had a local police bulletin issued for him in connection with the FBI search warrant."

"Keep it in play. I want our people to be looking for anything suspicious near the point of exchange."

66

LONDON McIntosh reviewed his notes one more time before the meeting. It was too early in the morning to be doing this sort of thing, but that was just the sense of urgency he was trying to create. He needed answers. The problem was they didn't even know what questions to ask. The investigation had hit a wall. There were no more leads to follow and no evidence to help them—no fingerprints, no DNA, no witnesses, no document, no Gilbert, no Gwyn, no Zeki and no motive.

This lack of evidence was pushing him to do something he tried to avoid, which was to build a case on assumptions. And, the only assumption that seemed to offer any hope as a starting point was Gilbert's claim that there was a rat on the police force. It was this lack of evidence that he now hoped to use as bait. Maybe they could coax the rat into the open.

The door opened. Bob walked in.

"Everyone's ready."

"Okay, great. What's the latest word on the interrogation of the fellow that was wounded and taken into custody in Gilbert's hotel room?"

"He is sticking with his story, sir."

"That he works for a private security company, which turns out to be bogus, and was accidentally sent to the wrong room to gather evidence on a divorce settlement case but doesn't know the name of the couple getting divorced?" asked McIntosh incredulously.

"Yes, sir."

"Even after we showed him the video Gilbert sent us?"

"Yes, sir."

"And, the fact that he cannot show us a single salary payment?"

"He says it was cash work."

"Well, good luck convincing a jury of that."

"How about numbers from his smart phone?"

"Sir, there was only one number on that phone. It belonged to a pre-paid card registered to a fictitious person."

"More dead ends."

"Afraid so, sir."

"I want us to tear this guy's life apart. Banking records, travel, purchases, associations. Go back as far as you have to. You're sure no one in the department is aware of the man's status, right?"

"Just me, you and internal affairs, sir."

"Good, let's keep it that way. Have we received those server records from the university's computers?"

"Not yet, sir. They say it'll take a few days."

"How about records for Dr. Brown's gmail address?"

"Google is promising to cooperate, but they are requesting that we file a formal request."

"Fine. Do we have the keyword filters in place?"

"Yes, sir. Phones and internet are all being monitored."

"What about city records, website date stamps, search engine caches, B.O.D. meeting minutes, bank accounts..."

Bob cut him off.

"It's all ready, sir. Don't worry. The organization looks legitimate. The tech guys have been on it for forty-eight hours straight."

"Great. Let's hope my B.S.er is working today. This needs to sound convincing."

He grabbed his notes and headed for the conference room with Bob in tow. It was hard to believe that any of the men in his department were rotten, but Gilbert's hint could not have been clearer. McIntosh opened the door and a hush fell over the room. The Chief Superintendent did not often take a direct interest in a case.

"Good morning, men. As you know, this case has been particularly frustrating. We are receiving a lot of pressure from the Ministry to gain some traction, especially since it involved the death of an important foreign national. However, it looks like we may have gotten a break. Today, we received an anonymous tip that we believe has some validity. A Turkish non-profit organization established here in London for the purpose of helping immigrants has been implicated. We do not have a motive or any connection outside of this anonymous tip, so we need to move carefully. However, if we can establish reasonable suspicion, the sooner we get a warrant issued the better. Drop whatever else you have going today and focus on this case."

Everyone looked around the room. McIntosh pursed his lips.

"Bob will give you the details."

<hr/>

In a small, white office with no windows in a separate wing of the complex, a single operator sat at a super-computer. Jack's only duty for the next week was to run a communications package developed by MI6 that would catch every occurrence of the words "Society for the Assimilation of Turkish Immigrants." The computer had been loaded with backdoor encryption keys from MI5 and SO15, so most encrypted traffic would be monitored as well. He was told nothing about the objective of his assignment, but the mission was plain enough. The order came from Internal Affairs. This was a rat-hunt.

Jack's job was simple. Capture chatter with concurrent sender, receiver, channel and time data, and then hand deliver this information to Bob Gaston every two hours. He was just starting his second twelve-hour shift, and so far, there had not been a single hit.

The only amenity in the bare room was a coffee pot. He walked over to refill his mug. It was going to be a long day, and he couldn't imagine a more boring assignment. He pulled an MP3 player out of his pocket, put in the earphones and walked back to his computer. He looked at the screen. *Holy shit!* He almost spilled his coffee in a rush to get situated at his desk. The filter was sending a constant stream of hits on the key term. Most of them were internet searches, but there were already two cell phone hits as well. Somebody somewhere had done something to bait the hook and now the fish were swarming. Now, all they had to do was wait for one of them to swim away from the school.

❧

VIENNA   Zeki walked out of the church, glad to leave the oppressive spirit of empire behind. On the other side of the square, he could see Patrick standing on the opposite corner, just under the arch leading to St. Michael's Plaza, staring at the Lipizzaner horses. Turning his back towards Patrick, he took a right hand turn and hit the speed dial. On the third ring, Patrick rejected the call. This was the all-clear signal. Patrick would follow at a safe distance.

The buildings on either side kept the narrow street in almost perpetual shadow. As he walked towards the Albertina Palace Museum, he passed a string of curio shops, all selling wooden puppets of Pinocchio. The irony hit him suddenly and out of the blue. Here he was, standing outside of the library that boasted the only extant copy of the entire G.O.B. in the world, and the first thing he sees is a shop dedicated to the lying puppet created by Geppetto. The universal recognition accorded to Pinocchio's story of human weakness was testimony to man's propensity for deceit. The G.O.B. was just another chapter in the sorry tale.

When he reached the end of Augustiner Street, Zeki stepped out into the bright sunlight of Helmut Zilk Plaza and dialed Yusuf. He clung to the right side of the small square, waiting for Yusuf to pick up.

"Hello."

"Yusuf, it's me, Zeki. Gilbert will be exchanging the document for his family tonight on the beach outside of Kısırkaya."

"So, you found what they needed?"

"Let's just say we have found ways to be persuasive."

"That sounds ominous."

"It went even better than I hoped."

"I'm afraid I have some bad news."

"What's that?"

"An Interpol bulletin has been issued for Gilbert O'Brien. He's wanted in connection with charges of corporate espionage."

"I already know that."

"Then you also know that I'm supposed to bring him in."

"And I know that you won't. He's not asking for your help. It would put his family at risk."

"Of course, but what about after the exchange?" asked Yusuf.

"That, my friend, is your call. I only want Gilbert to get his family back safely."

"What do you expect me to do?"

"What you always do. The right thing."

"I can guess that Gilbert is being set up. I can turn a blind eye to that without a problem. Letting the bad guys get away after the exchange, though, is not something I'm willing to do."

"If you move on them, you'll expose yourself. There will definitely be an inquiry. Their friends in the government will want to know where you got the intel."

"An anonymous tip."

"They won't buy it."

"No, but they can't prove it wrong either."

"They don't need proof."

"From what you've told me, they're guilty of kidnapping, extortion, the murder of two professors, the attempted murder of the young lady in Texas, and only God knows what else. I'm not going to let them get away. Besides, exposing this would set the organization back years. I'm not going to pass on this opportunity."

"You know the risks."

"I do, but I have sworn an oath to uphold the law and the Republic, both of which are threatened by these Islamists."

"I'm only asking that Gilbert's attempt to get his family back not be compromised."

"Fair enough."

"I'm going to be hard to reach for a long time," continued Zeki. "I've given Bahardır power of attorney to sell the summer house. It may take a while to sell, but he promised to send twenty thousand tomorrow. I appreciate you doing this for me."

"Don't mention it, my friend. What about the document? What shall I do with it when I recover it?"

"First of all, make sure no one knows about it. Leave a note on the blog and put it somewhere secret if you want to die a natural death."

"Are you kidding? I only joined the police force because I hated the idea of growing old," he joked. "Where are you going now?"

"There are some loose ends that I have to tie off."

"I'll follow you in the Interpol bulletins."

"Only if something goes wrong."

"Goodbye, my friend."

"Until we meet again."

Zeki terminated the call, and typed a short text.

CALL IN ANONYMS TIP TO METRO PLC. INSIST ON TALKING
W/ JOHN MCINTOSH, TELL HIM THIS NUMBER—07714 652222—
IS SUSPECTED OF BEING INVOLVED IN THE O'BRIEN MURDER.

He had reached the far end of the square and veered right onto the narrow side street of Operngasse. The travel agency was less than one hundred meters ahead on the right. That morning, he had called to reserve a ticket for Madrid. With any luck, he would be in London on Friday. Operations like this shouldn't be rushed, but he had to act quickly before his prey got away. *Ian's death cannot go unpunished and the only way to see something done right is to do it yourself...*

His thoughts were interrupted by an explosion. He saw all of the neon signs on the street go out. He didn't know it, but Bekir's boldest operation yet had just been launched. The banner of the Ottoman army recovered at the Battle of Vienna was housed in a museum less than two kilometers away. It would soon be making its way back to Istanbul.

426

67

LONDON   There was a knock at the door. Bob looked up to see Jack walk in carrying a thick folder.

"Do you have something for us, Jack?"

"In fact, I do."

"That was fast."

He placed a gray folder on the desk in front of Bob, who sighed when he saw how thick it was.

"Don't worry. There is no need for you to go through the whole thing. Your man is on page fifty-seven."

"How do you know?" he asked, flipping through the folder, looking for page fifty-seven.

"Can you think of another reason why someone in the IT department would be posting a one-sentence comment with the phrase Society for the Assimilation of Turkish Immigrants on a personal blog and then deleting it five minutes later?"

"Who is it?"

"Adam Parker."

"Parker!? That's impossible," exclaimed Gaston, in sincere disbelief. "We were classmates at university and went through the academy together. I've known him and his family for years. He's as solid as they come."

"Your sentiments are probably shared by many others in the department."

"Damn right they are!"

"Which is probably why he hasn't been caught. Being above suspicion is the best cover."

"I'm going to have to see this to believe it," Bob said doubtfully. "If he's dirty, then a worse judge of men never walked the earth."

Jack walked around behind Bob's desk and began to walk him through it.

"This is Parker's blog post," he said pointing to a line about halfway down the page. "The blog has a number of RSS subscribers, so this list you see below his post is the same information being forwarded to all of the subscribers. Five minutes later, Parker returned to the blog and deleted the post. If we hadn't been performing real-time surveillance, there is no way we would have caught it. So far, this is the only anomalous hit. The rest consists of internet searches, cell phone texts, emails and phone calls from the team you assigned and only with reasonable sources of information, such as the chamber of associations, municipal public records office and the like."

"Do we have any idea who received the RSS feed?"

"I was able to retrieve the list of email addresses, but they are all hotmail, gmail or ymail addresses. I'm sure any identifying information is bogus. However, I know that the feed was picked up less than one minute later, here," he said pointing to another line at the top of the next page.

Bob stared at the page for a minute. The discovery of a dirty cop always pissed him off, but the thought that it could be someone he would have trusted to watch his back shook him profoundly. The motive was usually money, and it invariably involved drugs, prostitution, or white-collar crime. But this? Why would Parker be involved in the deaths of two professors linked to Muslims?

"Good work, Jack. I'll handle it from here."

Jack turned to leave. Bob picked up the phone.

⊹──┉──⊹

Thirty minutes later, McIntosh and Gaston were sitting at a table with a very uneasy Adam Parker in a bare conference room. Gaston had convinced the Chief Superintendent that having Parker arrested in the middle of the department and sent down for interrogation would be bad for company morale.

"Adam, thanks for coming down," said McIntosh.

"What's this all about?" asked Parker, looking nervously at the Chief Superintendent.

"I'm going to shoot straight with you, Adam. You've served the department with distinction. Bob and I have both been very pleased with you, but today you got tangled up in the investigation of a non-existent entity called the Society for the Assimilation of Turkish Immigrants."

The color began to drain from Adam's face.

"Do you mind telling me why in the hell you posted the name of this bogus organization to a personal blog, and why you're so interested in monitoring the communications of the team investigating the murder of Prof. O'Brien?"

Adam pursed his lips and then took a half-hearted stab at a defense.

"Sir, my job is to ensure the security and integrity of communications, so obviously everything they do is passing through my system."

McIntosh didn't even respond. He just sat there waiting for an answer to his question. Parker fidgeted in his chair for a moment and then continued. "I'm afraid I'm not at liberty to discuss the matter with you, sir."

428

"Not at liberty!" exploded McIntosh. "Son, you'd better find the liberty and loosen your tongue. Whether you realize it or not, I'm doing you a favor here, but if you don't start talking I'll have internal affairs give your life a colonoscopy that leaves you with a funny walk for the rest of your life. Your career is finished. The only thing that changes now is how many years you spend deprived of female company."

"Sir, if you can allow me to make a phone call, I'll see if I can secure authorization to disclose the details of the case."

"A phone call? Bullshit!" yelled McIntosh, understanding the implications immediately. "Are you telling me that you are working for one of our own intelligence agencies?"

"I'm not telling you anything, sir. I don't have the authorization to do so."

"I'm your superior officer. I'm ordering you to tell me what the hell is going on. Who is the bastard that outranks me here? Who are you going to call?"

"I can't say, sir."

"Can't or won't?"

"Can't, sir."

McIntosh sat there fuming. Bob came to his rescue.

"Here, Parker," he said, sliding his phone across the table. "Make your call."

"I have to use my own phone, sir," he said apologetically. "Otherwise, no one will answer."

Bob gave McIntosh a nod, twisting his head slightly and blinking both eyes as if to say, let's see where this goes. McIntosh thought about it for a moment.

"Do you have Jack tracing all of this?"

"Yes, sir."

"Okay, you can make your call, but put it on speaker."

Parker pulled his cell phone out of his pocket and hit the speed dial number. A voice on the other end answered on the fourth ring.

"Code in please."

"Hornblower," said Parker.

"And, the grounds for your request?"

"Internal sting," said Parker simply.

"Please hold."

McIntosh looked at Bob in surprise. *The damn spooks have recruited one of our men.* They all sat there in an uncomfortable silence until the voice came back on the line.

"Request denied," the voice said simply. The line went dead.

Gaston took some consolation from the look of astonishment that came over Parker's face. Adam turned to the Chief Superintendent and said, "I'm sorry, sir. There must be a mix-up. I'm sure it'll get sorted out, but for now, I have no option but to remain silent."

Without a moment's hesitation, McIntosh's words poured out in rapid succession.

"Bob, I want you to personally take Parker down to human resources. His police ID is to be confiscated and all of his passcodes and logins must be changed or terminated." Turning to Parker, he said, "You are on unpaid leave and under house arrest effective immediately."

Parker started to protest.

"But, you heard…"

"I know what I heard," interrupted McIntosh abruptly. "But, unless someone at MI6, or whoever the hell it is you work for, is willing to vouch for you, you shall be charged with unlawful disclosure of confidential information."

There was a knock at the door, and Bob stood to get it while McIntosh continued.

"It's one thing to have you spying on your own colleagues, but it's quite another thing for you to refuse to talk to us when you get busted. Adam, I hope you're clean, but I can't take any chances."

Bob cleared his throat, and McIntosh turned towards the door.

"Sir, someone has called with information on a murder."

"Damn it, Bob. We're busy here. Have homicide handle it."

"Apparently, the caller is refusing to talk to anyone but you. It's about the O'Brien case. He said he'd call back in five minutes."

"Fine, we're done here anyway."

68

İSTANBUL   Four men playing a game of cards in the village teahouse watched a white TurkTelekom van circle the square and then park at the front gate of a five-storey apartment building directly across from them. Everyone else would have been watching too, but the haze of cigarette smoke and the dirty windows made it impossible for anyone not sitting at the front window to see anything outside. A man wearing a technician's uniform stepped out of the van, carrying a large toolbox, and pushed the button on the heavy iron gate.

A few minutes later, the apartment custodian, a thin, dirty man wearing a skullcap, crossed the tiny yard and opened the gate. In a voice calculated to communicate boredom and haste at the same time, the clean-cut technician said, "There's a problem with the ADSL connection in apartment fifteen on the fourth floor."

"That's the first I've heard about it," responded the custodian cautiously. "No one's home until six-thirty tonight, maybe later."

"Then we won't be bothering anyone," the technician replied flatly as he pushed past the man and headed for the apartment entrance. "Come on," he ordered over his shoulder. "I'll need you to open the door."

——

Yusuf looked at Murat across the table in the cramped temporary office they had been assigned at the Istanbul Police Intelligence Bureau. His friend wasn't smiling. When he spoke, it was in a whisper strangled by gritted teeth.

"You're telling me that after the exchange we let the American walk even though he's wanted by Interpol? Why in the world aren't we bringing him in?"

"Because he hasn't done anything. He's being framed."

"Framed? And, just how do you know this?"

"I have a reliable source."

"Well, I want to know who the source is."

Murat was raising his voice. Yusuf motioned with his hand for him to keep it down as he asked himself the question he had been contemplating all day. *How much danger will Murat be in if I tell him everything?* The question answered itself in his mind immediately. He looked down at the table, then over at the wall and drummed his fingers nervously.

"An old friend. That's all I can say."

Murat shook his head slowly.

"Forget it. I'm not going near this. I'm not sticking my neck out for a damned American."

"Look, all I'm asking you to do is turn a blind eye. I told you the organization we are targeting was behind the murder of two professors in London—one American, the other Turkish. I'm acting on the Interpol notice issued for them kidnapping this man's family. The only reason the American came to Istanbul was to get his family back."

"So, what were they kidnapped for? Is he being wanted because he broke the law to gain their freedom?"

"I think it's better if we not go into that."

Murat closed his eyes and turned his face away. Images of operations he and Yusuf had been involved with flashed before his mind. He had been to hell and back several times with Yusuf. They didn't make men like Yusuf anymore, which made it that much harder to say what he had to say.

"Captain, you know that I would follow you into a hail of automatic machine gun fire. But, I'm not going to risk my career doing something that violates my oath to uphold the law, especially when you give me no facts. You're asking for blind trust."

"That doesn't sound very different from following me into withering cross-fire."

Yusuf smiled in an attempt to allay his friend's concern. Murat wanted to return the smile to lighten the atmosphere but couldn't.

"Sir, that would be loyalty and affection, not trust. I wouldn't trust you to save me from the bullets, I'd just be willing to take mine fighting beside you."

"So, you don't trust me?" asked Yusuf quietly.

"I think I'm the one who should be asking that question," said Murat fiercely. "You've never kept anything from me before. Why start now?"

"To protect you," Yusuf said simply, unapologetically.

"Protect me? From whom?"

"Listen Murat, if you don't want to do it, I'll lead the operation myself and see if Bülent can run interference here to give us eyes in the field. It's imperative that no one outside of our team know about this operation."

"Damn it, Yusuf! I'm not asking to be sent home. You don't have to tell me all the details but give me something."

Yusuf brought his hands together so that his fingers interlocked. Murat had seen his friend do this many times. It was a sign he was deliberating something particularly weighty. He didn't take long to make up his mind though.

"What if I were to tell you that Fatih Gülben's organization was the group responsible for kidnapping the American's family? Would that be enough?"

Murat stared at his boss in disbelief. Then he pushed back from the table, stood up and started pacing the tiny office.

"Enough? Enough to scare the shit out of me!"

"So, you're in then?"

"I understand why you didn't want to say anything. Forget losing our jobs, this could get us killed…Yusuf, this isn't some marginalized radical like Bekir Kaya or Hizbullah. This is a man held in the highest esteem by millions of our countrymen. He's viewed as a saint. His sphere of influence reaches all the way to the White House. Bekir has guns. I can face guns. That is what we were trained for. But this man commands an army numbering in the millions. He has schools and training centers scattered across the globe with commercial interests that stretch from Kyrgyzstan to London. He has infiltrated the Police Academy, the Police Intelligence Bureau Headquarters, and," he lowered his voice, "We both know he has people in Counter-Terrorism…"

Murat's voice trailed off.

"If you think it's too risky, I understand," said Yusuf quietly.

"It *is* too risky," said Murat solemnly. "But so was opening that trap door in the brothel when you thought Bekir Kaya was on the other side. It didn't stop you."

"Everyone has to make their own call."

"You know they're going to come after us. They will have their lackeys over at the Ministry of Internal Affairs all over this."

"Most likely."

"Nobody touches this guy and escapes unscathed."

"So far, but that is no reason to shirk my duty."

"Count me in then. If you're willing to go down this rat-hole, I'm going down with you."

"One more thing, these men may be carrying a canister about fifty centimeters long. It's a document. If you find it, deliver it to me and me only."

"Sure thing."

"Alright, go ahead with the briefing then. I'll join you in a few minutes. I promised Bülent I'd give him a call."

"You haven't told me where we're going to rendezvous with the prisoners."

"I'm still working on that. I've got a friend in the Navy who may be able to help. Don't worry. I'll figure something out."

Murat stood up and extended his hand towards Yusuf, who grasped it between his own two hands.

"It's an honor to work with you, sir."

"I am the one who is honored, Murat. Be safe."

Murat left the room, closing the door behind him.

Yusuf's cell phone rang. He didn't recognize the number.

"Hello?"

"Hello. This is Matt Connor. I'm with The Coalition against Trafficking in Women, and I'm calling to speak with Captain Yusuf Demir."

"Speaking."

"Captain, I am trying to find some information about a Romanian girl named Bianca Ionescu. We believe she has been abducted and forced into prostitution here in Turkey..."

"Mr. Connor, I'm in Counter-Terrorism. The department you need is the Organized Crime Bureau. Call the Security Directorate. They can give you the appropriate contact information."

"Does the name Elvir Zubak ring a bell?"

"Mr. Connor, even if it did, you are talking to the wrong person. Who gave you this number?"

"I'm not sure you want to ask me that on the phone."

"On the phone? I don't understand."

"Let's just say we have a mutual friend."

"Mr. Connor, I don't know you or your organization, so..."

"Şanlıurfa 1986."

Yusuf stopped. This was the second time today a friend of Zeki's had contacted him.

"I spoke with the younger brother earlier this afternoon. Go on."

"I found out that you led a raid on the Black Sea almost two weeks ago. Apparently, there a number of women were rescued from traffickers. I'm wondering if your department might have learned anything about Bianca Ionescu?"

"You can obtain a list of the women from the Public Affairs Bureau."

"I just got off the phone with them. She wasn't on the list. Do you think I could have access to witness statements from the debriefing? Somebody might have referred to her. I'm here with her sister. As you can imagine, this is a horrible ordeal for the family."

Yusuf hesitated. Matt filled the gap.

"Captain, I've been tracking Elvir Zubak for a year. I know he works with Bekir Kaya, the terrorist you were hoping to capture. I'm in this for the long haul. We might be able to help each other."

Yusuf made up his mind.

"Mr. Connor, I'm going to give you a name and a number. There are some videos that might be helpful, though I must warn you they are not pleasant. The name is Bülent. The number is 0212 322 2114. I'm busy today. Let's talk next week after you've seen the videos."

"Thank you, Captain."

"You're welcome."

Yusuf terminated the call and dialed another number.

"Bülent? It's Yusuf...Yes, Murat is leading the operation. Are we ready?...I need you to get me in the building and down to the basement without having to swipe my ID...The Coast Guard cutters will only be given coordinates, no details about the op. Can you swing that?...If all goes well, we grab these guys, and nobody outside of our team knows what's happened...If it doesn't, well, I'm ready to face the music...No, I'm not just going to let them waltz away from this. These people can't be stopped if they aren't exposed...Listen, I just got off the phone with somebody named Connor. He's looking for a Romanian girl. I told him he could see the videos...Of course, you're protected. But, if anything should happen to me, I've left detailed instructions in the Akbank safety deposit box...Don't worry about me. I'll be fine."

<hr>

Murat put the last pin in the map, picked up a pointer and turned to the twenty rapid-response tactical officers sitting in the room.

"Everyone will get a copy of this to study on the way over. Make sure you know it by heart. If you have any questions, ask now. We've had to throw this together pretty fast. Last Saturday, two women and three children were kidnapped in Italy and brought to Istanbul. They are scheduled to be released tonight at sunset. Unfortunately, that means we won't have much daylight to work with. Planned that way on purpose, no doubt. We are under strict orders not to interfere with this exchange in anyway. If, for whatever reason, the exchange does not take place or any of the individuals are not returned, our operation will be called off."

The door at the back of the room opened. Yusuf slipped in and took a chair. Murat moved the tip of the pointer to a location a couple of miles west of where the Bosphorus joined the Black Sea north of Istanbul.

"Now, this is the beach where the exchange will be made. It's less than a kilometer long." He moved his pointer away from the sea to the south. "We will be in two separate choppers located here and here. We inserted a spotter half an hour ago in an apartment building in the village. He has a clear view of the beach and will tell us how many men there are, providing us with information about their movements. Once the women and children are safely away, he will give us the go ahead."

He moved the pointer over a large patch of green on the satellite image. "This is a heavily wooded hill overlooking the beach."

One of the team leaders raised his hand.

"Couldn't we insert a couple of snipers on that hill just to keep an eye on everything? It would make us all feel a lot better about this."

Murat nodded in agreement.

"Me too, but it's too risky. My guess is that they have had someone on that hill since the site was chosen. An insertion would risk alerting them to our presence. They may even have firepower of their own up there. If they do, we could come under fire as soon as we clear the crest of the hill. That is why you are all being issued body armor along with night vision equipment. We have to expect a firefight. Our choppers will come over the hill at the same time from opposite directions so that if they do fire at one of us, the other chopper can respond.

"Now, there are only two roads leading into the area; here, through the village on the east, and here, through the forest on the west. As soon as we move in, local police will be alerted and told to set up a road block with a loose perimeter along this line of approximately two kilometers." He drew the pointer across the narrowest part of the woods behind the hill.

Another hand went up.

"It looks like they're cornered. Why would they do that?"

"If they're operating from land," replied Murat, "They'd be cornered. I think they'll be arriving by boat. So, we'll have two Coast Guard cutters just over the horizon. One will be cruising here to the west to prevent them from entering Bulgarian waters. The other will be to the northeast. We don't want to spook them. If they make a dash for international waters later, we'll be able to intercept them. Our quick response on the water is going to be a long-range interceptor coming up the Bosphorus here—seven miles to the east, hopefully arriving just a couple of minutes behind us. The vessel will have to remain in the straits until we get the go-ahead because we have to assume that they will have at least one more vessel at sea looking for a trap. They would be suspicious of any boat loitering in this area," he said, drawing a five-mile semi-circle around the beach.

"This gives them more time than we would like, but it's the only way to ensure the safety of the hostages. If they've returned to the boat before we arrive, we'll pursue in the helicopter, directing the Coast Guard and our rapid response team at sea. We will only engage them if necessary."

Yusuf stood up and began walking to the front of the room.

"Thank you, Murat. Men, our job is to apprehend these kidnappers alive. Do not shoot to kill unless absolutely necessary. We need information, not dead bodies. I can get those at the morgue. Is that understood?"

"Yes, sir." The whole room responded in unison. These were good men. His Counter-Terrorism unit had one of the toughest jobs in the country and plenty of adversaries. The Kurdish PKK had waged a war of attrition for over thirty years. They fought religious fundamentalists and communists, taking on both sides of the ideological spectrum. The pay was not nearly enough for the risks they took.

"One more thing," he added. "We lost Bekir two weeks ago because somebody tipped him off, somebody in one of the agencies that knew about the operation. We all know that the enemy sometimes walks down the same halls we do wearing the same uniform. I'm not going to let that happen again. Only the people putting their lives on the line know about this assignment. No one outside of this room knows anything about this operation. Even the helicopters we will be using are, according to official reports, sitting in a maintenance yard south of the Marmara Sea. The local police will only be informed after the operation commences. Effective immediately, you are all dark. There is to be absolutely no communication with anyone outside of this team. If anyone violates this order, I'll shoot him myself. Is that understood?"

Again the room rang with the hearty response of men who loved and respected him. "Yes, sir!"

69

LONDON   There was a knock at the door. McIntosh didn't look up. He was too absorbed in the email he was writing to the Commissioner.

"Come in."

The door swung open. He heard people filing in and then the door closing. McIntosh raised his head to see Bob, Jack and Adam lined up in front of his desk.

"I thought I told you to escort Parker out of the building, Bob? I don't want to see the man until this investigation comes to a conclusion."

"Sir, I think you need to hear what Jack has to say."

"He could tell me Jesus is coming back tomorrow, and I'd still tell you to get Parker out of this building. I will not tolerate insubordination in my officers, nor will I speak with a man under suspicion of double-crossing his fellow officers. Do I make myself clear?"

"What if I told you we think Parker has given us a lead in the O'Brien case?"

"And what if I told you that I just received a scolding from the Commissioner of Police of the Metropolis for devoting so many resources to this homicide?"

Bob's eyes widened in surprise and then narrowed to slits.

"Then, I'd say it is even more important that you hear what Jack has to say."

"After Parker is out of my office."

Parker made for the door. Bob held out his hand to stop him.

"Sir, I've known Adam since university. We were at the Academy together. If you don't respect my judgment enough to let him stay in the room, I can tender my resignation effective immediately."

McIntosh put his head in his hand. Without looking up, he said, "What do you have, Jack?"

"Sir, I've tracked the emails that went out on the RSS feeds after Parker posted the message. There were five different emails, but they were all read from the same IP address today. That is strange enough, but after Parker made

438

his call, I sent a test message to all five. They all bounced. They've been shut down. The blog that Parker used to send messages is also gone."

"What is at the address where the emails were read?"

"It's a financial services company at 19 Nutford Place named Baraka. It's one block east of Edgware Rd. They specialize in *sukuk*, but they also operate several import-export companies and a real estate management firm."

"What the hell is *sukuk*?"

"Islamic bonds, sirs."

His ears pricked at the mention of another connection with the Middle East. McIntosh reached over and punched the intercom button on his office phone, "Jeff?"

"Yes, sir."

"Any luck tracing that cell phone number called in on the anonymous tip?"

"Sir, that cell phone has not registered on any towers since we received the call. They must have pulled the SIM card."

McIntosh stood up and turned to the city map that covered half of the wall.

"What did the retroactive usage profile show?"

"It was last used this morning at 8:43. Before that, the phone was generally connecting with towers north of Hyde Park, east of Paddington, south of A501 and West of Marylebone."

"Thanks, Jeff."

McIntosh turned back to Bob.

"That's interesting. The cell phone number provided by the tip was used in locations near this same address. What else did you learn?"

"The majority shareholder is a holding company named Waqf International Trading Ltd., incorporated in Beirut. I contacted a friend at MI6 and found out that they have had Baraka under surveillance for almost three months. He wouldn't give me any details, but Baraka has violated a number of corporate privacy laws and is under suspicion for sabotaging several British counter-terrorism operations."

"What's the connection with the O'Brien case?"

"Parker says his last instructions were all related to the O'Brien case. He relayed information on the bust at the hotel to his handler."

"So, how did the O'Brien boy know this?"

"That I can't say."

Adam cleared his throat and dared to speak.

"O'Brien must have had a tap on a communications link somewhere, sir. That's the only way he could have known."

"So, why the hell haven't we shut this Baraka establishment down?"

"Because every week there is a new revelation about how extensively they

439

have infiltrated our security system. MI6 is identifying each victim and rehabilitating them."

"Victim? Rehabilitation?" asked McIntosh, the words obviously coming as somewhat of a surprise.

"Sir, all of the inside assets that have been identified so far were aiding the organization unwittingly. Each believed they had been recruited by bona fide agents of the UK government."

McIntosh turned to Parker.

"What evidence can you offer me that you've been played and are not the one playing us?"

"Sir, with all due respect, there is no evidence except for my own testimony confirmed by MI6. I have been providing information about Muslim extremist groups. I was told that a Muslim group had assets on the inside here at the Metropolitan Police Force, that they were tampering with data and destroying evidence related to counter-terrorist operations. My job was to help find the mole."

"You were on a rat hunt?"

"Yes, sir."

"Only to find you were the one being ratted out?"

"Apparently so, sir."

"Bob, I want whoever is heading up this operation at MI6 over here in half an hour. That will be all."

Bob took a deep breath. McIntosh wasn't going to like what he had to say.

"Sir, Jack already asked his friend at MI6 to come over and brief us on the operation. They refused. I called myself to explain the gravity of the matter. They still refused. That's why I'm here. They say the operation is ongoing and that they cannot risk compromising it."

The smile that spread across McIntosh's face as he turned to Jack surprised him.

"Jack, you found the address, right? On your own and without any assistance?"

"Yes, sir."

"That is actionable enough for me. Spooks have their job, and we have ours. I want a low-profile surveillance team in place immediately. Find out what we are dealing with. Get specs on the building, an arrest warrant and run background checks on company officers and employees. Be ready to move at my command. MI6 doesn't dictate what happens here. I do."

━━━◆━━━

MADRID   Terminal 1 reminded Zeki of a bygone era, of a time when government projects were driven by functionality, and aesthetics were a luxury. It immediately conjured up images of the old Esenboğa airport in Ankara. The parking lot in front of the terminal was not the multi-storey structure found in a modern

440

airport, but rather a simple paved lot lined with cedar trees. The covered parking areas that lined the front of the parking lot were the best indication of the facility's age. They were essentially just rough sheds covered with corrugated tin. What surprised him most, however, was the long line of red and white taxis waiting for customers. He had never seen so many taxis sitting idle. The drivers didn't look like they expected the line to start moving any time soon either as most of them were standing outside their car smoking or talking on a cell phone.

He walked to the head of the line and addressed a fellow who looked to be twenty-something.

"¿Habla usted Ingles?"

"No," the young man replied with a simple shake of his head.

Zeki paused for a second, trying to form the sentence.

"¿Puedes llevarme a la Biblioteca Nacional de Madrid?"

"Si senor."

He looked down at his watch. It was 3:15 local time, giving him only one hour and forty-five minutes before the library closed.

"Podemos hacerlo antes de que la Biblioteca cierra ya que cierra a las 5:00"

"No hay problema."

The cabby put his bag in the trunk while Zeki slid into the back seat of the red and white taxi. Five minutes later, they were out of the airport and zipping down a highway on their way to the city center. The weather had been clear on their approach, giving him an excellent view of the countryside. They had crossed a range of mountains which gave way to a smattering of tidy farms in a pale chalky soil which, for some reason, he always associated with an arid climate. Olive groves and vineyards covered the gently sloping hills. Most of the fields were covered with the brownish-yellow stubble left after the wheat harvest.

This was his first time in Andalusia. He had traveled through most of Europe, but never to Spain. All he could think about during the forty-five minute drive were the stories his grandfather had told about how the cruel, heartless Spanish had forcibly converted the Muslim population to Catholicism after the conquest. How they had instituted the Inquisition to ferret out insincere converts, and after decades of torture and persecution, had finally decided that a multicultural society posed too much of a risk. So, they had uprooted Muslims who had lived there for centuries and sent them into exile.

The imams had drilled it into their heads. The most important duty of a Muslim after the five pillars of Islam was to reclaim any territory that had once been in the House of Islam and was later overrun by the infidel. Israel topped the list; Andalusian Spain was certainly second. In the airport, he had seen television coverage of the attack today in Austria. A large, electrical substation had been blown up, taking out security cameras over five city blocks. Five armed men had stormed Heeresgeschichtliches, the Museum of Military History. The news report gave no further details. Zeki didn't need them. He knew what the target was. It was the unnamed shame of the Turkish people—their defeat at the Battle of Vienna where the banner of Islam from Mecca was captured. *Had they recovered it?* He felt certain they had.

The centuries-old conflict continued and he was in the middle of it, but on which side? That was the problem. The middle didn't have a side. This middle ground he now occupied was contrary to everything he had been taught. Every instinct of culture and upbringing told Zeki he was a fool playing with fire, that he should be taking sides. But, how could one be on either side and still be on God's side when both were so obviously wrong?

The taxi came to a stop. Zeki handed the man a fifty Euro note and took the change. The taxi drove off, leaving him standing in front of the *Biblioteca Nacional de Madrid*. He walked in and looked around for an information desk. He found it to his right, tended by an officious looking lady in a white and blue uniform. He walked towards her and smiled when she looked up.

"*¿Se habla usted Ingles?*"

"Yes, I do," she replied. "How can I help you?"

"I would like to see and obtain a copy of a certain Morisco document, BNM MS 9653."

"Do you have a reservation?"

"I'm afraid not."

"Then I'm sure that it will be tomorrow at the earliest." She pointed over his right shoulder. "If you take the elevator to the second floor and talk to Mr. Santiago, I'm sure he can help you."

"*Muchas gracias, senorita.*"

He felt in his pocket for his cell phone and quickly typed a simple text.

VSS SNPR RFL. TWO CLPS OF SUBSONIC AMMNTN. INTRRGTION KIT. CONFIRM.

━━◆━━

LONDON   At the Chanbeli Indian restaurant, a waiter felt his cell phone buzz to herald the arrival of a new text. His eyes scanned the crowd and the buffet. The tandoori chicken was almost gone. He walked through the double doors into the kitchen.

"Aman, we need more tandoori chicken."

"The next batch is coming out in ten minutes."

"Okay," he replied, slipping out the back door into the alley where he retrieved his phone and read the text. His face registered no emotion. He thought about it for a minute. *Zeki's coming to London. Somebody's bridge is about to come tumbling down.*

442

70

BLACK SEA COAST, NORTH OF ISTANBUL   For over two hours, the man in the apartment had been watching four teenagers brave the waves in flirtatious horseplay. The two guys and two girls had only come out of the water once over the last four hours. The only other people on the short beach were two women who had brought their young children to play in the sand. It had been one of the most boring surveillance duties he had ever been given. That was good. When things got exciting, they got dangerous. Though he could not see them, he knew that a massive bank of thunderheads had formed in the east. The forecast called for severe storms that evening as they moved westward. Yet, from this window facing the setting sun, there was not a hint of the storm that was brewing.

It looked like the sun would sink peacefully in a sea of turquoise in the next fifteen minutes. In truth, it was cornered and retreating before the threat of darkness. At least, this was how the man felt. Something was wrong. There was no reason anyone would have chosen this place for an exchange and yet they had. This night was not going to be peaceful. The disappearance of the sun would even the playing field. He hated an even playing field. He would not be in the fray, but his friends would be.

With the monocular in his right hand, he zoomed in on the dirt road on the other end of the beach. It led to a rock quarry and was the only other way a land vehicle could access the beach. The road had been quiet. Nobody moved in the heat, especially during the fast. Only an occasional truck loaded with rock crawled along the road, raising a cloud of dust behind it.

He scanned the woods on the hill overlooking the beach. He had spent more time looking at that hill than he had the beach. Nothing was going to happen on the beach until sunset. If they already had company, it would be on the hill. He had looked in vain for any hint of movement. If there were a sniper or a lookout, they would need a break in the trees to see the beach. There was a small opening near the top, but nothing stirred. So, he turned his attention

443

back to the sandy strip. The family had packed up and was heading back to their car. The teenagers were out of the water too. From their gesturing and pointing to the east, it was obvious they could see the storm rolling in from the east. *Good, maybe this will encourage them to leave instead of using the cover of darkness and an empty beach as an excuse to consummate their flirting.*

The radio in his left hand moved to his mouth.

"Eagle's Nest, This is Hummingbird. Everything's quiet. No sign of either party."

"Things should pick up any minute now. Let us know as soon as you see anything."

The small red dot had been creeping across the screen of her smart phone for almost two hours. For now, the red dot was synonymous with Gilbert, but once the canister was handed off, she knew she would be watching the terrorists. She kept Gary updated on the progress as he struggled to find the proper dose of aggression and keep the minivan moving through the congested Istanbul traffic. Just when it had seemed that the red dot would plunge headlong into the Black Sea, it came to a stop.

"Well, at least he made it on time," said Gwyn, looking at her watch. "I wish one of us had gone with Gilbert," she said for the fifth time. "When that red dot starts moving again, all we will know is that these lunatics have the document. We won't know if Gilbert and Ginger are safe, if their bodies were left lying on the beach or if they've all been whisked away."

"He had to go alone, Gwyn. You know that. Let's just find the shopping mall. This will go down quickly. We're meeting them in a little over an hour."

Gary had gone over the plan with her a dozen times. It was amazing, ingenious, and precise, which was exactly what bothered her. Normal people couldn't throw this sort of thing together on the fly. He had whipped up the plan in less than half an hour, run into a couple of shops for the supplies and stuffed them into his backpack. That was it. Mission planned if not yet accomplished.

She looked out the window. Pine trees with a peculiar orange bark blocked her view. The monotony of the trees whizzing past had a hypnotic effect, creating a mental wind that whisked flimsy, extraneous thoughts from her mind like a March windstorm rips towels off a prairie clothesline. She wanted to think about something trivial, about planning a shopping trip with a girlfriend, treating herself to a home-cooked Thai meal or lounging in a hot bath with a good book until her skin got wrinkly. But she couldn't.

All she could think about was saying goodbye to Matt at the hotel. It wasn't anything like their parting several years ago. That had been different. It had been hard, but it had been right, too. This time it all seemed so wrong. He had changed. She wasn't sure exactly what the change meant, but after their last conversation, she had convinced herself to take a chance and find out. Now, he was gone again, carried off by a riptide of misfortune, an evil conjuncture. Her whole future was suddenly a black abyss opening up in front of her, and she was being inexorably carried forward by a current she couldn't resist.

No blueberry farm in east Texas, no settling down, no getting to know her mother's family, no quiet, peaceful life... She had put Matt out of her mind for years. She had thought she was over him. It was time to face the truth. She wasn't. She still loved his razor-sharp wit, the way he tackled problems head-on and his strong convictions, even when they were wrong. She loved his strong arms wrapped around her waist, his roaring laughter and sense of purpose. She thought back to their last few minutes together in front of the hotel.

Matt had told Gary he wanted to meet Angela and help her find her sister, so Gary had given him the girl's phone number and a picture of the two sisters. Gwyn couldn't help but feel a twinge of jealousy when she realized that Matt was literally walking off into the sunset to help another girl. She saw the picture when Gary took it out of his wallet. Both of the girls were gorgeous. Then, Matt had turned to her, given her a peck on the cheek and squeezed her hand. He hadn't said a word. *What was there to say?* She knew this had been her cue to respond in a way that would give him hope, but she had just sat there, unable to move, frozen by the black winds swirling around her. Ginger's kidnapping, her father's death, the prospect of a life in hiding... Now, this unexpected reconnection with the man she had thought was gone forever had slipped away. She had not given him any sign that her feelings might have changed.

"So, Zeki didn't say when he'd meet us?" she asked.

"Nope. All he said was that his plan had worked and he'd see us soon."

"And he didn't say where?"

"Nope."

"How are we going to get in touch with him?"

Gary was silent for a moment. He hated the thought of hiding anything from her, but it was too soon. There were still too many unknowns.

"He said to text him."

"Is he going to be here to help us get out of the country?"

Her nerves were getting raw.

"Gwyn, we've already gone over this."

"Yeah, well, I'm not very satisfied. Matt's rented a boat. We're going to cross the Sea of Marmara and navigate the straits of Gallipoli to the Aegean, where we'll just putt about until somebody comes up with a plan?"

"You can't risk any border checkpoints. Ginger and the kids don't have ID."

"So, why isn't that the first thing we do?"

445

"Because it's too risky to be in Turkey one minute longer than we have to. Zeki said the group has many sympathizers with the local police. He's convinced they will have government agencies searching for us."

"And so just how are we going to manage the ID on a boat in the Aegean? Let's just go to the US Embassy. Surely, we'd be safe there."

"I'm not so sure. Matt thinks the Interpol bulletin issued for Gilbert is almost iron-clad proof that this group is manipulating people within our own government."

"That's hard to believe. You said yourself that Gilbert probably crossed a line in that deal."

"Yeah, but somebody has known about that for weeks or months. Don't you find it strange that the Interpol bulletin was only issued after Gilbert disappeared?"

Gwyn's face said it all. She didn't find anything strange anymore. This realization was what prompted him to share with her what he had shared with no one else.

"Gwyn, have you ever felt like you had a premonition?"

"What do you mean?"

"I mean have you ever had the feeling that something really bad was going to happen?"

"Only every day of the past week," she retorted wryly. "Don't tell me you have a bad feeling about how all of this is going to turn out. I don't think I could take that right now."

"No, that's not what I'm talking about. I mean, it may be related but not directly." He stopped for a moment. How could he make her understand what he meant? "I'm talking about an experience, a hearing, a seeing, a knowing that you've been given a glimpse of the future, that the limitations of time and space were lifted, and that you saw truth, naked and dangerous, beautiful and pristine, horrible and full of despair."

Gwyn turned to look at her brother. His face was harder and at the same time more sensitive than it had been when he left home. He was different, but how? She couldn't put her finger on it.

"No, I can't say that I have. Do you want to tell me about it?"

"I want to understand it, to know if it's real, to figure out if I'm going crazy."

"What do you mean?"

"I had a disturbing dream the night Dad died. Of course, at the time, I didn't even know he had passed away. But, after Gilbert called me and before I flew to London, I felt like I had to talk to a friend of mine in Istanbul, an imam, who befriended me and taught me some important things. It was too late to see him, of course, but I walked by the mosque on my way home anyway. Imagine my surprise when I found him sitting at the door waiting for me. It was weird and it just got weirder. Before I could say a word about my dream, he stared into my eyes and said, 'A black noose of evil is tightening around you and your family, but do not be afraid, for you know that darkness can never overcome the light.' At the time, none of us could have known that any of this was going to happen. It was like he had divine insight."

Gwyn stared at her brother in shock. The thought that her own brother, her own flesh and blood, her childhood friend, could have anything in common with the people who had killed her father and kidnapped Ginger and the kids paralyzed her. Gary continued.

"Then, I told him my dream, how I had heard the sounds of cathedral bells, Buddhist gongs, the call to prayer sounded from minarets, a Jewish shofar, the chanting of African witch doctors, Hindu hymns... Before I was finished, he was down on his knees weeping. He said he had had the same dream for months but had no idea what it meant. People don't have the same dreams, Gwyn. That's not possible."

"No, I suppose it isn't," she replied tersely.

"Then, when I was in London, right after we thought that Zeki had killed you, I had an even more intense replay of the same dream, except this time I was wide awake. The whole world was in chaos—protests, war, famine, civil unrest, rioting... It was crazy. But, the worst part was the presence of evil, personal, malicious, intentional evil. I've never experienced anything like it."

He took his eyes off the traffic long enough to look at Gwyn. She was staring straight ahead, tight-lipped and silent.

"Gwyn?"

"I don't know what it means either, Gary, and to be honest, right now, I don't care."

"I understand," he said. "I just thought it would help to share it, and you're about the only one I can do that with, the only one who ever really cared about what I thought. I appreciate everything you did for me after Mom died. I know I probably didn't express that."

"No, you didn't."

Tears started streaming down her face. She turned away in an attempt to hide them.

"What's wrong, Gwyn?"

Without turning to face him, she said, "You've just reminded me of the only premonition I ever had."

"What was that?"

"The feeling I had when you left for India, an unspeakable dread that you were leaving and would never come back the same."

"No one ever stays the same, Gwyn."

"You know that's not what I mean."

"Let's assume I don't."

Gary saw their exit coming up, put on his turn signal and began to move the minivan slowly towards the solid line of cars in the right lane. He knew the only way was to muscle his way in.

"You stopped going to church. You didn't attend the memorial service when Mom died. You never send a card for Christmas. You've changed. It's like you've turned away."

"I have."

"I know."

"You know, but not what it means."

71

BLACK SEA COAST, NORTH OF ISTANBUL   "Eagle's Nest this is Hummingbird. The nectar has arrived. Still no sign of the bees, though."

"They'll start swarming soon enough. I'm sure they have their own lookout somewhere near to let them know the American has arrived. Did he come alone?"

"Affirmative."

"What about the other people on the beach?"

"The family is already gone. The young people look like they are leaving too."

"Good. The last thing we need is civilians caught in a fire fight. Keep us posted."

"Will do."

He watched the lone American walk the length of the short, rocky beach. Then he turned around, came back to the middle of the beach and stopped. He zoomed in on the man to get a better look. A job in the security forces was a study of human nature. He was essentially a psychologist with a gun. His job was to stay one step ahead of the deviant human psyche, whoever the particular host happened to be.

There was not a trace of fear, doubt or intimidation in the American's manner. He had the stiff bearing of a man facing incredible odds and determined to come out on top. Stress was something he handled well but did not hide. His face was covered with a five-day growth of beard, and he looked out of place on the beach, dressed in jeans, a button-up shirt and dress shoes.

He moved his monocular up and down the beach. There was still no sign of anyone coming to meet the American. The two young couples that had been swimming all day were walking back towards their car. They obviously didn't like the look of this stranger either and gave him a wide berth. The American paid them no mind. He just stood with his arms crossed in a stance of defiance and stared stolidly out at the sea. The last rays of a setting sun had turned the beach blood red.

The storm approaching from the east had begun to whip up the waves. He turned his monocular back to the sea and saw a single boat heading towards the beach. It was still several miles out, so he watched it for a couple of minutes to see if it would veer east in an attempt to take cover from the approaching storm in one of the two marinas located at the northern end of the Bosphorus straits. Two minutes later, there had been no change in course. It was headed straight for the beach.

He zoomed in with his monocular. There were three men on the deck, dressed in black wetsuits. Even though it was summer, they wore toboggans that he felt sure could be pulled down over their faces to make ski masks. One was driving; the others held assault rifles that looked like HK 91s. All of them had pistols strapped to their waists. He wondered how many more men were out of sight below deck.

"Eagle's Nest, this is Hummingbird. We have a boat approaching from the northwest at full throttle on a collision course with the beach. It looks like a Regal Commodore, one of those forty-footers. These are definitely the bees we've been waiting for. There are only three men visible, one is carrying an assault rifle, but who knows how many more are below deck."

"Copy Hummingbird. What is their ETA?"

"They're coming in fast, less than five minutes, just in time to make the transaction and get away under the cover of darkness."

"We'll see about that. A cruiser isn't exactly a get-away boat. Any markings?"

"No sir."

He kept his monocular trained on the boat. When it was about five hundred yards out, another man came on deck and began untying two inflatable rubber dinghies. By the time the boat finally came to a stop about fifty meters from the beach, all of the men had pulled the ski caps down to cover their faces. One lowered an anchor while the others lowered the rubber dinghies over the side. Two women and three children were brought up from below deck, followed by two more masked men carrying assault rifles. Two men boarded each dinghy; one took the oars while the other kept his weapon at the ready.

Then, the women were put into one rubber dinghy and the children in another. One of the women seemed particularly distraught at being separated. She tried to break free from her captors and throw herself into the water towards the dinghy that held the children. She was roughly shoved down on the floor of the rubber boat, which pulled away from the cruiser and was tossed on three-foot waves.

He moved back to the American to see how he was reacting to the drama. The man might as well have been a statue. Nothing in his demeanor had changed. His face was completely expressionless, a sign that all emotion had been compartmentalized. The only thing that moved was his hair. He looked like a mannequin with a toupee.

The man turned back to the rubber dinghies and refocused the monocular. It was impossible to tell if it was the oars or the wind at their back that was propelling them towards the shore. They were coming in quickly, and the waves were becoming more and more menacing. Returning to the cruiser was going to be a challenge in these rough waters. This meant Murat's team would have more time after the exchange before the cruiser could depart.

He turned his attention back to the mother ship. Now, there were five more men on deck, all armed. Two of them had their rifles leveled at the beach even though hitting anything from a vessel pitching in these seas would be a function of how much lead one could put in the air and not marksmanship. The extended magazines on the rifles indicated that the gunmen probably shared his assessment.

"Eagle's Nest, this is Hummingbird. They are rowing ashore. We have a total of nine hostiles, all armed and dressed in black wetsuits."

"Confirmed."

<hr />

Gilbert stood sphinx-like, watching the dinghy carrying his children pull ashore to his right while the one with his wife and Shelly beached to his left ,each about fifty meters away. A man from each boat converged on him from either side, weapons drawn. It was unnerving not to be able to see both his children and his wife at the same time, so he focused on the men. They were both tall and muscular.

The wind had grown steadily stronger. Rising away to his left, over Ginger's head, he could see thunderclouds mushrooming up into the sky. For a moment, he imagined the apocalypse approaching from the east. The noise of the waves crashing on the beach was so loud that when the first man reached him, he practically had to shout to make himself heard.

"Mr. O'Brien, I presume."

His English was almost perfect.

"That's right."

"Is that the document?" he asked, looking down at the canister Gilbert held in his left hand.

Gilbert nodded and pointed to the piece of paper he had taped to the top.

"I wrote the combination down for you. It's A clockwise E counterclockwise and H clockwise on the shortest mark."

The man took the canister from Gilbert. Keeping the muzzle of the assault rifle aimed at Gilbert's chest, he handed it to his friend.

"Open it," he ordered.

The man turned the cap as Gilbert had instructed, pulled the plastic page protector that held the document out of the canister and gently unrolled it. All Gilbert could make out was the Muslim star at the top. This was the document that had led to his father's death, the piece of parchment that had torn his family away from him and made him a fugitive. The man pulled out a cell phone, took a picture of the document and sent it as a text.

"We'll have this verified, and then you will be reunited with your family, Mr. O'Brien."

"How long will it take?"

Gilbert's voice was devoid of emotion. He was determined to maintain a steely aloofness and refused to even look at his wife and children.

"Not long," the man replied indifferently.

Gilbert said nothing. He simply returned their cold stare. The man with the document rolled it up, put it back in the canister and closed the lid, which automatically changed the combination. The other man seemed focused on the hill overlooking the beach. It took Gilbert only a second to guess that there was probably a sniper hidden in the trees.

He didn't hear the phone ring. The roar of the wind and waves was too great. He could only tell the man was talking because his lips moved. This was it. Gilbert could feel his whole body tense up. He was about to be reunited with his family. The man closed his phone and nodded to his companion.

"It's genuine."

"Good," the other man replied.

He turned to face the sea and waved both arms three times over his head, obviously a prearranged signal. Then, he turned to Gilbert and said, "Mr. O'Brien, in good faith, we have returned your family. You have ten days to resolve the mix-up in Vienna. My boss doesn't handle disappointment very well."

The man didn't even wait for a response. He slung his weapon over his shoulder, turned and began running towards his boat on the right while the other man peeled off to the left. Gilbert didn't move. He looked at his wife and then back to his kids, who were already running towards him. He wanted to run over and take them in his arms. But, he couldn't run in two directions at once. Emotions he had never experienced before were welling up inside. He fought them down. *No sign of weakness. Not in front of them.*

When Ginger saw the men begin to pull away in their boats, she simply melted on the beach, a heap of sobs. Shelly tried to pull her up, to no avail. Gilbert was on his knees hugging the kids. He quickly picked up the two smallest and began walking towards his wife with Garret in tow. When Ginger looked up, the sight of her husband crossing the sand in long, strong strides restored her sapped strength. She leaped to her feet, running like a gazelle across the beach. He set the kids down gently.

"Oh Gilbert! Thank God you came!"

She threw herself into his arms, buried her face in his neck and kissed him wildly. She could feel the terror melting away.

452

"Are you okay?" asked Gilbert.

Ginger said nothing. She only held him tighter. Gilbert looked at Shelly and repeated the question with his eyes. She only nodded. To speak would have been to burst into a fresh round of tears. The vacant look in her eyes told him the ordeal had taken its toll.

He whispered into Ginger's ear, "Honey, are you alright? Did they hurt you?"

"We're all fine, darling," she said. "But we wouldn't have been if you hadn't found us today. How did you do it?" she asked, pulling away from him and looking up into his eyes only to find hot tears of joy running down his cheeks and dripping on her face.

"It only matters that I did," he said softly.

"Where are we?"

"A beach north of Istanbul.

"Why did they kidnap us? What did you have to do to get us back?"

"Not now, my love. We'll have to save that for another day."

"But…"

He put his finger gently over her lips.

"Later. Why are your clothes all damp?"

"They hosed us down right before we boarded the boat to come here."

"Why?"

"That's something I'd rather explain later too."

He ran his finger gently along the cut on her chin.

"And this?"

"A mother's love for her children, that's all,

He saw her lip begin to quiver.

"Okay, save that story too," he said, bending down to brush his lips against hers. She closed her eyes and pulled his mouth into hers with passion, released as a physical expression of affection and gratitude. Somehow, her man had come through. That was all that mattered. The taste of his mouth suddenly reminded her of what had almost happened that morning, and she pulled abruptly away.

"Are you sure you're okay?" he asked, looking at her uneasily.

She pulled close to his ear and whispered.

"Shelly and I were almost raped this morning. I'm still trying to cope with that."

Gilbert pulled her close and looked over at Shelly, who was tying Garth's shoe. Now, he understood that look in her eyes. It was the shock of waking eyes that had stared a nightmare in the face. He wanted to sit on the beach and let them cry, wipe their teary eyes dry and assure them that everything was going to be alright. But he couldn't. It wasn't over. He didn't know the operational details, but Yusuf had told Gary that Turkish security forces would be all over this place ten to twelve minutes after the exchange. He had to get his family away. Ginger spoke before he could.

"But, we're safe now, aren't we? I hope you have plane tickets for us to go home? I just want to go home."

"We're going to take a cruise back. Let's get back to the car. It's at the end of the beach here," he said, pointing over her shoulder.

He looked out over the water. The waves whipped by the wind had the cruiser bobbing up and down like a cork. Men with guns could still be seen on the deck in the fading light. The rubber dinghies were still straining at the oars. A large raindrop struck him in the eye. He looked at the clouds to the east. The storm would be upon them in minutes.

+>==<=+

A little over nine hundred meters away, the monocular was laid down on the window sill. The sun had already set. It would be dark in fifteen minutes.

"Eagle's Nest, this is Hummingbird. Our targets will be boarding in the next couple of minutes. They are having a tough go of it. The wind has really picked up. The man and his family will be driving away any minute now. This storm should mask your approach by drowning out the noise of the rotors. Make your final preparations. You're a go in seven minutes."

"Hummingbird, stay in place. The Captain wants your eyes right up until the end."

"Understood."

72

In his headphones, Murat could hear the helicopter pilot asking for a weather update as the Sikorsky S-70B-28 Seahawk lifted off the ground. He didn't like flying in storms. It always made him queasy. Today was different though. Queasiness didn't seem to explain the sense of darkness and imminent danger he felt crowding in on his subconscious.

"The eye of the storm will be on top of you in minutes. Meteorological conditions are conducive for vertical wind shear up to thirty knots, golf-ball sized hail, and dangerous lightning. If possible, delay deployment."

Murat shook his head, telling the pilot that was not an option, as he watched the other bird, three hundred meters to his right, line up parallel with them. He addressed Yusuf on the radio.

"Captain, we're airborne. ETA in less than three minutes."

"I've notified the Coast Guard cutters. They are en route. ETA twenty minutes or less. Once they've boarded the ship, and the men have been apprehended, you can wait out the storm at Rumelifeneri. Then, take custody of the prisoners from the Coast Guard vessel. I don't want that vessel docking for the exchange. It's too risky. I've arranged transport to Ankara from the Topel airbase. I'll see you there. Be safe."

"You too, Captain."

Murat leaned forward in his seat as the two helicopters broke the crest of the hill, coming in low and fast. Approaching darkness and the heavy rain had reduced visibility to less than three hundred meters. There was no boat in sight.

"Hummingbird, this is Eagle One. What's our heading?"

"It should be about one o'clock, sir. It's too dark for me to see them now, but the last time I looked they hadn't moved."

The pilot altered course slightly and pushed the bird forward into the wind. Murat motioned further east.

"They'll want to put their nose into the wind."

He continued scanning the waves for any sign of the boat. They couldn't be far. In less than thirty seconds, Murat had spotted the boat at one o'clock, bouncing in seven-foot seas. It was too dark to see if there was anyone on deck until they got close enough to use the spotlight.

"Eagle Two, this is Eagle One. Target spotted dead ahead of you. Stay back and to the east side. Keep your guns trained on them. We'll move in for a closer look."

⊢━━⊣

CAIRO Ahmet's entire team sat frozen in the operations control room, listening to the report from the hostage team leader on the boat in the Black Sea. The computer monitors were all dark because the entire operation was via a sat-phone connection. Everything had been proceeding exactly as planned. This was no time for a complication.

"We had just retrieved our men from shore, weighed anchor and headed for open water when these two helicopters came over the hill."

The calmness in Ahmet's voice surprised everyone.

"Adnan, we've received no word of any operation." He turned to Jabbar. "Get on the phone with the Coast Guard in Istanbul. This might be a search and rescue operation in the area due to the storm."

Jabbar had finished dialing before Ahmet finished his sentence. Ahmet addressed the team leader.

"Stick with the plan."

"Sir, I don't think that's a good idea. The lead chopper has turned on its spotlight and is moving to cut us off."

"Run up the international maritime signal flags, Adnan. Communicate no distress, and see if they back off."

"Yes, sir."

Ahmet weighed the possible outcomes. This was his op. Every contingency had been planned for.

"Babek, do you copy?"

"Loud and clear, sir."

"Do you see any shore back-up?"

"No sir, it's been quiet up here all day."

"Well, they can't board the cruiser with a helicopter if the winds are as bad as you say. Be prepared to deploy the SAM at a moment's notice."

"Yes, sir."

"Listen team, if this turns ugly, the document must not be captured. If there is any danger at all, simply destroy it. Be ready to do this at my command."

He hit the mute button and turned to Jabbar, who had just hung up the phone.

"Sir, there is no search and rescue operation in the area, but two Coast

456

Guard cutters were given instructions to rendezvous near this location thirty minutes ago."

"On whose orders?"

"That's what is strange. Nobody at Coast Guard Command knew about it until I asked them to check with the vessels in the vicinity. The orders were conveyed through normal channels. All of the protocols were followed exactly."

"Perfect."

"Excuse me?"

"They've tipped their hand."

Ahmet hit the mute button again so he could address his men on the boat. The grin that spread across his face threatened to split it in two.

"Adnan, how did they respond to your signals?"

"They haven't backed off. One is still hovering less than fifty yards away, spotlighting the deck. The other is about 150 yards away with a .50 caliber gun trained on us."

"I need you to stall them for a few minutes while we finish our own little sting, but do let us know if they attempt to board."

"Yes, sir."

"Babek, do you copy?"

"Loud and clear."

"When I give the order, take out the chopper furthest from our men. We don't want it crashing down on our vessel. You'll have to move fast after that as the second chopper will take evasive measures."

"With pleasure, sir."

"Adnan, destroy the document. We don't need it."

"Sir, that may be a problem. The American delivered it in a stainless steel canister with a combination lock, but the combination he gave us isn't working."

Ahmet shook his head and smiled. He felt a grudging appreciation for the American.

"Throw it overboard."

He hit the mute button again and turned to his technical op team.

"All of you were assigned one name from the list Jabbar put together. We believe one or more of these men have been working against us. Now, it's time to find out who they are. Call your number. Any person involved in the operation at this moment will most likely refuse to take your call. Pinpoint the location of every person who doesn't take the call. Istanbul is standing by, ready to move. Let's go!"

Ahmet turned to Jabbar.

"The tracking device on the boy is working?"

Jabbar pointed to the screen on his smart phone.

"Yes, sir. The Americans have just entered Sarıyer and are moving south."

"And the physical tail?"

"It should be in place within five minutes."

"Fine. Now, call off the Coast Guard cutters. As soon as we've got a lock on where their instructions were coming from, send in Hamid with an inspector. Get the 2nd Istanbul Felony Court to draft the arrest warrant. I want this clean and legal. This has to be a senior officer. No one else could pull it off. Busting a high-ranking officer who opposes our movement in the act of helping Interpol fugitives will give us a lot of political mileage."

<hr>

BLACK SEA NORTH OF ISTANBUL   Murat looked down at the cruiser tossing in the storm. The ocean of air that buoyed the chopper was every bit as rough as the waves below, and it was starting to make him feel sick. He looked over at the pilot. The man's face was white and tense from the constant fight to keep the bird in the air. Twice, he had already said they should head back. He persevered only because Murat insisted.

On the boat below only one man was visible. He knew there were at least four more armed men in the hold. The entire situation made Murat uneasy. He had expected them to head for open water. Instead they had run up international maritime signal flags. The message was simple, 'VHF hailing channel has malfunctioned. No distress. Riding out storm.' It was a stalling technique. He knew that. What he didn't know was why, and that was what made him nervous.

"Captain, how far out are those Coast Guard cutters? I don't know how much longer our pilot is going to last out here."

"Hang on, Murat," replied Yusuf. "Let me check."

<hr>

POLICE INTELLIGENCE HEADQUARTERS, ISTANBUL   Yusuf switched to the Coast Guard frequency on the scrambled channel Bülent had set up for them. His friend had provided the impossible, a technical surveillance room in the Istanbul Police Intelligence Bureau Headquarters. It felt weird. He was concealing everything he was doing from the police, and yet he was surrounded by them. The room was actually used for storing obsolete communications equipment. Bülent had worked in this department years ago as a sergeant fresh out of the Academy. He had rigged the setup just that afternoon. Yusuf tuned the radio to transmit on the Coast Guard frequency and flipped the switch to turn on the microphone.

"Barbaros, this is Istanbul Coast Guard Command. What is your ETA to Kısırkaya?"

"Coast Guard Command? I don't understand. Those orders were cancelled five minutes ago. We're already moving back towards open water out of the storm's path."

Yusuf felt his stomach tighten.

"Sailor, this operation is still a go. I need you to turn around immediately."

"Meteorology says the storm will begin abating in less than an hour. We weren't told this was an emergency."

"Listen, I apologize for the confusion, but you need to rendezvous with another Coast Guard cutter to provide backup in a boarding operation. Please confirm your ETA."

Yusuf's cell phone vibrated on the table. This was the third call in the last ten minutes. He picked it up to look at the screen. Again, it was a number he didn't recognize it. He ignored it. The Coast Guard captain continued.

"Sir, this is all very irregular. I'm going to have to ask you to give me the operations passcode."

"I provided that with the initial order."

"I understand, sir. But, it was updated five minutes ago. I need you to confirm the new operations passcode."

Yusuf's heart skipped a beat. He looked back down at the telephone. *Three calls in the last few minutes, a new operations passcode in the middle of a shift. Is it coincidence?*

"One minute, Sailor. The duty officer is providing clarification."

He switched the microphone to mute, quickly pulled a different cell phone from his pocket and dialed his contact at Coast Guard Command. The man answered on the second ring.

"Captain, what in the hell is going on?"

The man's voice was strained.

"I don't know what you're talking about. I called for the new operations passcode."

"I can't give it to you."

"Why not?"

"Because I don't know it. A colonel from the Police Intelligence Bureau stormed in here a few minutes ago and put us in a lockdown. They're on to you."

"Thanks for the warning, friend."

He hung up the phone and terminated his connection on the Coast Guard frequency. There would be no cutter. They would have to board the vessel themselves, but the storm made boarding difficult if not impossible, especially if they were faced with armed resistance. *How much time do we have? Fifteen minutes? Half an hour?*

A knock at the door answered his question

"Open up. This is the police."

Yusuf tore his headphones off. He reached over and switched on the microphone to warn Murat, but before he could say a word, the door was kicked in, and he turned to see policemen streaming into the room weapons at the ready shouting,

"Hands in the air. Hands in the air."

Yusuf raised his hands, turned and smiled.

"Relax, boys. I'm one of the good guys."

"Put your weapon on the floor."

"What's going on here?"

"Weapon on the floor! Now!"

Yusuf unstrapped his belt and let it fall.

"Kick it towards us."

He obeyed. A police inspector walked into the room followed by Hamid, his niece's husband. Hamid was beaming. Yusuf's eyes narrowed to slits. It was the inspector who spoke.

"Captain Demir? What a surprise."

"I doubt it."

"I thought you were in Counter Terrorism."

"That's right."

"Then you'll forgive my surprise at finding you holed up in a room used for storage in the Police Intelligence Bureau's technical surveillance unit. I'm sure there is an explanation for this irregularity. The security logs have no record of you entering the building."

"Inspector, if you don't mind, we are prepping an operation."

"I checked with your office in Ankara. They have no knowledge of any operation. Smells like you are going rogue again. It wouldn't be the first time, would it?"

"We're acting on an anonymous tip about a group of terrorists making an exchange. The information indicated that certain members of the Security Directorate might be involved. Apparently, they were right. My team has been dark since the tip was received, and yet you still found us."

The inspector ignored Yusuf's insinuation.

"I suppose you will say this explains why even your own office has no knowledge of the operation."

"I don't think I have to say anything else to you."

"That's your prerogative, Mr. Demir. Indeed, you have the right to remain silent. This is an arrest."

Yusuf merely shrugged.

"On what charges?"

"You have the audacity to ask what the charges are, Captain? That takes a man with balls. But, that is how you built your reputation, isn't it? By inspiring

460

devotion with gutsy operations. You have used your popularity in the department to run roughshod over the law for years, ignoring protocol to win glory..."

"Inspector, are you here to arrest me or commend me for my leadership?"

"You're a cocky son of a bitch."

"What are the charges?" he asked again, with a calm that unnerved the
inspector.

"It's a long list, Captain. Aiding and abetting criminals sought by Interpol
in contravention of international treaty, neglect of duty and abuse of power for
conducting unauthorized operations and impersonating competent authorities, namely Coast Guard Command, and finally, conspiring with foreigners
to overthrow the constitutional government of Turkey."

"Those charges will never stick."

"That's for a court to decide."

Yusuf knew it was hopeless.

"I suppose you'll want to frisk me before you arrest me," he said, turning
his back on the policemen.

He placed his hands on the table and spread his legs. He addressed the
room speaking directly into the microphone, hoping that Murat was hearing
every word.

"By refusing to allow the Coast Guard to board this vessel, you are the
ones who have aided and abetted criminals. I'm sure the court can be made to
see that. Our job is to apprehend terrorists, even terrorists like these who have
friends in the government. We bring them to justice, alive if possible, dead
when that possibility no longer remains."

Before he had finished speaking, two policemen had holstered their pistols. One handcuffed him while the other frisked him for weapons. When they
were done, they spun him around. He was shocked to find Hamid directly in
front of him. He was a big man and his face was contorted with that leering
rage peculiar to metaphysical hypocrites on a soap box.

"You should have sought the commendation of Allah, instead you have
been a flunky of the Republic and blasphemed the religion of the Prophet.
You betray the ummah, scoff at the sharia and side with the infidel. You are a
disgrace to the uniform and a traitor to our people"

Yusuf held his tongue and smiled, which infuriated the man even more.

"You think that because Leyla is my wife's aunt you will be spared?"

Yusuf shrugged and said, "Funny, but the thought never crossed my mind.
I didn't rise to the rank of Captain because of friends in the government. I
earned it."

Hamid's face grew red, but he ignored the jab and pointed to the policemen in the room.

"The servants of Allah in this country are tired of being trampled by those

461

without faith. Allah is raising up a Golden Generation. We will bring back the golden era of the Ottoman throne, when faith made us prosperous, gave us peace and the strength to hold our heads high before our enemies. The blessing of Allah will rest on us when we obey His will and accept His law. It's not too late even for you, Yusuf."

"Hamid, maybe you could save the religious pep talk for your family visits while I'm in jail awaiting acquittal by the court."

"You will roast in hell first."

"No doubt you are right. My only consolation is that you and your friends will be the fuel for the fire."

Hamid's reaction was immediate. He landed a powerful open-hand blow to Yusuf's left ear that knocked him off his feet. The inspector jumped between Hamid and Yusuf.

"Let's not allow his provocations to upset us, Hamid. This is not personal."

Hamid turned without a word and left the room. The inspector pointed to the floor where Yusuf was trying unsuccessfully to sit up because his hands were cuffed behind his back.

"Help him up."

Two officers walked over and raised him to his feet. The inspector continued, "Captain Demir, you were entrusted with a sacred duty to serve the Turkish people. I'm disappointed that you have failed to perform it."

Yusuf wanted to spit in the man's face.

"Disappointing you, Inspector, is something I shall wear as a badge of honor. If I had known you were in league with these men, I would have used a larger net in this operation."

73

Black Sea, North of Istanbul   Murat couldn't believe his ears. The secrecy of their operation was blown and elements from within the government had taken the Captain into custody to protect Fatih Gülben's men. He and his men were on their own now. Murat's course was clear; the Captain couldn't have been more obvious.

"Eagle Two, this is Eagle One. I'm sending the team down to board this vessel. I need you sitting about fifty yards off the starboard side and close enough to observe the deck. Our men will be pretty helpless in the air, so you will be providing cover."

He switched channels on his headset so that he could communicate with the team in the back.

"Boys, we've got new orders from the Captain. We are going to have to board this vessel ourselves. This storm has gotten the Coast Guard's panties wet, so they've decided not to join the party. I think the wind has died down enough for us to do it without them anyway."

The storm hadn't abated a bit, and everyone knew it.

"It isn't safe to fast-rope down in this weather, so hook up the rappelling equipment and descend in pairs. Eagle Two will be covering you from starboard. Go down with weapons at the ready."

"Yes, sir."

Murat turned to the pilot and pointed to the boat.

"Take us as far aft as you can."

Murat watched the altimeter while the pilot maneuvered until he was about one hundred feet above the boat.

"You have to get lower," said Murat. "The rope is only ninety feet long."

"It's too windy, Captain. One gust of vertical shear could plunge us down on top of that boat."

"It could," Murat replied dryly. "And, that would be one way to keep them from getting away. Bring it down another fifteen feet."

"But, sir..."

"Just do it! That's an order," snapped Murat, removing his seat belt and moving to the back of the helicopter to man the .50 caliber machine gun so that his entire team would be free to board the vessel.

<hr>

CAIRO   Jabbar hung up the phone.

"Captain Demir has been arrested. He was running the op alone. We're working on how he got into the building."

"Excellent. He had to have help."

Adnan's voice burst into the room over the speaker.

"Sir, it looks like the helicopter is preparing to board."

"Hang tight," said Ahmet, "Babek? Do you copy?"

"Loud and clear."

"Adnan needs a little assistance. Take them out."

<hr>

BLACK SEA COAST, NORTH OF ISTANBUL   On the hill overlooking the beach, Babek sprinted towards the clearing with a shoulder-fired launcher and three infrared surface-to-air missiles. The helicopters were approximately a kilometer away. Time-To-Impact would be less than three seconds. The choppers were more like hovering hummingbirds than sitting ducks. The result, though, would be the same. The second helicopter would have almost a full minute to take evasive action before he would be ready to fire again. It didn't matter. They were so close their chance of getting away was less than one in ten thousand.

He raised the launch tube to his shoulder, took aim and partially depressed the trigger to activate the coolant on the infrared device. When the light flashed green, he depressed the trigger fully. The booster fired, and without even looking to see whether or not it would hit the target, he began preparing the second round.

<hr>

Murat had just strapped himself into the door gunner's seat and was watching the first two of his men rappel down to the boat when it happened. He heard the captain shout in the headphones, "Shit!" and less than a second later, the night sky was lit up by a fireball to his right. He spun around to see the burning Sikorsky list to starboard for a couple of seconds before losing power completely and plunging into the water below. All the while, the pilot was yelling in his ear, "Infrared SAM! The warning system went off right before it struck. Cut those men loose. We have to move NOW! We're too close for the counter measures to deploy in time."

Murat had seen his captain improvise a hundred times. Now, it was his turn, and he knew he had about a minute to make it happen.

"You can't outrun them either," said Murat. "Put that boat between us and the beach."

"Sir, that won't…"

"Do it, you son of a bitch, or I'll turn this .50 caliber on the cockpit. These bastards aren't going to get away."

The helicopter swung left as Murat continued giving orders.

"Maintain your elevation, keep us at two o'clock and about one hundred meters out."

"He was already giving the 'Go' signal to the other team members.

"Get in the water. Now!"

He turned the gun on the boat. He knew only seconds had passed, but his senses were so finely attuned that each one had seemed like an hour as his mind recorded every detail with the precision of a high-def camera.

"Let's see if we can give their infrared missile a bigger target."

Murat knew that, like every cruiser in its class, the hull of this vessel was made of fiberglass. Sinking it with a .50 caliber gun wouldn't be a problem. A concentrated stream of fire at any point would create an irreparable hole. But, he needed more than that. He needed to create an infrared signature big enough to cover their own. He needed an explosion.

Murat aimed toward the aft of the boat and pulled the trigger. The gun roared to life, firing at a rate of seven hundred and fifty rounds per minute, shredding the hull and sending debris flying everywhere. When five seconds and sixty-two rounds hadn't produced the explosion he sought, he moved to the other side of the vessel for another five seconds, in a determined search for the fuel tanks.

Murat didn't hear the shot, but he saw the muzzle-flash and felt the bullet hit him in the chest. His body-armor saved his life, but the impact was so powerful it would have thrown him from his chair if he hadn't been strapped in. Before he could turn the gun to take the man out, there were two more bursts of flame from the barrel of a handgun. The first one hit the outside of the helicopter right beside his head. He didn't know where the other shot went.

He sent a one-second burst of thirteen 225-grain bullets at the shadowy figure on the deck, perforating his body with enough holes to cause instant bleed-out. Before the man ever hit the ground, he had already returned to the stern of the boat, filling it with lead. In the light of the helicopter's spotlight, he could see the bullets chewing up everything in their path as he raked it systematically from one side to the other. The fuel tank had to have been punctured by now, which meant it just needed a spark. He zeroed in on the area he thought was the engine housing and a blossom of sparks ricocheting off of metal confirmed his suspicion. This was the engine. He pressed the trigger harder, willing it to detonate the fuel he could not see but desperately hoped was leaking everywhere.

Babek stood up with the launch tube and raised it to his shoulder. He couldn't believe the helicopter hadn't taken evasive action. It was futile at this distance, of course, but the instinct for self-preservation and the training of the pilot practically guaranteed that this was how they would respond. For some reason, they hadn't, and Cairo was not going to be happy about losing one of their best field ops teams. He pulled the trigger just enough to activate the coolant.

He could see the stream of tracer bullets disappearing into the cruiser. Their men were dead. He knew that. The .50 caliber gun would turn the boat into matchwood. He had seen what those guns could do first hand in Afghanistan, where he had fought for nineteen months with the Taliban against the Americans. He also knew this helicopter had to come down. The light in his sight turned green. He tightened his finger on the trigger and saw the explosion on the water a split second before his rocket booster fired. Babek let loose a string of curses and immediately began preparing his last round.

The second blast came just a couple of seconds after the first. If Murat hadn't seen the rocket streaking towards them, he might have thought the second louder explosion was a propane tank in the boat's kitchen. It had worked. The missile had been struck the burning boat. And he had carried out his captain's final order. Alive if possible, dead if not. The gamble had paid off, giving him another sixty seconds to think about his own life.

"How are the men?"

"They're all in the water."

"Kill the lights, head straight away from the beach, put it on autopilot, stay low and keep it at ten knots. We need to bail. They won't miss again."

Murat unlocked his seat belt, grabbed the handhold above his head to keep his balance and stood up. Before he could even get to his feet, a searing wave of excruciating pain shot up his left leg. He felt the bone give way as he collapsed back into the seat with the sickening realization that the third bullet had found its mark. His femur was broken. He ran his hand down his leg. It was too dark to see, and everything was so soaked from the rain he couldn't tell how bad the bleeding was.

Mechanically, but at lightning speed, he blocked out the pain and conducted the status assessment his training made second nature. Eight of his men dead, eight in the water. No backup. Possible pursuit. Unable to swim. Possible damage to the femoral artery, which would mean rapid bleed out. Five to six-foot seas, more than a kilometer from shore. The cover of darkness. He gritted his teeth and spoke into his headset.

"I'm hit. Bring a life-jacket."

He looked out the door. It was hard to gauge how high they were. A five-year old son and eight-year old daughter. Their mother, Jale. Everything went black. He felt the pilot shove the life jacket over his head.

466

"We've got to go, sir."

"How far is it to the water?" mumbled Murat through clenched teeth.

"As close as we dare."

"How far?" he repeated.

"At least thirty feet, which means we're going to have to knife the water."

The thought of a jumping from that height with a broken leg made him queasy.

"You go first. I'll follow."

The pilot didn't say a word. He simply moved behind Murat, grabbed him under his arms and heaved him to his feet. Murat screamed in pain.

"I can't stand!"

"You can, sir!"

"I can't jump."

"We'll do it together, sir."

The pilot moved to Murat's left side and pulled the man's arm over his shoulders.

"Alright, on three. Remember straight as an arrow. You can't tumble forward. You have to jump up and out. One…"

Murat closed his eyes. He felt like he was going to pass out from the pain. The anticipation of even more when his broken leg hit the water was even worse.

"Two…"

He thought of Jale, his children, his Captain, Fatih Gülben and his country.

"Three!"

With every ounce of strength and determination he could muster, Murat pushed up on his one good leg and jumped out the door into blackness.

—————

Babek finished connecting the trigger on the missile and raised his head to look over the water. Rain was coming down in sheets. He couldn't see a thing. He had seen the helicopter switch off its lights right after the explosion. The fire on the boat was already out. The stern had sunk low enough in the water for the waves to crash over it and douse the fire. He hastily pulled the infrared binoculars out from under his shirt and started scanning the darkness.

He spotted it almost immediately right over the top of the boat. Its powerful T700 engines were the only heat source strong enough to be detected in this storm. Because it was moving directly away from him, he couldn't judge how fast it was going, but assumed it was moving at top speed. He was surprised though at how low it was flying.

He grabbed the launcher and hoisted it onto his right shoulder. The sight was useless in the dark. It didn't matter. Precision was not necessary. It just needed to be close. He found the chopper again, pointed the launcher in the same direction, depressed the trigger partially and waited for the green light. This was his last missile, their last chance to tie this off neatly. The green light flashed in the sight, and he sent the third missile streaking across the sky. Another fireball lit up the darkness five seconds later.

74

ISTANBUL "Where are you guys?"

"I'm waiting right outside the entrance to Migros. White Hyundai van. I'll drive up to the curb as soon as I see you."

"And Gary?"

"He's in position. Where are you?" asked Gwyn.

"We're just pulling into the underground parking garage now. How many levels are there?"

"Four. Go to the very bottom. Gary said the third level is only fifty percent full, and that if anyone follows you down to the fourth level, you should assume it's a tail."

"Right."

"You'll be able to park very close to the elevators. There are two side by side. I'll call Gary now. He says the elevator will be open and waiting for you. Just remove the tape. He'll meet you on the ground floor. Remember to press Z and not 1. Their first floor is our second."

"Right. Thanks for the reminder."

"What about the stairwell?"

"Gary chained the doors on that level five minutes ago."

"We've got another problem."

"What's that?"

"Ginger and the kids were being held in some sort of shipping container. After I talked to her on the phone today, one of their captors came in and tried to force himself on Ginger. Of course, Garret tried to defend his mother. Apparently, they took him outside and beat him up pretty badly. He has several cuts on his face, and two on his arm."

"Oh my God! Is Ginger okay?"

"She's a bit traumatized, but she'll be okay."

"What about Garret? Does he need medical treatment?"

"Well, that's what's odd. All of his cuts, most of which seem minor, were stitched and bandaged. It's odd that they cared enough to do that."

469

"Maybe it was a gesture of good will?"

"I've questioned Garret at length. He says that during the scuffle he was hit hard several times, and that at some point, he blacked out. The last thing he can remember was a strong odor. He said it was not an unpleasant smell, but that it was sudden and unexpected."

"What are you saying, Gilbert?"

"I think he may have been knocked out with an anesthetic like sevoflurane or halothane. The whole thing may have been a ruse, so that they could implant a tracking device. After all, they don't want us to disappear. Ginger says they were separated for almost an hour. "

"What are you going to do?"

"Gary will take Ginger, Shelly and the kids out to you. I still want everyone to change in the minivan. Have Gary put all their clothes and shoes in a plastic bag and either stuff it in a trash can or hide it behind a car. I'm going to have to pick up some razors, or a sharp knife, some tweezers, bandages and antiseptic."

"You have to be kidding."

"I wish I were."

"We don't have time for this."

"Not much."

"I have to call Gary."

"Okay, see you in a few minutes."

Gilbert turned the phone off, and looked over at Ginger.

"Hang in there, honey. It'll all be over soon."

She hadn't said a word in the last ten minutes. She had thought the ordeal was over, that her family was safe. But, as she listened to Gilbert relate everything that had transpired over the last week, she had realized that it was their normal, comfortable lives that had come to an end. The ordeal was just beginning.

Gilbert looked in the rearview mirror. There were five cars behind him as he descended the ramp to the second level. He noticed the elevators were approximately twenty yards from the ramp. They would be the same on every level. He drove slowly across the length of the second level and watched two of the cars peel off in search of a parking space, while the other three followed him down to the third level.

On the third level, Gilbert drove even slower. Near the ramp, there were no empty spaces but he could see that the opposite end of the parking lot was mostly empty. As he passed the first row with empty parking spaces, he looked in the rearview mirror. The first car turned off immediately as did the second, but the third car, a dark-blue, European sedan he couldn't identify, didn't turn off. It continued to follow them, moving very slowly and keeping its distance.

"Ginger, we've got company. Remember what I told you. It is unlikely anyone will know English, and it will all be so unexpected that I'm sure it will give me plenty of time."

She nodded and turned to face her husband, her pensive look giving way to a broad smile.

"Gilbert, if this doesn't go well, I want you to know something."

"What's that?"

"That I'm sorry. Sorry for making your life so miserable these last few years. Sorry for not understanding the pressure you've been under. Sorry for making my love conditional."

"Ginger, that's not..."

She reached over and put her finger to his lips.

"Please," she said, still smiling. "I know what I need to say and how I've been. I just wanted you to know that I know. Forgive me, Gilbert."

He reached up and took her hand, folded it at the wrist and kissed her.

"I do, darling. I do."

"Good," she replied. "Now, let's do this thing and get it over with."

She turned to the back seat.

"Kids, are you ready?"

Everyone nodded in the affirmative. Gilbert started the turn down the ramp to the fourth level, and as soon as he rounded the corner out of sight, he pushed the pedal to the floor. Every second counted. He saw that the doors to one of the elevators were open, just as Gwyn had said they would be. He whipped into the parking space nearest the elevator, and everyone began piling out of the car. Shelly carried Gabriella, Gilbert took Garth and Ginger grabbed Garrett's hand as she raced to the elevator.

As soon as they were all in, Gilbert sat Garth down and spun around to look at the control panel. Over the control panel was the piece of packing tape Gwyn had told him about with a tube of super glue wrapped on one end. He shook his head at his brother's ingenuity. A giant piece of hard candy about the size of a quarter was taped firmly to the button that held the doors open. This had kept the elevator waiting for them. Gilbert ripped off the tape and pushed the Z button. Right before the doors closed, he saw the dark blue sedan come down the ramp to the fourth level.

When the doors closed, he took the lid off of the super glue and turned to Ginger.

"Remember I'll need at least ten seconds, maybe even twenty, after the doors open."

"We'll do our best."

Gilbert's heart was pounding in the stillness of the ascending elevator. Men who would love to see them dead were just a few floors below. He looked down at Garret. Images of what the terrorists were forcing him to do to his own son made him feel sick. A soft ding announced their arrival, and the doors opened.

Gilbert depressed the Door Open button and began squeezing super glue all around the edges to hold it down while Ginger and Shelly stood side by side in the door with the kids in front of them. The line they formed was a shield, blocking anyone from entering the elevator. They found themselves facing a small crowd of about fifteen people who had been waiting for the elevator. Ginger saw Gary at the back of the small group. He winked at her. It was just the boost she needed to begin her impromptu speech to this crowd of strangers. She forced a smile, cleared her throat and began.

"I'm sorry, but we are looking for the lost and found department. My friend sat her purse down on a bench and now it's gone. We've been wandering about for almost half an hour, and the children are too tired to walk anymore."

The small group of Turks exchanged questioning glances, obviously surprised by the spectacle of two foreign women and three children addressing them in English from an the elevator door. An elderly gentleman poked the young boy at his side, probably his grandson.

"Evladım, söylediklerini anlıyor musun?"

The boy raised his eyebrows and his chin while clicking his tongue to indicate 'No.' The old man looked around at the other Turks in the group.

"Anlayan var mı?"

The boy's actions were repeated with some variation by almost every person standing there. Ginger continued, but noted that a young girl at the back who looked to be about eighteen removed the MP3 player from her ears.

"It's getting late, and we have to get back to the hotel. Can anyone help us? We really need to find her purse. I'm sure someone turned it in."

The young girl was making her way to the front.

"You want to go to Lost Items?" she asked with a smile.

Ginger froze. She couldn't remember how Gilbert had told her to respond. She stood there speechless. She could feel herself turning red. The girl repeated her question more slowly as if she were unsure the foreigner could understand her accent. She was obviously eager to help.

"You want to go to Lost Items?"

Ginger just stared at her, unable to think of anything, anything but whether or not this young girl would have been this friendly if she knew some of her countrymen wanted her dead. *Would her humanity triumph or would her loyalty to the 'tribe' win out?* She was startled to hear Gilbert answer over her shoulder.

"Yes, that's right. If you could just point us in the right direction," he said, walking out of the elevator and gently prodding everyone forward.

"I take you there," she replied.

"Oh no, that won't be necessary. Just explain where it is," he replied with a smile.

The girl blushed.

"My English not very good. I can show better than explain."

"That's alright. I'm sure you have somewhere you need to be. Just show me which way to go."

The girl turned and pointed towards the other end of the mall.

"There is information desk on left side, across from main entrance. You ask there."

"Great. Thanks!"

Gilbert tugged on Ginger's arm to get her moving. The girl shrugged and turned back to the elevator with a puzzled look on her face. Gilbert kept everyone moving towards his brother.

"That was perfect, honey."

Gary closed the gap that remained between them.

"Boy, it's good to see you guys safe. We'll have to hug later," he said to Ginger. "Right now, we need to move. Mall security will be here any minute to find out what's wrong with the elevators."

Gilbert turned to see that the doors on both elevators were wide open. The one they had just exited was now full, and everyone was looking at the control panel.

"Gwyn said you had to pick a few things up at the supermarket. We'll all be waiting for you in the van."

Gilbert pulled his brother close, turned his back to Ginger and the kids and whispered in his ear.

"Garrett is coming with me."

"But, I thought…"

"I've changed my mind."

"If there really is a tracking device on Garrett, we can't risk putting him in the minivan. They could be on to us before we find it. We've thrown them off our trail, and I don't want them picking it up again. Those fellows we left in the parking garage will be up here in a few minutes. Besides, I don't think I can do this in front of Ginger and the kids. If we're not back in thirty minutes, you leave without us."

"I don't know…"

"I do. It's my family and my call. At least the rest of them will be safe."

"Ginger's not going to like it."

"I know. Is the boat ready for us?"

"Matt called two hours ago and said it was done. All we have to do is identify ourselves as the Lewis brothers. Matt refused to take the money though."

"And the signal? Are you still tracking the canister?"

"The signal disappeared about twenty minutes after your last call."

Gilbert ran his fingers through his hair. The document was the least of his worries, but he felt like a knight had just been taken in this game of chess. It was silly, the idea of winning the game without losing a single piece, especially when he was about to play a risky gambit to make sure his queen wasn't sacrificed. He turned to Ginger.

"Darling, I want you and Shelly to take Gabriella and Garth, and go with Gary outside to the van. Garret and I will join you in a few minutes."

Fear flamed up in her eyes.

"Gilbert, no..."

She grabbed both of his hands and looked into his eyes. What she saw scared her, making her plea even more desperate.

"I know what you're thinking, that you want at least some of us to get away, that this is the safest course of action, but I won't be separated from you again, Gilbert. Whatever lies ahead, I want to face it with you."

Gilbert pulled her close.

"Darling, we can't allow our emotions to cloud our thinking. We have to use our mind. This game is for keeps. We have to play to win. All of us dying together is not winning. This is only the first of many difficult choices ahead. Our safe and comfortable world is gone. The sooner you come to grips with that the easier it's going to be for all of us."

"Gilbert. I can't...Not alone. Not without you."

"You can! You have to. Now, take the kids and go. Even this discussion is a luxury we can't afford."

75

CAIRO   Ahmet stared blankly over the office. Rows of blank monitors stared back. He had never seen the place empty. It was an eerie feeling. Except for the two IT experts brought in to perform a complete system analysis and the four men he had kept to oversee the operation, the entire floor was vacant. The organization's Cairo headquarters had been effectively paralyzed. Everyone had been moved to the back-up site in Al Dokka. Anyone else would have viewed an operational failure of this magnitude as a huge setback, but not Ahmet. He was already plotting a way to turn the whole affair to his advantage and he was actually enjoying what was turning out to be the greatest challenge of his career. Jabbar interrupted his thoughts.

"Sir, our team lost visual contact at the mall when the American parked in the underground garage. He and his family took an elevator, but they must have disabled it somehow. Our men are stuck on the lowest level."

"Are they too good to use the stairs?" asked Ahmet, irritated that he had to make such a simple suggestion.

"They tried, sir. The doors have apparently been chained from the inside. Our men are driving back to the above ground parking."

Ahmet closed his eyes to think. A crowded shopping mall. Evasive action. They clearly know or suspect they're being tailed. It's all been planned. Switching vehicles will do them no good unless the American suspects a tracking device and finds the capsule. If he does, we will have no way of assuring that the Gospel of Barnabas is returned. Hope was not an operational parameter for Ahmet. He turned to Jabbar.

"What's the boy's location?"

"Still at the mall. In the southeast corner. It's impossible to tell what floor."

"Our team can track the device as well?"

"Yes."

"By involving Captain Demir, they've broken the agreement. I don't trust this American anyway. He's too wary. Who is the station chief at the Istanbul Smuggling and Organized Crime Department? Is he one of ours?"

"That would be Fahrettin Yıldırım."

"I remember him. Good man. We'll him send in uniformed police and an undercover team to arrest the American in connection with the Interpol bulletin. Get Chief Yıldırım on the phone."

Jabbar hesitated for just a split second. Ahmet knew why, but he waited to see if Jabbar would oppose his decision. Jabbar took a deep breath and began dialing the station chief's number, winning points with his boss in the process.

"I know what you're worried about, Jabbar. You think they won't return the Gospel of Barnabas and our organization will be implicated. I feel like a few days in a Turkish jail will make the American more than willing to cooperate. This evasive action proves he's suspicious. If they discover the tracking device, then we have no leverage at all. We will promise to release him when the Gospel has been returned. Meanwhile, let's get our people at Al Dokka to start working on the staff at the Österreichische Nationalbibliothek. In the worst case scenario, we'll have to bribe a librarian to change the register so that it looks like someone else stole it. This will be our back-up plan. Take no action unless necessary. There are too many risks, especially in Austria, where the people are already hyper-sensitive to Muslim integration."

Jabbar extended the phone.

"It's ringing."

Ahmet took the bulky sat-phone and looked at his colleagues. His men were accustomed to the stress of touch-and-go operations, but the constant stream of setbacks, the unknown repercussions of the security breach, the loss of sixty-two million dollars, the deaths of their colleagues on the Black Sea, and the possibility that their beloved leader might still be framed for the theft of the Gospel of Barnabas had taken their toll. He could see the despondency in their faces.

"*Alo.*"

"*As-salamu alaykum.*"

"*Wa Alaykum As-salam*"

"Chief Yıldırım?"

"Speaking."

"May the religion of the Prophet prosper."

"And the nations of the earth learn the virtue of submission. What is your code?"

"Hüdavendigar. 379-883-748"

"Cairo?"

"That's right."

"And, what are the orders of the Rightly Guided One?"

"There is an American by the name of Gilbert O'Brien at the Kanyon AVM in Levent with his family. He is wanted by the FBI and Interpol. We have a tracking device implanted on his son, but I suspect he will try to remove it. That will be bloody and require that he use a restroom. I need him taken into custody with all haste. We have one team there now, but it is a multi-storey building with over twenty-five restrooms if we include those in the restaurants and shops."

"Is he armed?"

"Not as far as we know, but he should not be underestimated."

"I understand. We can be there in twenty-five minutes."

"That may not be soon enough."

"I'll see what I can do."

Ahmet knew what that meant. He also knew that the American might find the capsule before then.

"Chief Yıldırım, the first thing I need you to do is call mall security, tell them you are on your way with uniformed teams, but that there is an undercover team on site tracking a terrorist from Monday's bombing. Tell them they are not to interfere in any way. Then, set up an ID check at all of the exits. If your team happens to apprehend them first, remember the detainees are not to be processed."

"Of course."

"Allah'a emanet ol."

"Siz de, efendim."

Ahmet handed the phone back to Jabbar and stood up.

"What is their position?"

"Northeast corner of the building, sir. I got the schematics from the Istanbul Security Directorate. There are public restrooms on every floor in that corner. As soon as our men are inside, they will go to the restrooms and begin working their way up."

"Excellent," replied Ahmet. "And, you've sent pictures of everyone to Mehmet and Ali?"

"Yes, sir."

Ahmet walked to the front of the desk he had been sitting behind and looked at his four most trusted mujahedeen. The last few days had dealt their vision and faith a severe blow. It was time to rally the troops.

"My brothers." His voice was robust. "This is no time to hang your heads. I know each and every one of you wish you had been on that boat tonight, that you had been martyred in battle with the enemies of the Qur'an. It was not the will of Allah. Our fate remains hidden, which can only mean that the Lord of the Worlds has seen fit to give us more time for deeds of valor and cunning. I have no doubt that the glory of martyrdom shall be ours, but it is not yet our time. We must also resist the temptation to mourn our loss. It is for them great gain. They are assured a place in the great hall of warriors. They will dine with

Zayd ibn Harithah, Ja'far ibn Abu Talib and Hüdavendiar. They will be served by black-eyed virgins with skin of ivory and ruby-red lips. The sea has become their grave, but their last rites shall still be performed in the land we dream of conquering by Fatih Gülben himself. May we be worthy of such an honor.

"The setbacks and difficulties we face are but a test of our faith, and even now, plans have been set in motion that you know nothing of. Plans that will turn these trying times into opportunity. Plans that will bolster our standing in the international community. We will condemn the bloody attacks by Bekir. We will assist the West in bringing him to justice and thereby prove our commitment to non-violence. We will unite the Muslim countries of the world with our commitment to education, technology, diplomacy and building good-will. We will increase our support for social initiatives in sub-Saharan Africa, Southeast Asia and the Americas as part of the Tolerance and Unity in a Multicultural World initiative.

"One must not lose heart on the eve of victory. The dark night of imperialism, idolatry and atheism is coming to an end. The bright day of truth and justice is about to dawn. The Rightly Guided One has already roused millions of Muslims from their spiritual slumber and lethargy. Soon the power of a united umma shall rule the world. We shall overcome the infidel. We shall see the nations of the world bow in submission to Islam."

76

ISTANBUL   Garret walked out of the supermarket into a milling crowd of Turks, clutching his father's hand and hoping that his dad didn't notice his sweaty palms. His father held a white plastic bag, a mop and a mop bucket in the other hand. Many of the men in the crowd looked like his captors. The thought that any one of them might be their pursuers, might grab him and send him back to the container was so nerve-wracking that the boy felt like he was going to throw up. The last thirty minutes in the car thinking about what was going to happen had been bad enough. Hearing the strange language of his captors spoken by everyone in the crowd almost paralyzed him with fear. He squeezed his dad's hand even tighter.

"What now, Dad?" he asked, hoping his father couldn't tell his voice was shaky.

"Now, we're going to the public restrooms around the corner," replied Gilbert, quickening his step.

His dad covered the last twenty yards to the bathroom at such a brisk pace that Garret had to run a couple of times to keep up. As his dad moved to open the door, Garret jerked back on his dad's hand.

"Dad, that's the ladies' room."

He pointed sheepishly to the stick-figure with a skirt on the door.

"I know, son. You have to trust me. No matter what happens, just go directly to the next to the last stall."

"So, you bought the mop to make it look like you're a janitor?"

"You're a smart boy. It won't be very convincing with two of us, but if it keeps some lady from screaming and running for mall security, that will be enough."

"Why not use the men's restroom?"

"No time to explain, son. We've got to hurry. Come on."

He followed his dad through the door. It was a labyrinth-style entrance, so they turned left and then right again to reach the restroom. They headed straight for the end of the row of stalls. Garret saw a woman in front of the mirror washing her face, but didn't think she even noticed them. His dad opened the door to the next to last stall, pulled him inside and locked the door.

"You wanted to be far away from the door so that if they come in here looking for us, you'll hear them coming, didn't you."

His dad nodded.

"But, why not the very last stall?"

His dad quickly put his finger to the boy's lips and leaned close to his ear.

"Son, we need to speak in a very quiet whisper and only if necessary. Understood?"

Garret nodded his head. He already knew that. He was desperately trying to avoid the silence because he could not keep himself from thinking about what was about to happen, which brought on waves of nausea. He watched as his dad opened the shopping bag, removed a package of yellow dishcloths, tore it open and began folding one of them lengthwise until it was a one-inch strip. Then, his dad took two more, tied one to each end of the folded strip and once again leaned close to his ear.

"Son, I'm not going to lie to you. This is going to hurt and not just a little either. I'm going to put this in your mouth and tie it around the back of your head. You need to bite down hard. It's very important that you not scream. Can you do that?"

Garret lowered his eyes and nodded slowly.

"Okay. Sit down then and open your mouth," said his dad.

Garret straddled the toilet and almost gagged as his dad pushed the strip of cloth into his mouth and quickly tied it with a square knot in the back. Then, he watched as his dad quickly made two more long strips from three dishcloths.

"I'll use these as tourniquets later," whispered his dad with a smile that was meant to be reassuring.

The boy didn't move. He watched as his dad opened the package of five box-cutters. He put one in each of his socks and one in his back pocket. He took another one, bent down to pull up Garret's pant leg, and stuck it inside Garret's sock. He removed the last box-cutter from the package, pushed up the blade and used it to slice through the tough plastic packaging that held the tweezers. His dad then stuck the closed end of the tweezers in his mouth, and turned back to his son.

Garret felt his stomach tighten. His dad had used his fingers to poke and prod around each of the cuts on his face and arm while they were in the car. The pain had brought tears to his eyes. The thought of his dad cutting them open again left him feeling dizzy and faint. He closed his eyes to keep his dad from seeing the fear in his eyes. The fear that he wouldn't be tough enough. The fear that he wouldn't be able to handle the pain.

⊹══◄╬

CAIRO   The sat-phone on the table rang.

"We're inside the mall and on individual coms."

"Okay, you have to move fast," answered Jabbar crisply, as he checked the

480

screen on his smartphone just to be sure nothing had changed. "We still show them to be in the northeast corner of the complex."

"That's what we are seeing too," replied Mehmet.

"According to the schematics that's the public restroom, but obviously you can't tell which floor. Split up. Mehmet, you check the ground floor and the first floor. Ali will go to the second and third floors."

Ahmet broke in.

"Remember brothers, a dead hostage is useless. The American will not go without a fight. Do you both have tasers?"

"Tasers and suppressed handguns with subsonic ammo."

"Stick with the tasers. Back-up from Smuggling and Organized Crime is on its way. Keep your coms live. It's the oldest boy we're after, but if you see any of the family members, apprehend them. Don't worry about mall security. We have that covered."

"Right."

The room fell silent. The whole thing would be over in minutes.

⊹━━⊹

ISTANBUL Gilbert looked at his watch. In just thirteen minutes, Gary would be driving off with his family, and it would take about two minutes for them to reach the parking lot. He put his hand on his son's head and whispered.

"Okay, son, let's do it. You can keep your eyes closed. That might make it easier."

He said this mostly because he wasn't sure he could do it with his eleven-year-old son staring up at him. All he could think about were the pictures of human sacrifice in his junior high history books, images of the ancients offering their children to the gods. Gilbert held his son's head in his hands and kissed him on the forehead.

"I love you, son."

Garret nodded nervously and closed his eyes again. A tear slipped out and rolled down his cheek. For the hundredth time, Gilbert wondered if he was just being paranoid. What if there is no tracking device? The thought of inflicting pain on his son for nothing had tortured him for the last half hour. He knew he would never forgive himself if he was wrong.

He took a deep breath, held the box-cutter like a pencil between his thumb and index finger, and cut the three crude stitches in the wound on Garret's forearm. He knew the fleshy part of the forearm would be better for concealing something than the lacerations on Garret's face. The boy winced as he quickly pulled the stitches out with the tweezers. Then, he grasped the boy's arm firmly and placed the point of the box-cutter at one end of the wound.

"Here goes," he said softly, quickly plunging the razor-sharp blade down into the flesh and slicing to the other side of the wound.

481

The boy's eyes flew open, and he instinctively tried to wrench his arm free from his dad's grasp. Gilbert was expecting this though. The eleven-year-old boy's strength was no match for his dad's. Gilbert mechanically noted that there was no rhythmic spurting. Still, the blood flowed in a steady stream out of the boy's arm and unto the floor. He knew there would be too much blood to see anything in the wound, which was why he had bought the tweezers. Without a word, Gilbert took them from his mouth and stuck the box-cutter between his teeth because there was no sterile surface he dared set it down on.

He knew that probing the wound was going to hurt the most, so he gripped the boy's arm as tightly as he could, braced it against his leg and pushed the tweezers down into the cut to start probing for a chip, a capsule, something hard. This time, however, the pain was so great and Garret's reaction so strong that the boy wrested his arm free and stumbled backed into the corner of the stall beside the toilet clutching his bloody forearm. Muffled sobs came through the dishcloth, tears flooded from eyes begging him to stop. The boy shook his head frantically side to side as if to say, *No, Daddy. Please, no!*

It was a trance-like moment. Within the span of a second, Gilbert saw a terrified and helpless boy cowering in the corner, his face covered with cuts and bruises, the blood-splattered toilet seat, and the red stain on the floor. Gilbert realized he couldn't do this alone. It was impossible without a second person to help hold the boy down, and there was no time for that now. Then, in a sur-realistic moment, he realized that the salty taste on his tongue was blood from the box-cutter, blood from his own son, and it was at that same moment that he realized what he had to do. He took a step towards his son and saw the panic in the boy's eyes change to absolute terror.

"Don't worry, son. I'm not going to hurt you. I have another idea. I need you to trust me. Can you do that?"

The blank look on his son's face told him the boy was too disconcerted to even process what he was saying. Gilbert slid his hands under the boy's arms, lifted him up, gave him a big hug and whispered in his ear.

"It's going to be okay. Remember, how you blacked out when the men took you out of the container? We're going to do the same thing. You just relax."

He sat down on the toilet seat with Garret in his arms, put his thumb and forefinger on either side of the windpipe and began pressing down, all the while whispering in his son's ear.

"I'm going to press pretty hard, so it may be a little uncomfortable, but it won't hurt. I promise. It'll just put you to sleep for about thirty seconds.

Gilbert could feel the carotid artery pulsing beneath his fingers. He knew he had to restrict blood flow and stimulate a parasympathetic response through pressure on the vagus nerve. Seven seconds later, he felt his son's body go limp in his arms. He now had less than one minute before Garret regained consciousness.

77

"This is Mehmet. The ground floor restroom was clear. I'm entering the restroom on the first floor now."

Ahmet frowned. He had felt sure the American would avoid the top floors. Ali reported next.

"I'm half-way through the second-floor bathroom now. Nothing so far."

This was followed by the sound of yet another stall door being kicked in and another man cursing for having been caught with his pants around his ankles. They had listened to this same routine already six times. They heard Ali apologize. He repeated what he had said every time. He told them that he was with Counter-Terrorism, that they had tracked one of those responsible for Monday's bombing into the mall, and ordered the person to remain where they were. More doors slammed. More curses. Forty-five seconds later, Ali's voice came over the sat-phone speaker.

"Second floor is all clear. Moving to the top floor now."

At the same time, they listened as Mehmet went down the row of stalls on the first floor. It took less than a minute for him to check the twelve stalls. Most were empty.

"First floor is all clear. Shall I wait for Ali or head for the parking lot?"

Ahmet looked at Jabbar.

"Has the device moved?"

"No, sir. It is still in exactly the same place."

"Negative, Mehmet. There has been no change in position. Did you see any blood anywhere?"

"No, sir."

Ali's voice came over the speaker.

"Entering the restroom on the top floor now."

Again, the room was filled with the sound of stall doors being kicked open. Ali was on the sixth stall when Ahmet began shouting at the sat-phone.

"Shit! Mehmet, they're in the ladies' room, not the men's! Go next door and check the ladies' room and then back down to the ground floor."

ISTANBUL   There had been nothing in the boy's forearm. Gilbert ripped the sleeve off of Garret's shirt so he could see the wound on his shoulder. There was no time to worry about removing the stitches. The box-cutter sliced right through them, opening up the second wound to a depth of two centimeters. He put the box-cutter back in his mouth, used the thumb and forefinger on his left hand to hold the incision open and began probing with the tweezers. He felt the capsule almost immediately. It was in the center of the wound embedded about one and half centimeters into the deltoid muscle.

He moved the tweezers until he was sure they were on either side and squeezed. The tweezers slipped off the round surface. He tried two more times with the same luck. Garret moaned, sending Gilbert into a panic. He had to get this out before his son regained consciousness.

Gilbert dropped the tweezers on the floor and took the box-cutter out of his mouth. Wiggling it back and forth in the wound, he located the capsule and followed it down to the end with the tip of the blade. Then, he turned the blade sideways and winced when he felt it scrape the bone. Garret groaned again. Gilbert began carefully prying upwards. The amount of blood flowing from the wound doubled. He couldn't tell if he was still under the capsule or not and was about to stop when he saw a white speck emerging from the red. Maintaining the same pressure and direction, he pushed it out far enough to grab with his fingers, and then pulled it out and dropped it into the toilet between his legs. He reached behind him to flush and realized it was an auto-flush toilet, so he stood up, holding Garret in his arms. Three seconds later, he heard the water being sucked down the drain. He sat back down and saw that Garret had opened his eyes.

"It's over son," he whispered, kissing him on the forehead. "Sit tight while I put a tourniquet on your arm."

The boy's face was sickly white. Gilbert wondered how much blood had been lost as he quickly took the second tourniquet, wrapped it twice around the gash in his son's shoulder and tied it off as firmly as he dared. The yellow cloth turned red immediately. Next, Gilbert untied the knot behind the boy's head and removed the dishcloth from his mouth.

"Are you okay, son?"

"My arm hurts, Dad. It hurts really bad."

"Well, it's over now. It'll feel better soon," he whispered as loudly as he dared. "We need to leave. Can you walk?"

"I'll try." The boy struggled to nod his head and closed his eyes again.

Gilbert set his son down on the floor gently. It was a bloody mess.

"Be careful," he whispered. "The floor's very slippery. Hold my hand."

Gilbert had just turned the lock on the door when there was a loud crash of metal hitting metal, then another, followed immediately by a woman's scream. He froze for a split second.

"Terrörle Mücadele. Sakin olun. Bir suçlu arıyoruz. Yerinizde kalın efendim."

The lady stopped screaming. Another stall door banged open. Gilbert relocked the door, grabbed Garret, whirled around and sat him on the toilet seat. He leaned close to his ear and whispered.

"Sit tight. When that door opens, I need you to scream as loud as you can and don't stop until I tell you to. Got it?"

The crack of another lock breaking was followed by another brief scream and more Turkish. Gilbert pulled the box-cutter out of his back pocket and pushed the blade up two inches. Another door slammed open. Six more stalls between us and them. He couldn't let his feet be seen sticking out under the stall door, so he sat down on his butt with his feet under the partition of the stall towards the entrance, slid across the floor until he had enough room to lay back and then used the partition to pull himself into the last stall. In the process, three more stall doors had been thrown open. He pulled himself up on his knees beside the toilet, but remained in a crouch low enough to let him see the floor of the stall his son was in. Another door was kicked open, followed swiftly by a second.

This was it. He heard the thud of a boot on metal, the snap of metal as the lock gave way and the door crashing into the partition. He waited for the scream. It didn't come.

"Oğlanı buldum."

Hearing the language of his captors pushed the boy over the edge. He let out a scream so blood-curdling it sent chills up his dad's spine. Gilbert saw the man step into the stall. Swiftly and silently, he opened the door to his own stall and turned the corner to find the man trying to put his hand over Garret's mouth to stop him from screaming. Gilbert threw his left arm around the man's head to pull it back and with one simultaneous motion pulled the box-cutter across his throat pushing down as hard as he could. At the end of the stroke, he felt the blade snap, but it had done the job.

Garret continued screaming, but the pitch and tone changed. Gilbert held the man's head in a death grip as he flailed wildly. A gurgling noise came from the man's severed windpipe. The diaphragm continued to do the work of inhaling and exhaling while blood from the jugular vein obstructed the flow of air. It was a full twenty seconds before the body went limp in his arms and Garret's screams finally subsided into sobs.

⊦═══◄╫

CAIRO   "Ali! Mehmet's down. Ladies' room, first floor!" barked Ahmet.

"On my way."

Jabbar grabbed the phone.

"Forget the ladies' room. The boy is moving. He has left the northeast corner and is heading due west."

"Copy that."

For several seconds, they heard nothing but Ali's labored breathing as he raced down the final escalator to the ground floor. Then, they heard the faint but unmistakable sound of a fire alarm, followed by the shrill screams of women.

"Ali, is that what I think it is?" asked Ahmet in exasperation.

"Yes, sir."

"The boy is now headed south by southwest towards what looks like the back exit," continued Jabbar.

They could hear Ali saying over and over again, "Excuse me, pardon me." He must have been rough. There several exclamations of "Watch where you're going, you son of a donkey!" Half a minute later, Ali came back.

"I'm at the exit heading into the parking lot, but it says the boy is headed west."

"That's right." replied Jabbar.

"But, that's impossible. There's a twenty-foot retaining wall on the west side of the parking lot."

78

İSTANBUL   The short, wiry man on the dock took the passport Gilbert held out and stood for a minute, studying the ragtag bunch in front of him. His eyes kept coming back to Garret. The boy was dressed in new clothes. He looked feeble, though, and the cuts on his face were fresh.

"What about ID for the rest of them?"

"Didn't our friend tell you I would be travelling with my family?"

"Yes, but you want to leave the vessel in Cyprus, so I should fill out a form."

"I'm sorry, but we left them at the hotel. Besides, my friend paid a bit of a premium for your help, not for you to set up a passport control booth."

Gilbert nodded at Gary, who immediately presented his passport as well. The man took it and opened to the first page.

"Duane Lewis?"

"That's right," answered Gary with a smile. "I'm Dan's brother. These are my two nephews, my niece, my sister-in-law and our sisters," he said pointing at each one.

The man still hesitated. Gary knew he had to resolve this quickly before the man's gnawing suspicion and fear of authority turned against them. He had to make an emotional connection. Gilbert's approach would never work.

"Abi, ben Istanbul'da oturuyorum zaten. Bunlar ailem. Ziyarete geldiler. Bir Mavi Tur yapsınlar istedim. Vakit kısıtlı olduğu için hemen çıkmaları lazım. Sorun oluyorsa parayı geri verin, başka bir tekne buluruz. Yani, bizden dolayı sıkıntıya girmeyin."

The man's face lit up. Foreigners never took the time to learn the language.

"You know Turkish! That's wonderful! *Tamam efendim. Sorun yok. Binsinler.*"

Gary turned to Gilbert.

"He says it's okay. You can all board now."

"Thank goodness," Gilbert replied.

Gary's knowledge of the culture and his amiable approach had just saved them. Gilbert turned to his family.

"Let's get moving. It's a long way to Cyprus."

He walked across the narrow gangplank, Ginger followed carrying Gabriella. Shelly held Garret's hand, Gary scooped up Garth and Gwyn boarded last. Their host stood holding the door to the quarters below deck. Gilbert motioned for everyone to enter.

Gary cleared his throat, put his hand on Gwyn's shoulder and said, "I need to have a word with you and Gilbert."

Gilbert responded impatiently.

"Gary, we can talk after we're safe at sea. We need to get moving."

"That's why we have to talk now. This is where we part ways."

Gwyn's mouth dropped open.

"Gary, you can't be serious. We are running for our lives. You can't stay here!"

"This is where I live," he replied softly. "Besides, Matt has a lead on Angela's sister. This afternoon, he obtained video recordings of girls who had been sold. Angela identified her sister. I'm going to start working on this case while he handles Dad's funeral arrangements."

"But, we may need your help," she protested.

Gary stuck his hand in his back pocket, withdrew a folded piece of paper and pressed it into Gwyn's hand.

"If you do, just let me know. All of my contact information, phone numbers, emails and Skype address, are on the back of this note from Matt. He asked me not to give it to you until you were aboard."

Gwyn grabbed the piece of paper and unfolded it eagerly to read the short paragraph in Matt's strong handwriting.

Dearest Gwyn,

I'm sorry for everything you have suffered recently. I too mourn the passing of your father. He was a great man. I am also very concerned about the difficulties your family now faces. You know that I will do anything I can to help any you. In spite of these recent troubles, I am glad that they brought us together again. I still cherish the hope that we might have a future. I don't know where your journey will take you, but if you are open to giving us another chance, I will be waiting for you at the Café Tortoni in Buenos Aires, Argentina on Avenida De Mayo 825 every day during the third week of February.

Love,
Matt

Gwyn crumpled the paper in her hands, threw her arms around her brother's neck and said through her sobs, "I'm so glad we did this together. Thank you for coming."

"Wouldn't have missed it for the world."

"Tell Matt I'll be there."

"I will."

Gwyn peeled herself away. Gary turned to his brother and stuck out his hand.

"Thanks for including me. I'd love to go with you, but this is where I belong."

Gilbert looked at the outstretched hand of the brother he felt he hardly knew. He shook his head, pushed the hand out of the way and wrapped his arms around his kid brother's neck.

"Why are you doing this? They're going to kill you if they find you."

"Don't worry about me. I have friends."

Gilbert drew back, put his arms on Gary's shoulders and said, "This is crazy. You're crazy. Why are you doing this?"

"I have responsibilities here."

"Gary, your students will find a new teacher! These people are not playing games."

"You think that's what I do here? Teach English?"

"That's what you told me."

"That's not the whole story."

"Then what is?"

"There's no time now."

"It's the same ol' thing, isn't it? Your hatred for the West, your utopian bullshit, your fascination with other cultures. Fine. Have it your way."

Gilbert turned to go. Gary grabbed his arm.

"I run an operation that protects Iranian dissidents. Turkey is used for transit. My job is to work with different non-profit organizations that give them asylum in the West. Most of these Iranians are followers of Messiah, escaping persecution."

Gary saw his brother's face soften, but he knew he was going to need some time to process this. Time they didn't have. Gary waited for his brother to respond. When he did, his voice was gruff.

"I guess we have a bit of catching up to do. Promise me you'll make time for that."

"Promise."

"Very well, then. We need to get going."

"Right."

Gary crossed the short gangplank. Gwyn shouted after him.

"Tell Matt to have Brittany read the second Psalm at Dad's funeral."

"Will do."

79

Friday, London Rush-hour traffic on the A5 had begun to subside, leaving the intersection of Forset Street and Nutford Place with an air akin more to aimlessness than tranquility. The primary school across the street wouldn't open for another week, so the lethargy of summer still hung in the air. The only threat it faced was from the Municipal Water Works maintenance crew that had been surveying on the street for the last two days.

Salih looked down on the scene with a peculiar sense of detachment. *Typical government planning. Waste the whole summer and then start a major project right before school starts. It will be a disaster when buses start delivering their cargo of kids.* The irony of wasting even a second on such a trivial line of thinking had not escaped him. Yet, over the last two days, he had found himself reflecting anxiously on the most insignificant things, things he would never have considered before. Things like whether he should forgo the elevator and take the stairs for exercise, or whether he should pass on the third cup of coffee. Subconsciously, he knew why it was happening, but a truth suppressed is a reality ignored.

For two days now, Ahmet had refused to take his calls. For over twelve years, they had served the organization together. They had put together a string of successes that circled the globe. Islam had a stronger foothold in western society than ever before, no small accomplishment in the face of such strident opposition, and his team had played an important part in achieving this victory. But, this morning he had received the call that confirmed his suspicions. Cairo had resumed operations. The London office was to be taken offline for cyber-disinfection. He had also been told to expect a visitor. Jabbar would be arriving that afternoon. Salih had known he was going to be replaced, but didn't intend to go down without making his case to Ahmet in person.

Outside, he could see two members of the maintenance crew cordoning off the south side of the building. It looked like the entire street would be closed to traffic. A backhoe which must have been brought in during the night was sitting idle on one corner of the intersection, waiting stoically for its work

490

of destruction to begin. Salih turned away from this mundane scene and sat back down in his chair. His team had isolated the key-logger on three computers in their office. For days, they had been engaged in the tedious task of sifting through every bit of information entered on the infected machines from the moment the key-logger had been installed. They had to review every email sent, every document opened, every website visited, every password entered and every article posted. It was the only way to complete the damage assessment Cairo was demanding by the end of the day.

+>=+=<+

Zeki walked briskly along Surrey Strand. The reflection of the sun on the river to his left was so bright he was squinting. His mind was fixated on a single dark thought—death. He pondered the death of George Sale almost three hundred years ago on this very street. *Was it poison that caused him to suddenly fall ill and die at the age of thirty-nine? No one would ever know...* His thoughts turned to Ian. He tried to imagine the final minutes of fear and panic his friend must have experienced, gagged and tied up by strangers in his own home in the middle of the night and then drowning in the fluid that gradually filled his lungs. There were few instincts that inspired terror like the feeling of asphyxiation, which was why waterboarding worked so well. He turned right on Bedford Street, and his thoughts turned from death to life, particularly the one he planned to take that afternoon.

He looked down at his watch. It was 10:29. He quickened his pace. He didn't want to keep Burhan waiting. As he picked his way through a group of tourists, he noted the security cameras on the modest four-storey Zimbabwean Embassy on the west side of the street. Zeki moved to the curb as he approached the restaurant, scanning the crowd in vain for a red shirt. Burhan was not there. He walked another ten meters and leaned against a No Parking sign. The man was never late. It was 10:32.

Without being obvious, he continued to comb the street, looking for any sign of his friend. Less than a minute had elapsed when he heard a car squeal its brakes behind him and turned to see a black Peugeot 308 driven by a man in a red shirt. It was Burhan. The look on his face told him to hurry. Zeki quickly crossed the street and got into the car.

"Good to see you in one piece," said Burhan, whipping out into traffic.

"Good to be in one piece. What's the hurry?"

"Are you aware that updated notices have been issued for you by Interpol, the FBI and the Metropolitan Police?"

"Everyone wants to be loved."

"Ankara is a hornet's nest of activity. They've declared you a rogue agent. The Interpol notice claims they have evidence proving that you helped organize the bombing in Istanbul on Monday and the theft of the Banner of the Prophet from Vienna."

491

"A sign of desperation… You still haven't told me what the rush is."

"I've had a tail on him since we received your message. This morning he bought a ticket for Cairo and paid with cash. I figured you might want to move up the timetable."

"Anyone likely to be there?"

"He lives with a pretty blonde. Wife or girlfriend, I don't know which. For the last several days, she's left around 10:30 every morning for an aerobics class and then gone to a Qur'an course in the afternoon over in Newham."

"Entry?"

"The old fashioned way."

"Alarm?"

"Yes, the code is 2318212."

"How did you manage that?"

"I didn't. Kiko did. And, I don't know how. She probably hacked into the security company. You know she doesn't share her secrets or her sources. Your bag is there in the back seat. It should have everything you need."

Zeki reached behind him, grabbed a black bag and opened it in his lap. He pulled out two passports, one Serbian and one Latvian.

"What are these?"

"Kiko thought it would be a good idea to supply you with some fresh ID. They'll be reviewing passport control surveillance tapes in four countries looking for you. It will take some time, but they'll eventually find some or all of your IDs and put them on a watch list."

Zeki reached for the money clip he kept inside his jacket. Burhan held up his hand.

"She said it's on the house."

"I suppose I'll have to thank her in person."

"I think she was hoping you'd feel obligated to do just that."

Burhan put on his signal to take the next right.

"I'll drop you off one block past the corner. You'll walk straight east for two blocks."

"Thanks for the help."

"I'll read about it in the papers."

"Don't you have anything better to do than read obituaries? You've been in the business too long."

"It's addicting, this job. The adrenaline, the intrigue, the chase, the danger… It's how men were meant to live. On a knife's edge, ever vigilant, constantly switching from hunter to prey and back again."

"Well, there's no problem as long as you get to switch back. I'm too old for this kind of stuff, and you will be soon."

"Nonsense. If you were too old, you'd be dead. What happened to your sense of destiny, of fate? When we're too old, they'll issue our final ticket. Until then, enjoy the ride."

Burhan pulled the car over to the curb.

"Be safe, old friend."

⊰−⋈−⊱

"It's open," said McIntosh, without looking up from the operational reports he had been poring over for the last half hour.

"Sir, the CO19 team is holding three minutes from the target, awaiting your final orders."

McIntosh took off his reading glasses and set them on his desk.

"Good work, Bob. Have there been any updates in the last thirty minutes?"

"No, sir. At the moment, we think there are around twenty people in the offices. We have no reason to suspect they're armed. The microphone and cameras we placed on the windows have not given us any new information other than confirming a frenzy of activity and the company's close connections with Cairo, DC, Brussels and Istanbul."

"I see here that communications from the office all but ceased this morning. No email, no internet, no cell phone or landline communications."

"That's right, sir. It happened at 7:27 this morning after the office manager received a call on his encrypted sat-phone. It's there in the report."

"I must have missed that," said McIntosh flipping back through the pages trying to find the relevant section. "Were we able to decipher it?"

"Yes, sir. Parker cracked it. The caller said, 'Cairo is back online. Halt operations. Finalize system recovery and send damage assessment by 18:00 hours.' It also said someone would be visiting the office, but I don't remember the name."

McIntosh cocked his head. This was huge.

"That's independent confirmation of the email we received yesterday!"

"It seems to be. The attachment was obviously information captured with a key-logger. Apparently somebody managed to get spyware onto their system."

"By 'somebody', we mean O'Brien, don't we?"

"Given his profession, the FBI warrant for his arrest on charges of corporate espionage, and the initials G.O.B. at the bottom of the email, I would say he is the most likely source of the information, sir."

"You know that email is going to start a firestorm in the diplomatic core and intelligence community."

"Or, get us killed."

"We need collaborating evidence…"

"We need a vacation."

"Any idea why the email was sent from Spain, and how O'Brien got there?"

"There's no record of him entering the country. The email was sent from

493

an internet café in Madrid. There are security cameras both inside the café and on the street outside. We've reviewed the footage, but cannot identify O'Brien."

"Then, it wasn't O'Brien," said McIntosh slowly, his mind searching desperately for that one thing he knew was being overlooked.

"What about the symbol at the top of the email?"

"It's called Rub el Hizb. It's an Islamic symbol. That's about as far as we've gotten. We haven't been able to make a connection yet. It's peculiar. Obviously meaningful. Parker is working on a couple of leads right now."

"Okay," replied McIntosh curtly. "How long will it take to empty the building?"

"Ten minutes at the most, sir."

"Let's do it then. They know they've been compromised. We need to secure any evidence before it gets deleted. I'll meet you in the operation room in five minutes."

"Yes, sir"

Parker shut the door on his way out. McIntosh pulled a thumb drive from his computer, slipped it into his pocket and picked up the phone. It was time to put the pieces together.

"Jack, has the university not responded to our subpoena? I need those server records."

"They arrived in the morning mail. I'll get on it right away."

"Did you have any luck cross-referencing past records on that cell phone number we received from our anonymous tipster with any of the individuals in the case file?"

"We had one match, but it could be coincidence. The guy looks clean."

"Let's talk after the raid."

80

LONDON When the door finally opened, Zeki picked up his bag, slipped into the apartment and closed the door. Normally, the control panel would have been on the wall just inside the door. Instead, he found himself staring at a portrait of Tariq ibn Ziyad. Zeki quickly scanned the entryway. There was no control panel, only a coat rack and a shoe rack, both of which gave evidence of female habitation. He had been on jobs before where the security control panel was intentionally hidden, so this was not unusual. The difference was that on those missions he had been informed of its location in advance. Now, he had the security code, but no way to enter it, and less than sixty seconds to find something that wasn't meant to be found.

The beads of sweat that had formed while he was picking the lock grew as he looked around the living room, trying to determine the most likely place to conceal a control panel. His roving gaze stopped on the wall directly opposite him on the other side of the living room. Bookshelves covered it from top to bottom. He felt a drop of sweat finally gain enough mass to begin trickling down his neck. If it was hidden on a wall, this was the most likely one. Dropping the bag, he crossed the room in quick strides and working from left to right, he began emptying the two middle shelves, hurling the books to the floor. Twenty seconds later, he was standing on the other side of the room with nothing but bare wall in front of him.

Without wasting a moment's time, he started down the adjacent wall, removing both of the picture frames that hung there. Still no control panel. He was running out of time. He turned to the opposite wall, which also had two pictures hung directly opposite the ones he had just taken down. Halfway across the living room, he stopped, looked at the entryway for a moment and sprinted for the door. *Of course! The key to Europe, the conqueror of Spain. Tariq ibn Ziyad.* Zeki took the frame and pulled on both sides. The right side swung open to reveal a control panel with a flashing yellow light. 2-3-1-8-2-1-2. He repeated to himself as he punched the numbers in. Flashing yellow turned to steady green, and he gave a sigh of relief.

Zeki picked up his bag, locked the door and turned the deadbolt before checking each of the rooms. In the end, he decided the study would be the best place to set up. Five minutes later, the contents of the bag were all neatly arranged on top of the desk. He sat down in the high-back leather office chair and gazed at his surroundings. More books. Three of the four walls were solid bookshelves from floor to ceiling. Several of the shelves across from the desk were decorated with ceramic vases of Middle Eastern origin, one of which bore the characteristic blue patterns of the Ottoman style developed in Iznik. The only wall without book shelves was covered with examples of Islamic calligraphy tastefully framed. To the uninitiated, the flowing Arabic script was more like a Rorschach inkblot than anything else.

The center-piece of the collection was twice as large as the others, and Zeki found himself tracing it out. Deciphering the flowery characters was almost as hard as drawing them. He patiently followed the lines to separate each word. *Murat…son of…Orhan…* Zeki stopped. The style was different, but he was clearly looking at a modern-day rendition of the royal seal of Murat I, the *tuğra* of *Hüdavendigar.* The same *tuğra* under the text on the document Professor O'Brien had found. *Something to ask him before I kill him.* Zeki looked down at the papers on the desk. There was a stack of essays marked with corrections and grades, a book entitled *Islam in the Modern World* and several utility bills. He picked up the bills and began looking through them. This was when he noticed the top of the desk. In the very center was the Rub el Hizb executed in beautiful mother-of-pearl. The circle in the very center was a snake swallowing its tail.

+)=(+

Salih was standing in front of his desk, looking at a system analysis report, when the door at the far end of the office burst open. He turned to find CO19 officers streaming into the labyrinth of cubicle work stations in navy blue uniforms and ceramic helmets, guns at the ready.

"Hands in the air! Everybody! Now!"

There were at least five rows of cubicles between Salih and the door. He dropped to his knees and began crawling as fast as he could. Everyone knew the drill. They had rehearsed it the first Friday of every month for six years. In seconds, the commotion and shouting were over. No one offered any resistance. Careful not to raise his head above the desk, Salih began feeling on top of the desk for his cell phone, silently cursing himself for breaking protocol by taking it out of his pocket. He heard the team leader speaking.

"You are all under arrest. You will be escorted to a police van that is waiting outside. You will be processed individually at the station. Let's make this easy on everybody."

Salih found his cell phone and quickly began punching in the number. He wished it had been a speed dial number, but that was just too risky. His movements were quick and sure. His fingers weren't trembling. He could hear the man giving instructions to his colleagues.

"Do not touch, I repeat, do not touch any of the equipment in this office. As of this moment, it is all State's evidence."

From his position under the desk, Salih started chanting the *tekbir* slowly, with feeling and conviction.

"*Allahu ekber, allahu ekber…*"

He was immediately joined by every employee in the office.

"*La ilahe illallahu allahu ekber. Allahu ekber ve lillâ ilhamd.*"

He solemnly pushed the call button on the cell phone and began repeating the *tekbir* again. One of the officers began shouting for them to stop. In seconds, several other policemen had joined him, screaming out orders for the employees to remain silent. It had to be unnerving to hear the Islamic confession of faith recited so calmly in this tense situation. One of the officers bolted for the door. None of the employees paid them any mind. They had all turned to a mark on the wall which indicated the direction of Mecca and were prostrating themselves in prayer.

Salih looked over at the block of C4 attached to the back of his computer. An identical set-up could be found under every desk in the office. On the fifth ring, the embedded detonators would be activated. The block of plastic explosive wrapped in ball bearings was less than three feet away. He knew he was looking at the gates of paradise, the face of God in a lump of plastic putty. *La ilahe illaallahu…*

⊹

The explosion could be heard five kilometers away. Windows rattled in buildings over two kilometers away. From a distance, Londoners saw only a small cloud of dust rise slowly into the air. Up close, it was messier, a gangly pile of rubble, nowhere near as tidy as a controlled demolition. But no one in that building cared about aesthetics anymore. The live feed in the operations room went dead, and the only thing McIntosh heard was silence. Silence more deafening than the roar of the explosion. It was the hush of forty-seven souls being unplugged, severed from their connection with the material world.

"Damn it! Bob, I'm going down there myself; you coordinate from here. Send in our search and rescue teams. Alert the fire department and local hospitals. Plus, I want a search warrant for the homes of every single employee at that company before any evidence is destroyed."

"Yes, sir."

There was a knock at the door. It was Jack. McIntosh waved him in.

"Sir, is everything alright? You don't look well?"

"Our raid just turned into a mass suicide."

"Shit! The CO19 team?"

497

"They were inside."

"Damn!" he said, dropping his eyes.

"What do you have, Jack?" asked McIntosh.

"Remember how Professor Brown said that he hadn't received the emails sent from the secretary? Well, that's not true. The server records show that those emails were both delivered successfully."

"Whatever," replied McIntosh, waving his hand as if batting at a gnat. "Maybe he lied to keep from getting entangled in a murder investigation."

"The Google report came back too. It confirms that he read them," replied Jack. "Sir, we made it pretty clear that the document was a central piece of evidence."

"Fine. Pay him a visit. We've got bigger problems right now."

"That's not all," continued Jack. "Remember the cell phone number we received on that anonymous tip?"

"The one that was disconnected before we had even started tracking it?"

"Yes. Well, it still hasn't registered on the network, so obviously the SIM card is not being used, but there was a call, or rather several calls, to that number. Two yesterday and one today."

"And?"

"All three calls came from Professor Donald Brown."

The expression on McIntosh's face hardened.

"Are you saying the professor was connected with the office we just raided?"

"It certainly looks that way, sir."

"Get a warrant," snapped McIntosh. "I want him in my office this afternoon."

81

Professor Brown fumbled for half a minute, trying to line the key up with the key-hole, before realizing that he had the key upside down. This was when he noticed his hands were shaking uncontrollably. He flipped the key over, slid it into the keyhole and turned the lock. When the door did not immediately respond, he felt a moment of alarm, which quickly subsided. It was only the deadbolt. Seconds later, he had found the proper key. When the door finally swung open, he slipped into his apartment, locked the door, and leaned back on it with a sigh of relief, glad to be off the street where he had felt naked and exposed.

His anxiety was understandable. Cairo had called half an hour ago to inform him of the raid on Salih's office and told him to go to a safe house in Newham. They didn't say anything about the explosion. They didn't have to. He knew what protocol was. It was what they didn't say that bothered him. Nothing was said about how Salih had been compromised or why they thought he might be in danger. He held up his hand up to see if it was still shaking. It was.

Then, he remembered the security alarm, turned to his right and swung the picture of Tariq ibn Ziyad away from the wall. There was no blinking light to indicate that the alarm was armed, but he never noticed that anyway. A prickly chill ran down his spine, raising goose bumps on a balmy August afternoon. He was staring at a sticky note over the keypad with two short handwritten lines:

Why_Hüdavendigar?
Is MS 9653 real?

"Holy shit!" he said, reaching for the note.

A voice came from the study behind him.

"Turn around slowly and keep your hands where I can see them."

Brown jumped in fright and spun around to find Zeki Öztürk standing sideways in the doorway of the study. He closed his eyes and said, "Allah help us," as he raised his hands.

499

"You look a bit distraught, Professor."

Brown struggled to regain composure.

"How did you get in here?"

"The door."

"If you don't leave right now, I'm calling the police."

"That is the one thing I'm quite sure you will not do."

"That's preposterous," said Brown, lowering his hands to retrieve his cell phone from his pocket.

Zeki raised the Vintorez sniper rifle concealed at his side, slipped off the safety and pointed it directly at the man's chest.

"Hands in the air! I won't say it again. The next time you reach for a phone, the only thing your downstairs neighbor will hear is the thud of your dead corpse hitting the floor."

"Listen, I don't know what's going on here. Who are you and what are you doing in my house?"

"But, I asked my questions first."

"I beg your pardon..."

"Why Hüdavendigar?"

"I don't know what you're referring to."

"The *tuğra* at the bottom of the document Professor O'Brien found, the center piece of the calligraphy display on the wall in your study. The seal of Murad I. Why does your group use that symbol?"

"My group? Listen, if you'd only put down that gun, I'm sure we can sort this out. There must be some mix-up."

"Stop playing games with me, Dr. Brown. You know who I am. You've seen pictures of me in your briefings. The new bald look may have been a surprise, but I'm confident you see past that. There is one thing, though, that you may not have learned about me. I'm an impatient man, especially with liars and cowards. I'd rather shoot you than listen to your sniveling denials."

Zeki paused to give the man time to process the warning and then continued.

"Though Fate has ordained that I should be your executioner, you get to decide how quick and painless it will be, and that is no small thing."

"My executioner?" returned Brown with dismay. "I had nothing to do with Professor O'Brien's death."

Zeki sighed, "You also seem to have forgotten that I was with Turkish intelligence before the Europeans interfered with all their nonsense about human rights and how ineffective torture is. I might be a little rusty, but it's like riding a bike. You never forget how to break somebody."

Zeki stepped away from the study door and motioned with the barrel of the gun.

"Into the office."

500

"You have to believe me. I'm innocent. Can't we just talk about this in a civilized manner?"

Brown's attempt to mask his fear with a calm tone failed. His voice cracked.

"I like that suggestion. I'll ask the questions and you answer, fully and as calmly as you are able."

"You're making a mistake," protested Brown.

"It wouldn't be the first time, though it would be unfortunate for you."

Brown walked into his study to find his chair had been moved to the front of the desk.

"There is one zip tie in the chair," said Zeki. "Sit down and secure it tightly around both feet. There is another loosely attached to each armrest. Slide one arm through and tighten it with the other hand. Then, slip the other arm through the loop and tighten it with your teeth."

Brown stood for a moment with his back to Zeki. Then, he walked over to the chair, turned around and sat down with a look of defiance.

"I'll answer your questions, but I'm not going to restrain myself."

Zeki pointed the gun between the man's legs, squeezed the trigger and sprayed several bullets into the wood floor. The sound of splintering oak was much louder than the whisper of the rounds being fired.

"Subsonic 9 mm rounds," said Zeki matter-of-factly. "I could shoot you in a crowd and no one would even know a shot had been fired. Next time, I'll put a round in both shoulder joints."

Without a word, Brown did as Zeki had instructed him. When he was finished, Zeki pulled up a simple wooden chair he had brought from the kitchen and sat down in front of Brown.

"Now, why do you have the seal of *Hüdavendigar* featured so prominently in the display on that wall?" Zeki asked, pointing at the large center piece.

"I don't understand why it matters," returned Brown dryly.

"Because, like you, I'm a scholar and inquiring minds want to know."

Brown said nothing. Zeki cleared his throat.

"Do you know how Professor O'Brien was killed?"

"I told you I don't know anything about that."

"But, what you *mean* is that you weren't there when it happened, which is different from not knowing anything."

Brown was silent. Zeki stood up, walked to the desk behind him and continued.

"Professor O'Brien suffocated from a fluid buildup in his lungs caused by an adverse reaction. The sodium thiopental your people gave him proved to be lethal when combined with his prescription medication."

"That sounds like an accidental death, not murder," replied Brown, straining to see what Zeki was doing behind him.

"Don't be antsy, Professor. I assure there will be no accidents here."

Suddenly and without warning, Zeki pulled a clear plastic bag down over Brown's face. He placed his hands on top the man's head and slid them down, squeezing out any air pockets and then twisted it tightly at the back of his neck. Brown struggled violently, a wild look of terror in his eyes. Zeki held Brown's head back against the chair and silently counted to forty. Brown swung his legs back and forth and rocked the chair in an attempt to knock it over, but Zeki held him tight. Then, he bent down close to Brown's ear and said:

"This, Professor, is similar to what my friend Ian was feeling in his last moments, fighting for air, just like you are doing now, but unable to get any. I'm only going to take this bag off one time. If you don't start talking to the point, it goes back on to stay. Are we clear?"

Brown nodded his head vigorously. Zeki removed the bag, walked back to his chair and sat down, leaving Brown bent over in the chair, gasping for breath.

"I started with the easy question and will not go on until I've received an answer. Why Hüdavendigar?"

"You know as well as I," said Brown laboring for breath.

"I can guess. To know, I need you to confirm my suspicions."

"Consider them confirmed."

"Isn't that interesting? I am here to avenge the death of Ian O'Brien, who was murdered because your group is still avenging the death, seven hundred years ago, of a Turkish Sultan. Vicious cycle, isn't it?"

"It was treachery. The Serbian infidel feigned allegiance."

"Apparently, he was fighting according to your rules!" responded Zeki, his voice dripping sarcasm.

"It was *Iblis*, who goaded the Christian to take the life of Allah's warrior on the field of victory. Sultan Murat I symbolizes who we are. He was the founder of the empire, the first sultan, a visionary who longed for the emancipation of Europe from superstition and idolatry."

"You mean a tyrant who taxed his Christian subjects in gold and blood, taking their brightest and healthiest children and raising them as Muslim soldiers or harem decorations."

"It was a magnanimous policy that elevated them to many high positions they would have never have achieved without Islam."

"I doubt their parents viewed being the Sultan's whore as upward mobility. Nor do I suppose it pleased them that their sons were the Janissary forces used to crush dissent and expand the empire."

"They were proud of their sovereign and faithful to his religion. You speak like an infidel!"

Zeki shrugged off the slur.

"All dreams of empire end because day breaks in the hearts of the slaves used to build it. What about Manuscript 9653?"

Brown held his tongue.

"Was the plot hatched in Tunis or Istanbul?" asked Zeki.

"I don't know. No one does."

"That was the point, wasn't it? *Erase every trace*... Oh well, tell me about your London organization."

"I have only one contact."

"Phone number?"

Brown looked at the plastic bag in Zeki's hand and wished it were the gun instead.

"07714 652222."

Zeki removed a slip of paper from his shirt pocket.

"Let me check that," he responded coolly, unfolding the paper and dropping the plastic bag to retrieve the pen from his pocket as well. "You see, I can verify much of what I'm asking. Yes, that number is correct. Keep going. I want to know everything."

"I know very little. Everyone in the order is insulated from the others for security. The only man I ever spoke with or met was Salih. That was his telephone number."

"What else?" said Zeki patiently.

"I maintained three blogs under different aliases. Coded messages were left in the comments."

Zeki wrote down the names of the websites as Brown coded them out.

"What else?"

"Those are my only connections in London, I swear."

"Your mission?"

"I'm in academia. My job is to write and teach objectively about the virtues of Islam."

"That explains why you went to such great lengths to cover up the fact that your organization rewrote the Christian Bible, I suppose. What's your real job?"

"That's it."

Zeki picked the plastic bag off the floor and stood up with a sigh.

"I thought you were going to tell the truth. If that were your only duty, Cairo wouldn't have contacted you about Professor O'Brien."

Brown spat out the words as if they were poison.

"I contacted them. O'Brien has been under surveillance for several years. His obsession with the Moriscos concerned us."

"What did you do besides babysit O'Brien?"

"Disinformation."

"I see. Professional bull-shitter. And, your modus operandi?"

"Influencing opinion leaders, building a reputation and following in academia, long-term social integration, image management..."

"How many of you are there in London?" asked Zeki, sitting back down in his chair.

"I don't know...Honest."

"Guess."

"A hundred maybe."

"So, probably closer to five hundred. Give me some names."

"I told you we don't have contact with each other."

"No contact with operations. Believable. No contact with the other bull-shitters like yourself. Impossible."

"Give me twenty names, or the bag goes back on."

Brown started rattling off names. Zeki wrote them down without a word. When he was finished, the interrogation continued.

"So, you weren't on the team that took out Professor O'Brien?"

"I only heard about it later."

"Salih. Is he the head of the organization in London?"

"As far as I know."

"What about Cairo?"

"I have no contact with Cairo."

"I thought we had agreed you would tell us the truth."

"I swear. I have no contact information for the Cairo operations."

"But, you spoke with Ahmet."

"He called me. Encrypted line, no caller ID. I've never met him."

"What did you discuss?"

"He asked about the document. I told him what it was. He said they would take care of it. I had no idea there would be any physical harm done. I thought they just wanted to secure the original order. We believe in reason, not violence."

"What about the fifteen thousand dollars he wired you?"

Brown's eyes popped with astonishment.

"I...I don't...I'm not..."

Zeki cut him off.

"What was the money for?"

"It was a grant to fund the work of certain scholars."

"I'm sure you've confused scholarship with propaganda, but let's not get into semantics. I need a name."

"It was not an individual. It was a group, the UN Committee for the Protection and Promotion of Diversity in Cultural Expression."

"Interesting," said Zeki, refolding the paper and placing it in his pocket. "I was hoping you knew enough to save yourself, enough to be useful, but you're a pathetic pawn in this game. I'm tired of playing."

He stood up with the bag in his hand.

"You are the person who told the organization about the document Professor

O'Brien discovered. He was a true scholar and gentleman who never thought ill of anyone. You are the one I hold responsible for his death. Your time is up."

"Wait! We can help each other. You don't want me anyway. You want the real killers."

"But, you don't know them, remember?"

"That's true, but I know how they work. I can tell you everything you want to know about recruitment, the psychological profiles they run on high-level diplomats, who they target and how they get people on the inside. Surely, that is worth something," he said, his eyes pleading.

Zeki sat back down, tossed the bag on the floor and pulled out pen and paper.

"I doubt it's worth your life, but I'll give you a chance," he said, happy that his plan was working. "I'm listening."

For the next half hour, Brown talked non-stop about everything he had learned during his six-month orientation in Germany. Money laundering, influence peddling, educational initiatives, cultural awareness programs, inter-faith dialogue, business acquisitions through capital infusions, sleeper cells, immigration, population growth strategies…When he finally paused, Zeki raised his hand.

"I think that's enough for the authorities to work with."

He picked the bag up. Brown immediately began shaking his head from side to side.

"But, I've told you everything."

"Indeed, you have. Fear seems to have been quite the antidote to your faith."

"So, why the bag?"

Zeki didn't respond. Instead he found the corner of the bag and tore the tip off, leaving a hole about one centimeter in diameter.

"If my calculations are correct, this should provide just enough oxygen to keep you alive. Be careful not to collapse the bag though. Otherwise, you will certainly suffocate before the authorities arrive."

Now, he was standing at the desk behind Brown, who was sweating pro-fusely. He took a long piece of cloth and put it in front of Brown's face.

"Open your mouth."

Brown complied silently. Zeki tied the gag tightly behind his head. Then, he slipped the plastic bag down to his neck and tied it securely in the back.

"While you're sitting here waiting for the police, you might just pray that I get to Ahmet before he gets to you."

82

McIntosh was standing in front of the collapsed building, talking with the head of the search and rescue team when his cell phone rang.

"McIntosh."

"Superintendent, it is nice to finally hear your voice."

"Who is this?"

"Allow me to offer my condolences for the loss of your men. I'm truly sorry. I would have called earlier, but I was helping you with another part of your investigation."

"What investigation?"

"The O'Brien murder. If you'll send a team to Professor Brown's house, you'll find the man restrained and waiting eagerly for your arrival. There is a taped confession on the desk as well as copies of documents you will need to continue your investigation. If you want him to stand trial, he's going to need serious protection."

"And, to whom do I owe this debt of gratitude?"

"A friend. That should be enough for now."

"How do I know I can trust you?"

"Because today's events have already proven my email was accurate. Good day, Superintendent. Watch yourself."

The line went dead. McIntosh looked at the devastation in front of him. There was no hope that any survivors would be found here. He turned to the rescue team leader.

"Mark, I've got a very important arrest to make. Please carry on without me."

83

VIENNA Zeki heard the shuffling steps coming up behind him on his left. It was one of the library attendants in Prunksaal, an elderly man who had spent the entire day muttering to himself in German as he arranged and dusted the ancient volumes housed in this splendid room. Zeki shouldn't have been there at all, and he felt a tiny bit guilty for indulging his passion for history.

The original plan had been to meet Patrick early that morning, give him the Gospel of Barnabas and then supervise its return to Augustinerlesesaal from a safe distance in the reading room. When that was done, he was supposed to catch a flight to Amsterdam for a meeting that afternoon. He had promised himself that he would return in the near future and treat himself to a full week in General Eugene Savoy's library. But, on his way out of the reading room, he had passed by the Prunksaal entrance and decided life was too uncertain to postpone his intimate acquaintance with the General. He had cancelled his appointment in Amsterdam and spent the entire day browsing through the library, marveling at Savoy's mind and the vast assortment of books the man had managed to collect.

In his study of European military history, Savoy had always been the general he admired the most in terms of tactical and logistical skill on the battlefield. As a younger man, Zeki had often wondered why Allah had given the infidel such a brilliant general when the Ottoman Turks had been so close to expanding their empire. He knew now that the reason was in the question itself.

A little after noon, he had found a copy of *History of the Wars* on the library shelves, the same book Ian had given him as a gift shortly before his death. The lady at the desk had been kind enough to let him examine it, which was how he had spent the rest of the afternoon.

The shuffling feet stopped behind Zeki and to his left.

"Excuse me," the man said apologetically. "We'll be closing in fifteen minutes, so you'll need to return your book to the desk."

Zeki raised his eyes in a smile for the wizened old man.

"I thought the Prunksaal was open until five o'clock?"

"Normally it is, but there is a special state function here tonight, so there are preparations to be made."

"That's too bad. It's not easy parting with such a wonderful manuscript especially when one has the pleasure of reading it in the library of the general himself."

"What is it you're reading?" asked the old man politely.

"*History of the Wars*," replied Zeki.

"By Procopius of Caesarea?" returned the old man.

"Why yes, it is."

Zeki could barely hide his shock. "I'm surprised to find someone who knows anything about it."

"The wars of empire, be they Christian or otherwise, should be known by all, don't you think?"

"I do. I do indeed."

The old man shuffled off. Zeki picked up the book and a massive manila envelope sitting on the chair beside him. It was time to go.

A few minutes later, Zeki was on the ground floor of the building, sitting on the bottom step of the massive stone stairway that led up to Prunksaal and Augustinerlesesaal. He put the manila envelope beside him on the step and began to wait. A number of people walked past on their way up the steps, but he didn't like the look of any of them. Fifteen minutes later, he was starting to get impatient when he saw a tall, young man with blonde hair approaching the door. He looked about eighteen. When the youth headed for the steps instead of turning right to the rooms on the ground floor, Zeki stood up, coughed violently, and put his hand on the wall as if to steady himself.

"Good afternoon, lad."

"Good afternoon, sir."

"Would you be so kind as to do an old man a favor?"

"Sure. What is it?"

"I think I'm having an asthma attack, so I'm afraid to climb these stairs. I need to give this envelope to one of the librarians in Augustinerlesesaal. Would you mind doing it for me? It's just one flight up."

"Sure. I'm going there myself."

Zeki picked the manila envelope off the step and handed it to him.

"The lady's name is Elizabeth. She has a lazy eye."

The boy nodded as he took the envelope and continued up the stairs. Zeki waited until he was out of sight and then dialed his cell phone as he walked away.

"Patrick. I'm still in town. I cancelled my meeting in Amsterdam. How would you and Sally like to have dinner?

†━━━†

"Excuse me, I am looking for Elizabeth, one of the librarians here."

Without even raising his head, the man behind the counter motioned to

508

the opposite corner of the room with that lassitude peculiar to civil servants. He turned to find a young woman straightening books on a shelf, and walked over to her with a smile.

"Excuse me. Elizabeth?"

"Yes, that's right."

He noted immediately the physical feature that confirmed she was the intended recipient.

"This is going to seem as strange to you as it did to me. On my way up here, a fellow stopped me on the stairs and asked me to give you this envelope. He said he was having an asthma attack and couldn't climb the stairs."

He held out the bulging, oversized, padded manila envelope. She took it from his hand and looked at the front. It said simply 'For Elizabeth.'

"What is it?" she asked cheerfully.

"I have no idea."

"Well, thank you for bringing it up here."

"Not at all."

She watched the young man walk towards the counter and request a book from her colleague. *What a hunk.* She breathed a heavy sigh. *And, I have a lazy eye.* She walked back to her desk and opened the envelope. Inside she found two seemingly identical and strangely familiar volumes with a sticky note on the front cover.

> Have discovered and foiled, at great personal risk, a plot to steal your library's copy of the Gospel of Barnabas. The two volumes you hold in your hand are the fakes prepared for this very purpose. Recommend heightened security for this important work, as well as repositioning the security camera at the front desk and installation of a metal detector. G. O. B.

A shiver went down her spine, followed immediately by a wave of panic. Spinning around in her chair to look at books on their way back to the archives, she quickly located the codex that had been returned that same morning and removed it from its gray cardstock cover. Then, she laid the three books on the table side by side. They all looked identical. She picked up the phone and dialed the archive director, and then with her free hand began flipping through the library sign-in sheets to see who had checked out the book last.

"Hello."

"Hello, Director. This is Elizabeth in the reading room. If you have a moment, there has been a delivery I think you should see."

"Sure. I'll be down in a few minutes."

She hung up the phone and looked down at the registry. The person that had checked out and returned the book that same morning had identified himself as Gilbert O'Brien. G.O.B.

84

RURAL EAST TEXAS   The buzzing insects were no more monotonous than the droning country preacher's sermon, which she found more irritating than the flies and mosquitoes she swatted at with her fan. It was a fan she had thrown in her suitcase on a whim, inspired by popular tales of the American south and romantic notions of what a Southern belle was like. Now, she realized that a hand fan was not an accessory in the South. It was part of any woman's personal survival kit. That anyone would have a graveside service in this heat was, to her mind, positive proof that these people were perverse in their adherence to tradition. The heat was stifling for the natives, but for Judith Heron, the professor in the ankle-length black dress who had flown from London to attend the funeral, the situation bordered on life-threatening. A pavilion had been set up to provide shade, but it was barely big enough for family, so she stood with everyone else in the sun, sweat pouring into her eyes, dripping from her nose and drenching her underclothes.

Her elegant wrist whipped the fan like a dragonfly's wings while the preacher's canned consolations for the grieving family wafted over the crowd on heat waves billowing up from the ground. She was surprised at how many people were in attendance, given that Ian had spent most of his life abroad. In addition to friends and family, there were also a number of academicians present. Professor Jones from King's College had cornered her before the service with questions about forming a search committee to replace Professor O'Brien. He hinted at her coming back to the university and probably would have pressed the point, but she was rescued from his tedious torrent of questions by the arrival of the family.

She had walked up to Randolph O'Brien, who bore a striking resemblance to his older brother Ian, and introduced herself as a colleague and intimate friend from King's College in the UK. He had been polite but cool. When she had inquired about Professor O'Brien's children and said she would like to offer her condolences, the man's wife broke down sobbing, at which point Randolph had simply thanked her for coming and begged to be excused.

There was a ripple in the crowd. She noticed that the preacher's sermon had ended and his tone had become more conversational.

"The family has requested that Brittany Kirkpatrick read a Scripture."

He moved away from the podium that had been set up behind the casket where Ian's body lay, and a young woman stepped up to the microphone.

"Losing someone we love is always tough; losing a man as kind, compassionate and wise as Uncle Ian is tougher, but the toughest thing of all is knowing that this gentle soul was murdered, taken away from us prematurely. Our heart goes out to the family. The situation is made even worse by the fact that his children cannot be present. My dear friend Gwyn O'Brien and her brothers Gilbert and Gary should be here today, comforted by the support of friends and family, allowed to grieve and mark the passing of their father. I don't know why they're absent, where they are, or even whether or not they're safe."

Her voice cracked. Judith could tell the young lady was fighting to keep back the tears. They came anyway, but through some tremendous exertion of willpower, she managed to keep her voice steady.

"Two days ago, I received a message from Gwyn. She asked that I read Psalm 2 in loving memory of her father. For some of us, it is particularly meaningful given the circumstances."

She cleared her throat, and began reading.

"Why do the nations conspire and the peoples plot in vain? The kings of the earth rise up and the rulers band together..."

Judith's thoughts turned to Ian O'Brien, the man she had tried so desperately to win because there were so few people who had as much to offer the cause as he did. The problem had been simple. The man had been an idealist with no political aspirations, an intellectual with no passion for the practical application of his scholarship. Early on she had learned to mask her own political convictions. Professor O'Brien had been so buried in the past and mankind's failures that he couldn't comprehend the new world she and her friends at the UN wanted to build.

Though she didn't hear it, someone must have said 'Amen' to a closing prayer because the crowd relaxed and began to stir. Some people began picking their way through the gathering to greet friends, most moved off in search of air-conditioning. There was no point sticking around, so Judith walked quickly back to her rental car. She opened the door and sat down in what was a veritable sauna, cranked the car and turned on the air-conditioning. Then, she pulled out her cell phone and dialed the number Senator Giovanni's office had provided.

"Hello."

It was a rough, masculine voice.

"Hi Tate, it's me, Judith."

"What happened?" his voice softening immediately.

"None of O'Brien's kids showed up at the funeral. We've hit a dead-end."

"What about Connor?"

"I didn't see him either."

"Damn!"

"We knew they wouldn't be here."

"Yeah, well, Fatih called this morning and said he can't afford to pay us our share of the Libya deal unless we can help him recover the money the O'Brien brothers stole."

She could feel the strain in his voice.

"The Senator's not going to like this," he added quickly.

"He should be thanking his lucky stars that the info the brothers sent to the Metropolitan Police didn't implicate him. But, if I'd known Ian's sons were going to screw things up this bad, I would've killed them in London when I had the chance."

He loved the detached professionalism she exhibited when referring to her work.

"What's Cairo doing?" she continued.

"Relocating their entire operation to Istanbul. They're too compromised to stay in Cairo. Gülben isn't happy about it either."

"As long as he funds the initiative, I don't really care if he's pleased with his harem or not. That's the price he pays for tolerating incompetence in his organization."

"Well, at least they kept the Gospel of Barnabas connection from being exposed."

"So, their team destroyed the document as soon as they recovered it?"

"That's what they said."

"I sure hope they're telling the truth…"